THE SHADOWS SERIES BOX SET BOOKS 1-5

A CHRISTIAN ROMANCE

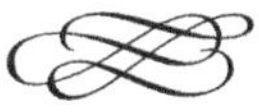

JULIETTE DUNCAN

Cover Design by http://www.StunningBookCovers.com

Copyright © 2018 Juliette Duncan
All rights reserved.
The books that form The Shadows Series books 1-5 are all a work of fiction. Names, characters, and incidents are all products of the author's imagination or are used for fictional purposes. Any mentioned brand names, places, and trade marks remain the property of their respective owners, bear no association with the the author, and are used for fictional purposes only.

THE HOLY BIBLE, NEW INTERNATIONAL VERSION®, NIV® Copyright © 1973, 1978, 1984, 2011 by Biblica, Inc.™ Used by permission. All rights reserved worldwide.

PRAISE FOR "THE SHADOWS SERIES BOX SET"

"I loved each of these books. I could hardly put them down."

— AC

"This set of book gives tribute to the grace of God and he miraculously works in our lives through difficult and joyous times. His grace is sufficient."

— CAROL V.

"Great read. True to life. I really enjoyed following this couple and sharing in their trials and triumphs. Would like to read more from this author."

— VERONICA G.

"This series is an excellent love story depicting grace and commitment. Love this and can't wait to read others written by her."

— LGORDON

FOREWARD

Note from the Author:

Hello! I'm so glad you've picked up a copy this Box Set, and I do hope you enjoy it. Just a forewarn - Book One can be quite confronting, but Books 2-5 show God in all His glory, so push on! Also, if you haven't already got my free book, "Hank and Sarah - a Love Story, get it for FREE, and to be notified of future releases by clicking here.

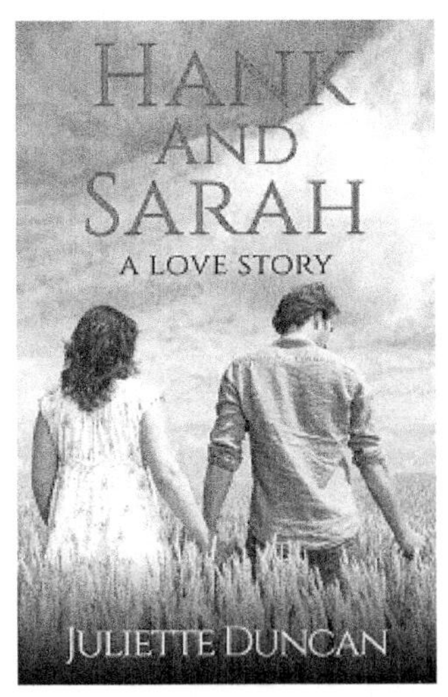

BOOK 1 - LINGERING SHADOWS

CHAPTER 1

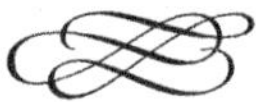

North East England 1981

Marrying Daniel O'Connor was a risk, no two ways about it. Lizzy still didn't know why she'd agreed to marry him, but tomorrow at midday, come what may, she would be saying "I do".

Although impetuous, she was also loyal, and while her actions were highly irregular, she *would* see it through, and she *would* be a good wife to Daniel, regardless of what anyone thought. And she'd prove her father wrong.

She would also ask God to bless their marriage, even though Daniel didn't yet share her beliefs.

The past week had been busy, keeping her mind off tomorrow, and now she had to collect Sal, her best and most loyalist of friends, from the station. Lizzy glanced at her watch and tapped her fingers on the steering wheel as the traffic stalled in front of her.

"Come on, you lot! I don't want to be late. Move!" She thumped the wheel, and then sped around the car in front that had completely stopped and was going nowhere.

The train pulled into the station just as she entered the car park. She zipped into a spot someone had just vacated, jumped out of the car, slammed the door, and sprinted to the entrance, taking the stairs two at a time. People of all sizes and shapes were already piling out of the train onto the platform, but Sal's carrot red hair stood out amongst the crowd, making her easy to spot.

"Sal!" Lizzy waved and called out, not worried in the slightest what the people around her would think. Running down the stairs against the general flow of traffic, she bumped into anyone who wasn't fast enough to get out of her way, and almost knocked Sal off her feet when, finally reaching her, she threw her arms around her best friend with uncontrolled abandon.

"I'm so glad you could make it, Sal. It's great to see you!" Lizzy whirled her around and hugged her again.

"Wow Liz! It's great to see you too, but it's only been three months!" Sal drew her eyebrows together and tilted her head slightly, curiosity loitering in her smile as she searched Lizzy's face. "Are you okay?"

Lizzy pulled back, annoyed at Sal's perception. "Of course I'm okay. What makes you think I'm not?"

"Oh, you just seem a little on edge."

Lizzy's eyes narrowed and her lips flattened into a thin line as she picked up Sal's dark brown carry all.

"I'm fine."

"Okay then." Sal glanced at Lizzy from the corner of her eye before tucking her arm through the crook of Lizzy's elbow as they walked back along the platform. "I still can't believe you moved all the way up here. Couldn't you have gone somewhere just a little closer?"

"You know why I did." Lizzy breathed in deeply. "Oh, but Sal, I do miss home." Lizzy fought back the sudden tears that pricked her eyes, and then turned her head to Sal, a forced smile planted on her face. "But enough of that. Tell me everything that's been happening."

All the way to the car, the girls chatted like two long lost friends, and Lizzy's mind was taken off the events of the morrow yet again.

The traffic hadn't lessened, and as she pulled out of the car park, Lizzy turned on the wipers. *A wet day. Great. That's all I need.*

She slammed on the brakes as a car pulled out in front of her, and blasted the horn while she shouted at the driver, a futile exercise, but it made her feel better. Her nerves were a little on edge.

"You haven't told your parents yet, have you?"

Lizzy bristled and held the steering wheel a little tighter. *Why did Sal have to bring my parents up?* She shook her head without looking at Sal.

"Don't you think you should?"

Lizzy clenched her jaw. *Why can't she let things be? Maybe asking her to come was a mistake.* But Sal was her best friend.

She put her foot down to beat the lights that had just changed to amber. "No. And I don't feel bad about it. They'd never agree to me marrying him, so I'm just going to do it. I know they'll be angry when they find out, but it'll be too late to do anything about it then. They shouldn't have been so horrible to him."

"Are you sure you know what you're doing, Liz? Have you prayed about it?"

Sal's eyes bored into her. Lizzy wasn't game to look. *Maybe I should tell her how I'm really feeling.* But if she knew the truth, Lizzy was sure that Sal would try her best to stop her from marrying Daniel, and it wasn't worth the risk. Having set her path, Lizzy was determined to stick to it. She'd actually contemplated calling it off a few times over the past couple of weeks, but the prospect of being alone again made her banish those thoughts immediately. It had to be better to be with someone than to be lonely.

Lizzy took a deep breath and calmed herself. "Yes, I've prayed about it. And yes, I do love him. I know what I'm doing, Sal, even if you think I don't." She slowed down to take the next corner. "He's a bit of a lad, so different to Mathew, but I love him. He makes me laugh and smile. I feel happy when I'm with him." She turned her head and glanced at Sal. "I know what you're thinking, and you might be right. I probably am marrying him on the rebound, but you know what? I don't care. I can't handle being on my own any longer." She wiped the tears from her eyes and hoped Sal hadn't seen them.

Sal looked at her intently. "I hope you'll be happy, Liz. I really do."

They sat quietly the rest of the way to Lizzy's apartment on the outskirts of town. The street lights had come on early, and the drizzle had increased to light rain. The windscreen wipers were doing their thing, and their squeak reminded Lizzy she needed to get new blades.

"This is it. Home sweet home." Lizzy pointed to the block of apartments on the left as she reversed into a small gap on the narrow street lined with cars. Four storeys high, and spanning half a block, the complex's only redeeming feature was the garden that ran between the brown brick walls and the footpath. "It's better on the inside," she said as she saw the look on Sal's face.

"I would hope so!" Sal raised her eyebrows. "A bit of a come down, Liz. "Are you going to live here once you're married?"

"For a while. It really is much better on the inside." Lizzy opened the car door and climbed out. She zipped her jacket and covered her head with its hood before grabbing Sal's bags out of the boot and directing her up the flight of stairs. Opening the door to the apartment, she held her breath as she waited for Sal's reaction.

"Wow, Liz! You weren't wrong! This really is nice!" Sal entered the living room and fell onto the new sofa Lizzy had picked up recently at a sale. "You always did have an eye for nice things."

"Thanks Sal." Lizzy's face expanded into a broad grin. "I'll just put these in your room and then make us a drink."

Lizzy placed Sal's bags in the spare room, and then busied herself making a cup of tea. She glanced at the clock. Daniel would be here any minute.

~

"LIZ! I know you told me he was good looking, but you didn't tell me how much!"

"Shh! He'll hear you!"

"Okay, I'll just sit here and drool."

"He is pretty cute, I have to agree." Lizzy laughed and glanced over to where Daniel was standing at the bar, and her heart warmed. Maybe she did love him after all.

"Here you go, my lovelies! Two shandies with flair!" Daniel placed the glasses on the table and winked at Sal.

"Daniel! You shouldn't do that! What will she think!" Lizzy said with a laugh in her voice.

"Oh, go on," he said in his best Irish accent. "I was just having a bit o' fun!"

"It's okay, Liz." Sal patted Lizzy's leg and then looked up, a warm smile on her face. "Thank you, kind sir."

"My pleasure." He bowed, and then took his seat beside Lizzy. He placed his arm around her shoulders, and pulled her close. She didn't resist, instead, she snuggled closer.

"Good of you to come up for the wedding, Sal," Daniel said. "Lizzy's told me a lot about you."

"Has she just?" Sal glanced at Lizzy with a glint of mischief in her eye. "And what exactly has she been saying?"

"Oh, only good things," Daniel replied.

"I'm pleased to hear that!" Sal said.

"And what has she told you about me?" Daniel raised his eyebrows.

Sal hesitated and stole a glance at Lizzy before replying. "Only good things!"

Both girls burst out in laughter at Sal's attempt to copy his accent. Lizzy sat up and smiled at Daniel. As their eyes met, a tingle of excitement ran through her body. Cheeky he might be, but he was also lovable. And he was going to be her husband.

"Come on you two! You'll have enough time for that tomorrow!" Sal said.

Lizzy turned her head and grinned at Sal. "Yes, you're right. Let's order, shall we?"

As Lizzy laughed and reminisced with Sal over dinner, her heart lightened and her anxiety over her forthcoming wedding lessened. For a while at least.

When she climbed into bed a few hours later, however, her active mind kept her awake. Did she really know what she was doing?

CHAPTER 2

Lizzy woke early from her restless sleep and peeked out the window. The sun was nowhere to be seen, just thick black cloud hovering in the sky, just like the cloud that hovered in her heart.

She propped her pillows behind her and sat up. She reached for her Bible, but could only stare at the cover. What if she read something she didn't want to hear? No, she couldn't risk that. Closing her eyes, Lizzy tried to pray, but instead, she drifted off to sleep.

She woke with a start when Sal placed a cup of tea on the dresser beside her bed some time later. Sal sat down and took her hand.

"Hey."

"Hey yourself." Lizzy looked at her friend and smiled warmly. The knot in her stomach she didn't know was there loosened. No need for words. They knew each other so well after all they'd been through. Her heart lifted knowing Sal was here to support her on this day. Lizzy wished she could talk honestly, but probably had no need. Sal knew.

"Come on, kiddo. We need to get you ready for your big day." Sal stood and opened the curtains. "I think that man of yours is champing at the bit to marry you."

Lizzy laughed at the thought. How many times had he suggested they run off and get married at Gretna Green? And how many times had she told him they were almost doing the same thing, anyway?

She straightened herself and sipped her tea. This was it. She would go ahead with the wedding, right or wrong. She lifted her head and her eyes met Sal's. "Okay, kiddo, let's get this show on the road."

THE HOUR or so she and Sal spent at the beauty salon having their hair and make-up done had been relaxing, but now they were back at the apartment, and the time had come to get ready.

"Do you want something to eat before we begin?" Sal called out as she put the kettle on. "I think I'll have a cup of tea and some toast."

"Mmm, maybe not." Lizzy rubbed her stomach. "I don't know I could eat anything."

Sal looked at her tenderly. "Are you sure you're okay?"

Lizzy paused for a moment and took a breath. "Yes, I'm fine. It's just hard to believe it's all happening." She smiled at Sal and reached for the cross hanging around her neck. "I'll go fetch my dress."

She'd chosen a simple dress to get married in. After all, it was a morning wedding at the Register Office. A full blown wedding gown would have been over the top.

"Come on, let me do that." Sal placed her tea and toast on the table and took over from Lizzy.

Maybe she could have done it herself, but Lizzy's hands were shaking, and she was having trouble doing up the little buttons on the front of the bodice. As she stood there while Sal battled with each tiny button, she was aware of the clock ticking. *Not much longer now...*

"There you go! Let me look at you." Sal stepped back and Lizzy turned around slowly. "Beautiful!"

"Thank you, Sal." Lizzy looked at herself in the mirror. Maybe she did look beautiful today. Well, almost. Beside Sal she often felt very plain, but today, with her hair done nicely and her make-up done properly, and wearing the dress the shop attendant had insisted suited her perfectly, maybe she did look beautiful.

The taxi arrived and Lizzy and Sal walked carefully down the stairs and climbed into the back seat. The rain that had been threatening still held off, and although the sky was still grey, small patches of blue were visible in the distance. Maybe the sun would beat its way through the clouds and shine down on this day after all. She could always hope.

"Are you nervous?" Sal asked as the taxi made its way along the streets towards the town centre.

Lizzy looked down at her hands before replying. "A little."

"I'm not surprised. It's not too late, you know." Tears formed in Lizzy's eyes at Sal's gentle, caring tone. Sal reached out and squeezed Lizzy's hand. "You don't have to go through with it, you know."

Lizzy looked out the window, forcing her tears to stop. It wouldn't do to turn up at her wedding with red eyes and mascara blackening her cheeks. She pulled a tissue out of her purse and dabbed her eyes.

With the flow of tears stopped, she took control of herself, and turned back and looked at Sal. "I'm okay. I know it's not what I wanted, but Daniel loves me, and I do love him. It's just last minute nerves, that's all."

"Okay then." Sal squeezed her hand again. "If ever you need to talk, you know where I am."

THE TAXI PULLED up outside the Guildhall. On a sunny day, the dark coloured sandstone building would have looked more appealing, but on this dreary winter's day, it looked cold and unwelcoming. A sudden gust of wind hit as they alighted from the cab. Lizzy shivered and pulled her coat tighter.

"This is a beautiful old building, Liz," Sal said as they entered the foyer. Looking around at the plush furnishings and artwork, Lizzy had to agree it was indeed a much nicer building inside than out.

Sal's gaze settled on Lizzy. She stepped closer and tucked a piece of hair that had been blown in the wind back into place. "Are you sure you're okay, Liz? Last chance."

Lizzy stood steadily and reached for Sal's hand. "Yes, I'm sure. Let's go find everyone."

They found the small room that had been allocated for the ceremony without any problem. Before they entered, Lizzy stopped and inhaled deeply. For a moment, she wanted a crystal ball. Was she doing the right thing? Was she really ready for this? Neither she nor anyone else had one, so she held her head high and entered the room with Sal beside her.

THE FIRST PERSON she saw was Daniel. Always the life of the party, today he was no different. The fears of her heart melted away when he winked at her. She looked into those cheeky blue eyes and saw the man who had swept her off her feet only months before.

She'd first laid eyes on him at his cousin Nessa's thirtieth birthday party. A fine autumn evening, Lizzy had been looking forward to getting out after being house bound with all her school work. Nessa had befriended her at church, and was keen for her to make some friends. This was the perfect opportunity, she'd said.

The party began with cocktails in Nessa's garden. Lizzy wore a long Indian type skirt and felt almost bohemian. She stood with Nessa, chatting to a couple of girls she'd just been introduced to, when Nessa called a dark haired young man over to join the group.

"Everyone, this is my cousin Daniel from Belfast. Daniel, this is Susan, Lizzy and Brianna."

"Pleasure to meet you lovely ladies." He bowed with a flourish, and then asked if he could get the girls a drink.

"Thanks, but I'm okay at the moment," Brianna replied. Lizzy just shook her head and laughed. She'd never heard such an intriguing accent before. She thought it suited him. He was far too attractive to just sound normal.

"How long have you been here?" Susan asked.

"Oh, going on two weeks now. Bonny place."

"You really think so?" Brianna asked. "I've always thought it was rather a boring backwater type town, myself."

"I guess it's what you compare it with. I think it's grand. There's the river, and the sea not far away, and the pubs. A lot of pubs." He cocked one eyebrow and grinned. "Are you girls from here?" He looked at each of the girls in turn, but his cheeky eyes caught Lizzy's and she was mesmerized by them for a fleeting second.

She let out a huge breath when Susan answered first, because it took her a moment or two to gather herself. Susan and Brianna had both replied, so now it was her turn. She didn't want to tell him she was from the south, but Lizzy figured he'd know as soon as she opened her mouth.

"Oh, we've got a posh one here." His eyes sparkled and then he winked at her.

"I'm not really." Lizzy lifted her chin to a haughty angle and glared at him. "My family might be, but I'm not. I'm just an ordinary person, doing an ordinary job."

"Posh **and** fiery! And what job might that be?"

"I'm a teacher." She looked him straight in the eye.

"That's a grand job. Teachers are the backbone of our society, don't you agree?" Susan and Brianna both nodded. They appeared to be fascinated by this gregarious, cheeky man, but it was Lizzy he was interested in, so it turned out. He took her arm when dinner was announced, and led her to a table where they dined together and engaged in friendly banter for the next hour or so.

When the music started, he led her to the floor, and literally swept her off her feet.

"You dance very well, Elizabeth," he whispered in her ear, causing her pulse to race. Being from a 'posh' family, she certainly knew how to dance, but she'd never danced like this before. What would Mother think if she could see her now? Casting that thought aside, Lizzy decided to enjoy the moment. Perhaps he was holding her just a little too close, but she didn't push him away.

Lizzy didn't know what he saw in her. She was plain, nowhere near as attractive as either Susan or Brianna, but he was taken with her, and she with him. Maybe her rebellious spirit had attracted him. Whatever it was, they spent the rest of the evening together, and when it came time to leave, he asked if he could see her again. She didn't hesitate. She was ready for this. *Maybe at last I can forget Mathew.*

"LIZZY! There you are! And what a treat for sore eyes, might I say!" Daniel strode towards her and was about to wrap his arms around her when his mate, Johnno, stepped between them.

"Uh, uh - none of that yet. Wait until you've tied the knot, man."

"Get outta here, Johnno. Can't I give my lady a peck on the cheek?"

"Wait until you're legally wed. It's bad luck if you kiss her beforehand."

"Says who?"

"Says me."

"Okay then. Well, let's get this show on the road, and then I can kiss her all I want - right?" He looked at Johnno, and then at Lizzy. "Lizzy, you ready?"

"Yes Daniel, let's do this." She smiled at him. How handsome he looked in his pin striped suit. He loved wearing nice clothes, but the suit made him look suave and sophisticated. A thrill of excitement ran through Lizzy's body at the thought of being alone with this man later in the day.

Only ten people were present, plus the officiating celebrant.

Daniel, Lizzy, Sal, Daniel's cousin Nessa and her husband Riley, Daniel's mate John, Lizzy's fellow teachers, Janine and Robert, and her friends from church, Colin and Linda. Colin had agreed to give her away.

"Colin, let's go." She hooked her arm in his as Daniel and Johnno took their places beside the celebrant. Sal led the way, and stood to the side when she reached the front. Lizzy walked the whole ten metres with her eyes glued on Daniel's. Colin's hand on hers helped to steady her pounding heart, and she tried not to think of anything apart from marrying Daniel, but in those fleeting moments, images of Mathew and her parents flitted through her mind. *Oh God, not now. I can't deal with it. Later. I promise. Later.*

Colin placed her arm in Daniel's when they reached the front, and gave her a reassuring squeeze before taking his place beside Linda. She heard very little of the ceremony. Like an out of body experience, happening to someone else. Not to Elizabeth Walton-Smythe of Wiveliscombe Manor in Taunton Deane.

The familiar words pulled her out of her trance, and back to the here and now. She'd heard the words many times before at the endless weddings of distant relatives she'd been forced to attend, but now it was her turn.

"Do you, Elizabeth Anne Walton-Smythe, take Daniel Rorey O'Connor to be your lawful husband, to have and to hold from this day forward, for better, for worse, for richer, for poorer, in sickness and health, until death do you part?"

She looked at Daniel and saw the sparkle in his eyes. She took a deep breath.

"I do."

DANIEL GOT his way at last, and kissed her long and hard in front of everyone. She felt her cheeks flush, and pushed him away gently. He stole one more brief kiss before he turned her around and pumped his arm in the air.

Someone wolf whistled. She thought it was Johnno, and then everyone clapped. She saw the smiles on Sal's and Nessa's faces. It was real. It had really happened. She was now Mrs Elizabeth O'Connor.

THE WEDDING BREAKFAST was a noisy occasion. Daniel was in his element, and Lizzy could tell he was happy. He kept hugging and kissing her, and whispering words in her ear that made her blush. She knew it wouldn't be long before he'd want to leave, but to be honest, she wasn't in that much of a hurry now the time had come.

Sal sat on the other side of her, looking stunning in her green suit. Lizzy reached out and squeezed her hand.

"I wish you could stay longer, Sal." Lizzy's eyes teared up a little, and she quickly wiped them away, hoping Sal hadn't noticed.

"Oh sweetie, we'll catch up again soon enough." Sal returned her squeeze and smiled tenderly, almost causing Lizzy's tears to break free.

"I wish I could have come up earlier. Such a bother, this work business!" Sal's laugh lightened the moment, and Lizzy breathed easier.

"I agree. At least we've got a week off now. We'll have to catch up again soon, Sal. I don't know I can bear not seeing you."

"Come on, Liz. You've got Daniel to keep you company now." Lizzy caught Sal's eyes, and in that instant, what she'd done hit her like a ton of bricks. She was now married, for better or for worse, to Daniel O'Connor.

CHAPTER 3

Daniel and Lizzy left soon after. Daniel had planned their honeymoon, and all he'd told her was not to bring much. That wasn't very helpful, so she'd packed for almost all possibilities, just in case. As it turned out, she really didn't need much at all, as they stayed in their hotel room most of the following week.

He was a skillful lover, tender and kind, and their first week together was bliss. Lizzy had never imagined that married life could be so wonderful. Her mother had never spoken to her about what happened behind closed doors. The limited information she had as they began their marriage had been gleaned from the odd magazine and hushed whispers amongst her circle of friends at University. Never in her wildest dreams had she thought she could be so close to another human being.

They ventured out once or twice to get some fresh air, but the chill wind of the north east coast soon drove them back inside into the warmth of each other's arms.

The week passed all too quickly, and before long they headed back into town to start their real life together.

Not once had she thought of Mathew.

"Come on Daniel, I'm going to be late!" Lizzy grabbed her coat off the hook and opened the door. "I'll go without you," she called out playfully.

"Coming! Just give me a minute."

She looked back inside and saw him tying his shoe laces. His hair was rumpled and his shirt still undone, and as he stood, the sight of his bare chest made her insides quiver. She almost forgot she was in a hurry.

"I'm sorry, Lizzy. I'll be right there." He raced into the bathroom and she soon heard water splashing, and thought with dread about the mess he was making. Living with a man was certainly different to sharing a flat with a girlfriend, but it did have its benefits. Her mind started to replay their lovemaking of the previous night whilst she stood at the door waiting for him. Daniel had completely won her over with his constant tenderness and eagerness to love her at any hour of the day or night. It was no wonder he slept in.

"Well come on then, what are you waiting for?" He snatched a quick kiss as he flew past her.

Lizzy locked the door and ran down the steps, catching him as he reached the car.

She threw him the keys.

"You'd better drive today. I might be a bit late finishing this afternoon."

They climbed into the car, and took off towards Hull Elementary. She looked at her watch. They might just make it. The traffic seemed to be getting worse every day, but maybe it was because they were late every day. She'd never been late to school when she was single, but now, most mornings the bell was ringing as she jumped out of the car and sprinted to her classroom in an effort to beat the children.

Lizzy's preparation was suffering. How long would it be before she was spoken to about it? She muddled her way through each day, but she wasn't doing the best she could. Now Kids' Club was starting up again. Why had she agreed to it? Lizzy raced, yet again, into the classroom just ahead of the children.

"Good morning class." Lizzy stood with her hands on her hips, taking a number of slow, deep breaths, and surveyed the class of eight year olds standing before her.

"Good morning Mrs O'Connor." Her heart jumped as she once again heard the name. Still not used to it, every time Lizzy heard it, she thought of Daniel. A mental image of him pushing a trolley at the hospital flitted through her mind. It was the perfect job for him. He lit up anxious people's lives every day with his wit and humour, and he could whistle and sing as much as he wanted. The faintest of smiles played on her lips at the thought.

"Take a seat, class." She opened the folder on her desk and glanced inside. Normally she would have asked them to sit quietly, but this morning she let them talk amongst themselves for a few moments while she planned the day.

Daniel arrived before Kids' Club had wrapped up. He leaned on the door frame of the activities room as she sat in front of the children, strumming her guitar whilst they sang a song she'd just taught them. His arms were folded, and the twinkle in his eyes suggested he was enjoying himself.

The children gave her a strange look when she stumbled over some words and played the wrong chord. *Drat him for having this effect on me.* She tried to concentrate on the job at hand, all the while aware of him taunting her from the back of the room.

At the end of the song, the children turned around when they heard clapping. Lizzy shook her head as he came closer.

"That was lovely, children, and Mrs O'Connor."

She knocked the music stand over in her hurry to get up. "Children," Lizzy sighed and straightened her skirt. "this is Mr O'Connor. Say good afternoon."

"Good afternoon, Mr O'Connor," they all said in a sing song chant.

"And good afternoon to you, too," he replied in a similar fashion, making the children laugh.

"What are you doing?" she whispered sharply.

"Just thought I'd come and meet some of your little protegees. That's alright, isn't it?"

"Not really." She turned her back so the children couldn't hear. "Best if you wait outside in the car. We're finishing up now." She leaned closer. "I could get into trouble with you here."

"Okay, I'll go. Don't stress your pretty little head. Bye children. Nice to meet you." He waved as he walked back the way he came.

"Nice to meet you, too," they all called out.

"Miss, he sounds funny," a little blond haired girl said after he'd gone. They all laughed again.

"He's Irish, that's why," Lizzy said, quickly tidying up and dismissing the children.

The parents were all waiting outside, and once the children were handed over safely, Lizzy headed for the car. She'd calmed down a little by the time she reached it, but she still gave Daniel a good talking to.

"You just can't do that. You can't walk into a classroom full of children and take over." She folded her arms and glared at him.

"There there, Lizzy. I'm sorry. I just couldn't help it. I heard your sweet voice and the guitar music and it drew me in. I won't do it again, I promise." The twinkle in his eyes got her again. How did he manage it? Every time they had a disagreement, he'd sweet talk her and apologise; she'd forgive him, and then she'd end up in his arms.

It was hard to be angry with Daniel O'Connor for long.

THE FOLLOWING DAY, two things happened that rocked their almost perfect world.

CHAPTER 4

Lizzy had just stepped into the shower when she heard the phone ring.

"Daniel, can you get that?"

"Sure, sweetie."

When he appeared in front of her several moments later with a startled look on his face, she wondered what had happened.

"You'd better get out. It's your mother."

Lizzy's mouth fell open and her body stiffened. They stared at each other for a moment. How could she have been so stupid? Her mother often called on a Friday morning.

"What am I going to say?"

He shrugged and shook his head. For once he had no words.

"You're a great help." She walked past him and picked up the receiver, taking a deep breath before speaking.

"Mother, how are you?"

"I'm fine thanks. How are you, Elizabeth?"

"Fine."

Her mother wasted no time.

"What's he doing there this time of the morning? I'm surprised at you, Elizabeth. We brought you up better than that."

"It's not what you think, mother."

"I thought we'd made it clear he was no good for you. Your father and I hoped we'd seen the last of him."

"No Mother. We're still together."

"I have to say I'm disappointed, Elizabeth." What was new? She always seemed to disappoint her parents.

"I'm sorry to let you down, Mother."

"Very well then. I was calling to say that your father and I would like to see you next Saturday on our way to Edinburgh. Maybe we could have luncheon together."

Lizzy paused before she answered, her mind racing as she digested this request. "It would be nice to see you, Mother. But Daniel will need to come. I hope you'll be okay with that."

"No, Elizabeth. Please don't bring him. You know what your father would be like. We'd much rather have luncheon just with you."

"Well, I'm sorry, Mother, but I won't come without him."

She heard her mother sigh on the other end of the line. Silence hung in the air between them. Lizzy pressed her hand hard against her chest and felt for her cross.

"If that's the way it has to be, I guess we'll just have to tolerate him." Lizzy rolled her eyes and looked at Daniel.

"Thank you, Mother. Do you have anywhere in mind?"

"You choose. But make sure it's a reputable place, will you?"

"Yes, Mother. I'll find somewhere suitable."

And with that, she ended the call. Lizzy held the receiver in her hand for a moment before replacing it. It had to happen eventually, but she'd successfully avoided having to tell her parents the truth for three whole months. There was no escaping it any longer.

Daniel stood and stared at her, his eyes wider than normal.

"What did she say?"

"Lunch next Saturday. They're going to stop in on their way up north."

"And what did she say about me?"

Lizzy hesitated. How could she repeat her mother's words to Daniel? Why did her parents always consider themselves to be above everyone else? What right did they have?

"She said it would be alright."

"That's a lie, Lizzy, I can tell. What did she say?"

Lizzy grimaced and took a deep breath. She'd have to tell him.

"She said they'll tolerate you being there."

"Tolerate! Who do they think they are? I've a good mind to give them some of their own back."

"Oh Daniel. Don't be like that." She reached out to him, but he pushed her away. "You know what they're like. We've just got to be better than that and not let them get to us." She reached out again, but this time he backed away. "We're going to have to tell them. We can't put it off any longer."

He turned and thumped his hand against the wall.

"God help me, Elizabeth. I'm going to need patience."

Lizzy needed to sit down. She felt faint. The last time she'd seen Daniel like this was the day they'd stormed out of her parent's place at Christmastime. Her heart fell as she recalled that moment.

It wasn't as if he'd done anything wrong. Her mother and father, particularly her father, were snobs. How they professed to be Christians was beyond her.

They were an intimidating couple at the best of times. She thought Daniel had handled himself very well, but they'd obviously thought differently.

"He's just an uncouth Irishman, Elizabeth," her father had said as they stood in the morning room where she'd been summoned half an hour earlier. "I don't know why you're wasting your time with him." She held her hands together to stop them from shaking. His cold eyes were fixed on hers and he looked her up and down before continuing.

"For God's sake, Elizabeth, we've brought you up better than this. Find yourself a real man for once." Roger threw his hands up in despair. "First you gallivant around with a Theology Student and now you degrade yourself with this, this…." He turned and looked at her mother, who'd been standing there allowing him to continue with his tirade. Lizzy was disgusted.

"You deal with her, Gwyneth. I can't handle this ludicrous nonsense."

Lizzy glared at her mother and dared her to continue.

"It's not that we don't like him, Elizabeth. It's just that we think you can do much better for yourself. Don't we, dear?" Her mother's subservience to her father angered her so much.

Lizzy breathed deeply and tried to control herself. How dare they talk about Daniel like that. She shook her head in disgust and turned away.

"He's not welcome here, Elizabeth," her father said sternly. "Don't bring him back."

"Don't worry. I won't." She strode across the room and slammed the door behind her.

Despite her outward bravado, her hands shook and she burst into tears as she fled for the sanctity of the garden, which was where Daniel found her.

"What's wrong with you, sweet girl?" She'd turned her head so he couldn't see her face, but he sat beside her on the garden bench and made her look at him. More tears fell and he wrapped her in his arms.

Lizzy sobbed into his chest, unable to speak. She didn't want to tell him about the confrontation she'd just had with her parents. They could be so horrible. What wasn't there to like about Daniel O'Connor? He was funny and outgoing. He was friendly and courteous. He might have drunk a little too much at dinner, but she put that down to nerves. Who wouldn't be nervous meeting Roger and Gwyneth Walton-Smythe?

Her sobbing eventually eased, and she lifted her head. Daniel handed her a handkerchief and she dried her tears before facing him. She studied his dark curly hair and his crystal blue eyes. Why did her parents have to ruin everything? She reached out and gently caressed his face with the back of her hand.

"We've got to leave, Daniel."

"Why? What's happened?" The concern in Daniel's eyes warmed her heart.

She felt for the cross hanging around her neck.

"I've just had words with Mother and Father."

He tilted his head and narrowed his eyes.

"What about?"

She shook her head. How could she tell him?

"No, I don't want to repeat it, Daniel. Let's just go."

Lizzy gritted her teeth and dug her fingernails into the palms of her hands. Their eyes locked together for what seemed an eternity.

"Was it about me?" Daniel finally asked.

Lizzy lowered her eyes and nodded. Tears began to well up again, and one after the other rolled down her cheek.

"What did they say, Lizzy?"

She sniffed, and wiped her face before slowly lifting her head. She couldn't speak.

Daniel's eyes had darkened, and his brow was furrowed. Lizzy's heart thumped in her chest. What would his reaction be if she told him? She couldn't imagine him accepting it happily. Who would? Maybe she should just tell him. Get it out in the open. It said more about her parents than anything else, although it would still be hurtful.

"Lizzy?" Daniel tilted his head.

She breathed in deeply and swallowed. *Oh God, please help me.* "They said I'm not to bring you back here."

Daniel leaned back and placed his hands on his thighs. His face darkened and his whole body tensed. Lizzy waited for the explosion.

"The two faced hypocrites. Who do they think they are! I've been nothing but nice to them. If they didn't like me, they should have told me to my face, not via you. I've a good mind to have it out with them." He jumped up and pummelled his fist into his other hand. A vein in his forehead pulsed.

She pulled on his arm.

"No Daniel. Let's just go. It would only make it worse if you saw them." She paused, hoping he'd see sense and calm down. She could only imagine the scene that would erupt if he confronted them.

Her eyes pleaded with him. "Please Daniel. Please."

Daniel's breathing calmed a little, but she didn't like the steely look on his face.

She placed herself in front of him and grabbed both his hands. Her heart thumped as she looked into his eyes.

"Daniel, I won't be coming back either. Let's go."

Lizzy exhaled slowly as she felt the tension in his body fall away. He pulled her close and wrapped his arms around her. She rested her head against his chest. Did she really mean what she'd just said? Could she choose Daniel over her parents? At this moment, yes, she could. Daniel loved her. She felt safe wrapped in his arms. Her father had never hugged her or made her feel loved. To him, she was just someone to control, to manipulate. Not the precious daughter she longed to be. No, she'd choose Daniel any day.

They held hands as they re-entered the house to collect their belongings. If she'd seen either of her parents, Lizzy would have turned away from them, but they were nowhere to be seen.

Taking one last look at the home she'd grown up in as they drove back down the driveway, Lizzy turned to Daniel and smiled, willing her tears to disappear.

Just outside the gates of Wiveliscombe Manor, Daniel stopped the car and took her hands in his.

She looked at him with puzzled eyes. "What are we doing, Daniel?"

"Shh." He lifted his right hand and slid a finger along her chin and traced her face slowly, all the way to the corner of her eye. The touch of his finger made her weak.

"Lizzy, I love you. I feel very honoured you chose me over your parents. I hope you won't regret it."

Lizzy shook her head slowly, captivated by his mesmerizing eyes.

"From the moment I saw you at Nessa's party, I knew you were the one for me. I know your parents don't think I'm good enough for you, but Lizzy, I love you, and I want to marry you." He squeezed her hand gently as he took a deep breath. "Lizzy, will you marry me?"

Lizzy's mouth fell open and her hand flew to her chest.

"Oh Daniel. Do you really mean it? Are you really sure?" She could hardly speak.

"Sure as I could be about anything."

She gazed into his eyes. Was this really happening? Did she love him enough to marry him? Could she say yes, knowing her parents would have nothing more to do with them? Knowing his relationship with God was doubtful? But he loved her, and he'd made her forget Mathew. If she said no, what would happen? Would he leave her? If he did, she'd be beyond despair. Her mind was made up.

"Yes Daniel. I'll marry you."

~

LIZZY PULLED her towel tighter and looked up at Daniel, her eyes pleading with him to calm down.

"It had to happen sometime, Daniel. We knew that. We couldn't hide it forever." Her gaze lowered to her wedding ring. What would they say?

Daniel pulled her up and wrapped her in his arms.

"I'm sorry, sweet girl," he whispered as he kissed her neck. "We'll get through this."

It was going to be a long week, but at least they had each other.

THE OTHER EVENT was much happier. Unbeknown to Daniel, Lizzy had booked a doctor's appointment for that afternoon. She'd told him she'd be a little late as she had a few errands to do, and that she'd make her own way home.

She had her suspicions. She'd been sick just about every morning for the past two weeks, although she'd tried to hide it from Daniel.

Lizzy poured herself a second glass of water while she waited in the doctor's surgery. She couldn't sit still for long. Why did doctors always run late? Finally it was her turn. Dr Richardson poked her head in the door and looked around at the waiting patients.

"Elizabeth O'Connor?"

Lizzy nodded and stood, and followed the doctor into her consulting room. She took a seat, and clutched her hands together.

The doctor gazed at Lizzy over the top of her glasses. "Well, young lady, your test has come back positive. You're going to be a mother. Congratulations!"

Lizzy's hand flew to her chest. She couldn't believe it. She was expecting!

"I hope your husband will be pleased," the doctor said.

"Oh yes, I'm sure he will be. I'll go home and tell him straight away. How far am I?"

"Eight weeks. And everything looks fine, but you need to come back for a check-up in two weeks' time."

LIZZY WALKED on air as she left the surgery. Surely this news would make it easier with her parents. It couldn't have happened at a better time. She thanked God for this miracle on her way home, and apologized for neglecting Him of late.

She couldn't wait to tell Daniel the news. He'd be so excited. She stopped at Tesco on her way home and picked out a nice piece of meat to cook for dinner to celebrate. She pictured it in her mind. Some pretty flowers picked from the garden in front of the apartment block to brighten their table, and a candle or two lit to create a romantic atmosphere. Quiet music playing in the background. She'd hold his hand, look into his eyes, and tell him he was going to be a father. His eyes would twinkle, and he'd wrap her in his arms and kiss her passionately. *He doesn't need an excuse to do that.* She giggled as she walked to the bus stop.

The bus ride home was uncomfortable. Friday afternoon rush hour, and there was no spare seat. If only the people around her knew she was a mother-to-be maybe she would have been offered one, but it was early days, and it definitely wasn't obvious yet to anyone apart from herself. And she really didn't need a seat. She was young, fit and healthy, but the smell of body odour from the man in front of her made her feel nauseous. She didn't want to make a spectacle of herself, so she peered out the window as best she could to take her mind off it.

The day had certainly thrown up some surprises. Whilst she'd been almost certain the doctor would officially announce her pregnant, the news that her parents were visiting next Saturday was a shock. She'd played the scene over in her mind a hundred times or more already, but she still didn't know how she would tell them their daughter had run off and married the man they'd evicted from their home only months before, and that they were also going to be grandparents.

THE GARDENERS HAD BEEN BUSY, and the array of spring blooms adorning the footpath was enough to brighten anyone's day. Lizzy checked to make sure no-one was watching, and quickly picked a few brightly coloured geraniums and petunias before heading upstairs to the apartment. She hoped Daniel had stopped for a pint on the way home, as she wanted to have everything ready before he arrived. She wanted it to be perfect.

The apartment was quiet when she entered a few seconds later. It didn't take her long to unpack the groceries and put the meat in the oven. Walking into her bedroom to change out of her work clothes, she thought about what she should wear. Maybe the long Indian skirt she'd worn the night they met? Or perhaps the low cut summer shift she'd bought recently but hadn't worn yet. She decided on the shift. Maybe she'd even wear a little make-up. Yes, some blusher, mascara and lipstick. Not bad, Lizzy thought, as she stepped away from the mirror to get a better look. *Should I put my hair up?* She twisted it into a messy bun and secured it with a clip. *Yes, that's better.* She ran her fingers over her neck and down her chest, and closed her eyes, imagining they were Daniel's hands caressing her. She sighed in anticipation.

The smell of roast meat cooking suddenly hit her and brought her back to reality. She just made it to the toilet in time, and promptly brought up the whole contents of her day's food intake. She'd heard about morning sickness, but this wasn't morning. She never knew it would be like this.

Lizzy cleaned herself up, and headed back to the kitchen with a little less enthusiasm for cooking than before. Nevertheless, she still had important news to impart to Daniel, and so she set about preparing the vegetables and the table in readiness for his imminent arrival.

Everything was almost ready. She checked the clock. He should be home any minute. One last glance in the mirror. Yes, she still looked okay. A little pale maybe, but still more attractive than normal.

She put on her favourite music, the one they often made love to. She thought with a giggle that they might not even make it to the table. She glanced at the clock again and checked the meat and vegetables. Very nicely cooked. Maybe she should cut the meat and have it completely ready. It wasn't a job she liked, but she thought she could do it this time. Lizzy put her apron back on and carefully took the meat out of the oven and placed it onto the cutting tray. She attempted to control her breathing as another wave of nausea hit her. There was nothing left to bring up, or so she thought. Once again, she just made it, but this time she just heaved liquid into the toilet bowl. She almost cried. *When will Daniel be home?*

THE KEY in the door woke her, and she pulled herself up with a start. Lizzy didn't know what time it was, but she knew it was late. She'd turned the lights off hours before, and she must have fallen asleep in front of the television. She touched her eyes and knew they were puffy without even looking at them. Her hair had fallen out of its bun, and hung loose around her shoulders.

And then she remembered. Daniel hadn't come home for dinner.

She peered at him through the semi-darkness. He was trying to take his boots off. He was struggling, but she didn't get up to help. He was drunk. Tears rolled down her cheeks. Their perfect evening had been ruined.

He staggered towards the couch, and stopped suddenly when he caught sight of her.

"Lizzy." His whole body swayed. "You startled me, girl. What are you doing up?" He lurched forward and almost fell on top of her. She quickly moved out of the way before he landed on the couch beside her.

He was a mess. She recoiled from the smell of cigarette smoke and alcohol that oozed from his body. Lizzy had never seen him like this before. In fact, she'd never in her whole life been this close to an intoxicated person. She didn't like what she saw. This wasn't the Daniel she knew and had fallen in love with. She swallowed hard and fought back her tears.

"Where have you been, Daniel?" Lizzy narrowed her eyes and breathed heavily.

"Just havin' a few drinks wit the boys." He reached out for her arm, but she pulled away.

"I think you've had more than a few. And you can leave me alone, thank you very much."

"Oh Lizzy. I love you when you're angry." His eyes closed momentarily but then opened with a start. "I won ten quid."

"Well that's nice. On what, may I ask?"

"I beat the boys at pool. Ya shoulda seen me….." His eyes closed again.

She thought he'd fallen asleep, and she inched herself away from him. She'd almost made it, when he grabbed her and pulled her on top of him.

"Not so fast, Mrs O'Connor." His breath on her face made her queasy. "You haven't finished for the night. Come 'ere an give yur ole man some love." Lizzy recoiled as he fondled her breasts and tried to undress her. She resisted as much as she could, but he was strong. Stronger than normal. Maybe it was the drink. She succumbed and gave him what he wanted. But her heart and body were numb.

CHAPTER 5

During Lizzy's disturbed night, images of Mathew floated through her mind, and she didn't stop them. In fact, she relished them. Somehow they helped that horrid night to pass. Mathew would never have come home drunk. He didn't drink.

Lizzy allowed herself to relive the week she'd spent at his home in Portsmouth, almost three years ago.

HAVING COUNTED the days until she could see him again, Lizzy's heart burst with anticipation and excitement as the day finally came, and she drove the hundred or so miles from her family home in Taunton, where she'd spent most of the summer break, to Portsmouth, where his mother lived.

She tried to calm the butterflies in her stomach as she parked her car in front of his home, a semi-detached, less than ten paces wide, three streets from the harbour. For a few moments, Lizzy sat and studied the house, pulling herself together before she climbed out of the car and walked to the front gate. A whiff of fresh paint suggested that Mrs Carter, *Hilary,* had been doing some last minute preparations for her visit.

Taking a deep breath, Lizzy straightened her skirt and rang the bell. Her eyes lit up as Mathew opened the door. They gazed at each other for a moment, and then he smiled and hugged her. All the tension in Lizzy's body floated away as she hugged him back.

"So good to see you, Lizzy." His eyes sparkled and Lizzy's heart warmed. "Come on in. Mum's waiting to meet you."

He took her hand and she followed him into the tiniest kitchen she'd ever seen, well, apart from the one in her bed-sit accommodation at college, but that didn't count. And there she was. The mother she'd heard so much about. The mother who'd raised her two boys alone after their father had died in a traffic accident years ago. The mother who'd brought them up in the ways of the Lord and encouraged them both to go to Bible College to study for the ministry.

Hilary Carter greeted her with a warm kiss, and directed her to the table.

Lizzy relaxed and smiled at her. She took a seat beside Mathew, and reached for his hand, her heart beating faster as their hands joined. Hilary offered her tea and freshly cooked scones, and asked how her trip had been. Lizzy could see where Mathew's temperament had come from. A dainty, quiet, and particular lady, but also serious and perceptive. Lizzy felt scrutinized.

"How long have you lived here, Mrs Carter? It's a lovely home." Lizzy's heart fluttered as Mathew squeezed her hand.

"Since my wedding day. Thirty-three years next month," Mrs Carter replied wistfully, glancing at the photo taking pride of place on the wall directly opposite the kitchen.

"Let me show you to your room, dear."

Lizzy followed her up the stairs, with Mathew trailing behind. The room was tiny, *and so close to Mathew's*. She sighed in frustration. It wouldn't be a problem. They rarely got any further than holding hands.

The week passed all too quickly. Every morning they ate their breakfast at the small round kitchen table. No radio. No television. No children. Occasionally she caught Mathew's eyes, and her heart exploded with love for him. Sometimes their legs touched under the table, but she was unaware of his mother noticing any of this.

They spent the week wandering around the harbour, discovering hidden coves and all sorts of remnants left over from the war. They read, talked, played games, and occasionally watched television.

But it was the memory of their last night together that brought tears to her eyes.

"Come on Lizzy, let's go for a walk." Mathew stood suddenly and grabbed her hand after dinner that night. She looked at him quizzically, and jumped up and followed him to the door. "Won't be long, Mum," he called out to Hilary in the back of the house.

"This is unexpected, but nice!" Lizzy snuggled closer as they strolled arm in arm along the street. The night air carried a slight chill, a wonderful excuse to cling to him.

They reached the park running along the water within minutes. The Gosport ferry's horn blasted into the night air not far away. Such a busy harbour. The old street lamps shed just enough light on the pathway, and cast strange shadows either side. Lizzy thought they'd head towards the main harbour area, but Mathew led her the other way along a path meandering through garden beds filled with perfumed roses and summer annuals. The heady smell assaulted her senses and made her think how nice it would be if he would only stop and kiss her. As she snuggled closer, his arm tightened around her and she breathed in his manly scent. Drawn by the mesmerizing sound of splashing water, they strolled towards the central fountain.

Taking a seat near the fountain, Mathew placed his arm around Lizzy and she rested her head on his shoulder.

"I know this week's been difficult for you, Lizzy." Mathew reached out and gently lifted her face. His lips were so close she could taste his sweet breath. Her heart pounded.

"I'm going to miss you, Elizabeth Smythe." His sparkling eyes looked deeply into hers as he traced her face with the tip of his finger. Her heart beat even faster as he lowered his head and brushed his lips against hers.

"Lizzy," he whispered as he held her face in his hands and kissed her gently.

If only this moment would last forever.

SUNLIGHT FILTERING through the flimsy curtains woke Lizzy the following morning. She opened her eyes just enough to see Daniel sleeping beside her, and then curled her body into the fetal position and squeezed her eyes closed again.

Their honeymoon was over.

Tears rolled down her cheeks onto her pillow. *Drat you, Mathew. Why did you break it off?* Daniel grunted and rolled over. Lizzy turned her head and looked at him. If only it was Mathew lying there instead of Daniel. More tears trickled down her cheek. She wiped them away. But it wasn't Mathew she'd married. It was Daniel. A sudden wave of nausea hit her and she threw off the bed covers and raced for the bathroom. For a moment she'd forgotten she was pregnant.

WHEN LIZZY RETURNED to the bedroom, Daniel was leaning against the pillows. Considering the state he'd been in when he arrived home, she was surprised he didn't look worse. His hair was rumpled, and his eyes were bleary, but other than that, he didn't look much different to any other morning.

Lizzy stood in the doorway with arms folded, and glared at him.

"Well?" She broke the silence.

"I'm sorry Liz. I only meant to have a couple. I just got carried away." He tilted his head and reached his arms out. "Come and give me a cuddle."

Still upset, she wasn't prepared to forgive him that quickly.

"Was it the phone call that did it?" Lizzy's eyes narrowed.

He shrugged and breathed deeply, shaking his head.

"I don't know, Liz." He looked at her with puppy dog eyes. "Come here, sweet girl. I'm sorry."

Lizzy pursed her lips and sighed before climbing back into bed with him. He wrapped her in his arms and kissed her neck. He lifted his face and looked her in the eye. "I really am sorry, Elizabeth. Will you forgive me?"

He looked sincere. Maybe she could forgive and forget this one time. She nodded and snuggled in close, but chastised herself for letting him off so lightly.

As they lay satisfied in each other's arms a little later, Lizzy sat suddenly and wrapped the covers around her.

"Daniel. I need to tell you something."

"What is it, sweetie?" He sat up and looked at her with concern in his eyes. "Are you okay?"

Lizzy looked into his eyes and nodded, her face alight. "I've just been a little sick in the mornings. You might have noticed?"

He shook his head, but then his eyes widened.

"You're not…?"

She nodded her head and grinned, but she was unsure of his reaction.

"God be with us! I'm going to be a father! Come here you little beauty. Oh you precious thing." As she rested her head on his shoulder, tears welled in her eyes. *Perhaps if I'd told him last night, he wouldn't have been so rough...*

Lizzy watched in amazement as Daniel ran around and did everything. He made her rest while he cleaned the apartment. He made her cups of tea, and he even made dinner. Well, he didn't actually make it. He re-heated the dinner she'd cooked the previous evening. She lay on the couch reading a magazine, watching him out of the corner of her eye buzz around like an excited child. It was a strange but pleasant sight, and love for him smouldered and took root in her heart.

What a difference the news of their impending parenthood had made. At least for now, her parent's visit had faded into the background.

"I'll be able to teach him to ride a bike! I can take him fishing. I'll be able to play football with him. Oh, Lizzy, this is the best news yet!" It went on like that for the whole weekend.

THEN MONDAY CAME. Most days, Daniel dropped Lizzy at work and picked her up in the afternoon. She always had plenty to do in the classroom, and so was never too worried if he was a few minutes late. That Monday afternoon, she glanced at the clock and expected him to be there at any minute. She wanted to finish her planning for the next day, so she focused on what she was doing, trying to get it done before he arrived. The next time she looked at the clock, another hour had passed.

Lizzy stood and looked out the window. Neither Daniel nor the car were in sight. She packed up anyway. As she walked the short distance to the car park, she shivered and put on her jacket. Taking a seat on the brick retaining wall surrounding the car park, Lizzy checked her watch and looked out onto the road. All of a sudden her hands felt clammy. *What if he's had an accident?*

She stood and ran closer to the road. The cars were almost at a stand-still in the rush hour traffic. Lizzy peered both ways. He usually came from the left, but the white Ford Escort wasn't amongst the cars trundling along in either direction. Maybe she should call the hospital? The phone box was just over the road. She took a deep breath to calm herself down. Just about to cross the road, her hand flew to her chest and she breathed a sigh of relief as the Escort came into sight.

"I'm sorry, sweetie, I lost track of time." Daniel reached over and opened the door for her.

Lizzy climbed in and looked at him. "You've been drinking." The relief she'd felt a moment earlier instantly disappeared.

He feigned a sad look and his cheeky eyes almost made her forget how annoyed she was. But it didn't work. Lizzy shook her head and narrowed her eyes. The memory of him coming home drunk just the other night was too fresh in her mind to allow her to forget that easily.

"The boys shouted me a few when they found out I was going to be a dad. That's all. Don't be angry, Lizzy love." He reached out and squeezed her leg.

"You'd better let me drive." She climbed out and strode around to the driver's side and opened the door. "Come on, Daniel… You're not driving like that. Get out."

"I do love you when you're angry, Lizzy." He planted a wet kiss on her cheek as he brushed past her.

She shook her head and climbed into the driver's seat. She was tempted to drive off without him. Her hands clenched the steering wheel as she entered the long line of traffic. She shot him a glance and gripped the wheel tighter. "I hope this isn't going to happen every day, Daniel."

He reached out his hand and placed it on her leg. "No Lizzy. It was just a one-off. I won't do it again." He squeezed her leg. She glanced at him again. The cheeky grin on his face made her think she was married to a naughty child.

CHAPTER 6

Only it did happen every day. Lizzy grew angrier as Daniel returned later and later as the week progressed. The prospect of her parent's visit weighed heavily on her mind, and she guessed it weighed on Daniel's as well. Talking about it was impossible given his state of inebriation every night, and every morning they were in a hurry, and so it never happened.

Six pm Friday evening, she gave up waiting and called a taxi.

Home alone, Lizzy heated a can of spaghetti for dinner. She didn't feel like anything at all, but she had to eat something for the sake of the baby. She took her plate and sat on the couch, put her feet up and flicked on the television. A tear rolled down her cheek as she stared at the screen.

How could she sit with her parents in the restaurant of the Grand Hotel tomorrow lunchtime, and convince them she'd made the right decision, when she herself was not convinced? Would Daniel even turn up? She grabbed a tissue and blew her nose. Maybe it'd be for the best if he didn't come. That way, she could put off telling them.

She put her bowl of hardly touched spaghetti on the side table and then slumped against the cushions. Was that a coward's way out? Probably. But right then, she didn't care.

DANIEL SAT AT THE BAR, cigarette in one hand, a pint in the other. He'd lost count of how many he'd had, and now he didn't care. At one stage, Johnno had encouraged him to go home, but Daniel shook his head and told him he couldn't do it.

"I can't go, Johnny, I just can't. I'm no good for her…" His voice was slurred and his eyes had glazed over. Hunched over his drink, he almost fell off the stool.

"Come over here, then." He looked up as Johnno helped him off the stool and into an alcove.

"What will you tell her?"

Daniel pulled out another cigarette but struggled with his lighter.

"Here, let me help."

Daniel leaned forward and allowed Johnno to light it for him before taking a long drag.

"Dunno mate. But she'll probably throw me out."

LIZZY HARDLY SLEPT, drifting in and out of conscious thought and desperate pleas to God. Her anger grew. Anger with herself. With Daniel. With her parents. The very thought of her parents caused heart palpitations. She didn't want to see them.

Sleep must have come at some stage, as daylight peeping through the curtains woke her. Pulling herself up, she looked around. No sign of Daniel. It was cold and empty without him. Where was he? Where had he slept? Was he okay?

She picked up her spaghetti bowl and placed it in the sink. As she stood gazing out the window, she caressed the small baby bump that had recently appeared and breathed in slowly.

The colourful spring blooms in the garden below caught her eye. Her mother's garden would be in full bloom right now. The garden she loved playing in as a child. Her mother's pride and joy - an award winning garden overflowing with colour and design. A young girl in hot pink lycra jogged past, catching her attention. An elderly couple out for a morning stroll with their equally old overweight labrador made her smile.

Then her gaze was drawn to the spot where hers and Daniel's Ford Escort was normally parked. The spot was empty. She closed her eyes and gripped the bench. *God, I need you today. I know I don't deserve your help, but please help me.*

She turned around and walked to the shower.

LIZZY WAS RELIEVED that Daniel hadn't returned before she left. It made it easier. She dressed herself in a skirt and blouse her parents would approve of, rather than the hippy type clothes they abhorred but she preferred. The little baby bump was hidden, and she hoped she'd put on enough make-up to complete the facade. She glanced at herself in the full length mirror in her bedroom, and was pleased with the transition from Lizzy O'Connor to Elizabeth Walton-Smythe. Before she left, she removed her wedding ring and placed it on her dresser.

She checked her watch and called a taxi. Her heart pounded as it pulled up outside the Grand Hotel. She paid the taxi driver, climbed out, and stood on the pavement. How she wished she was anywhere but here at this very moment. But she had no choice, so she steeled herself and walked towards the entrance of the hotel where she'd agreed to meet them at midday.

. . .

IT TOOK a moment for her eyes to adjust to the dim lighting inside, but it didn't take her long to find Roger and Gwyneth Walton-Smythe. Seated in overstuffed arm chairs that looked like they'd been there since the hotel opened two hundred years before, her mother's back was rod straight as always, and her father looked every inch the country gentleman in his tweed jacket and highly polished brown leather slip-ons.

She tightened her grip on her handbag and clenched her teeth before stepping forward to join them.

"Mother, Father." She stood before them, her eyes steady and her face expressionless.

"Elizabeth. There you are!" Gwyneth Walton-Smythe stood and smiled warmly at her daughter. She held out her hands. Lizzy took them and then leaned forward, placing a kiss on her mother's cheek.

Her father had also risen. Lizzy, aware of his eyes on her, turned and looked at him. "Good afternoon, Father."

"Good afternoon, Elizabeth." He nodded at her, but with no welcoming arms, she merely returned his nod.

"I see you're on your own," her mother said. "We had expected to see Daniel with you, from what you said on the telephone."

"Daniel couldn't make it. He sends his apologies."

"That's very good news, Elizabeth. I have no desire ever to see that young man again," her father said. "Let's find our table, shall we?"

He called a waiter, who led them to their table in the restaurant. It was all so formal. Daniel would have been out of his comfort zone here. Just as well he hadn't come. The waiter removed the fourth place setting, and took their orders.

The silence was uncomfortable. It had been over four months since 'that' day. Their telephone conversations during that time had been civil, but now face to face, Lizzy was tempted to speak her mind. But no. She had to maintain the facade for now. It also wouldn't be proper to make a scene here.

"What are you going to Edinburgh for?" she asked instead.

"Your father has some business dealings to attend to, and I thought I would go along for the trip," her mother replied. "It's been a long time since we visited Edinburgh, or been away together, for that matter. We're looking forward to it, aren't we, Roger?" Gwyneth reached out and touched Roger's arm lightly, her eyes seeking his.

Lizzy tilted her head, slightly puzzled. What had she seen in her mother's eyes? Could it be longing?

"Yes. It's a lovely old city, Edinburgh." Roger sipped his wine and looked Lizzy in the eye. "And you, Elizabeth. What are you doing with your life? I believe you're still cohorting with that good for nothing Irishman?"

His eye was cold and piercing, but Lizzy held it for as long as she could. "Yes, Father, Daniel and I are still seeing each other. I'm old enough to make my own decisions as to who I see and associate with. If I choose to 'cohort' with Daniel, you will just have to accept that." Her heart pounded in her chest, and she couldn't believe she'd just said that, but it gave her strength to continue.

"You're wasting your life with him, Elizabeth. You could have done so well for yourself. Terence Allsopp still asks after you. He'd marry you tomorrow, I'm sure."

"I'm not interested in Terence Allsopp or any other high-browed son of the well-to-do, Father. You know that." Lizzy's muscles tensed, and she fought hard to control her anger.

"Be it on your own head, then, is all I'll say. I don't know what you see in him."

Lizzy held her retort as the waiter arrived with their meals. Her mother had ordered fish, and the smell of it immediately made her nauseous. She took a sip of her water. *Oh God, please help me control this.* She herself had ordered the simplest, blandest item on the menu. A chicken sandwich.

"Aren't you hungry, Elizabeth?" her mother asked a few minutes later. Lizzy's sandwich lay there, barely touched.

"Please excuse me," she said as she stood. She placed her napkin neatly on the table, and then walked briskly to the bathroom, hoping she'd make it.

~

"I'M CONCERNED FOR HER, Roger. She doesn't look well." Gwyneth said to Roger once Lizzy had left the table.

"It's hanging around with that lout that's doing it." His eyes narrowed and he breathed heavily. "I've a good mind to find him and give him a piece of my mind."

"You can't do that, Roger. As much as we don't like him, Elizabeth obviously does. Perhaps in time she'll come to her senses. We can only hope." She reached out and touched his arm. "Don't be too hard on her, Roger. We don't want to lose her."

Roger Walton-Smythe looked into his wife's eyes. Maybe she was right. Elizabeth was their only daughter, after all. Such high hopes he'd held for her when she was younger. He'd pictured her riding at Royal Windsor, graduating from Oxford University with Honours, and marrying Terence Allsopp. But now... now... He shook his head and looked away.

~

"ARE YOU ALRIGHT, DEAR?" Gwyneth asked when Lizzy returned.

Lizzy had tried to freshen herself as best she could, but how much longer could she keep it up? She took her seat and placed her napkin on her lap. "Yes, Mother. I'm fine, thank you." Picking up her sandwich, she forced herself to take a bite.

When she looked up, she followed the direction of her mother's eyes and froze. They were fixated on her left hand. *A ring mark.* Her body sagged. She slowly lifted her eyes and looked at her mother.

"Elizabeth, please don't tell me you're married," Gwyneth stammered. Lizzy felt so sorry for her mother in that moment. The colour drained out of her mother's face, and Lizzy feared she might faint.

But Lizzy couldn't deny it. She lowered her hand onto her lap and breathed deeply. "I know you'll both be disappointed, but yes, Daniel and I are married. We were going to tell you, but then Daniel couldn't make it..." Her voice trailed off.

Silence sliced the air like a knife. Lizzy's heart pounded in her chest. What would they say?

"Get out of here immediately, Elizabeth! You disgust me!" Her father stood so fast he knocked his chair over. The waiter ran to help, and every diner in the restaurant stopped eating and gaped at the spectacle.

Lizzy looked at her father and rose. His nostrils flared, and his face had reddened.

"Very well, Father. But you might also like to know you're going to be a grandfather." And with that, she spun on her heels and strode out of the restaurant.

GWYNETH GASPED at Lizzy's announcement and reached out to her, but it was too late. Lizzy had disappeared out the door.

Gwyneth stood unsteadily and grabbed Roger's arm. "We need to go after her, Roger. We can't just let her go like that."

"I don't know why we should. I don't understand her at all, Gwyneth. Why would she do such a thing?" Roger ran his hands through his hair and paced on the spot.

"For a number of reasons I can think of." Gwyneth took a deep breath and squared her jaw. "Pay the bill, Roger, then we'll go look for her."

Roger's eyes darted around the restaurant. The others diners had resumed eating and talking, almost as if nothing had happened. He straightened his jacket, lifted his chin, and paid the bill.

Outside the hotel, Roger and Gwyneth stood together on the pavement, their eyes scouring the immediate area for any sign of Lizzy.

"She can't have gone far. Maybe she's in the park," Gwyneth said, pointing across the road.

Roger looked at his watch and drew in a long breath.

Gwyneth stared at him. "How dare you, Roger! She's your daughter. And she's pregnant. We might not like it, but if we don't want to lose her completely, we need to find her."

Roger narrowed his eyes and pursed his lips, but followed Gwyneth across the road.

"I think I see her." Gwyneth grabbed Roger's arm and pulled him along the path to the right to where Lizzy sat on a park bench.

Lizzy's head hung low with her arms wrapped around her stomach. She looked up as her parents came to a standstill in front of her.

"I won't talk unless you're civil." She crossed her arms pertly and pulled herself up.

"We'll try, Elizabeth. We'll try." Gwyneth sat beside her daughter and placed her arm gently around Lizzy's shoulder.

Lizzy fought the impulse to pull away, but remained still.

"Are you really expecting?" Gwyneth's voice was surprisingly soothing, and her touch calming. Lizzy hadn't been this close to her mother for many years. Her perfume was still the same. Chanel No. 5. It's distinct, fresh smell evoked so many memories. But right now it made her queasy. She tilted her face slightly to her mother's as she inched away and nodded, her eyes glistening.

Tears rolled down Gwyneth's cheeks. How long had it been since she'd seen her mother cry? Lizzy fetched a tissue from her bag and handed it to her.

"I'm sorry, Elizabeth. It's just such a shock." Gwyneth dabbed her eyes and took a deep breath before continuing. She squeezed Lizzy's hand and searched her eyes. "How are you, dear? Are you feeling okay?"

Lizzy inhaled deeply, and blinked back her own tears. She had to remain strong. "Yes, thank you, Mother. I'm keeping reasonably well."

Gwyneth squeezed Lizzy's hand again, a warm smile growing on her face. "We couldn't leave without finding you, Elizabeth."

Gwyneth tilted her head and looked to Roger for support.

The scowl on Roger's face left no doubt about his feelings. "This is a sorry mess you've got yourself into, girl. I assume you married him because he got you pregnant?" He studied Lizzy with thinly veiled disapproval.

Lizzy looked at him and narrowed her eyes.

"No Father. I wasn't pregnant when we married." She straightened her shoulders defensively. "In fact, you might be surprised to learn I was unblemished when we married."

"I find that hard to believe." Roger turned his back and folded his arms, his head lifted high and his back as straight as a rod.

"Believe it or not, it's true." Lizzy stood and spoke to her father's back, hands defiantly placed on her hips. "I also happen to love Daniel. I don't care what you think, Father, but Daniel and I are married, and we are having a child. Deal with it in whatever way you see fit." She turned and looked at her mother, her demeanour softening. "Mother, I hope you're happy about the news. I'm sure you'll be a wonderful grandmother." Lizzy smiled warmly at her and then took a deep breath.

Gwyneth returned Lizzy's smile, and wiped another tear from her eye. She reached out her hand to Lizzy. Lizzy took it and squeezed it before walking off. In that moment, Lizzy knew she had an ally in her mother.

CHAPTER 7

Lizzy hailed a taxi and climbed in. Having snatched one last look at her parents before turning the corner, she settled herself into the back seat and took stock of the turn of events. The words she'd spoken to her father played on her mind. Yes, she was married to Daniel, and they were having a child together. But did she *really* love him?

Moments passed, her mind racing through endless scenarios. Was she with him only because she had no choice now they were having a child? If she did have a choice, would she choose to stay and love him? Or would she still choose Mathew over Daniel if there was the slightest possibility of that happening?

Finally, Lizzy acknowledged she did love him. They weren't just words she'd spat at her father. It was the truth. She loved Daniel, and she'd defend him against her father time and time again.

If only he wouldn't drink.

When Lizzy entered the apartment, she sighed and trudged to her bedroom. She threw her bag on the bed, walked to the dresser and picked up her wedding ring. Just a simple gold band, yet it tied her to Daniel, for better, for worse. It had also given her secret away. She slipped it onto her finger and held it up.

When would he come home? How she needed his arms around her.

HER BODY TENSED when she heard the key turn in the lock. Sleep had eluded her once again, and she glanced at the clock, even though she already knew it was past midnight. Where had he been all this time?

She jumped as one of his boots flew off and hit the wall. He lumbered into the bedroom and undressed clumsily. The stench of alcohol permeated the room and made her nauseous. She remained still but her heart beat fast. *Oh God, please protect me.* She tensed when he climbed into bed, but relaxed a little as he settled in close to her and wrapped his arm gently around her. His body shuddered as he wept. She rolled over and hugged him.

LIZZY ROSE EARLY despite the late night. She glanced at Daniel sleeping soundly, and tip-toed out of the room so as not to wake him. Standing in the kitchen, waiting for the kettle to boil, she picked up one of their few framed wedding photos. How much had changed since that day when she so naively married him.

The kettle whistled and she poured herself a cup of tea. Sitting on the couch, she glanced at her Bible laying unopened and neglected on the side table. She picked it up and opened it, the familiar feel of the pages warming her heart. *It's been too long, Lord. Please forgive me.*

Lizzy flicked through several pages before settling on Psalm 42, one of her favourites. She read the words before humming them, and as she sang, tears streamed down her face. *'Yes Lord, as the deer pants for the water, so my soul longs after you. You alone are my heart's desire and I long to worship you. You alone are my strength, my shield, to you alone will my spirit yield. You alone are my heart's desire and I long to worship you.'*

Closing her eyes, Lizzy prayed for forgiveness for marrying Daniel while she still loved Mathew. She prayed for Daniel, that he'd come to know God's love in his life, and that he'd learn to face his problems without the need for alcohol. For their baby, that it would be healthy and strong, and wrapped in love. For her parents and their relationship. And for herself.

Lizzy felt God's presence in the very depths of her soul. She felt renewed, refreshed.

The alarm brought her back to the present. She jumped up and ran to the bedroom to turn it off, but she was too slow - Daniel was awake and pulling himself up as she entered the room. The smell of stale alcohol made her gag, and she brought her hand to her mouth.

She stopped and looked at him. His eyes were bleary and he needed a wash and a shave. Lizzy bit her lip and decided there and then, she'd love him as she'd promised...

He leaned against the pillows and looked at her with sorrow in his eyes. "Lizzy, come here my sweet girl. I'm sorry."

She walked to the bed and climbed into his arms. He kissed the top of her head and pulled her tight.

THEY SAT at the table and shared the breakfast Lizzy had prepared. Not that she ate much, but she needed to be near him. She leaned back in her chair and studied the outline of his face, wondering at the turn of events that resulted in her sitting here with him like this. Eventually she spoke the words he had to hear.

"They know, Daniel. My parents know about us and the baby."

His hand stopped midway to his mouth and his eyes widened.

"Oh..... Lizzy, I'm so sorry." He lowered his fork and reached his hand out to her. The genuine sorrow in his eyes touched her heart. "Tell me what happened."

As she told him about the meeting with her parents, the need to discuss his actions of the week leading up to it pressed on her. It couldn't just be ignored. It was wrong of him to have left her to face her parents on her own. He was her husband, and he should have been there to support her. Instead, where was he? She could get really angry if she wasn't careful. Maybe she needed to. Just because she loved him, it didn't mean he could get away with treating her like this.

She swallowed before looking him in the eye.

"Daniel, we need to talk about why you weren't there."

He looked startled and didn't answer straight away. His body was rigid, she'd rattled him. She didn't care. They had to talk about it.

Lizzy's gaze remained on Daniel. Silence filled the air with only the ticking of the clock interrupting it.

He put his toast down and folded his arms before finally responding. "I know I let you down this week, Lizzy, and I feel bad about it." He sighed wearily and lifted his eyes. "I'm sorry. I should have been there." He took her hand and looked into her eyes. "I promise I'll never let you down again."

Lizzy thought for a moment. He'd apologised, but could she trust him? She tilted her head and tapped her fingers on the table.

"That's a big promise, Daniel. What makes you think you can keep it, when every day this week you said you were sorry after you'd been out drinking, but then you still did it again?" She straightened her head and regarded him with a steady gaze. "I don't see that anything's changed, really."

He sighed and dipped his head, his whole body slumping. "You're right, Lizzy. It was the thought of seeing your parents. It was just easier to drink and disappear than face them."

"Well, that's a start, I guess. But it doesn't excuse your behaviour. You let me down, Daniel." She sat back and crossed her arms pertly, almost savouring his discomfort. "I hope next time we have a difficult situation you'll be man enough to face it."

Lizzy's eyes were unwavering. Daniel averted his face and stared out the window. Had she said too much? Her heart thumped in her chest.

At last he turned back and let out a long, low sigh.

"I don't know, Lizzy. All I can do is try."

Lizzy eased off just a little. Really, that was all she could ask for. "Well, you need to try hard, Daniel. For the baby's sake, and mine." She stood and placed her hands on the back of the chair. "I'm going to church today. Maybe you should come with me." She walked to the sink and began washing the dishes.

Daniel remained seated. His head hurt, but Lizzy's words had hurt him more. He didn't want to lose her. He loved her too much. But could he go to church? Maybe he needed to.

He closed his eyes and leaned on his elbows. What kind of a man was he to let his wife go through what Lizzy had just gone through? He really was no good for her. But he loved her.

He stood and walked to the bedroom.

"Wait, Liz, I'll come with you."

Lizzy peered from the bathroom to where Daniel was seated on the bed, slipping his boots on. She'd been wondering as she got ready if he'd come. Maybe God was answering her prayers already.

She looked at him and smiled, and sent up a quick prayer of thanks.

Standing in church a little while later with Daniel beside her, Lizzy felt at peace. Ever since she'd committed her heart to the Lord when she was at University with Sal, she'd loved going to church. Sure, she knew

God was with her constantly, and she could pray to Him wherever she was, but there was something special about joining together with other believers in praise and worship. And she'd really missed it. But now, it was like the Holy Spirit was breathing new life into her heart.

She prayed that Daniel would also feel God reaching out to him, and that his heart would be open. It would be so wonderful if they could be on the same path. Marrying Daniel when he didn't share her faith was just another mistake on her part, so now she needed to trust God to work it out for them. It did make her wonder, however, how many of her mistakes she could expect God to fix up. Was it presumptuous of her to ask God to fix the situations she'd got herself into? Time to think more about later. For now, she would just enjoy being in God's house. She squeezed Daniel's hand as they took their seats, and snuggled closer to him.

At the end of the service Nessa came over and hugged her. It'd been a while since they'd seen each other, and Lizzy chastised herself for letting their friendship slip. It was Nessa, after all, who'd introduced her to Daniel. It crossed her mind that Nessa most likely knew about Daniel and his drinking.

When Nessa invited them to lunch the following Sunday, it gave the perfect opportunity to talk to her about him.

CHAPTER 8

The week passed without event, much to Lizzy's relief. She did, however, check the clock every few minutes from about four o'clock onwards, and often jumped up to look out the classroom window to see if Daniel had arrived. She knew she was being overly anxious, as he'd promised he'd be there by half four. So far he'd arrived on time or early every day.

When half four came on Friday and he wasn't there, she started to panic. She was packed and ready to go, so she locked the classroom door and headed out to the car park. She bit on her lip as she walked to the wall where she'd sat so often the previous week. She sat down, but stood again straight away. *I'm **not** going to do this. I said I wouldn't wait.* She sighed and clenched her fists. *Oh God, where is he?* She walked to the edge of the road. The angrier she became, the faster her heart beat. She'd just put her hand out to hail a taxi when she saw the Ford Escort trundling along the road towards her.

She let out a huge sigh, and shook her head at Daniel as he pulled up.

He leaned over and opened the door. "Sorry sweetie. The traffic was worse today." He kissed her as she sat beside him. Why had she doubted him?

Gwyneth called that night. Lizzy took the phone and sat on the couch. Daniel was still eating his dinner, but he shifted his chair so he could see her face.

"Mother, how was your trip?"

"Edinburgh was lovely, dear. And your father's business dealings were successful. But how are you? How is your morning sickness?"

"Not so bad this week. I've been feeling better most days, thanks."

"Your news surprised us, Elizabeth, I have to say. We'd certainly never expected it."

"I'm sorry I shocked you, Mother. I hope Father will come around."

"He'd like a word, if that's okay."

Lizzy's chest tightened. She glanced at Daniel before answering. "Okay. Put him on."

"Elizabeth."

"Father."

"Elizabeth, as your mother said, your news shocked us." He paused. "Your mother and I have been talking. We don't approve of your choice. I dare say we never will, however, you are our only daughter, and we would like to give you a proper wedding. Please think about it."

Lizzy's eyes widened and she stared at Daniel, unable to speak.

"Elizabeth, did you hear me?"

"Ah, yes, Father. You took me by surprise this time. I'm not sure what to say. I'll need to discuss it with Daniel."

"Very well, then. I guess that was to be expected. You'll need to think about it quickly, given your condition. Good-bye, Elizabeth."

"Good-bye, Father."

Lizzy placed the receiver on the hook and leaned back on the couch, deep in thought. Daniel joined her. "What did he say?"

She took a deep breath and looked at him. His eyebrows were drawn together and his gaze intense. "Father and Mother would like to give us a proper wedding."

His mouth gaped. "You mean, with all the bells and whistles?" Lizzy nodded. "Forget it. I'm not going to be paraded around for his benefit. That's all he'd be doing it for. To save face. I'm sorry, Lizzy, I can't do it." He shook his head vehemently.

Lizzy wasn't sure what she wanted. She'd always dreamt of a fairy-tale wedding, especially when she thought she'd be marrying Mathew Carter. It was tempting. But Daniel was probably right. Father wouldn't be offering this for their benefit. And she wouldn't want to expose Daniel to all the dramas of a society wedding, with all its snobbery and melodrama. No, she didn't want this either.

"It's okay, Daniel. I'll say no."

He hugged her and whispered in her ear, "I love you, Elizabeth O'Connor."

They remained in each other's arms for several minutes before Daniel pulled away. "Let's go out, Lizzy. Let's go dancing."

Her eyes lit up and her smile broadened to a grin. "That would be lovely, Daniel!"

"IT'S wonderful to be out, Daniel. I'd started thinking my dancing days were over," Lizzy whispered into Daniel's ear as he led her around the dance floor of the Mariat Hotel.

"We need to do it more often, while I can still get my arm around you."

She threw her head back and laughed. "I can't say I'm looking forward to being fat."

"You'll look beautiful, Mrs O'Connor." Daniel leaned forward and planted a kiss on her cheek.

The music picked up, and they transitioned easily into a jive. Lizzy didn't care they were being watched. She was out with Daniel, and she was going to enjoy herself.

"I think I need to sit," she said breathlessly when the music finally stopped.

Daniel helped her to a seat. "I'm sorry, Lizzy. That was stupid," he said as he poured her a glass of water.

Lizzy took a gulp before looking at him. "But it was fun." She laughed and her eyes twinkled.

"Yes, it was fun." He leaned back and smiled at her.

"Let's take a walk, Daniel. I'm not ready to go home yet." Lizzy stood and took his arm, and led him outside towards the river. She clung to him, breathing in his manly scent - a mixture of sweat, after-shave, and cigarette smoke. The intoxicating mix sent a shiver through her body.

"Are you cold?" Daniel wrapped his arm around her and pulled her close.

She looked up at him, her eyes full of love. "No. It's just what you do to me."

He spun her around and looked deeply into her eyes before he kissed her.

"Maybe we should go home." His breath on hers was warm and inviting.

"Not yet," she whispered. "Let's walk a little further."

She leaned close as they strolled along the path. *If only this night could go on forever.* She squeezed his arm and when he kissed the top of her head, Lizzy thought she was in heaven.

"Let's never have a week like last week ever again," she said as she leaned her head on his shoulder.

THE FLASHING NEON lights ahead caught her attention. "Oh look, Daniel, an ice-cream stand! Can we get one?"

"Of course, sweet girl."

As they sat on a bench watching the boats puttering up and down the river, licking their ice-creams, Lizzy turned her head and asked Daniel in a soft voice, "Why did you decide to come to church with me last Sunday?"

Daniel stopped mid lick. "Where did that come from?"

"It's just been on my mind this week, that's all. You said you didn't like going, so I'm curious about the change of heart."

Daniel slumped on the bench. Her question had thrown him. Maybe she shouldn't have asked.

He sighed heavily. "I'm not sure, Lizzy. It was a spur of the moment decision. I think I just wanted to be with you." He pulled her close and hugged her.

Lizzy leaned her head on his shoulder, her heart fallen. That wasn't the answer she'd hoped for.

CHAPTER 9

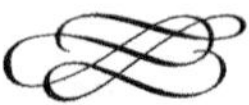

"Don't forget Nessa asked us to lunch today," Lizzy said as she climbed out of bed the following Sunday morning. "Are you coming to Church again?"

Daniel rolled over and stared out the window while she stood waiting for his answer.

"It's okay, you don't have to come. No pressure." *But God, I pray he will.*

She jumped into the shower and while she washed her hair she prayed. *'What a week, Lord. I'm so glad we're back on talking terms. Please be with Daniel. I know he's got stuff going on inside. He needs you, Lord. I don't know what's worrying him, but he needs to let go of whatever it is. Please help him. And help me to help him too. And please can you help my parents, especially my father, accept our situation? And lastly, Lord God, bless this little baby. Keep him or her safe and well. Thank you Lord God for this day and for loving me.'*

She caressed her tummy and began to hum, allowing the Spirit to cleanse her soul while the warm water cleansed her body.

. . .

Lizzy smiled when she re-entered the bedroom. Daniel was up and dressed and looking as charming as ever.

"I guess you're coming, then?

"Yes, I'm coming. I can't let you go on your own. Too many single men prowling around."

Lizzy's heart fell a little. "Well that's an interesting reason for going to church. I don't think any man would be interested in me if they knew my condition, though." She looked down at her baby belly which was still barely noticeable.

"Lizzy, any man would find you attractive, regardless of your condition."

"Are you flirting with me, Daniel O'Connor?"

"Maybe." She shook her head when he winked at her.

Sitting in church a little while later, Lizzy looked around and saw her good friends, Colin and Linda, and also Nessa and Riley. Two people she didn't know sat beside them. She guessed they were Nessa's brother and sister. Having just sung an old hymn and holding Daniel's hand, her heart was full. She turned her head and smiled at him. *Mmm, I could easily get used to this.* God had a lot of work to do, both in her own life, and in Daniel's, but it was a start, and for that she was thankful.

"It seems a long time since we met at Nessa's party," Lizzy said to Daniel in the car on the way to Nessa and Riley's a little while later.

"I'm glad you were there, Liz. You captured my heart the moment I saw you." He glanced at her and winked.

She laughed at him. He was so easy to love when he was like this. Playful and funny. Easy to get on with. She leaned back in her seat and relaxed. *But how long will it last if he doesn't deal with whatever's worrying him?*

For now, she would just enjoy the moment, and leave the rest to God.

"NESSA, THANKS FOR INVITING US!" Lizzy said as Nessa hugged her and showed her and Daniel into their living room.

"A pleasure, Lizzy. It's good to see you both. And you're looking well. As are you, Daniel."

Lizzy couldn't help but notice the look that passed between the two of them. *I need that talk with her. See if she can fill me in on anything I should know.*

"Come and meet my sister, Lizzy. She's visiting with my brother for a week. I think you'll like her." And with that, Nessa drew Lizzy away from Daniel.

Lizzy's mind wasn't on what Nessa or her sister, Fiona, were saying. She was focused on what Daniel was saying to Riley, and hoped she replied appropriately at the right times.

She held her breath when she overheard Daniel asking Riley for a beer. *Why is he asking for a beer? He hasn't had a drink for a whole week.* Her body relaxed a little at Riley's reply.

"Why don't we just stick to the soft stuff today?"

But then she could have throttled Daniel when he pressed Riley further.

"Oh, come on Riley. What's wrong with you? Just get a man a beer will you?"

She stared at Daniel, not caring if Nessa or her sister saw her. Lizzy's body tensed as Daniel walked to the refrigerator and helped himself to a beer.

"Are you okay, Lizzy?" Nessa asked. "Do you want to sit down? You're looking very pale all of a sudden."

Lizzy quickly turned back to Nessa and Fiona. "Sorry Nessa. I'm fine. I was just a little distracted. Where were we?"

"I was just saying we should go for a girls' night out while Fiona's here. Are you up for that?"

"Ah…I guess so. Depends on when." She glanced at Daniel before continuing. "I've got a busy week at school, but I'll see if I can make it."

Daniel had been joined by the man who'd sat beside Nessa in church, who she assumed was Nessa's brother. Nothing tangible, but a bad feeling settled in her stomach.

"Can I help you with lunch, Nessa?" Lizzy asked once having pulled herself together. It was only one beer, after all. But it was the way he'd demanded it that concerned her.

"It smells wonderful, Ness. Lasagne and garlic bread. Lovely!"

"Yes. It's Fiona and Liam's favourite. Some help would be good, thanks Liz. Your morning sickness must be better?"

"Mainly. I still get a little queasy now and then, but much better than a few weeks ago. Where are your two, by the way?"

"Oh, they're in their rooms. Liam brought them over some new games. They haven't stopped playing with them since."

Nessa put the tray of vegetables back in the oven after checking them, and then stood with her arms folded, looking at Lizzy. "So how are things really, Liz? Has Daniel been behaving himself?"

Lizzy looked up, trying not to look startled. How much should she say? Should she tell her everything? Maybe not. Not the time or the place, anyway. But then, Nessa obviously knew more than she was letting on. And she did want to talk to her. She sighed heavily and looked away.

"Please tell me he's not mistreating you."

Lizzy turned her head back with a surprised look on her face. "No. He hasn't been perfect, put it that way, but he hasn't mistreated me. He's been great this past week." She paused, and took a deep breath. "Not so good the week before. My parents stopped in last Saturday, and I think he was anxious about it. So was I, to tell the truth."

"Mmm. He's never been too good in sticky situations. I'd hoped he'd improved. But you're good for him, Lizzy. And he loves you. You can tell just by the way he looks at you. Be patient with him."

Lizzy felt tears well up in her eyes and tried to push them back, but when Nessa walked over and hugged her, they began to fall.

"If ever you want to talk, Liz, just let me know." She pulled her closer and then grabbed some tissues.

"Now, let's get this lunch sorted."

LIZZY SQUEEZED Daniel's hand while Riley gave thanks. Now seated beside him, she could keep an eye on him, and maybe encourage him to stick to the soft stuff. He seemed okay at the moment. Happy and jovial, the life of the party. But maybe it was just a facade, a cover up, and underneath he was actually insecure. *Where did that thought come from?* She looked at him. Was he being slightly louder than normal? *Oh Daniel. What's going on inside you?*

"This is a lovely meal, Nessa," Fiona said. Yes, it was a lovely meal. She should just relax and enjoy the fantastic spread Nessa had prepared, and enjoy being outside on such a lovely summer's day. But something wasn't right. An underlying tension, but she didn't know what was causing it.

"My pleasure, Fiona," Nessa replied. "It's lovely to have you all here. Eat up everyone. There's plenty to go round."

Lizzy began to eat, but looked up when Liam, sitting opposite Daniel, spoke to him directly.

"You haven't properly introduced me to your wife yet, Daniel."

Liam's eyes held a glint. How many had he drunk? More than a few, by the looks of it.

Daniel straightened, his body tense beside her. What would he say? His words played back in her mind. Was he thinking that Liam was one of those prowling single men he meant to protect her from?

"Liam, this is Elizabeth, my wife." Their eyes locked. "Keep your hands off," Daniel leaned forward and hissed.

Lizzy stiffened as everyone stared at Daniel.

Riley broke the silence. "Come on everyone. Don't let Nessie's good food go to waste. Eat up."

Lizzy breathed a sigh of relief when Daniel picked up his fork and began to eat.

"DANIEL, we need to go. I've got preparation to do for tomorrow." He was swaying. How many had he had? She'd only left him on his own while she helped with the dishes, but he must have downed one after the other in quick succession if his demeanour was anything to go by. A sickness developed in the pit of Lizzy's stomach.

"Just let me finish this one, Lizzy love." He draped his arm around her shoulder and pulled her close. She resisted him, and instead sent him an unwavering glare.

"I think you've had enough, Daniel," she hissed into his ear. "We need to go." Riley and Liam stood together, watching. She turned her head quickly so they couldn't see her face. "Daniel, we really need to go."

She grabbed his arm. It was going to be awkward. She guided Daniel towards the gate, and called out to Nessa through the door as they passed. Riley offered to help, but she thanked him and continued on her own.

Lizzy directed him into the passenger's seat, although he put up a fight. He wanted to drive, but there was no way she'd let him. Once she'd pulled out onto the road, she turned her head and took a quick look at him. She didn't like what she saw. His whole manner had changed, and she didn't feel comfortable or safe with him. She remained quiet, hoping he'd fall asleep on the way home.

She fought to control her tears. How had this happened? What had gone on between Daniel and Liam? She wanted to shake him. This wasn't her Daniel.

He moved beside her and sat forward. His eyes bored into her. Lizzy gripped the wheel tighter.

"Why d'you make a scene like that for, Lizbeth?" he spat at her. "Didya want to impress that young cousin of mine? I saw the way he looked at you."

Lizzy glanced at him. His eyes were glazed, and she didn't like the way he was talking.

"Don't talk rot, Daniel. I just needed to get home, you know that." She looked straight ahead, and concentrated on driving, but her heart was racing.

"Tell me what was going on, Lizbeth."

"What do you mean? Where?"

"Don't give me that nonsense," Daniel spat at her.

"I don't know what you mean, Daniel." She tried to remain calm on the outside, but inside her heart pounded.

"I don't believe you." He moved his face closer to hers. "What was going on?"

"With what? I really don't know what you're talking about."

"With that cousin of mine, that's what. I saw the way he looked at you. You stay away from him. I'm warning you."

"You're talking rubbish, Daniel. Nothing was going on." Lizzy gripped the wheel tighter to steady her shaking hands. What had gotten into him? Maybe she should pull over.

Seconds passed. Would he let it go? She daren't look at him. When Daniel at last sat back in his seat, she exhaled slowly.

What had happened to make him act like that? The look in his eyes had scared her. She liked nothing about the Daniel she'd just seen. Tears rolled down her cheeks as she drove the remaining distance home.

. . .

LIZZY WAS TEMPTED to leave him asleep in the car when they pulled up outside the apartment a short while later. Her arms slumped over the wheel, she closed her eyes and wiped the tears that had continued to fall. *God, where are you in all of this? I don't know what to do. I don't know how to cope. Please help me.*

Daniel stirred beside her. She sat up and studied his face. Would he remember what had happened? She certainly would. It didn't make any sense at all. What did he think she'd done? What if he did remember and apologised? Could she forgive him again? Should she consider leaving him? But what about her vows? She'd promised to love him, in good times and bad. Even though they hadn't said their vows in a church in front of God, to her it was as if they had. She was married to Daniel, for better or worse. And this was certainly worse. But how could she go on? How could she forgive him? Expecting his baby made it worse. Maybe she should leave for the baby's sake. But no, maybe the baby would help Daniel come to his senses.

Wiping her face, she drew a sober breath, and hung her head. *I don't know I can forgive him, Lord. You've got to help me. I really don't know how to handle this.* She looked at her hands. Their shaking had lessened, but her heart was heavy.

Daniel shifted in his seat and her body tensed. His eyes opened and he turned his head to look at her.

"What are we doing here?"

Lizzy hesitated before answering. It was all too fresh in her mind. It'd be so easy to respond angrily, but then what would he do? She was no match for him. She breathed deeply and stilled herself.

"Waiting for you to wake up. I can't carry you up the stairs."

"Let's go then." His voice still held a slur but had lost a little of its sting. He opened his door, but before he got out, Daniel turned and looked at her with dark eyes. "Stay away from Liam, Elizabeth."

. . .

When Lizzy woke the following morning, her heart was still heavy. As she'd expected, Daniel apologized and went to bed early, but she had trouble sleeping. She couldn't shake off the utter shock of it all. How could she ever forget? Or forgive?

She sat on the edge of the bed with her head in her hands.

Daniel stirred, and she held her body rigid. She relaxed a little when he seemed to be back to his normal self.

Instead of getting up, Lizzy lay back on the bed and curled up in a ball.

"I don't feel too well, Daniel. I think I'll stay home today." She pulled the bed covers around her and closed her eyes.

"I'll make you a cup of tea, Liz. Stay there. Stay in bed all day if you need."

Tears squeezed their way through her closed eyes and landed on her pillow. How could a person be so different one minute to the next?

When he left for work, she reached for the phone and made a call.

"Nessa, can we go for coffee today?"

CHAPTER 10

An hour later, Lizzy sat opposite Nessa. Once she'd made up her mind to make the call, her body had responded and she felt better immediately. The hope that she might gain some insight into his past spurred her on.

"I'm glad you could make it, Nessa. And at short notice. I hope Fiona didn't mind you going out without her?"

"No, she had some things to do today, so no problem." Nessa looked at her intently. "I assume this is about Daniel?"

Lizzy nodded and lowered her eyes.

"I had hoped he'd sorted himself out. But seems not."

"I need to know about him, Nessa." Lizzy looked up and leaned forward. "I need to know what makes him tick. He won't tell me much about his past. Just snippets here and there." She took in a deep breath and sipped her coffee. "I'm not coping too well with his changing moods. Sometimes he can be so loving and kind, and other times he can be so horrible. Usually when he's been drinking." *Like yesterday on the way home.* She glanced outside and saw people scurrying in the rain. The sun had definitely gone.

When Nessa squeezed her hand, Lizzy struggled to hold back her tears.

"You poor girl. He should be treating you like a precious princess. I know he loves you, but yes, he does have a past, Lizzy." Nessa's eyes bore into hers. "Do you really want to know?"

Lizzy nodded, her eyes unmoving.

"Daniel's one of eight children. The second eldest. I assume you know that already?"

Lizzy nodded again.

"His father drank heavily, and treated his mother badly. It wasn't uncommon in our area of Belfast. His father disappeared when he was ten, leaving his mother to bring up the children on her own. She always made sure they were well dressed and went to church. She did the best she could." Nessa stopped and took another sip of her coffee.

"His mother, my aunt, got sick a few years later. She died of cancer not long after, and the kids were all split up. Daniel came to live with us." *Come on Nessa, I know all of this. Move on.*

"Everything was fine for the first few years, but you could tell he was angry about losing his mother. He wouldn't go to church with us. He said he blamed God for letting her die. He was a bit younger than me, and I kept a look out for him. He was always loud, funny and charming. Just like he is now most of the time. He hasn't lost that. But when he was sixteen, he started drinking. It was the done thing. Most of the lads did it. We all knew, but couldn't do anything to stop it. One night he got so drunk he ended up in hospital. My parents told him if he didn't stop, he'd have to leave. They didn't want him setting a bad example for my brothers." She paused before continuing and glanced out the window. "He agreed to stop, but they also said he needed to go to church with them if he wanted to stay. He reluctantly agreed, and that's where he met Ciara."

Lizzy leaned forward and rested on her elbows. "This is the bit I don't know. He never talks about her to me."

"I'm not surprised," Nessa said. "The whole thing messed him up pretty badly." She leaned forward, their heads almost touching. "Ciara was lovely. They were inseparable, but he got her pregnant. He was seventeen, and she was sixteen. Her parents were shocked. They were good Christian people, and they thought she was too. My parents were more angry than shocked. They made him marry her, even though they were so young. They lived in the back room of our house. They didn't have any money. Daniel tried to find work, but could only get the odd job here and there. Not enough to support a family."

Nessa leaned back and crossed her arms.

"I feel bad making you remember all of this, Nessa." Lizzy reached out and squeezed her hand. "Are you okay?"

She met Lizzy's gaze. "Yes, I'm fine. It's just a sad story, that's all." She took a deep breath. "The baby was born. It was a little girl. They called her Rachel, and she was perfect. Daniel was a changed person. He doted on her, and being a father made him grow up. He got a job, and they moved into their own place. Everything was perfect until the night Rachel died in her sleep. There was no real explanation. Just 'cot death'.

"Daniel began drinking again. He lost his job, and often he wouldn't come home for days on end." Nessa leaned forward and sighed. "One night when he did come home, Liam was there. He had his arms around Ciara, and she was crying on his shoulder. Daniel grabbed him and punched him. He punched him until Liam could hardly move. He probably would have killed him if Ciara hadn't hit him with a saucepan."

Lizzy's eyes widened and her body slumped a little.

"She didn't want to call the police, but Liam was hurt so badly he needed to go to hospital. Daniel was charged with assault, and he was sent to jail for twelve months."

"Oh goodness, Nessa. I had no idea." Lizzy's mind reeled with this information. She rubbed her temple with her fingers and then looked up. "What happened to Liam?"

"He had some broken ribs, and was covered in bruises. He recovered."

"So was he with Ciara, or did Daniel get it wrong?"

"Liam said he'd just gone round there to see Daniel, and found Ciara crying. No-one really knows apart from him. He maintains they weren't together."

"What happened to her?"

Nessa sighed sadly. "She went back home to live with her parents. She was never the same though." Nessa brushed tears away from her eyes and gulped. "She took her life a few years later. Her family was devastated. They blamed Daniel. They still do."

Lizzy grabbed Nessa's hand. "That's a terrible story, Nessa. No wonder he doesn't want to talk about it. But now I understand why he acted like he did yesterday."

Nessa pulled out a tissue and blew her nose. "Yes, well. He shouldn't have been drinking, that's for sure." She inhaled deeply and checked her watch. "There's more. Have you got time?"

"I have if you have. Do you want another coffee?"

"Yes please."

Lizzy called the waiter over and ordered two more coffees. "Okay, tell me the rest."

"When Daniel got out of jail, he was a mess. He went straight back onto the bottle and almost drank himself to death. We were all worried about him, but there wasn't much anyone could do. One night he got picked up by the Salvos. They took him to a home and cared for him. He must have been really bad, because they convinced him to get help. He started going to AA. It worked for a while. We couldn't believe it was the same person when we saw him a few months later. It was like having the old Daniel back, but better. He patched it up with Liam, and apologised for beating him up. That was five years ago.

"By that time I'd married Riley. We moved over here not long after, so I didn't see much of him after that, but I heard he was doing well most of the time. He got himself a job at the hospital, but then all of a sudden he just packed up and disappeared. The next thing I know, he's knocking on our door several years later. He said he needed to get out of the place. Too many memories, and so he went travelling, as you know. He went lots of places, and got jobs where he could. I think he might have been drunk a lot of the time, because he can't remember much about the places he went to."

The waiter arrived with their coffees and Lizzy thanked him.

"When he arrived on our doorstep, it seemed he was ready to settle down. We took him in, on the condition he didn't drink. He was older, obviously, but he also seemed more mature. He wouldn't come to church with us, though. Seemed like he still blamed God for both his mother's and Rachel's deaths. And Ciara's too, for that matter. But apart from that, he seemed to have sorted himself out. He got the job at the hospital, and he wasn't drinking. And then, that's when he met you."

Lizzy sat back in her seat and took a few moments to digest all of this information. She glanced out the window. It was still raining. She turned and looked at Nessa. "Why didn't you tell me any of this before, Ness?"

Nessa held her eyes for a moment, but then looked away. She took a deep breath before answering. "I guess because you seemed so happy together. We didn't really expect it to get so serious so quickly, but by the time it did, it was too late. We just hoped and prayed he was a changed man, and that he'd look after you properly. We assumed he'd tell you in his own time. But obviously, he didn't."

"Why did you ask us over yesterday when you knew Liam would be there?"

"They've seen each other a few times since that day, Liz. Daniel apologised, as I said before, and they haven't had any problems that I know of since. We had no reason to think it would cause a problem." She stopped and tilted her head, her eyes narrowing. "Did something happen last night?"

Lizzy looked her in the eye. *Do I tell her, or do I just let it pass?*

"Not really. He was just a little agitated for a while."

"I'm glad. I didn't realize he'd drunk so much until after you'd left. Too busy with cooking I suppose. I'm sure he'll be fine, Lizzy. Especially with the baby coming. He really does love you."

"I think I need some time alone, Ness."

Nessa's head shot up, her eyes wide open.

"Oh, I don't mean, go away, if that's what you're thinking. I meant now. I think I need to go for a walk, even though it's raining." Lizzy glanced outside again. The rain had stopped, but the sky was still grey. "I need to gather my thoughts. Knowing this puts a whole different slant on everything."

"I understand, Lizzy. It's a lot to take in. I'm sorry I didn't tell you earlier." Nessa reached out and squeezed Lizzy's hand. "I really am." She looked into Lizzy's eyes. "Would it have made a difference if I had?"

Lizzy leaned back and folded her arms and thought for a moment before answering.

"I don't know. But it's irrelevant now. I married him."

She looked up when the waiter came over and asked if they'd like another drink.

"No, but thanks for asking. We're just about to leave."

Lizzy stood and straightened her skirt. "Thanks for coming, Nessa. And for sharing. Now I've got to process it."

Nessa hugged her. "God bless you, Lizzy."

They walked out together. Lizzy shivered.

"Here, take my jacket if you're going to walk."

Lizzy smiled at her. "Thanks Ness."

LIZZY TURNED left and crossed the road. It wasn't raining as such, but a fine mist had settled in the air. Although it was refreshing, she slipped Nessa's jacket on anyway. She didn't want to get sick on top of everything else. She walked along the river, unaware of the activity carrying on either side of her, both on the water and on the road. Lizzy's mind was in turmoil. She'd never dreamt that Daniel could have been hiding so much of himself from her. Why hadn't he told her? Weren't husbands and wives supposed to share everything with each other and not keep secrets? How could she have been so naive when she married him? She'd jumped blindly into marriage with a man she hardly knew anything about. *Was I really that desperate?*

She kept walking, but couldn't get the picture of Daniel being in jail out of her mind. *Jail?* What would her parents say if they ever found out? And poor Ciara. She must have been so brokenhearted and depressed to have taken her own life. Lizzy stopped and sat on a bench seat and bowed her head.

Oh God. This is too much to bear. No wonder Daniel's in turmoil most of the time. He needs you, Lord. Really needs you. Only you can take his hurt and anger away. He needs to forgive himself, Lord. He's been through so much. Please touch him in a special way today. And show me how to love him. Really love him.

An image of a dove settling on her shoulder flitted through her mind and peace flooded through her being. She also knew what she must do.

CHAPTER 11

Lizzy stepped back to inspect her handiwork and smiled. The table looked perfect. And the smell of roast chicken made her feel hungry. How good it was not to feel queasy anymore. She was just unsure about how to broach the subject with Daniel. Should she just come straight out and tell him she knew everything? That she'd plied the information from Nessa, or should she press him to tell her, and not let on she already knew? Either way was fraught with danger.

Lord God, you need to be with me in this. It could go really well, or it could end really badly. Please give me wisdom.

She glanced out the window. The car wasn't there yet. *What if he doesn't come home?* Lizzy rubbed the back of her neck and breathed deeply. Checking the table once more, she adjusted the small bunch of daisies she'd picked on the way home, and then looked at her watch. *Where is he?*

She'd just about given up hope when she heard the key in the door. Her body tensed. He was an hour late. Did that mean he'd been drinking? His treatment of her in the car the previous afternoon was still fresh in her mind. She looked up as he entered, and sent up a silent prayer of thanks when he appeared to be sober.

Lizzy stood slowly, and walked over to him. Lifting her arms, she wrapped them around him and caressed his back, then pulled away slightly so she could look at him.

"Daniel O'Connor, I love you." Then she kissed him.

"Jaysus woman! What are you trying to do to me?"

"Shh! And don't swear…"

She led him to the bedroom and made love to him.

"I DON'T KNOW what got into you, Liz, but if this is what a day at home does to you, maybe you should stay at home more often." Daniel rolled over and looked deeply into Lizzy's eyes. "I don't know what I did to deserve you, Elizabeth O'Connor, but I'm very glad you're my wife." He kissed her gently, and then pulled her close. "I'm sorry for yesterday, Lizzy. Forgive me?"

She nodded, her face expanding into a beaming grin before she planted another kiss on his lips.

"COME ON THEN, dinner will be ruined if we don't get up and eat," Lizzy said as she sat up and pulled on her loose fitting shift.

"It smells great, Liz. I could eat a horse after that frolic!"

She led him to the table, and dished out the roast chicken and vegetables she'd prepared earlier. She lit the candles, and then sat and took his hand.

"Daniel, will you give thanks tonight?"

He squeezed her hand and then he prayed. She wiped tears away with her other hand as she listened to his words that for once sounded genuine.

"This is grand, Lizzy. Thank you," he said as he picked up his knife and fork and began to eat.

Now the time had come, she hesitated. What if he thought she'd just done all of this to trick him, to lure him into talking about his past? No, she couldn't think like that. She'd been genuine in her loving. Surely he would know that. She played with her food a little, and then took a deep breath.

"Daniel, I had coffee with Nessa today. I asked her to tell me about what happened with Ciara and Liam."

His hand stopped midway to his mouth. He turned his head and stared at her.

Her heart thumped. *Oh God, here we go...*

He put his fork down and leaned back in his seat.

Lizzy reached over and touched his hand. "Please Daniel. Don't be upset. It was time I knew, don't you think?"

"Is that what this is about?" He indicated to the plates on the table and narrowed his eyes.

She sighed in frustration and shook her head. "Daniel. We're married, for better or worse. I don't want it to get worse, but it might if we're not honest with each other. I know you'd rather try to ignore what happened, but seeing you with Liam yesterday, it was obvious you've still got issues. The way you reacted yesterday when you saw him.... I wanted to understand, but you kept on refusing to talk to me about it. I needed to know, especially after what you did to me. I'm sorry Daniel, but I had to know."

He folded his arms, his lips pressed into a thin white line. "What did she tell you?"

"Everything."

Their eyes locked. Lizzy's heart pounded. What would he do? It had definitely been a risk talking to Nessa without him knowing, and she wouldn't blame him if he got angry. She just hoped he wouldn't become violent.

"Everything?" His eyes narrowed and his breathing was heavy.

Lizzy nodded, her eyes round as marbles.

He thumped the table and Lizzy jumped, her hands flying to her chest.

"She had no right. And you… you, Lizzy. How dare you go behind my back."

"I'm sorry Daniel. But someone had to tell me. Don't you agree it's better to have everything out in the open?" She grabbed his arm again and pleaded with her eyes.

Time stood still. Lizzy held her breath.

Daniel lowered his head a little and crossed his arms, his lips pinched.

"I don't know, Lizzy." He shook his head then looked out the window.

Lizzy prayed silently.

He finally turned back but avoided her gaze. His body had sagged. "I didn't want you to know all the terrible things I did. But then the way I treated you yesterday, maybe nothing's changed." He lifted his face slightly. His eyes had lost their spark. "I can't do this, Lizzy. You shouldn't have married me, your father was right. I'm no good for you."

"No, Daniel." Lizzy gripped his arm. "We can do this together. Now I know, I can help. And we can ask God to help. I'm not letting you go that easily."

Tears welled in his eyes and he wiped them away with his hand. "I don't deserve you, Lizzy."

CHAPTER 12

The next few weeks passed quietly. Lizzy and Daniel spent their free time talking and sharing more of themselves with each other. They went for long walks along the beach, where the gale, whipping off the North Sea, invigorated them and breathed life into their marriage. They huddled in cozy nooks of quaint old pubs they discovered in nearby villages, and they went to church.

Lizzy was frustrated, though. She prayed daily that Daniel would find God. Really find God. He said the right words, and did the right things. They even prayed together sometimes, but there was no depth to his prayers, and she sensed he still didn't really know God. Not the living God she knew and had experienced first hand. She tried to talk to him about it, but he always skirted around the main issue. She never once got the feeling he'd ever cried out to God or wept for forgiveness. Maybe he'd done it in private, but she didn't think so. She continued to pray for him.

One day as they were out walking, she suggested they take a holiday. Her heart lifted when Daniel agreed, and so they made their plans.

. . .

"WHAT A LOVELY FEELING, to be heading away for three weeks," Lizzy said as Daniel pointed the Ford Escort southeast on the M1. "It's going to be so good to see Sal again." She glanced at Daniel and sighed wistfully. "Maybe not so good seeing my parents, but we should be able to cope with one night."

"Mmm. I don't want to think about it. I'm not looking forward to seeing your old man, and I guess he's not looking forward to seeing me either. It's surprising they asked us to stay after you turned the offer of the wedding down."

"I think Mother talked him around. I feel really sorry for them both, especially Father. He's so caught up with what people think and putting on a show to all their friends and neighbours, he can't see there's more to life. I'm not sure how I managed to escape from it, but I'm glad I did." She leaned back in her seat and looked out the window.

"They wanted me to marry this guy called Terence Allsopp. His family are just as bad, maybe even worse. I couldn't imagine being married to him and living like they all do in their big fancy manor homes." She turned her head and looked at Daniel. "You know, I think I'd be happy living in a tent in the middle of a desert as long as we loved each other enough."

Daniel laughed and threw his head back. "You never cease to amaze me, Lizzy. I can't see you living in a tent anywhere, let alone in a desert." He glanced at her. "Do you even know what a desert's like?"

She grinned, and her eyes lit up. "Maybe not. I was just making a point." She paused for a moment, as she pictured her and Daniel trying to put up a tent in the middle of a sandstorm in a hot desert. "Maybe not in a desert, but you know what I mean. I don't want a huge house. I just want a house that's a home, with lots of children running around playing happily because they feel loved. That's really all I want."

"And just how many children are you planning on?" he asked playfully. "Do I have a say in this?"

She laughed and her eyes sparkled. “Oh, I don’t know. Maybe a dozen?”

He chuckled and shot her a cheeky glance. “And we’re not even Catholic!”

Lizzy settled back into her seat and relaxed as the miles slipped by. She tried not to think about the night ahead, and instead looked forward with anticipation to seeing Sal and to the cottage by the sea they’d booked for their holiday.

“HERE IT IS...” Lizzy said hours later as they reached the stone pillared entrance to Wiveliscombe Manor, the impressive manor house she used to call home. Nothing seemed to have changed. The gardens looked immaculate as ever. Not a single dead head on the roses that filled the circular garden beds, nor a stray weed in sight. Everything in its rightful place. Her chest tightened as images of their last visit flitted through her mind.

“Let’s stop for a moment, Daniel.” She reached out and grabbed his hand. “I’m not sure I’m ready for this. Are you?”

He shook his head. “Don’t think I’ll ever be.”

“I wish we could just drive on, but we’ve got to do it.” She turned her head and sighed heavily as she looked at the house. “I guess we’d better go.”

Daniel put the car into gear, and they slowly made their way up the long gravel driveway towards the house.

HAVING PULLED up in front of the house, Lizzy climbed out and was stretching her arms when she saw her mother walking towards them.

“Elizabeth, dear, how good to see you.” Gwyneth reached out her hands and studied her daughter carefully before pulling her close and hugging her. "And Daniel." She turned to look at him, and hesitated. Her smile grew warmer and she reached out her hands to him.

"Mrs Walton-Smythe. How are you?" He shook her hand gently.

Lizzy rubbed her arms and looked around. "Where's Father?"

"He's in his study. He's finishing some business, and then he'll be out."

"I hope he's going to behave," Lizzy said, rolling her eyes.

"He's trying his best to accept the situation, dear. Come on, let's go inside."

Daniel carried their bags and followed Lizzy and Gwyneth into the entry.

"I've put you in your old room, Elizabeth. I hope that's suitable."

"That will be fine, Mother. Is Jonathon at home?"

"Yes, he's home for the holidays and will be joining us for dinner. He said he's looking forward to catching up with you."

Lizzy turned and saw her father standing at the foot of the spiral staircase. Was he pleased to see her or not? *Why can't he just relax and be normal for once? Why does he always have to put on an act?*

"Father. Good to see you." *Okay, I have to play act as well, it seems.* She walked over and kissed his cheek.

"Elizabeth." *Why can't he smile?*

Roger turned his head to Daniel. Lizzy held her breath and prayed silently. He held out his hand.

"Daniel." Lizzy took note of the look that passed between them. It definitely lacked warmth, but at least they'd shook hands.

"I think I'd like to freshen up before dinner, if that's okay," Lizzy said, mainly to her mother. "It was a long drive."

"You must be tired, dear. But you're looking good." Gwyneth smiled, and stretched out her hands to Lizzy again. "It's lovely to see you. But run along, and I'll call you when dinner's ready."

. . .

DANIEL CLOSED the door behind them, and placed their bags on the floor. "Just as well it's only one night. What's wrong with the man?" He sat in the plush green armchair and rested his feet on the matching footstool.

"So this is your bedroom. It's almost as big as our apartment."

Lizzy glanced around at the furnishings and old fashioned wallpaper, and the image of herself as a young girl seated at her dresser brushing her hair flitted through her mind.

"I don't miss it, Daniel. It wasn't a happy home. Mother tried, but it was always uncomfortable when Father was around." She'd opened her case and was pulling out some fresh clothes.

"We don't have to get dressed up for dinner, do we?"

"Probably best to put on a clean shirt. Don't worry about a jacket."

"Good. I wasn't going to."

"Don't start, Daniel. Please." She sighed, and walked over to the chair. She sat on his lap and wrapped her arms around him. "We've just to get through tonight. That's all." She leaned her head against his, and then stroked his hair. "We can do this. I know we can."

LIZZY HELD Daniel's hand as they entered the dining room a short while later. The table was laid beautifully. She would have been surprised if it was any different. Her mother directed them to their seats in front of the fireplace. Not that it was on. Jonathon sat opposite, beside his mother, and her father sat at the head of the table in his normal place.

"You've excelled yourself, Mother," Lizzy said as Gwyneth served up a roast dinner with all the trimmings.

"Thank you, dear. I'm a little out of practice, now that it's just your father and me."

"It smells wonderful, Mrs Walton-Smythe," Daniel added.

"Please call me Gwyneth, Daniel. Mrs Walton-Smythe sounds so formal. And I am your mother-in-law," she said as she placed several roast potatoes on his plate.

"Thank you, Gwyneth," he replied, smiling at her.

"So Daniel, how's married life?" Jonathon asked.

Daniel glanced at Lizzy and squeezed her hand before answering. "Your sister is an amazing woman, Jonathon. Married life is good."

Her father had said nothing apart from grace, which had sounded stilted and lacked any real thankfulness. Lizzy glanced at him. He held himself straight, and his jaw was clenched. *Oh God, please let this dinner go smoothly.* She had a feeling, though, that a miracle might be needed for her prayer to be answered.

Lizzy's whole body tensed when her father put down his napkin after wiping his mouth, and looked directly at Daniel. His superior manner sickened her to the core.

"What plans do you have, Daniel, for bettering yourself? Being a hospital orderly is hardly a job to aspire to."

Lizzy glared at him. *Why are you doing this, Father?* She waited for Daniel's reaction with dread in her stomach. She glanced at him. His eyes had narrowed, and his chest was heaving. Her heart went out to him. *Daniel, please don't. Please don't react.*

"I happen to enjoy my job, Roger. It might not be as financially rewarding as some, but it's what I do." His knuckles had whitened as his grip on his knife and fork tightened. "I resent your insinuation that it's not an acceptable job for your daughter's husband."

"I didn't say that. But I do wonder if you'll be able to support her and a baby when she stops work. She is my daughter, after all, and I have a right to be concerned. Do you not agree?"

"Lizzy's my responsibility now, Roger. You have no need to worry yourself."

Lizzy smiled inwardly. *Go Daniel! Not many are brave enough to take on Father! And you're controlled. Thank you God.*

The conversation continued, a little strained, until Jonathon asked Daniel how the mood was in the north.

"Thatcher's definitely not popular. Things are getting tough. Jobs are disappearing." He glanced at Lizzy. "Not as bad where we are, but you can feel it. I think there's trouble ahead."

"You'd be used to that, wouldn't you, Daniel? Coming from Belfast," Roger said, his voice full of contempt.

Daniel lowered his knife and fork and placed them neatly on his plate before looking Roger in the eye. "There's nothing wrong with standing up for what's right. It's the likes of you, all of you who lord it over everyone else, thinking you're better than them, that's the problem. The upper class disgusts me."

Roger's nostrils flared.

No! Please don't start!

"How dare you speak to me like that. Don't forget you're in my house!"

"I don't care where I am. I'll speak my mind. I'm not going to be put down by the likes of you." Daniel pulled himself up in his chair, the vein in his neck pulsating. "Who said you were better than anybody else? You're just an arrogant high brow aristocrat who doesn't have a clue."

Lizzy gasped as her father pointed his finger at Daniel.

"You're not welcome at this table. Remove yourself immediately."

"With pleasure." Daniel stood and pushed his chair back. "Are you coming, Lizzy?"

Lizzy's pulse raced. *Oh God, why did this have to happen?*

Daniel breathed heavily, and his eyes had darkened. What should she do?

"I'm sorry, Mother. I'm going to have to go." Lizzy stood and placed her napkin neatly beside her plate. As she left the room with Daniel, she struggled to keep her anger at bay. *Why couldn't he have just let it go?*

. . .

"WHY DID YOU DO THAT?" Lizzy asked Daniel back in their room. "Just one night! One dinner. That's all we had to get through. You should have just let it go." She stood inside the door with her hands on her hips.

"He goaded me, Lizzy. I didn't mean to have a go at him."

"Well, it's done now. Either you apologise or we'll have to leave." Her chest heaved and her eyes bulged as she glared at him.

Daniel held her glare and pursed his lips. "I'm not apologising, so I guess we're going."

Lizzy's heart fell as Daniel grabbed his bag and started throwing his clothes into it. She shook her head, and tears began to roll down her cheeks. Why couldn't they have got through just one night?

"Can't you find father and apologise? Please Daniel?"

He stopped packing, and looked at her. "You can stay if you want, but I'm going. Please yourself."

Tears streamed down Lizzy's face as she watched him open the door. "Wait Daniel. I'm coming."

AS DANIEL PUT the car into gear and spun the wheels on the gravel, Lizzy struggled to fight back her tears. She glanced back and saw her mother standing under the portico with outstretched arms. Her father was nowhere to seen.

Lizzy fell back in the seat and threw her head against the head rest. How did this happen? Tears streamed down her face.

"Where's the closest pub?" Daniel demanded as he skidded to a halt in the gravel at the end of the driveway.

Lizzy shook her head and pulled herself up. "No Daniel. Don't go out drinking. Please."

"Don't tell me what I can and can't do. Just tell me which way to go." He sat with his arms draped over the steering wheel, peering both ways.

Lizzy breathed deeply. Her body shuddered as she tried to control herself and think logically. She didn't like the sound in his voice one little bit. Where was the Daniel she'd been planning their dozen children with just hours before?

"We could drive on to Sal's. It's not that far, and I'm sure she wouldn't mind."

"No Lizzy. I need a drink. Which way do I go? Just tell me."

Lizzy sighed and inhaled deeply. "There's a pub about two miles down the road on the right that has some rooms."

Daniel put the car into gear, and turning right, he drove until they reached the Red Lion Hotel where they took a room for the night. He was still angry. He'd hardly said anything since they'd walked out, and he had that rigid look on his face she'd learned to detest.

"I'm going down for a drink. And don't try to stop me." The look on his face made her wince. She knew it was no use saying anything.

"Wait. I'll come with you."

Daniel stopped in his tracks and turned around slowly. Lizzy inched back, feeling for the bed. What made her say that? Her heart thumped.

"Well, come on then." Daniel pursed his lips and grabbed her hand.

THE DOWNSTAIRS BAR was already noisy. Daniel led Lizzy into the lounge area and left her at a corner table while he went and got their drinks. He returned with three - a squash for her, and two pints for himself. This didn't bode well. She refrained from commenting. Any wrong word could tip him over the edge.

She still had half a glass left by the time he'd skulled both. Lizzy's heart fell when he came back with another three drinks.

"Don't." He said as their eyes met.

Lizzy's body tensed. This wasn't going to end well.

After the next round, Lizzy said she needed to go to bed.

"Come with me, Daniel? Please." She hated pleading with him.

He walked her to the bottom of the stairs, and then pulled her tight and kissed her aggressively. His beer breath and wet lips revolted her, but she responded, not wanting to aggravate him further.

His eyes were already glazed, and his words slurred.

"I'll be up soon. Be ready for me."

Lizzy pushed back her tears as he slapped her on the bottom. Once back in her room, she fell on the bed and sobbed.

THE NOISE downstairs kept her awake. Lizzy turned on the light and checked the time. It was past ten o'clock, so last drinks would have been called a while before. That wouldn't have stopped Daniel from stacking them up, though. She sat up in bed and stared at the smoke stained wall. How did it all go so wrong? It was always going to be hard, but they'd agreed not to let her parents get to them. Easier said than done. *This wasn't supposed to have happened.* And on the first day of their holiday. A tear rolled down her cheek and landed on the bedcovers.

She got out of bed and poured herself a glass of water from the jug on the dresser. *What am I doing here?* She leaned against the wall and closed her eyes, her hands resting on the baby growing inside her. She longed to feel it move, to know it was real.

The airless room was suffocating. Why wasn't Daniel here with her? Why couldn't they have helped each other deal with it? Wasn't that what marriage is about? Helping and supporting each other? Not running off and leaving the other partner in despair and turmoil, while you go out and drink yourself silly. Maybe she should have stayed downstairs with him. *Oh Daniel. Daniel...*

She laid back on the bed, and sobbed into the pillow. She wanted him to come back, even though he was drunk. It had to be better than being in this horrid room on her own.

. . .

Her heart pounded when she heard the door squeak open sometime later. His heavy step and the stench of alcohol pervading the room turned her stomach. How many more had he had? She clenched her hands to her chest and prayed silently he'd forgotten his parting words. She just wanted him to hold her. That was all.

But he hadn't forgotten. In fact, he was rougher than normal. Lizzy could only explain his behaviour by assuming he was taking the aggression he felt for her father out on her. That night, she rued the day she set eyes on Daniel O'Connor.

CHAPTER 13

The sun, peeking its tentacles under the door, woke her before she was ready. Lizzy opened her eyes, and remembered. She reached up and felt her face, then her neck, and then her chest. She closed her eyes as tears rolled onto the pillow.

When she came to again, Daniel wasn't there.

Lizzy dragged herself out of bed, and carefully cleaned herself. She put on fresh clothing and went looking for him.

He wasn't far away. Seated on the river's edge, his legs dangled down the grassy embankment. His head hanging low, his clothes dishevelled, he looked like the drunk that he was.

She contemplated walking away. Going back to her parents, and asking for help. But she could never do that. Her pride wouldn't let her. Besides, Daniel would come after her, she just knew it. He wouldn't let her go that easily. *But would she leave if she could?* Her emotions running rampant, she was torn between leaving and staying.

Lizzy looked out to the fields in the distance beyond and prayed.

Lord, I have no idea what to do. Tears rolled down her cheeks. *I know it's my fault. I made foolish decisions and didn't trust you. I know that now. I really do.*

She turned and looked at Daniel. *Oh God, what do I do? What do I feel for him? We were so happy. But now, I don't know. I don't know if I can get past this.* She hugged her unborn baby, and closed her eyes. *I can't go on like this, Lord. Please help me. Please.*

SHE WALKED SLOWLY to the edge of the river and sat beside him, saying nothing. She stared at the water, so clean and clear as it flowed across the pebbles and the sand below. *Just what Daniel needs.* Living water flowing through the innermost part of his being, washing him clean, making him new. *But he has to want it.*

She finally looked at him. "We can't go on like this, Daniel."

Moments passed. Her heart was heavy. He looked up and briefly caught her eye before turning his head away.

"You need help. You're going to destroy us otherwise." She wiped the tears from her eyes.

More moments passed.

"You're right, Lizzy. I'm a failure."

"No you're not, Daniel." She looked at him intently. "You're not a failure. You just need God in your life. He can help you. But you have to want Him deep down."

He shook his head and gave a half-hearted shrug.

"I don't know, Lizzy. I'm beyond help."

"No! No-one's beyond help, Daniel. Don't think like that!"

He turned and looked at her, his eyes dull and lifeless. "I know you don't think I mean it, but I'm sorry, Lizzy. I really am. I don't know what got into me."

She looked at him, and for the first time in their relationship she felt pity instead of love.

"Okay, Daniel. Just this time. But believe me when I say that if you ever treat me like that again, I will leave."

She held his gaze until he averted his eyes and looked away.

THE SHORT DRIVE to Sal's house in Exeter was quiet. Lizzy had little to say. Although she drove, her mind was elsewhere, and the familiar countryside passed by without her really seeing it. She occasionally winced when she moved in her seat and her body reminded her of Daniel's treatment the night before. The thought crossed her mind that she could report him. But would anyone believe her? Her word against his. And then, where would that leave her? Daniel would probably never forgive her, and it would only be worse. No, she wouldn't do that.

She'd have to tell Sal. She wouldn't be able to pretend that everything was okay with her. Sal would know. But how would Daniel feel about that? He never talked about his problems with anyone. She sighed in despair. *God, please help us.*

The flashing lights ahead brought her focus back to the present. A broken down car, that was all. She looked at Daniel. She'd need to wake him up. They were almost there. She paid more attention to her whereabouts. It was all so familiar. Was it wise to have come back here so soon? The place where her heart had been broken? Where so many memories were waiting to be relived. She'd have to be careful. If Daniel knew the extent of her heartbreak, who knew what he'd accuse her of? Especially since Mathew lived nearby. Had she suggested they come here because of him? Just to be near him? *No. Definitely not*. This was her home, where she belonged. She wanted to come because of Sal. No other reason.

Daniel stirred beside her as she slowed down for a red light. She turned her head and looked at him. Sleep had done him good. At least he now looked human. His day old growth was dark and stubbly, and he needed a hair cut. Once again she wondered what lay ahead of them.

Would they ever be happy again? Would Daniel ever find God and true peace and forgiveness? And would her threat of leaving be enough to prevent him treating her like that again?

"SAL!" Lizzy squealed like a school girl as she fell into Sal's arms.

"Well, look at you with your little baby bump!" Sal exclaimed when they finally pulled apart.

Lizzy glanced down and rubbed her tummy before grinning at Sal. "I didn't think it was that obvious."

"It's not really, but you're so skinny, it does stick out a bit."

Lizzy's grin gave way to a broad smile. "It's so good to see you, Sal. Have I missed you or what!"

"I've missed you, too, Liz," Sal said as she peered around Lizzy and looked in the car. "Is Daniel alright?"

Lizzy's heart raced. *No, he's not alright, and neither am I. We're a mess.* But now wasn't the time to say anything. There'd be time for that later. Hopefully.

Lizzy glanced at him and was relieved to see him combing his hair. At least he was making an effort. "Yes, he's fine. He just fell asleep on the way here."

"You must have had a late night at your parent's place, then. Did it go okay?"

Lizzy sighed and lowered her eyes. "Not really. I'll tell you later."

Sal peered at her with a puzzled look. If only Lizzy could tell her everything right now. Get it off her chest. Get some perspective. But it was too fresh. Too raw. And besides, she couldn't tell her in front of Daniel.

Moments later, he joined them.

"Sal! Good to see you," he said as he hugged her.

"Good to see you too, Daniel. What's this then?" Sal asked as she stroked his day old beard.

He reached up and felt his face. "Forgot to shave this morning. I might keep it while we're on holiday. What do you think?"

Lizzy and Sal looked at each other and shook their heads and burst out laughing.

"Well I guess that sorts it then," he replied.

"Enough!" Sal said. "Let's grab your gear and head inside. Got the gang coming over tonight for a get together. Hope that's okay with you."

Lizzy's smile wavered and her heart fell. Did that mean Mathew would be there? One part of her longed to see him. The other part knew it would be asking for trouble. Big trouble.

"YOU LOOK like you both need a rest," Sal said once they were inside her small semi-detached she shared with another teacher.

"I'm okay for now," Lizzy said, "but I might need a short nap before everyone comes tonight." *Dare I ask who's coming?*

"Let me make coffee, then. I guess you've had lunch?"

Lizzy nodded and winced as she took off her jacket. "Coffee would be great." She took a seat in the kitchen, and was relieved to see Daniel sit on the couch and flick on the television. *Maybe he'll fall asleep again, and then I can talk to Sal.*

"It's a pity you're not staying longer than a couple of nights, Lizzy. But I might be able to get down to the cottage for a day or so. Two nights just doesn't seem enough."

"I know. I wish we were staying longer, but Daniel wanted us to spend as much time as we could at the beach." In light of what had happened, Lizzy now wondered how wise that was. She picked up her mug of freshly brewed coffee and wrapped her hands around it. She inhaled deeply, allowing the sweet aroma to tickle her senses. She brought the mug to her lips, and savoured the warm creamy liquid as it slid down her throat. "This is wonderful, Sal. Thanks."

"Is everything okay, Lizzy? You don't look your normal, happy self."

Lizzy looked into her friend's eyes. *How much could Daniel hear?* She shook her head a little. Her gaze darted to him. His feet were up, and he'd finished his coffee. He seemed engrossed in the programme he was watching, and wasn't paying any attention to them. She leaned in closer to Sal and whispered, "Let's go outside."

She picked up her coffee and joined Sal outside in the garden. Leaning back on the bench, she closed her eyes and soaked up the warmth of the sun.

"You're not okay, are you?"

Lizzy slowly opened her eyes and shook her head. Sal reached over and hugged her. Tears streamed down her face as her pent up emotion finally escaped.

"What's happened, Lizzy?"

Lizzy wiped her face and blew her nose with the tissue Sal handed her. "It's the drink, Sal. He can't handle it. It makes him do things he wouldn't normally do." Tears streamed down her face again. "Last night he and Father had an argument, and we ended up leaving." Her body shuddered. "We stayed at a hotel, and he got drunk." Lizzy closed her eyes and paused, inhaling deeply. "He was rough with me, Sal. I didn't do anything to upset him. I don't know why he did it." She sniffed and wiped her eyes.

"You poor thing." Sal hugged her again, and this time held her until her sobbing had eased. "He has no right to treat you like that. Especially in your condition."

Lizzy sniffed and fought back a fresh wave of tears. "I know." She closed her eyes for a moment. "We talked this morning. He needs help Sal, but mainly he needs God. He's so insecure, and he says he feels like a failure, even though he puts on a good front."

"Yes, but what he did to you, it's not right at all. I've got a good mind to confront him about it." Sal's nostrils flared and her eyes narrowed. "He could have seriously hurt you, Lizzy."

"I know." *Do I tell her about him doing time for assault?* Lizzy's mind raced. *Maybe not. Who knows what she'd do if she knew.* She breathed deeply and wrapped her arms around her stomach. *Oh God, how did I get myself into this mess? Why couldn't I have just married Mathew? It's not fair.* Tears threatened to start falling again, but she took control of herself. *No, I can't think like that. God, please forgive me.* "We've just got to pray for him, Sal. Only God can heal him and make him whole."

"Yes, I agree. He needs to talk to someone. Get some counselling."

"Maybe. But I don't know he's ready. He doesn't like talking to anyone about it, even me. But we can ask God to bring the right person into his life when he's ready. Until then, I'll just have to trust God to protect me and the baby. He's not like it all the time. And I told him I'd leave if he treated me like that again."

"Good on you, Liz, but shouldn't you consider leaving now? What if he does do it again? It might be too late then."

Lizzy shook her head and sniffed. "No, I'll give him one more chance. I'm not ready to leave. I know it sounds stupid, but I need to stay with him. I really believe God's going to work in his life."

Sal squeezed her hand. "As long as you know what you're doing." The look in Sal's eye made Lizzy shiver.

Did she really know what she was doing? Or was she making a big mistake?

A LITTLE LATER, when they were in their room together, Daniel grabbed Lizzy's arm and glowered at her. "What have you been telling her?"

"She guessed, Daniel. I didn't have to tell her." Lizzy looked up into Daniel's dark eyes and took a deep breath to calm her pounding heart. Daniel didn't move.

"Daniel, what's happened?"

He glared at her, but he was controlling himself. Finally he let go of her arm and slumped on the bed.

"Come here, Daniel." Lizzy's voice trembled. She stretched out her arms to him. "Something's troubling you. Please, Daniel. Come." This wasn't the Daniel she knew. This was a different person. A hardened, unhappy person. And he wasn't even drunk. *Lord, what's going on?*

Her heart raced as she slowly walked towards him. *God, please help me...* When she reached him, he looked up. The hardness had gone from his face, and the Daniel she knew and loved had returned. *But for how long?*

LATER, seated outside in Sal's garden, Daniel took her hand.

"I don't know what happens, Lizzy. It's like something snaps in my head and I become a different person. I don't mean to get like that. It just happens. I don't ever want to lose you."

She looked at him with a combination of pity, love and frustration all at once. "I know. But Daniel, it mainly happens when you've been drinking. That seems to be the trigger." She had to tread carefully.

He stared at the garden. "You're probably right. But I hadn't been drinking when we were at your parent's place."

"No, but you let Father stir you. And then you went out drinking. So maybe it's what causes you to drink in the first place that's the issue."

"Maybe I'm just a failure."

She sighed in frustration. "How many times have I told you before you're not a failure? You've just got a problem, Daniel. And you need to get help. Underneath you're a caring, loving person. You're funny, friendly and intelligent. You just can't drink, because then you become a monster."

"But I like a drink, Lizzy. How can a man not take a drink?"

"Because you can't stop at one, Daniel, and that's the problem." She paused for a moment and looked at Sal's garden while she gathered her thoughts. Should she talk to him about God? About how he could be freed from his inner demons? She couldn't keep putting it off, but was now the right time? *Lord?* Her heart raced as she turned her head and looked him in the eye.

"Daniel. I don't think drinking's the main issue. I think you're carrying guilt about everything that's happened, and whenever you get in a tricky situation, you drink to deal with it."

Daniel pulled back and opened his mouth to speak, but Lizzy continued. "Let me finish, please. I know you've said you blame God for taking Rachel and Ciara from you, but I truly believe that if you'll let Him, God can help you deal with it all. He can take away the guilt, and He can help you stay off the drink. He can make you into a new person on the inside if you'll let Him. He loves you Daniel, and so do I. But you've got to be open to Him, and want Him in your life. He won't force you."

Daniel straightened himself. "You know I'm not into all that God stuff, Lizzy. It might be alright for you, but he wouldn't be interested in me. And even if he was, I don't know I'd be interested in him. I'll sort my own problems out." He leaned closer and kissed her cheek as he squeezed her hand. "We'll be okay, Liz. I promise I'll try harder in future. I'm sorry."

All Lizzy could do was smile. Daniel's attempt to console her was comforting, but without God's intervention she was confident there was little chance they'd be okay. All she could do now was pray for the Holy Spirit to soften his heart and for another opportunity to share with him.

She leaned her head on his shoulder and closed her eyes, allowing the late afternoon sun to warm her body.

LIZZY SHOULD HAVE BEEN EXCITED to see all of her old university and church friends again, but she wasn't. They used to be so close, but now, what did they have in common? She'd already heard from Sal about their successful careers and marriages. As far as she knew, they were all happy. How could she maintain a facade in front of them, and pretend everything was wonderful when it wasn't? She didn't want to pretend, but she didn't want their sympathy, either. Could she ask Sal to call it off? Probably not. It was too late for that.

Out of all their friends, she was the only one who'd moved away, and they bombarded her with questions all evening. Answering the same questions over and over again was tiring, especially when she had to skirt around the issue most of the time to avoid lying.

"And how's married life?"

"Oh, it has its ups and downs."

"I bet it does!"

How many times had she heard that?

"When's the baby due?"

"What's it like living in the north?"

"Do they speak English up there?"

"Where did you meet *him*?"

"What does he do?"

"Are you going to keep working after you've had the baby?"

"What do your parents think of him?"

"Why didn't you invite us to your wedding?"

"Have you got any wedding photos?"

"Sal said you were married at a Register Office. Is that true?"

"Why?!"

"Why not!!!!"

A few of the husbands had come, but they had little in common with Daniel. He made an early exit. He said because it was mainly all girls and he felt out of it. 'Have time alone with your friends,' he'd said. But she knew it was really because his heart wasn't in it either. They had much more serious business on their minds.

At least Mathew hadn't come.

. . .

Lizzy flopped onto the couch after everyone had left, put her feet up, and closed her eyes.

"You look tired," Sal said, as she sat beside her.

"Yes, I am a bit." Lizzy pulled herself up and yawned. "Thanks for organising it, Sal. It was good to see everyone. Strange, though. Living up north is so different to down here. It's like a different world. I got the impression they thought I was crazy choosing to move up there."

"They don't know the reason why you moved, Lizzy. Some of them guessed, but most just think you wanted a change, which is partly true. I wouldn't worry about it. You've got more important things to worry about."

"Don't remind me." Lizzy rolled her eyes and hugged a cushion. "I don't even know if Daniel's here. He said he was going to bed, but for all I know he could've gone out." She sighed and glanced at their bedroom door. *God, let him be there, asleep.*

Lizzy tiptoed into the bedroom and breathed a sigh of relief when she heard Daniel snoring. Even though she was exhausted, she spent a few minutes in prayer before falling asleep.

CHAPTER 14

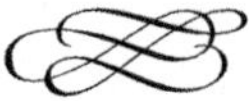

When Lizzy awoke next morning, her mind was in turmoil. Normally she would have been ecstatic if Daniel wanted to come to church with her, but this morning she was half hoping he wouldn't. What if Mathew was preaching? How would Daniel react if he met him? More importantly, how would she react if she saw him? Maybe she shouldn't go.

Daniel stirred beside her and as she looked down at his tousled black hair, her heart warmed with love for him, despite everything. Maybe this would be the day Daniel would hear from God. She'd go, and prove to herself and anyone else who was interested that she was over Mathew Carter, and that she was in love with her handsome, gregarious Irishman.

As they took their seats towards the back of the church, the familiar surroundings of the church stirred Lizzy's heart. It had been in this very building she'd come to the Lord, and the memories she held were precious. It felt like home, even though it was only a building. Not much had changed. The well used hymnals still graced the back of the dark timber pews, but were now accompanied by the newer praise and worship song books some of the older parishioners didn't like. The organ played quietly as people continued to take their seats. Lizzy looked around discreetly and saw a lot of familiar faces. Her heart suddenly fell as she realised there might be a repeat performance of the question and answer time she'd suffered through last night. Maybe they should sneak out during the last hymn.

They stood as the music from the organ rose and began to play the first hymn. As she sang, the words of Blessed Assurance warmed her heart, and she was truly grateful that Jesus was indeed hers. Beside her, Daniel sang the words too. At the last moment, he'd decided to come, and she stood proudly with him, holding his hand. She prayed that one day soon he'd also be able to claim this as his story.

Her pulse raced when Mathew walked to the pulpit. She hoped Daniel wouldn't notice. Her eyes took in every one of his features. He so looked the part. She breathed deeply in an attempt to control the emotions she didn't want to be feeling and knew were wrong. She prayed for forgiveness and asked for strength, and then focused her attention on the content of the sermon rather than the speaker.

Despite her previous decision to sneak out, she couldn't do it. Mathew stood at the exit, shaking everyone's hands as they left. Her heart pounded as she followed Sal towards him. Her hands shook, and were clammy. She'd have to introduce Daniel to him. But would she be able to speak? She felt like a bumbling, nervous school girl about to go on her first date, not a mature married woman carrying her first child. *Oh Lord, please help me. This was a stupid idea. We shouldn't have come.*

Then he was there, standing right in front of her. The dimple on his right cheek appeared as he smiled, causing palpitations in her heart.

"Lizzy!" He stretched out his hands. The hands she'd held so lovingly in the past. The hands she could now only shake. She looked into his eyes, and for a moment time stood still. How she longed to wrap her arms around him, but instead, she turned and introduced Daniel. Had Mathew sensed any hesitation? Did he see the turmoil she was in when he looked into her eyes? She hoped not.

She laughed too loudly, and her voice was too high as she tried to cover her nervousness with meaningless chatter. Her eyes lingered on his as they walked away, and her heart felt like it was being ripped out of her. She prayed Daniel wouldn't notice.

"I NEED TO GO THE BATHROOM," Lizzy said to both Sal and Daniel as they reached the outside grassed area. "I'll be right back."

Standing in front of the mirror, she saw how flushed her face looked. She turned the tap on and splashed cool water on it until she felt normal and had regained control of herself. There was no towel, so she rummaged in her bag and found a tissue. That would have to do. She patted her face dry, and wiped away the mascara that had run and was making her eyes look like Alice Cooper's. She brushed her hair and breathed deeply, thankful that nobody else had come in.

She straightened her skirt, and turned sideways. She could just see her baby bump if she stood on tiptoes. Had Mathew noticed it? *Stop it, Lizzy. You can't think about him like that anymore. It's wrong.*

Thankful it was a bright sunny day, she hid behind her sunglasses as she opened the door and stepped out.

"So, what have you got planned for us for the rest of the day?" Lizzy asked Sal a little too brightly when she returned a few seconds later. She grabbed hold of Daniel's arm and gave it a squeeze.

"How about we show Daniel the highlights of Exeter? Are you up to riding, Liz?"

Lizzy hesitated for just a moment. "Yes! It'll be fun to ride. What do you think, Daniel?"

"Fine by me." But he didn't sound fine.

"Great! There are two bikes at home, and we can borrow one from next door."

Lizzy took one last lingering look at Mathew before they walked to the car.

It was a lovely day for a ride around town. They visited the cathedral and the university, and rode past the flat Lizzy had lived in whilst she was a student. Although she found it difficult, she didn't allow her mind to dwell on any of the memories that included Mathew. Finally, they rode along some of the canal paths and ended up at an old pub sitting on the edge of the River Exe.

They chose to sit on the terrace overlooking the river, and were lucky to get a table. The late afternoon sun cast its golden glow over the weeping willow trees standing on the opposite bank, creating a peaceful setting. Keen rowers were taking advantage of the good weather, as were a number of families out for a leisurely Sunday afternoon stroll.

Lizzy pulled her chair closer to Daniel's and took his hand. She needed to make an effort to keep things right between them. He was, after all, like it or not, the man she'd married.

WHILE LIZZY and Sal chatted away, Daniel sat quietly, contemplating the looks that had passed between Lizzy and her ex beau that morning. She'd told him it was all over, but Lizzy's demeanour suggested otherwise. *A man could get really jealous if he wasn't careful.* The all familiar aroma of the ale house wafted around him, tempting him to order a real drink. But he'd promised Lizzy, so he fought the temptation.

He lit a cigarette, and fidgeted with the car keys as he studied his wife. She was too good for him, if he was honest with himself. Why she'd ever agreed to marry him was beyond his understanding. They came from different worlds, he and Lizzy. What could he offer her? A hospital orderly's wage was never going to be enough to keep her happy. And before long, she'd be stopping work to have their baby. How would they survive on his wage alone? *It would have been better if she'd stayed with that preacher.* He was obviously more her type than him. Educated.

Well behaved. Probably never been drunk in his life. Maybe he didn't even drink.

He stubbed out his cigarette and stood up. "I'm getting a drink. Do you girls want another?"

~

LIZZY LOOKED at Daniel in alarm and grabbed his hand. "No Daniel. Please don't," she pleaded.

His eyes had that unsettled look she'd come to hate. Why hadn't she noticed he was on edge?

Her heart cringed when he glared at her and pulled his hand away. "I'm only having one. I'm not getting drunk. Do you want another drink or not?"

Lizzy glanced at Sal, and then shook her head. She had that sinking feeling in her chest, as if a heavy weight was pulling her down and she could do little to stop it. She closed her eyes momentarily and inhaled deeply in an attempt to still her racing heart.

Sal reached out and squeezed her hand. Lizzy looked into Sal's caring eyes and fought back the tears triggered by her friend's concern and understanding.

"Oh, Lizzy." Sal squeezed Lizzy's hand tighter. "I'm here for you. Just remember that."

Lizzy nodded and wiped her tears.

Sal withdrew her hand just before Daniel returned. Lizzy's heart was heavy, but she made sure she involved Daniel in their conversation.

Daniel was true to his word and only had one drink, although the number of cigarettes he smoked suggested he was still on edge and could easily have had more. They ordered a meal, and then rode back to Sal's place in the dark.

As they prepared for bed later that night, Lizzy watched every word for fear of saying something wrong, and jumped at every slightest movement Daniel made. She just wanted the tension between them to disappear, and tried several times to wrap her arms around him and tell him she loved him, but he pushed her away every time. The silence between them killed her.

Her pulse quickened when he turned and glared at her. His eyes had narrowed and the vein in his forehead bulged. She leaned back as far as she could as he spat into her face. "I saw the way you looked at him, Lizzy. Tell me, do you still love him?"

So he had noticed. A bolt of alarm ran through her body and for a moment she was unable to reply. Was he going to hurt her? Her heart rate increased even further and she tried to stop her hands from shaking. She shook her head. "No. No, I don't love him, Daniel. It's over." She inhaled deeply as she waited for his next move.

He leaned so close she could feel his breath on her face. "It had better be."

She inched back on the bed as far as she could. Her chest heaved. They stared at each other for what seemed minutes. Tension hung in the air between them. Should she scream out for Sal, or just sit it out and see what he'd do? Rooted to the spot and unable to speak, Lizzy held her breath and waited.

Finally she spoke. Her voice was quiet. "Daniel, it really is over." She gulped and reached out to him. "It was just a shock seeing him again this morning. But it really is over. You need to believe me." She inched closer to him. "It's you I love, Daniel. We've got stuff to sort out, but believe me, I love you, not him." But was it the truth, or was she just saying it to placate him and diffuse the situation?

The clock in the living room chimed ten. Moments passed. Lizzy gulped. She stood and slowly walked to the end of the bed where Daniel had remained. His eyes had lost their dark intensity, and his body was less rigid. She wrapped her arms around him and pulled him tight. She ran her fingers through his dark curly hair and kissed his neck. She turned his head to face hers and kissed him slowly.

CHAPTER 15

The following morning Lizzy prayed a prayer of thanks when it seemed her peace offering of the night before had worked, and she smiled as Daniel sang in the shower. In some ways she wished they could stay with Sal for the rest of their holiday. How would it be in a cottage on their own, with no-one around to call for help if she needed it? No, she'd be okay. She'd make sure Daniel got all the attention he needed. And God was with her.

Her chest was tight as goodbyes were said a little while later. "Make sure you come and see us soon," she whispered into Sal's ear. She waved all the way down the street until Sal disappeared into the distance and could no longer be seen.

It wasn't a long drive to Blackpool Sands. The directions provided by the landlady were detailed, and although they made a number of turns along narrow country lanes, they didn't get lost once. When they reached the cottage that was to be their home for the next two weeks, they were rewarded with the most beautiful of views. Perched high on a hill overlooking the brilliant blue sea, the 16th century whitewashed stone cottage stood like a sentinel guarding the beach below.

Lizzy climbed out of the car and stood, arms outstretched, breathing in the clean fresh air and taking in the amazing view. As she looked out on God's creation, her heart lifted. She turned around and smiled at Daniel.

Inside, Lizzy ran around like a small child checking out each room, opening and closing cupboards and investigating every nook and cranny of the quaint cottage.

"Come and look at this, Daniel! We can sit here to have our meals. Isn't it wonderful?" She hugged him as he came outside to see what she'd found. They sat for a few minutes in the summerhouse just outside the kitchen, breathing in the heady scent of the jasmine vine covering the trellis. Sitting there with Daniel, gazing out at the azure blue sea, Lizzy began to hope that maybe they'd be okay after all.

Time passed all too quickly. Leisurely breakfasts taken outside, walks along the beach below, drives around the coastline checking out quaint villages and rocky headlands. Lunches in pubs where history was etched in each wall, and dinners either at home or out, each day held its own magic, almost as if they were on their honeymoon again, apart from an underlying feeling that Lizzy had that something was still not quite right between them.

Even when they were laughing and enjoying each other's company, she was aware that one wrong word could send Daniel off on a drinking binge. Although he hadn't had a drink since that last night with Sal, and hadn't been drunk since the night they'd stormed out of her parent's place, his restlessness was evident by the number of cigarettes he smoked and his inability to fully relax. She steeled herself constantly for another interrogation over her feelings for Mathew, and mentally prepared answers just in case.

One day as she was preparing breakfast, Lizzy felt a flutter in her stomach. She wasn't sure what it was at first. Such a strange sensation, but then she realised. She hugged her tummy and called out to Daniel. She guided his hand to where she'd felt the movement. She looked into his eyes, and warmed at the love she saw there for her and the baby. He didn't feel anything, but it didn't matter. She'd felt it. The baby had moved. It really was there. Their own child. Maybe this child would help Daniel face his problems. But then her heart dropped. He was probably anxious after what happened to baby Rachel. *If only he'd allow God to wash away his guilt and anger.*

Every morning as she sat outside having her quiet time, Lizzy hoped and prayed that one day Daniel would join her. How she longed to share this most important facet of her life with him. It was like they were walking two separate but parallel roads, and she wondered if those roads would eventually merge or separate. She pleaded with God for them to merge. She prayed that Daniel's heart would be softened and he'd be open to receiving God's love in his life. But he never wanted to talk about it. He dismissed it immediately whenever she even broached the topic, so she just prayed.

The morning before they were due to leave, her heart fluttered when Daniel joined her. Maybe today would be the day. She smiled as he sat beside her and lit a cigarette. The morning sun was warming and welcoming on her body, and the sea below glistened as it basked in the new day. She breathed in the fresh air and thanked God for His creation and for His presence in her life, and for Daniel joining her. She remained silent so as not to spoil the moment, but prayed silently that Daniel would also feel God's presence as he gazed upon His beautiful creation.

The peace was broken when Daniel stubbed out his cigarette and asked her unexpectedly if she ever regretted marrying him. The question took her completely by surprise. Here she was, thinking he might want to talk about God, but instead, he threw this at her. How could she answer him honestly? Her body slumped, and her mind raced as she tried to work out how to respond.

"Well, do you?" His eyes were intense and unsettled her.

"Oh Daniel. Where did that come from?" She sighed and shook her head. "Surely you know how much I love you. Is it really necessary to ask that?"

"I think it is, Lizzy. You see, I don't really know why you married me or what you see in me, so it makes me wonder if you're still hankering after that preacher, even though you say you're not." He leaned back and crossed his arms, his eyes fixed on her.

Lizzy fidgeted with her hands and felt her wedding ring. She wanted to look away to gather her thoughts, to be free for a second from Daniel's intense gaze, but instead, she held it. "Okay. If you want an honest answer, there have been a few times I've regretted marrying you. The times you were drunk and mistreated me. But they were just immediate responses to your actions, not necessarily to you as a person. Maybe we married a little too hastily, but I do love you, Daniel, and I don't regret being married to you. Do you ever regret marrying me?" She raised her eyebrows and tilted her head. Two could play at this game.

Lizzy smirked as Daniel struggled to answer. "See, not so easy, is it?"

He narrowed his eyes. "You have no idea what's going on inside me. You think you know what makes me tick, but you don't. You want to shove this God nonsense down my throat, thinking it'll make everything better. What a load of rubbish. There's no way he could change anything, if he exists at all." He sat up and lit another cigarette. "I regret a lot of things, Lizzy, but marrying you isn't one of them. I regret I'm not good enough for you. I think you'd rather have married that preacher, but because he didn't want you, you just married the first man that came along to try to get back at him. And that just happened to be me. But I guess you'll never admit that. I worry one day when you realise what a no-hoper you married, you'll just pack up and leave." He leaned forward and held her gaze. "If ever you do that, Lizzy, I won't let you take the baby away from me."

Lizzy gasped and her hands flew to her chest. That thought had never occurred to her. How could Daniel expect her to leave the baby behind? But hopefully it wouldn't come to that.

She moved closer to him and took his hand.

"I'm not planning on leaving you, Daniel, unless you mistreat me again. We'll work through our issues together, but we need to be honest with each other. Talk to me if you're troubled, and we can work it out. I just want us to be a happy family. You, me and our baby." She glanced down and hugged her stomach. "Okay?"

He stared at her for a few moments. She wanted to know what he was thinking, and what really made him tick, but would he ever let her get that close?

"Okay Lizzy. I'll try. For the baby's sake. But I can't promise anything."

Lizzy exhaled slowly and squeezed his hand. Another bomb diffused.

DESPITE THEIR CONVERSATION THAT MORNING, Daniel was quiet and withdrawn for the rest of the day. Lizzy felt like she was walking on egg shells and wondered why. Why wouldn't he tell her what troubled him, especially after promising he'd try. She really didn't understand him, that was obvious.

After lunch, Daniel said he was taking a nap, so Lizzy took the opportunity for a walk on her own. She picked up her Bible and headed along the top of the headland. Reaching a seat that some thoughtful person had placed there years before, she pulled her scarf tighter while she breathed in the salty sea air.

Her thoughts turned to God. How she needed Him right now. Although she'd assured Daniel she didn't regret marrying him, seeing Mathew again had unsettled her, and if she was truly honest, she had to admit that Daniel was right. She would rather have married Mathew.

The truth of that statement filled her with guilt. She lowered her head, closed her eyes and cried out to God. *"Oh Lord, I'm so sorry. I'm sorry for being so impatient and not trusting you to lead me, and for taking matters into my own hands. It wasn't fair of me to marry Daniel when I still loved Mathew. Please forgive me."* Tears rolled down her cheeks. How could she ever make it up to him?

She stared out to sea, not really seeing anything, but in her heart, she heard the still, quiet voice of God.

'My dear child, your sins were forgiven at the cross. I hear your cries of repentance, and I know you mean them. My loving arms are wrapped around you. Draw on my strength, Elizabeth, not your own. True love is an action not a feeling. Go back and choose to love your husband. He needs you. But know that you can't change him. Love him as he is. Don't dwell on the past, Elizabeth, but learn from it. Whatever happens, don't forget that I'm with you.'

Tears fell from her eyes as the assurance that the God of creation loved her flowed through her body. All her wrong decisions were forgiven, and her slate was clean. And God had his arms wrapped around her.

She remained for some time, lost in the peace and love that filled her heart and soul, and prayed for Daniel and their baby.

CHAPTER 16

The next day as she packed their bags, Lizzy's heart was heavy, despite her experience with God the previous afternoon, and her earlier misgivings about being in the cottage on their own. If only they could stay here, cocooned in this lovely cottage, away from the real world with all its troubles and temptations. But no, the time had come to leave, and she just had to trust God to be with them.

The street lights flickered on as they turned into their street. The sun had set behind gloomy grey clouds, and Lizzy sighed as Daniel parked the car in front of the apartment block. More graffiti had appeared while they'd been away, and a gang of unkempt youths in torn jeans and flannelette shirts sat on the brick wall smoking cigarettes.

"It'd be great to live in our own little house," Lizzy said as they carried their bags towards the entrance. "What do you think, Daniel?"

He held the door open for her and glanced at the youths. "It'd be great, but I don't know we can afford it."

"Yes we can. We've got money saved up. Come on Daniel, can we please take a look?" Her eyes pleaded with him.

He looked at her and sighed. "Maybe."

Lizzy's heart lifted, and as she climbed the stairs, she pictured a beautiful terraced house, with a garden filled with sweet smelling forget-me-nots and daisies, and a swing where she could sit with their baby in the afternoon sun. It'd be wonderful. They'd have an upstairs and a downstairs, and they'd have space! Nowhere near as much space as she'd had when she was growing up, but that was decadent, almost obscene. How much space do three people really need? A terraced house would do just fine.

Daniel bent down and picked up the pile of mail that had built up while they'd been away. He ripped open one of the envelopes and the colour drained from his face.

"What's wrong, Daniel? What's happened?" Lizzy looked at him with concern.

He hesitated before answering. "I have to meet with the supervisor tomorrow at ten am."

"What on earth for?"

Daniel glanced at Lizzy before looking back at the letter. "It doesn't say."

"Maybe it's just to catch up on something that happened while we were away." Lizzy leaned closer to take a look. "What else could it be?"

Daniel shrugged half-heartedly.

"I don't know."

The following morning, Lizzy leaned over and kissed Daniel tenderly on his cheek before climbing out of the car.

"I hope your meeting goes well." She smiled at him and gazed into his eyes. Their holiday had done them good.

She watched him drive off, wondering why he spun the wheels, and then surveyed the cold, uninviting walls of the brick building in front of her. *Only seven more weeks of school to go.*

Aware of the children's eyes on her as she walked along the corridor to her classroom, she knew the time had come to tell them. She'd definitely miss the children, but to not have any preparation or marking... she couldn't wait.

She looked down fondly at the little blond haired girl tugging on her arm.

"Miss, are you having a baby?"

Lizzy grinned and ruffled her hair. Yes, she definitely would miss the children, especially this one. "Yes Hayley. I'm having a baby." Hayley giggled, and ran off to tell her friends.

Lizzy laughed to herself as she opened the door.

DANIEL'S FACE dropped when Lizzy left the car. He watched her walk into the school yard and wondered how to break the news to her that he was out of a job. Because that's what he fully expected to hear when he attended the meeting. Her words of the previous evening rang in his ear. How could he tell her there'd be no house? She'd be devastated. And she'd be furious when she found out why.

He thumped the steering wheel and started the car. He put his foot down, spinning the wheels as he entered the traffic. Who had it been? Who reported him? *It must have been that cow of a woman at reception.* He thumped the wheel again and cursed her.

Sitting in the car park with his head on the steering wheel, his chest was tight and his breathing laboured. The meeting wasn't until ten am. Two hours away. Two whole hours. He sighed, leaned over the back and picked up his lunch bag. Not that he'd need it. He opened the door, climbed out, and went to work.

"Morning, Danny. Have a good break?" *Why did they have to be so happy and chatty?* He held up his hand and waved as he walked past the reception area.

"It was grand, thanks. Good to be back." His trade mark whistle was missing.

And there she was, walking right towards him. He glowered at her as their paths crossed. His eyes bore into hers, and he had a good mind to pull her aside and have it out, but thought better of it at the last moment.

He reached his locker and took out his key. Looking both ways, he held his breath and opened it. It was still there. He gulped, glanced over his shoulder, and reached in. Time stood still when he heard heavy footsteps stop behind him.

"What have you got there, O'Connor?"

Daniel slowly put the bottle down and turned around. His supervisor stood with his arms crossed and a smirk on his face.

Daniel's muscles tightened. Highly skilled at covering things up, he had no idea how to talk his way out of this. He'd been caught red handed.

"Move." The supervisor stepped forward and reached for the bottle. "Follow me."

He led Daniel to his office, where the Head of HR was already seated at a solid timber desk surrounded by dark panelled walls covered in diplomas and certificates, obviously designed to impress and intimidate. Just like the Headmaster's office at St Pat's. Daniel could see no positive outcome from this meeting.

"Well, Mr O'Connor, take a seat." His voice was steady, clear and decisive. He locked eyes with Daniel for a moment before continuing. "You can't say you haven't been warned."

Daniel knew there was no way out. Yes, he'd been warned. No alcohol was to be in his possession at any time, and that included his locker. He'd been caught three times already. Twice drinking on the job, and once being under the influence at work. This was the fourth time.

"I was removing it from the premises, Sir." Memories of being hauled in front of the Headmaster on numerous occasions flitted through his mind. How often had he succeeded in avoiding punishment back then? Rarely, although he'd always tried hard to talk his way out of it. What were his chances now?

"Very commendable, O'Connor, but too late. Your employment is terminated. Take your belongings, and don't come back."

Daniel's gaze darted from one to the other. "But Sir, my wife's due to give birth shortly. We won't survive if I'm not working." He leaned forward and spoke quietly. "Could I please have another chance?" He looked from one to the other. "I'll get rid of the bottle, and you have my word I won't bring any more in." His eyes lit up and he clasped his hands together in his lap.

The Head of HR drew himself forward, his unsmiling determination showing clearly in his eyes. Daniel's shoulders slumped.

"I'm very sorry for your situation, Mr O'Connor, but it's your own making. Your employment here at this hospital is terminated immediately."

Daniel held his gaze for a moment before he stood and was accompanied to the exit by the supervisor.

He was tempted to ask if he could at least have his bottle.

Had it only been twenty minutes since he'd climbed out of the car? And here he was again, but this time, knowing for sure he didn't have a job. Daniel thumped the steering wheel with his fist several times. *How do I tell her? She's going to kill me.*

He lit a cigarette and stared out the window. Time stood still. Cars came and went all around him, but he didn't hear or see them. Neither did he hear the wail of an ambulance approaching the hospital. His head spun and his thoughts were jumbled.

Somewhere through the fog that was his brain, a solution came to him. He wouldn't tell her. He'd spend his days looking for work, and only tell her once he'd found a job.

Daniel turned the key in the ignition, and drove towards town.

CHAPTER 17

As Daniel expected, Lizzy's first question when he picked her up that afternoon was about how the meeting had gone. He'd been thinking about his answer all day. He didn't wanted to lie, but there was no way around it.

"Oh, it was nothing really. Just a few changes to procedure, that's all. Nothing to be worried about." He quickly glanced at her, avoiding her eyes.

"That's a relief," she said as she settled in the seat beside him. "What a day! I didn't get to sit for a minute. My feet are killing me. I have to say, I'm looking forward to finishing. I think I'll be counting the days."

Daniel focused on driving in the wet weather. How long could he keep the facade going? He figured he had two weeks. She'd find out anyway when his pay didn't come in.

"Sounds like you need a hot bath, Mrs O'Connor. I'll cook dinner tonight."

Lizzy's eyes widened. "Really? That would be wonderful, Daniel." She leaned back in the seat and smiled at him.

Day after day for the next two weeks, Daniel looked for work. As far as he knew, Lizzy never suspected anything. Worried that someone he knew would see him, he'd prepared answers that would dismiss their curiosity. He'd tried everywhere, including his local pub, but even they didn't have any vacancies. No jobs were to be had anywhere.

On Friday afternoon, he took himself for a walk along the river. It was driving him crazy. He couldn't keep it from Lizzy much longer. He could maybe get away with saying there'd been a problem with their pays - that would buy him a few days, but no more. He'd played it over and over in his mind how he'd tell her, but it always ended badly, regardless of which way he did it. He'd become jittery. Not having a drink for the last four weeks had been almost a record. He was proud of himself, but now, with so much time on his hands, he continually thought how good a drink would be. He could taste the bitterness of the liquid sliding effortlessly down his throat, and he longed for the immediate relief it would bring. *No, I can't think about it. Don't go there.* He walked on. *God, if you're there, you'd better help me.*

He found a rock on the water's edge and sat on it. The water flowed slowly, grey and uninviting, reflecting the colour of the sky. He picked up some pebbles and threw them in. *"You know, God. I don't think you're there at all. If you are, you've done nothing for me. Nothing."* He thought for a moment. *"Well, maybe you brought Lizzy into my life, but that's about all."* He threw more pebbles into the river and watched them sink out of sight. *"Stuff it. I'm going for a drink."*

He stood, and drove straight to his local.

WHEN DANIEL WASN'T there to pick her up by five pm, Lizzy knew something was wrong. She'd actually been surprised at how punctual he'd been since they'd returned from their holiday, but hadn't thought much more about it. She'd just been relieved he wasn't drinking, and that he was helping her out more at home.

The one main thing that still worried her, though, was his resistance to God. She continued to pray for him every day, but she was impatient. She longed for them to share a common journey, to pray together, to read the Bible together, and more importantly, to bring up their child together in a loving Christian home. Although he came to church with her, she knew his heart wasn't there even though his body was. He'd even agreed to attend a small group meeting with her during the week, but she got the feeling it was just to keep her happy, not because he wanted to learn about God.

But there was always hope, and so she continued to pray.

Sometimes she felt like shaking him. Why couldn't he just let go of all the things he kept bringing up as arguments? He still blamed God for allowing little baby Rachel to die, and for Ciara's death. He often referred to the fighting between the Catholics and the Protestants in Northern Ireland, and said in no uncertain words that if that's what religion's all about, he wasn't interested. It didn't matter how often she told him that God wasn't interested in religion either. 'He's just interested in you, Daniel, and what you think of Him. Religion is just what man has made up.'

Daniel wouldn't budge. He blamed God for all the bad things that were happening in the world. 'If God's so powerful, why doesn't he stop it all?' he'd ask. It didn't matter how many times she tried to explain that whilst He could stop it all, if He did, it wouldn't fix the root cause which was sin, sin that could only be dealt with when individuals repented and accepted the forgiveness that could only be found in Jesus. He didn't want to wave a magic wand and force people against their will to serve Him like robots.

But Daniel couldn't get past all the negatives, and see the grace and mercy God was offering him though Jesus. He couldn't see the forgiveness and freedom that was his for the taking. All he could see were wars being fought over religion, people killing each other in God's name, people starving and dying. His heart had been hardened by years of conflict and hurt, and he was unwilling to open it, and it frustrated Lizzy to the core.

It also annoyed her that God didn't seem to be listening. How much longer did He expect her to wait?

So, where is he? She peered down the street, but couldn't see him in the line of traffic. A feeling of dread gathered in her stomach like a ball of thick heavy mud. She looked at her watch. *He should have been here half an hour ago. Where is he?*

She had to do something. She couldn't sit and wait patiently any longer. What if something had happened to him? Lizzy walked to the crossing and waited for the flow of traffic to stop, and then crossed and walked to the telephone box. She rummaged in her bag and found the number for the hospital. She placed the coins into the slot, and dialed the number.

"I'M SORRY MRS O'CONNOR, Daniel hasn't worked here for the past two weeks." *How could that be?* Lizzy's mouth fell open and she felt giddy. Unable to formulate a reasonable response, she thanked the receptionist, and then slumped backwards against the wall. Her grip on the receiver loosened, and it was left dangling like a thick hairy spider in front of her. She closed her eyes. The noise in her head deafened her.

She couldn't move. This confining dirty telephone box had all of a sudden become her haven. Her protection from the world outside. If she remained here, she wouldn't have to face the horrible realities that awaited her outside. Outside, where everything had changed in an instant. *How had this happened? Why hadn't he told her? Where was he?*

The fog in her brain slowly cleared, and she realised it must have been that meeting. *But why had he lied?*

She turned her head when she heard knocking on the door. How long had that been going on? She made out a middle aged man through the filthy glass door making pointed gestures. She pulled herself up and gathered her belongings, and took a deep breath before opening the door.

She kept her head low as she passed him. The only person she wanted to look in the eye right now was Daniel O'Connor. She uttered a few words of apology as she left her haven.

DANIEL KNEW it was too late. From the very moment he'd entered the doors, the familiar aroma of fermenting beer and cigarette smoke calmed his mind. The four pints he'd downed in quick succession hardly touched his throat, and now he'd lost count. In the back of his mind, he knew he had to be somewhere. He stood to leave, but staggered and fell. Johnno helped him up and ordered another.

THE TAXI DRIVER dropped Lizzy outside their apartment block. She'd thought about looking for him, but had no idea where to start. And how degrading would that be? No, she'd go home and make herself dinner and wait for him to come home. And then have it out with him.

But he didn't come home that night or the next. By Sunday morning she was ready to go out and find him. She couldn't wait any longer.

She telephoned all the hospitals in the area. No Daniel O'Connor had been admitted in the past forty-eight hours. She telephoned the police. No accident involving a Daniel O'Connor had occurred. He was not in their custody, but she was told she could lodge a missing person's report. She thanked the constable politely and then slammed the phone down.

She took a shower, dressed herself in the maternity jeans and smock she'd recently bought, and left the apartment.

CHAPTER 18

Lizzy didn't know Daniel's favourite pub. There were so many, how was she going to find him? Plus, she was on foot. Daniel had the car. Her blood boiled. How dare he do this to her! Not only had he lost his job, he'd lied to her and disappeared with their car. Not normally an angry person, this time she'd had enough. Enough of his pathetic promises, of his insipid excuses. What was it about men? First Mathew and his pathetic reasons for breaking up. And now Daniel, unable to keep a promise, and wanting to blame everyone apart from himself for his problems. His weakness of character appalled her. Why couldn't he stay off the drink and face his problems head on like most normal people? What was wrong with the man? How had he so easily forgotten their agreement to talk about their problems?

She needed to calm down and think rationally.

Standing on the pavement, she wondered which way to go. The light drizzle dampened her hair and clothes but didn't dampen her resolve. She would find him, even if it took all day. A decision had to be made. *Okay God, we're in this together. You need to help me.* She took a deep breath and turned left towards the river.

. . .

Lizzy felt uncomfortable and conspicuous walking past the neglected semi-detached houses that lined the streets leading to the dock area. What had drawn her here she wasn't sure, but she'd trusted her instincts and believed this was where God had led her. It was the kind of area she imagined people went to if they wanted to hide, and she guessed that Daniel was indeed hiding.

The street looked dreary. The front gardens, if they could be called that, were overgrown with weeds that flourished in this damp climate. Gates hung off broken hinges and were left half open. Some of the places looked completely derelict, not fit for human inhabitation. She hoped Daniel wasn't inside any of them. The smell was different, too. Maybe it was the mixture of diesel and rotten fish drifting up from the trawlers docked nearby, but whatever it was, it was pungent and stung her nostrils. The drizzle had increased to a steady downpour, and although it was summer, she shivered in the biting wind that blew down the desolate street.

She pulled her coat closer, and increased her pace. She passed a Chippy that was already doing a fair trade, probably not surprising since it was close to midday. The smell of frying fish and chips reminded her she should eat, but not there. Definitely not there. Just past the Chippy, the first pub came into sight. It was as she expected. A run down establishment that had seen better days. She really didn't want to do this, but she had to.

Lizzy strode to the door and pushed on it, only to find it wouldn't budge. Stepping to the side, she peered through the windows. *Empty.* She looked at her watch and remembered. Opening time was twelve pm on Sundays. Only ten minutes to go. But what were the chances of Daniel coming here at twelve anyway? He could go to any number of similar establishments in this area. Or maybe he wouldn't be at any of them. But there was no way she'd give up before she'd even started.

Maybe she should get something from the Chippy after all. She turned around and walked the short distance. The looks she received as she entered made her feel she didn't belong. Was she really that much different? Lizzy looked around at the waiting customers and thought that maybe she was. She stopped herself immediately. Wasn't that the kind of attitude she despised in her father and that she'd vowed to never emulate? But she had to admit that sometimes she struggled to see people as God saw them. She smiled at the shopkeeper, and ordered a packet of hot chips.

She just wished her voice hadn't given her away. A young lad sitting backwards on a plastic chair jeered at her. "Listen to her - poshness in our presence..." She cringed as his mates joined in laughing at the lad's apparent wittiness.

Walking out the door with her bag of chips, she wished she could find a place she really belonged.

Like worms coming out of woodwork, at twelve o'clock on the dot, men appeared from all directions and converged on The Sailors Tavern. From her position outside the Chippy, Lizzy watched closely. What was the attraction? Didn't they have families? What made these men, who on the whole looked clean and neatly dressed, flock to this dismal, uninviting, run down building? She really didn't understand. She watched for several minutes. Her heart pounded inside her chest. She couldn't eat any more of the chips. The grease made her feel ill, or was she just nervous about seeing Daniel and what she'd do when she did?

But Daniel wasn't amongst them. Her shoulders sagged as the stream of men petered out within minutes of opening time. Had she really expected to find him so quickly? She breathed heavily, and threw the remainder of the chips into the bin, then strode down the street to the next pub.

From a distance, The Hairy Hog had a similar appearance to The

Sailors Tavern, although as she got closer, it did seem to be in slightly better condition. The outside walls looked recently painted, and unlike The Sailors Tavern, the colourful annuals trailing over the sides of the window boxes gave the place a much cheerier feel. As she approached, the raucous laughter flowing out from the public bar stopped her in her tracks. What was she doing? What made her think she could go in there and look for Daniel?

Lizzy retreated to the safety of a small park opposite the pub. Maybe she could sit there and watch and wait without submitting herself to the humiliation she'd feel if she entered the public bar. Maybe Daniel wasn't there yet and she'd be able to catch him before he went in. The bench seat provided a good view of the main entrance. Her eyes darted left and right, checking out every tiny movement that caught her attention. How long could she sit there? She rubbed her back and stretched. It was useless... she'd have to go in, she was just wasting her time otherwise. She pulled herself up and walked back across the road. Her heart pounded as she opened the door and walked in.

The air was heavy with cigarette smoke and the stench of beer. She squinted her eyes to get her bearings. Had she imagined it, or had the din slowly decreased? She became aware of eyes following her. She walked slowly past the row of bar stools where men perched, leaning on the bar with a pint of ale in one hand and a cigarette in the other. And then she saw him.

It was obvious he hadn't seen her. She stopped directly behind his stool and glared at the back of his head. A general hush descended upon the bar. Daniel stopped mid-sentence and turned around, only to look directly into the eyes of his wife.

CHAPTER 19

Lizzy's eyes bore into Daniel's. There was no need for words… he knew he was in trouble.

"Lizzy! What are you doing here?" He jumped off his stool and grabbed her arm. He needed to get her out of there.

"Get your hands off me, Daniel." She jerked her arm out of his grip and glared at him. She leaned in closer and hissed at him, "What are *you* doing here, more to the point?"

"Alright, alright. Let's go." He skulled the rest of his drink and stubbed out his cigarette. He glanced around at his drinking companions, and rolled his eyes to their jeers. He walked with her past the row of men who slapped him on the back as he passed.

OUTSIDE, Lizzy breathed in the cool damp air and crossed her arms. "What do you think you're doing, Daniel?" Her eyes narrowed. "I know about your job. Why didn't you tell me?"

Daniel hung his head and shuffled his feet. "I didn't know how to tell you, Lizzy."

"Look at me, Daniel." She waited until he lifted his head and his eyes met hers. The eyes that had caught her attention not that long ago were now bloodshot and fidgety. "Two whole weeks! Two whole weeks you've known, and you didn't tell me!" She leaned in closer to his face and wagged her finger at him. "And then you just disappear." The harshness in her voice surprised her. She took a step back. Her heart raced, and she knew for the baby's sake, if not her own, she needed to calm down.

"We need to talk about this, Daniel. But not here. Where's the car?"

He hesitated and then looked around. "It's down one of these streets. Not sure which one."

"What do you mean? Not sure which one! This is our car, Daniel, and you've just gone and left it lying around somewhere? Unbelievable!"

"At least I didn't drive it, Lizzy. That would've been worse, wouldn't it?" She jumped back and almost slipped as he stepped forward aggressively towards her.

She ignored him. It looked like he'd been sleeping rough. His clothes were filthy and his body odour mixed with the stench of stale beer and cigarettes made her sick. His shirt hung over his pants, half tucked in and half out, and his two day old beard made him look like the drunk that he was. She couldn't believe he was her husband. He disgusted her.

"Let's go find it," she said angrily. She grabbed his arm to make sure he didn't disappear. She felt his resistance as he tried to pull away from her.

"I'm coming. You don't need to drag me."

THEY FOUND the car two streets away, parked outside a derelict semi-detached house. Although it wasn't the street she'd walked down earlier, it could have been. She was surprised the car was still there, and appeared to be undamaged. She didn't even ask him if he had the keys.

She'd brought her own set, and walked straight to the driver's side. She gave him no opportunity to drive.

He slumped into the passenger seat, and was silent the whole way home. She was concerned about how they'd get into the apartment without being seen by any of their neighbours. In the end, she decided she didn't care. She walked in front of him up the flight of stairs, and opened the door to let him in.

"I think you'd better get straight to the shower. How long since you've eaten?"

He shrugged dejectedly. "Can't remember."

Lizzy shook her head and breathed deeply. She'd need every inch of patience she could muster not to lose her temper.

"I'll make something, though you don't deserve it."

"Thank you." He looked up. "And Lizzy, I'm sorry."

Lizzy pursed her lips and took another deep breath. She stared at him before turning and walking into the kitchen.

Daniel allowed the warm water to run over his body, its soothing effect slowly clearing the fog in his brain. As his mind cleared, the sudden realisation of what he'd done hit him hard, and he wondered how he was going to get out of it this time.

He turned the water off and climbed out of the shower. Looking at himself in the mirror, he saw the dark stubble on his chin and rubbed his hand over it. Maybe he should keep it? No, Lizzy probably wouldn't like it, and he couldn't afford to make anything worse at the moment. He opened a drawer, pulled out his razor, and proceeded to shave it off.

He felt much better, but hesitated before opening the door and facing Lizzy. He hoped she'd calmed down a little. He stretched his neck and shoulders, and breathed deeply.

~

LIZZY WAS MAKING coffee when Daniel entered the kitchen. She glanced at him. He looked almost normal again. His eyes had lost their redness, and he'd shaved that horrible stubble off, thank goodness. He also smelt much better.

He came around behind her, and before she could do anything to stop him, his arms were around her, and he was kissing the nape of her neck. She was tempted to allow him to continue, but her resolve was strong, and she turned around and pushed him away.

"Daniel, not now. We need to talk. This is serious."

"Oh Lizzy. Come on. I'm sorry." She side-stepped when he tried to grab her again. She almost gave in when she saw the playful look on his face.

"No Daniel. Stop it. Sit down. We need to talk about what happened."

She put the plate of toasted sandwiches on the table and grabbed the mugs of coffee she'd made and sat down. She needed to eat, but she needed to talk to him more. She took a bite of her sandwich and washed it down with a mouthful of coffee. She used those few moments to settle herself. It was going to be more difficult than she thought it would be now he was home, clean and freshly dressed. It had been easy to say the words out loud when he wasn't sitting in front of her. When her anger was at its height and she could have almost killed him. She prayed for strength to carry her plan through.

She took another sip of coffee and placed her mug on the table and leaned back in her chair. "I know you lost your job, but I don't know why. I can guess, but I think you should tell me."

She sat, poker faced, as Daniel relayed to her about how he got caught with the bottle of spirits in his locker at work, and how he believed he'd been set up.

"They wouldn't have sacked you if that was the only time, Daniel. Have you been caught before?"

He nodded and lowered his head.

"Yes. I was never drunk, though. I just had a swig every now and then to keep me going. It didn't hurt anybody."

"Maybe not, but it's against the rules. And you would have known that." Lizzy shook her head and took a deep breath. "Daniel, we can't go on like this. I know you'll say you're sorry and you'll promise you won't drink again, but how many more times can you say that? You need to sort yourself out, and I don't think you can do it with me around, so I'm going away for a while."

She saw the look of shock in his eyes but continued. "During that time, you need to make a decision. I don't believe you can do that on your own, even if you want to. The only way you're going to be able to do it, if you decide you want to, is to get proper help." She paused and took a breath. Her hands shook and her heart pounded in her chest. He leaned back in his chair and crossed his arms. His eyes had narrowed and she felt his anger building. Not a good sign, but she had to continue now she'd started.

"You need to get help, either with AA or the Salvos at one of their Rehab places. I won't come back until you're sorted." She gulped. There, she'd done it. Her heart beat even faster as he rose from his seated position and towered over her, hand in the air.

"You'd better pack your bags then and get out of here before I throw you out. How dare you speak to me like that!"

She stared him down. "Daniel. Don't." Her voice was firm and determined.

He lowered his hand, glared at her, then turned around and stomped out.

. . .

LIZZY SLUMPED in her chair and sobbed. Her heart ached. What had she done? *Oh God ...* She grabbed a tissue and wiped her eyes. *Maybe I should have been easier on him.* She sniffed and then lifted her head. *No, I believe You led me to say that. I have to trust You to work in his life, Lord. Please go with him. Keep him safe, and bring him to yourself, I pray. And Lord, work in my life too. Help me to grow and trust You more.*

She recalled the verse from Romans she'd read recently, and claimed it as her own: '*And we know that in all things God works for the good of those who love him, who have been called according to his purpose.*'

Lord, I trust you to work this out for good, in whatever way you will. Amen.

BOOK 2 - FACING THE SHADOWS

CHAPTER 1

Lizzy rapped her fingers on the table, telephone held tightly to her ear. "*Come on Sal, pick up.*" She glanced at the door slammed by Daniel only minutes earlier as he stormed out. Would he come back? And if he did, *what would he do?* Her hands trembled. She had to leave immediately, just in case. But why wasn't Sal picking up?

She threw the telephone back into its cradle, pulled the curtain back, and peered out the window to the street below. At the sight of the Ford Escort fish-tailing down the street into the distance, the reality of what she'd just done hit her like a ton of bricks. A sick feeling flooded her body, and she let out a desperate gut wrenching wail as she fell into the nearby chair and burst into tears.

With her arms wrapped tightly around her stomach, and her body racked by uncontrollable sobs, Lizzy tried to reign in the jumbled thoughts writhing formlessly inside her head.

It hadn't gone to plan. Daniel shouldn't have taken the car, *and where was Sal?* She should have been home. *Now what am I to do?*

A fresh wave of tears assailed her. Sal's mother had taken ill. *How could I have forgotten that?*

She pulled herself slowly up and dried her tears. That left only one option. She'd have to go home, but the very idea filled her with dread.

SHE NEEDED TO GO, or else the temptation of staying might be too great. Standing up, Lizzy straightened her dishevelled clothing and surveyed the apartment with a heavy heart. She picked up the wedding photo sitting on the coffee table and gazed into Daniel's sparkling, mischievous eyes. He'd been so happy and carefree that day. She smiled at the cheeky grin on his face. Then her heart fell. What had happened to them? She hugged her unborn baby and forced back the fresh wave of tears that threatened to besiege her.

Returning the photo to the table, Lizzy sighed dejectedly and walked to the hall cupboard. Her bags were already packed. Deciding what to take had been difficult. Where would she be when the baby was born? By then, hopefully Daniel would have sorted his problems, but three and a half months wasn't a long time, and there was no guarantee. One thing for sure - she wouldn't come back until he had.

Without a car, it was going to be challenging. Lizzy glanced at the clock. If she hurried, there might be time to catch the afternoon train to London. And then... well, she'd think about what to do when she got there.

She picked up the telephone and called a taxi. There was no way she could bring herself to call her parents just yet. Taking one last look at the apartment, Lizzy wondered if she'd ever be back. Before opening the door, she grabbed the photo and squeezed it into her case.

THE RAILWAY STATION was busier than Lizzy had expected. Taking a train was a new experience. Her family always had a car, and she even remembered when she was little, they also had a driver. These days, Father drove himself.

Maybe going by train would be better anyway. If only she didn't have this heavy suitcase. She thanked the taxi driver as he lifted it out and placed it onto the pavement for her, but then she looked at the stairs.

Inhaling deeply, Lizzy picked up her case, and joined the queue for tickets, her heart rate increasing the closer she got. Could she really do this? Could she really leave Daniel and return to her family home? *Yes.* She had to.

If there was any hope for her marriage, there was no option. Yes, it was a risk, but staying was riskier. Daniel had to sort himself out. She couldn't do it for him. If he loved her as much as he said he did, surely he'd take action and seek help. But would leaving him like she had be enough?

Lizzy moved forward and gulped. It was her turn. The lady behind the counter looked over the top of her glasses with a bored expression on her face as Lizzy hesitated.

"Single to London, thanks. 2nd class." Lizzy's voice wobbled. She handed over the money and took the ticket. When would her heart stop pounding?

Although she'd left most of her belongings behind, her suitcase was still heavy, and the prospect of carrying it up all those stairs was daunting. But she had to do it. She grabbed it with her right hand, and held the rail with her left. *One step at a time.* She could do this. Where was Daniel when she needed him?

Totally focussed on reaching the top, Lizzy jumped as a hand touched her shoulder. *Daniel? No, it can't be.* She turned around and looked into the eyes of a brown haired young man wearing glasses a little too big for his face.

"Here, let me help you." He reached out and took the case from her hand, warding off her protests. He carried it effortlessly to the top and waited for Lizzy to join him. "What carriage are you in?"

Lizzy took out her ticket and inspected it before answering.

"Number three. But I should be alright from here." She smiled at the softly spoken young man who seemed more than eager to help.

"No, no. Let me carry it for you. You shouldn't be carrying it in your condition."

In her condition! She allowed a small grin to show on her face.

"Thank you. That would be lovely." Lizzy babbled about inconsequential things all the way to her carriage. What would he think if she told him she was running away from her husband? It didn't matter. He was only carrying her suitcase.

He helped her onto the train and lifted the suitcase onto the luggage rail above the seats.

"Thank you so much." Lizzy gave the young man an appreciative smile. "There was no way I could have lifted that up there by myself."

"My pleasure. I'm just down the other end of the carriage. I'll come and help when we reach Doncaster."

"There's really no need…"

"It's fine. I don't mind." His sincerity warmed her heart. There really were some nice people in the world.

She smiled at him. "Thank you. That would be wonderful."

He left, and she settled herself into her window seat for the first short leg of her journey.

Alone at last, Lizzy leaned back and breathed in the strange smells. People were still entering, and she hoped no-one would take the seat beside her. The last thing she wanted or needed right now was to engage in idle chatter.

Lizzy's head hurt. Not quite as much as her heart, but a trillion thoughts were running around in her brain, fighting for attention. She took out a notebook and a pen, and started a list. So many things to do, phone calls to make. *Nessa.* She needed to tell her she'd left, and ask her to keep a lookout for Daniel. *The school.* She felt terrible about leaving her class and Kid's Club at such short notice. She'd have to tell the principal it was unlikely she'd be back. He wouldn't be happy about that. She sighed and glanced out the window.

She'd have to call the hospital. Her next checkup was in two weeks. Then she'd have to call her parents. Or maybe she could just turn up unannounced? Was that a coward's way out? Maybe. She'd think about that one. She'd need to pay the rent on the apartment. Daniel didn't have any money as far as she knew. It was either pay it or risk losing all her belongings. She'd have to be careful with her money. The last thing she wanted to do was ask her parents for any.

And where to stay in London? It'd be too late by the time the train got in to go any further, and besides, a day and night in London on her own held some appeal. Maybe she could stay two nights. No-one knew where she was, after all.

Now that her brain had settled, Lizzy closed her eyes and fell asleep to the clickety clack of the train.

She woke with a start as a loud voice boomed through the speaker. *"Doncaster. Doncaster next station. Change here for Kings Cross London."* She pulled herself up and stretched. How she'd slept in that uncomfortable seat was beyond her.

The train slowed and she gazed out the window as it passed the outskirts of the town. The steeple of the centuries old cathedral was just visible in the distance, but was then blocked by a coal train with seemingly endless carriages.

Once the train had pulled to a stop, she stood and looked up at her suitcase. No, she'd better wait. It'd be stupid to try to get it herself. She smiled at the friendly young man making his way around the other passengers towards her.

"Thank you so much. It's very kind of you." The young man reached up and lifted the case down into the passageway.

"My pleasure. I'll help you onto the next train, but I'm getting off before London. Is someone meeting you at the other end?

Lizzy shook her head. "No, I'm afraid not. I'll manage somehow."

Lizzy followed the young man to the end of the carriage, where he helped her down the step and over the gap between the train and the platform. But how *would* she manage? Her heart began to race as she gazed at the platform that stretched into the distance. And this was only Doncaster.

"The train to London goes from the platform over there. No easy way, I'm sorry. Up the stairs and then back down."

"Why do they make it so hard?" Lizzy grimaced as she looked in the direction he was indicating.

Shrugging, he picked up his own bag before picking up hers, and started walking. "Who knows? I'm Scott, by the way."

"Lizzy. It's nice to meet you, Scott." She smiled warmly at the young man and then walked beside him all the way to the next platform.

The London train was already there and filling up with passengers. Scott helped her into her seat in the seventh carriage, and wished her well. As he walked away, Lizzy was sad she'd never see him again, but content to be left to her own thoughts.

CHAPTER 2

Darkness had fallen by the time the train arrived at Kings Cross Station. Lizzy spent the hours reading, thinking, praying and dozing, but now having arrived, being in London on her own caused her stomach to flutter.

The man seated opposite offered to help with her case, and she smiled thankfully at him. She waited for most of the other passengers to alight, and then followed behind. Without Scott to help her, she'd have to take her time.

Even on a Sunday night, London was a noisy, bustling city. Shivering in the cool night air, Lizzy pulled her coat tighter and walked slowly towards the exit, past vendors selling anything from hot dogs to cream buns and ice-creams. The combination of smells assaulted her senses, and she was thankful her morning sickness had passed.

A debate raged in her head most of the way. Should she find a cheap place to stay near the station, or should she go to the fancy hotel her parents always stayed at when they came to London? She'd be safer at The Kensington for sure, but could she afford it? Lizzy glanced at her watch. Eight o'clock. No, she couldn't risk blowing all her money in one go. She'd find somewhere closer and cheaper.

She made her way to the taxi rank and joined the queue. She'd have to trust that the driver would know a suitable place. Whilst waiting, she looked around at the bustling city. It was the strangest feeling being in London, with absolutely no one knowing she was there. At least Daniel wouldn't be able to find her, if he was even trying. He was probably drunk. Her heart ached for him. *Oh Lord, please be with him.*

A black cab pulled up in front of her. The driver, a short jolly looking, middle aged man wearing a brown flat cap, got out and helped with her bag, she assumed because of her 'condition', as she hadn't seen any other drivers do this.

"Where to, Madam?"

The question she'd been dreading. *Where to, indeed?* Lizzy straightened herself and gulped.

"I'm really not quite sure..." She looked into the cab driver's friendly eyes and relaxed a little. "Would you be able to suggest a hotel near here that's not too expensive?"

"Sure, I can help with that. I think I know just the place." He smiled and closed the door before climbing into the driver's seat.

Lizzy watched the lights of London flash by without really seeing them. *What was she doing here?*

Safely inside the small but comfortable room at the Great Northern Hotel, Lizzy placed her bag on the rack and took off her jacket and scarf. She rubbed her back as she stood at the window, looking down on the busy road below. It had been a long day. Too long. She needed a shower. She turned and pulled her nightgown out of her bag and headed to the bathroom. As the warm water from the shower flowed over her body, Lizzy marvelled at how God had provided for her. First Scott, and then the cab driver. She closed her eyes and the tension of the day was washed away.

. . .

Maybe it was the unfamiliar bed or the noises of the city, or just because Daniel wasn't beside her, but Lizzy had trouble sleeping. Daniel dominated her mind. All she could do was pray for him, but her heart was heavy as she imagined him coming home to the empty apartment. Did he expect her to be there? Did he expect her to keep her word? Maybe he hadn't even come home. That was more likely.

Morning finally came. How easy it would have been to stay in bed all day, to hide from the world, but she had phone calls to make, so she got up. Sitting on the edge of her bed, her hands shook as she dialled the school's number. In some ways, this was the easiest of all the calls. When the school's receptionist answered, she asked to be put through to the principal. Maybe he wasn't there yet. Lizzy closed her eyes and breathed deeply. She could do this. She had to do this.

"Elizabeth. This is unexpected," the principal said when Lizzy explained she wouldn't be coming in that morning, or anytime soon.

"Yes, I know. I'm so sorry for the short notice, Harold. Family problems. I don't expect to be back before the end of term, and then I'll be on maternity leave. I'm so sorry to do this to you."

One down. Two to go.

Lizzy then dialled Nessa's number. She'd be busy with the children, but she had to be told. How bad would it be if she found out through someone else?

Four rings. Would she answer?

"Hello." Nessa sounded as if she'd been running.

"Nessa. It's Lizzy."

"Lizzy. Are you alright? You don't sound good."

Lizzy gulped and held back her tears. "Yes, kind of." She sniffed and took a breath. "I've left Daniel."

Nessa's exclamation of shock flowed through the phone.

"Not forever, God willing." Lizzy closed her eyes and felt for her cross. "Just until he sorts himself out."

"Where are you, Liz? You can stay here if you want."

"Thanks Nessa, but no, I left yesterday afternoon. I needed to go further away. But can you do me a favour?"

"Sure sweetie. Anything."

"Can you keep an eye on Daniel?" Lizzy wiped her eyes. "I don't know what he'll do. He lost his job, Ness. And he didn't tell me for two weeks." She burst into tears.

"Oh Lizzy. You poor thing. I'm so sorry. I wish I could hug you."

Lizzy sobbed, unable to reply.

"Let me come to you. Where are you?"

Lizzy sniffed and took a deep breath. "No Ness. I'll be alright. Just look out for him."

"Absolutely. Stay in touch, hey?"

Lizzy's grip on the receiver tightened. She squeezed her eyes to stop her tears from flowing.

"Okay."

She fell back on the bed and curled into a ball. Her parents could wait.

LIZZY WOKE two hours later with a growling stomach and checked her watch. If she hurried, she could just make breakfast. She dressed quickly, pulled her hair back, and dabbed on a little make-up to cover her blotchy face. The image staring back at her from the bathroom mirror wasn't flattering, but what did it matter? She grabbed her purse and headed down to the breakfast room.

Only two people were there - an older couple who looked up as she entered. Lizzy smiled at them, and then headed straight for the toast and tea. That would have to do. There was very little left that appealed. At least her hunger pangs would be kept at bay for a while.

When the older couple left, her body relaxed. Why she'd been on edge she wasn't sure. Nobody knew her or why she was on her own, but nevertheless, she'd been awkward and self-conscious with them there.

She poured herself another tea and drank it slowly, allowing the sweet warm liquid to revitalise her.

The main dilemma now was whether to stay another night, or go straight home. The prospect of facing Father answered the question. She'd stay another night, and go tomorrow morning. That way, there was no need to telephone until later.

A day in London. No point shopping. She couldn't carry anything. Maybe she could pretend she was a tourist, and just wander around. Catch a bus. Walk through Hyde Park. Maybe even go to the theatre if she could get a ticket. She'd always wanted to see 'The Mousetrap'. But could she do that guilt-free when she'd abandoned her class and had no idea what Daniel was doing, or even if he was okay?

Lizzy's body sagged. Would it be like this the whole time she was away from him? Hadn't she asked God to look after him and do whatever was necessary in his life to make him face his problems? Yes, so what was the problem? Lizzy swallowed the painful lump in her throat. *The problem was her.* She had to let go and trust God. But could she? She wrapped her hands around the still warm cup and leaned back in her seat. *"Okay God, teach me to trust You. I'm sorry for asking You to look after him and then worrying about him straight away. I need to learn how to do it. Please teach me."*

With a much lighter heart, Lizzy returned to her room and prepared for her day out.

London put on a lovely autumn day for her. Warm enough to not be bothered with a heavy coat, Lizzy enjoyed the freedom of wandering around the city she hadn't visited for many years, and never on her own. The experience was liberating. Later that afternoon as she sat in the upper circle of St Martin's Theatre, she immersed herself in Agatha Christie's suspenseful murder mystery, and was shocked, along with the rest of the audience, when the murderer was finally revealed.

Maybe she could stay another day… *no, that would be decadent.* She was really just putting off that phone call. Lizzy caught a bus back to the hotel and arrived in time for dinner, and then headed to her room where she took a shower. Her feet ached and her body was tired, but she'd had a great day. Making that call would spoil it. Could she put it off until the morning? Yes, she'd do that. She'd watch some television tonight, and get up early. With that settled, she leaned back on her bed and flicked on the television.

EVEN THOUGH HER room was on the third floor, the rumble of traffic below was enough to waken Lizzy the following morning. Peering out the window, the grey clouds that filled the sky made her thankful for the lovely day she'd had yesterday. She sat up straight and grabbed her Bible. She needed to stay close to God. Daniel was constantly on her mind, and she longed to know where he was. Had she done the right thing? How easy it would be to forget the reasons for leaving now she was away from him. *'God, please help me stay strong. It's less than two days, and already I want to go back. I know that would be foolish, so please give me strength and wisdom, and please work in Daniel's life.'*

She read a few chapters, and then spent some more time in prayer before taking a shower and preparing for the day. As she brushed her hair, she glanced at the telephone beside the bed. Her chest tightened. Why was it so hard to make this call? If only Sal was home. She closed her eyes and breathed deeply. Maybe it'd be better just to turn up and tell them face to face.

With that decided, she went to the dining room for a quick breakfast before checking out.

CHAPTER 3

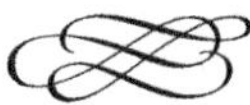

Daniel couldn't believe it. Who did she think she was? Telling him to sort himself out. *How dare she!* She's the one who needs sorting. He slammed the door as he left and thumped the wall of the staircase. He'd show her. He found the car and sped off. Maybe Johnno would still be at the pub.

He checked his watch and thumped the steering wheel. Too late. He'd have to wait until the next session. He'd go to Johnno's place instead.

Pulling up outside the run down semi-detached several minutes later, Daniel turned the ignition off and leaned back in his seat. He lit a cigarette and turned the radio up. What was she up to? Would she really leave him? He took a long, slow drag and held his breath before exhaling. *It was that big, fat cow of a woman.* If she hadn't dobbed him in, he'd still have his job, and everything would still be sweet with Lizzy. He held his head in his hand. The throbbing was getting worse… his head felt like it would explode any minute. He needed a drink.

Daniel opened the car door and headed inside. He poked his head into the living room, drawn there by the haze drifting out into the hallway. "Danny, brother, come on in." Johnno sat with four, maybe five others, some on the floor, others sprawled on the couch. Bob Dylan played in the background.

"Whad'ya do with your missus?" Johnno clapped his arm around Daniel and handed him the bong.

Daniel lit the cone and inhaled deeply, allowing the magic weed to calm his head before he answered. "She kicked me out. No. Not true. She said she was leaving, so I left first." He snickered and leaned back on the couch. "Have you got a drink, Johnno?"

"I'll get you one, Danny. We'll drink to your freedom, hey boys?"

Daniel grinned at his mate, but his heart was heavy.

NESSA RACED to the door when Riley turned his key in the latch late Monday afternoon. She was still in her pyjamas but she didn't care. She'd been pacing and praying all day, ever since Lizzy's call that morning. Several times during the day she'd considered looking for Daniel herself, but then better judgment stopped her, and she returned to pacing. But now Riley was home, they could take action.

Immediately he walked in, she grabbed his arm.

"We've got a problem, Riley. Lizzy's left."

Riley stood still and tilted his head, eyebrows raised. "She's left? What do you mean? Where's she gone?"

Nessa sighed heavily as she shook her head. "I don't know. She wouldn't say. But she asked us to look out for Daniel." Nessa grabbed Riley's arm tighter. "I feel so bad. We should have warned her about him. It's our fault, Riley. What are we going to do?"

Riley hung his coat on the hook and loosened his tie. "Calm down, Ness. Do you know what made her leave?"

"She said Daniel lost his job two weeks ago but didn't tell her. I think she had enough. She said she needed to go away so he could sort himself out."

"Well, that's not such a bad thing then, if it makes him wake up to himself. Depends on how much he wants her." Riley stepped around her and headed towards the living room. "Let me have some dinner then I'll go look for him." He fell onto the couch as two noisy toddlers jumped on top of him.

BEFORE HE LEFT, Riley stood in front of Nessa and gazed into her eyes. How lucky he was to have her. If it hadn't been for her, he could well be where Daniel was today. Yes, they probably should have warned Lizzy. Now it was their duty to help them. First, he needed to find Daniel.

He brushed Nessa's hair with his hand. "I don't know how much luck I'll have, even if I find him. But I'll do my best. I promise." He leaned forward and kissed her gently before opening the door and leaving.

"Lord God, You need to direct me. I need your wisdom. Please forgive us for not warning Lizzy. Be with her and give her Your strength. Comfort her, Lord Jesus. She must be really hurting right now. And Lord, be with Daniel, wherever he is. Please work in his life and bring him to Yourself. And use me in whatever way you will, Lord. You know I'm your servant. I'm sorry for failing You so often, but Lord, I'm Yours. You know that. Thank you for saving me, and for bringing Nessa into my life. I'm forever grateful. Thank you Lord."

Riley turned the key in the ignition and drove to 'The Hairy Hog'. As he pulled into the car park, he kept an eye out for Lizzy and Daniel's Ford Escort. He assumed Lizzy had taken it, but didn't know for sure. No, not there. He climbed out of the car and walked around to the front door. What was it about old pubs? They all smelled the same. How many years had it been now? And yet, if he had even one drink, he'd be a goner. He steeled himself and pushed the door open.

Being a Monday night, the bar was quiet. Only a few regulars by the look of it. An old joker who looked like he lived there, poor old sod. A couple of workers on their way home, another one or two in the corner. No Daniel.

He sat on a stool and ordered a squash, not caring what they thought. It was unlikely the young bar maid who'd served him would know, but no harm in asking.

"Looking for a friend of mine. Irishman. Dark hair. Laughs a lot. Seen him lately?" She continued drying glasses, but looked up at him. Her long dark hair made her pale face look even paler. What was a good looking girl like her doing in a joint like this? Surely she could find herself a better job. Riley sighed inwardly.

"Maybe. Think he was here yesterday." She stopped wiping and leaned on the counter. "I think the guy you're talking about got hauled out by his lady."

"Mmm. So, he hasn't been here today?"

"No, sorry. Haven't seen him, or his mate Johnno. He's normally a regular. Surprised he's not here."

Johnno. Of course.

"Thanks Love." Riley skulled the rest of his squash and gave her a tip as he jumped off his stool.

Riley climbed back into his car and sat for a moment, trying to remember where Johnno lived. He'd only been there once when he'd dropped Daniel off not long after Daniel had arrived in town. Riley knew the area, so he started the car and drove, praying he'd find the place.

He turned his lights on, and headed slowly along Wellington Parade, peering down each street as he passed, but they all looked the same. He turned down Bradley Street and drove slowly between the cars parked on either side. None of the houses stood out. He stopped at the next intersection and peered both ways. More of the same, but maybe this was it. Indicating right, he turned into Kingston Street. The Chippy on the corner looked familiar. And there's the Escort. *Yes, this is it.*

The first available spot to park was fifty yards away. After squeezing into it, Riley stood on the pavement and looked around, thankful he and Nessa had been able to settle in a better area. The houses were tiny, and on the whole, run down, with front gardens overgrown with weeds taller than any of the plants that were hardy enough to survive. He walked back along the pavement towards the Escort, checking each house as he passed.

The semi-detached the Escort was parked in front of looked familiar. Nothing really distinctive to make it stand out, but surely it was the one. He paused before entering, taking a moment to pray, both for himself and for Daniel. What state would he be in?

Riley walked to the front door and knocked. No answer. He knocked again, this time a little louder. The door opened slowly, and Johnno poked his head out. His long straggly hair looked like it could do with a wash, and dressed in faded baggy jeans and an off white T-Shirt with a peace sign on the front, he looked like a left over hippy.

Johnno stood and peered at Riley, a confused look on his face.

"Riley. Come in, man." Johnno opened the door wider and extended his arm. "Guess you're looking for Danny. He's in here."

Johnno led Riley into the living room where Daniel lay on the couch, hands behind his head and eyes closed. A bong sitting on the coffee table looked like it'd been used recently.

Riley stood in the doorway and sighed despondently. *At least he's not drunk.* He walked over to the couch and leaned down and gently shook him. "Hey Daniel. Wake up."

Daniel sat slowly and steadied his bloodshot eyes on Riley. "Hey man. What are you doing here? Sit down." He indicated the spot beside him. A grubby throw covered the couch, and an array of assorted cushions and pillows were scattered both on the couch and on the floor. Riley sat, but declined the offer of a cone.

"So Daniel … I believe Lizzy's gone."

Daniel hung his head.

"Yeah. I stuffed up big time."

"Don't you want her back?"

"She won't come back." Daniel lifted his head and found Riley's eyes. "I'm no good for the likes of her."

"You're right on the ball there, mate, with the state you're in. Look at yourself." Riley shook his head and sighed heavily. "Ness and I had hoped you were past all of this." He glanced at the bong and then back at Daniel, who smelt like he hadn't washed in days.

"I'm sorry, Rilo. I'm a failure." Daniel turned to Johnno. "Can you get us some food, man? I've got the munchies big time." He looked back at Riley. "Do you want something to eat?"

"No thanks, mate." Riley stood up. "Come back with me, Daniel. Ness and I will help get you sorted. It's not too late to get Lizzy back."

Daniel slumped and shook his head despondently. "Nuh. She's gone." His stare was directed at the pile of records sitting on the floor opposite him.

"Well, let me know if you change your mind. I'll drop by again later in the week, and we can talk about it more then. Try to stay off the weed, man. It's no good for you."

Riley walked back out to his car with a heavy heart. It was going to be a long road home.

CHAPTER 4

Lizzy hailed a cab to take her to Paddington Station. If only another Scott would appear on the scene to help with her bags, but everyone seemed to be in a hurry and took no notice of her. After buying her ticket, she checked the board. Fifteen minutes before the train was due to leave. Not long really. Not long enough to grab a coffee, especially with more stairs to tackle. Her chest was heaving by the time she arrived on the platform, and she headed straight for a seat where she rubbed her back and took some slow, deep breaths. If only Daniel hadn't taken the car.

She looked up as the train came into view. Only a few more hours and she'd be standing on her parents' door step. Lizzy stood and looked for her carriage. Relieved it was only a short walk, she picked up her bags and headed slowly towards the door.

"Here, let me help you with that." She turned and looked at the tall, dark haired gentleman dressed in a navy suit carrying a brief case reaching out for her bag.

"Thank you very much." Lizzy smiled warmly at the man and accepted the offer of help gratefully.

"My pleasure. Let me put it on the rack for you as well."

God had once again provided for her, and she was thankful.

Lizzy tried to read, but with every station the train passed bringing her closer to her destination, there was no way she could concentrate. She really didn't want to face her parents, particularly her father. A heavy knot took residence in her stomach, weighing her down.

She looked out the window at the all too familiar scenery. Clusters of houses, and horses grazing happily despite the damp weather, dotted the green rolling fields that resembled home-made patchwork quilts. Small villages centred around churches with steeples visible before anything else came into view. Grand old manor homes perched on hill-sides, displaying the prosperity of their owners.

Too quickly the train slowed for her stop. Lizzy stood, and was relieved when the same gentleman once again offered to help. A pity he wasn't getting off here.

Standing on the platform a few moments later on her own, Lizzy determined to carry her own bags the rest of the way. There didn't appear to be as many steps, and besides, she couldn't rely upon strangers all the time. She could do this. It would help build the courage needed to face her parents.

She pulled her shoulders back and stood as straight as she could before making her way down the stairs and through the subway. A young girl with long straggly hair playing a guitar caught her attention, and she dropped a few coins into the girl's hat as she passed.

She hoped her own guitar would still be in one piece when she returned. If Daniel got really angry, that might be the one possession he'd take revenge on. She sighed and continued walking. There was nothing she could do but pray. It was only a guitar when all was said and done, and could easily be replaced.

Two taxis waited at the rank. She gulped and fought the fluttery feeling in her stomach. This was it. The final leg of the journey.

"Where to Ma'am?" The jollier of the two cab drivers walked towards her and reached for her bag.

"Wiveliscombe. Do you go that far?"

"Yes Ma'am. No problem. To a hotel there? Or visiting friends or family?"

Lizzy winced inwardly. Just her luck to get a happy chatty driver again. "Family. My parents own Wiveliscombe Manor." The driver lowered his head and raised his brow just enough for Lizzy to notice. She was sure he would have whistled if it wasn't inappropriate.

Sitting in the back of the cab, Lizzy clutched her handbag the whole way. The closer she got, the faster her heart raced.

AS THEY REACHED the gates to the manor, Lizzy leaned forward and instructed the driver to go through and drive right to the house.

Had it only been a month since she and Daniel had driven up this same driveway? It seemed so much longer. She shivered at the memory of that night. The night he beat her. Maybe it was good to have that memory. Although she'd forgiven him, it helped justify her decision to leave, and to remain resolute in her decision not to return until he addressed his issues.

The few seconds it took to reach the house weren't long enough. Lizzy wanted to tell the driver to turn around and take her back, but before she could, he'd jumped out and opened the door and that option was gone. She breathed deeply and stepped onto the gravel which crunched under foot. The driver lifted her bag out of the boot, and placed it under the portico in front of the double wooden doors. She thanked and paid him. Her mouth went dry as he drove away.

. . .

The rose gardens either side of the driveway caught her attention. The bushes, heavy with blooms of gold and crimson and salmon were putting on a dramatic display in defiance of the winter chill threatening to extinguish their flame. Lizzy breathed in the heady scent and tried to calm her pounding heart.

The click of the door made her jump. With her hand to her chest, Lizzy turned and looked straight into the eyes of her mother.

"Elizabeth! What are you doing here?" Gwyneth hurried towards Lizzy and threw her arms around her daughter.

Tears streamed down Lizzy's face. She couldn't help it. All that pent up emotion flowed out of her uncontrollably as she was comforted by her mother.

Gwyneth helped Lizzy into the house, and led her to the summer drawing room. Seated in front of the bay windows with a view of the rose gardens, Lizzy composed herself. She had to explain her unexpected appearance and uncontrolled emotion. It wouldn't be easy, but at least her mother was on her own.

Lizzy breathed deeply and clenched her hands.

"I suppose you might have guessed already, Mother." Lizzy looked up and held her mother's gaze as she fiddled with her wedding ring. "I've left Daniel." The words she'd never wanted to say to her parents stabbed at her heart. Lizzy forced back the tears that threatened to flow again.

"Oh darling." Gwyneth stood and moved quickly to Lizzy, placing her arm around Lizzy's shoulders. "I had hoped this would never happen."

Lizzy sobbed, her heart at breaking point. "I hope it won't be for long, Mother. Only until Daniel sorts himself out."

"Oh my poor girl. Do you really think he will, Elizabeth?" Gwyneth stroked Lizzy's hair with her free hand, as Lizzy tried to control herself.

"I hope so, Mother."

"I know your father would be pleased if you just forgot about him."

Lizzy pulled back, "Oh Mother, no, I can't do that. I love him. And he's the father of this baby." She looked down and hugged her stomach. "I couldn't do that to him. I'm confident he'll sort himself out. I just don't know how long it will take." She jumped a little and moved her hand to the side of her stomach, and then smiled shyly at her mother.

"The baby just moved. Would you like to feel it?"

Gwyneth hesitated, but then nodded, a faint smile showing on her face. Lizzy gently guided her hand to where she'd felt the movement, and looked into her mother's eyes expectantly as they waited for another movement. Lizzy's smile grew wider as her mother's eyes widened and glistened.

They sat together in warm silence, and for the first time in a long time, Lizzy felt close to her mother.

CHAPTER 5

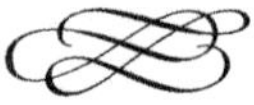

"When will father be home?" Lizzy asked her mother as she and Gwyneth sat in the sun room drinking tea.

"He's away on business for the night, so he won't be back until tomorrow evening."

Lizzy let out a huge breath, and her body relaxed. "I'm not looking forward to seeing him, but at least I've got another day to prepare."

"He's not that bad, Elizabeth. He really does love you."

"He's got a funny way of showing it." Lizzy stood and walked to the window. The clouds had cleared and the late afternoon sun cast shadows over the fields, throwing a yellow tinge over the whole vista. She glimpsed a rider on a horse in the distance bobbing up and down. It'd be nice to go for a ride, but now wouldn't be the right time. She caressed her baby, and wondered what Daniel was doing.

"I'll get your bags taken up to your room," Gwyneth said as she joined Lizzy at the window.

. . .

As Lizzy sat on the bed, she recalled the last time she'd been in this room. Daniel had been so angry with her father that night. *Why couldn't he have just let it go?* She fingered the heavy brocade bedspread her mother had bought when she was ten as her mind drifted. Things might have been so much different if they hadn't come that day and had gone straight to Sal's instead. But they had come, and she couldn't turn the clock back.

She'd call Nessa in the morning for any word on Daniel. In the meantime, she needed to unpack.

"You look nice, dear." Gwyneth looked up as Lizzy came downstairs a little while later. Wearing a light blue smock with herringbone embroidery on the bodice and a pair of white maternity slacks, Lizzy was self-conscious under her mother's watchful eye. "You must have bought a whole new wardrobe."

"Kind of. Nessa, that's Daniel's cousin, lent me some of her maternity clothes, so I didn't need to buy everything." Lizzy took a seat on a stool at the breakfast bar as Gwyneth peeled some potatoes. "Can I help?"

"No, but thanks for asking, dear. I wasn't going to bother cooking for myself, but now you're here, I thought I should." Gwyneth put down the peeler and walked to the sink. Her dark brown hair was done neatly in a bun as it had been for as long as Lizzy could remember, but the tinge of grey was new.

"It was a shock seeing you at that door, Elizabeth. I'm glad you came, though." Gwyneth wiped her hands on a towel and then walked back to where Lizzy was seated before placing her hand lightly on Lizzy's shoulder. "Are you really alright, Elizabeth?"

Lizzy lifted her head and looked into her mother's eyes, and for the first time in a long time she saw the mother she remembered from childhood. The mother who she'd snuggled up to every night as she listened to the Bible stories Gwyneth read to her and Jonathon, the mother who waged battle with Lizzy's unruly hair every morning before school, and the mother who used to hug her and make her feel loved.

Maybe she hadn't changed that much after all.

Lizzy shrugged and tried to hold back the tears that welled up behind her eyes. "It wasn't meant to be like this. Daniel is a great guy, he's just got a few problems. I'm praying he'll sort them out and I can go back before the baby comes."

"And what if he doesn't?"

Lizzy's mind raced. She hadn't really thought that far. *No, he had to sort himself out. There was no option.*

She held her mother's gaze. "He will. I'm sure of it."

"Your father won't want you to go back. I'm sure of that."

"What's with Father? Why is he so horrible to everyone?"

Gwyneth walked back to the counter, and picking up a knife, began to slice the vegetables. "He's a hard man to understand, Elizabeth, but most of what you see is just a front. He worries too much what people think, but that's because he's never felt as if he belongs here. You know he got left this estate by a distant relative?" Gwyneth stopped slicing and looked up.

Lizzy nodded and encouraged her to continue.

"Well, what you probably don't know is that before he inherited the estate, he had very little. No job, no money, no name. His parents lived in the poorest part of Exeter, and worked at whatever jobs they could find. His father signed up for the war, but came home a broken man. He took up drinking and became a recluse. Your father left home soon after. Both his parents died within a few years of each other."

Gwyneth walked over and picked up the kettle. "Another cup of tea?"

"That would be nice, thanks Mother."

"Your father was only twenty-three when his great uncle Sydney died and left him the estate. He didn't really know the man. He'd only met him once or twice when he was young, but Sydney had never married, and had no family apart from your father. When your father came to live here, he had to learn the ways of the privileged very quickly, but he's always felt like an outsider, trying to justify his position. He still feels like that, although he hides it well.

Lizzy took the hot tea from her mother and took a sip.

"That explains a lot, but not why he's so distant from us. You'd think he'd relax when he's at home.

"I think he's tried so hard to be someone he's not, he's forgotten who he is." Gwyneth wore a faraway look on her face, and Lizzy's heart went out to her.

"That must have been difficult for you, Mother. I know it was for Jonathon and me growing up. It still is."

"Oh, I've just come to accept that's the way he is." Gwyneth returned to her vegetables.

Lizzy looked up and tilted her head. "How did he get the name, 'Walton-Smythe'? Surely that wasn't his parents' name?"

"Ah yes. I always wondered when you'd ask about that. When your father inherited, his last name was just plain old 'Walton', but Sydney's last name was 'Smythe'. Your father thought if he combined the two, he'd have a better chance of being accepted, so he changed his name by Deed Poll."

Lizzy chuckled, and her eyes lit up. "Funny that. You know I went by plain 'Miss Walton' at school?"

Gwyneth shook her head and looked up, knife in hand. "Really? Why did you do that?"

"I would have been given a really hard time by the other teachers and most of the children if I'd kept my full name. You don't know what it's like up there, Mother. It's a different world."

"I guess I don't." Gwyneth put the knife down and looked Lizzy in the eye. "Elizabeth, what was the real reason you chose to move up there?"

Lizzy gulped and looked away. This was getting a bit too close to home now.

"You don't have to tell me if you don't want to." Gwyneth tilted her head. "But did it have something to do with Mathew Carter?"

Lizzy swung her head around. How had her mother guessed? She sighed with resignation and nodded. "Yes. It was mainly because of him. I couldn't get over him, as much as I tried, so I thought the further away I could get the better. It drove me crazy being in the same town as him, and seeing him almost every other day. I had to go."

"Do you regret it?"

Oh God. How do I answer this? Since when has my mother asked me such personal questions? Lizzy folded her arms and leaned back on the stool.

"I sometimes wonder what would've happened if I'd stayed. I probably would've been sent to a local school, and I'd still be pining after him." Lizzy rubbed the back of her neck and inhaled deeply before looking up. "He still hasn't got another girlfriend, you know."

"No, I didn't know that."

Lizzy glanced out the window and reined her thoughts in before turning back to her mother.

"To answer your question - I needed to get away, so no, I don't regret it. I just wish he'd never broken it off." Lizzy's voice wavered as she spoke.

"You poor girl. I had no idea it had affected you so much." Gwyneth's gentle caring tone tugged at Lizzy's heart.

"Tell me, dear, did you love Daniel when you married him?"

Lizzy's shoulders dropped. Why was she asking all these questions? How could she answer that?

An awkward silence hung between them.

Lizzy gulped and took a deep breath.

"That's difficult to answer, Mother. If you mean, was he all I ever thought of, and did he turn my night into day, kind of." She paused and looked out the window. "But I think, no, I *know,* I would have chosen

Mathew over Daniel if I'd had the choice. I didn't, so I chose to love and marry Daniel." Was she really saying this to her mother? How could this be?

"Love is something you choose to do, so I'm learning, even when you don't feel like it. But I'm guessing you know all about that?" Lizzy lifted her eyes and looked directly into her mother's.

Gwyneth had tears in her eyes. Lizzy had been right. Her mother had chosen to love her father, despite everything. Lizzy leaned forward and reached out her hand to her mother, as tears welled up in her own eyes.

"Look at us! What a pair! Just as well Father's not coming home tonight." Lizzy pulled a tissue out of her pocket and wiped her face, as her mother reached for the tissue box on the kitchen bench and did the same.

"How did you get to be so wise, Elizabeth?"

Lizzy frowned and shook her head. "I'm not wise. I've made some really stupid decisions."

"We all have, Elizabeth." Gwyneth drew in a long breath, and straightened herself. "You're a strong girl. It won't be easy, but if you've chosen to love him, that's half the battle."

Lizzy's lips tightened. If only that was true. She let out a breath.

"Maybe you're right, Mother. I hope so." Lizzy picked up her tea and took a sip. "I wonder what Daniel's doing now?"

"Is there anyone you can call to find out?"

"I asked Nessa to keep an eye on him. I thought I'd call in the morning, but maybe I could call now."

"Go ahead, dear. You know where the telephone is."

CHAPTER 6

The phone rang while Nessa was bathing two year old Cindy and three year Jake. Leaving the children for a moment, she grabbed the phone and answered it, all the while keeping one eye on the shenanigans going on in the bath.

Nessa's eyes widened at Lizzy's voice. "Lizzy! How are you? I've been thinking about you all the time."

"I'm okay, Nessa. Oh, not really. I can't stopping wondering how Daniel is and what he's doing. Have you seen him?"

Nessa glared at the children who'd just tipped water all over the floor and were giggling about it. "Sit down you two! Not you, Liz - Jake and Cindy are in the bath, and they're standing up pouring water everywhere."

"Sorry to have caught you at a bad time, Ness. I can call back later."

"No, it's fine. They're just doing what they normally do. I'm just going to ignore them." Nessa leaned against the door but kept one eye on the two young children. "Riley went out last night looking for Daniel, and found him at Johnno's." She stopped. *How much should she say?* She grimaced as her mind raced through the options. How to tell her without telling her... she gulped before continuing. "He wasn't drunk, but he wasn't quite with it."

"What do you mean? What was he doing?" Nessa cringed at the despair in Lizzy's voice, but wanted to protect her from the truth if she could. Lizzy could do without hearing that her husband was stoned out of his brain.

"Riley said that Daniel thinks you've left for good, but it's just his initial reaction. He's obviously in shock. Give him some time, sweetie. We'll keep a good watch on him, don't worry about that. Hopefully he'll come to his senses quickly - for your sake and the baby's."

"I hope so too, Ness. I feel really bad about leaving him the way I did, but I didn't know what else to do."

Nessa jumped as one of the children poured water on the floor, splashing her. She glared at them, but they just giggled. Why did they always misbehave when she couldn't do much about it?

"You did the right thing, Liz. He needed a shake-up, and if this doesn't do the trick, I don't know what will. So, where are you? I'm guessing you went south?" Nessa grabbed the bath toys out of the bath to noisy cries by the two children.

"I'd rather not say, Ness. Then you won't have to lie to Daniel if he asks. I'll ring every couple of days if that's okay?"

"Yes, poppet. No problem at all. We're both praying for you, Liz. Hang in there."

LIZZY TOOK a few moments to ponder Nessa's words before returning to the kitchen. *What did Nessa mean? 'Not quite with it?' What was he doing?* At least Riley had found him. That was something. She'd just have to keep praying, and trust that God would work in his life, *'but sooner rather than later would be good, please God.'*

Lizzy wandered back into the kitchen, only to find that her mother was no longer there. Dinner was in the oven, and smelled good. She opened the back door, grabbed a jacket from the hook, and stepped outside. The sunset had faded to a gentle line of orange on the horizon, and directly overhead, stars were starting to appear in the sky. She pulled her jacket tighter as she breathed in the cool evening air.

So many things to take in. She walked along the path through the vegetable garden and found the seat where Daniel had found her the first time she'd brought him here. The day he'd proposed. It'd been so simple back then. Daniel's exuberant personality had taken her mind off Mathew and helped her forget him. But why hadn't she taken the time to get to know Daniel properly before making such a huge commitment? She was paying the price for that oversight now.

Lizzy sighed and gazed at the darkening sky, its beauty drawing her focus to its creator.

'Oh God, creator of heaven and earth, I come to you with a heavy heart. Please help me. You know I'm committed to Daniel, but I can't live with him the way he is. God, please let him open his heart to you. May he come to know the breadth and depth of your love. Soften his heart, Lord, I pray. And Lord, do whatever You need in my life to make me a better person and a better wife. Let the fruit of your spirit grow in me, Lord, I pray. I really do want to be like You, but I know I fail so often. Please forgive me and breathe your spirit into my life.'

She paused and gazed at the night sky, now strewn with a myriad of stars glittering and twinkling like polished diamonds, and her thoughts drifted to her parents, and the story her mother had told her. *'Lord, thank you for helping me understand my parents a little better. Help me love my father, and to not get upset with him when he says hurtful things. Help me show him your love. And thanks for my mother. Seems she's a lot stronger than I ever thought she was.'* Lizzy chuckled and her heart softened further as she recalled her mother's tears.

'Oh God, thank you for loving me, and for bringing me into your kingdom. Please give me strength and wisdom for the days ahead. In Jesus' name, Amen.'

As Lizzy continued gazing at the night sky, breathing in the perfume from the lavender growing around the seat, she was at peace with herself and with God.

After dinner, Lizzy and her mother sat in the main living room together, Lizzy flicking through old photo albums and her mother reading a novel. Duchess, Gwyneth's much loved Persian cat, purred gently on her owner's lap.

Lizzy, leaning on a pile of cushions, tucked her feet under her body and took a trip down memory lane. She smiled at the old black and white photos of her and Jonathon dressed up in their Sunday best outfits when they were only about five or six. Her long white socks with frills around the elastic tops, and the pretty yellow dress with the huge sash around the middle. And her hair! What did she look like! The matching yellow ribbons in her pigtails brought a smile to her face. But even then, Father had been so stern. She studied a photo of him standing with Mother. His face was unsmiling and so hard. How had Mother ever loved him?

Lizzy kept turning page after page, stopping every now and then to take a closer look, and putting one album back and replacing it with yet another and another. As she picked up an older looking one, a piece of note paper poked out between the pages. She opened the album to that page and looked at the photos.

She leaned closer. They were photos of Father when he was much younger, but he was with another woman. And they appeared to be taken in Exeter. She recognised some of the buildings and the surroundings, and there was one taken in front of the same church that she and Sal went to when they were at University. She didn't know her father had gone there. And who was the woman? Lizzy glanced at Gwyneth, but as she was engrossed in her book, Lizzy didn't interrupt her, and kept flicking through the pages.

The photos showed that her father and this woman had been close. And her father looked different. In some of the photos, he was actually smiling. *Smiling!* Had she ever seen him smile? It must have been before he inherited, when he was just plain old Roger Walton.

She fingered the note paper. It had that old world look and feel about it, slightly discoloured and quite thin and fragile. Dare she open it? Even years later, it exuded a slight perfume, suggesting it may have been a note from this woman. Lizzy breathed deeply and her hands shook a little as she carefully opened it. The writing was old fashioned but very neat, and although faded, was just legible. Her heart beat faster as she sat up and began to read…

Dear Roger,

My heart weeps as I write this. I don't even know if I can put into words how I feel, but I'll try. To say I was devastated when you broke our engagement is an understatement.

We had such grand plans, you and I. I loved you so much, Roger, and I thought you loved me. But you changed. Sadly, you're no longer the man I fell in love with and wanted to spend the rest of my life with. Inheriting that estate changed you, and not for the better, I'm sorry to say.

My heart's broken, Roger, and I'm angry with you. I don't understand how you could so easily turn your back on all that we had. I don't think you'll ever know how much hurt you caused by telling me I wasn't good enough to be your wife. How dare you! I pray God will forgive me for my anger, I know it's wrong, but I can't help how I feel.

I beg you to reconsider. Don't throw everything away just because you've come into money.

That's all I have to say. I don't know if I'll ever see you again, Roger. I don't know if I could bare it. I can't believe it's come to this.

Your heart broken ex-fiancee,

Hilary

Lizzy's mouth fell open and her heart beat faster. She re-read the letter, and then looked more closely at the photographs of the woman. No, it couldn't be. *But it was.* It was Hilary Carter. Lizzy bit her lip and her skin tingled. *Her father had been engaged to Mathew's mother.*

Gwyneth glanced up at that moment and Lizzy caught her eye. Did her mother know about this? It was too much to take in. Lizzy's mind raced. Surely Hilary Carter must have recognised her the moment she'd walked in her door all those years ago. The daughter of the man who'd jilted her. Why hadn't she said anything? *Oh goodness. This is major.*

"Are you alright, dear? You look a little off colour".

Lizzy took a deep breath. Her eyes were wide open and she was having trouble controlling her thoughts. She gulped and took another deep breath. "I've just discovered something that threw me a little."

Gwyneth tilted her head, slightly puzzled. "That's your father's album. I haven't looked at it in years." She drew her eyebrows together. "What did you find?"

Lizzy hesitated. Should she tell her mother? Her heart beat faster as she thought about what to say.

She had to say something. Best just get it out. Lizzy took yet another deep breath and lifted her eyes to meet her mother's. "That he was engaged to someone else." She waited for her mother's reaction.

Gwyneth put her book down and sighed, closing her eyes for a brief moment before opening them and looking at Lizzy.

"It all happened before I met your father. He told me he'd been engaged to a girl he'd met at church, but that it all fell apart when he inherited and moved in here. Apparently she didn't want to live here."

That's not what the letter said....

Gwyneth's eyes had a distant look.

"I always felt he still loved her, and that he'd only asked me to marry him to save face." She looked back at Lizzy. "That's why I asked if you loved Daniel when you married him. I'm glad you said you did. At least there's hope for you."

Lizzy stood and put her arms around Gwyneth's shoulders. "Oh Mother. I'm sure he loves you. He can't still be pining after her all these years."

Gwyneth pursed her lips together and shrugged.

"I'm not sure. I feel like I've been living in her shadow all our married life. I never met her, but he compared me with her all the time when we were first married. Why they broke up is beyond me. He obviously still loved the woman."

"That must have been so difficult for you, Mother. How unfair of Father!"

Lizzy's heart fell. Was that how she was with Daniel and Mathew? She'd never said it out loud, but she'd thought it plenty. How often had Daniel noticed?

"Do you know who the woman was, Mother?" Lizzy gulped. Did she really want to have her suspicions confirmed?

Gwyneth reached for the album and studied the photos before lifting her head.

"A girl he met at church. Hilary. That's all I know." Gwyneth's eyes glistened and her voice wavered. "She must have been an amazing person, though, the way he talked about her."

It must be true. Too unlikely there was another Hilary. The woman must be Mathew's mother. This was too much to take in. Lizzy's heart pounded in her chest. Finally, she found her voice.

"Very strange they broke up, then."

Gwyneth sat straighter and took control of herself. "Yes, I always wondered if there was more to it than he told me. He asked me to go out with him soon after. I really think it was to make her jealous and to save face, but I think he loved her so much she almost became saintlike in his mind. But then he slowly hardened into the man he is today."

Lizzy sat beside Gwyneth and looked at her. "I think the woman is Mathew's mother. Hilary Carter."

Gwyneth's eyes widened and she tilted her head. "Really? What makes you think that?"

"There were photos of them standing outside Exeter Baptist. I remember Mathew telling me that his mother used to live in Exeter before she married. And it looks like her. She's very short, and the woman in the photo is short. I'm sure it's her." Lizzy's head spun, loose ends flying everywhere.

"What a small world we live in. Who would have thought?" Gwyneth grabbed a tissue out of her pocket and blew her nose. "I wonder if Mathew knows?"

Lizzy returned to the couch with the album and take another look. "I don't think so. I'm sure he would have said something if he did." She looked up, her eyes a little brighter. "Maybe I should ask him."

Gwyneth looked at her over her glasses. "Do you think that would be wise, dear?"

Lizzy shrugged and closed the album. "I don't know. But maybe I need to see him anyway to find out the real reason he ended our relationship. I never really believed what he said, and I don't know I'll ever be able to move on properly if I don't know. And I do want to move on, Mother. Especially with the baby coming." Lizzy sighed deeply. "I just hope and pray Daniel sorts himself."

Gwyneth smiled at her affectionately. "You really do love him, don't you?"

Lizzy nodded and lifted her eyes, revealing her answer before she spoke it. "Yes, I do. I do love him, Mother."

CHAPTER 7

Daniel woke with a start. His heart pounded heavily in his chest, and his head spun. Awareness of his whereabouts dawned slowly. Then it all came back. *Lizzy's gone!* A wail, full of lament and heartache, rose from deep within his body and escaped in a long, deep moan. Whimpering like a dog that had just been kicked, Daniel curled into the fetal position and hugged a cushion to his chest. If only he could sleep, maybe it would all go away.

Images of Lizzy floated through his mind, tormenting him. Why had he got involved with her in the first place? She was too good for the likes of him. But he loved her. Lizzy was the most beautiful thing to come into his life since he'd lost Ciara and Rachel. And he was going to lose her too. He imagined holding her, kissing her, making love to her. She was doing his head in. He'd never get her back.

Daniel sat and ran his hands through his hair. He licked his lips, but his mouth was dry, and his throat hurt when he breathed. Grabbing the half empty bottle on the floor beside him, he took a mouthful, but winced at the taste of the warm, flat beer. Maybe he should go home. She might still be there. But no. Riley said she'd gone. *Riley*. That's right.

He was here. Where's Johnno? He looked around, but the place was empty.

He stood and made his way to the bathroom. Looking in the mirror a few moments later, he jerked his head back, not recognising the face looking back at him. Maybe Johnno had a razor. Opening the bathroom cabinet, he found one, and proceeded to shave off the stubble. If Lizzy happened to be home, he should at least look respectable. Maybe he should shower as well.

Once clean, Daniel wandered into the kitchen to look for food. He opened the cupboards and looked in the fridge. Not much to choose from. *Johnno really needs to do some shopping.* He found some bread and a toaster, and cooked two slices, which he buttered and smothered in jam. There was only beer to drink, so he took one and opened it.

He cleared a space at the table and sat down to eat, but couldn't stomach it. The beer helped, so Daniel tipped the toast in the bin, and took the beer to the living room and flicked on the television. Just reruns of the Royal Wedding and a Faulty Towers episode. He left it on Faulty Towers.

What day was it? He rubbed his hair and tried to remember all that had happened since he'd stormed out of the apartment.

He stood and turned the television off. *Now, where are the keys?* He felt in his pocket. Yes, they were there. Daniel grabbed them, opened the front door and walked outside. Lucky it was still warm, because he didn't have a jacket.

Relieved the car was where he'd left it, he unlocked it and climbed in. His head was still spinning, so he sat for a few moments to steady himself. Then he turned the key and started the engine.

At the apartment, Daniel tentatively opened the door, hoping she'd be there waiting for him, but the emptiness that met him revealed that not only had she left, she'd also taken a lot of her things. A heart wrenching ache settled deep inside of him and almost tore him apart.

Her words came back to him as he pictured her sitting opposite him at the table. *'You need to sort yourself out, Daniel. I'm going away for a while.'* He swayed and reached for the wall before slumping onto the couch.

"Lizzy, I'm sorry. *I'm sorry.*" He thumped the couch and buried his head in the cushions, moaning like an injured animal. Her smell was all around him. On the rug, on the couch, in the cushions. Tears welled in his eyes. *"Lizzy, where are you?"*

He couldn't stay here, not without her. He sat and composed himself. His gaze travelled slowly around the room before he stood and headed to the door.

CHAPTER 8

Lizzy's body ached and she longed for sleep, but her mind wouldn't rest. About midnight she gave up trying and climbed out of bed. Wrapped in one of her mother's dressing gowns, she tiptoed downstairs, put the kettle on and made herself a cup of tea, which she took into the main living room. She turned on one of the table lamps and pulled a rug over her knees as she settled against the cushions.

The baby was active, digging her in the ribs and making her uncomfortable. Maybe it sensed something was going on. She'd need to call the hospital in the morning and organise her next check-up. How terrible if something went wrong.

She sipped her tea and her mind drifted. So much had changed in such a short time. Had it only been yesterday she'd been in London? It seemed such a long time ago.

And now she'd found out that Mathew's mother had been engaged to her father. *Her father!* It was difficult to imagine them together. She'd have to see Mathew. They had unfinished business. There had to be more to the break up than he'd told her. But what would it really achieve? It wouldn't do anything to help Daniel, well, maybe it would.

Getting Mathew out of her skin once and for all would have to make a difference, surely.

'Oh God. Please settle my brain and calm my spirit. And this baby...' Lizzy hugged her stomach and waited for another kick. *"Pour your blessings out on this little one, and protect it from harm. And God, please be with Daniel. Let him know I love him, wherever he is.'*

Lizzy put her tea down, leaned back on the cushions and closed her eyes.

As Gwyneth walked along the hallway towards the kitchen the following morning, she passed the entrance to the living room and stopped, her eyes drawn to the figure asleep on the sofa. Standing in the doorway, her heart ached for her daughter.

She'd been glad, but surprised, Elizabeth had chosen to come home. She'd need to speak with Roger as soon as he arrived. Maybe she should telephone him at the office. Yes, that would be best. Forewarn him, and plead with him to be understanding, if that was possible.

Gwyneth continued quietly along the hallway so as not to disturb Lizzy. When she reached the kitchen, she smiled at Duchess who jumped off her bed, stretched, and began to rub herself against Gwyneth's leg. Gwyneth reached down and scratched the cat behind its ear.

The kettle was still slightly warm. Elizabeth must have made herself a drink. Gwyneth reheated it, and once her tea was ready, carried the cup and saucer into the morning room, placing it on the side table beside her Bible.

Gwyneth breathed in the peace and serenity of the early morning and began her quiet time. She poured her heart out to God, and prayed for her family, especially Elizabeth and the unborn baby. She prayed for Daniel, that he'd sort himself out, and that he'd find peace with God.

She prayed for their marriage, that they'd be reconciled, and that they'd learn to love and respect each other. And she prayed that somehow, Roger would remember his roots and become that loving, caring man she'd seen in those photos. *'I know you can do all these things, Lord God. Please bless my family. In Jesus' precious name.'*

GWYNETH LOOKED at the clock on the mantlepiece. Still too early to call. In fact, it'd be best to wait until Roger returned to his office in Taunton later in the afternoon. He wouldn't appreciate being called at the Bristol office.

She peeked into the living room. Elizabeth was still sleeping. *She must have needed it, poor girl.* It was Gwyneth's normal shopping day, but she'd put it off - more important to be here for Elizabeth. She took a coat and a hat off the hook, and opening the door very quietly, went outside to do some gardening.

She wandered around to the rose garden, stopping on the way to inspect the Camellia Sasanqua she'd recently bought at the local nursery. The bush was already covered in soft pink blooms, with even more buds bursting to open. She snipped a couple of the blooms and placed them in her basket. The sun hadn't quite reached the rose garden. Dew sat heavy on the bushes which were doing their best to defy the change in season. Gwyneth began the never ending task of dead heading. She didn't mind. It gave her time to think. And pray.

Time disappeared when she was in her garden, and so she was surprised to see Elizabeth standing before her when she lifted her head.

She wiped her forehead with the back of her hand, and then took off her gloves. "Elizabeth dear. I hope you had a good sleep."

Lizzy's smile lit up her face. "Yes, I feel much better now. Thanks for letting me sleep in, Mother."

"You must have needed it. I'll just clean up and I'll make you some breakfast."

"Oh, no need, Mother. I can look after myself. I think I can remember where everything is." Lizzy let out a small chuckle and her eyes glistened.

"Alright then. I'll come in shortly anyway. It's just about time for coffee."

~

LIZZY STOOD for a moment taking in the beauty of the garden. Sadness took hold of her heart as she remembered that she and Daniel had been planning to look for a house. How much she'd been looking forward to having her own backyard and garden. That wasn't going to happen now. But no use brooding over it, there were more important things to be concerned about, like Daniel sorting himself out. If he did that, they'd be more likely to get a house anyway.

She turned and walked back inside. Lizzy would have been happy to stay here if it wasn't for Father. But at least now she understood him a little better. But would he understand what she'd done when she saw him later today? Only time would tell.

Lizzy filled the rest of the day with menial tasks such as calling the hospital and washing, but she did spend some time at the piano, playing tunes she thought she'd forgotten, but which came back easily once she began.

Even as she sat and let the music pour through her fingers, Lizzy worried about her Father's reaction, and even more, how Daniel was doing.

LIZZY WOKE from a nap to voices filtering up from the kitchen. *Father.* Her heart beat faster, and although tempted to pull the covers up and go back to sleep, Lizzy got up and went to the bathroom.

She splashed her face with warm water, and brushed her hair before pulling it back into a messy bun. That would have to do. She looked at herself in the mirror and took a deep breath. *'Okay, this is it, God. Please be with me. Give me patience and understanding, even if he doesn't have any.'*

"ELIZABETH. Your mother has just told me. It's about time you left that good for nothing Irishman." Lizzy looked at her father standing in the kitchen and felt nothing but pity for him. Hiding in there somewhere had to be love and compassion. She'd seen it in the photos with Mathew's mother, but it certainly wasn't evident now.

"Nice to see you too, Father." Lizzy held his gaze, waiting to see if he'd realise how cold his words had been.

"I'm sorry, Elizabeth. How are you?" Roger shifted his weight and crossed his arms. His ever so slight smile appeared forced.

"That's better. I'm fine, thank you Father." Lizzy walked up to him and placed a kiss on his cheek. If it made him squirm, she didn't care.

She glanced at her mother, and drew on the strength she'd gained from their rediscovered relationship.

"I'll make coffee for us all, shall I?" Lizzy looked from one parent to the other, and then busied herself under their gaze, far less confident than she looked. Father was not going to bully her anymore if she could help it.

"So, what did Mother tell you?" Lizzy asked as she handed a tray holding the mugs of steaming coffee to her father. He looked uncomfortable, but took it anyway.

"She said you arrived on the doorstep unannounced yesterday afternoon, and that you'd left Daniel."

"Did she also tell you it wasn't permanent?" Lizzy raised her eyebrows as she took a seat in the sunroom.

"Ah, she did mention something like that." Roger sat stiffly in his chair and glared at Lizzy. "You'd be daft if you went back."

Lizzy shook her head and sipped her coffee.

"I know you don't understand, Father, but I love him, and I do plan to go back. He just needs time to sort some things out."

"Yes, you're right. I don't understand. You could have had anyone you wanted, and you chose him." Roger's eyes narrowed. "You've thrown your life away, Elizabeth. After everything we've done for you, and this is what we get in return." He shook his head in disgust. "First you go off teaching, and then you get hooked up with this good for nothing character, and now you're having his child, I really don't understand." He leaned back in his chair and crossed his arms.

Lizzy dug her fingernails into the palms of her hands. She needed to remain calm and not reply in kind, but it wouldn't be easy. *How dare he talk to her like that!* She took a deep breath and exhaled slowly.

She lifted her chin and held his gaze.

"I'm sorry you feel that way, Father. It'd be nice if you respected my decisions for once, and allowed me to be myself instead of forcing me to be someone you want me to be." She paused and slowed her breathing before continuing. "I'm not a child anymore. I know I've made mistakes, but isn't that how you grow and learn?"

Lizzy tilted her head and her voice softened. "I don't believe I've thrown my life away. Just because I don't want to live how you want me to, doesn't mean I'm any less a person. I'm learning more each day about who I am. About who God wants me to be. I wish you'd be happy about that."

There. She'd said it. She held his gaze and waited for his response. Lizzy remained perfectly still waiting for his response. She hardly dared breathe or move a muscle. Her mother also sat still and upright. Such a different person when Father was around.

"Well, it certainly sounds like someone's got in your ear, Elizabeth, and filled your head with all this nonsense. Why you'd choose to throw away all this is beyond me."

"Father, if that's how you choose to live, I respect that. But I don't want it for myself. Maybe one day in the future I might, but for now, I want the freedom to be myself, to experience life without having everything done for me. But, can we let all that go for now, and just try to be friendly to each other? Especially if I'm going to be here for a while."

Roger sat back in his chair and pressed his hands together. It must be upsetting for him to hear those words from his daughter, but she had to say them... no longer would she allow herself to be pushed around by him.

When he lifted his eyes, they looked a little less cold.

"I don't agree with what you've said, Elizabeth. I do believe you've made a mistake, but I guess it won't hurt to be civil." He sat forward and picked up his coffee. "How long do you expect to be here?"

"I'm not sure, but I hope to be home before the baby comes." Lizzy considered her father carefully. "Are you looking forward to be grandfather?"

Roger shifted in his seat uncomfortably and crossed his legs.

"I haven't really thought about it." He looked up and caught her gaze. "Are you keeping well?"

At last ... a reasonable question! "Yes, I am, Father. Thank you. Much better of late. I just get tired a lot." Lizzy turned her head as her mother stood.

Gwyneth picked up the tray and started collecting the mugs.

"I'll make a start on dinner, but you two can stay here if you like."

"I'll come and help, Mother. I'm sure Father has things to do." Really, she just needed some space. Speaking to Father was exhausting.

Lizzy followed Gwyneth to the kitchen and relaxed.

"IT WAS brave of you to speak to your father like that, Elizabeth, but I'm glad you did." Gwyneth paused while washing the cups and glanced at Lizzy.

"I had to do it, Mother. I hope I didn't go too far." Lizzy pulled out a stool and took a seat.

"No, I don't believe you did. Maybe it'll cause him to think about his attitudes."

"Hopefully it will, but I'm not convinced. Now, what can I do to help?"

"Oh, it's okay, dear. Dinner's mainly ready. But tell me, have you made any plans?"

"I was thinking of visiting Sal for a few days, but I need to find out if she's back. I need to keep busy, or else I'll go crazy." Lizzy crossed her legs and gazed out the window into the distance where the fading daylight was softening the landscape. She turned back to her mother and fingered the cross hanging around her neck. "It's hard to keep my mind off Daniel. I wish I knew what he's doing."

"Be patient, dear. And stay strong."

Lizzy sighed deeply and gritted her teeth. Her mother was right. *Patience.* How she hated that word.

CHAPTER 9

Daniel sat in the car not knowing where to go. He felt like just taking off and driving, with no particular destination in mind. No one would miss him. He could go back to Belfast and look up his mates. No, too many skeletons there. He could try to find Lizzy. She'd probably gone to her parent's place or to Sal's, but fronting up at either place didn't appeal, and what was the likelihood of her coming back anyway? He could go to Riley and Nessa's. But they'd only preach at him. He didn't want any of that.

He could try to find another job. But he'd looked for two whole weeks and found nothing. What would be any different now? No, no use doing that. He could go to the Salvos like Lizzy suggested, but he wouldn't be able to have a drink if he did that. No, that one's out, too. *I'll just go to the pub.*

~

THE BAR MAID glanced up as Daniel entered. He plonked down on a stool in front of her.

"What can I get you?"

"Two pints and keep them coming."

She threw him a sidewise look as she pulled the two beers. She should have got that guy's details. It was going to be a long night.

DANIEL STAGGERED out of the pub. The cold breeze off the river slapped him in the face but did little to lift the fog in his head. He found the car and poked his key at the door. The blasted hole kept moving. Once the door opened he fell in. The roar of the motor startled him, he didn't remember starting it...

How close was that car behind? Daniel got out and looked, and stumbled as he tried to get back in. Pulling himself up, he climbed back in, and put the car into reverse. There was plenty of room. The car took off backwards. He slammed his foot on the brake, but it was too late. The sudden stop jolted him into action, and thrusting the gear stick into first, he took off down the road.

Daniel's heart raced. The lights confused him and it was difficult to make out the lines on the road. He needed to stop. He pulled over and pushed open the door just in time. Once the contents of his stomach had been poured out onto the road, he leaned back in his seat and passed out.

The next morning, he headed for the pub, as he did the morning after that, and the one after that, and the one after that, until he ran out of money.

Several times Riley turned up, trying to get him to go home with him, but he just pushed him away. "Leave me alone, mate. I'm no good to anyone. Let me be."

He got into some fights, once with Johnno, once or twice with some old drunks who hassled him for money. He drank more to stop the pain that racked his body and his heart. He slept in the car, in fact, he didn't even bother driving it anywhere. He just slept where it was, parked on the side of the road. Images of Lizzy floated through his sub conscious from time to time, but whenever conscious thought entered his head, he drank more to escape from the pain it brought.

THE PHONE RANG on Thursday night as Nessa was cooking dinner. She half expected it to be Lizzy, and she was right. Her heart sank. She had no good news to tell her. Riley had found Daniel the night before at the pub, blind drunk. He couldn't talk straight, and refused to come home with him, so Riley had to leave him there. The bar maid had told Riley Daniel had been there the previous day as well. How could she tell Lizzy all of this? But would it do any good to protect her from the truth? Maybe not. It was probably best she knew.

"Lizzy! How are you, poppet?"

"I'm okay. Missing you all. How's Daniel?"

She wasn't mucking around. She must be really missing him. Nessa sighed deeply and sent up a quick prayer.

"He's not in a good way, Lizzy. He's been drinking, and we don't know where he's staying. Riley saw him last night, but he didn't want to come back with him."

"Oh... I'd hoped he might have got some help by now." Nessa's heart went out to Lizzy on the other end of the phone. The poor girl must be doing it tough.

"It'll probably take a while for him to come to his senses, Liz, but we're sure he will. We just don't know how long it'll take. He's in shock, and drinking's his way of dealing with it. He'll come round, but even then, it's going to take a while for him to get clean, assuming he decides to get help."

"But you really think he will?"

"He loves you, Lizzy. But there's a battle going on inside him. I can't promise you anything, but we think he loves you enough to do something about it when he finally hits rock bottom."

"What do you mean? Rock bottom?

Nessa closed her eyes and chastised herself. Why did she say that? She took a deep breath.

"Usually that's how it goes with alcoholics, Liz. Daniel's on a bender, and sometimes they last for days, if not weeks. Often something happens that makes them stop all of a sudden. We just have to pray that whatever happens will make him realise he needs help. Especially if he wants you to come back."

"Oh… I hope he'll be okay, Ness." Lizzy's voice sounded very fragile and she seemed close to tears. "How do you know all of this?"

Nessa stopped stirring the dinner and took a deep breath.

"Because Riley's an alcoholic too."

"But he doesn't drink."

"No, not any more. He's been sober for five years now, but we went through this as well, Liz. That's how I know."

"Oh Nessa. That gives me such hope. If Riley could do it, that means Daniel can too."

"Yes, but everyone's different, Liz. It has to be Daniel's choice. No-one can do it for him. And there's no guarantee."

"But we can keep praying for him. God can do it. God can do anything."

"Yes, but you know He won't force anyone. It still has to be Daniel's choice."

"Nessa, I just want to be with him. It's killing me being away. And it's been less than a week."

"I know, sweetie. But you've got to hang in there. If you come back too soon, you'll only go through it all again another time. Believe me, I know. I left three times. If you stay strong and let it take its course, there's more chance he'll decide to get help and you'll be back before you know it."

"But it's so hard, Ness. I think about him all the time."

"Have you got people around to support you?"

"Yes, kind of. But it's not the same. It's been good talking to you about it, Ness. I wish you could be here with me, but at least I know you understand. That helps."

"We're praying for you both every day, Liz. And Riley's looking out for Daniel. He gave the bar maid his details last night, and she said she'd call if anything happens to him. He'll be okay, Liz. Call as often as you want. I don't mind."

"Thank you Nessa. I'll call again soon."

After Nessa hung up the phone, Lizzy sat down and prayed.

'Oh God, I don't know I'm strong enough for this. Please help me.'

CHAPTER 10

Lizzy struggled for days following her phone call with Nessa. The conversation itself played over and over in her mind. No one had ever said that Daniel was an alcoholic before. Yes, it may have been alluded to, but it had never been stated out loud. That cold hard fact was like a blast of arctic air in Lizzy's face, alerting to her to the enormity of hers and Daniel's predicament. Learning that Riley was also an alcoholic shocked her, but provided comfort since he and Nessa had been through similar trials themselves.

Every day Lizzy tried to call Sal. She desperately needed to talk with her friend, and finally this morning Sal answered. She spent a good half hour on the phone, pouring her heart out to her, and was now looking forward to catching up in person later that day.

Lizzy looked up when Gwyneth joined her in sunroom, and smiled warmly at her mother.

"I heard you on the phone earlier, Elizabeth. I assume you were speaking with Sal?"

"Yes, finally. She just got back from Bristol last night." Lizzy put her coffee mug down and relaxed in her seat. "She has to go back to school on Monday, but has nothing planned before then, so I'm planning on going down there today and will spend the weekend with her."

"I'm sure that will do you good, dear. Will you see Mathew while you're there?"

Lizzy picked up her cup of coffee and took a sip, and then wrapped her hands around the cup as if for support.

"Yes, I think I need to. I know it won't change anything, but maybe it'll help me move on once and for all." She glanced out the window and breathed deeply. "He never really gave me a proper reason for breaking it off, and maybe that's why I found it so hard to get over him. I think there's more to it than he told me, especially now it seems it was his mother in those photos."

"You still have feelings for Mathew, don't you?" Gwyneth leaned forward and squeezed Lizzy's hand.

Lizzy gulped and looked away. Tears welled in her eyes and she wiped them with the back of her hand.

"It's okay, Elizabeth. I think I've known all along. But the question is, what are you going to do about it?"

Lizzy turned her head and looked at her mother.

"He doesn't want me, Mother, so there's nothing I can do but let him go. But even if he did, it's too late now." Lizzy looked down at her wedding ring and fingered it. "I know it's over, and I want my marriage to work, but I think I need to see him one more time."

Gwyneth tilted her head and pursed her lips.

"As long as you know what you're doing, dear."

As THE BUS approached the outskirts of Exeter, Lizzy was deep in thought. Did she really know what she was doing? Would seeing Mathew again really help put him behind her once and for all, or would it only stir up all the old feelings she thought she'd almost left behind? And what would Daniel think if he knew what she was doing?

Just the prospect of seeing Mathew again caused her pulse to race, not a good sign. *Oh God, what should I do?*

The bus was pulling into the bus station, so she gathered her belongings and looked out the window to catch a glimpse of Sal. And there she was. Sal could never hide in a crowd with that red hair. Lizzy waved out the window to her, and when the bus finally came to a stop, stood and made her way to the front.

"Sal!" She wrapped her arms around her friend and fought back the tears that came from nowhere. Why did she have to be so emotional all the time?

"I didn't expect to see you again so soon! Here. Let me take your bag." Sal reached out and took the bag from Lizzy, and guided her towards her car. "How are you holding up, Liz? Are you really alright?"

"I think so, Sal. I sometimes wonder how it all happened, but I'm hopeful it'll work out. I'm really missing Daniel, even with everything that's happened. I just hope he gets himself sorted quickly."

"At least he's got Nessa and Riley looking out for him. It must have been bad for you to have left. I can't believe he didn't tell you he'd lost his job. That's pretty low."

"Yes, I know. I was so angry when I found out. He could have just told me, but no, he hid it from me and then went on a bender." Lizzy's lips compressed into a thin flat line.

"Here's the car." Sal unlocked it and opened the door for Lizzy. They both climbed in.

"Do you really think he's going to change, Liz?"

Their eyes met and Lizzy cringed.

That was the question that haunted her day and night. Would Daniel ever be any different? Could he stop drinking? Would he ever allow God to change him? And if not, would she be able to live with him the way he was?

Lizzy shrugged dejectedly. "I hope so, Sal. I pray for him all the time. But like Nessa said last night, there's no guarantee."

Sal reached out and squeezed her hand. “Chin up, Lizzy. He’d be mad to let you go.”

Lizzy smiled weakly and let Sal’s words encourage her. Sal always knew what to say.

“SORRY THE HOUSE IS A MESS. I just dropped everything when I got the call about my mum, and Lauren’s hopeless with housework.”

“It’s not a problem, Sal. It doesn’t look too bad, anyway.”

“Always the diplomat! So, what do you want to do? We’ve got all weekend to ourselves.” Sal turned the kettle on and busied herself making coffee.

Lizzy pulled out a seat and sat at the table. “Maybe some fun things to get my mind off Daniel for a while. Go to the cinema perhaps, but mainly just hang out. I don’t really want to see anyone. I couldn’t handle all the questions.”

“Yes, I guess not. We can hide out here, it’s okay, Liz. No one knows I’m back yet.” She carried the two coffees to the table and sat down.

“I do want to see Mathew while I’m here.” There, she’d said it.

Sal’s eyes widened, and her mouth fell open.

“Why, Lizzy? What good will that do?”

Lizzy sighed and picked up her mug.

“I just need closure, Sal. I don’t think he told me the truth about why he broke it off. I’m hoping that if I know, I’ll be able to put it behind me once and for all, and move on properly. It just nags at me. I know it’s over, especially now.” She looked down at her tummy and her lip twisted into a sardonic smile. “Maybe it’s stupid, but I just need to know. We’d been planning our future, Sal. *We were so happy.* You know that. It’s hard to understand why he changed his mind all of a sudden with no real reason. Is that stupid or not?”

Sal squeezed her hand. “No Lizzy, it’s not stupid. If it helps you to move forward, you should see him. I can ask him over if you like.”

Lizzy flashed her a smile. "That would be good. Thanks Sal. There's one more thing. Take a look at this." Lizzy pulled the photo she'd removed from her father's photo album out of her bag. "Do you know who that is?"

Sal took the photo from Lizzy and inspected it before shaking her head. "I'm guessing that's your father. But who's the woman?"

"It's Mathew's mother."

"No way! Get out of here!"

"I'm pretty sure. I found a letter from that woman to my father, signed Hilary. That's his mother's name. And it looks like her. I don't understand, though, if it's her, why she didn't say anything to me when I stayed there. She must have known who I was."

"Maybe she didn't know."

"She must have. Father broke off their engagement when he inherited the estate, and that's when he changed his name, so she must have known. I want to ask Mathew if he knew."

Sal rolled her eyes.

"You might be opening a bag of worms."

Lizzy leaned back and grimaced.

"I know."

CHAPTER 11

Lizzy listened as Sal arranged with Mathew to come for lunch the following day. Sal told him Lizzy was in town and wanted to see him, but didn't fill him in on all the details. They'd agreed it'd be best to leave that to Lizzy.

All night, images of Daniel and Mathew flitted through Lizzy's mind, and when the early morning sun peeked through the blinds and woke her, she turned over and went back to sleep. It was close to nine o'clock when she stirred again, and she had a sudden panic attack when she glanced at the clock. Mathew would be here in just over two hours. Her pulse raced at the thought of seeing him again. How would she survive?

She pulled herself up and calmed her breathing before climbing out. It wouldn't do her or the baby any good to be so on edge. She pulled on a dressing gown and headed to the kitchen to make a pot of tea. The house was very quiet. Neither Sal nor Lauren were around.

Lizzy took her tea and piece of toast outside to get some fresh air. It wouldn't be long before it'd be too cold to sit outside, so best enjoy it whilst she could. How nice it was to have a garden. Sal definitely wasn't a gardener, but still, it was much better sitting out in the sun in a slightly overgrown backyard than in an apartment where you could only look out the window. She sighed and wondered where Daniel was. Was he even missing her? She fought back the tears that threatened to fall, and prayed for him. How long could she stay away? *God, please give me strength.*

She heard a door close and some clanging and banging coming from inside. Sal must be back. Lizzy picked up her mug and plate and headed inside. Sal was unpacking grocery bags, and looked up as Lizzy entered.

"There you are, sleepy head."

"Sorry Sal. You should have woken me."

"No, you looked too peaceful, I didn't want to disturb you."

Lizzy smiled kindly at her. "Thanks. I had a fairly rough night. Couldn't get either of them out of my head."

"Mathew and Daniel, you mean?" Sal glanced up at her.

Lizzy nodded as she washed her mug and plate.

"Yes, they haunted me all night, but they got all mixed up in my dreams. It was really weird." She shook her head and let out a small laugh.

"Are you okay?"

Lizzy stopped and took a deep breath. "I think so…" She put the mug she was wiping down and turned to look at Sal. "No, I'm not alright, Sal. I'm nervous about seeing Mathew. I don't want to make a fool of myself."

"It's not too late to call it off."

Lizzy closed her eyes briefly and steadied herself.

"No, I need to see him, but I need to calm myself before I do."

Sal walked over to Lizzy and wrapped her arms around her, pulling her close.

"I'm sure you'll be fine. Why don't you shower and get dressed while I make a start?"

Lizzy wiped her eyes and nodded. Thank goodness for Sal.

. . .

Not having brought many clothes with her, Lizzy had limited choice of what to wear. In the end, she decided on a light blue pinafore over her white stretch jeans. Not the most flattering of outfits, but it would have to do.

She couldn't stop checking the clock as she helped Sal with the finishing touches for lunch.

"Will you stop that! You're driving me crazy!"

"What am I doing?"

"You're fidgeting. Sit down and talk to me. Tell me about your holiday."

Lizzy sat and folded her arms. "No, I can't think about that right now."

"Okay, then talk to me about something else. Tell me what you did in London."

Lizzy began to tell Sal about her day or so in London, but stopped mid-sentence as the doorbell rang. She sat up and placed her hands on the table, her gaze meeting Sal's. She inhaled deeply.

"I'll go." Sal took off her apron and placed it over the back of the chair, and squeezed Lizzy's shoulders before walking to the front door.

Lizzy straightened her shoulders and lifted her chin. This wasn't going to be easy. She listened intently as Sal opened the door and let him in. The sound of his quiet gentle voice made her skin tingle. She grabbed the cross around her neck and looked up. *'God, please give me strength.'* She squeezed her hands to her chest, and then stood.

Her pulse raced and her skin went clammy. Could she really face him again? She closed her eyes for a moment and calmed her breathing.

And then he was there. Standing right in front of her. His eyes met hers as he held out his hands.

"Lizzy. So good to see you."

Lizzy reached out and took them, and gazed into those eyes. The years apart slipped away and it was like time had stood still. If only he would pull her close and wrap his arms around her, all would be right. But that would never happen, and it was wrong to even think that way.

"Mathew." She smiled shyly and then tilted her head slightly. "It's good to see you, too. Thank you for coming over." She let go of his hands, and moved out of the way to let Sal through.

"I was surprised to hear you were down, especially after seeing you and your husband so recently. But I couldn't refuse Sal's invitation of a free lunch." His eyes sparkled as he grinned at Sal before turning back to Lizzy. "She said you wanted to see me."

Lizzy lowered her eyes and gulped.

"Why don't I leave you two together?" Sal interrupted them. "Lunch is all ready, you just need to serve yourselves. I've got some work to do, so I'll grab a plate and take it to my room."

"Sal… you don't have to leave." Lizzy grabbed Sal's arm. Her eyes were startled. "Stay?"

Sal eyes were firm and she held Lizzy's gaze.

"No, Liz. I really do have work to do, and you two have things to talk about. I'll just be in my room."

Lizzy let go of her arm and glanced at Mathew, who still stood just inside the doorway. What would he be thinking? This wasn't a good start.

Sal took her plate and left the room. Lizzy's heart beat rapidly. She looked up at him.

"I'm sorry Mathew. I wasn't prepared for that. Come and sit down." She took a seat and indicated for him to take the one opposite. Now he was here, she didn't know what to say.

"Would you like a drink?"

The corners of Mathew's mouth curved into a smile.

"It's okay, Lizzy. No hurry. Just relax."

She returned his smile as she breathed in slowly and leaned back in her seat.

"Thank you." Outside the sun shone in the sky with only a few wispy clouds in the distance. "Why don't we sit outside for a while? It's nicer out there."

He nodded agreeably and stood, and then helped her out of her chair.

"Are you keeping well, Lizzy?" he asked as they headed outside.

"Yes, thank you." She hugged her tummy. "Just over three months to go now."

"You must be getting excited."

Lizzy grinned as love for her unborn baby warmed her heart.

"Yes, I am. A little scared, though." Her shoulders fell slightly and she let out a small sigh.

"Is everything alright, Lizzy?" Mathew turned to face her once they'd taken their seat. He was so close, she could almost feel his heart beating beside her. How wise had this been?

Lizzy looked into his eyes and gulped. *Lord, I need you right now. Help me to stay strong.*

"Not really." She proceeded to tell him about Daniel's drinking problem, and how she'd made the decision to leave him until he got help. Lizzy surprised herself, and despite the heaviness in her heart as she spoke about Daniel, her eyes remained dry.

"I do love him, Mathew, and I pray every day that he'll find God and that he'll sort out his problems and we can be together again, but there's something else that's bothering me." Lizzy inhaled deeply and gazed at the garden before turning to look at him.

"What's that?" Mathew tilted his head and looked at her quizzically.

"What was the real reason for our break up?"

Mathew frowned, drawing his brows together.

"What do you mean, Lizzy? It was just as I said."

Lizzy's heart raced and she clenched her hands together to stop them from shaking.

"No, there has to be more. You couldn't have just woken up one morning and thought, *'Lizzy's not the one'*, after all we'd been planning. What didn't you tell me, Mathew?"

Mathew squirmed in his seat and folded his arms.

"It won't change anything," Lizzy said, "I realise that, but Mathew, it haunts me, not knowing. Maybe it shouldn't, especially now I'm married, but don't you owe it to me to be honest?" Her eyes pleaded with him. "You might not be aware of this, but the reason I left was to get away from you. I couldn't handle being in the same town as you. Seeing you in the distance every day or so was driving me insane. I didn't have an option, really. But our breakup changed my life, Mathew, and not knowing why hasn't helped."

He lowered his head and sighed. He remained silent for what seemed an age before looking up.

Lizzy hardly dared breathe. Her heart beat so loudly he must have heard it. Her hands were clammy and her throat hurt when she gulped.

"Lizzy, I'm so sorry for hurting you like that. And yes, you're right. There was more to it." His eyes had watered and a pained expression sat on his face. "I didn't want to break up, Lizzy. Believe me. I loved you, and it was the most difficult decision I ever had to make."

"Well, why did you, then?"

He stared down at his feet and shook his head slowly.

Lizzy held her breath. This was the moment she'd been waiting for for almost three years. What would he tell her? Her heart thumped and her hands began to shake.

He lifted his head and looked into her eyes.

"It was my mother." He gulped and blinked rapidly.

"Your mother?" Lizzy's mouth fell open.

"After your visit, she called me every second day to tell me you weren't the one for me. She was incessant. In the end, I had to decide between you or her." Tears rolled down his cheeks. "I'm sorry, Lizzy."

Lizzy's breathing quickened and she felt faint. Hilary must have known who she was. But what caused her to dislike Lizzy so much she made Mathew break it off? Lizzy's body shook and she buried her head in her hands. Hilary had never shown any dislike to her the whole time she'd been there. It was too much to bare.

Mathew moved closer and wrapped his arms around her. She sobbed into his shoulder. His heart beat loudly, and she could feel his chest rising and falling. What had they done to deserve this? *Torn apart by his mother.* But why did Mathew choose her instead of Lizzy? Surely he could have stood up to her?

Lizzy's tears subsided and were replaced with anger. Her heart beat faster and she pulled away. She looked at him accusingly.

"Why didn't you stand up for me if you loved me so much?"

Mathew looked crest fallen.

"You don't know her, Lizzy. She might seem quiet and gentile on the outside, but underneath, she's a force to contend with. I don't know why she took a dislike to you, but she said she knew you weren't the one from the moment she met you, and she wouldn't let it go. She made it impossible for me to be with you without thinking of her. It would never have worked."

Lizzy pursed her lips and fought back her tears. This was too much to bare. Why hadn't he stood up for her? He loved her, after all. He'd said so.

"It makes me really sad you didn't fight harder, Mathew. You obviously didn't love me enough." She folded her arms. He had a hurt look on his face. Maybe he'd been suffering too. "But I also don't understand how anyone has the right to tell anyone else who they should or shouldn't be with. It's wrong."

She hesitated before pulling the photo out of her pocket and handing it to him.

"Take a look at this."

Mathew took the photo and held it up. He studied it closely, his eyes widening.

"That's my mother." He pointed to the woman. Then he turned his head and stared into Lizzy's eyes. "That's not your father, is it?"

Lizzy nodded and took a deep breath. Her suspicions had been confirmed. She looked at him intently.

"Did you know?"

"No, I had no idea."

"They were engaged. My father broke it off when he inherited." Lizzy grabbed his arm. "She must have known who I was as soon as she heard my name. I think she turned you against me out of spite."

Mathew jerked his head up. "She'd never do that."

"Are you sure? Did she ever give you a good reason?"

Their eyes locked together and time stood still. If it was true, how could Lizzy ever forgive her for putting Mathew in that situation, for ruining their hopes and their dreams? Did Hilary despise her father so much that she would do this?

Mathew shook his head slowly.

"Maybe you need to go and see her."

He shrugged dejectedly and peered sadly into her eyes. "It's not going to change anything, Liz. It's too late for us."

"But if that's what she did, shouldn't we at least know? It's not right, or honest, if she did. You never know, she might be feeling guilty but hasn't been able to tell you. You'd think that something like that would eat away at you."

"Mmm. Maybe I should. I did ask her why, but she always said it was just something about you, but she really believed she was right, and never wavered." He crossed his arms and narrowed his eyes. "Now I think of it, she did say once or twice she thought being a minister's wife would be too much of a come down for you."

Lizzy's shoulders slumped. That was all she'd ever wanted. To be Mathew's wife, supporting him in his ministry. *How dare that woman take her dreams away!* It wasn't fair or right."

"I think you need to talk to her."

"Yes, I think you're right, Lizzy. I will. I'll go and see her." He breathed slowly and deeply and his face softened as he gazed into her eyes. “I'm so sorry, Lizzy. I should have stood up to her.”

The tears that Lizzy had been holding back now flooded down her cheeks. If only he had, everything would have been different. But it was too late.

She grabbed his hand and held it to her face as he wiped her tears away with the back of his other hand. She had to let go, but she clung on for just a moment longer. As she slowly pulled away, their eyes locked together, and in that moment, all the love they'd held for each other passed between them in unspoken words, but they both knew it was over.

Lizzy took his hand. “Come on, Mathew, let's have lunch.”

CHAPTER 12

"We'll always be friends, Lizzy," Mathew said as their gaze lingered on each other at the door. Her knees weakened as he bent down and kissed her gently on the cheek, before turning around and walking away.

Sal wrapped her arm around Lizzy's shoulder as they stood together watching him disappear into the distance.

"Come on, I'll make you some coffee."

Lizzy could hardly stand. Her heart felt like it had been ripped out of her. There could have been no other outcome, but oh, it was so hard to let him go.

She smiled weakly at Sal. "Thank you."

Retreating to the living room with their coffee a few minutes later, they curled up on opposite couches. Lizzy remained quiet for some time, lost in her thoughts. Her heart was heavy. Finally, she recounted the conversation she'd had with Mathew. Talking about it made her feel better, stronger, and slowly, indignation replaced her heart ache.

"It just doesn't seem right, Sal. What makes people, including our parents, think they can control who you marry? Why can't they just respect your choice? Sure, they should be free to say what they think, but in the end, shouldn't the decision be ours?" Lizzy shook her head and sighed deeply. "I just don't understand it. First my father, and now Mathew's mother, I just don't get it."

"I guess they just want the best for their kids, and think they're doing the right thing, but I agree, they shouldn't make it such that you're left with no say." Sal grimaced, and picked up her coffee.

"But they've made their decisions based on prejudices and resentment. Father's so caught up playing the part of an English gentleman he'd never accept anyone who wasn't in the same league. He also thinks all Irishman are good for nothing."

Lizzy sat up and leaned forward. Her body tensed and her pulse quickened. "It's simply not true. And then there's Mathew's mother." Tears welled in her eyes.

"Lizzy, calm down. It won't do you any good." Sal sat up and moved to the couch beside Lizzy and hugged her.

"I know you're angry, but you've got to be bigger than this." She gently stroked Lizzy's hair. "Let it go, Liz. What's done is done, and the most important thing now is to forgive and move on. You've got Daniel and your baby to think of now." She pulled her tighter as Lizzy sobbed into her chest.

LATE AFTERNOON, they went to the cinema, and on their way home, Lizzy told Sal she wanted to go to church in the morning.

Sal raised her eyebrows. "Are you sure? Mathew's preaching."

"Yes, I know." Lizzy took a deep breath. "I feel stronger, Sal. I'll be alright."

"Even if people ask questions?" Sal glanced at her as she parked the car outside the house.

Lizzy took a slow deep breath and pursed her lips. "Yes, I'll deal with it."

"Okay then," Sal said as she opened the car door. "As long as you know what you're doing."

"Not really, but I'm getting there." A faint glimmer of a smile grew on Lizzy's face. "Thanks for everything, Sal." She grabbed Sal's hand and squeezed it. "I mean it. You've been such a good friend to me. I don't know what I would have done without you."

"Come on, Liz, don't get all soppy on me again." Sal's grin was infectious as she threw Lizzy's hand off.

BEFORE SHE WENT TO BED, Lizzy pulled her Bible out of her bag and opened it. She had business to do with God, but was she ready? She'd been cheated, even though she loved Daniel and would return to him. But letting go of what might have been and forgiving those who were instrumental in changing the course of her life wasn't going to be easy.

How different life would have been if she and Mathew had married. She would have been beside him, supporting him in his ministry, and they would have been happily married, without all the issues she and Daniel were having to work through. But maybe they would have had other issues. She'd never know.

The hurt in Mathew's eyes when he'd learned the truth of what his mother had done made her weep. If only he'd stood up to her.

He seemed so lonely. Why hadn't he found someone else? She prayed that God would bring the perfect person into his life, and that he'd be happy. As she prayed for him, her heart lightened. Maybe this was the first step to full healing. Forgiving his mother wouldn't be that easy, of that she was sure.

Before going to sleep, Lizzy picked up the wedding photo she'd brought from home and gazed at Daniel. Such a handsome man, with his cheeky eyes that could light up a room. *Oh Daniel, please sort yourself out. Please.*

She hugged the photo to her chest, and curled up in bed. Sleep came easier that night, with only Daniel occupying her thoughts.

. . .

As Lizzy entered the church, her mind was drawn to the last time she'd been there, not much more than a month before, but in such different circumstances. How she longed to have Daniel beside her again. The week apart seemed more like a year, and she just wanted to hold him. She'd try to call him soon, and pray that he'd taken steps to deal with his drinking problem.

But right now, she'd join in worship with Sal beside her, and trust that God would be working in his life. The organ played and they stood to sing the first hymn. Lizzy squeezed Sal's hand and smiled warmly at her. Just like old times.

The moment Mathew stood to commence his sermon, Lizzy held her breath. Would she be able to look at him without her heart racing or her hands shaking? Would his hold over her be finally broken? She looked at him standing behind the pulpit. So confident in a quiet way, and his smile lit his face, exuding warmth and love to the whole congregation. He'd make a wonderful husband for some lucky girl. He caught her eye, and for a moment time stood still. How was it possible that so much could be conveyed through just one look? But Lizzy knew in that moment she'd always love him. Not as a lover or a husband, but as a dear friend.

She breathed deeply and relaxed, and listened intently as he began to speak.

"If we're to walk closely with God, we must forgive. There is no choice. Why? Because Jesus commanded it. As simple as that."

Lizzy's body went goosy. Had the topic been a last minute choice, or had God planned it all along? She shivered, and pulled her coat tighter.

"But how can a person whose heart has been trampled on, and whose emotions are in tatters because they've been wronged by somebody, find it within themselves to forgive that person?"

Oh Mathew, how are you doing this? It must be tearing you apart. Lizzy struggled to control her own tattered emotions.

"How can they let go of the hurt and the anguish caused by this person and not only forgive them as Jesus commanded, but also love them?"

Lizzy closed her eyes and tried to settled herself. The words Mathew spoke were coming straight from God, and it was almost too much to bear.

"Only Jesus can enable us to forgive the one we deem to be unforgivable. It's the forgiveness we receive through Jesus that makes it possible for us to forgive others. True forgiveness acknowledges that a genuine wrong has been performed, and it doesn't belittle the pain that this wrong has caused.

"Instead, forgiveness says, *'although I was truly wronged, I won't allow that wrong to control my life. Although I was deeply hurt, I won't let the hurt fester and harden my heart. Instead, I'll release the wrong, and the wrong doer, and hand them both over to the Lord.'"*

Lizzy's heart beat faster. God was speaking directly to her.

"The act of forgiveness is something you choose to do. By allowing the love and grace of God to permeate your heart, you can then live a life free of bitterness and resentment. Rely on God's strength and grace to help you release the person and to love them, with no strings attached.

Let me finish by reading Ephesians 4:31-32, which sums up beautifully how we can be free to love and serve God with all our hearts with our consciences clear: *'Get rid of all bitterness, rage and anger, brawling and slander, along with every form of malice. Be kind and compassionate to one another, forgiving each other, just as in Christ God forgave you.'*

Please pray with me today if there's someone in your life you need to forgive. Let's bow our heads.

Dearest Father, thank you for the forgiveness you offer us through Christ. Thank you for the undeserved grace and mercy you pour out on us every day.

Thank you for the joy and freedom we experience when we confess our sins to you and in return are forgiven for those sins. And thank you that as we experience your forgiveness, you enable us to forgive others.

But Heavenly Father, sometimes it's hard to forgive. "Yes, it is, God. It's hard." Sometimes the wrongs are so hurtful and the wounds so deep that forgiveness seems almost impossible. Your instruction to forgive is clear, but sometimes we don't have it within us to do so. And sometimes we simply don't want to.

So, loving Father, we ask you for help. May our own experience of your grace and mercy both heal and change us, and give us the courage and strength to forgive, even when we've been terribly wronged."

Lizzy couldn't hold it any longer. Tears she'd been holding back rolled down her cheeks as God touched her heart.

"Today, I pray for those who are struggling to forgive. And Lord, I include myself in that. Open our hearts to your love. May we comprehend the majesty of your mercy. Help us trust you, even to the extent of forgiving those who've hurt us so very deeply that we may not want to forgive. May we know your healing and love in our lives when we follow your example and choose to forgive.

All praise to you, God of mercy and grace, God of healing and love and forgiveness. Amen.' "

LIZZY WIPED her face and remained still with her head bowed. Her heart was pounding. Sal reached out and squeezed her hand. God, through Mathew, had nailed it perfectly. He'd met her right where she was, and challenged her to forgive. To forgive Hilary, her father, Mathew. Yes, she would forgive them, and she'd let go of the hurt and the disappointment she'd been holding in her heart for so long. She'd grasp God's love with both hands, and trust Him to fill her with his peace as she moved forward in His strength.

She lifted her head. She wasn't the only one in tears. God had done a mighty work in a lot of lives. A quiet hush had fallen over the congregation, and instead of the normal conversations at the end of a service, people filed out slowly and quietly.

When Lizzy reached the door and faced Mathew, she held out her hand to him. His eyes were slightly red, and he looked tired. No words were required, but Lizzy had something she needed to tell him.

"There's no need to ask her, Mathew. It's okay. Let it be."

He gave her a beautiful, thankful smile.

"Thank you, Lizzy. I'll pray about it." He looked deeply into her eyes as he gently held her hand. "You take care now." As she withdrew her hand slowly and turned to leave, their gaze lingered for just a second longer than it should before it was broken and she and Sal walked away.

"WHAT A WEEK," Lizzy said to Sal as they walked arm in arm back to Sal's car. "This time last week I was out looking for Daniel. It seems so much longer than that."

"You're missing him, aren't you?" Sal stopped in front of the car and reached into her bag for her keys.

"Yes, I am. I just wish I knew what he was doing." Lizzy tilted her head and sighed wistfully. "I think I'll call Nessa again tonight, if that's okay."

"Sure, no problem, Liz." Sal unlocked the car and they climbed in. She put the keys in the ignition and then looked at Lizzy. "How about we go somewhere for lunch?"

Lizzy's eyes lit up. "Yes, that would be great! How about we go to that pub we used to go to at Woodbury Salterton?"

"Done. Let's go." Sal started the car and pulled out of the car park onto Wonford Street, before turning right onto Butts Street and then joining the B3183 towards Woodbury Salterton. Being a Sunday, the traffic was light, and it would only take about twenty minutes to get there.

"That was some sermon today," Sal said, glancing at Lizzy as she slowed down for a red light. "I don't think there was a dry eye in the church."

"Yes, it was certainly a powerful message." Lizzy looked at Sal and crossed her arms. "You know, I think Mathew was almost as surprised as I was when he found out what his mother had done. Maybe I shouldn't have shown him that photo, or pressed him for answers. I feel really bad now that I might have ruined their relationship. Maybe I should've just let it all go, and dealt with it myself."

"It's done now, Liz. You can't change it, and really, he did owe it to you to explain why he ended it. Especially when you were so close. I'm sure he'll do the right thing, and you never know, it might make his relationship with his mother stronger."

"Maybe." Lizzy stared out the window, deep in thought, as they drove the last few miles. Had she done the right thing leaving Daniel as she had? Yes, he'd wronged her, there was no question about that, but should she have forgiven him and stayed? Nessa said she'd done the right thing, but after today's sermon, she wasn't so sure.

"Here we are," Sal said as she pulled into the car park of the Diggers Rest a few minutes later. "Full house today."

"I hope they haven't run out of their chicken pies!" Lizzy said, opening her door and sliding out onto the gravel.

"Let me help you, you poor old thing!" Sal ran round to Lizzy's side, but it was too late. Lizzy had already regained her footing and steadied herself.

"I'm not poor and I'm not old, thank you very much!" Lizzy was indignant and pushed off Sal's arm.

"No, but you did have trouble."

"Well, you shouldn't have a car that you need a step ladder to get in and out of."

Sal chuckled as she closed the door and locked the car. "Maybe I'll replace it one day, just for you."

Lizzy shook her head and grinned. "That'll be the day."

"Come on then, let's go get some food before there's none left."

THEY FOUND a table in a cosy corner and ordered their meals. Lizzy ordered the Chicken and Leek Pie and Sal ordered the grilled fish, just like old times. They both ordered a lemon squash.

Lizzy took a sip of hers, and then put her glass down. She leaned forward and rested her folded arms on the table.

"Sal, do you think I did the right thing, leaving Daniel?"

Sal's head shot up. "What brought that on?"

"Oh, I was just thinking after the sermon this morning. Maybe I should have just forgiven him and stayed."

"No Lizzy." Sal reached out and grabbed Lizzy's arm. "He needed a good wake up call. The way he was treating you wasn't acceptable."

"But I feel like I'm blackmailing him, telling him I won't go back until he gets help." Lizzy leaned back in her seat, her arms still folded. "I don't feel right about it, Sal."

Sal sighed and ran her hands through her hair. "Oh Lizzy. I wish I could wave a magic wand and fix it for you, but I don't think it's that simple. I don't think you're blackmailing Daniel. He might see it like that, but if he loves you enough, surely he'll see that he really does need to get help."

Lizzy shook her head and glanced at the young couple sitting at the next table. They were holding hands and looked so in love. She and Daniel used to be like that. She grimaced and her body slumped.

"Lizzy, you've just got to stay strong. Look at me."

Lizzy turned her head back and lifted her gaze to Sal's.

"You can't go back and put yourself and the baby in danger. I saw what he did to you when you were down here before. If he's done it once, he can do it again, and maybe even worse."

"But he promised he never would." The picture of Daniel lifting his hand to her when she told him she was leaving flitted through her mind. *But he put it down. He didn't hit me.*

"Didn't he promise to talk to you about his problems too?"

Lizzy lowered her head and breathed deeply. *Yes he did.* Why couldn't he have just told her he'd lost his job instead of hiding it from her?

"You can't go back yet, Lizzy. Not until he's done something about it. If you do, you'll be asking for trouble."

Lizzy looked up as the waiter delivered their meals, thankful for the diversion. She placed her napkin on her lap and picked up her knife and fork.

"Okay, you win. But I'd like to at least talk to him sometime soon."

"Alright. I'll let you do that. Now, let's give thanks."

The two girls spent the rest of their time chatting about other things. Sal told her about a new male teacher who'd just started at the school, and who had caught her attention.

"It's about time, Sally Anne Wheatley. I was frightened you were going to be old maid." Lizzy's eyes sparkled as she teased her best friend.

"And what's wrong with that? I quite like being single. I can do what I want, when I want. It has its benefits."

Lizzy shrugged and placed her knife and fork together on the plate and leaned back in her chair. "I guess so. I have to admit I enjoyed my day in London. But I don't know I'd enjoy it forever." She took another sip of her squash and then folded her arms. "You know, I thought you and Mathew might have gotten together."

Sal's eyes widened and she let out a laugh. "And you would have been alright with that?"

Lizzy chuckled as she shook her head. "I don't know. It would have been a bit strange."

"Well, it's unlikely to happen." Sal leaned forward. "I didn't want to tell you this before, but Mathew's started seeing someone."

Lizzy jolted upright. "Who?"

"Remember that girl at College who was a bit older?"

"The quiet one who had that funny hair style?"

Sal nodded, her eyes bright. "It's her."

"Really? I wouldn't have thought she was his type."

"Lizzy, no one has been his type since you. I think it took him as long as it took you to get over it."

LIZZY SIGHED and looked at the young couple who were just leaving. "All I can say is just as well we had that sermon this morning." And with that, they also stood and walked arm in arm to the car.

CHAPTER 13

That evening, Lizzy called Nessa. *Please let there be some positive news and tell me it's okay to come back.* The weight in her stomach argued against the possibility. Even with Sal's reassurance, what she was doing to Daniel screamed 'blackmail' in her conscience. Nessa would agree with Sal, but it didn't lift the heavy guilt from her heart.

As she picked up the receiver and dialled the number, her fingers shook and she almost rang the wrong number. The phone rang for ages, and Lizzy was just about to hang up when Nessa answered, sounding quite breathless.

"Sorry to have made you run, Ness."

"No problem, Lizzy, we've just come in and I heard the phone. I thought it might have been you. I'm sorry, Liz, but there's no news of Daniel."

Lizzy slumped in the chair. That definitely wasn't what she wanted to hear.

"In fact, Riley couldn't find him when he went out last night to look for him."

Lizzy forced her tears back and tightened her grip on the receiver.

"Do you have any idea where he might be?" Her voice was faint and weak, and a feeling of dread flooded through her.

"Not really. The bar maid at the pub said she hadn't seen him for a couple of days, and Johnno hasn't seen him either, so we're not sure. Riley will go out again tomorrow after work and try to find him."

Lizzy gulped and took a deep breath. This was even worse.

"He has to be okay, Ness. I feel really bad for leaving him the way I did. He must hate me right now." Lizzy sniffed and slumped further in the chair.

"Oh Lizzy, stay strong. He's probably feeling a lot of things right now, but that's a good thing. One day soon he'll wake up and see sense. I'm sure of it.

"I hope you're right, Ness. It's so hard being away. Harder than I thought it'd be." She gulped and took a deep breath. "You know, sometimes I think that being with him the way he is would be better than not being with him at all."

"I can understand how you're feeling, but Liz, you're really only thinking about the short term. Just think what it would be like in all the years to come if nothing changed. Do you think you'd cope, let alone be happy, especially when you have a baby around?"

Nessa had a point. Would she be able to cope living with him year after year if nothing changed? Maybe not. A day or a week possibly, but not years and years.

"So, what should I do if he decides not to get any help? Because that's a possibility, isn't it?"

"Mmm. That's a hard one. But yes, I guess it's possible. If that happened, you'd have to really think seriously about how much you want to be with him."

Lizzy pulled herself up. "But we're married, Ness. I've never considered not going back. But I almost feel like I'm blackmailing him, telling him he needs to get help before I will."

"You really are doing it tough, aren't you, you poor thing? There'll be an answer, Liz, one way or the other. God won't leave you high and dry. But if you did come back and he hadn't got any help, you'd have to agree on very clear boundaries. You'll have to do that anyway, even if he does get help, but it'll be harder if he hasn't. Anyway, you need to give him more time. And no, I don't think it's blackmail. It was a reasonable thing to do, given the circumstances."

Lizzy sniffed and wiped her nose.

"Thanks Ness. You always seem to know what to say."

Nessa gave a half-laugh. "I don't know about that. I just wish I could do more."

When Nessa ended the conversation, Lizzy hugged the receiver to her chest. It was her only form of contact with Daniel, as tenuous as it was, and she wanted to hold that thread as long as she could. *Where was he?* Not knowing was horrible. All she could do was pray that God would be with him, wherever he was, and that He would draw Daniel to Himself.

She looked up when Sal entered the room sometime later.

"Any news?"

Lizzy shook her head, and the tears she'd been holding back started to slide down her cheeks.

"Oh Liz." Sal bent down, and wrapping her arms around Lizzy, comforted her until her tears stopped.

WITH DANIEL so much on Lizzy's mind, sleeping was always going to be a challenge, so she and Sal watched a James Bond movie on television to get her mind off him. The choice was limited, and although not great Bond fans, they agreed it was a better option than 'The Way We Were'.

Curled up on the couch with Sal, munching on popcorn and sipping on hot chocolate, Lizzy tried to concentrate on what was happening. For a while she lost herself in the world of espionage, but every now and then an image or a thought would pop into her head and remind her that Daniel was missing. No, not really missing, just no one knew where he was. *But God knows where he is. Oh God, please be with him.* How was she ever going to sleep?

Once the movie was finished, it was way past bedtime, especially for Sal who had to get up and go to work the following morning. Lizzy climbed into bed and pulled out the Janette Oke novel Sal had given her to read. Maybe it wasn't the best choice to be reading right now, but she was loving Marty's journey, and the way God showed His love to her through all her trials and troubles.

She read into the small hours of the morning, devouring Marty's story, clinging to the hope that if God had blessed Marty like He had, maybe He would also do the same for her. By the time she put the book down, her mind had settled, and she rested in the assurance that God wasn't just watching over her, but over Daniel too.

"LIZ... ARE YOU AWAKE?"

Lizzy stirred and forced her eyes to open, shielding them from the sunlight pouring in through the flimsy lace curtains. Where had the night gone? She pulled herself up and focussed her attention on Sal. How did she always manage to look so fresh?

"I am now. What time is it?"

"Eight o'clock... I've got to go, Liz, or I'll be late." Sal walked over and gave Lizzy a big hug. "I'll be praying for you, kiddo. Come back whenever you want. I'm always here for you, you know that, don't you?"

Lizzy's heart burst with love for her friend. How blessed she was to have Sal in her life.

"Yes, and thank you, Sal. I don't know what I'd do without you."

"Go on. Enough of that nonsense. Lock the door on your way out, will you?"

"Of course."

Sal turned to leave.

"Sal…"

Sal stopped and turned around.

"Thank you. I mean it."

Sal met Lizzy's gaze, and an unspoken understanding passed between them. They would always be there for each other.

CHAPTER 14

As the bus took Lizzy ever closer to her home and her father, she breathed in and tried to hold on to God's strength. Mathew's sermon remained fresh in her mind, as did her resolve to forgive her father. As hard as it was to say she forgave him, to live it out would be harder still. She'd never really considered what she'd forgiven him of. There were so many things. She'd been under his control most of her life, from being on display at riding shows, to him trying to marry her to Terrence. Becoming a teacher instead was her first time she'd stood her ground.

Lost in her thoughts, Lizzy almost missed her stop. Luckily for her, the bus driver stopped and called out, otherwise she would have ended up in town. She climbed down the steps and thanked the driver. Gwyneth was there waiting for her as promised, and got out of the car to greet her. Lizzy had told her not to bother, but Gwyneth had insisted, saying it was too far to walk in her condition.

"How was your weekend, dear?" Gwyneth asked after giving her a warm hug.

"It was good, thank you, Mother. I got a lot of things sorted."

"Including Mathew?" Gwyneth raised her eyebrow and studied her daughter.

"Yes, including Mathew." Lizzy smiled inwardly, glad that at last she was able to think of Mathew without an aching heart. She settled herself into the seat and looked ahead. "We spent several hours together on Saturday." She turned her head to her mother and gulped. "I found out why he broke it off, and he also confirmed it was his mother in that photo."

"That must have been a difficult few hours?"

"Yes, it was. It was upsetting, to be honest, but I'm glad I know." Lizzy paused, tilting her head and taking a deep breath. "It was because of his mother. She took a dislike to me from the moment we met, but I had no idea, she hid it that well. It must have had something to do with her relationship with Father. Mathew didn't know about that either. She just kept telling him I wasn't the one for him, and put so much pressure on him that in the end he had to choose between her and me." Lizzy lowered her head and played with her wedding ring. "He chose her."

"Oh my poor darling. That's so sad," Gwyneth said as she stopped the car just outside the entrance gates. One of the gates had become unhinged and was blocking the driveway. Gwyneth climbed out and moved the gate back.

Lizzy spent the few moments alone to reign in her emotions. No room for self pity or regret any longer.

"Sorry sweetie, I didn't mean to interrupt you," Gwyneth said when she re-entered the car.

"Not a problem, Mother."

Lizzy took a deep breath and fixed her gaze on the rose garden as the car crunched its way up the gravel driveway.

"I was angry with Mathew for not standing up to her, but it's too late for anything to change now, so we just have to get on with our lives." She turned to look at her mother. "Sal told me he's started going out with a girl from college. I'm pleased for him. He seemed so lonely."

Gwyneth smiled at her warmly. "And you've finally let go of him?"

"Yes, I believe I have, at last. Now I just want to get home to Daniel."

"Have you had any news?"

"I called Nessa last night, but no one's seen him for several days. She said Riley would go looking tonight. I'm concerned about him, Mother. I almost wish I hadn't left."

"It must be hard for you dear, but stay strong. I'm sure it will all work out in the end."

"I hope so, Mother. I really do."

Gwyneth parked the car in the garage and they both climbed out.

"Come on, let's go inside. I've got lunch ready."

THE PHONE RANG while Lizzy and her mother were seated at the table having lunch. Gwyneth put her sandwich down and walked to the counter to answer it. Gwyneth's face paled and she gripped the counter tightly.

"Yes, she's here. I'll just put you on."

Lizzy looked at her mother quizzically and mouthed, "Who is it?" Her heart beat rapidly. Something had happened to Daniel. She just knew it.

Gwyneth covered the mouthpiece. "It's the hospital."

Her eyes held deep concern as she passed the receiver to Lizzy.

Lizzy took a deep breath to calm herself before answering. "Hello, Elizabeth O'Connor here."

"Mrs O'Connor," a woman with a clear business like voice responded. "Dr Henderson here, from Hull General Hospital. I'm glad we were able to locate you. Your husband had an accident last night, and he's in Intensive Care. He's in a coma, and has multiple injuries. I don't want to alarm you, but we think you should come as quickly as possible."

Lizzy slumped and her hand flew to her chest. Her heart raced. This couldn't be happening.

"Will he ... will he be alright?"

"We honestly don't know, Mrs O'Connor. He's not in good way. We won't really know until he comes out of the coma. If he comes out at all."

What did she mean? 'If he comes out of it at all...' It couldn't be..... Lizzy fought to gain control of her emotions. It would achieve nothing to break down on the phone to a doctor she didn't know. She took a deep breath and gulped, clinging onto the receiver with both hands.

"I'll come right away, but I may not get there until tonight." Lizzy straightened herself and held out her hand to her mother.

Gwyneth wrapped her arms around Lizzy, and supported her physically.

"Can you tell me what happened, Dr Henderson?"

"He had a car accident. Ran into a pole from what I hear."

"No one else was hurt?"

"Not that I know of."

Lizzy let out a sigh of relief. She'd had visions of a multi car pile up with bodies strewn everywhere. At least he hadn't hurt anybody else.

"Thank you for telling me, Doctor. I'll organise myself and get there as soon as I can."

Lizzy hung up the phone and collapsed into her mother's arms.

"I'll drive you, Elizabeth. I can't let you go on your own. He's not in a good way?"

Lizzy shook her head and sobbed uncontrollably. She clutched her chest and felt for her cross. *Oh God, I can't lose him now.*

Gwyneth pulled her tighter and stroked her hair.

Lizzy packed in a daze, and before she knew it, she and Gwyneth were on the M5 heading north.

An empty feeling sat in the pit of her stomach the whole way. *What if he dies?* It didn't bear thinking about. She pleaded for God to keep him alive. Had she caused this? Maybe not directly, but indirectly? How could she live with the guilt if he died? *Oh God, you've got to let him be okay. Please.*

The cold darkness that settled over Hull as they entered the outskirts of the city reflected Lizzy's mood. Heavy mist rolled in from the mountains, enshrouding the city in a cold damp blanket. Lizzy shivered as she climbed out of the car in the hospital car park.

She and Gwyneth walked to the main entrance and stopped in front of the directory board. The Intensive Care Unit was on the third floor, and as reception was closed, they took the lift directly there.

Lizzy held onto Gwyneth's arm for support. Not knowing what to expect was the hardest thing. She should have asked the doctor for more details. Standing in front of the Nurse's station, Lizzy clung to Gwyneth and waited until one of the nurses stopped what she was doing and peered over her glasses at them. Her friendly eyes and demeanour provided Lizzy with some encouragement.

"Yes, can I help you?"

"I'm Elizabeth O'Connor. My husband Daniel is here..." Lizzy's voice wobbled and caught in her throat.

"Oh, Mrs O'Connor. We've been expecting you. Take a seat and I'll call a doctor."

Lizzy and Gwyneth took a seat, but all Lizzy wanted to do was to see Daniel.

Lizzy spent an eternity waiting for the doctor. Fear immobilized her, while the tortuously hard seat meant she couldn't sit still. Waiting would kill her. How bad was he? Maybe he hadn't made it. Her heart beat faster and her pulse raced. *No God, please let him be okay.*

Finally a young male doctor appeared, dressed in a white coat and looking like he should still be in school. Lizzy had hoped Doctor Henderson would've been there.

"Mrs O'Connor?"

Lizzy nodded and gulped. The moment of truth had arrived.

"Come this way, please." He led them into a small clinical room with a round table and four plastic chairs. They took a seat and waited for the young doctor, who had introduced himself as Dr Miller, to speak. Lizzy grabbed Gwyneth's hand.

"Your husband has been seriously injured, Mrs O'Connor." Lizzy let out a slow breath. *At least he's alive. Thank you God.*

"He's still in a coma, and he has swelling on his brain. We're hopeful he won't have any significant brain damage, but we'll have a better idea when the swelling goes down. He also has severe bruising on his chest and abdomen, and has several broken ribs. He's lucky to be alive, Mrs O'Connor." Dr Miller looked Lizzy in the eye.

Lizzy grimaced. *Poor Daniel.*

Gwyneth squeezed Lizzy's hand.

"How long will he be in a coma?"

"Impossible to say. It could just be a matter of days, but it could stretch out for weeks, even months."

"Can we see him?" Lizzy leaned on her mother for support.

"You can, but he's not a pretty sight. Just a warning."

"It's okay. I just want to see him." Lizzy looked at Gwyneth. How would she have survived without her mother's strength and support?

She followed Dr Miller along the corridor until they reached the room where Daniel lay. The doctor opened the door and ushered them in. Lizzy gasped at Daniel lying in the bed with tubes of all sorts attached to his body. He didn't look like Daniel at all. His face was bruised and swollen, and a deep gash low on his forehead had been stitched. His right eye was black and his head wrapped in bandages.

Lizzy's heart melted at him lying there, so broken and damaged, and she raced forward and sat beside him, taking his hand gently. As she peered into his face for some sign of life, tears rolled down her cheeks.

"Daniel, I'm so sorry. Please come back to me," she whispered to him as she squeezed his hand, but his lack of response only made her tears fall harder. She took the tissue her mother held out and wiped her eyes. Her mother's hand on her shoulder was comforting, but didn't alleviate her pain.

"Can he hear me, doctor?" Lizzy finally asked when she was able.

The doctor was checking the monitor, and stopped to answer. "Probably not, but best to assume he can. Just speak to him normally. It often helps when comatose patients start to come out of their coma to have someone they know there for them."

"Thank you." Lizzy turned back to Daniel. She'd stay here with him until he woke up. She couldn't live if he didn't. So lost in her grief for Daniel, she'd forgotten her mother was standing behind her until Gwyneth squeezed her shoulder and suggested they get something to eat.

"You need to look after yourself, Elizabeth, for the baby's sake. Come on, let's get some dinner, and then we can come back for a while."

Lizzy almost had to be dragged away, and only agreed to leave when Dr Miller promised to let them know if there was any change.

Gwyneth guided Lizzy out of the room and down to a large cafeteria where she bought sandwiches and cups of tea. Being quite late, there was little choice, but in reality, Lizzy wasn't hungry. Worry over Daniel sat heavy in her stomach, leaving no room for food.

"He's in good hands, dear," Gwyneth said as she unwrapped her egg and lettuce sandwich a few minutes later.

"But he's such a mess. I don't know what I'll do if he doesn't survive."

"I'm sure he'll pull through, dear. They'll do everything they can for him."

"I need to stay with him, Mother." Lizzy leaned back in her seat and looked at Gwyneth.

"I understand, sweetie, but you should sleep tonight, and then come back first thing in the morning. They'll let us know if there's any change."

"I guess you're right, but I feel so bad." Lizzy gulped and wiped her eyes with the back of her hand. "He wouldn't be here if I hadn't left him."

"Oh Elizabeth, don't say things like that. You did what you thought was best at the time, and Daniel made his own choices. You're not responsible for that. You didn't put him in that bed. He did it himself. You have to accept that, because it's the truth."

Lizzy sighed as a wave of guilt washed through her body. She wrapped her hands around her cup of tea. "But I know I didn't help. Maybe if I'd been a better wife we could have worked things out and this wouldn't have happened." She sniffed and glanced at the nurses who had just entered. "I just want the opportunity to make our marriage work, Mother. He needs to pull through. He really does."

Gwyneth reached out and took Lizzy's hand. "I'll pray that he will, dear, and trust that God will work it out for good."

Lizzy nodded and gave her mother a half-smile. How full of surprises she was. Fancy her being so spiritual and encouraging.

RETURNING TO DANIEL'S ROOM, Lizzy hoped for some improvement. Just something little. Anything would do. But nothing had changed. Nothing at all. Daniel lay there, hooked up to those hideous machines, still and lifeless. How could she leave him alone in this cold, clinical room?

"But Elizabeth, you need to get some sleep. We'll come back first thing in the morning."

Gwyneth was insistent. Lizzy finally gave in, but before she left, she squeezed Daniel's hand and gently kissed his cheek.

"I love you Daniel," she whispered as she skimmed her lips over his battered and bruised face. "Please come back to me."

CHAPTER 15

"You'll need to tell me how to find your place, Elizabeth," Gwyneth said as the BMW sprang to life in the hospital car park.

When Lizzy realized her mother had never been to the apartment, her chest tightened. *Had Daniel been staying there?* She'd gathered from Nessa that he probably hadn't been, but then, maybe he'd been there at some stage, and who knows what he might have done. As there was nothing she could do, she gave her mother the directions.

The street lamps shed a fuzzy yellow glow through the heavy fog. Not surprising really that no one was about when they pulled up outside the apartment a short while later. It was surreal, being here with her mother and not with Daniel. Lizzy could only imagine what her mother would think of it. The building lacked any street appeal, in fact, it was ugly, but Lizzy was proud of how she'd decorated and furnished the inside of the apartment, and hoped it would gain her mother's approval. Not that her mother's approval really mattered. But it would be nice.

Lizzy held her breath as she slowly opened the door and peeked inside before switching on the light. It appeared that everything was as she'd left it, and she slowly exhaled.

"Come on in, Mother. Welcome to our humble abode."

Gwyneth looked around as she undid her coat.

"This is very nice, dear. Small, but homely." Lizzy took her mother's coat and hung it on the hook.

"Thank you, Mother. We were going to start looking for a house, but then all this happened. I guess we'll be stuck here for a while now. If Daniel survives, that is." Lizzy's shoulders slumped and a sudden wave of fear gripped her body, sending a cold shiver up her spine. *What if he didn't survive?* She couldn't imagine what it would be like if he didn't.

"Oh darling." Gwyneth pulled Lizzy close and comforted her. She gently stroked Lizzy's hair and whispered to her. "God's looking after him. Trust Him, dear." She slowly released her hold on Lizzy and held her at arm's length. "Come on now Elizabeth, dry those tears and show me to my room."

Lizzy sniffed, a faint smile growing on her face. "Thank you for being here, Mother."

Gwyneth's eyes watered, and she squeezed Lizzy's hands.

WITH GWYNETH SETTLED in the spare room, Lizzy ventured into her own bedroom. Her and Daniel's bedroom.

Everything was as she'd left it the morning she'd gone looking for Daniel just over a week before. Her heart ached. *Oh God, please let him pull through.* She fell onto the bed, not even bothering to change, and clutched Daniel's pillow to breathe in his scent.

LIZZY WAS WOKEN by her mother at six o'clock the following morning with a cup of tea.

"Elizabeth! You slept in your clothes!" Gwyneth said as she placed the cup on the bedside table.

Lizzy looked at the crumpled smock she'd had on since leaving Sal's place the previous morning and grimaced.

"I must have fallen asleep without realising." She pulled herself up and reached for the cup of tea. "Thanks for waking me, Mother."

"I thought you'd be anxious to get to the hospital, dear. Although I'm sure you'd also benefit from a sleep in."

"Yes, I am anxious. I wonder how Daniel is this morning?" She put her tea down and slid out of bed.

"I doubt there's been any change," Gwyneth said as she walked back out to the kitchen, followed by Lizzy.

"I want to be there when he opens his eyes." Lizzy stood looking out the window and drank her tea. "I'll finish this and get ready quickly." She glanced at her mother, who was already dressed and ready for the day. "You must have been up early, Mother."

"No earlier than usual, dear."

"Oh… I hope you slept well?"

"I won't complain," Gwyneth replied, taking a seat and picking up a piece of toast.

Lizzy tilted her head to her mother as she washed her cup and placed it upside down on the draining rack. So strong and stoic. Love for her mother warmed Lizzy's heart.

"That sounds like you didn't…"

"Yes, well. Strange bed and all. It's not a problem, dear."

"Okay then. As long as you're okay, I'll leave you to your toast and jump in the shower."

Fifteen minutes later, Lizzy was showered, dressed, and ready to leave for the hospital.

. . .

When they arrived they went straight to the ICU and stopped at the Nurses' station, where they learned Daniel was still in the same room, and that his condition was unchanged.

Lizzy led the way, and stopping at the door, she took a deep breath to still the shaking in her hands before opening it slowly. The nurse was correct. Daniel lay in the same position, his face empty of expression. Only the bandage on his head looked any different. Everything else about him was just as it had been the night before.

She walked swiftly to the chair beside the bed and took his hand, saying good morning to him before placing a gentle kiss on his cheek. She had to be strong for him, but inside she was a mess. She pushed back the tears that stung the back of her eyes and took a slow, deep breath.

"Well, Daniel O'Connor. What are we doing today?"

When he didn't answer, Lizzy proceeded to tell him about their trip into the hospital that morning in rush hour traffic. It had taken twice as long to get there that morning as it had taken to get home last night.

"And you know what I discovered when we got home? You haven't been sleeping in our bed!" She leaned closer to him. "Where have you been, Daniel? What have you been doing?" She peered into his face, hoping for some reaction. Just a flinch or a twitch. Just something to let her know he was okay. But there was nothing. Lizzy's heart fell, and she pulled back a little, her body slumping. "Well, you're not going to get rid of me that easily. I'm going to stay here until you wake up, so you'd better make it snappy. I don't want to have the baby while I'm sitting here."

Gwyneth placed her hand gently on Lizzy's shoulder.

"Elizabeth, I think you need some time alone with Daniel. Do you mind if I go off for a while?"

Lizzy looked up startled. How could she have forgotten about her mother? "Where will you go, Mother?"

"Just for a walk. The hospital gardens looked particularly lovely. I'll grab a coffee and find a seat and read for a while. I'll come back later in the morning and check on you."

"Okay Mother. I'm sorry." Lizzy held her hand out to Gwyneth and smiled weakly.

"Nonsense, dear. Daniel needs your attention, not me."

Lizzy let her hand drop and thanked her mother. When Gwyneth had gone, she turned to Daniel, and as she gazed at him and gently stroked his hand, love for him flowed through her body like warm honey.

"Daniel. I don't know if you can hear me or not, but I'm sorry for everything. I know I didn't love you as I should, but that's all sorted now, and I just want you back. I love you, and I promise we'll work everything out together." She leaned in closer to him and kissed him on the cheek. "Just come back to me, please." She closed her eyes and squeezed back the tears that threatened to fall. She had to stay strong, for both their sakes.

As she sat beside him stroking his hand, she told him all about her week, including the meeting with Mathew and how she'd finally been released from his hold on her. She told him about the church service, and how she'd forgiven Mathew and his mother, and that she'd also forgiven her father. It all came off her lips so easily, but would she have been able to talk to him like that if she knew he could hear?

"It's like a clean slate, Daniel. We can start again, without any of those shadows hanging over us. I know we can do it, Daniel. I just know it."

Lizzy sat quietly, and prayed for Daniel and their marriage. She pleaded with God to bring Daniel back to her, whole and undamaged, and that she'd learn to love him more, and to be the wife he needed. One that would support and encourage him, through thick or thin. One that would love with him with God's love, unconditionally.

She studied his face. The bruising and cuts told a story, and not a nice one. *But how will it work if you keep drinking, Daniel? How can I love you unconditionally if you continue to drink and lift your hand to me?* Nessa's words came back to her as she reflected on this seeming disparity. *'Lizzy, you'll need to set boundaries...' Boundaries...*

Nessa! Does she know Daniel's here? Lizzy sat up, her heart pounding. How could she have forgotten about Nessa and Riley, especially after all they'd done?

She stood up and was about to go looking for a phone when a woman doctor walked in. She had a friendly face and short ginger wavy hair, and Lizzy knew instantly this was Doctor Henderson.

"Mrs O'Connor?" The doctor stretched out her hand towards Lizzy's.

Lizzy nodded and took her hand.

"Doctor Henderson. The nurses told me you were here. It's nice to meet you."

"It's nice to meet you too, Doctor." Lizzy shot Daniel a glance. "He doesn't look too good, does he?" Lizzy's voice faltered. "Please tell me he'll be alright."

"We certainly hope so, but it's a matter of waiting. Apart from looking after his physical injuries, we can only wait for him to come out of the coma himself. Hopefully it will only be a matter of days."

The doctor picked up Daniel's chart and inspected it.

"Everything seems fine here. He'd be very sore if he was conscious, so maybe it's best he's unaware of it all for now."

The room started spinning, and Lizzy fumbled for the seat.

"Are you alright, Mrs O'Connor?" Doctor Henderson strode over and helped Lizzy to sit.

Lizzy looked up gratefully and nodded.

"Yes, I think so. It was just such a shock seeing him like this, but hearing it from you ..." She reached out to Daniel and took his hand. "It must have been a bad accident. Do you know what happened?"

Doctor Henderson stood with her arms crossed low in front of her and tilted her head. Her face softened further as she spoke. "Not all the details, but I believe it was a single vehicle accident, and he was intoxicated at the time. I hate to tell you this, dear, but the police will want to interview Daniel when he regains consciousness."

Lizzy closed her eyes. It was as she'd feared. Why had Daniel been driving when he'd been drinking? She could throttle him. He knew better than that, surely. But maybe this was the rock bottom Nessa had referred to. At least he hadn't injured anyone else. She inhaled deeply and opened her eyes.

Squeezing her lips together, Lizzy nodded acknowledgment. The doctor placed her hand gently on Lizzy's shoulder.

"Can I call someone for you?"

Lizzy sniffed and shook her head. "My mother's not far away. But thank you."

"'No problem, dear. It looks like this couldn't have happened at a worse time for you. Make sure you look after yourself."

Lizzy nodded and smiled gratefully at the doctor.

"I will."

When the doctor left, Lizzy remained seated to calm her nerves. Having the Police involved was something she hadn't anticipated, and the very prospect filled her with apprehension. Leaning forward, she clenched her hands together and controlled her breathing, inhaling and exhaling slowly.

She was interrupted by a nurse who had come to check on Daniel, so took the opportunity to visit the bathroom and then to call Nessa.

"Nessa, Lizzy here." Lizzy gripped the receiver with both hands, and leaned against the wall for support.

"Lizzy! We've been trying to contact you. Where are you?"

"I'm at the hospital. We left as soon as we heard and got here late last night. Oh Nessa, it's horrible!"

"I know sweetie. We were there yesterday for a while. He's a mess."

Lizzy sniffed and wiped her nose with a tissue.

"He's in good hands, Liz. He'll pull through."

Lizzy nodded and closed her eyes. "I hope so," she said weakly.

"Stay strong, sweet girl. Is somebody with you?"

"My mother at the moment. But she has to go home today."

"Come and stay with us then. You won't want to be on your own."

Lizzy sniffed and gulped before replying feebly. "Thank you, Ness."

"I'll come to the hospital this afternoon, and we can sort out what to do then."

Lizzy nodded, her heart overflowing with an array of emotions, including a sense of relief to be able to share her grief with Nessa.

"Thanks Nessa," Lizzy whispered before hanging up.

LIZZY PULLED a tissue out her pocket and wiped her eyes, annoyed with herself for not even being able to make a simple phone call without bursting into tears. Why couldn't she be strong like Sal or Nessa?

Once she'd regained control of herself, she returned to Daniel's bedside, where she remained until Gwyneth returned half an hour later.

"How was your walk, Mother?" Gwyneth's cheeks looked flushed and her normally tidy hair slightly out of place.

"Quite relaxing, dear, although a chilly wind was blowing." She pulled her jacket off and placed it over a chair. "And how are you?"

Lizzy pulled herself straighter, determined to be strong.

"Good. I met Doctor Henderson, and I've spoken to Nessa. And there's been no change with Daniel." She looked at him, longing him to wake him. Nothing, not a single thing, had changed. How much longer would it take?

Gwyneth smiled warmly at Lizzy and held out her hand. "Be patient, dear. It's early days yet."

That word again. Her mother was right. She'd always wanted things to happen straight away, patience not being one of her strong points.

"Nessa said I can stay with them."

"That's a nice offer, dear. Better than being on your own. I feel bad about leaving you, but I promised your father."

"It's okay, Mother. You drove me here." Lizzy stood and gave Gwyneth a warm hug.

"It was the least I could do, dear." Gwyneth leaned back and held Lizzy at arm's length. "I'll be praying for you both, Elizabeth. Despite what your father thinks, I believe Daniel is a fine young man, and I'm sure once he's faced his problems, he'll make you a wonderful husband."

Despite her resolve to be strong, Lizzy couldn't control her tears. Her mother's words warmed her heart and gave her hope for their marriage. Yes, Daniel was a fine young man, and he would make her a wonderful husband. Despite all the odds, they would have a future to look forward to together. *You just need to wake up, Daniel.*

CHAPTER 16

Day after day Lizzy sat beside Daniel's bed, holding his hand, talking to him, reading to him, and praying for him. Day after day there was no change, apart from the fresh dressings the nurses applied. They washed and shaved him, making him comfortable, but the expression on his face remained unchanged.

Lizzy ran her fingers over his body when no one was watching, imagining what it would be like to be in his arms again, to have him love her like he had when they were first married. She remembered their honeymoon and how affectionate he'd been, and she laughed at how many clothes she'd packed but hadn't needed.

She whispered to him and told him how much she loved him, and made promises she hoped she could keep if ever he came back to her.

She read to him from the Bible, praying that the words might filter into his heart, even if his ears were unable to hear.

AND THEN ONE DAY, as Lizzy read aloud from the book of John, his monitor sent out a series of piercing beeps. Startled, she dropped her

Bible and stood, her heart beating faster as panic set in. Moments later, two nurses flew in through the door.

Lizzy stood back, her eyes wide and pulse racing, as the nurses checked the monitor and pressed the alert button. Within seconds, two orderlies appeared and transferred Daniel, with all his tubes, to another bed, and wheeled him out with Lizzy following, her arms reaching out to the trolley.

Lizzy frantically tried to get past a short, stocky middle aged nurse who stood in her way, but the nurse held out both arms and prevented her from going any further.

"You can't go with him, dear. He's had a haemorrhage in his brain, and we need to operate straight away. You can stay here or in the waiting room, but you can't go with him."

"Please let me follow him." Lizzy's eyes popped as she pushed harder to get past the nurse.

"Walk with me."

Lizzy walked with the nurse down the hallway until the orderlies pushed the trolley with Daniel lying on it through a pair of swinging doors with a 'No Entry' sign very obviously placed above, and disappeared. The nurse directed her to the waiting area, and then left.

On her own, Lizzy's heart raced out of control and she thought she would faint.

"Are you alright, Mrs O'Connor?"

Lizzy looked up with a pained expression on her face. "I just need my husband to be alright."

"It's too early to tell, I'm sorry, but we'll let you know the moment we have news."

Lizzy inhaled deeply and clenched her hands together. *God, why did you let this happen?*

The nurse placed a cup of hot tea in Lizzy's hands without her noticing. Lizzy stared at the swinging doors, and every time someone came out, her heart lifted, but then fell when they walked past her.

She turned when someone sat beside her. Nessa placed her arm around Lizzy's shoulder and pulled her close. Time inched forward slowly and painfully, one slow second at a time.

WOULD DANIEL SURVIVE? *Oh God, he has to. Please be with him.* Lizzy remained in Nessa's embrace, suspended somewhere between hope and despair. Her mind drifted briefly from time to time, but then she'd be brought back to the horrible reality of the situation as the sound of the doors swinging open reached her conscious mind. How much longer could this go on for?

Finally a doctor she hadn't seen before stood in front of them. Lizzy looked up expectantly, desperate to hear that Daniel had pulled through, but scared to hear he hadn't. The look on the doctor's face didn't tell her anything. Her eyes pleaded with him for an answer.

How long can he just stand there for? Her heart screamed out for an answer, and yet she was unable to speak. Everything happened in slow motion.

Through the thick fog, his voice came to her.

"Mrs O'Connor, your husband is one lucky man. We got it just in time."

It was a dream. Had he really said that Daniel was going to be okay? Why had she doubted? Lizzy slowly came out of her fog and absorbed the wonderful news. Daniel had survived! Tears of joy and relief rolled down her cheeks as she hugged Nessa tightly. Her heart felt like it would break, such was her elation.

ALTHOUGH DANIEL HAD SURVIVED the blood clot, he was still in a coma. Lizzy determined to stay at his bedside, and despite pleadings from Nessa to come home and sleep, she stayed there, night and day, only catching a few hours' sleep here and there in an armchair the nurses brought in for her.

Two weeks after Daniel's accident, Lizzy felt a twitch in his fingers while reading to him. She jerked her head up, wondering if she'd imagined it, much like the first time she'd felt the baby move. She peered into his face as she called out to him, but there was no reaction. Maybe she'd imagined it.

She continued reading, but then it happened again. This time she called a nurse.

It was true. Daniel was starting to regain consciousness, and Lizzy was delirious with joy. Her prayers had been answered! But then, her elation was short lived when the doctor told her it could still take days, possibly even weeks, for him to fully regain control over his body and mind, and they still weren't sure if he'd suffered any lasting brain damage.

But it didn't matter! He was coming back, and she didn't care how long it took. When the doctor left, she leaned her head gently on his chest, and carefully draped her arm over his body. Her smile stretched from ear to ear and her heart filled with love for him as she caressed his body and listened to his strong heartbeat.

That evening, Daniel opened his eyes, and Lizzy was ready for it. She'd been waiting all afternoon, ever since she'd felt that first movement. But she wasn't prepared for the empty stare she received when she looked into his eyes. Yes, the doctor had warned her not to expect too much too soon, but shouldn't there be at least be some sort of recognition? But there was nothing. Her heart cried out for Daniel to see her. Really see her.

Once again, she'd need to be patient. It seemed God was using Daniel's injuries to work on her own issues.

Daniel's eyes didn't remain open for long, but Lizzy remained alert for any further movements, and was rewarded as he occasionally lifted an arm or twitched a finger. She whispered to him constantly, encouraging him to come back to her. She fell asleep with her head beside him on the bed and her arm draped over his chest.

Sometime during the night, she was woken by a nurse checking on him, and she moved back into her chair. The baby must have been squashed, as it began to kick once she sat up. Lizzy gently rubbed her tummy, and her heart warmed as she thought ahead to the time when the three of them would be a real family together.

Over the next few days, Daniel gradually regained consciousness, and Lizzy was elated. Very slowly, he became aware of her and his surroundings, and with every improvement, Lizzy gained hope that he would make a full recovery. She continued to read to him from the Bible, even though she knew he might tell her to stop at any moment. But she couldn't think of any better book to read. She prayed that God's word would be embedded in his soul, and would breathe new life into his heart and mind.

As she read, God was also speaking to her. Verses 2 and 3 in James 1 pointed directly at her. '*Consider it pure joy, my brothers and sisters, whenever you face trials of many kinds, because you know that the testing of your faith produces perseverance.*'

Maybe God was indeed growing her through the trials she and Daniel were experiencing, but how did He expect her to 'consider it pure joy'? Did it really mean she should be welcoming these trials in order to grow in perseverance and character? But who in their right mind would welcome suffering in their life? She would have preferred to grow without it, if truth be told.

Maybe this was part of the journey she was on, and she should be open to whatever God wanted to teach her. How could she expect God to work in Daniel's life if she wasn't open to Him working in her own?

TWO DAYS after he first opened his eyes, Daniel spoke to her. Lizzy wasn't sure at first, but she stopped reading, and waited to hear it again.

Daniel slowly reached his hand out, and as she looked down and gently took hold of it, he spoke her name. It was faint, but it didn't matter. Daniel had spoken to her.

She looked into his eyes and knew in that moment he'd be okay. His body was still a mess, but his eyes held a promise that he would be coming back to her. Lizzy couldn't hide her joy. Her face beamed, and warmth radiated through her body.

The next day, he spoke a few more words, and by the end of the week, he was able to put together a sentence. The doctors were confident he didn't have any permanent damage, and once his physical injuries had improved a little more, they'd try to get him up. In the meantime, they would move him to a lower care ward.

Lizzy called her mother and told her the good news. Gwyneth was ecstatic, and said her father would also be pleased.

"Will he really?" Lizzy asked, hoping that somehow this might actually be the case.

"Yes, dear. I had a good talk to him when I returned, and I believe he's now a little more accepting of the situation. I think he's realising he might have judged you both a little too quickly."

Could this really be happening? Could God be at work in her father's life as well? It was too much to hope for but it sure sounded as if He was!

"Mother, that's great news! I'm so pleased to hear that." The grin on her face stretched from ear to ear.

Nessa and Riley were also regular visitors at Daniel's bedside, and encouraged Lizzy to come home for a good sleep. Lizzy agreed to think about it, but she had no choice. The privileges she'd enjoyed in the Intensive Care Ward weren't extended to the lower care ward and she wasn't allowed to stay with him over night.

LIZZY WENT HOME with Nessa the day Daniel was moved.

"We're so glad Daniel's pulling through, Lizzy," Nessa said as she drove towards her home. "He certainly had us worried for a time."

"Not as glad as I am!" Lizzy sat quietly for a moment before continuing. "I hope this is the rock bottom you mentioned he'd have to hit, Ness. I can't imagine it getting any worse."

"I think so, Liz, but there's still no guarantee he'll stop drinking. You'd think if something like this happened to you, it'd really make you stop and think about what you're doing, and hopefully it will, but it's still totally up to him to make the decision." Nessa shot Lizzy a glance as she turned a corner. "Don't push him, Liz. Be patient. Let him go at his own speed."

Lizzy grimaced. What Nessa was saying was right, but oh so hard.

"That's my problem, Ness. I just want everything to happen straight away. I think God's trying to teach me to be patient."

She took a deep breath and looked at Nessa. "You'll need to talk to me about those boundaries you mentioned, but maybe not now. I'm just happy he's awake and improving every day. He'll probably still be in hospital for weeks anyway."

"Hopefully he'll be out before the baby comes," Nessa said as she pulled up in front of their house.

"That would be good - very good!" Lizzy opened the door and climbed out.

ALTHOUGH SHE WOULD HAVE ENJOYED Nessa and Riley's company, the sight of a proper bed was too much, and as soon as she'd eaten, Lizzy excused herself and went to bed.

The pillow felt so soft, and she snuggled into the blankets, pulling them right up to her neck. Within minutes, she was sound asleep, and didn't stir until the following morning when the sounds of young children jolted her awake.

Lizzy spent some time with Nessa and the children, but couldn't keep her mind off Daniel.

"Ness, I need to go back to the hospital. Do you mind?" Lizzy asked when she could get a word in over the din the children were making.

"Of course not, sweetie. We'll get ready and go."

CHAPTER 17

When Lizzy arrived at the hospital mid-morning, Daniel was sitting and looking much better. The bandages around his head had been replaced with smaller patches, and the stitches had been removed from the cut on his forehead. He was clean shaven, and his hair had been brushed. But best of all, he was reading the Bible Lizzy had left behind.

He started as she walked in and put it down. Was he embarrassed, or did he just put it down because she'd turned up? She recalled Nessa's words. *'Take it slow. Don't push.'*

Lizzy walked over to him, and bending down, kissed him gently on the lips, allowing them to linger on his just a little longer than they possibly should in public, but she didn't care. Daniel was alive and well, and no one was going to stop her from kissing him.

She pulled up a chair and took his hand. Leaning close, she traced the outline of his face with the tip of her finger, her eyes not letting go of his.

"You don't know how much I've waited for this day, Daniel O'Connor."

He squeezed her hand and the faintest of smiles grew on his face.

Lizzy rested her head against his chest, and he lifted his hand and stroked her hair. Warmth radiated through Lizzy's body as all the tension of the previous weeks slipped away.

THEY COULD HAVE STAYED like that forever as far as Lizzy was concerned, but eventually she had to sit up. The baby was making itself known, and she was in discomfort.

Daniel was asleep, so she carefully extricated herself from his body and once standing, gave her back a good rub. Was she ready for this baby? Her preparation had certainly been interrupted, but all seemed to be going well, although she was behind in her check-ups. She made a mental note to call the clinic. But what did she know about being a mother? The thought concerned her now the time was coming near. She really knew nothing about caring for a baby, but then, she'd have Daniel to help her, and he should know. She looked down at him and her heart overflowed with gratitude to God for bringing him back to her.

He stirred, and his eyes opened. She took his hand and gently squeezed it.

A SHORT WHILE LATER, once Daniel had eaten the lunch he'd been given and Lizzy had been to the cafeteria to get a sandwich, the time had come to ask Daniel for his version of what happened. She'd heard from various people that he'd been on the A63 heading west when he veered off the road and hit a pole. But where was he going, and why?

She sat beside him, leaning slightly forward, his hand in hers. Her heart rate had increased slightly, and it took a while for her to speak, being unsure of where it would lead.

"Daniel, do you remember anything at all about the accident?"

His eyes lifted and his body tensed.

"It's okay. I'm not angry, Daniel. I just want to know what happened, and where you were going, that's all." She stroked his hand with her thumb and leaned her arm on the bed beside him.

He looked away and Lizzy's heart fell a little.

"If you don't want to talk about it, it's okay, Daniel." She continued stroking, but pulled back a little. Maybe he wasn't ready just yet, and she'd have to put some of that patience into practice.

Just when it seemed he wasn't going to answer, he cleared his throat. She lifted her head and her gaze caught his. His mouth was downturned and he shook his head.

"I don't know Lizzy. I really don't. It's a blur in my mind." His eyes had that faraway look, as if he was in another place and time. "I remember being at the pub. I'd had a few, and I decided to go and find you." He looked into her eyes. "That's about all I remember."

Lizzy didn't know what to feel. Part of her was elated that he wanted to find her, but then she also carried guilt that she'd indirectly caused his accident. No, she couldn't let herself think like that. She recalled her mother's words - *'it was his choice to drink, not yours'.*

She squeezed his hand and her smile grew warm.

"Thanks, Daniel. At least I know where you were going." She took a deep breath and grimaced. "The Police want to talk to you."

Daniel closed his eyes and hung his head. Lizzy sat still, her heart beating rapidly.

Opening his eyes a few moments later, he lifted his head slowly.

"I've wrecked everything, haven't I?"

She leaned forward and clutched his hand. "No, you haven't, Daniel. Please don't think like that. As long as we're together, we'll be okay. We can work it out, I promise." Her eyes pleaded with him, and her breathing was heavy. She just wanted to hug him and assure him of her love, but his ribs hadn't quite healed.

Tears welled up in his eyes.

"I don't know what I've done to deserve you, Lizzy. You had every right to leave me." The remorse in his eyes was genuine and warmed Lizzy's heart. "But I was so glad to see you here. I didn't ever expect you to come back."

"Oh Daniel. I said I would. It was never in my mind to leave you forever. I just didn't know how to cope with your drinking, not being used to it and all."

"I'm sorry Lizzy. I really am. We're in a mess now because of me." He turned his head to the side and gulped.

"Daniel, look at me." She waited until he looked at her before continuing. "It doesn't matter. It really doesn't matter. We can sort out the mess. The main thing is that you're okay and we're together."

Daniel held her gaze and then nodded slowly. He held out his arm and she leaned into him gently. Yes, as long as they were together, it would be alright. It might not be easy, but they'd be alright. *Thank you, God.*

DANIEL'S RECOVERY CONTINUED SLOWLY, but each day he grew stronger. He asked Lizzy to read to him, as he couldn't keep his eyes open long enough to read much for himself. She was surprised when he asked her to read from the Bible. "But don't get your hopes up," he said when she raised her eyebrows and smiled excitedly.

"I'm just figuring it didn't work my way, so maybe I should try a different way. But I don't want you preaching to me, right?"

Lizzy nodded her head vigorously.

"Right. I promise."

She chose to read the book of John to him, but had to stop regularly to answer his questions. When she got to the story about Nicodemus, he asked her to read it again, and wanted her interpretation of what it meant to be born again.

This was really putting her on the spot. She'd expected God to somehow just change Daniel, but now he was wanting her to explain things. If she stuffed up, she'd lose her chance. No, she couldn't think like that. God was here with her. She loved Him, and her faith was strong. She'd never doubted Him, ever since she'd committed her life to Him when she was at university.

But her faith had been more private. Apart from praying for people and going to church and reading her Bible, she'd never really shared her faith with anyone. Would she be able to get the right words out so they made sense, or would she make a mess of it and as a result, lose Daniel's interest?

No, she had to trust God to give her the words. After all, she really just had to share what in her heart she knew was true. If she was honest and genuine and sincere, surely God would bless that.

Okay, here goes... "When Jesus was talking to Nicodemus, he tried to make it easy for him to understand by using an illustration of a newborn baby entering life. What He was saying is that to begin a new life with God, we have to start again. Jesus called it being 'born again', but these days it's also called 'being saved'. We don't literally have to go back to being physical babies, but in a spiritual sense, we do. Being 'born again' or 'being 'saved' is the actual moment we start that new life, but understanding how God made it possible is the first step."

"Alright, I think I've got that. I guess you'd better tell me how, now that we've started." Daniel straightened himself a little and then settled back against his pillows.

Lizzy smiled inwardly. How exciting it was to be sharing about Jesus with Daniel after all this time.

She breathed deeply before continuing.

"The simple answer is just a few verses down, in John 3:16: *'For God so loved the world that he gave his one and only Son, that whoever believes in him shall not perish but have eternal life.'*

"There must be more to it than that. Just believing doesn't sound enough."

"Well, yes and no. I guess it comes back to what *'believes in him'* actually means. It doesn't mean just head knowledge. It means that you really believe in everything about him. How he came, why he came, and why he died. Oh, and also that he rose again. Just a minor point." Lizzy lifted her eyes and realised she may have confused Daniel. Why had she joked at a time like this? She quickly went on to explain.

"Not really. Jesus rising from the dead is the key to it all, because if it's not true, and he didn't, well then, all the other stuff is meaningless."

Daniel tilted his head.

"Why did he die in the first place? I know it has something to do with being saved, but it's never made sense to me."

"Well, basically it's because without his death on the cross, no one could have eternal life. The whole reason for His birth, death, and resurrection was to provide the pathway to heaven for sinful mankind who would never get there on their own. It all goes back to Adam and Eve."

Daniel rolled his eyes.

"Stop it!" She waved a hand at him. "Hear me out!"

"Okay then. This might be interesting, I guess." He crossed his arms and looked at her with a glint in his eye. It was good to see the old Daniel coming back. "Do you really believe in them?"

"Yes I do. There's a lot to take in, Daniel. But it's also really simple. The gospel in a nutshell is that God created man without sin, but Adam and Eve, the first man and woman, stuffed it up by listening to the snake, who was really the devil in disguise. They disobeyed God, and as a result, all of mankind was tarnished with sin and condemned to death, both physically and spiritually.

"But it hurt God so much that his perfect creation was now imperfect, he made a way for mankind to come back to him. And that was to have his perfect Son, Jesus, come to earth as a human, to live a perfect life, and then to become the ultimate sacrifice for all of mankind by dying on the cross. Jesus, who was without sin, chose to take on the sin of the world, my sin, your sin, so that we could be sinless again in God's eyes. Now, when God looks at me, or anyone else who believes in him, he doesn't see our sin. He sees a new creation, pure and clean because of Jesus.

"Oh, and he rose again. He came back from being dead. That proved He was God, and that He just wasn't any old person. Jesus coming back from death shows us that we don't have to worry about dying physically, because Jesus conquered it for us. If we believe in him, we have everlasting life. With God." Lizzy stopped and looked at Daniel. "So, what do you think? Did I do alright?"

Daniel reached out his hand and squeezed Lizzy's, an encouraging grin lighting up his face.

"You did good, Liz, but I'm going to have think about it some more. It kind of makes sense, but it's a lot to believe in. Especially when you can't see God or Jesus."

"Yes, I know. That's where faith comes in, but there's a lot of information you can read that proves Jesus was actually a real person. A lot of people have tried to prove he didn't exist, only to go on not only to believe in him, but to become Christians. And like I said before, it's not just head knowledge. I know deep down in my spirit, or my heart, or whatever you want to call it, that it's true, and that Jesus lives in me. It's just so real. It's hard to explain, but *I know*. I might not be able to touch Him, but He's with me all the time. Anyway, maybe that's enough for today?"

"I think so. I'm feeling a bit tired. But maybe we can read some more tomorrow?"

Lizzy smiled and squeezed his hand. This was way more than she'd ever hoped for, and her heart overflowed with expectation.

"That would be great, Daniel."

. . .

THAT NIGHT AT DINNER, Lizzy shared with Nessa and Riley about how Daniel seemed to be softening towards God. Even as she spoke, she had to pinch herself to make sure it was real.

"It's only a start, but it's amazing how open he's become. I can hardly believe it."

"That's wonderful news, Liz. We're so happy for you." Nessa said as she gave Lizzy's hand a squeeze.

"Thank you. I know that even if he does give his heart to the Lord, which I'm really hoping and praying he will, it's still not going to be easy for him, but at least he'll have God in his life and that will make a huge difference."

"Yes, it will. He'll still have a long road ahead of him, but I'm sure once he decides, God will give him the strength he needs."

There was still no guarantee that Daniel would give his heart to the Lord, Lizzy knew that, but there was hope, and she clung onto that with both hands.

CHAPTER 18

Lizzy continued to read the Bible to Daniel every day, and every day Daniel had questions for her. She discovered he actually continued reading for himself after she left at night, and often he'd bombard her with questions as soon as she walked in. His hunger to understand was insatiable.

After days of this, the time had come to ask Daniel if he was ready to do something with all this knowledge. Was he ready to accept Jesus for himself? She'd prayed about it the night before, and was confident it was the right time.

Nessa dropped her off at the entrance to the hospital, and she made her way to Daniel's ward. As she turned the corner, her heart fell. A policeman stood at the end of Daniel's bed. She knew it had to happen, but she'd almost forgotten about it.

Lizzy paused, hesitant to interrupt, and turned when a nurse called out to her.

"Mrs O'Connor, you can sit here if you like," the nurse said as she pointed to some chairs not far from the Nurses' station. Lizzy smiled and thanked her, and took a seat.

"How long have they been here?" Lizzy asked as she glanced at Daniel's room.

"About ten minutes I think."

"They didn't want to see me?"

The nurse shrugged her shoulders. "I'm not sure. I'll let them know you're here, just in case."

Lizzy sat demurely with her hands in her lap and her ankles crossed while she waited for the nurse to come back, but inside she was a bundle of nerves. Why did this have to happen today of all days? *God, what's going on? Did I get it wrong?*

The nurse reappeared a few moments later and told Lizzy they didn't need to see her, but they were just leaving, so it was fine for her to go in.

She passed them in the corridor, a burly older man with short bristly hair who walked with a slight limp, and a thinner younger man with dark hair, cut short. Neither looked terribly friendly.

Unsure as to how Daniel would have coped with this meeting, Lizzy paused before she entered his room and took a deep breath. Would he be angry, or would he have just accepted it as an inevitable consequence of his poor choices? She was about to find out…

Daniel sat in bed with his head down and his arms crossed. He looked up briefly as Lizzy entered, but slithered down the bed slightly and lowered his head. Not a good sign.

"Daniel, it's okay," Lizzy said as she leaned over and kissed his cheek. "Whatever happens, it's okay. We'll work through it." She lifted his chin with her finger and kissed him on the lips. Their eyes connected, but Lizzy's heart fell. The glint had gone and his eyes were now dull.

"No Lizzy. It'll never work." He sighed dejectedly and shook his head slowly. "You won't want to be married to me once I've been hauled before the court."

"Don't make decisions for me, Daniel. You're not the only one who's ever been convicted of driving under the influence, you know. We'll survive this, but we have to be together on it. I'll support you, but don't shut me out, okay?" Her eyes pleaded with him, and she moved closer.

His shoulders sagged further.

"Who knows what they'll give me when they find out about my past. Are you ready for that?" He leaned forward as he spat the question at her.

Lizzy gulped. She'd forgotten Daniel's prior conviction and his time in jail. Maybe it wouldn't come out, given it had happened in Ireland, but it was highly likely it would.

"We'll get through it, Daniel. I promise. Whatever they give you, we'll survive."

Silence hung between them, Lizzy's body rigid as she waited for Daniel's next move.

After several tension filled moments, he lifted his eyes.

"You're persistent, Lizzy, I'll give you that." He paused and pulled himself up. "You know I might get jail time again?"

Lizzy's heart fell. No, she didn't know that. She took a deep breath as she gripped his hand. "I didn't know that Daniel, but I'll stand by you, whatever. I promise."

"Why would you do that, Lizzy? Your father will completely disown you when he finds out."

"Daniel, everyone's responsible for their own actions and reactions. If Father doesn't agree with my decisions, that's his problem, not mine. But I won't hold it against him. You're my husband, for better or worse, and I'll stand by you, even if he disapproves."

Daniel's face softened to a grin and he squeezed her hand.

"I always knew you had spunk, but now you're proving it." He pulled her close and hugged her gently.

Lizzy rested her head on his chest as he stroked her hair, and tried to force the thought of jail out of her mind.

When she sat up, Lizzy asked Daniel when he was due in court.

"There's no date yet, but it'll be soon after I get out of here."

Lizzy nodded, and fought against the nausea building in her stomach. If Daniel was sent to jail, she'd most likely be without him when the baby was born…

"So Lizzy. How does your God fit into all of this?" His arms were crossed as he once again put her on the spot.

Lizzy took a moment to pull her thoughts together. Why had she ever thought it would be easy? But really, if Daniel was going to make a decision to follow Jesus, it would never work if his commitment was shallow and only made to please her. It had to be real. And he had to see that her own faith and belief was real and could survive the toughest of tests. But would she pass this test? *Oh God, I pray I do.*

She inhaled deeply, and let out a pained chuckle.

"It's like I'm on a quiz show, but the stakes are much higher." The glint in his eye had returned and her body relaxed.

"It's okay Lizzy. Take your time. I'm not going anywhere."

She shook her head at his cheek, but the grin on her face broadened.

"Well, God never promised an easy life with no troubles, even for those who believe in him." The verse she'd read just a few days before came to mind, and she immediately saw God's wisdom in drawing her attention to it at that time. "But He gives us the strength and ability to get through them if we let Him, and as a result, we become better people.

"Giving your heart to Jesus is only the first step. The journey from then on is all about growing more like Him, but we don't have to do it on our own, because He's with us all the way. We just have to be open to Him and allow Him to teach us how to live. It's just like we're little children learning from our parents. It's a life long journey, and sometimes the best way we can learn is by going through tough times.

"So, to answer your question, God will help us through this if we let Him. He's not going to fix it so that it goes away. He doesn't do that. But if we let His Spirit into our lives, and accept the outcome without being angry or bitter, He'll give us His peace and love instead, and will help us handle whatever we have to."

"You really believe this, don't you?" Lizzy looked up into Daniel's eyes and her heart filled with love for him. God was working in his life, she could feel it.

"Yes, I do, Daniel. I can't imagine my life without Him in it. I thank Him every day for saving me and for being with me. I know I let Him down all the time, but He's always there for me."

Daniel remained still and quiet. He was deep in thought, and Lizzy sensed God was touching his heart and reaching out to him.

"Daniel," she said a few moments later. "Do you want to ask Jesus into your heart?"

Lizzy held her breath as Daniel looked deeply into her eyes. Her heart raced. This was the moment she'd been waiting for. *What would his answer be?*

His gaze, steadfast and sincere, held her captive. She couldn't move. *Come on Daniel, please answer...*

He took her hand and patted it gently.

"Yes Lizzy, I do. I want to ask Jesus into my heart."

Lizzy didn't even try to stop the tears trickling down her cheeks. Her heart soared and she hugged him as tightly as she dared.

She slowly pulled back, and wiped her face. "Okay then, Daniel O'Connor. Today you become a child of God - let's do this!"

"What do I have to do?"

"It's simple really. You first have to believe, and I think you do?"

"Yes, thanks to you, I believe."

Lizzy's body tingled. Daniel really believed!

"Then you have to repent." She gulped. *This was going to be a challenge.* "Repentance means that you confess you're a sinner and that you're in need of saving. But it has to be genuine. You have to really mean it, and that's the hardest thing for most people to do, because it makes them face up to their real self."

Lizzy's heart beat rapidly as she waited for Daniel's response. Would he humble himself and confess his sin before God? Or would this be the stumbling block?

"Lizzy, I really am sorry for all the wrong I've done. For the way I've treated you and other people. I can see I've got sin in my life, and I need to get rid of it, so yes, I'm ready to confess."

The remorse revealed in Daniel's words was genuine, and Lizzy thanked God with all her heart.

"Well then, all that's left is to tell God all of that. And then he'll do the rest." She squeezed his hand. "Are you ready?"

His eyes glistened as he returned Lizzy's squeeze.

"Yes."

"Let's pray, then." Lizzy closed her eyes and began.

"Dear God, thank you so much for your love for us. And thank you so much for sending Jesus to earth to die for us so that we can be with you. We don't deserve any of this, but we gratefully accept it. And today, Lord, Daniel wants to accept you as his Lord and Saviour. Please fill him with your love and your peace as he gives his heart to you. Thank you Lord God."

"Daniel, just say this prayer after me, okay?"

Daniel nodded.

"Dear God, I need You to sort me out. I've done some bad things in my life, and I'm truly sorry for them all. Not just things I've done, but things I've thought. I want to turn away from my old life, and instead live for You. Will You come into my life and cleanse me from the inside out? Make me a new person, Jesus. I know I don't deserve You, but I know You love me just as I am, and for that I'll be forever grateful. Thank you Lord Jesus. In your precious name, Amen."

After Daniel had finished praying this prayer, Lizzy stood and gave him the biggest hug she dared. Tears streamed down both their faces, but Daniel was sobbing. Lizzy held him as God washed him clean from the inside out, just as He had done with her many years before, removing the debris and dirt from all the years he'd lived for himself, and replacing it with His love and forgiveness.

A nurse came in while Lizzy was holding him, but Lizzy shook her head and the nurse left quietly. When Daniel's tears finally subsided, he lifted his head and looked into Lizzy's eyes.

"Thank you, my sweet girl. Now I know what you've known all along. That I'm nothing without God in my life. Thank you for showing me that." He pulled her close and kissed the top of her head.

CHAPTER 19

When Lizzy left the hospital early that evening, Daniel had time to revisit the events of the day. He'd never anticipated he'd feel so different inside, but it was like a weight had been lifted from him, and he felt new and refreshed. Lizzy had shown him 2 Corinthians 5 :17 which explained what he was feeling: *'Therefore, if anyone is in Christ, he is a new creation; the old has gone, the new has come"*, but it was still a little unreal.

He opened his Bible and started reading, but unlike before, it now seemed to make so much more sense. Lizzy suggested he keep reading through the book of John, so that's what he did, and he was blown away by the way Jesus was treated while He was here on earth, and how most people still didn't believe in Him even though He did all those amazing things right in front of their very eyes.

It was like Lizzy said, that unless people want to believe, they won't. Instead, they'll choose to go their own way and do their own thing, even though the God of all creation stood right there in front of them, offering them a whole new way of living. People's stubborn hearts held them back from all they could be in God. Which is exactly what he'd been doing all his life. Until now.

He was still reading when the nurse came to check on him later that evening. Looking up, he smiled at her, and wondered if she'd notice any difference in him. He closed his Bible and placed it on the dresser before holding his arm out.

"You seem chirpy tonight." She glanced at him as she held his wrist. "Must be almost time you left us, I'd say, from the look of you."

It must have been obvious.

LIZZY SHARED the good news with Nessa and Riley that night, and like Lizzy, they were ecstatic. They'd seen the hurt and bitterness he'd been carrying for years eating away at him and showing itself in his unpredictable behaviour.

"We're just so pleased, Lizzy. It's wonderful news," Nessa said, giving her a big hug. "We've prayed for him daily, and now, well, this is great! *Thank you Jesus!*" she said as she lifted her eyes heavenward.

The mood that night was very upbeat. Lizzy called Sal and told her the good news, but something held her back from calling her parents. Her mother would understand, but she wasn't sure about her father.

She found it difficult to sleep, not because she was worried, but because she was overjoyed and her mind was active. It didn't matter. Instead, she prayed and read, and prayed some more, before she finally succumbed to sleep.

THE NURSE WAS RIGHT. When Daniel was visited by the doctor the following morning, he was told he was well enough to go home. The news filled him with relief and concern. Whilst it was great he'd recovered so quickly, it meant leaving the security of the hospital ward, and going back into the real world with all its problems and temptations. But this time he'd have God with him. And he was determined to not let Him down.

When Lizzy arrived, she found him already dressed and packed. The doctor wanted to see her to go through his follow up care with them both, but then they were free to go. As Nessa had already left, they called a taxi and went home.

It had been almost ten weeks since they'd been in the apartment together, since that day Lizzy had made that ultimatum with Daniel. She'd never imagined it would end like this, but she couldn't have been happier. It didn't matter that they didn't have a house. This was their home, and as she'd joked with Daniel on their holiday a few months earlier, she'd be happy living with him in a tent.

After Daniel unlocked the door and they were both inside, he pulled her close and kissed her like she'd been wanting him to for so long. She gave herself to him willingly, and revelled in the closeness she'd feared might never have been theirs again.

CHAPTER 20

The day after arriving home, Daniel received his notice to attend court on Friday of that week.

"They didn't waste any time, did they?" Lizzy said as she stood behind him looking at the piece of paper.

"No, not at all. Are we ready for this?" Daniel faced her and pulled her onto his lap.

Lizzy wrapped her arms around his neck, and leaned against him. "I don't want you to go to jail, Daniel, but we'll survive it if you do. Maybe they'll take one look at me and decide to just give you a fine and a suspension. You never know."

"I'll hate it if I'm not around when the baby comes." He kissed the side of her face, and brushed her hair with the back of his hand.

Lizzy took his hand and placed it on her tummy. "Here, feel for yourself. I think it's in training for a marathon the way it's kicking."

Daniel chuckled and agreed.

The rest of the week was spent catching up on everything, as well as meeting with the solicitor in preparation for Friday's court hearing, and plenty of Bible study and discussion. Daniel wanted to know everything. Lizzy was amazed at his thirst for the Word, and the way he just didn't accept what he read without trying to understand what it meant for him.

DANIEL'S BODY still had some healing to do, so even if he avoided jail time, it was unlikely he'd be able to return to proper work for some time. This knowledge made them take a look at their finances. Their savings had dwindled now that Daniel's pay had stopped and Lizzy had taken leave without pay. Once her maternity leave payment kicked in, they might just survive for a while, but Daniel would need to find a job. They didn't even think about what would happen if he went to jail. And they needed to buy another car. The insurance company refused to pay out as Daniel had been charged with driving under the influence.

"Who's going to give me a job now?" Daniel asked one night as they sat together discussing their situation. "I couldn't find one before, so what's the chance of finding one now?"

His dejected look brought back memories of the old Daniel and sent a shiver down Lizzy's spine.

"You can't think like that anymore, Daniel. We'll pray about it and ask God to open some doors. You never know what He's got in store for you. We just have to trust Him, not only with a job, but also with the court appearance, and with our money. With everything, really. But that doesn't mean we sit back and wait for Him to wave a magic wand and hand us everything already done. You still need to go out looking for a job, but this time, you know that God's on your side. Maybe you'll still get twenty rejections, but you keep going because you know that God has something special for you. And in the meantime, He'll provide for us, somehow, as long as we're trusting Him."

"You sound so confident, Lizzy. I don't know if I can be like that."

"I just know that God won't leave us high and dry. He loves us, Daniel, and He'll look after us."

"I do love you, Lizzy." He pulled her close and kissed her gently.

THURSDAY MORNING, as Daniel was reading aloud from the Bible, Lizzy sat back and rubbed her neck. The change in Daniel had amazed her, and her heart was full of gratitude to God for turning his life around, but she couldn't help wondering how Daniel would cope when he went back into the real world. Would his new found faith be enough to withstand the pressures he'd face?

"Hey you, what are you thinking about?" Daniel closed the Bible and looked at Lizzy with a puzzled expression on his face.

Lizzy looked at him and took a deep breath. They had to talk about it.

"I was just thinking about how wonderful this week has been, Daniel, but I'm a little concerned."

Daniel cocked his head.

"Go on, my love. What are you concerned about? Apart from my court appearance, that is…"

"It's just that we've been protected here, Daniel. Just you, me, and baby Dillon. But there's going to be battles ahead, especially when you go back out to work. Your battle with alcohol isn't over. You'll be challenged by it again and again at some stage, and I really believe you need to get some help before then."

Daniel straightened himself, and drew his eyebrows together.

"No Lizzy. I've got you, and I've got God. And I'm determined not to drink. That's enough. I don't need outside help."

Lizzy cringed inside. Why did he have to be so adamant? But it wouldn't do to force the issue... she'd just have to pray.

She reached out her hand to his, and forced a smile onto her face she didn't feel. A lump sat heavily in the pit of her stomach.

"Okay then. I guess I have to let it go. You know I'm here for you, Daniel, and I'll support you in any way I can."

"Yes, my love. Thank you. I'll be alright, you'll see."

Oh God, I pray that will be the case...

THAT NIGHT, the night before Daniel's court appearance, Riley telephoned and asked to come over as he had something to talk to them about. They agreed, and waited for his arrival.

Daniel let him in, and ushered him to the lounge where Lizzy was resting.

"Don't get up, Lizzy," Riley said as he leaned down and kissed her on the cheek.

"Thanks Riley. Good to see you." She smiled at him as she squeezed his hand.

"Well, I won't keep you long. I've got a proposal to run past you." He cleared his throat and glanced at both Daniel and Lizzy before continuing. "I've heard about a job that might suit you, Danny. A Bible College in the Lakes District is looking for a maintenance person. It's a live-in job, and they're prepared to accommodate a family. The pay isn't great, but you wouldn't have to pay for housing, so it could be a good option. Plus, it's run more like a community, so you get to mix with the students and teachers, and you can sit in on any classes you want. I can put in a good word for you if you like the sound of it."

"Daniel, it sounds perfect!" Lizzy sat up and grabbed his hands.

Daniel laughed and shook his head. "Lizzy, look at you! You're just like a little kid wanting an ice-cream!"

"I'm sorry, I can't help it." She calmed herself a little. "Don't you think it's perfect?"

"Maybe. But we hardly know anything about it." Daniel turned to Riley and tilted his head. "Do you really think it's a job I could do?"

"Easy. It's just mowing lawns, a bit of gardening, keeping things running, all things you've done before. Nessa and I both think it would be the ideal job for you."

"Well, I guess I'll trust you on that. So now it's just a little matter of that court appearance..."

"Yes. That's the sticking point. But we're hoping for a good outcome, Danny. Bill's a legend, and if anyone can get you a lighter punishment, it's him. But you'll have to agree to rehab."

Daniel leaned back and crossed his arms over his chest.

"Why are you so against rehab, Daniel?" Lizzy drew her eyebrows together. "Anytime rehab's mentioned you put up a wall. I don't understand." Memories of their earlier conversation about him getting help came to the fore.

"Do you really want to know?"

She nodded eagerly. "Yes, I do."

Daniel sighed and took a deep drag on his cigarette. "When I was in last time, I went cold turkey. Not just alcohol, I'd been taking some hard gear as well, and it's left a bad taste in my mouth. I don't have fond memories of the place. I don't want to be locked away for weeks on end away from you." He tapped the ash into the tray in front of him and crossed his legs. "I know it works for some people, but just not me. I don't need it, anyway."

Lizzy grimaced and struggled to remain positive. It couldn't all fall apart just because Daniel wouldn't agree to rehab, surely?

"Can't you agree to regular counselling without being admitted? That would surely help?"

Her eyes locked with his as an unspoken battle waged between them.

Riley leaned forward and spoke quietly. "I think you should agree, Daniel. It can't hurt, and might just help. And it might keep you out of jail."

Daniel turned his gaze to Riley. Moments later, he threw his arms up.

"Alright. You both win. I'll agree to counselling."

Lizzy cast her eyes heavenwards and sent up a prayer of thanks as tears welled up behind her eyelids. She squeezed Daniel's hand and a broad smile grew on her face.

LIZZY COULDN'T GET the news of the possible job for Daniel out of her mind. Although little information had been given, she felt it was from God, and thanked Him for providing for them. Yes, there was a long way to go, but she was confident, and so when it came time to go to court the next morning, she was far less nervous than she might have been, although she'd been battling a persistent headache all night.

That morning, Daniel deliberated over what to wear, but in the end agreed with Lizzy's suggestion of black trousers, white button up shirt and black jacket, although he wasn't happy about it.

"I look like a waiter," he said as he looked at himself in the mirror. "Can't I wear something a bit trendier?"

"No. You look smart and presentable. Just how you need to look in court. I think you look very nice." She reached up and planted a kiss on his lips. "Come on, Riley and Nessa will be here any moment."

She grabbed his hand and pulled him out the door. Riley and Nessa had just pulled up outside the apartment block as they reached the bottom of the stairs. Lizzy held Daniel's hand in the back of the car for the short trip into town. He was fidgety, and she knew he was nervous. There was every possibility he wouldn't be coming home with them.

Nessa must have been nervous too, as she was chatting away in the front about anything and everything. Lizzy did her best to listen and respond when appropriate, but her head hurt, and she just wished Nessa would stop.

THE COURT HOUSE car park was almost full, but there were a few spots towards the back. Once parked, Riley turned around in his seat and looked at Daniel. Thankfully Nessa had stopped talking.

"Hey Danny, would you like to pray before we go in?"

Lizzy squeezed Daniel's hand again and tried not to tear up when he agreed.

"Let's pray, then," Riley said as he reached out his hand to Daniel. "Heavenly Father, God of mercy and grace, we know You want the best for Daniel and Lizzy. We don't know what the outcome will be today, but we trust that whatever it may be, You will give Daniel and Lizzy peace and joy. We pray that they will trust You to lead them and be with them in the days ahead. We dare to ask that Daniel might avoid jail time, but we pray that Your will be done. Lord Jesus, I commit Daniel and Lizzy into your hands, and ask that You bless them with your mighty love. In Jesus' precious name, Amen."

The moment passed all too soon, but God was with them, and they knew that whatever happened, they'd be okay. When Riley turned back and opened his door, cold air raced into the car, making Lizzy shiver. She pulled her coat and scarf tighter before she climbed out with Daniel's help.

Hidden between the open doors, Lizzy faced Daniel and gently put her hands on his chest after straightening his collar. "Are you okay, Daniel?" She looked into his eyes and her heart filled with love and respect for him as he looked back at her with strength and determination.

"Yes, I'm more than okay." He brushed her hair with his hand, and held her gaze. "I'm ready for this, Lizzy my love. I'll trust God whatever the outcome, even if it's jail. It won't be forever." Lizzy's heart pounded as he pulled her close and kissed her gently.

"Come on you two," Nessa said with a laugh in her voice. "Anyone would think you'd just got married!"

Lizzy turned her head and gave her a cheeky grin. "Give us a break, Ness. It *is* like we've just got married..."

"I know, I know.... Sorry to break it up, but we do need to go in."

"Okay Ness, settle down. We're coming." Daniel released Lizzy and took her hand as they headed towards to the courthouse.

DESPITE THE FACT they'd only just committed the whole proceedings to the Lord, Lizzy's stomach had an empty feeling, and she gripped Daniel's hand.

Bill McIntosh, Daniel's solicitor, had arranged to meet them at nine thirty in the foyer. Of medium height, he stood erect, giving the appearance of a much taller man. He looked impressive in his dark suit and navy blue tie, and Lizzy prayed he'd be successful in obtaining a lighter sentence for Daniel.

Bill smiled broadly and held out his hand.

"Good morning Daniel, Lizzy." His voice was deep and commanding, and filled Lizzy with confidence. He nodded to Riley and Nessa before turning his attention back to Daniel.

"You're towards the top of the list, so I suggest we wait here." He pointed towards the waiting area where others were already seated.

Daniel and Lizzy took a seat, with Daniel sitting beside Bill. Lizzy was having trouble breathing and didn't feel too well, but hid it from Daniel. She wanted to be so strong for him. As Bill talked to Daniel, she tried to focus on what was being said, but she was feeling light headed and her headache hadn't gone away. *Oh God, please help me get through this, for Daniel's sake.*

She sipped the coffee Nessa handed to her a few minutes later and felt a little better.

Nessa sat beside her.

"Are you okay, Lizzy?"

"Not really, but don't say anything, Ness. I just want to get through this."

"I don't like the look of you. You're all puffed up."

"I'll be okay." Lizzy smiled weakly, and looked up expectantly when Bill said Daniel had been called.

Nessa helped her up and held her arm as they followed behind Bill and Daniel, who were deep in conversation.

Taking her seat in the court room, Lizzy wished she was anywhere but here. Would she be able to focus on what was happening? She really didn't feel too well at all. In fact, she might be sick at any moment.

The magistrate called Daniel to the front. Daniel stood and stated his name, and pleaded guilty to the charge.

She had to get out. Sweat oozed from her forehead, and she felt clammy all over. She attempted to stand, but swayed. Nessa steadied her.

"I need to go to the bathroom," Lizzy whispered to Nessa while holding her hand over her mouth. As Nessa helped her out, Lizzy's gaze settled on the back of Daniel's head, and her heart ached for him. Why was this happening right now? *God, why?*

"I think we need to get you to hospital, Lizzy," Nessa said once Lizzy had been to the Ladies. "You're very pale, and your face is swollen. I'm really concerned."

"No Ness. I need to be here for Daniel."

"No Liz. Listen to me. You need to look after yourself right now. We're going to the hospital."

Lizzy gave in when she swayed and almost fell. She waited in the foyer while Nessa got the car, and then sat slumped in the front seat while Nessa sped to the hospital.

One look at her, and she was admitted straight away. It was all a blur, as she was prodded and poked by a variety of doctors and nurses. Nessa remained by her side the whole time, holding her hand, assuring her everything would be alright.

"Mrs O'Connor, can you hear me?"

Lizzy tried to focus on the person speaking. She nodded to the vague outline of a male doctor standing over her.

"We need to deliver your baby, Mrs O'Connor."

The words jolted her. *No. This couldn't be happening.* It was too early. She was semi-aware of Nessa beside her, but nothing else made much sense.

She jumped slightly at a prick in her arm, and then she was being pushed through a tunnel. A tunnel with no end. Bright lights flashed overhead, and jumbled sounds of voices and wheels and metal touching metal whirled in her head. Then it all went blank.

CHAPTER 21

Daniel held his hands together tightly in front of him to keep them from shaking. As much as he wanted to trust God, he'd still be devastated if he was sent to jail. How could it be otherwise when it'd mean being separated from Lizzy when she was so close to having their baby?

He turned his head slightly at a noise that came from behind. *Lizzy!* He gripped the back of the chair but it was too late. His case had begun.

WHEN LIZZY CAME TO, she struggled to remember where she was. A nurse stood above her with a baby in her arms. Lizzy glanced at her stomach, and realized with a start it was her baby. She tried to pull herself up, but winced as searing pain tore through her lower abdomen.

"Don't get up, Mrs O'Connor. Stay right there. May I introduce you to your new little son?"

She must be dreaming. It wasn't real. But no, it was real. She looked down at the tiny bundle that had just been placed beside her. This was unbelievable. She had a son. But how had it happened? And where was Daniel?

She glanced around, but he wasn't there. Her heart fell when the fog in her brain cleared and she remembered he was in court. Slowly it all came back. The trip to the hospital, the lights, the noise, and being told her baby had to be delivered.

Lizzy's heart swelled with love for her tiny son. He was perfect, and the mop of black hair was so Daniel. She gently touched his little pink face and kissed the top of his head as she held him in her arms.

She glanced up as Nessa walked in, smiling from ear to ear.

"Lizzy! Congratulations!" Lizzy smiled tearfully when Nessa leaned down and kissed her on the cheek before gazing at the tiny bundle lying beside her. "He's beautiful, Liz." Nessa's eyes sparkled and held tears of her own.

"Thank you, Nessa." She shook her head and looked up. "I don't believe it's happened." Lizzy's eyes widened and she grabbed Nessa's arm. "What happened to Daniel?"

Nessa shrugged and had a painful look on her face.

"I don't know yet, Liz. I haven't been able to find out. I left a message at the courthouse to tell Riley where we were, but I haven't heard anything yet."

"Oh Ness, I'm so worried about him."

Nessa leaned down and hugged her as Lizzy began to sob. "Try not to worry, sweetie. We'll know soon enough."

Lizzy sniffed and tried to calm herself. Every time she moved, it hurt. It was almost too much to take in.

"Here, let me take this little one," the nurse said, leaning down and gently picking up Lizzy's baby. "I'll bring him back shortly once you've had a little more recovery time, Mrs O'Connor. It mightn't hurt to get some sleep if you can." The nurse was right. Maybe it was the after effects of the anaesthetic, but whatever it was, she was very drowsy.

"I think I'll have a little sleep, Ness, but wake me the moment you hear anything from Daniel. Promise?"

"I promise." Nessa smiled at her and squeezed her hand before leaving the room.

"LIZZY, ARE YOU AWAKE?" Lizzy blinked at the sound. "Lizzy, I've got a surprise for you."

Lizzy opened her eyes wide as she recalled where she was. Nessa was standing over her. Was there news of Daniel?

"Here, let me help you up." Lizzy leaned on Nessa's arm and wriggled herself up until she was sitting. Her eyes questioned Nessa, but her gaze averted round her as she caught a glimpse of blue helium balloons being held by someone standing in the doorway.

Lizzy's skin tingled and her grin broadened when she realised it was Daniel.

"Daniel! Oh my goodness! You're here! I can't believe it!"

Daniel raced towards her and hugged her gently as she sobbed in joy. "My precious Lizzy. Thank God you're alright." He kissed the side of her cheek before pulling slowly away. "And I believe we have a son…"

"Yes Daniel. We have a son. And he looks just like you!"

"Poor little baby! Fancy looking like his daddy!"

"It was a compliment!"

"I know, I was only joking, sweet girl. When can I get to meet him?"

"We can call the nurse. But Daniel," she grabbed his hand and peered into his face. "Tell me - what happened in court? You're here, so I'm guessing you didn't get jail?"

"Yes, thank God. Bill was brilliant. I got off with a fine and a suspension. No jail." Daniel's smile was infectious, and tears welled up behind Lizzy's eyes as all the built up tension fell away.

"Daniel, that's wonderful. I'm sorry I wasn't there."

"Go on with you. You had other business to attend to… So, where is he?" He turned as the nurse entered the room with a tiny bundle in her arms. She leaned down for him to see, and then placed the tiny bundle in Daniel's arms. Lizzy's heart filled with love for the two men in her life as Daniel gazed in wonderment at their son, and she revelled in God's goodness.

Daniel sat gently on the side of the bed with his son in his arms. "What are we going to call him?" He glanced at Lizzy as he allowed the tiny baby to wrap his fist around his finger.

"How about 'Dillon', after your brother?" Lizzy suggested.

Daniel's face expanded into a wide grin. "That's perfect, Lizzy. A perfect name for a perfect boy!" He leaned down and kissed his little son. "Welcome, baby Dillon."

Lizzy leaned over and looked at the baby.

"I think it's my turn," she said with a mischievous grin on her face.

LIZZY SPENT the days following the early arrival of baby Dillon getting to know him, and learning how to care for him. Daniel was brilliant. He had it down pat when it came to changing Dillon, and showed Lizzy a trick or two. Every time she saw him with the baby, she smiled.

She telephoned her mother and told her the exciting news, and she also telephoned Sal. Both were ecstatic. Sal said she'd try to get up to see her, and Gwyneth also promised a visit as soon as she could.

Meanwhile, Riley helped Daniel apply for the job he'd mentioned, and organised for his counselling sessions to start. Daniel told Lizzy he was really looking forward to finally kicking his old habits, even though he wasn't looking forward to the sessions. He said he felt bad that they didn't have a car, but even if they did, he wouldn't be able to drive for another year.

"But I guess it's my fault. I can't blame anyone else."

"We'll be alright, Daniel. We'll sort it somehow."

NOT LONG AFTER she'd been allowed to go home with baby Dillon, her parents told her they would pay a visit the following weekend.

DANIEL, although nervous about meeting Lizzy's father again, was determined to prove to him that he was worthy of being Lizzy's husband, and that he was fully prepared to take responsibility for her and Dillon. It just would have been better if he had a job. He'd been waiting to hear whether his application had been successful, and had been checking the mail box every day. The interview had been the week before, and he'd been told he should hear within the week. The interview had gone well, and he was surprised at how keen he was to get the job.

Yes, it would mean living in a community environment, and yes, he may feel a little threatened, but it didn't matter. It'd be an opportunity to learn and grow, and to mix with Christians who could provide support as he learned to live his new life with God and without alcohol. He'd told Lizzy all about it, and they'd prayed about it, and although they agreed they'd trust God for the outcome, he was still on tenterhooks about it.

The Friday before Lizzy's parents came, Daniel picked up the mail and it was there. He carried the envelope to the kitchen where Lizzy was making tea, and stood before her with the envelope in his hand.

"This is it, Lizzy love."

"Well, go on. Open it." She stopped and studied him. "You're nervous, aren't you?"

Daniel nodded as he stared at the envelope.

"You're not going to find out if you don't open it. Do you want me to do it?"

He held her gaze and breathed deeply.

"No, I'll do it." His heart pounded in his chest as he carefully opened the envelope and took out the piece of paper. Lizzy bent her head so she could see, but he turned it away from her. "Let me look first."

Lizzy didn't need to see it, however, as a moment later, Daniel's whole face exploded into a huge, beaming grin.

"I got it! I got it!!" He wrapped his arms around her and planted a kiss on her cheek as they jigged up and down together.

"Daniel, that's wonderful news! Congratulations!"

THE FOLLOWING day when Roger and Gwyneth arrived, Lizzy's heart expanded with pride when Daniel was eager to tell them his good news. Her father also appeared to be making an attempt to be friendly, and was less officious looking than normal. Maybe holding his tiny grandson for the first time softened him a little. Whatever the reason, there was hope that Daniel and Father might at last be able to remain in each other's company without an argument.

AS ROGER and Gwyneth prepared to leave, Gwyneth caught her husband's eyes and tilted her head as if she was trying to tell him something. Lizzy caught sight of this and wondered what was going on.

Roger coughed and cleared his voice.

"Elizabeth," he paused and glanced at Gwyneth before turning to look at Daniel. "And Daniel... we have a gift for you."

Lizzy raised her eyebrows and glanced at her mother, puzzled. They'd already given them a huge basket full of baby clothes and baby items. What more could there be?

"Best come downstairs," Roger said, pointing to the doorway with his outstretched arm.

"I'll wait here with little Dillon," Gwyneth said, walking over to look at the sleeping baby.

"Are you sure, Mother?" Lizzy asked.

"Yes, off you go." Gwyneth shooed them out the door.

"What's all this about, Father?" Lizzy asked as they walked down the stairs together with Daniel following.

"Just be patient, dear. You'll see in just a few moments."

He led them to where his car was parked, but surprised Lizzy by continuing past it before stopping at a red Ford Fiesta hatchback.

Lizzy looked at him, and then back at the car, her mouth and eyes gaping as he handed her the keys.

"Go on. It's yours."

Lizzy couldn't stop the stream of tears that began to flow as she threw her arms around her father.

"Thank you, Father! I don't believe it," she said as she bent down and inspected the car. Stepping back, she reached out for Daniel, and put her arm around his waist. This could go well, or it could cause an argument between him and her father. The old Daniel would never have accepted a gift like this from him, but what would the new Daniel do?

She looked at her father and then turned her head to look at Daniel as tension filled the air. Their eyes locked together. Daniel was fighting a battle, there was no doubt about it. Everything within her pleaded with him to accept the gift graciously. Her heart stopped while time stood still.

She breathed out slowly when he broke the silence.

"Roger, you needn't have done this."

"I know, Daniel. But we wanted to. Please accept it as a gift for you both. A peace offering?"

Roger held out his hand towards Daniel.

Lizzy held her breath again and then let it out as Daniel slowly reached out and shook Roger's hand.

"Well, go on then. Take a look." Roger walked over to the car and unlocked it for them. Lizzy hesitated before climbing in, and relaxed when Daniel chose the passenger side. She inhaled the new car smell before inserting the key into the ignition and starting it. It was so quiet compared to the old Escort. Turning her head, she smiled broadly at Daniel. How much more could they take?

When they walked the stairs back up to the apartment, Lizzy hugged her mother and planted a kiss on her cheek.

"Thank you so much Mother. It's beautiful!"

"Our pleasure, Elizabeth. Consider it a wedding gift."

Lizzy chuckled and caught her mother's eye. It was so good to be on better terms with her parents after all this time.

"Thank you so much for coming all this way," Lizzy said to her parents as they made their way to the door. As a last minute thought, she asked, "You wouldn't consider staying would you?"

Roger and Gwyneth both stopped and looked at each other before turning back to Lizzy.

"It would be alright," she assured them when they hesitated. "The bed's made up, and we'd fit somehow. I can't promise a good night's sleep, however." She grinned as she glanced at little Dillon lying peacefully in Daniel's arms.

Gwyneth smiled warmly and squeezed Lizzy's arm.

"That would be lovely, dear. Roger?" She tilted her head towards him and raised her eyebrows.

"I don't think I could say no. She'd never forgive me." He shrugged with resignation and then grinned at Lizzy.

"So I take that as a yes?" Lizzy glanced from one parent to the other.

"Yes, dear, we'd love to stay," Gwyneth said, before giving Lizzy a hug.

. . .

LIZZY WAS AMAZED at how well behaved her father and Daniel were that night. What a difference a few months had made. No longer were terse words spoken, in fact, they were deep in conversation for a good part of the evening. Her mother had been working on him, and at last he'd seen sense. Lizzy wondered if the time would ever come when she could quiz him about his relationship with Hilary Carter, or maybe that would be going too far. Time would tell.

DANIEL WAS due to start his new job in two weeks, just before Christmas. In that time, he and Lizzy packed up their apartment, and arranged for their belongings to be moved to the small cottage that was to be their home. Riley and Nessa helped as much as they were able, and Riley told Daniel his counselling sessions would be transferred to one of the staff members at the college.

Moving day finally came, and Lizzy was as excited as a small child about to go to the spring fair for the first time at the prospect of moving into a proper house, after she'd feared so recently it would never happen.

Although Daniel had described the cottage to her, she was in no way prepared for her reaction when it first came into sight.

"Daniel, it's simply perfect! I couldn't have wished for a lovelier place!" Lizzy jumped out of the car and ran with her arms wide open towards the white picket fence surrounding the small thatched roofed cottage. Window boxes overflowed with bright yellow pansies and dark blue lobelia, and all sorts of other pretty flowers that somehow managed to bloom despite the chill of the season. She reached the fence and turned around, stretching her arms behind her and threw her head back, allowing her long unruly hair to fly freely in the breeze, and her heart soared.

"You like it, then?" Daniel looked at her with a cheeky grin on his face.

"Like it? I love it!" She turned around and opened the gate, before remembering one little thing. Dillon. *Dillon! How could I forget him?*

Lizzy spun on her heels and began to head back to the car, when Daniel caught her in his arms.

"He can wait. This can't." Daniel wrapped his arms around her and gazed into her eyes. With one hand he brushed the hair from her face. "Lizzy, what a happy man am I. A beautiful wife, a handsome son, a cottage of our own, a job to die for, and new life in Jesus. What more could a man ask for?"

Lizzy's heart swelled with gratitude to God for blessing a marriage that seemed doomed for failure not that very long ago, and for taking her and Daniel, and little baby Dillon, by the hand and bringing them to this place where they could grow closer to each other and to God.

She held his gaze and looked into his eyes. Yes, they still held mischief and a glint, but they also now held purpose and resolution. Life with Daniel O'Connor would never be boring, but he was a changed man, and she longed to make a start.

"Kiss me, Daniel." Her eyes drew him in, and his hold on her tightened before he lowered his mouth over hers.

BOOK 3 - BEYOND THE SHADOWS

CHAPTER 1

Lakes District UK February 1982

DANIEL THREW the telephone receiver back into its cradle and thumped the wall.

How dare Da return! Twenty years gone, and he waltzes on in, and expects everyone to come running. The hide of the man! Inhaling slowly, he shook his head and fought the anger swelling up inside him. *Not on your life, Da. Not on your life. Even if you're dying.*

Clenching his fists, he stared out the window at the mountains in the distance without seeing them. Just when everything was falling into place. He'd been doing so well. Three months sober. Hadn't even felt like a drink. But now… no, he must stay strong, for Lizzy's sake. He ran his hands through his hair. *God, give me strength. I can't handle this.*

Life had never been so good - he and Lizzy loved living at the College. Why should Caleb expect him to drop everything and come running back to Belfast to see the man he hated most in this world? How did Caleb even get the number?

So many memories. So much pain and hurt. He'd pushed their ugliness away for so long. Why should he be forced to revisit the past? He had a new life. A life full of happiness and peace. Going back was the last thing he wanted to do.

Daniel looked up and clenched his muscles. *That's it. I won't go. Nobody can make me. Not Caleb. Not Da. Not anyone.*

~

"Look Dillon, Daddy's home."

Lizzy held their three month old baby to the window as Daniel drove the tractor towards the shed and excitedly pointed out his daddy. Her heart skipped a beat as she caught sight of Daniel's strong, masculine frame atop the tractor. Wearing his heavy sheepskin jacket and colourful beanie, even from a distance he caused her heart to flutter.

Although almost two months had passed since Daniel began his job as a groundsman at the College in the Lakes District, Lizzy was still in awe of the way God had provided for them. She adored the little cottage where she and Daniel lived. Yes, it was small and basic, but compared to the apartment in Hull, it was paradise. She'd already planned what flowers and vegetables she'd plant when spring came, but until then, she'd busy herself making the cottage into a home.

As much as she loved being a mother and a homemaker, Lizzy missed her friends and her job as a teacher. With Daniel gone early each morning, and the weather too cold to venture outside with baby Dillon, her days were long. Daniel's homecoming was the highlight of each day.

Daniel had surprised her with his devotion to his job and to the Lord. Since giving his heart to the Lord several months earlier while recovering in hospital from his car accident, he'd been hungry for the word and so keen to learn how to live as a Christian. Every day he asked God to give him strength to withstand the hold of alcohol on his life, and every day he gave thanks for one more day of sobriety. He'd also recently made the decision to give up smoking. Lizzy had suggested he wait. It wasn't a problem for her, and besides, staying sober was way more important. But Daniel believed he should. He'd been convicted about how badly he'd abused his body over the years before coming to Christ and was committed to making amends.

Daniel's new found vigour for life warmed Lizzy's heart. The memories of the old Daniel had faded, and rarely, if ever, did she worry about how he'd treat her when he came home from work or whether he'd been drinking. Instead, she yearned for his company more than ever.

He'd taken the responsibility of being the head of his family very seriously, too seriously, Lizzy sometimes thought. Whenever she broached the topic of her going back to work when Dillon was a little older, Daniel stated emphatically there was no need. It was his job to look after her and Dillon. For now, she willingly complied. No use putting undue pressure on their relationship. It was like he needed to prove he could do it.

Lizzy accepted that for now, this was her life. Spring would soon arrive, allowing her to venture out more often. At least they'd gone to town to celebrate their first anniversary just a few days ago. Although Lizzy looked forward to it, leaving Dillon for the first time made Lizzy anxious. She had no qualms about Robyn's ability. After all, being the Principal's wife, and a grandmother of three, Robyn's experience spoke for itself, but Dillon was so tiny, and so dependent. Lizzy knew he'd be fine for the few hours they were out, but it felt strange not to have him with her.

They enjoyed a lovely meal at the Gardens Restaurant in Ambleside, the nearest town to the College. The restaurant adjoined the Lions Head hotel, and Lizzy breathed a sigh of relief when Daniel only briefly glanced at it on their way in. Every time he passed a hotel he was tested, and so far he'd passed with flying colours.

. . .

TONIGHT AS DANIEL walked in the door, something was wrong. Normally he'd be happy and his eyes would light up as he reached out for Dillon, but tonight, trouble sat on his face, and Lizzy's heart fell.

She pulled Dillon tighter and followed Daniel to the bedroom. He hadn't even kissed her. Standing in the doorway, she watched with dismay as he pulled off his work clothes and put on a pair of jeans and his favourite rugby jumper without even showering.

She sat beside him on the bed as he pulled on his boots. "Daniel, what's the matter? Talk to me."

"I need to go out, Lizzy. Please don't try to stop me."

LIZZY FOUGHT HER ALARM. It wouldn't pay to over react. This was the exact situation they'd planned for, but hoped would never happen. Before they left Hull, Nessa and Liam explained what could happen as Daniel weaned himself off alcohol, and helped them formulate an action plan. Lizzy found it challenging to step back and allow Daniel to take responsibility for his decisions, and to trust he'd make good ones, especially after all they'd been through. It would've been so much easier for her to take control, but Nessa advised against that.

"You have to give him room, Lizzy. But don't make it easy for him to drink. If he asks you to drive him to town for that purpose, you have to refuse, unless you feel physically threatened. That's a whole different ball game. He's made the commitment to stay sober, but if he does drink, it's not the end of the world. You just go back to square one and start again. Hopefully he'll be strong, and that won't happen."

But it was happening. Why else would he go out on his own? Lizzy breathed in slowly. Her heart pounded in her chest. She held onto Dillon, cradling him into her shoulder. She had to stay strong for his sake.

"Do you want to talk about it?" Lizzy placed her hand gently on

Daniel's leg. If only he'd share the reason for this sudden change in behaviour.

Daniel finished tying his laces then stood, pulling Lizzy into his arms.

"I'm sorry Liz. I need to be on my own for a while. It's not you. It's me. I need some space."

It took all her strength not to cry as she gazed into his troubled eyes. If only she had the right words to stop him. Her hands trembled and a sick feeling grew in the pit of her stomach. Somehow she had to retain control of herself. Nessa had said not to plead with Daniel, or to over react. *Easier said than done.*

"Okay. I won't stop you, Daniel, but please don't do anything you'll regret. Just remember, God's with you, and you can draw on His strength to help you get through whatever it is that's troubling you."

"I know that Lizzy. And I'll try." Daniel's normally confident voice strained with emotion. He pulled back from her and sighed dejectedly. "I guess you won't drive me to town?"

Lizzy's shoulders slumped. It was tempting. Maybe he'd change his mind on the way, and he'd come back home with her. But she had to carry out the plan. That's what they'd agreed.

"No, Daniel, I won't drive you. I'm sorry."

"Okay then. I'll walk."

Lizzy bit her lip and blinked back her tears. *God, please give me strength.*

How easy it'd be to give in. She could agree to pick him up at a set time. But that wasn't what they'd agreed. She wasn't to do anything that made it easier for him to drink. Besides, walking might give him time to sort out the problem. *Whatever it was.* But why couldn't he share it with her? Memories of Daniel's deception when he lost his job flashed through her mind. He'd promised never to hide anything from her again. And he'd been such a different person since giving his heart to the Lord. The old Daniel had reappeared, and she didn't like it.

"I'll pray for you." She reached out her hand and gently touched his cheek, her eyes searching deep within his. His eyes flickered. Was he weakening? But then he spun on his heels and headed out the door.

Every bone in her body wanted to follow him, but she remained strong, and instead of racing after him, she cradled Dillon and pleaded to God to keep Daniel safe.

LIZZY'S HANDS shook as she tended to Dillon. Once he'd settled, she picked up the phone and called Paul. As head of the College, Paul provided the counselling to Daniel that was a condition of his rehabilitation program agreed to by the court. Calling him was part of their plan.

"Paul, it's Lizzy here." She gulped as she tightened her grip on the receiver. "I hope you don't mind me calling, but something's happened, and Daniel's walking to town." She bit her lip and forced herself to stay calm.

"I had a feeling that might happen. He got a phone call at lunch time and was in a dark mood all afternoon. Didn't want to talk about it."

Lizzy's mind raced. *A phone call?*

"Did he say who it was from?"

"No, he didn't say a thing. Didn't even finish his lunch."

"That's strange. I have no idea who would have called him. I'm trying to think."

"I tried to talk to him several times during the afternoon, but he just retreated into himself. It's the first time I've seen him like that. I was surprised, because he's normally been quite open."

"So, what do we do, Paul? I'm really concerned about him." Lizzy held the receiver tightly with both hands. She had to stay calm, but it was so hard.

Paul sighed heavily on the other end of the phone. "Well, first we pray. There's obviously a battle going on inside him. We knew he'd be tested at some stage. We'll leave him alone for a while, and trust he'll work it out for himself. I'll go to town and look for him in a couple of hours. By that stage he might be prepared to talk."

"Thank you, Paul. I don't know what I'd do without you." Lizzy bit her lip, forcing herself to hold it together.

"It's all I can do, Lizzy. We're in this together. Daniel has a good heart, and he loves God. He's just got to learn to trust Him, as we all do. Let me know if he comes home, otherwise I'll leave about eight o'clock. In the meantime, Robyn and I will pray for him, and I encourage you to pray too."

"I will. Believe me, I will."

CHAPTER 2

Daniel, blind to the deepening darkness around him, trudged along the road toward Ambleside. His head hurt, and a weight, heavy as lead, sat in his heart. He should reach out to God. He knew it deep down, but his body craved the release that alcohol would bring. *Just one drink, that's all I need to clear my head. And then I'll think about Da.*

Reaching the outskirts of town half an hour after leaving the cottage, and knowing Lizzy would have called Paul, Daniel sought the least likely place Paul would look. Despite not visiting any of the drinking establishments in town until now, Daniel had kept his ears open. The small tavern on Stockghylle Lane would suit his purposes.

He pulled the hood of his jacket over his head, not only to keep the cold from biting his face, but to avoid being recognised. The tavern could only be reached through the town centre. The few people out scurried about their business, not paying him any attention. He glanced inside the Gardens Restaurant as he passed by, the memory of his dinner with Lizzy flashing through his mind. *She'll be so angry if I come home drunk. I won't. Just one drink. That's all I need.*

The lights from town slowly faded until he was back in almost complete darkness, with just the occasional lamp glowing from an outside porch providing some indication of where the lane headed. In the distance, the lights from the tavern beckoned. Drawing nearer, Daniel glanced back. No-one was following.

A cold chill ran through his body as he reached the door. The familiar alehouse aroma pulled at him, drawing him in. In the darkened room, Daniel paused to steady his nerves and get a feel for the place. A haze of smoke permeated the stale air, stinging his eyes. Only one room. Several men perched at the bar, and another couple huddled in a corner, deep in conversation.

The stool scraped against the floor as Daniel pulled it out and took a seat. The barmaid approached. His heart thumped. Could he really go through with this? *Am I strong enough to stop at one drink?* He reached for the packet of cigarettes hidden in his jacket pocket and lit up. *Should have thrown them away.*

Instant relief. His heart steadied. Slow, deep breaths. Maybe he could sit on a squash. Let the cigarette do the job. Better than risking getting drunk. *But just one pint...*

"What'll it be, love?" The barmaid stood, hands on hips, her silky voice and voluptuous curves providing a momentary distraction.

Daniel gulped. Was one drink worth jeopardising everything he'd worked for over the past few months? His relationship with God, his relationship with Lizzy, his job? *What am I thinking?*

His hands shook as he drew deeply on his cigarette before grinding it out in the ashtray. Looking up, he held the barmaid's gaze.

"Nothing. Changed my mind."

The bar maid raised her eyebrows. "You sure about that, love?"

Daniel straightened and held her gaze before jumping off the stool. "Yes, I am. Sorry."

Shaking off the eyes staring at him, Daniel opened the door and slipped back into the quietness of the night. He walked a short distance and then stopped, slumping against a light pole. He slid down the pole until he landed on the ground. Relief and anger flooded his body.

What was I thinking? I know better than that. I don't need alcohol.

But something had gripped him deep inside and dragged him towards the abyss. But thanks be to God, he hadn't jumped.

The phone call triggered it. The phone call....

A thousand thoughts swirled in his head. How long since he'd seen Da? He hardly remembered the man who'd deserted Mam and left her to rear him and his seven siblings on her own. He'd assumed Da was dead, but now, to discover he was still alive, and wanting to see him, was too much. Daniel had done his best to put his past behind him and focus on his future with Lizzy and Dillon. But now, here it was, throwing itself in his face.

His eyes drifted closed. Thoughts of God, Lizzy, Da and Mam tumbled together, over and over. Cold seeped into his body, its invisible fingers penetrating into his very depths. He curled into the foetal position, and remained there, oblivious of the danger he was in, until he awoke to someone shaking him.

Daniel sat with a start. Paul? No, it couldn't be. Not Paul... Daniel's heart fell. How would he explain this to him?

"Hey Danny. Here, put this around you." Paul wrapped a thick woollen blanket around Daniel's shoulders, and remained crouched beside him.

Daniel shivered and pulled the blanket tighter. How long had he been lying there? He glanced up the road towards the tavern. The lights were still on, so not long. He shivered again. He could have frozen to death. How had he been so stupid? But he hadn't given in. A surge of warmth trickled through his body. He fought back his tears and lifted his head.

"Thanks Paul. I'm sorry."

"It's not a problem, Danny, I'm glad I found you." Paul squeezed his shoulder. "Come on, let's get you out of this cold. Have you eaten?"

Daniel shook his head.

"You haven't had a drink either, have you?"

"No, I haven't." Tears welled in his eyes. *But I came so close.*

Paul hugged him. "Well done, Danny. Well done."

Daniel nodded. *Must have been God. Couldn't have done it myself.*

Paul helped him stand and led him to the car.

"Let's get something to eat, Danny."

Paul drove back into town and parked outside Pamela's Pantry. From the outside it appeared no-one was there, but inside, the cafe hummed with background music and hushed conversations.

Daniel inhaled the aroma of freshly cooked pizza. His stomach growled. How long since he'd eaten? Lunch... the phone call had come while he was eating lunch...

"Pizza?" Paul asked as they sat at a table on the far wall, well away from the other late diners.

"That would be great. Thank you."

Paul ordered the pizzas and two coffees and leaned back in his chair.

Under Paul's scrutiny, Daniel lowered his eyes and fidgeted. He had nothing to fear from Paul, but to a degree he'd failed. He hadn't taken a drink, but he'd reacted badly to the phone call, and treated both Paul and Lizzy miserably. *Lizzy.* She must be worried sick. He looked up and sucked in a breath.

"I need to call Lizzy. Is there a phone here?" Daniel's gaze darted around the cafe.

"Don't worry about Lizzy, she's okay. You'll be home soon." Paul's voice was so reassuring.

Daniel relaxed and settled into his chair. The waitress delivered their coffees, steaming and hot, just what he needed. Daniel sipped the sweet liquid greedily, wrapping his hands around the brightly coloured mug.

"So what happened today, Danny?" The deep timbre in Paul's voice should have been soothing, but Daniel gulped and stared at the bright red coffee mug. His heart rate quickened. Time to confess. But could he?

Drawing in a deep breath, he slowly lifted his eyes to meet Paul's.

"I'm not sure." He cleared his throat and took another breath. "Everything got confused after I got that phone call. It was like something got into me and dragged me along, and I had no control over it. My head was really scrambled, and all I could think about was having a drink."

"Who was the phone call from, Danny?"

Daniel placed his mug on the table and folded his arms, stalling for time. Talking about it would make it real. Was he ready for that? To revisit his past, to rip open old wounds that had haunted him for years. Wounds he'd successfully buried of late?

Maybe it was time to face his past. But did he have to? *God???*

He pushed down the swelling pain deep inside his chest. Yes, he had to.

"It was from my brother. Our Da's come back, and he wants to see me." Daniel narrowed his eyes and pursed his lips. "I don't want to go. I hate the man. Maybe I shouldn't, but I do."

Paul tilted his head and studied Daniel.

"There's a lot of hurt, isn't there, Danny? I can see it in your eyes."

Daniel squirmed in his chair as a wave of anger took hold.

"He deserted our Mam. Left her with eight kids and no money." Daniel held Paul's gaze. "He used to beat her. Us kids'd huddle together in the room next door while he did it to her. The little ones'd cry and want to go to her when they heard her screaming. They didn't know what was going on." Daniel paused, clenching his teeth. "Me and my brother did, though. We hated him for what he did to her. She didn't deserve to be treated like that." Breathing heavily, Daniel's muscles tensed as he fought to control his anger.

"Truth was, we were glad he left, but then we had nothing. Mam did everything to make sure we always had food to eat. She worked the skin off her hands, and it killed her. That's what we reckon. So basically, he's responsible. Maybe not directly, but it was his fault she died." Daniel pulled himself up and leaned forward. "So you see why I'm not that keen to see him?"

Paul drew in a deep breath. "Daniel, I had no idea. I'm sorry." He held Daniel's gaze before continuing. "Something like that goes deep, and I can understand your reaction, especially when it was totally unexpected. No need to make a hasty decision. Take your time to work through it. I'll help you. Whatever it takes."

"Don't have much time to decide. It makes me so angry." He clenched his fists. *Control, Daniel. Control. Breathe...* "He's dying. That's why he wants me to come. How dare he come back just so he can feel better before he dies! What right does he have?" Daniel's chest heaved as he spat the words.

"Danny, calm down. We can work through this together. You don't need to handle it on your own. Okay?"

As Daniel held Paul's gaze, his breathing steadied. Paul really did care. Just like a father should. If only Da had been like Paul, everything would have been different. The tension in Daniel's body eased. He could rely on Paul. That was a good thing. And Paul was offering to help him. *Maybe I should accept.*

Daniel sighed, his shoulders sagging. Time to let go. But his stomach churned. Thinking about Da made him sick to the core.

"Okay. But I'm still not happy about it."

"That's okay, Danny. It's a start. You can grow through this if you're open to God and allow Him to teach you." Paul gave Daniel a warm smile. "He's got great things in store for you, I just know it. He loves you, Danny, and He doesn't expect you to handle this in your own strength."

Tears sprang to Daniel's eyes. Paul had a knack for turning things around.

"There's a verse in 1 Peter you should memorise, Danny. In Chapter 5 verse 7, Peter says to *'Cast all your anxiety on Him because He cares for you'*. And He really does. God cares for you so much, Danny, and He doesn't want you to handle your cares and troubles on your own. You've been learning a lot over the past few months, but this is the first big challenge you've had. Don't let it beat you."

Daniel gulped. No, he wouldn't let Da beat him. Wouldn't give him that satisfaction. *But how do you 'cast all your anxiety onto God?' It's not like you can see Him.*

Leaning back in his chair, Daniel folded his arms.

"Okay. I'll memorise it, but how do you do it?"

Paul let out a small chuckle. "That's a great question, Danny." Paul looked up as the waitress delivered their pizza. "Thank you." He smiled at her and then directed his attention back to Daniel. "Let's give thanks before we eat."

The aroma of the bubbling mozzarella and pepperoni was more than Daniel could bare. His stomach rumbled, but he lowered his head anyway.

"Lord God, thank You for today, and for the challenges that have come our way. Thank You that You're bigger than any challenge we might meet, including this one Daniel's facing right now. Use it to grow him, Lord. Let him open himself to You and allow You to mould and shape him so You can use him to bring glory to Your kingdom. And Lord God, bless this food to our bodies. We are truly grateful for all the good things You give to us, including this pizza. In Your precious Son's name. Amen."

"Amen." Daniel opened his eyes and glanced at the pizza that had been taunting him. "Can we eat now?" He tilted his head and chuckled as he placed a slice on Paul's plate and then one on his own without waiting for an answer.

"Mmm…" Daniel licked his lips as he devoured his first slice in extra quick time. "How good is this?" He flicked the mozzarella that dangled off the edge of his second piece onto its top and took a bite.

Paul nodded his head, his mouth too full to answer.

Paul came back to Daniel's question after he'd eaten his first slice and washed it down with a mouthful of coffee.

"Okay, so how do we 'cast our anxiety on God'?" Paul leaned back and crossed his arms. "Firstly, we need to really know and accept that God is bigger than all our worries and problems put together. Our view and understanding of how big God is determines how much we trust Him. We often limit His ability to work in our lives because our view of Him is too small. The more we learn of God and appreciate His absolute enormity, the more we learn to trust Him. Does that make sense?"

It was a lot to take in, but it did make sense. Daniel inhaled deeply and nodded.

"Good. The second thing is to understand that everyone has difficulties. They come in all different shapes and sizes, but we all have them. Not all the time, and some are more challenging than others, but we all have them. That's life. People often think that problems come their way because of sin in their lives, that it's God's way of punishing them, and they carry guilt and shame that weighs them down, and separates them from God's love and mercy. But that's Satan's trick. God cares for His children. He doesn't punish. He forgives and cleanses, and offers strength and support to get us through any trial that comes our way. If we let Him." Paul smiled at the waitress who came to clear their table. "May we have two more coffees, please?"

The waitress smiled as she wiped the table. "Coming right up."

"But *how* do we let Him?" Daniel asked after the waitress had left. It all sounded good in theory, but how did it play out in reality?

"Well, it's really quite simple when you break it down. Feelings come from thoughts, so even if we can't change how we *feel*, we can change how we *think*. And that's what God wants us to do. Romans 12 verse 2 says, *'Do not conform to the pattern of this world, but be transformed by the renewing of your mind. Then you will be able to test and approve what God's will is—His good, pleasing and perfect will.'* The more we immerse ourselves in God's word, the more our thoughts are transformed, and the less anxiety we have about the troubles we face, because we know God's working in our lives, and that every problem we face is an opportunity for Him to teach us and grow us. So, when it all boils down, it's a decision you make. When problems, worries, and challenges of life come along, you ask Jesus to carry the burden for you. You hand it over to Him. And then you don't take it back. Trust Him to work it out for good in your life, and be prepared to learn and grow as the situation unfolds."

"Okay then." Daniel leaned forward, resting his forearms on the table. "So when I got that phone call from my brother, you're saying I should have just prayed about it and handed it over to God?" He tilted his head and narrowed his eyes. It sounded too simple.

"In a nutshell, yes."

"But my head got all scrambled, and I couldn't think clearly. How was I supposed to do it?"

"It takes practice and commitment, Danny. You're a new Christian, and no-one expects you to react like someone who's been trusting Jesus for many years. The main thing is that you learn from it, so next time something happens, and it will, you'll be more aware, and you can give it to God straight away. But He's not going to judge or condemn you, Danny, and neither will I, or Lizzy, or anyone else for that matter. And you shouldn't beat yourself up either. You didn't take that drink, and that's a huge achievement." Paul leaned closer. "Danny, I really believe God has something great planned for you and Lizzy. I just know it. His hand's on your life, and He's going to lead you into something exciting. I want to encourage you to keep learning and trusting, and keep your heart open to Him. And He'll definitely help you work through this situation with your father."

Daniel gulped. *He's so genuine and sincere. He really does believe what he's saying.*

Paul reached out his hand and gently placed it on Daniel's arm. "Can we pray about it?"

A stirring, deep in his soul, took Daniel by surprise, causing tears to prick his eyes. Never before had anyone offered him so much encouragement. Not Nessa or Riley, or even Lizzy. Paul really believed that God had something special planned for his life. And Daniel wanted it, whatever it was.

"Yes, please." Daniel wiped his eyes and bowed his head, not caring what anyone thought.

"Dear God, thank You for Daniel, and for giving him new life in Jesus. And thank You for being with him right now. We know You'll help him through the days ahead, as he works through the situation with his father. Let him welcome Your thoughts and Your love, and Your forgiving grace and mercy. Help him to cast all his worries onto You, and to allow his mind to be transformed by You so he can see Your good, pleasant and perfect will at work in his life. And Lord, we rejoice that today You gave Daniel the strength to turn down that drink. What a major milestone that is! I ask You to bless him, and Lizzy and little Dillon, and to guide and lead them as they grow closer to You each day. In Jesus' precious name, amen."

Daniel gulped and took a deep breath. "Dear God, everything that Paul said and more. I don't deserve Your love, and I'm sorry for failing You. Please help me do better next time. I want to, I really do." Daniel paused and wiped his tears. "Lord God, You're going to have to work hard if You want me to see Da. You know how I feel about him, but I give it to You, and ask for Your help and guidance. I'm sorry for the way I reacted. Please show me the way. Amen."

"Amen." Paul raised his head and squeezed Daniel's hand. "Danny, you did good. Now, let's get you home to that wife of yours."

LIZZY HAD BEEN PRAYING on and off since her phone call with Paul earlier that evening. Despite her original anguish and the fact that

Daniel hadn't returned, she had peace in her heart, and confidence that God was with him.

Well after ten o'clock, tyres crunched on the gravel outside the cottage. Jumping up, she pulled the curtain back and glanced out the window. She let out a small sigh. It was Paul's car, and Daniel was climbing out. She closed her eyes briefly and held her hands to her chest. *Thank You God. Thank You.*

She raced to the door and threw it open. As Daniel walked slowly towards her, Lizzy pushed back the tears that threatened to fall. She held out her arms and threw them around him, pulling him into a tight embrace. His body relaxed in her arms, and as she held him, she closed her eyes and gave thanks once more that he'd come home, whole and sober.

"I'm sorry, Lizzy. I really am. Please forgive me." Daniel spoke softly, as if he was having trouble speaking.

Lizzy lifted her head and searched his eyes. "It doesn't matter, Daniel. Whatever it was, it doesn't matter. You're home, that's the most important thing."

"Yes, it is. Thank you, Lizzy." Daniel pulled her closer, and enclosed in his arms, her heart overflowed with love for him.

"Come inside, Daniel, before we die from the cold." Lizzy took his hand and led him inside into the warmth of the cottage. "Sit down and I'll make some hot chocolate, and then maybe we can talk. Only if you want." As she turned to walk into the kitchen, Daniel pulled her around to face him.

"I love you so much, Lizzy, and I'm sorry for going off like I did."

"Daniel, it's okay. Really." Reaching up, she held his face gently between her hands, and as she kissed him, she made sure he knew he was forgiven.

CHAPTER 3

Lizzy and Daniel talked deep into the night. Lizzy's heart ached as Daniel opened up more than he ever had before about his childhood.

"Oh, Daniel. I'm so sorry. Your Da was such a horrible brute." Lizzy's chest heaved. Daniel's story made her sick to the stomach. "Your poor Mam. Why did she stay with him?"

Daniel shook his head. In the dim light, his eyes watered, and Lizzy grabbed his hand.

"I wish she'd left, Liz, but it wasn't the done thing." Daniel inhaled deeply. It tore her apart watching him relive this nightmare. "Women were expected to put up with whatever treatment their husbands dished out back then. Plus, she had nowhere to go, no money of her own, and a handful of bairns to look after. She was tied to him, and that was it." He looked up into Lizzy's eyes. "But we hated him for what he did to her."

"Oh Daniel." His eyes had darkened. The hate was real, tangible. She didn't blame him - it would be hard not to hate a man like Thomas O'Connor.

"I feel so sorry for her, Daniel. She must have felt trapped." Lizzy gulped. *But wasn't that how I felt when Daniel started hurting me? Trapped, confused, alone.* That gut wrenching pain she'd long forgotten clutched at Lizzy. How terrible to have suffered that pain year after year. *How did his Mam survive?*

"It makes me so angry when I think of all she put up with." Daniel's breath came fast, and his hold on Lizzy's hand tightened.

"But Lizzy," he peered into her eyes, "it hurts me even more when I think of how I treated you. I so hated Da and how he treated Mam, and yet I was going down the same track." He gulped and took a deep breath. "I'm so sorry, Lizzy."

Lizzy reached out and gently wiped the tears rolling down Daniel's cheeks before taking his hand.

"Daniel, I forgave you long ago for all of that. God's changed you. You're a caring, kind man, and I love you with everything I have."

"But I treated you so badly, Liz. I should never have hurt you." More tears welled in his eyes. "I'm so sorry."

"I know, my love. I know you are." Pulling him close, Lizzy rested her head on his. Love for Daniel overflowed from her heart.

Slowly pulling himself away, Daniel wiped his eyes with the back of his hand.

"I could so easily have ended up like him, Lizzy."

"But you didn't, Daniel. You didn't. God's changing you from the inside out, and I know you love me and will never hurt me again. And for that, I am so very thankful." She had not felt quite so much love for Daniel as she did at that moment, and as he kissed her, every nerve in her body tingled as she lost herself in his love.

Nearer to dawn than midnight, sleep finally came, but Dillon had other plans. Lizzy tried to ignore the small cries that would soon escalate to full-blown screams, and snuggled closer to Daniel, pulling the pillow around her ears.

"I'll go." Daniel lifted his head but then dropped it. Lizzy snuggled closer. As Dillon's cries grew louder, she forced herself up. Daniel rolled over. Her head hurt. *If only he'd take a bottle.*

"Come here, little man." Lizzy sighed heavily as she lifted Dillon out of the cradle. His crying stopped and the distraught look on his face changed to a cheeky smile that melted her heart. She pulled him close. "How could I get angry with you?"

Sitting in her chair, with Dillon suckling at her breast, Daniel's heart-wrenching story of his childhood years played through Lizzy's mind. No wonder he'd struggled after getting that phone call. It had been difficult enough for her to forgive her own father who wasn't guilty of any of the atrocities Daniel's father had committed. She couldn't comprehend Daniel's anguish. But God was bigger than all of this, and she knew, beyond a shadow of a doubt, that He'd give Daniel the ability to work through it, just like He had with her.

And He'd already started. Lizzy rejoiced when Daniel told her how close he'd come to ordering a drink, but at the last moment had walked out. Such a major milestone in his rehabilitation, and for that, they'd both given thanks. Of course, more temptations would follow, but for now, this achievement was worthy of celebration. Lizzy decided there and then to surprise Daniel. She'd invite Nessa and Riley and their two children for the weekend, and they'd have a party. The timing was perfect. Daniel turned thirty on Sunday. And maybe, just maybe, Nessa and Riley could help him work through the situation with his father.

Lizzy smiled to herself as she lifted Dillon and gently patted his back. Yes, it would be wonderful to see Nessa and Riley. It may be short notice, but surely they'd come, especially when they knew the reason.

LIZZY'S MIND clicked into gear. No use going back to sleep now. Too early to call Nessa. She made herself a cup of tea and opened her Bible to the book of 2nd Corinthians, Chapter 12.

The words grabbed her as soon as she started reading. *"My grace is sufficient for you, for my power is made perfect in weakness. Therefore I will boast all the more gladly about my weaknesses, so that Christ's power may rest on me. That is why, for Christ's sake, I delight in weaknesses, in insults, in hardships, in persecutions, in difficulties. For when I am weak, then I am strong."*

Just what Daniel needs. He might not like to think he's weak, but if he could grasp the truth of this message, that the God of the universe was offering His strength to help him cope with this situation with his Da, it would be life changing.

Lizzy closed her Bible and folded her arms. *That may be true, but why have You allowed this to happen now, when everything's been going so well?*

Why did You let Daniel's Da come back and upset it all? I don't understand.

I'm really sorry, God but I can't help it. I'm with Daniel on this - why did You let his Da come back now? If it makes him start drinking again...

Still deep in prayer, arguing with God, Lizzy jumped when the alarm buzzed. *Bother! I meant to turn that off.* She raced into the bedroom. Too late - Daniel was awake and pulling himself up.

"I'm so sorry, Daniel. I was going to let you sleep in, but I forgot to turn the alarm off."

"Thanks love, but I need to get up. Too much to do." Daniel stretched his neck and arms, and then stopped abruptly, his face paling.

"Are you alright, Daniel?" Lizzy raced to him and placed a hand on his shoulder, searching his face.

He ran his hands through his hair. His eyes flickered. "I just remembered what happened. It's all come back..."

"Oh Daniel. It's okay." Lizzy wrapped her arms around him. "Maybe you should take the day off? I'm sure Paul won't mind."

Daniel sighed deeply. "No, I need to go. Paul also wants to see me this morning." He lifted his head and looked into Lizzy's eyes. "I'll be alright. Talking about everything last night helped. Thank you, Lizzy." He drew in a long breath and then kissed her gently on her forehead. "I'd better get ready."

As Daniel showered, Lizzy prepared breakfast and tended to Dillon who had also just woken again. She put him in his bouncer and gave him some toys to play with, every now and again bouncing him with her foot.

Lizzy had little idea of what Daniel's job would entail before he started at the College just before Christmas. She soon discovered he was expected to keep everything running, and by everything, they meant everything... from water which tended to freeze in the pipes, to the generators which provided power for the main college building and all the staff accommodation. He was also expected to tend to the cows and chickens the college kept. Lizzy had laughed when he told her that.

Every time Daniel ventured out she prayed for him. Despite being less than half a mile to the main college buildings, at this time of year the road was slippery, and occasionally piled with snow. Although the tractor looked at home as it trundled around the property with Daniel at the wheel, it didn't matter how often he told her it was as safe as houses, she wouldn't relax until he pulled up outside the cottage and turned the tractor off.

The job was perfect for him. He loved tinkering with things, but he also had plenty of contact with people. People who cared about him, especially Paul. Thank God for Paul. He always had time for Daniel. And Daniel always talked about Paul. Almost as if they'd known each other for years, not just a couple of months.

Lizzy smiled at Dillon's chuckles. He was growing so quickly. God had really blessed them with this little man. Her heart swelled with love for him.

"Feel better?" Lizzy smiled at Daniel, her body unexpectedly tingling as he stood there in his work overalls looking spunky. A spark of life had returned to his eyes, much better than yesterday's steely hardness.

"Yes, thank you, love." He bent down and allowed Dillon to grab his finger. "Hello little man. My, how you're growing." Daniel lifted the baby out of the bouncer and sat him in his lap as he ate breakfast.

"You're getting very skilled at that," Lizzy said. "Watch out! He'll steal your toast!"

Daniel chuckled, a warm smile growing on his face. "He's just got a good appetite. Here. Take this, little man."

"He can't eat that yet, Daniel. He's only three months old!"

"He can suck on it if he wants to, surely. It won't hurt him." His eye twinkled with a hint of mischief.

Lizzy shook her head and laughed. "How can I win against the two of you?"

"You don't need to, my love. You have us both eating out of your hand."

"If only..." Lizzy rolled her eyes, but the grin on her face reflected the joy in her heart at having Daniel almost back to normal.

"Here, you'd better take him, and I'll be off." Standing, Daniel drained his mug, then passed Dillon over to Lizzy before placing both his hands on her shoulders and looking deeply into her eyes. "Lizzy, thank you. I mean it. I truly don't deserve you." He leaned forward and pressed his lips against hers. "I love you." He pulled away slowly and held her gaze for a moment before leaving.

Lizzy stood at the window and watched him walk to the shed. Normally he'd be whistling and have a spring to his step, but today he walked in silence with his shoulders slumped. *Must have his Da on his mind. Poor Daniel.* He climbed into the tractor, reversed it out, and then waved before trundling off down the track. Lizzy's heart ached. How she hated to see him struggling like this. They'd been so happy since they'd been here. It wasn't fair.

WITH THE TRACTOR out of sight, Lizzy put Dillon down and picked up the phone to call Nessa. She let it ring longer than normal, but was about to hang up when Nessa finally answered.

"Nessa! Lizzy here."

"Lizzy! Good to hear from you. I hope all's well..."

Lizzy inhaled deeply before relaying the events of the previous day and night.

"Oh Liz, that must have been horrible for Daniel. We always wondered what happened to his father. I guess we assumed we'd never see him again. But now, to turn up like that, poor Daniel. He was such a mean man, Lizzy. No-one held any respect for him whatsoever. It's a wonder I haven't heard from my side about him turning up. But then, I haven't talked to anyone for a while."

"I'm not sure how long he's been back, but Daniel's refusing to see him. Can't say I blame him. He's so upset about it all, but the best thing, Ness, when he went to town last night, he didn't drink! I was so relieved when Paul brought him home, sober."

"Oh Lizzy, that's wonderful! He's making progress then."

"Yes, he is." Lizzy smiled to herself as unexpected warmth flowed through her body. He really was making progress.

She grabbed the receiver with both hands. "Ness, do you think you and Riley and the kids could come and visit over the weekend? It's Daniel's birthday on Sunday, and I thought we could surprise him. I know it's short notice, but what do you think?"

"Sounds great, Liz. I think we can manage it - we don't have much planned, and it won't be a problem to put off Riley's work mate until next weekend. How about we come tomorrow morning? If we leave early, we should get there by about eleven."

"That's perfect, Nessa. You'll stay the night? There's enough room for you all." *Just...*

"Yes, why not? That would be lovely. I've always wanted to see the Lakes District, so I'll look forward to it."

"Great, Ness. We'll see you tomorrow! Safe trip."

WITH THAT SORTED, Lizzy began to plan for their visit. She'd have to squeeze them all into the spare room, but they wouldn't mind. And she'd have to go shopping for extra food, and plan what they'd do. Maybe they could go on a boat ride on the lake. It was still cold, but it'd be fun. If they rugged up well, they'd be okay. The kids would probably like the Aquarium at Lakeside. She'd heard about it, but hadn't been there. And then they could have a birthday dinner for Daniel. Lasagne. Yes, that's what she'd make. His favourite. And a big chocolate birthday cake. She'd better get moving! This was going to be fun. And hopefully Nessa could talk to Daniel about his Da...

Daniel arrived at work and went straight to the workshop. One of the generators had broken down and needed urgent attention. For some unknown reason, the College board wanted to keep the College as self-sufficient as possible, but the old equipment certainly provided a challenge. Not his problem, as long as they kept paying him.

As Daniel worked, the phone call from Caleb played through his mind. He hadn't seen his eldest brother for over ten years, and the unexpected call had scrambled his brain, that was for sure. How close he'd come to taking that drink. Truly amazing he'd baulked at the last minute... or maybe it had been God who'd stopped him? Either way, he hadn't. But having his past dragged up...

But what about Da? Maybe he should go? The churning in his stomach answered his question. But then, talking to Caleb had stirred something deep inside. As the two eldest boys, they'd been the ones who'd stuck together the most against Da, and had helped support Mam. It'd be good to meet up with him and Caitlin again, and meet their two little girls. But what about Da? Daniel thumped the generator. Why wouldn't it do what it was meant to?

Daniel glanced at his watch. Time to meet Paul. Need a break from that monster, anyway. He cleaned up and headed over to the main college building. Paul stood on the walkway outside a lecture room.

"Hey, Paul."

Paul waved as Daniel took the steps two at a time.

"Hey Danny. How are you today?" Paul clapped an arm around Daniel's shoulder and smiled warmly at him.

"Not too bad, considering Lizzy and I stayed up most the night talking."

"Glad to hear that, Danny. All okay, then?"

Daniel shrugged and let out a small sigh.

"Kind of. Still not keen about seeing Da."

"Let's sit down and talk about it. I've got some coffees coming."

Paul's office had a great view of the lake and mountains, but this morning Daniel didn't pay any attention to it. He took a seat on the couch opposite Paul and leaned forward, his body tense.

"I don't understand how he has the gall to come back after all this time. Why couldn't he just leave us alone?"

Daniel fixed his eyes on Paul's and tried to steady his breathing.

"I feel your pain, Danny. But let's talk about it. Maybe your Da wants to make amends before he dies. People often do that. The finality of death puts everything into perspective, and the need to apologise for wrong doings, to sort out relationships that have soured, especially with family, take on an urgency that was never there before."

Daniel gritted his teeth and folded his arms. He shouldn't have come. Da had no right to intrude on his and Lizzy's life. Even if he was dying. Why should he be allowed to feel better about everything when it was him who'd destroyed their lives? No, he really didn't want to hear this. Not even from Paul.

"Sometimes it's selfish. They just want to feel better, to cleanse their consciences. But if the person's genuine, it can be a wonderful experience for everyone. Forgiveness is liberating, Danny. Yes, it's challenging and confronting, but sometimes you only get one chance. Once he's dead, it's too late." Pausing, Paul leaned closer. "Danny, if you don't see him, you might regret it for the rest of your life."

Daniel narrowed his eyes. His chest heaved. How could Paul be talking about forgiveness? He hadn't even decided to see Da, let alone considered forgiving him. And he seriously doubted there'd be any regret.

"No. Can't do it."

"Just think about it, Danny. And pray about it. Forgiveness won't change what happened, but it will change your future. God can begin to heal you deep inside when you're willing to let go of past hurts and forgive those who've wronged you, including your Da. You just need to be open to God and allow Him to do the rest. Will you think about it?"

Daniel sighed heavily. How did Paul always manage to put the guilts on him? He didn't want to hear what Paul was saying, but deep down, Daniel knew it to be the truth.

"I guess so, but to be completely honest, right now, I don't want to."

"I know that Danny. But if you run away from this, you'll miss out on a great opportunity to grow. Growing is never easy. All I'm asking is that you be open to God." Paul looked up as a young girl with long, dark hair walked in with a tray laden with an array of sweet treats and steaming hot coffee.

"Ah, thank you Alicia. Just put it on the table." Paul smiled at her as she lowered the tray and then retreated towards the door. "Coffee smells great, Alicia. Thanks."

The girl smiled in appreciation and closed the door behind her. Paul offered the plate of fancy treats to Daniel. "They know I have a sweet tooth."

"So do I…" Daniel said as he chose a chocolate eclair and took a bite. Cream oozed down his chin.

"These are so good." Paul wiped his face and sipped his coffee before placing the mug on the table. He leaned back in his seat.

"How are you finding it all, Danny? Are you enjoying living here?"

Daniel breathed a sigh of relief. A change of focus was good. His head hurt with all the talk about Da and forgiveness.

Placing his plate on the table, Daniel looked up.

"Yes, it's been great so far. Lizzy's looking forward to the warmer weather so she can get out more, but she loves the cottage."

"She could get involved here. She's always welcome to attend any lectures that interest her, and I'm sure Robyn would only be too happy to look after the baby."

"I'll let her know. She might like that."

Daniel and Paul continued chatting while they finished their coffee. Returning to his generator soon after, Daniel tried to focus on the job, but after a while he got so annoyed with the voices in his head, he threw a spanner on the ground and stomped out.

Standing outside the workshop, he reached inside his jacket pocket and pulled out the packet of cigarettes he still hadn't thrown away and lit one. He inhaled slowly as he gazed through the trees to the lake in the distance. The mountains from the other side of the lake reflected in the water, just like in the post cards at the local newsagent's stands.

As he leaned against the workshop wall, he exhaled slowly, his breath creating little puffs of cloud in the chilly air. He needed this moment - it was so peaceful here. If only his head would settle.

He finished his cigarette and returned to the generator, pushing all thoughts of Da and God out of his mind.

By mid-afternoon, Daniel had the generator re-assembled. He stood back and studied the beast which had tested all his mechanical know-how and pushed his patience to its limit. He had some basic mechanical knowledge, but wasn't formally trained. Only what he'd picked up from some of the jobs he'd had whilst traveling, but it was enough to do the job. Daniel carried the generator to the side of the shed and tried it out on a pump. It worked.

He cleaned himself up, tidied the workshop, checked that everything was in order, and climbed back into the tractor to head home. He stopped to top up the feed for the cows and the chickens, and then trundled back down the track towards the cottage. His stomach rumbled, reminding him he'd skipped lunch. He needed a good feed and a sleep. His body and mind were exhausted.

LIZZY LOOKED up as the tractor disappeared into the shed and her heart fell. *Bother!* She'd hoped to have finished cooking before Daniel got home. If only Dillon had behaved... She stood at the stove stirring the sauce for the lasagne. Why wasn't it thickening? No time now either to tidy up. Dirty bowls, saucepans, bags of rubbish... how would she explain it all to Daniel without giving away her secret? At least the soup smelled good.

Finally the sauce bubbled. She gave it one last stir and took the pan off the stove. A few seconds to clean up. She gathered the garbage and threw it in the bin, and stacked the dishes in the sink. Not great, but better.

As Daniel took his boots off on the step, Lizzy patted her hair and pulled her apron off, planting a smile on her face as he opened the door.

"You made it home early, Daniel." She leaned forward and kissed him as he pulled her into his arms.

He peered around her. "So what's all this, Liz? I'm starving..." Pushing her aside, Daniel walked to the stove and lifted the lid on the soup. "What's all this for?" He dipped a spoon in and brought it to his mouth.

Lizzy sighed and folded her arms. "Just never you mind, Daniel O'Connor. There might be a little surprise happening for your birthday, but that's all I'm saying. And don't put the spoon back in! Who brought you up?!" She sucked in a breath. *Why did I say that?* A shadow passed over Daniel's face.

"I'm sorry, Daniel. I shouldn't have said that." Lizzy slid her arms around his waist, leaning her head on his chest. "Did you have that talk with Paul today?"

Daniel sighed heavily. "Yes, I did, but Lizzy, I don't want to talk about it right now. I'm tired and hungry. Can we leave it for now?" He pushed her away and held her at arm's length. "I just want something to eat, and then chill out in front of a movie. Okay?"

"Of course, Daniel. Have some soup now and I'll get some dinner ready shortly." She reached up and kissed him gently. He'd be asleep in front of the television within the half hour. Then she could finish everything in peace.

CHAPTER 4

When Lizzy rose the following morning, the clear sky warmed her heart. The world always looked better with blue sky. While Daniel slept, she'd finished preparing most of the food, including his birthday cake. All she needed do now was decorate it. Dillon also was in a much happier mood. Why wasn't he like that yesterday? The challenge now was to get Daniel out of the house so she could finish the final preparations without him becoming too nosy. Maybe she could ask him to take Dillon for a long walk. It'd probably do them both good. Yes, she'd do that.

To her surprise, Daniel happily agreed. Lizzy rugged Dillon up and sent them off soon after breakfast. She might have an hour or so before they returned. One hour… a lot could be achieved in that time without Dillon to care for. Retrieving the cake from its hiding place in the pantry, Lizzy mixed up the icing and decorated it with Daniel's favourite sweets. That done, she made up the beds in the spare room and gave the bathroom a quick clean. Having guests was exhausting!

. . .

THE KITCHEN CLOCK CHIMED. Lizzy stared at it. Surely it was wrong. How could two hours have gone, just like that? Lizzy's hand flew to her chest. *Daniel and Dillon should have been back. What if something's happened to them?* Lizzy opened the door and peered down the road but they weren't in sight. Maybe they'd bumped into someone - Daniel was always up for a chat. *Breathe, Lizzy. They'll be fine.* Why did she always think the worst?

The kettle was still hot, so Lizzy made a cup of coffee and went outside. Sitting on the steps, she breathed in the clean, crisp air, shivering slightly as a cool breeze brushed her cheeks and neck. The lake would be glistening in the sunshine this morning. Pity the cottage was tucked in a hollow, hiding the lake from view. Never mind. At least she could see the mountains shimmering against the soft blue of the sky. Lizzy inhaled deeply, thankful for such beauty.

A car approached in the distance. Lizzy turned her head. It had to be Riley and Nessa, but where was Daniel? *Surely nothing bad's happened?* As the car came into view, Lizzy stood and waved. Moments later, Riley parked the car in front of the cottage, and he, Nessa and the two children piled out. Lizzy embraced them all warmly.

"Great to see you, Lizzy. And what a lovely cottage!" Nessa pulled back a little to get a better view, and then called out to four year old Jake who was already running around, enjoying his freedom after being cooped up in the car for four hours. "Don't go outside the fenced area, Jake."

Lizzy chuckled. All of this was ahead of her. But where were Daniel and Dillon? She peered back along the track, trying to cover up her concern, when she saw Daniel running towards them, pushing the pram.

Nessa followed Lizzy's line of sight and reached out her arm.

"I meant to tell you we bumped into Daniel on the way in. No room in the car, so we had to leave him." Nessa laughed as she glanced back over her shoulder.

"Lizzy! Why didn't you tell me we were having company?" Daniel asked when he finally joined them. Panting, he leaned over and rested his hands on his knees to catch his breath. "She's a dark horse, that one." He tilted his head to Lizzy, but his eyes held a twinkle.

They all laughed, and then headed inside with their bags.

Lizzy showed Nessa and Riley to their room, and suggested an early lunch to make the most of the day. They all agreed to her suggestion of a trip on the lake, and so, after a quick lunch of soup and bread, headed off to Ambleside to wait for the ferry.

Lizzy had a quiet word with Nessa while they waited on the wharf. Daniel and Riley stood together with Jake and Cindy playing chasings around them. Nessa cuddled Dillon while she and Lizzy stood a little distance away from the men.

"Daniel seems okay, Lizzy." Nessa turned her head and shot a glance at Daniel.

Lizzy winced, letting out a small sigh.

"On the surface, yes, but it's all bubbling underneath." Lizzy folded her arms and leaned back against the railing, pulling her scarf tighter around her neck to ward off the chilly breeze. "He doesn't want to talk about it at the moment, but it's on his mind. He hasn't said a word since the other night." Lizzy turned to face Nessa. "What he told me about his Da... no wonder he's struggling."

"Daniel's Da was a horrible man, Lizzy." Nessa stepped closer to Lizzy and spoke quietly. "After your call yesterday, I did some checking of my own. It's true he's dying, but Caleb said he's changed, and he wants to put things right with his family before he dies. Riley and I both think Daniel should see him."

Lizzy held Nessa's gaze. "He doesn't want to, Ness. He despises the man." Tears pricked Lizzy's eyes. "I'm kind of with Daniel on this, although I know the right thing is to see him. Maybe you can talk it through with Daniel? He respects you."

Nessa squeezed Lizzy's arm.

"Oh Lizzy. It'll be okay, poppet. You'll see. I don't want to cause any problems, but I'll pray about it, and if it seems right, I'll bring it up, okay?"

"Thanks Nessa. It's so good to have you here." Lizzy's voice caught in her throat.

"And it's good to be here." Nessa patted Lizzy's hand and then glanced at the ferry chugging towards the wharf. "Are you okay, Liz?" Nessa's smile turned tender. Lizzy swallowed the lump in her throat and nodded. Why was it so hard to control her emotions?

Nessa slipped her arm through Lizzy's and walked with her to join the others.

Fares paid, they boarded the old wooden ferry along with a dozen or so other passengers. Riley grabbed Jake's hand to stop him from running around, and Nessa handed Dillon back to Lizzy before taking Cindy's hand. Daniel followed behind Lizzy with the push chair.

"In or out?" Daniel called from behind.

Lizzy glanced at Daniel over her shoulder. Did he sound annoyed, or was she just imagining it? She pushed the thought aside.

"In? It's a bit cold outside."

Daniel pulled her back.

"Lizzy, did you ask Nessa and Riley to come just to talk me into seeing Da?"

Lizzy's heart sank. Gulping, she raised her head and looked into his darkened eyes. How could she convince him it wasn't one of the reasons when she knew full well it was? It wouldn't pay to lie, in fact, it could make it worse.

Reaching out her hand, she gently touched his arm, but he pulled it away.

"I knew it." Daniel glowered.

"Daniel, I'm sorry. It wasn't the only reason. It was mainly for your birthday."

"I don't want to be hassled, Lizzy. You should have left me to make my own decisions."

Lizzy bit her lip. She'd been caught out.

"I'm really sorry, Daniel. I didn't mean it to be a problem. I was just concerned, that's all, and I thought talking to them might help."

"You need to learn to trust me, Lizzy, and not force things. Let me work through things in my own time."

"I'm sorry, Daniel. I really am." Lizzy reached out again for his arm, and this time he didn't pull away. She searched his eyes, hoping to see some softening. "Will we be okay? I'd hate them to feel unwelcome after driving all this way."

"Yes, it'll be fine." Daniel narrowed his eyes. "But don't push, Lizzy. Okay?"

Lizzy nodded, swallowing hard.

"I really am sorry, Daniel." Lizzy took his hand and walked with him to join the others.

For the rest of the trip, Lizzy clung to Daniel. She had to make things right between them. Why had she thought she could fix everything for him? She still had so much to learn.

The afternoon passed pleasantly enough, although Lizzy struggled to keep her mind focused. She prayed that Riley and Nessa would sense Daniel's reluctance to talk about his Da and not push him. The last thing she wanted was to cause problems between them. She should forewarn them…

The opportunity to speak with Nessa came when they reached the Lakeside Aquarium and the men took charge of the children. Lizzy fell back and joined Nessa. She grabbed Nessa's arm.

"Ness, Daniel's upset."

Nessa faced Lizzy, her head tilted.

"What do you mean?"

"I thought I was doing a good thing." Lizzy's shoulders slumped and she bit her lip.

"Lizzy, what's happened?"

Lizzy took a deep breath and clenched her hands.

"Daniel thinks I asked you here just to talk him into seeing his Da."

"Ouch..." Nessa's eyes widened. "I wondered what you were talking about on the ferry." Nessa slipped her arm around Lizzy's waist. "Don't worry Liz. We know Daniel, but God's also working in all of this. If Daniel doesn't want to talk at the moment, that's fine. We'll just wait for him to be ready. In the meantime, we'll just enjoy being here with you." Nessa smiled warmly and squeezed Lizzy tightly. How did Nessa always have the right words?

Lizzy pulled herself together and determined to enjoy the outing. She and Daniel hadn't been out much, mainly because of the weather. They strolled through the Aquarium, marvelling at the different types of sea creatures, and laughing at Jake and Cindy's delight at seeing a huge octopus. They ended up at the cafe where the adults enjoyed a Devonshire tea and the children had an ice-cream each. Lizzy stayed close to Daniel and held his hand as often as she could. She wanted him to know how sorry she was for upsetting him, and how much she wanted everything to be right between them. Maybe she was overdoing it, but what else was there to do?

The children fell asleep on the ferry ride back, and by the time they reached the wharf, the sun had disappeared behind the mountains and the chill of early evening began to bite.

"You might have to help me chop some more wood," Daniel said to Riley as they shivered on the way back to their cars.

"No problem, Danny. A good workout will do me good." Riley chuckled as he grabbed Jake and Cindy's hands and led them to the car.

LIZZY HAD ANOTHER SURPRISE, one she hoped Daniel would be happy about. She'd asked Paul and Robyn for dinner as well. She and Nessa quickly bathed and dressed the children, and Lizzy was doing last minute preparations when Paul and Robyn arrived. Daniel and Riley were still out chopping the extra wood, but came in soon after.

Following the introductions, Lizzy asked Daniel to sort out drinks for everyone. She caught a whiff of cigarette smoke on his breath. It didn't matter. As long as he wasn't drinking. She held his gaze for a moment. Had he forgiven her? She wasn't sure.

Despite the underlying tension that possibly only Lizzy was aware of between her and Daniel, dinner was a joyous occasion. Pleased everyone was getting on well together, she relaxed and enjoyed the friendly banter at the table. Maybe Daniel was just putting on a good show, but he was in good form, as he and Riley competed for the funniest joke. Paul didn't even try to compete, he just joined in with the laughter.

Following dinner, Lizzy brought out the birthday cake and placed it in front of Daniel. His eyes lit up at the assortment of sweets adorning it.

"Happy birthday, my love." Lizzy pressed her lips against Daniel's cheek and squeezed his shoulder. He had to know how sorry she was.

She hoped the sparkle in his eye meant she was forgiven and that everything was fine between them. She'd hated walking on eggshells in the past and certainly didn't want to start again.

Riley began singing 'Happy Birthday' and then everyone joined in. Lizzy beamed at Daniel and clapped her hands as he blew out the candles.

Then Riley pressed him for a speech. Lizzy stiffened and held her breath. *No, not a speech. Please...*

Daniel cleared his throat, shot Lizzy a quick glance she couldn't read, then stood. Lizzy's pulse quickened. She clenched her hands together to prevent them shaking.

~

DANIEL'S GAZE travelled around the table. He didn't deserve such good friends and family. They'd each stood beside him, supporting him when he needed it the most, even when he'd treated them badly. And then there was Lizzy. He'd been way too hard on her. He hadn't meant to react the way he had - she was only trying to help. And he loved her so much. Daniel swallowed hard. What would he do without her?

He inhaled deeply and lowered his eyes, his fingers resting on the table. He owed it to each of them to be honest, but could he really share what was on his heart? Bare all? How could he do that? Maybe he should just thank them for coming and leave it at that. It'd be the easiest way out, but no, it wasn't enough. He closed his eyes and took a deep breath. *God, I really need your help...*

His mind calmed as Lizzy took his hand and squeezed it gently. *Yes, he could do this.* He needed to. For Lizzy.

Daniel lifted his gaze and smiled warmly at Lizzy. He cleared his throat again.

"Thank you all for coming, especially Nessa and Riley for coming so far, and for Lizzy for organising this without me knowing." He paused for a moment and swallowed hard. "I haven't been the best lately, and I'm sorry for my bad behaviour. I haven't been handling things too well since I got that phone call. It was the first big challenge I've had since becoming a Christian, and I blew it."

Paul started to interrupt, but Daniel held up his hand.

"Let me speak. I owe everything to God and to you people. You've all been so patient, and have shown love when I haven't deserved it. Being forced to think about my childhood and Da stirred up old emotions that have been eating away at me. I know you all believe I should see him, and forgive him, but it's not that easy when all I see when I think of him is a despicable man who beat my Mam." Daniel breathed slowly as he clenched his fists. *Control yourself, Daniel. Don't lose it in front of everybody.*

He steadied himself. He had to do this. "Each of you have had something to say, and God's been pricking me, even though I've been trying to ignore Him. But it's eating away at me, and I can't ignore Him forever, I know that, so despite how I feel," Daniel paused and gulped, "I've decided to go."

Daniel held Lizzy's gaze, her tears causing a lump to appear in his throat. She squeezed his hand.

"I have no idea how God can change the hate I have for Da into anything else, but I'm willing to give it a go and trust Him. You'll all need to pray hard, because He's going to have a difficult job."

Lizzy stood, and in front of everyone, wrapped her arms around him and kissed him.

"Daniel, we're all behind you." He squeezed back the tears that threatened to fall. He didn't deserve this much love. Breathing deeply, he hugged her back.

"Daniel, can we pray for you?" Paul asked as he stood and placed his hand on Daniel's shoulder.

Unable to utter a word, Daniel nodded.

"Lord God, thank You for working in Daniel's life. Such a special and much loved man, and one whom I'm convinced You have Your hand on. Bless his decision to trust You, and I ask that You change his hate for his Da to love and forgiveness. Do a wonderful work in his heart, Lord God, and use this to bring him closer to Yourself. Guide and lead him in the days ahead. Thank you Lord God. In Jesus' name, Amen."

"Amen."

Daniel inhaled deeply as a wonderful sense of calm flowed through his body. Why had he struggled so hard against God? He had so much to learn about living as a Christian.

THE FOLLOWING MORNING, Paul was the guest speaker at the church in Ambleside, and Daniel looked forward to hearing him preach. Making the decision to see Da had changed everything. Like a light switch being flicked on in his head, all the negative thoughts he'd been harbouring had been replaced with positive ones, and he felt much happier.

Daniel and Lizzy took their seats in the small stone church, with Riley and Nessa alongside. The children had gone to Sunday School, so only Dillon was left to care for, and so far he was behaving.

Daniel took Lizzy's hand. He'd never believed church could be so enjoyable. In the past, he'd gone just to keep Lizzy happy, but now he went because he wanted to. And now he was back on speaking terms with God, Daniel sensed the presence of the Lord and it warmed his heart.

Paul stood to begin his sermon. *God, please speak to me this morning. I need to hear from You.* Although it was the right decision to see Da, Daniel had no idea how to handle it. If it was up to him, he'd probably end up punching Da, but that definitely wouldn't go down well in anyone's eyes, let alone God's.

Paul began by reading from Mathew 5, verses 43 - 47, *"You have heard that it was said, 'Love your neighbor and hate your enemy.' But I tell you, love your enemies and pray for those who persecute you, that you may be children of your Father in heaven. He causes his sun to rise on the evil and the good, and sends rain on the righteous and the unrighteous. If you love those who love you, what reward will you get? Are not even the tax collectors doing that? And if you greet only your own people, what are you doing more than others? Do not even pagans do that? Be perfect, therefore, as your heavenly Father is perfect."*

As Paul spoke about God's undiscriminating love to all people, Daniel listened intently. God wanted him to show the same undiscriminating love not only to those who were easy to love, but to those he didn't like, or even hated, i.e. Da. *Can I do that? God, I'm sorry, but I'm not ready for this...*

Paul continued; "Jesus instructs us to live by a higher standard than what the world expects, a standard that's impossible to attain through our own efforts. A standard that can only be achieved through the power of God's Holy Spirit working in our lives.

"What's impossible for man, becomes possible for all those who give their lives to Jesus Christ through the power of the Holy Spirit living in their hearts.

"And there's more... God not only expects us to love those we find hard to love, He also wants us to pray for them. In my experience, I've found it's infinitely easier to love someone I dislike when I've prayed for them, because when we pray, God's able to open our hearts to seeing people the way He sees them, instead of the way we naturally see them.

"Loving your enemies, and praying for those who grieve you leads you into release, freedom and happiness..."

Maybe that's what I can do. Pray for Da. Even if I don't feel like it. God'll have to do the rest, because I can't.

Daniel squeezed Lizzy's hand. This would be the hardest thing he'd done in his life.

AFTER CHURCH ENDED, they had lunch in town before Riley and Nessa headed back home. As they were leaving, Riley took Daniel aside and handed him an envelope, telling him not to open it until they'd gone.

Daniel gave Riley a puzzled look.

"What's this?"

"Just wait until you open it."

Daniel obeyed and put the envelope into his top pocket.

Driving back to the cottage after waving Riley and Nessa off, Daniel reached into his pocket and took out the envelope. His eyes popped. Two hundred pounds! This was too much. Opening the note, he read it aloud.

"Daniel and Lizzy, we want you to put this toward your trip to Ireland so that all three of you can go. Please accept it as a gift that doesn't need repaying.

We give it to you in love, and pray that God will work His way in your lives as you obey Him. All our love, Riley and Nessa."

Daniel's eyes blurred with tears. "Liz, pull over." A sudden breathlessness took hold, along with a fluttering in his chest, as if a small bird were inside trying to escape. He couldn't believe it. No-one had ever been this generous to him. What had he done to deserve this?

Lizzy pulled over and wrapped her arms around him.

"Daniel, are you okay?" Lizzy's voice was gentle and concerned as she whispered in his ear and stroked his hair.

Daniel nodded and slowly controlled himself.

"I just can't believe it, Liz. I'm in shock."

Lizzy laughed softly. "I think it's God's way of telling you you made the right decision."

Daniel let out a huge breath. He still couldn't believe it. *Two hundred pounds!* It would have taken him months to save that much.

He took Lizzy's hands. "Seems like God really wants us to go, so I guess we'd better book our tickets."

Lizzy beamed a smile at Daniel and threw her arms around his neck before planting a huge kiss on his lips.

CHAPTER 5

Lizzy rose earlier than normal the day they left for Belfast. With so much still to do, her mind had been active all night and she had trouble sleeping. After Daniel had made the decision to go, everything happened quickly, leaving little time to organise it all. Boat from Liverpool was the easiest and cheapest way to get there, but it meant an early start to arrive in time for the 10.30 a.m. sailing. Dillon had to pick that day to be difficult, and it didn't help that Daniel still couldn't drive. The year without his license was dragging.

"Come on, Daniel, we have to leave. Turn it off." *How does he have time to watch television?* Lizzy huffed as she did a last sweep around the kitchen and lounge. "Dillon's ready. His pram's in the car. The bags are all at the door."

"Okay, love. Calm down. We've got plenty of time."

She stopped and glared at him. "No, we haven't. What if we get lost?"

"We won't. Trust me."

Lizzy rolled her eyes. That was the problem. Every time Daniel navigated, they took twice as long to get anywhere. But she daren't say that.

She bent down and picked up Dillon, his little face still red from crying. She needed to calm down for his sake. "Come on, little man. Please be good." Patting his back, Lizzy carried him to the car and placed him in the baby seat. She sighed with relief as the front door closed and Daniel appeared with the bags.

Sliding in beside her, Daniel extended his hand and placed it on her leg. "Sorry Liz. I haven't been much help."

Lizzy gave an exasperated sigh. "It's okay, Daniel. I know you're nervous."

"I guess we've got everything?"

"Yes, Daniel, we've got everything."

Lizzy pulled out the choke and sent up a quick prayer of thanks when the car started first go.

"Just as well we don't have the Escort anymore, hey love?"

She threw him a wry look as she thrust the gear stick into first and sped off down the track. *Yes, but I miss my old car...*

Once on the open road, Lizzy gave the Fiesta a good workout. Daniel turned the radio up and leaned back in his seat, humming to the music. Dillon thankfully had fallen asleep soon after leaving.

She shouldn't have been so short with Daniel. He was nervous about meeting up with his family, especially his Da. She knew that. Despite all the discussion they'd had, and all the praying they'd done, he was still nervous. Who wouldn't be? She should be grateful he hadn't turned to drink as he would have in the past. Yes, she should've been more patient and understanding. Lizzy sighed as she sped past a slow lorry. *God, will I ever get it right?*

Lost in her thoughts, and with Daniel and Dillon both fast asleep, the miles slipped away. Everything was fine, and they made good time until they hit a foggy patch. Lizzy slammed on the brakes as the cars ahead came to a standstill. Daniel jolted forward and almost hit his head on the dash.

He straightened himself and faced Lizzy. "Whoa, love. You trying to kill us?"

"No Daniel. But look at this!" Lizzy raised her hand and waved it around. "If it doesn't start moving, we won't get there in time."

"Calm down, love. You can't do anything about it."

"I know, but what if we miss the boat?"

Daniel peered out the window. "Where are we?"

"About half an hour out. Can you check the map? I think we turn off soon. That's if we ever get moving again." Lizzy gritted her teeth and tapped the steering wheel.

Daniel opened the map and studied it as the traffic began to slowly move again.

"Have you found where we are?" Lizzy glanced at him. "I think I can make out a sign up ahead."

"Not sure, love. Still looking."

"The lorry's covering the sign. I need to make a decision. Left or right?"

"Give me a minute..."

"We haven't got a minute, Daniel!" Lizzy's pulse quickened. Why couldn't he read a map? How he'd managed to get himself around the world was beyond her. Too late to get across, no choice - she had to go right. She sighed heavily. *God, I hope this is the right way...*

She breathed easier when a sign for the port showed up ahead.

"See, nothing to worry about." Daniel's grin was infectious and she couldn't help letting out a small laugh as she shook her head.

"Yes, but we're still cutting it fine."

"Maybe, but we'll be right, Liz. You'll see."

"Ten minutes until check-in closes. We'll have to run when we get there."

Reaching the car park, Lizzy frantically searched for a spot. Finally finding one, she pulled in and brought the car to an abrupt halt.

Grabbing a trolley, Daniel placed their bags on it as Lizzy picked up Dillon and almost threw him into his push chair. He needed a feed, but he'd have to wait. The ferry wouldn't.

People milled about, the din hurting her ears. So many counters. So many people. She scanned the area frantically.

"Over there, Liz." Daniel pointed to the check-in counter to his right, and steered the trolley towards it.

"I never want to do that again, Daniel. Two minutes more and we would've missed it."

"But we made it, love, that's all that matters." Daniel winked, dispelling her angst in an instant. It worked on her every time.

"Yes, we did. Just. I've got to feed and change Dillon before we board, but I can't see anywhere to sit. Can you find somewhere, Daniel?" Lizzy lifted Dillon out of his pram and gagged. "Poor little man. No wonder you've been upset." She wanted to comfort him, but held him at arm's length.

"I'll take him to the bathroom to change him. I won't be long." Lizzy reached up and kissed Daniel on the cheek. "I'm sorry for losing my patience, Daniel."

Daniel smiled and brushed her cheek with his fingertips. "It was both our faults, Lizzy. I'm sorry too."

Lizzy smiled as she walked to the bathroom. She hated being angry with Daniel.

She found the bathroom easily. The whole area needed a clean, but at least it had a changing bench. Laying Dillon on his back, she tried to placate him as she battled to clean him.

"Come on little man. Work with me. The sooner you do, the sooner you can be fed."

With Dillon finally cleaned and smelling much better, Lizzy hurried back to Daniel, now standing alone with the bags.

"Boarding's begun, Liz. Here, let me take him."

Lizzy handed Dillon over and followed Daniel to the end of the slow moving queue.

"Where do we go, Daniel?" Lizzy called once aboard the ship. She didn't like the way she was being jostled. Everyone seemed to be in a hurry.

"Follow me," Daniel called out over his shoulder.

She followed him to a quiet area with sofas on the left side of the ship.

"We can stay here all day if we want. I'll put our luggage in one of the lockers."

Lizzy sat on one of the sofas, thankful Daniel knew his way about, and began to feed Dillon.

As the ship pulled out of port, Lizzy realised she had no idea whether she'd get sea-sick or not, never having been on the open sea before.

She soon discovered she wasn't a good sailor. Not long out of port the ship began to roll and a wave of nausea hit her. Her body instantly felt clammy. She threw Dillon into Daniel's arms and sprinted for the bathroom, just making it.

She wasn't the only one who spent most of their time in the bathrooms heaving up green bile.

Morning sickness has nothing on this. Maybe I won't make it to Ireland after all.

WHILE LIZZY SPENT most of her time either in the bathroom or laying prostrate on the sofa, Daniel walked up and down the boat with Dillon, often in his arms, and occasionally in the push chair. Every time he passed one of the bars, his taste buds played havoc on his brain, and he had to tear his gaze away from the kegs holding the amber liquid.

If it hadn't been for Dillon, it would've been so easy to give in. *Maybe Lizzy being sick is God's way of keeping me sober.* Daniel grinned at God's sense of humour. He'd have to tell Lizzy when she was well enough to understand. She might not appreciate it after being so sick, but oh well. Tell her anyway.

The first few hours passed slowly. Dillon didn't want to sleep. Daniel had hoped the movement of the boat might've settled him, but it had the opposite effect, and Dillon had also been sick once or twice. By mid-afternoon, Daniel was at his wits' end. Lizzy was in no fit state to help - she could hardly even feed the baby, let alone do anything else. After Dillon had been fed, Daniel decided to try again, and put Dillon in the push chair and walked him briskly up and down the deck. Not daring to stop, Daniel guessed that Dillon might have finally fallen asleep after five or so minutes. He continued walking for another few minutes and then slowed down enough to take a look. Yes, the wee little man had finally given in. Hallelujah!

Daniel retraced his steps and lay down on the sofa opposite Lizzy, half lying, half sitting, one leg on the sofa, the other slowly rocking the push chair. He'd just rest his eyes for a few moments while Dillon slept...

Although his body rested, his mind was active, and strange images flitted through, jolting him into semi-awareness every now and then. A picture of Mam sitting at the dinner table peeling vegetables flashed through his mind. Mam...

Da had been sent home from work again that day. Every day he went, hoping to get a day's work, but more often than not, he and many others were sent packing without any work or pay. On those days, Da would spend his time out back, drinking with Micheal O'Leary from next door. And on those days, Mam would more than likely suffer at Da's hands.

Summer in the Cregagh Estate offered many opportunities for two eight year old boys to fill their time. Daniel and his best mate from next door, Colin O'Leary, spent most of their summer holidays fishing down at the River Lagan, or tramping along the river's edge and canal paths, stopping now and then to throw in a line. They'd set off in the morning, and wouldn't return until late afternoon, usually with at least a couple of good sized trout to give to their Mam's, who depended on the boy's efforts to help feed their families.

That day started like any other...

"Daniel, now don't you go getting yourself into any mischief, you hear?" Mam handed him a brown paper bag containing two large oat cookies. Mary O'Connor was so short, that at eight years of age, Daniel almost stood eye to eye with her. He couldn't help but notice how big her belly was getting. He sighed. Another bairn on the way. Another mouth to share their food with.

"No Mam, we'll be good. Promise."

"Off with you then. And make sure you bring home a good catch today." Daniel chuckled at his mother's words. Exactly the same as every other day's.

"We'll try, Mam." He flashed her a cheeky grin and darted quickly out of her reach. Mam had an annoying habit of ruffling his hair, but she did it because she loved him, not to annoy him. He didn't mind, really, but it was still better to escape it if he could.

Daniel ran out the door, leaving the chaos of his home behind him, and jumped over the piles of assorted objects lying discarded in the backyard and into the yard next door to meet up with Colin.

"Hey Colin, you ready?" Daniel called out through the back window where he knew Colin would be. He daren't go inside. Colin's Mam was worse than his own. Her humongous body smelt, and she had long hairs coming out from under her arms. Despite that, she was quite a nice person - from a distance.

"Coming," Colin replied.

A moment later, the short red headed boy with freckles appeared on the door step. He too held a brown paper bag in his hand.

"What have you got today?" Daniel asked.

"Strawberries and cream."

"Go on with you, Colin O'Leary. Let me look."

"No. It's all mine."

"You've got oatcakes, the same as me."

"No I haven't."

"Yes you have."

"Doesn't hurt to pretend."

"S'pose."

The two boys continued their friendly banter as they headed off towards the river for their day of fishing and exploring.

"Hope we don't see those crazy Catholics today," Colin said as they took their spot on the bank of the river. In the distance, army helicopters hovered over the city as they did every day, but the boys ignored them.

"If we do, we'll shoot them with our sticks." Daniel held up the long stick he used for fishing and pretended it was a gun, shooting the hated Catholic kids they sometimes had the ill fortune of meeting.

"Yeah, we'll get 'em good." Colin joined in, and before long, they'd killed all the Catholics that dared to walk along their path.

Later, sitting on the edge of the bank with their legs dangling close to the muddy water, they munched on an oat cookie each, pretending they were strawberries and cream.

"Do you even know what strawberries taste like?" Daniel asked Colin.

"Yeh. Like a Gobstopper."

"No they don't. I had one once. It was all soft and sweet and tasted like heaven."

"What does heaven taste like?"

Daniel thought for a moment. "Like a Gobstopper." He peeled over backwards in laughter, and Colin joined him.

Sitting up suddenly, Daniel looked at Colin. "We'd better catch some fish. I'll get a backhander if I go home empty handed."

"Yeah, me too."

For the next hour or so, the boys concentrated on fishing, and between them caught five good sized trout.

"Guess it's fish for dinner again." Colin's shoulders slumped beneath the weight of his bucket. "Don't like fish."

"Better than broth."

"Guess so."

The boys trudged back to their homes. They would've stayed out longer, but if they did, they'd expect a hiding from their Da's for being late and for getting up to no good. Not that their Da's ever asked what they actually did. Their Da's just assumed the boys always got up to mischief.

At their front gates, the boys separated. From the front, the brown brick terraced houses looked exactly the same. Two storeys high, and stretching as far as you could see, the row of houses was cold and lifeless. Daniel hated the brown brick, and wished he could paint it a bright colour, but he'd never be allowed.

He paused before entering the house to listen for Da. The coast was clear. He tiptoed in and placed the fish on the kitchen sink. So far so good. He snuck out of the kitchen and had his first foot on the threadbare step when a heavy hand landed on his shoulder. He froze. *Not again, please, no.*

He turned around slowly and looked into Da's bloodshot eyes.

A SHRIEK ROUSED Daniel from his sleep. He sprang up, dazed. Where was he? Shaking his head, he looked at the source of the noise. Dillon was awake and screaming, his little arms thrashing in the air. Lizzy wasn't about.

Standing, Daniel undid the clip on the push chair and lifted the screaming baby to his shoulder.

"There, there, little one. Da's sorry."

Daniel froze. Where had that word come from? He never, ever used it for himself. He'd been dreaming about his childhood. And Da... A sickness developed in the pit of his stomach. Tomorrow he'd be seeing him again - face to face.

Daniel sat back down and held Dillon close to his chest, gently patting him on his back. Maybe it'd been a bad idea to come back. Could he really face that man again after all he'd done? How many beatings had he and his brothers and sisters suffered at the hands of that cruel man? And how many times had Mam been so battered she could hardly get out of bed? And now he'd come back, wanting to make amends. *Twenty years too late, Thomas O'Connor. Twenty years too late.*

"God, you're going to have to give me the strength to do this. I can't do it on my own. There's just no way."

Daniel sighed deeply. "There there, Dillon. It's okay." He looked up as Lizzy came towards him, still a little green, but better than before.

"How are you feeling, my sweet?" Daniel pushed thoughts of Da away for the moment and gave Lizzy his full attention.

Sitting beside him, she reached for Dillon. "I've had better days. I never knew anyone could be so sick. And the boat's even stopped rolling." Shaking her head, she smiled weakly at Dillon.

"What's all this nonsense, then, my little man?" Dillon calmed down as soon as he was in her lap. Amazing.

"We're almost there, love. Should be docking within the half hour." Daniel placed his arm gently around her shoulder and pulled her close. "I don't know if I can do this."

Lizzy pulled away slightly and held his gaze. "No, you can't, Daniel, but God can. He's brought you this far, He'll be with you the rest of the way."

He gazed into her eyes, so strong, and so right. God was here, and wouldn't let him down.

~

As THE SHIP sailed towards the dock, darkness settled over Belfast, the lingering colours of twilight slowly giving way to the artificial lights of the big city.

Lizzy stayed close to Daniel as they lined up with all the other passengers jostling for position to get off first. She felt claustrophobic with so many people so close.

"I need to get off," she whispered to Daniel. Slapping her hand over her mouth, she attempted to calm her nausea.

"Are you going to be sick?" Daniel's voice was gentle and full of concern.

She nodded, and then pushed her way through the crowd to get to the side of the boat, immediately feeling better as she gulped in the fresh air. She turned her head slightly as Daniel laid his hand on her shoulder.

"Are you alright, love?"

She smiled weakly. "Yes. I just couldn't handle being in that crush. Let them go. There's no hurry, is there?"

Daniel shook his head. "No, not really. We can stay here until it clears." He paused, placing his arm around her shoulder. "Lizzy, do you mind if I have a smoke?"

Lizzy slipped her arm around his waist and held his gaze. "You're nervous, aren't you?"

"Yeah, you could say that."

"Go on, then. Have a cigarette if it'll help."

"Thanks love." Daniel pulled the packet from his jacket pocket and lit up. "I will give up, Lizzy, I promise."

When he planted a kiss on her head, she leaned in to him. It didn't matter. She loved him just the way he was.

CHAPTER 6

"I feel bad we've made them wait," Lizzy said as she and Daniel walked along the corridor towards the Arrivals Hall at the end of the long line of passengers.

"Don't, Lizzy. It's only a few minutes between first and last off."

"They might think we're not coming."

"It's okay, Lizzy. Stop panicking."

"I'm not panicking." Lizzy shot Daniel an angry glance and straightened her shoulders defensively.

"Yes, you are."

But her grip on the push chair tightened the closer they got. What would his family be like? Would they have anything in common? As much as she tried, her English accent was impossible to hide. What would they think of her? Would they see her as someone who considered herself better than them, just because of her accent, even though that's not what she thought? Was she over-thinking it? They were just people, after all. And God was with her. She should never forget that. As long as she remained open to Him, His love and kindness would shine through her. She inhaled deeply. *God, please help me get along with them. Let your love shine through me, I pray.* Her heart pounded, nevertheless.

And there they were - standing together in a group holding a 'Welcome, Daniel & Lizzy' placard in the air. Lizzy hung back slightly to the side of Daniel, allowing him to take the lead. She squeezed his arm as he paused and shot her a quick glance. Their eyes met for a brief second. *Yes, they could do this.*

CASTING his eyes over the small group standing before him, some faces familiar, others, not so, Daniel's gaze settled on a tall, lanky man, not much older than himself wearing a pair of black high-tops, acid washed jeans, white T-shirt and denim jacket. The man's neck, adorned with a tattoo of a cross, suggested his body could well be a work of art under his clothes. His dark hair, shaved on the sides, was spiked on top. Daniel recognised him immediately.

"Caleb!" Daniel strode to his brother and wrapped him in a bear hug before holding him at arm's distance. "You haven't changed a bit, man, apart from maybe this." Daniel tilted his head to get a better look at the tattoo.

"Yeah, that's new. Grand to see you, Danny. It's been too long." Caleb grabbed Daniel's hand and shook it vigorously, his dark eyes lighting up.

"Yes, it has. Way too long."

The tall young woman on Caleb's right caught Daniel's attention. *No, it can't be... or can it?* "Grace?"

The young woman's dark smoky eyes were familiar. Yes, it was Grace. His little sister had morphed into a classy beauty. Slightly overdressed in dark designer jeans, knee-length boots and fitted red jacket, she could have just come off the cat walk. Her immaculate make-up accentuated her naturally good looks, and was topped off with heavily permed dark brown hair.

Grace nodded as her eyes watered. Daniel held her tight, squeezing back his own tears. How long had it been? She must have been twelve when he'd gone to live with Nessa's family, and Grace and their next sister down, Brianna, had been sent to live with Aunt Hilda in Londonderry. He hadn't seen either of them since.

He pulled away and held her at arm's length. Her tears had escaped, and black streaks spiralled down her cheeks. Pulling a clean handkerchief from his pocket, Daniel gently wiped her face.

"Grace, I don't believe it. Look at you! You're all grown up. I wouldn't have recognised you on the street."

"You've changed a bit too, Danny, you know." Her eyes sparkled as a cheeky grin grew on her face. Taking the handkerchief from him, Grace continued dabbing her eyes, and once composed, turned to Lizzy and held out her hand. "And you must be Lizzy. Welcome." She smiled broadly at Lizzy, continuing to exude such confidence Daniel was amazed. Grace had always been outspoken, but he'd never expected this.

Lizzy returned Grace's smile and took her hand. "Thank you, Grace. It's lovely to meet you."

Daniel cringed at the look on Caleb's face. He'd almost forgotten how Lizzy sounded, but here with his siblings, her well-bred English accent was blatantly obvious. He placed his arm gently around her shoulders.

"Lizzy, this is Caleb, my brother, and Caitlin, his wife." He directed Lizzy's focus to the young woman to Caleb's left. She'd changed in the years since he'd last seen her too, which in fact had been at their wedding, not long before he'd packed up and left. Although she'd put on weight, Caitlin's round jolly face would cheer anyone.

Lizzy smiled at them both and said hello before her gaze dropped to the two young girls standing between them.

"And this is Imogen and Tara." Caitlin lowered her eyes to the twin girls and gently pushed them forward. "Say hello to your Uncle Danny and Aunt Lizzy, girls." Dark eyes gazed up, but the girls clung to Caitlin's legs and wouldn't budge.

"It doesn't matter," Lizzy said to Caitlin before stooping to the girls' level. "You have very pretty hair ribbons. And I love your sparkly shoes."

The girls looked down at their shoes before inching closer to their mother.

Caitlin shook her head and rolled her eyes. "One day they'll learn to be social."

Lizzy let out a small laugh as she stood. "They're very cute. I wouldn't worry about them."

Dillon let out a huge cry. Daniel bent down and picked him up from the push chair. "And this is our little man. Dillon Patrick O'Connor. He obviously didn't want to be left out!"

Everyone laughed, and then Caleb finished introducing the other family members. He apologized for not being able to gather all the siblings together, but said he'd fill them in on the others later. At first glance, Daniel would never have recognised the two youngest girls, Aislin and Alana, who'd only been six and seven when the family had been torn apart. On second glance, he gasped. Maybe it was their eyes, or the shape of their faces, he wasn't sure, but their resemblance to Mam unnerved him. The two girls held back and clung to their partners. Had they only come out of curiosity? Probably. It'd be up to him to make a move - standing there like a stunned mullet wouldn't achieve anything. He leaned forward and kissed them, trying to avoid thoughts of Mam before shaking hands with their partners.

"Hey Danny, we thought we'd stop at Molly's Tavern on the way home to get a bite to eat. You up for that?" Caleb asked as the group moved slowly towards the exit.

"Sounds good." Daniel looked to Lizzy and raised his eyebrows. "Liz?"

Lizzy nodded as she took Dillon from him. "I'll need to feed this little man soon, but he can wait a little longer." She glanced around quickly. "Nowhere to feed him here anyway. So, yes, that would be nice."

"Great. Grace has room for you in her car. Let's go." Caleb picked up one of the little girls who'd been pulling on his leg as he tried to walk. "What's up Immi? Can't you walk today?"

The little girl shook her head and put her thumb in her mouth, her large round eyes fixed on Lizzy and Dillon as she peered at them from the safety of her father's shoulder.

LIZZY SHOT Daniel an amused look as they approached Grace's car. Why wasn't she surprised to see a hotted up red sports car?

"Don't worry... Caleb will take your luggage." Grace laughed, her grin widening into a full, easy smile that lit up her face.

"Phew! I did wonder how we were all going to fit," Lizzy said, warming to Grace's unexpected sense of fun.

Caleb, Caitlin and the girls had been tagging along behind, and stopped in front of a less trendy but more practical Ford Escort parked beside the sports car. Lizzy reached for her cross. Twice in one day, memories of the not too distant past had surfaced, bringing with them a sense of nostalgia.

Caleb grabbed the luggage and squeezed it into the boot.

"We'll see you there," Grace called out and waved as the sports car sprang to life and surged forward. In the back, Lizzy held on tight. Grace drove fast, but had complete control. She obviously loved driving. Or was she trying to impress?

"You've done alright for yourself, Grace." Daniel shot her a sideways look as he caressed the leather seats.

Lizzy studied the two of them. They must have been close when they were young, there was an ease between them you wouldn't expect after so many years apart.

"You could say that. I decided to make something of myself, so I went to University." Grace shifted down a gear as the lights changed, and the car gurgled to a stop. She turned her head and gave him a playful look. "Your little sister's a lawyer."

Daniel's eyes popped and he let out a low whistle. "Wow. You've certainly done more than alright. So, is there a Mr Grace anywhere?" Daniel's eyebrows lifted and he wore a cheeky grin.

Lizzy winced and glowered at him. *Don't ask questions like that, Daniel!*

Grace straightened her shoulders defensively and lifted her chin to a haughty angle. The playfulness disappeared from her face.

"No. Not interested in men." Her voice was crisp and measured.

An uncomfortable silence took over for several seconds. Lizzy bit her lip as she watched from behind. *Come on Daniel, be sensitive.*

"Sorry, Grace. I didn't mean to upset you." He sounded apologetic. But would Grace let him off that easily?

Grace looked him up and down. Lizzy held her breath.

"Apology accepted."

Lizzy exhaled slowly and her body relaxed. *Thank goodness for that.*

Moments later, Grace made a hard left before screeching to a stop in the Tavern's car park. "Looks like we're the first ones here."

"I'm not surprised." Daniel's grin held warmth and affection.

"What do you mean, Daniel? Don't you like my driving?" Grace threw out the challenge.

"I didn't mean that. Your driving's grand, Grace. Just teasing." Daniel chuckled and shook his head.

Lizzy, relieved the tension had diffused, smiled to herself before handing Dillon over to Daniel so she could squeeze her way out of the back. This was going to be a good week.

The others arrived within minutes, and they all wandered into the Tavern together. Lizzy walked beside Grace and tried to strike up a conversation. She'd like to get to know her. Lizzy couldn't quite put her finger on it, but despite Grace's outward confidence, Lizzy was convinced she was hiding something.

The group stopped in front of the menu board. Main meals were still being served, but had they been any later, only the snacks' menu would have been available. A table, large enough to accommodate the whole group, was available, but Lizzy excused herself before taking her seat and took Dillon into a quieter, more private corner to feed him.

From her vantage point, Lizzy studied the group. Each of them had a story, beginning in their family home all those years ago.

Caleb and Caitlin appeared happy enough, and so did Grace, on the outside. And the two girls who'd hardly said a word? What was going on there? There were still three more. Brianna, and the twin boys, Shawn and Brendan. And then there'd been Dillon, who'd only lived a matter of hours, and who they'd named their own little man after.

Daniel appeared with a menu in his hand, interrupting her thoughts.

"How's the little man doing?" Daniel lowered his gaze to Dillon, moving the cover Lizzy had placed over him slightly so the baby's face was visible.

"Almost done. Another few minutes should do it." But Dillon stopped sucking as he caught sight of Daniel, his big round eyes lighting up. He kicked his legs and pulled his mouth away, letting out a huge chuckle.

"Well, that's it. No more for you." Lizzy propped him up and patted him gently on the back. "You can go to your daddy in a minute."

"Let me order first, Liz. I'm just getting a burger and chips. Here's the menu."

"Just get me something light, Daniel. I don't feel like much after being sick all day. Maybe a plain sandwich?"

"Okay love." He stood and squeezed her shoulder. "Are you alright?"

Lizzy sighed deeply and nodded. "Yes, kind of. It's been a long day."

"I know. My mind's spinning." He glanced at the group seated behind him and leaned closer to her. "I don't really know any of them."

"I gathered that." Lizzy looked up at him, searching his eyes. "Do you think we've been sent here for a reason, Daniel?"

"I was wondering that. Seems Grace has something going on, that's for sure."

Lizzy put Dillon back in his push chair and straightened her top.

"Yes, I agree. The more I've thought about it, the more I believe God's brought us here, Daniel. It might be an interesting week."

Daniel nodded as he pulled his finger away from Dillon's grip.

"Yes, I agree. I hope I'm up to it."

"You will be, Daniel. God's with you, don't forget."

"Just as well He is. I wouldn't be here without Him." Daniel gently ruffled Dillon's head, causing the baby to gurgle and kick. "I need to place our orders." He gave Lizzy a peck on the cheek before turning and walking away.

"Don't be long. Dillon wants you," Lizzy called after him.

Daniel turned his head and grinned. "I'll be as quick as I can."

Daniel ordered the meals and returned to the table, picking Dillon up from the push chair and placing him on his lap. He picked up his squash and took a sip. If only it was a Guiness. Was he really strong enough to do this? He sighed resolutely. He had to be. For Lizzy and for Dillon. For himself. *God, please give me strength.* He took Lizzy's hand. Her squeeze assured him he wasn't in this alone. *Thank you God.*

The conversation around the table was mainly directed at them. Daniel's siblings knew very little about where he'd been since he'd left Ireland over ten years before, nor how he and Lizzy had met, nor what he was doing now. He answered their questions as best he could, deferring to Lizzy at times, and asked them what they'd been doing too, since he knew less about them than they knew about him.

Caleb had married Caitlin just before Daniel had left and still worked at the shipyards where their Da had worked until he lost his job. They still lived in the Cregagh Estate, not far from the house they'd all lived in as kids. Grace had returned to Belfast to study, and now lived in an apartment in the city on her own, near to where she worked. The two girls, Aislin and Alana, lived together in a flat with their boyfriends, Joel and Conall, and were shop assistants. Joel was a carpenter, and Conall a painter. They all seemed to get on well together, but it soon became apparent they saw little of the family. It was only at Caleb's insistence they'd come.

"We don't know where Brianna is," Caleb said. "She took off with some dude a while back and hasn't been in touch since. We're worried about her, aren't we, Grace?"

Grace nodded. "We tried to find her, but I don't think she wants to be found." Her face paled. "She didn't get on too well with Aunt Hilda, and ended up mixing with a bad crowd." Tears welled in her eyes. "I'm sorry." She took the handkerchief Daniel had given her earlier out of her pocket and dabbed at them.

"Don't apologise, Grace," Lizzy said, squeezing her hand. "You obviously care about her."

Grace nodded and sniffed. "Yes, very much. I hope she'll come back one day."

"I'm sure she will. We'll pray for her."

A faint smile appeared on Grace's face but disappeared quickly.

"And Shawn and Brendan - that's another story." Caleb took a sip of his drink. "Shawn took off overseas with his girl a year ago - last we heard, they were in America. Brendan - well, he's a no hoper. Drinks way too much, and he's in and out of trouble all the time. He's in the clink at the moment for assault." Caleb shook his head and shrugged. "Not much we can do for him. Not that we haven't tried, hey Grace?"

"Yes, we've tried just about everything, but he doesn't want any help." Grace sighed heavily.

"Well, I know what that's like," Daniel said. "If there's one thing I've learned, it's that you can't make people do something they don't want to do. I hate to say this, but it might take something bad to make him wake up to himself."

"Did something bad happen to you, Danny?" Grace asked, touching his arm lightly.

Daniel hesitated. How much should he say? They would all have known about his own stint in jail after he'd assaulted Liam, Nessa's brother, but they knew very little about his journey since then. How could he sum everything up in a sentence?

"Well, yes, it did. I almost killed myself in an accident a few months back, didn't I Liz?"

Lizzy nodded as she linked her arm through his.

"Almost losing everything made me come to my senses, and I haven't had a drink since."

"I wondered why you were drinking squash and not the Black Stuff," Caleb said.

Daniel paused for a moment, shifting in his seat as all eyes turned on him.

"Yep. I can't afford to drink." His gaze quickly travelled around the group. "It's not easy. I'd love to have a drink, but that's the way it is." He drew in a deep breath. "But I'm okay with it now."

"Good on you, Danny," Caleb said. "I'm glad everything's worked out for you. I've had a few problems myself, haven't I, Caity, and I've cut back." He put his arm around his wife and gave her a kiss on the cheek. "But we're good now. I had to behave once these two came along." He tilted his head towards the two little girls sitting on his other side, colouring in quietly.

"Seems like our Da left his mark on a lot of us," Daniel said as the meals began to arrive.

While they were eating, Daniel continued his conversation with Caleb.

"I got really down about five years back and hit the grog hard. Almost lost my job, and I hate to say it, I almost lost Caity too, but she stuck by me and helped me get myself together. We go to church every week now, and I've only had the occasional slip up since."

"Stop the lights! You serious?"

"Yeah man. We're regular church-goers. Does that surprise you?"

"Not really. It's just that Lizzy helped me find God too." Daniel shook his head and chuckled. "Who would'a thought…"

"Yeah, my mates were all gobsmacked, I tell you. They still give me a hard time, but I don't care. My life's much better now."

"I'd have to agree with you. I'm only a few months down the track, but I couldn't imagine life without God anymore."

The buzz around the table lowered. The others were listening, but Grace leaned back with folded arms and narrowed eyes. *Something's definitely going on with her.*

Daniel squeezed Lizzy's hand and caught her eyes for a second. Yes, it really did seem that God had brought them here this week.

A short while later, once the table had been cleared, Caleb stretched his neck and yawned. "You both must be tired. I know I am. Call it a night?"

"Yes, it's been a long day," Daniel replied.

"Let's get you home, then." Caleb reached over and picked up one of the girls. Following his lead, everyone else stood and began to stroll out to the cars. Before they all went their separate ways, they all agreed to catch up again in the next day or so, even the two girls who'd hardly said a word.

Grace dropped Daniel and Lizzy at Caleb and Caitlin's home and promised to see them again the following night after work. As Daniel climbed out of the car, Grace hugged him tightly and planted a kiss on his cheek.

"It's been good to see you again, Danny. I'm sorry I got short with you." Her eyes twinkled, but he couldn't read what lurked behind her well-groomed facade, which he was now sure it was. Daniel smiled warmly and hugged her back.

Grace then turned to Lizzy and held out her hand. "It's been lovely meeting you, Lizzy. I'll look forward to seeing you again tomorrow."

Lizzy took Grace's hand and smiled affectionately. "I'll look forward to it, too, Grace." She then leaned in and gave Grace a hug.

Daniel placed his arm around Lizzy's shoulder and waved to Grace as she sped off. Waiting for Caleb and Caitlin to climb out of their car, a wave of nostalgia swept through Daniel. It was all so familiar. Under the dim street lamps, the brown brick was as cold and unwelcoming as ever, although the small garden out front did help to soften it.

They followed Caleb and Caitlin inside. The layout was exactly the same as the house he'd grown up in, but the modern furnishings and light clean colours gave it a totally different feel. Daniel breathed a little easier.

Caitlin led them upstairs to the spare room. Decorated in warm yellow, a double bed dominated the space, along with an old chest of drawers standing on the wall at the foot of the bed. A cot for Dillon was tucked in beside the bed.

"I hope you'll have enough room," Caitlin said as she pulled the blind down and closed the yellow polka dot curtains. "I know it's a bit tight."

"I'm sure we'll be fine," Lizzy said. "It looks very homely. I just hope this little man doesn't wake everyone up in the night." Lizzy smiled at Dillon and grabbed his hand and gave it a waggle.

"Oh, don't you worry about that. We're used to it with our wee ones. They still wake up sometimes." Caitlin chuckled as she fussed with the bed covers.

"Leave that, Caitlin. We can sort it," Lizzy said, giving Caitlin a warm smile as she bounced Dillon in her arms.

Caitlin stopped fussing and squeezed her way back towards the door. "I'll go downstairs and put the kettle on, but if you'd like to freshen up first, the bathroom's through here." She pointed to the door beside the bedroom at the end of the hallway.

"A shower and a cup of tea before bed sounds great, doesn't it, Daniel?"

"Yes. Grand idea. It's been a long day," Daniel replied with a yawn.

Caitlin chuckled. "I'll leave you to it. Come down when you're ready."

After Caitlin had disappeared down the stairs, Lizzy took out their night things and suggested Daniel have first shower while she changed Dillon.

When she looked up, Daniel was peering out the window.

"Are you okay, Daniel?"

"Yes, it's just strange being back. Come and have a look, Liz." He pulled her gently to his front and slid his arms around her waist. "See that house over there? The one with the street light out front?"

Lizzy followed the direction he was indicating and nodded.

"That's our old house."

As Daniel stood with his arms around Lizzy, gazing across the roof tops, the years fell away, and for a moment he was transported back to a far less happier time. He sighed deeply.

"Are you alright, Daniel?" Lizzy leaned back and tilted her head towards him so their eyes met.

He spun her around gently and traced his fingertips along her hairline. "Yes Lizzy. As long as you're with me, I'm more than alright. I couldn't imagine being here on my own."

"Oh Daniel." Lizzy searched his eyes as she lifted her free hand and gently caressed his face. "I can't imagine how you're feeling. But God's with you too, and He'll be there to help."

"And for that, I'm forever grateful." He lowered his head towards hers, and just as their lips met, Dillon let out a cry.

Daniel pulled away and poked Dillon's little chest. "You, little man, have great timing…" He shook his head and chuckled. "I guess we can pick up where we left off later." He flashed Lizzy a grin full of promise, and picked up his clothes before walking to the shower.

CHAPTER 7

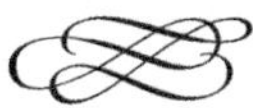

Daniel tossed and turned. Sleep eluded him. Dillon let out the occasional whimper and Lizzy breathed steadily beside him. Throwing off the covers, Daniel slid out of bed and put on the dressing gown Caleb had lent him before tiptoeing out the door and into the hallway. The floorboards creaked on the steps even though he purposefully only trod on the edges. A wonder the noise didn't wake anyone.

Outside, the cold night air took his breath away. He pulled the dressing gown tighter and lifted the collar around his neck. If only he'd put on a heavier coat. Too late now. Walking briskly, Daniel reached the end of the street and turned left. The streets were silent, but in the distance a dog let out an occasional bark and a car horn blasted.

Reaching Teldarg Street, Daniel's heart raced. So many memories. *This is stupid. Shouldn't have come.* He gulped and fought to remain calm. What had Paul said? *'Doing the hard thing is the way to grow...' Okay, God, I'm willing, I think, help me grow...*

As he walked slowly along the street, memories of the day Mam died floated through his mind. Mam'd been sick for a while, but none of the kids really knew she was dying. She kept saying God would heal her.

But He didn't. None of the kids could understand what had happened when they were separated. Daniel looked up. *God, why didn't You heal her? I know You could have.* Daniel wiped the tears pricking his eyes.

He stopped in front of the house. Very little had changed. Ugly brown brick. A shiver ran down his spine. Such a cold house. No-one ever wanted to leave the only fire and venture upstairs to their cold beds. No, the house held few happy memories. If only Da hadn't drunk so much, things might've been different. Daniel closed his eyes and inhaled slowly, trying to control the tension growing in his body.

Clenching his hands, he looked up. His whole body quivered. *"God, how do You expect me to face Da? You know I've been praying for him, but right now, I despise the man. I'm sorry, but that's how I feel."* Daniel took a deep breath. *"I'll be honest - I don't want to be here, God. I know I'm fighting against You at the moment, so You're going to have to help me. Okay?"*

Daniel took one more look at the house before turning and slowly retracing his steps. Could he face the man who'd destroyed their family?

When he slipped back into bed a short while later, Lizzy stirred and wrapped her arms around him. He closed his eyes and finally, sleep came.

"Well Danny, you ready?" Caleb asked as the four adults sat at the table finishing breakfast.

Daniel tensed. *I'll never be ready.* He breathed deeply as his heart pounded in his chest. Was it too late to pull out?

Lizzy took his hand and squeezed it. *No, this is stupid. I've got to do it. Get a grip, man.*

He looked into Caleb's eyes. "Don't think I'll ever be ready, but I'll go anyway. We'd better leave before I change my mind."

"Why don't we pray before you leave?" Caitlin asked, looking at Daniel, her round face warm, jolly and caring.

Lizzy squeezed Daniel's hand again and smiled at Caitlin. "That would be wonderful."

"Let's pray then."

Daniel bowed his head with the others. Caitlin began, praying for God to be with Daniel as he met with his father. Caleb continued, and thanked God for bringing Daniel back to them, and asked that he might find it within himself to forgive Da.

Daniel hesitated. He should pray, but a lump had formed in his throat. His heart beat faster, and then Lizzy began to pray. He breathed out a slow breath. *God, thank you that Lizzy knows exactly how I'm feeling.*

"Lord God, we ask that You meet Daniel exactly where he is, and that You expect no more of him than he's capable of right at this moment. Reward his willingness to be obedient, even if he's struggling with it. Let him draw on Your strength, Lord God, and may he know Your peace and love deep in his heart."

Daniel squeezed back tears. He needed God's touch more than ever. What was expected of him was more than he could do on his own. And to be honest, he didn't understand why he should forgive Da. The man didn't deserve anything from him. *God, You really need to work this out in my life. I'm sorry, but I can't say something I don't mean. You'll have to perform a miracle.*

THOMAS O'CONNOR WAS in a Rehab place run by the Salvation Army. As Caleb parked the car, Daniel steeled himself. Too many things in his head - his time in the building next door intruded into his mind.

"Not sure if I can do this, Caleb." Daniel sat, frozen in his seat.

He closed his eyes and breathed slowly. He'd let everyone down, God included. Why couldn't he just trust God like Paul had encouraged him to do? Why was it so hard?

Maybe Lizzy should have come. She gave him strength. *No. I need to do this on my own.*

Daniel turned his head and studied Caleb. He would never have expected his brother to be so solid.

"How did you manage it, Caleb? I'm really struggling with going in there." Daniel reached into his jacket pocket and took out a cigarette. "Mind if I smoke?"

"Go ahead."

Daniel offered the packet to Caleb, but he refused. Daniel lit up and inhaled slowly.

"I felt much the same as you, Danny. When Da first made contact a few months ago, I straight out refused to see him. He kept ringing. Every night. I refused to speak to him." Caleb shifted in his seat. "Caity spoke to him though. Asked her not to, but she ignored me. She finally convinced me to see him."

Daniel leaned his arm on the window sill and tapped the ash onto the ground.

"What d'you do when you saw him?"

Caleb drew in a long breath and chuckled quietly.

"You might not believe this, but I cried."

"Go on. You cried?"

"Yep. Balled like a baby." Caleb's eyes twinkled.

Daniel shook his head. "That's the last thing I'll be doing."

Caleb leaned forward and looked Daniel in the eye.

"You might be surprised, Danny. He's not the git you remember. There's hardly anything left of him, and he really does seem sorry for what he did. Says he's found God." Caleb winced and took a breath. "Don't know whether he has or not, but me'n Caity, we decided to believe him. You decide what to do, but we figure he doesn't have much time left, and it's better to let it all go. Grace doesn't feel the same. She won't have anything to do with him."

Daniel took another drag on his cigarette and then folded his arms. "Guess we'd better go in. Get it over with. You might need to hold me back though."

"You'll be okay, Danny. I think you'll be surprised."

"We'll see."

WHILE THE TWO little girls entertained Dillon, Lizzy helped with the breakfast dishes.

"Daniel seemed very nervous," Caitlin said, hands deep in suds.

"Yes, I'm concerned about him. He's been struggling with the whole thing ever since Caleb called." Lizzy stopped wiping and stared out the window. *God, please be with Daniel... he must be there by now...*

"I'm sure he'll be fine, but would you like to pray again?" Caitlin stopped washing and faced Lizzy.

"That would be great, Caitlin." Lizzy smiled warmly at Caitlin. Such a wonderful surprise to discover they shared a common faith.

Caitlin dried her hands and then sat at the table. Lizzy took the seat opposite, and with their hands joined and heads bowed, they prayed for Daniel and his father.

"God's with him, Lizzy." Caitlin's eyes sparkled as she raised her head.

Lizzy nodded, pushing back the tears that had welled in the corners of her eyes. "Yes, I know He is."

Caitlin squeezed Lizzy's hand, and then turned her attention to the little girls standing before her.

WALKING along the corridors of Calder House, a cold, nauseating lump sat heavily in the pit of Daniel's stomach. Every step brought him closer to Da. He recalled the verse Paul had asked him to memorise ... *'cast all your anxiety onto Him because He cares for you...'*

'Okay God, I'm casting my anxiety onto You now. You've got me this far, which is a miracle, but I don't know how much further I can go.'

Daniel glanced inside each of the rooms he passed. The beds were full of men. Thin, sickly men, older than he, but any one could've been him in the years ahead. But God had saved him from this. How close to the edge he'd come, but God had stopped him tipping over, and given him new life full of hope and purpose.

And now he had the opportunity to reunite with Da. Was it possible Da was truly sorry for what he'd done? Daniel needed to be open to that possibility. To give Da the benefit of the doubt, like Caleb had done. But could he really do that?

'God, I'm really not ready for this...'

The closer Daniel got, the harder his heart pounded. Caleb stopped in front of the last door on the left.

"This is it, Danny. You okay?"

Daniel inhaled deeply and shook his head. He couldn't do it. How had Caleb made himself walk through that door the first time? Must be made of stronger stuff.

"Give me a few minutes..." Daniel walked to the end of the corridor and leaned against the door frame. Shivers ran up and down his spine and his hands shook. Why had he agreed to come? What would Lizzy think if he didn't go in? To come all this way and baulk at the last moment?

Daniel turned as Caleb placed a hand on his shoulder.

"Take your time, buddy. There's no hurry."

Daniel looked up and nodded. If anyone understood how he was feeling, it was Caleb. He took some deep breaths and gritted his teeth. He had to do this.

Lifting his chin, Daniel forced himself to speak words he didn't want to say.

"I don't want to see him, Caleb, but I'll do it. Once. That's all."

Caleb squeezed Daniel's shoulder and held him at arm's length.

"That's all that's expected of you, Danny. No more, no less."

Daniel followed Caleb into the darkened room. Six beds in total, three on each wall. Five occupied. Daniel scanned each bed. His eyes rested on the last bed on the right. It had been almost twenty years, but he would've recognised Da anywhere. Yes, his body had shrunk, and his face was bony and thin, but there was no denying this man was Thomas Rory O'Connor, Da.

Caleb reached out and gently touched his arm. "Da, wake up."

Da slowly opened his eyes, the whites no longer white, but yellow, like the rest of his body. He had trouble focussing, but his face lit up a little as he recognised Caleb.

"Caleb. Good to see you, son." He held out his thin arm to Caleb.

Caleb helped him to a sitting position and placed several pillows behind his back. Daniel was shocked at the tenderness his brother was showing Da. He would never have expected it.

But then, although this man looked like Da, the similarity ended there. This man was weak, his voice no more than a raspy whisper, not loud and churlish as Daniel remembered. Difficult to tie the two together.

"Da, I've brought someone with me." Caleb held Da's hand and glanced at Daniel.

"Who's that?" Da peered at Daniel, but there was no recognition on his face.

"It's Daniel, Da. Daniel's here."

Until that moment, Daniel could have turned and walked away, but now it was too late. He had no choice. He had to face Da.

His chest tightened and he couldn't speak. His mouth wouldn't work. Gulping, he tried to steady his pounding heart.

Da sat straighter and peered at Daniel more intensely.

"Daniel, you say?" He glanced at Caleb and then back at Daniel.

"Yes, Da. It's Daniel." *Just as well Caleb could speak.*

"Ah, Daniel, my boy. Come here." Da reached out his hand, and Daniel had no choice but to take it.

Da's fingers were long, thin and bony. His grip, weak but warm. Daniel pushed back the tears that pricked the corners of his eyes.

"What a handsome boy you are. Come closer so I can take a better look at you."

Daniel obeyed and sat on the chair beside the bed.

"I never thought I'd see you again, son. This is a real surprise." The man's face softened into a grin, the warmth in his voice throwing Daniel.

How can this man be Da? Got to say something... but what?

Daniel took a deep breath. "Da..." His voice faltered. He gulped. Caleb's hand on his shoulder helped steady him.

"It's okay, son. I know it's a shock." Da patted his hand. "I've seen the light. I'm not the same man anymore."

Daniel blinked his eyes. This was too much to take. He didn't know this man, and he had no idea how to respond. Da was a drunkard. A bully. This man was neither.

God, please help me. This is too hard.

"Da, Daniel lives in England. He's married and has a little boy."

A faint smile grew on Da's face and his eyes lit up. "Is that right, son? You'll have to bring them in." He coughed and wheezed. "I'm sorry, son. This body, it's giving way on me." Another coughing bout interrupted them.

He didn't look good, that was for sure. *How long did Caleb say he had left?* Daniel recalled his words...

"If he doesn't get a liver transplant, he's probably only got three or four weeks..."

Not very long at all. But this wasn't Da. He didn't know this man. How could Da have changed that much?

"I'm glad you came, son." Da's breathing was slow and measured. "I don't deserve to see any of you. I was a terrible father." Another coughing bout interrupted him. "I'm truly sorry for the way I treated you and Mam." He struggled for breath, but continued anyway.

"I could blame the drink, but I won't." He paused, a far-away look in his eyes. Turning his head and looking directly at Daniel, he continued, "I was a bully, and the drink just made it worse. It's a pity I didn't see the light earlier, son. All those years, wasted." His eyes watered. Daniel gulped.

"You probably won't believe me when I say I'm sorry, son. And I don't blame you, but I am sorry. I don't deserve to be your Da."

Da was apologising? No way. Words like that could never come out of that drunkard's mouth. But it certainly sounded like it.

Daniel's heart thumped. Unable to move, let alone speak, he had to respond. But what would he say? *'It's okay, Da, what you did is forgiven and forgotten? Beating Mam until she couldn't move was nothing - it's okay?'* No, he wasn't ready to forgive and forget. Maybe he never would be. How could God ever expect him to do that?

"I'm sorry, I can't cope with this. I need to go." Daniel stood. Backing away, he cast another look at the emaciated stranger lying in the bed before fleeing for the sanctuary of the corridor.

What would Lizzy think? He'd let her down, but there was no way he'd let Da off that lightly. Da had destroyed their family, and now he says sorry, and it should be okay? *What a load of shite. 'Sorry God, I didn't mean that.'*

Daniel reached inside his pocket and took out a cigarette, ignoring the 'No Smoking' sign on the wall. His hands shook so much he had trouble lighting up. The first drag helped to calm him, and he inhaled slowly. He caught sight of Caleb coming out of the room and turned away. He'd let Caleb down too. He really was a failure.

"Hey there, Danny." Caleb placed his hand gently on Daniel's shoulder.

Daniel shrugged it off. "Just leave it, okay? I couldn't do it." He took another drag of his cigarette. "Let's get out of here."

"No problem, Danny."

So annoying how cool Caleb is about everything.

"Want to get a drink?"

Daniel shrugged. He couldn't care less. He'd blown it, and all he wanted to do was crawl into a hole and hide. Or punch someone. Da, probably. *That pathetic git of a man. How dare he apologise!*

Caleb started the car and drove a short distance before pulling up in front of a snack bar.

"This do?"

"Guess so." *A pub would be better.*

Daniel climbed out of the car and followed Caleb inside.

"What'll it be?" The young girl behind the counter stood waiting, chewing gum and looking bored.

"A chocolate milkshake and a pastie for me. How about you, Danny?"

He didn't care. But no use taking his frustration out on Caleb and this girl. Sighing, he pulled himself together.

"The same, thanks."

Daniel followed Caleb to a table in the corner of the shop. He leaned back and crossed his arms, staring at the grubby red and white plastic tablecloth.

"It was a shock, wasn't it, seeing him like that?"

Daniel glanced up and considered his reply. Not only had Da changed, but Caleb had too. It'd been a mistake coming back. He didn't know any of his family anymore. Lizzy and Dillon were his family now - he should be with them. But how could he face Lizzy? He'd failed. Let her down. Let God down. Let himself down.

He lowered his head and squeezed back the tears stinging his eyes. It was too much. Paul had told him to face his challenges head on, and to lean on God for strength and wisdom. He thought he'd tried. Maybe he hadn't truly let go. He'd been so determined to hate Da. But that's not what God wanted, of that Daniel was now certain. But it rankled so much. He clenched his fists. What right did Da have to come back and upend everything? That git's intrusion into his new life with Lizzy and

Dillon wasn't welcome. But it was real, and had to be faced. Daniel took a deep breath and looked up.

"Yes." Daniel held Caleb's gaze. "You warned me, but I didn't believe you. That man wasn't Da."

"You're right. He's not the Da we remember, that's for sure." Caleb lifted his gaze to the young girl placing the milkshakes and pasties on the table. "Thank you, love."

She smiled and walked away slowly, her hips swaggering a little too much.

"You'd better tell me about him. Now I've seen him for myself, I need to know how he got to be like that so I can try to understand." Daniel sat straighter in his seat.

"No problem." Caleb took a long suck of his milkshake. "After he left, he hit the grog pretty hard, and he can't remember much of those years. He lived on the streets mainly, and was in and out of rehab, but he always went back to the bottle." Caleb took another slurp before continuing. "About twelve months ago a street worker took an interest in him and convinced him to dry out for good. Not sure how it happened, but I guess Da was sick of his life, and agreed to go to the centre. They helped him get off the grog for good. He said it was the hardest thing he's ever done, and he almost gave in, but he's been off the drink now for almost a year. Sometime during all that, he found God."

Daniel shook his head and glanced out the window before looking back to Caleb. He narrowed his eyes and sighed.

"That's what I don't understand. How can a person who's lived a life like that, who beat his wife and kids, and has been a drunk all his life, suddenly say they've found God, and then everything's supposed to be okay?"

"That's exactly what Grace says. She won't accept he's changed. I keep telling her to check for herself, but she won't. But you saw him. He's different. You can't deny that."

No, Daniel couldn't deny Da was different. But it might be a put on. He didn't trust the man.

"I don't buy it. He was certainly different. But I reckon he could be faking it. He must want something."

Caleb shook his head. "I don't think he does. I've been seeing him now for a few months and haven't noticed anything to make me think he's pretending. He really does seem genuine."

"So we're supposed to say it's alright, and let him back into our lives, after all he did?"

Caleb took a deep breath and held Daniel's gaze.

"I can't tell you what you should do, Danny, but that's what I've done. As a Christian, I believe God wants me to do that. Especially since Da's asked for our forgiveness, and he seems to genuinely mean it. It'd be wrong of me to not forgive him."

That's exactly what Lizzy said I should do. Daniel sighed heavily.

"I'm not ready to forgive, Caleb. I'm sorry. Maybe because I'm a new Christian and I'm still learning, but it's all too quick. I don't see how a person can just say they're sorry and then get let off the hook for everything they've done."

"But isn't that what happened when we became Christians? We're all guilty of bad stuff, Danny, but God forgave us, regardless of what we'd done. There really isn't any difference. And besides, he's already paid a hefty price. He lost his family."

"But how do we know he means it?"

"We don't. Only God knows what's in a man's heart. But *we're* in the wrong if we don't forgive."

Caleb was right. But he couldn't do it. Not yet.

"I need a smoke."

Caleb pushed his chair back. "Let's take a walk along the river."

Strolling along the edge of the River Lagan, memories of when he and Colin came down here as lads flitted once again through Daniel's mind. Last he'd heard, Colin had left the estate and moved to the other side of town. Maybe he should look Colin up – shouldn't be that hard to find him.

"Just like old times, hey Danny?"

Daniel turned his head and caught Caleb's eyes before letting out a small chuckle.

"Yeah. Nothing much has changed." Daniel opened his cigarette packet and offered one to Caleb.

Caleb hesitated, but then took one. "Caity won't be happy." He leaned forward while Daniel lit it for him.

"Special occasion." A slow grin grew on Daniel's face.

Caleb chuckled, his whole face expanding into a beaming smile. "Yes, it is." He threw his arm around Daniel's shoulders.

"So what's it like being back?"

Daniel exhaled slowly, blowing puffs of smoke into the air.

"Strange. Very strange. Not sure what to make of it all, to be honest. Have you ever thought of leaving?"

"Nah. Too hard. And Caity wouldn't leave her family. Can't imagine living anywhere else."

"Don't know if I could move back. Too many memories." Daniel took a long drag on his cigarette and stared at the river. A barge, laden with assorted drums, chugged slowly upstream towards the city docks.

"You've done good for yourself, Danny. Looks like you've landed on your feet. Lizzy's something special."

Daniel laughed and shook his head. "I'm still amazed she married me."

"Look after her, man. She's a good one."

"You're telling me? I almost lost her. I was an eejit. You know, I could've easily turned out like Da." Daniel gulped. The image of Da's emaciated body sent a shiver down his spine. Would have been him in years to come if God hadn't touched his life when He did. If only Da had 'seen the light' earlier.

A wave of pity floated over Daniel's heart and tugged at his conscience. Maybe he should go back and see Da. Daniel took a deep breath. *Tomorrow. Maybe.*

"Come on, man. Let's get back to our girls." Caleb clapped his hand on Daniel's back.

Daniel stubbed out his cigarette and nodded. God was at work, but would he have the strength to do what was being asked of him?

Passing a bin, Daniel took the packet of cigarettes from his pocket and threw it in. "There weren't many left anyway."

CHAPTER 8

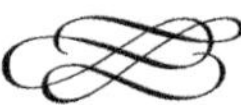

As Daniel entered the living room, Lizzy studied him carefully. Had it gone well? She'd hoped Daniel would be relaxed and happy, but he walked slowly, his shoulders sagging, and his eyes dull. Lizzy's heart fell. There it was again. She'd expected everything to be sorted straight away. *When would she learn?* Hadn't she prayed that God would let him go at his own speed?

Her heart ached for him. She walked towards him, and brushing the hair from his forehead with her fingertips, placed a gentle kiss on his lips.

"Are you okay?" Lizzy searched Daniel's eyes, trying to read what was going on inside him.

Daniel placed his hands on her hips and held her gaze.

"Getting there. Slowly." Pulling her close, he hugged her tightly. The tension in his body eased as she caressed his back with her fingertips.

"Thank you, Liz." He pulled away and held her at arm's length. Her pulse quickened as he leaned forward and kissed her.

Caitlin appeared from the kitchen holding two mugs of steaming hot coffee.

"Oh, I'm sorry! Didn't mean to interrupt… just thought you might like these." She let out a small laugh as she placed the mugs on the coffee table.

"Thanks Caity." Lizzy smiled fondly, and then, after taking a deep breath to steady herself, moved away from Daniel and picked Dillon up from his bouncer.

"Any plans for the rest of the day?" Caleb asked of no-one in particular.

"We can catch a bus into town and show Lizzy the city." Caitlin pulled the curtain back and glanced out the window. "The weather's not too bad."

Lizzy looked at Daniel and lifted her eyebrow. Was it safe to wander around Belfast? Hadn't he said there was still trouble?

Daniel turned his head to Caitlin. "Sounds good, Caitlin, but Lizzy's worried about how safe it is."

Lizzy narrowed her eyes and glared at him. "Daniel! Thanks for that!"

Caitlin chuckled. "It's okay, Lizzy. Most people think that way. It's true. There are problem areas, and you do have to be careful, but generally, everyone just goes about their business as normal. Promise we'll bring you home in one piece."

Lizzy smiled, relieved offense hadn't been taken. "That would be nice, then. I'd like to see Belfast. Have I got time to feed Dillon?"

"Yes, go ahead. Easier to feed him here," Caitlin replied with another chuckle. "I'll get the girls ready while you sort him."

HALF AN HOUR LATER, the group stood at the bus stop at the end of the street. Lizzy's heart warmed at the sight of Daniel carrying Dillon in a pouch on his front. You couldn't ask for a more doting father. Daniel loved Dillon with all his heart. Almost too much, if that were possible. Memories of little baby Rachel must be floating through his mind now he was back here, near where he'd lived with her and Ciara all those years ago. Nessa said Daniel had doted on the baby girl too, but rarely since Dillon's birth had he mentioned her. Would he say anything about them? Would he point out the house where they lived? Would he want to visit their graves?

His mind must be a jumble of thoughts and memories. Lizzy took his hand as they sat together in the bus and leaned in close. She caught his eye and smiled. This trip was good for him. Confronting the past and letting go of all the hurt and sadness would free him to move forward if he allowed God in. She prayed he would, *but in his time, not mine...* That was the difficult bit.

If only the visit with his Da had gone better. But at least Daniel had said he might go back again tomorrow. That was promising. Warmth radiated through Lizzy's body, and she smiled to herself. Life was good. She gazed out the window and took in the run down area they were passing through. They'd had such different upbringings, she and Daniel. But it could have been so different. It was only Father's inheritance that had resulted in her being brought up with privilege. In fact, if he hadn't inherited, Father probably would have married Mathew's mother. What a strange thought! Really weird how things happen. How just a moment in time can change everything.

Lizzy's musings came to an abrupt end when the bus driver slammed on the brakes, throwing all the passengers forward in their seats. She held on tightly as the tyres squealed and the bus skidded out of control. Her heart thumped, waiting for the bus to come to a stop. When it did, the sound of shattering glass and passengers' screams sickened her. Throughout the bus, pandemonium reigned.

Her head hurt. She reached up and touched it. Must have hit the steel bar on the seat in front. A huge lump had appeared, but apart from that, she was okay. No broken bones or blood. She reached over to Daniel. Blood oozed from his head.

Lizzy's heart raced. "Daniel! Are you alright?" She wrapped her arms around him. *He has to be. How could this have happened?*

Daniel reached up slowly and felt his head. When he pulled his hand away, it was covered in blood.

"Here, take this. Hold it against your head." Lizzy handed him one of Dillon's nappies and helped him press it against his temple. Dillon was screaming. How he hadn't been hurt was a miracle. Daniel must have shielded him, but he wasn't responding now to Dillon at all. Daniel just sat, staring ahead in a daze. Lizzy helped him sit back in the seat and carefully extracted Dillon from the pouch.

"Oh my little man." Lizzy showered Dillon with kisses and tried to calm him. His little face was distraught. "It's okay, Dillon. There, there. We're safe." Lizzy cradled him in her arms and rocked him back and forth, gently caressing his head with her hand. Her heart raced, but she had to hold herself together for his sake.

In the few moments Lizzy had spent settling Dillon, Daniel had recovered and had moved forward to check on Caleb, Caitlin and the girls. Lizzy inched her way across the seat to reach them as well. Sirens wailing in the distance sent shivers through her body. Glass was strewn everywhere. She had to be careful. When she finally managed to pull herself forward, what she saw made her ill. The front of the bus had crumpled, and she couldn't see the passengers in the front seat. Tara and Imogen had been in those seats.

Caitlin crawled on hands and knees through the debris, trying to reach the girls. Lizzy's heart went out to her. She couldn't imagine the terror Caitlin would be feeling. Caleb was in front, Lizzy could just see his back. At least they were okay. *But what about the girls?*

"Daniel..." Lizzy held her hand out. When he turned, her eyes sought his. She needed his arms around her. He inched his way back and pulled her tight. She sobbed into his chest. "Thank you." Lizzy tilted her head and searched his eyes. "Are the girls okay?"

Daniel's eyes held grave concern. "I don't know, Liz. It doesn't look good."

Lizzy pushed back her tears, her stomach clenched with dread. She took a deep breath. "Let's go to them, Daniel." She glanced forward to Caitlin and Caleb who were both reaching into the space on the floor under the seat where Tara and Imogen had been sitting.

The wail from Caitlin sent chills through Lizzy's spine. *No, God. Please no. Let them be okay.*

LIZZY GRABBED Daniel's hand tighter as they made their way together through the debris strewn all around. Caitlin sat on the floor, reaching out to Imogen who lay on the floor under the seat, limp, lifeless and covered in blood. Caleb held Tara in his arms. Her eyes were open, but her face was bruised and bloody.

Lizzy bent down and wrapped her free arm around Caitlin's shoulders and prayed. "Oh God, be with Caity and precious little Imogen. Comfort her, I pray. Wrap them in Your arms. Oh God, please help them. Give them strength."

The wail of sirens stopped, and a woman in a blue uniform appeared. She moved Caitlin out of the way and reached for Imogen. The woman glanced back at her partner and yelled for oxygen. Gaining access, the paramedic felt for a pulse.

Lizzy reached for Caitlin's hand and gave it a gentle squeeze.

"Stay positive, Caity," Lizzy whispered into her ear. *Oh God, let Imogen be okay.*

The paramedic worked on Imogen as Lizzy held Caitlin tightly. Daniel reached down and took Dillon. Lizzy caught his eyes and unspoken words passed between them, memories of Daniel's near death experience so fresh in her mind. As the paramedics worked, time stood still as life and death hung in the balance.

All around, other passengers tried to escape the wrecked bus, some on their own and others with help, but for Lizzy and Caitlin, the only thing they heard were the words of the paramedic, "She's going to be alright."

Caitlin sobbed into Lizzy's chest as tears welled in her own eyes. *Thank You God. Thank You.*

"WE'LL HAVE to take her to hospital, but she's going to be alright." The paramedic gave Caitlin a warm smile as she squeezed her arm. "Would you like to come?"

Caitlin nodded, her eyes glistening.

She tried to stand, but was unsteady. Daniel caught her before she fell. The door of the bus had crumpled. The only way out was through the front where the windscreen had shattered, leaving a gaping hole. Caitlin followed the paramedics who'd placed Imogen on a stretcher, and was helped out by several men who'd come to the rescue.

Police cars, ambulances and firetrucks surrounded the bus and the car it had collided with. Lizzy gulped as she looked at the crumpled mess. No-one could have survived.

A waiting ambulance whisked Caitlin and Imogen away, leaving Lizzy, Daniel and Caleb, standing, dazed and in shock, on the pavement. They were all attended to, with temporary bandages applied where necessary. A nearby cafe provided hot cups of tea.

Clinging to her daddy, Tara refused to allow anyone to look at her injuries.

"Come on Tara, it's okay. They just want to clean you up," Caleb said, but she hid her face in his neck and sobbed.

Lizzy stroked her head. "Tara, are you okay, sweetie?" Lizzy leaned in close and lifted Tara's chin. "Your mummy and sister are going to be alright, sweetheart. Is that what you're worried about?"

Tara nodded, her big brown eyes full of fear and uncertainty. Blood from her face had smudged Caleb's shirt. One of the cuts on her face looked quite deep.

"Will you let me clean your face?" Lizzy asked. "Make it all pretty again?"

Tara nodded slowly and allowed Lizzy to take her from her daddy. Lizzy sat down and placed Tara beside her. A paramedic handed Lizzy a swab, and Lizzy gently wiped the blood off Tara's face. She also picked out the small slithers of glass stuck in Tara's hair.

"Show me your hands, sweetie." Tara reluctantly opened her hands and Lizzy cleaned them with a fresh swab. "There you are princess. All clean!"

Tara lifted her head, her big brown eyes melting Lizzy's heart. Lizzy forced back the tears pricking her eyes and gave Tara a gentle squeeze. Dillon had settled, and Daniel appeared unharmed now his cut was bandaged. Caleb, too, appeared to have escaped unharmed. Such a miracle.

As Lizzy stood, her head spun and she broke out in a sweat. Without any warning, she vomited on the road. She couldn't breathe. Daniel was talking, but his voice came to her as if through a tunnel.

His arms were around her, warm, safe and strong, and then a blanket was placed over her, but she was cold, oh so cold, and she couldn't stop shivering. *So sick... God, what's happening?*

The next thing Lizzy was aware of was being sat up and having her blood pressure taken. Everything was hazy. It was still daylight, and people still scurried around.

She grabbed Daniel's hand and looked into his eyes. Her breathing had steadied. "What happened, Daniel?"

"You went into shock, Lizzy." Daniel gently brushed her hair with his hand, his eyes filled with love and concern.

"Oh..." Lizzy leaned her head on his shoulder and gazed around. Slowly, it all came back. She bolted upright, her heart thumping.

"Tara. Where's Tara?"

"She's with Caleb, just beside you. She's okay, Lizzy, no need to worry. Here my darling, take a sip." Daniel held a cup to her lips. The hot sweet liquid slid down her throat, warming, calming.

"I don't believe that happened. I feel so embarrassed, Daniel."

"Don't be, Liz. We've all had a shock." Daniel hugged her gently as she leaned against him.

Lizzy reached for Dillon and rocked him in her arms, her heart breaking with love for him. What would she have done if something had happened to him? No, she couldn't even think about that.

In Lizzy's arms, Dillon squealed and kicked. Lizzy fought back tears as she rocked him. The more she relaxed, the calmer he became. So much a part of her. She kissed the top of his head and closed her eyes, calm settling deep in her soul. *Thank You so much God for looking after us all.*

"Dillon's fine, Liz," Daniel said, pulling her close. "We're all fine."

Lizzy lifted her head, searching his eyes. "Yes, we are." She drew in a deep breath. "I pray Imogen pulls through." Tears pricked her eyes.

"She's in good hands, Lizzy."

"Yes." Lizzy straightened herself. "I feel very thankful, Daniel. It could have been so much worse. If I'd lost either of you after all we've been through..."

"Hush, Lizzy." He kissed her cheek and pulled her closer.

Sitting there on the pavement, wrapped in Daniel's arms, and surrounded by what could only be described as a disaster zone, Lizzy wondered at the irony of it all. Only a short while ago she'd been worried about walking around Belfast for fear of being bombed, but here they were, lucky to be alive after a traffic accident. She snuggled closer to Daniel. Life was so precious and unpredictable. Her heart filled with love for her husband and little boy, and for God who had brought them together and had kept them safe.

. . .

LIZZY LOOKED up as a young red-headed paramedic bent down.

"You worried us there for a second." He took her arm and checked her pulse.

"I feel fine now." Lizzy gave him a warm smile as she straightened herself.

"You seem okay, but you both need to get checked out properly, just in case."

The paramedic stood and reached out a hand to help Daniel up.

"Thank you. We will." Daniel helped Lizzy to stand, quickly placing his arm around her when she wobbled.

"You can go to hospital in an ambulance, but you'll need to wait, unless you can get there by yourselves..."

"We'll be right." Caleb appeared with Tara still clinging to him. "I've just called my sister - she'll be here shortly."

WITHIN MINUTES, Grace pulled up in her red sports car. All eyes turned towards her as her long shapely legs peeled out of the tiny car. Elegantly dressed in a navy blue designer suit with stilettos to match and her make-up and hair coiffed perfectly, she looked very much out of place amongst the mayhem.

Her eyes widened as she surveyed the scene. Stepping around the glass and other debris scattered everywhere, Grace headed straight for the small family group huddled together on the pavement. She stopped in front of Caleb and wrapped her arms around him and Tara.

"Thank goodness you're alright." Grace's voice faltered and she brushed tears from her eyes.

She straightened, and then turned to Daniel, hugging him tightly.

"This is terrible, Danny. Are you okay?" Her eyes went straight to the cut on his forehead.

"Yes, I'm fine, thanks, Grace." He smiled appreciatively.

"Come on, let's get you to hospital." Grace ushered them all towards her car.

"We're not all going to fit. Take Caleb and Tara first, Grace - there's no hurry for us," Daniel said, taking Lizzy's hand.

Caleb gave Daniel a bear hug and clung a little longer than normal. Caleb's hands shook and his eyes twitched. *He must be so worried about Imogen...*

"Thanks Danny." Caleb let go of Daniel and then walked towards the car with Tara still in his arms.

"We'll be praying for you..." Lizzy called out as they reached the car. Her voice caught in her throat, and her eyes filled with tears.

As Caleb turned and caught her gaze, his pinched face made her gulp. *What if Imogen doesn't make it?*

Daniel placed his arm around Lizzy's shoulder as the sports car roared off. She leaned in to him. "He must be so worried, Daniel."

LEFT ALONE, Daniel and Lizzy sat on the pavement clinging to each other. What if he'd lost her? He couldn't imagine life without Lizzy now, after everything they'd been through. Daniel's heart hurt with love for her. Lizzy, the most precious thing to come into his life, ever. Lizzy, his best friend, his lover, his companion. *No way do I deserve her, but oh God, I'm so thankful You brought her into my life.*

Deep in Daniel's soul, an overwhelming ache grew. God had done so much for him, and once again, he'd failed. What kind of person walks out on their own father, especially on his death bed? Da had been so humble and honest, so different to what Daniel had expected.

But I threw it all in his face. I rejected his plea for forgiveness. How could I have done that? What kind of person am I?

A hard lump formed in his throat, and a wave of nausea rose from within. His breath came fast and hard, he shivered, but sweat beads formed on his forehead. He let go of Lizzy's hand. He'd never felt so sick in his life. Not even when he'd been drunk. But it wasn't physical sickness - his soul was ill. Daniel hung his head between his knees as sobs racked his body. *Oh God, I'm so sorry. I'm sorry... please forgive me...*

Lizzy placed her arm over him and held him. He was so ashamed... *how could I have done that? God forgave me for everything, and so has Lizzy. She didn't need to. She could have just left me in a heap. That's what I deserved. And yet, she stood by me, nursed me, loved me when I didn't deserve it. Despite all the love and forgiveness shown to me, I couldn't forgive my own Da. What a pathetic person I am.*

Oh God... what have I done? More heart wrenching sobs tore through Daniel's body. Lizzy's arms tightened around him. His chest heaved. *Need to make this right, God... please help me.*

Resting in Lizzy's arms, Daniel's breathing slowly steadied. He knew what he had to do.

Daniel gulped and inhaled deeply before lifting his head. He gazed into Lizzy's eyes.

"I'm so sorry, Liz."

"Daniel, it's alright." Her eyes glistened with tears as she ran her fingers down his cheek.

"I'm not sure what happened... it all just hit me ... Da, you, this accident..."

"Shh, my love, it's okay." Lizzy pulled him close and rocked him like a baby. He clung to her.

"I love you, Liz. With all my heart, I love you."

"I know that Daniel. I love you with all my heart, too." She pulled him closer and there he remained, cocooned in Lizzy's arms until Dillon interrupted, demanding attention.

"Are you okay, Daniel?" Lizzy asked as she straightened herself and sat Dillon on her lap.

Daniel took a moment as he considered his reply. Yes, he was okay.

Inside he was calmer, and confident that God would give him the strength to do what needed to be done.

He nodded slowly as Grace's car turned the corner and came to a halt beside them.

As Grace slid out and closed the door, Daniel drew in a deep breath. In those few minutes, God had done something deep inside him, and as he looked at Grace, dressed to impress, beautiful, intelligent and world-wise, his heart went out to her. *Yes, she might appear to have everything, Lord, but she needs You. Just like I need You.*

Before he made a move, Daniel squeezed Lizzy's hand and caught her eye. They were in this together, and God was with them. And for that, he was eternally grateful.

CHAPTER 9

"You really have done alright, sis," Daniel said as he and Lizzy entered Grace's apartment on the fourth floor of an ultra-sleek complex not far from the city centre. Through the expansive glass sliding doors leading out to a large balcony, the city sprawled into the distance. On the inside, the living room was furnished elegantly, but was clinical, like a hotel room, not a home. Everything was modern and crisp, but lacked any warmth or personal touch. The lone photograph on a shelf in the kitchen of Caleb, Caitlin and the two girls was the only indication a real person lived here.

"I've worked jolly hard, and it's mortgaged to the hilt." Grace placed her handbag on the marble kitchen bench and turned the kettle on. "What can I get you?"

"Just a cup of tea, thanks Grace. I'm still feeling a little off," Lizzy said, handing Dillon back to Daniel. "May I use your bathroom?"

"Of course, Lizzy. Just through here." Grace showed Lizzy to the bathroom, and then returned to the kitchen.

"I wish she'd stayed in overnight," Daniel said quietly. "Lizzy's so stubborn sometimes."

"I'm sure if they were worried they would've made her stay."

Daniel sighed heavily. "Guess so, but I'm still worried." He lifted Dillon onto his shoulder and rubbed the baby's back.

"How did your visit go with Da?" Grace took three china mugs from the shelf above the bench and placed them in front of her before settling her gaze on Daniel's. Her eyes held a smirk that churned his stomach.

The question he'd been dreading… Daniel pulled a stool from under the bench and sat, pondering how best to reply. How could he admit he'd stomped out when he wanted to be a witness of God's love to Grace? What would she think of him? *If only I'd been prepared to forgive Da this morning…* Sighing deeply, Daniel tried to steady the thoughts swirling in his head. *Lord God, what do I tell her?*

The truth...

Daniel gulped. Where had that come from? *The truth?* Daniel took a deep slow breath and held Grace's gaze. He had to answer. An empty feeling grew in the pit of his stomach. *God, You need to give me the words...*

His heart pounded. *Okay, here goes...* He swallowed hard. "I have to be honest, Grace, I didn't handle it too well." Daniel shifted in his seat. "Caleb had warned me about what to expect, but I wasn't prepared." He paused, holding her gaze. "Grace, you might not believe this, but Da apologised."

"I wouldn't believe a word that came out of that decrepit man's mouth." Grace spat the words with such vehemence it threw Daniel. His eyebrows furrowed. What was going on? Had something else happened he wasn't aware of?

"Yes, well, I didn't believe him either. I couldn't tie together the man we knew as Da, and the man lying in that bed." Daniel closed his eyes tightly, and pulled his mind from the past to the present.

Shifting in his seat, Daniel rocked Dillon in his arms. The baby was restless and had started to whimper. *Come on, Lizzy...*

He lifted his head and looked straight into Grace's eyes. "I couldn't handle it, Grace, and I raced out of the room without speaking to him."

Daniel's voice caught in his throat. "I feel so ashamed." He paused and inhaled deeply. "I've had time to think, though, and I've decided to go back tomorrow and make it right." He gulped. There, he'd said it...

Grace rolled her eyes and shook her head. "Don't tell me Caleb's been in your ear with all his religious nonsense. He's gone soft, he has."

Daniel slumped a little on his stool. "What's happened to you, Grace? You never used to be so cynical." His heart went out to her. She'd been hurt, that was obvious. *But will she talk to me?*

Their eyes locked. Daniel held his breath.

"Just...things."

"Like what? You can talk to me, Grace. You know that."

Grace busied herself with making tea.

Daniel reached out his hand and grabbed her arm. As she lifted her eyes, a lone tear rolled down her cheek. He reached out and pulled her towards him as Lizzy reappeared. Grace quickly wiped the tear away and patted her hair before turning to face Lizzy as if nothing had happened.

"Feel better?" The smile planted on Grace's face was too cheerful.

"Yes, thanks. I couldn't believe what a wreck I looked." Lizzy let out a small laugh as she took Dillon from Daniel's arms.

Had she noticed Grace's tears?

"There, there, little man. Look at you! You need some cleaning up too if that smell's anything to go by." Lizzy sat on the leather couch, placing Dillon on her lap. "Is it okay to change him here, Grace, or would you rather somewhere else?"

"There's fine, Lizzy. No problem."

"What kind of law do you practice, Grace?" Daniel asked, settling back on his stool. A change of topic was needed.

"I work for the Prosecutor's Office as a junior barrister."

"You'd be good at that." Daniel let out a small chuckle and smiled teasingly at Grace. He wouldn't like to be prosecuted by her, that was for sure.

"I do alright. Should make senior barrister in the next year or so."

"Never thought of changing sides?"

Grace gave a mirthless laugh. "And what, help all those criminals get off? No way."

"Hit a touchy point there…"

Grace shot him a wry look and placed her mug on the bench.

"You wouldn't believe the cases that come through. Some sick people out there."

"I know. But some of them just need help. Like me." Daniel gulped as the memory of his most recent court appearance flashed through his mind. "I have no doubt I'd be in jail right now if it wasn't for my lawyer. Instead, I got put on probation and landed this amazing job. It was a real answer to prayer, wasn't it, Lizzy?"

Lizzy nodded and smiled, her eyes lighting up.

Grace sighed and shook her head in disgust. "How do you believe all that nonsense, Daniel? God doesn't answer prayer. Doubt he even exists."

Daniel let out a nervous laugh. "I know what you mean, Grace. I didn't think He existed until recently, but now, I know He does. I know it in here," Daniel said, placing his hand on his chest. His heart raced - he was completely out of his depth, but God was giving him the words, and he really did mean them. *If only Grace could see that.*

"Seems to me like religion has a lot to answer for. If God exists, why hasn't he stopped all the fighting?"

"That's the same question I asked for years. Lizzy helped me understand, didn't you, my love?"

Lizzy stood and joined Daniel and Grace, slipping her free arm around Daniel's waist.

"Yes, but it took a while. Not until you were ready to listen. Before then, it wouldn't have mattered what I'd said, you wouldn't have believed it." Lizzy's voice was calm and steady, and her eyes held warmth and sincerity.

"So what about our Da? Caleb says he's found God too." Grace narrowed her eyes. "Seems to me it's just a crutch for people to lean on when they can't sort themselves out." Grace faced Lizzy, her eyes widening as she reached out her hand and touched Lizzy lightly on the arm. "I didn't mean you, Lizzy. Sorry. But people like our Da, and even Caleb and Danny with their drink problems. They should be able to sort themselves out without leaning on a God that probably doesn't exist. I think they're just fooling themselves." Grace leaned against the bench and folded her arms.

"Everyone's entitled to their own view, Grace." Lizzy took a stool beside her. "But for many, faith in God is real, and it changes their lives. It's just unfortunate that religion has given God a bad name, and turned a lot of people away from seeing the real God. But nobody can force anyone else to believe." Lizzy lifted Dillon onto her shoulder and gently patted his back.

How does she talk so calmly?

"Believing comes from an open heart, Grace, and a desire for truth. Then, and only then, does everything start to make sense and God can be seen for who He really is." Lizzy's eyes lit up. "A God who's real, and loving and caring. But He never forces Himself on anyone. It's a personal choice, and religion has nothing to do with it."

Lizzy reached out and squeezed Grace's hand. "Sorry if I've preached to you, Grace - I didn't mean to come over like that." Lizzy's smile was genuine and warm. If Grace couldn't see that Lizzy really meant what she said, his sister really must have blinkers on.

Grace remained silent, seemingly lost for words. She picked up her mug and took a sip before replying.

"It's okay, Lizzy. You're right, I've just been turned off religion by all I've seen, even from when I was little and our Da would come home drunk and beat Mam. Mam believed, but look what good it did her." Grace's breathing quickened. "Our Da basically killed her. And all the religious hypocrites make me sick. I guess I've turned my back on religion and God, as I can't see that any good has ever come of it." She paused and steadied herself, then looked first at Lizzy, and then at Daniel. "But I do sense something different in you two. You seem genuine, Danny, but I'm not ready to even consider it. And don't ask me to go see our Da with you. I won't go."

Daniel chuckled. His sister was fiery, that was for sure. "Don't worry, sis, I won't."

"Good." Grace collected the empty mugs and placed them in the sink. "We'd better check if Caleb and Caitlin are ready to be picked up," she said, effectively changing the topic as she wiped the bench and tidied everything away.

GRACE COLLECTED Caleb and Tara from the hospital and dropped them at their home so Caleb could get his car. Imogen's injuries weren't life threatening, but the doctors wanted her to stay in hospital overnight, so Caleb planned to return with a change of clothes for both Caitlin and Imogen.

On her way back, Grace briefly stopped in at the Prosecutor's Office to tell them she wouldn't be back in that day, and possibly even the next. She had so much work to do, but needed to spend time with her family, especially after this accident. Grabbing some files, she squeezed them into her briefcase. She'd stay up all night if needed. Sleep was overrated.

The accident, though unfortunate, had provided more time to spend with Daniel and Lizzy. Such an odd couple, but somehow it worked. She could probably enjoy their company, *but not if they begin preaching.* Lizzy's words had touched a chord, but Grace didn't want to go there. She had everything she needed. A good job where she was highly in demand, her apartment and car, a few good friends, and enough money to do whatever she wanted. She lacked nothing, not even male company. Any number of young men were at her beck and call, and she did occasionally call, but not often. It didn't pay to let any of them think they had a chance. After her one serious relationship had ended badly, she now kept any interested men at arm's length.

Grace pulled up outside the local store to grab some supplies - she'd have to play hostess with Caitlin out of action, and she wasn't prepared. Most nights Grace would grab a take-out meal on the way home from work, or eat at her desk. By the time she finished each night, she was in no mood to cook. Besides, she didn't know how.

Entering the store, Grace grabbed a trolley and began to walk the aisles. *What do you feed your siblings and their partners? Meat and veg? Frozen pizza?* The more she looked, the more confused she became. She picked up some frozen meals and then promptly put them back. *Party pies, sausage rolls, frozen pasties....?* Her pulse quickened. *Have to get something...* After ten minutes, all her trolley held were drinks and crisps. *I can't do this.* She glanced at her watch. *Too long already - have to order in.* Her heart rate immediately steadied as she strode to the checkout.

"Having a party, love?" The middle aged woman behind the register glanced quickly at Grace as she rang through the bottles of Coca Cola and Fanta and the packets of crisps and sweets Grace had piled up.

"Kind of. Just a family gathering." Grace fidgeted with her purse and took out enough cash to pay the woman. She couldn't wait to get out of there. Reaching the car, Grace placed the bags on the front seat before climbing in and speeding off. She'd never get sick of the sound of her sports car, nor the heads it turned. She'd never fit into a normal life. Ever.

Moments later, Grace pulled up in the underground car park and headed upstairs, hesitating a moment to steady herself before opening the door. She'd need her wits if any of them started talking about God again. She steeled herself and opened the door.

"Grace, here, let me help with that." Daniel jumped up and took the bags out of Grace's hands as she struggled to get in.

"Thanks Danny." She'd half expected to see Aislin and Alana there, but breathed with relief when they weren't. Not that she didn't like them - she hardly knew them, but she wanted to spend more time with Danny & Lizzy. Something about the couple intrigued her. Maybe it was how well they got on. Rarely had she seen a relationship that worked, and where both partners were happy, but Daniel and Lizzy really seemed to like each other. Grace smiled to herself. Yes, that was it - they actually liked each other! And it was contagious. She felt immediately happier around them, even if they did talk about God. She'd just have to overlook that for now.

"Aislin and Alana not here?" Grace asked Daniel as she began to unpack the bags.

"No, just us. Lizzy's having a lie down with Dillon - the accident took it out of her. She's still feeling a little shaken."

"Maybe she should go back to the hospital."

"She won't go." Daniel pinched his lips together.

Grace stopped unpacking and leaned back against the bench, folding her arms. "I really like Lizzy. Make sure you look after her, Daniel."

"Planning on it, sis. Learned my lesson big time, and I'm not going to blow it."

"Glad to hear it." Grace gave a soft laugh. "Let's grab a drink and have a chat before everyone gets here. I'm going to have a gin and tonic… oh dear, maybe that's not a good choice, and I should just have coke."

"It's okay, Grace. If you want a G and T, have one. I'm learning to deal with it. Can't allow my problem with drink to affect everyone else."

"You sure?"

"Have what you want, Grace, it really is okay. But I'll have coke."

Leaning forward, Grace kissed him on the cheek. "Proud of you, Danny. If only our Da had your strength when he was younger." Lowering her eyes, Grace pushed down the growing ache in her chest. "Everything would have been so different if he hadn't drunk." Grace's voice caught, and tears stung her eyes. *Again.* Quickly turning, she grabbed some glasses from the shelf above as she tried to regain control.

"Grace, what's the matter? Look at me." As Daniel placed his hand gently on her shoulder and turned her slowly to face him, she fought hard to push back the unwanted tears.

"It's nothing. Really Danny, it's nothing." Grace stood stiffly and turned her head away, wiping her face with the back of her hand. *Drat Daniel for having this effect.* She hadn't shed this many tears in years, but just being with him revived memories she'd shoved to the back of her mind, never to be thought of again. But now they threatened to be her undoing.

As Daniel wrapped his arms around her, she lost control and convulsions racked her body. Her eyes burned from tears she'd refused to shed until now.

Daniel held her tight. "Grace, whatever it is, it's okay," he whispered quietly as she continued to sob uncontrollably.

Grace nodded, but it wasn't okay. *How can it ever be okay?* The ache in her heart wouldn't leave. But she could never talk about it. Aunt Hilda had made her promise. Had threatened her...

Drat you Daniel. Drat you! She pounded his chest.

Daniel grabbed her hands. "Whoa Grace! What's going on?"

She raised her head slightly. "Nothing."

"Right."

Grace slowly straightened and pulled herself together, wiping her face with a tissue Daniel gave her.

Daniel pulled back and lifted her chin. She avoided his eyes.

"If you don't want to talk about it now, Grace, it's fine. Lizzy and I are here for you, whenever you're ready, okay?"

Grace shrugged and turned her head. Her insides churned and her head hurt. *I'll never talk about it.*

She closed her eyes and inhaled deeply. Never again would she let this happen.

. . .

Moving away from Daniel, Grace headed straight for the drinks' cabinet and took out the bottle of gin. With her back to Daniel, she poured a measure, and then just a little more, before adding the tonic.

Daniel had grabbed a coke and was seated on the sofa. "Come on, Grace, come and join me." He held his hand out, his eyes soft and caring. How was she supposed to hold it together? No, she needed space.

"Come outside, Danny." Out there she could hide.

Leaning on the railing, Grace concentrated on the city lights. Breathing in the cool night air, she allowed the G and T to do its job. She had to regain control. She refused to let the others see her like this. The hardened, cool-headed lawyer no-one got close to, a blubbering mess? No. No-one would see her like that.

The doorbell rang. Grace downed the last of her drink and walked inside, pausing in front of the hallway mirror. Her face had lost its flush, but her eyes were still slightly puffy and red. No time for eye drops, she'd just have to get by. Lifting her chin, she took a deep breath before opening the door.

"There you are!" She flashed a warm smile at Caleb and Tara. "I was beginning to wonder where you were!" She inched back to let them through.

"Took a bit longer than planned, sorry Grace. Immi didn't want Tara to leave and I had to tear her away. Was a bit awkward."

"I should have brought Tara back with me. Sorry Caleb - I didn't think..." Grace looked up at Caleb apologetically before bending down and giving Tara a cuddle. It was true - she didn't think often enough when it came to things like that.

"No problem, Grace."

A moment later Lizzy reappeared with Dillon in her arms.

"Feel better, sweetie?" Daniel asked, reaching out for Dillon.

"Heaps, but my neck's a bit sore." Lizzy rubbed her neck and moved her head from side to side.

"Hope it's not whiplash, Lizzy," Grace said, standing up and joining her. "Might be best to get it checked."

"You may be right. I'll see how it is in the morning."

The doorbell rang again. This time it was Aislin and Alana, without their partners who'd been conveniently delayed at work. Although she felt a little guilty, Grace was relieved they hadn't come.

"Come in girls. Good to see you." Grace hugged each girl in turn and then offered them a drink.

Now they were all here, she'd take control and ensure her walls stayed up. Because that's what she did. Even with family.

DANIEL KEPT an eye on Grace all night. The small peek she'd allowed him into her real self had been unsettling. He'd seen an inkling the previous night, but he'd put most of that down to the excitement of meeting up again after all this time, not something deeper inside. Out of all his siblings, Grace had been his favourite. Sure, he and Caleb were close, and often it'd been left to them as the two eldest to do all the things Da should have done, but it was Grace he'd had the most connection with. They understood each other, even as children.

Daniel looked at her now. Talking with Lizzy, Aislin and Alana, Grace was confident and in control. Not an inkling of the breakdown he'd witnessed earlier in the evening. His heart ached for her. *Grace, what's going on?*

SOON AFTER, Caleb suggested they call it a night. Daniel was last out, and hung back to have a word with Grace.

"I'm going to see Da again tomorrow. Come with me, Grace. " He took her hand and held her gaze.

Grace shook her head, her lip twisting into a sardonic smile. "Sorry to let you down, big brother, but there's no way I'll ever see that man."

Daniel held up his hands. "Sorry - just thought I'd ask. Don't get all snarly."

Leaning forward, Daniel placed his hands gently on Grace's shoulders. "Grace, don't let whatever the problem is destroy you. Something's causing you pain. I don't have all the answers, but I know Someone who does, so please talk to me when you feel able."

Grace's eyes welled. Daniel pulled her close. "Promise me?"

Grace held herself erect and didn't respond.

Lying in bed that night, Daniel held Lizzy tightly. His body craved sleep, but his mind was once again active. His heart ached for Grace. It must have been horrible to be sent away as a young child. They'd never talked about how they all felt when Mam died. It wasn't the done thing. With no parents to care for them, they'd been told to be grateful they had family willing to take them in. They could have all been sent to a children's home. *Might've been better if we had...*

Daniel knew how he coped. He'd turned to drink. What had Grace done to survive those years? What had happened to her heart and mind? A twelve year old girl needed her mother. Had Aunt Hilda understood that and helped her, or had she just told Grace to 'get on', the most common way local folk had of dealing with life? Would she ever let her guard down long enough to allow him, or anyone else, into her tightly walled life? Would she open her heart to God's love and healing?

Daniel nuzzled Lizzy's neck. "We need to pray for Grace."

"Mmm. Yes, we do." Yawning, Lizzy wriggled and stretched, then pulled herself up slowly and turned on the bedside lamp. "You really feel for her, don't you, Daniel?"

"I do, Lizzy. I've never felt like this before. It's like God's opened the eyes of my heart, and I can feel her hurt. I just want to help her, Liz."

Lizzy squeezed his hand. "I know. And I think it's wonderful. God's working in your life, Daniel, I see it with my own eyes, and it makes me so happy."

Daniel pulled her close and kissed the top of her head as she leaned into him.

"I'm sure He'll use you to help bring Grace to Himself, when she's ready," Lizzy said, peering into his eyes.

Daniel slumped and let out a slow breath.

"I know, but I want her ready now."

Lizzy chuckled quietly.

"I know what that's like!"

"Let's pray for her, Liz."

They joined hands and prayed that the Holy Spirit would soften Grace's heart and that she'd be open to God's healing touch. They prayed she'd hand over all the hurt from the past to Him, and learn to live in the freedom of new life in Jesus.

Lizzy hugged Daniel and wiped the tears rolling down his cheeks with a tissue.

"What about your Da, Daniel? Are you going to see him again?"

Daniel leaned back and took a deep breath.

"Yes, I am, Liz. God's been pricking my conscience all day, ever since I walked out of his room. I think I'm ready to forgive him." Daniel gulped. Never had he expected to hear those words come out of his mouth. "I've finally understood what you and Paul have been telling me all along. That absolutely everyone's a sinner, and that no-one deserves God's forgiveness. And that it doesn't matter how old they are, what they've done, what their life was like before, God's love and forgiveness is open to them. So, if Da has asked for my forgiveness, I need to let go of the hate I have for him, and try to see him as God does. A sinner, just like me, who's been forgiven. I don't think it'll be easy, but I'm prepared to try. It hit me today when I was talking with Caleb, that Da's already paid for all the bad things he did. He lost his family, and he lost his health. He basically lost his whole life."

Daniel turned his head and gazed into Lizzy's eyes.

"I'm so glad you stood by me, Liz, and that you didn't give up on me. If I'd lost you, I think I would have killed myself. But because of you, I've got new life in Jesus, and I've got the most beautiful wife and son a man could ever wish for."

Lizzy wrapped her arms around Daniel and held him. His body relaxed, and now he'd finally made the decision, he felt at peace with himself and with God.

CHAPTER 10

Daniel stirred in his sleep. *Was someone calling?* He turned over. Must be dreaming.

"Daniel." There it was again. Someone was calling out and knocking on the door.

Daniel sat up, immediately alert. *Caleb, and he sounds distressed.* Lizzy stirred. He peered at the bedside clock. Five am. What was Caleb doing, waking him so early? Dillon wasn't even awake yet.

Slipping out of bed, Daniel pulled on his robe and tiptoed to the door, opening it quietly before slipping out.

Caleb stood in the hallway, rubbing his arms and bouncing on his feet.

"What's up, Caleb?" Daniel whispered, pulling his robe tighter.

"The hospital just called. Da's body's shutting down." Caleb's voice faltered, and his face, in the pale pre-dawn light, was ashen.

Daniel felt faint. *No! This can't be happening.* Not now, not when he'd just made up his mind to see Da. *God, what are You doing?*

"Did they say how long he has?"

"No, but they said to come quickly, so it mustn't be long."

"We'd better go then. I'll tell Lizzy - she can stay with Tara."

Daniel crept back into the bedroom, trying not to disturb Dillon, and gently shook Lizzy.

Lizzy's eyes snapped open, and she pulled herself up, grabbing Daniel's arm.

"What's the matter, Daniel? Is Dillon okay?"

"Yes, it's not Dillon - it's Da."

Lizzy's eyes widened.

"Is he…?"

"No, but the hospital said to come quickly." Daniel forced down the lump in his throat. "Are you okay to mind Tara? We'll call as soon as we know anything."

"Sure, sweetie." She squeezed his arm. "Are you alright, Daniel?"

"I'm not sure. If anything happens and I don't get to speak to him, I don't know what I'll do." Daniel raked a hand through his hair. "I need to go, Liz." He quickly threw on his jeans and a clean T-shirt. Grabbing his jacket, he leaned over and kissed Lizzy gently on the top of her head.

She reached for his hand and looked up as he stood. "I'll be praying for you both."

Her words tugged at his heart.

"Thanks…" Daniel's voice trembled. He swallowed hard as he bent over and touched Dillon's cheek with his back of his hand. The baby had stirred and opened his eyes. Love for his little son flooded through Daniel. Had Da ever looked at him this way? *Unlikely.*

He kissed Lizzy again and then joined Caleb downstairs. Caleb looked as distressed as Daniel felt. How could he be feeling this way about a man who until yesterday he hadn't seen for almost twenty years, and who he'd only held bitterness and hate for? Now, with the very real possibility Da might die before they got there, a deep sense of loss already sat heavily on his soul.

"Come on man, let's go." Caleb pulled Daniel out of his thoughts and opened the door. Exiting quickly to stop the chill of the early morning air creeping inside, Daniel pulled the door closed and followed Caleb to the car. Caleb pumped the pedal several times before turning the ignition. The Escort sprang to life, the sound of the engine reviving memories of his and Lizzy's Escort. The one he wrecked. Daniel gulped and closed his eyes. It was all too much. *God, I don't know how to handle this.*

Caleb manoeuvred out of the tight car park before heading off down the street shrouded in semi-darkness.

"Planned on seeing him today." Daniel glanced at Caleb before returning his gaze to the slow moving traffic ahead, the red tail lights barely visible through the heavy fog.

"Thought you might. Bad timing, hey?"

Daniel slumped in his seat and sighed. "Yeah, could say that." He lifted his head. "Can he get a new liver?"

Caleb stared straight ahead and gripped the steering wheel tighter. "Doesn't want one."

Daniel's head jerked up. "What? He doesn't want one? Why not?"

Caleb sucked in a breath. "Said he doesn't deserve one."

Unbelievable...

Daniel balled his fists and tried to control the anger growing inside him. How could Da do that! Come into his life out of the blue, and then just disappear without a fight. *It's not on, Da. It's not on.* He pulled himself up and drew in a deep breath.

"We've got to get him one, Caleb."

Caleb shook his head. "He's already told the hospital he doesn't want one, so fat chance they'd go against his wishes, even if there was one to be had."

Daniel inhaled deeply. No use getting angry. He had to control himself.

"The best thing is to be there if he comes to."

Caleb was right, but Daniel wanted more. Now he'd decided to let Da back into his life, he wanted to spend time with him. Get to know him. Not say goodbye. *This wasn't meant to happen.*

The lights changed to green and Caleb let out the clutch. The car lurched forward and then took off as he pressed down heavily on the accelerator. The car had seen better days.

"Hope we get there in time." Daniel stared straight ahead. "Should we call Grace?"

Caleb glanced at Daniel and let out a heavy sigh.

"She won't come, but we can let her know. Aislin and Alana might. We'll call as soon as we get there." Caleb slowed down to take a left-hand corner. "I'll need to check on Caity and Immi too."

"At least they're in the same hospital."

"Yeah, that's a plus."

The hospital loomed ahead, stretching as far as the eye could see. Caleb parked, and he and Daniel strode to the main entrance where they checked the directory. Da was in the second last building on the right. They marched down the corridor, and reaching the end of that building, followed the path to the Intensive Care ward.

A short cheery nurse with a round face looked up.

"Can I help you?"

"We're looking for Thomas O'Connor." Caleb's voice faltered.

"Ah - Mr O'Connor. Down the corridor, third bed on the right. Go ahead - I'll check if the doctor's around."

"Thank you. How is he?"

"Not good, I'm sorry. He's had a few lucid moments, but I'll let the doctor fill you in."

Daniel's heart raced. He had to be there if Da came to. Striding ahead of Caleb, he found the bed. Faded blue curtains had been drawn to provide privacy. He took a deep breath, and finding the join in the curtains, he carefully pulled them apart and entered slowly, closing them behind him. There lay Da, just a skeleton of a man. Daniel swallowed hard.

"Da..." Daniel's voice was just a whisper. Seated on the plastic seat beside the bed, Daniel took one of Da's hands and rubbed it gently with

his thumb. Da's skin was so thin, he had to be careful. And so yellow. Da was having trouble breathing, his body shuddered with every laboured breath. Mustn't have much time left. Daniel glanced at Caleb as he entered. Caleb's eyes glistened as he took Da's other hand, causing Daniel's eyes to fill with angry tears.

Daniel knew what death looked like. He'd seen it plenty. How many bodies had he wheeled to the morgue as part of his job at the hospital? But he hadn't come to farewell Da. He'd come to forgive him. To talk to him. To get to know him. Not to lose him. There was little time left.

Daniel sprang from his seat. "I'm going to call Grace."

Caleb lifted his head, a surprised look on his face. Daniel didn't care if Caleb thought it useless. He had to call her. Encourage her to come. It may be her last chance.

Daniel left the bed, not taking his eyes off Da until the curtain fluttered back into position. Sprinting to the telephone box at the end of the ward, he glanced at his watch. Grace might not be up yet. Then again, she probably was. The phone rang three times before she answered.

"Daniel! What do you want at this time of the morning?"

"It's Da, Grace. He's dying. Probably only has hours left, if that." He paused, waiting for a response, but none came. "Will you come?"

Grace let out a heavy sigh. Was she considering it? *Please God, let her come.* Daniel started as Caleb opened the door of the phone box and peeked in. His heart raced. Had something happened? Drawing his eyebrows together, Daniel placed his hand over the mouthpiece as he asked the question of Caleb. When Caleb shook his head, relief flooded Daniel's body.

"Just going to get Caitlin."

Daniel smiled weakly and then turned his attention back to Grace.

"No, Daniel, I won't come." Grace's answer was measured and controlled. *How can she not come?* He didn't understand. Daniel's shoulders slumped.

"Grace, please. You'll regret it if you don't." He didn't want to plead. He wanted her to come of her own will, but he had no choice.

"Daniel, I'm not coming, and that's that. I have no wish whatsoever to see that man." Her voice had grown even more determined.

Daniel sighed dejectedly. He had to leave it. It was no use. She wasn't coming.

"Okay then. But I pray you'll change your mind."

"I won't."

GRACE HUNG up the receiver and fell back on her pillows. It was time to get up, but she needed a few minutes to steady the thoughts swilling in her head. *Maybe I should've agreed to see Da. Could Daniel be right? Will I regret it if I don't? Once he's dead, it'll be too late.* Her head hurt. *No, I can't. There's no good reason to see that man, dead or alive. He destroyed our family and caused Mam's death. Mam could still be alive if it hadn't been for him.*

And Brianna and I wouldn't have been sent to Aunt Hilda's...

Grace squeezed her eyes shut and buried her face in a pillow. Her heart thundered in her ears. *I'd rather kill the man myself than watch him die peacefully.* No, she would not see Thomas O'Connor. And she wouldn't regret it.

That decided, Grace slid out of bed and stepped into the shower, turning the heat up until her skin reddened like a cooked lobster. She'd push all thoughts of Da out of her mind and focus on the day ahead.

LIZZY'S HEART WAS HEAVY. Although Tara and Dillon were both awake and demanding her attention, her thoughts were totally focussed on Daniel and his Da. She pleaded with God to give Daniel time to say what he needed. She prayed for Daniel's emotional well-being, and that he wouldn't blame God for taking his Da away from him right now. That he'd see the bigger picture, and be happy his Da was going to a better place where there'd be no more pain or suffering. Above all, Lizzy prayed for peace for Daniel, his Da, and the rest of the family. And that those who didn't know Him, like Grace, might catch a glimpse of heaven because of the way God had blessed and changed Thomas O'Connor in the last year of his life on earth.

She couldn't physically go to the hospital with two small children, but in every other way, she was there. She needed to be strong for him, to support him in every way possible. She closed her eyes and inhaled deeply. *God, please help me be the wife Daniel needs right now.*

DANIEL TOOK a moment after hanging up the phone and leaned his head on the wall of the telephone box. Grace needed to come. The other girls had little memory of Da, and besides, he himself didn't really know them. Grace was his main concern. Always had been. *'God, I don't know what it'll take, but I plead with You to work in Grace's heart. Soften it, Lord God, and let her come. And Lord, please let me have just a minute with Da. That's all I need, and all I ask for. I'm sorry for reacting so badly before. He's a child of God, and regardless of what his life was like before, You've forgiven him, and so must I. Please help me see him with Your eyes. Thank you Lord God. Amen.'*

Daniel pushed the door open and let it swing behind him as he headed straight back to Da. His heart was still heavy, but he had to leave Grace to God. That's what Paul had told him to do. But it was hard. He felt like screaming, or punching someone, but that wouldn't do any good.

As he passed the nurses' desk, the nurse they'd spoken to earlier stopped him.

"The doctor will be here in about half an hour and can speak with you then." Her voice was warm and caring. Daniel managed a half smile and thanked her.

He hesitated outside the curtains. All was quiet. Caleb hadn't returned. It was just him and Da. Daniel steeled himself. It was now or never. He prayed Da would have just one lucid moment. That's all he needed.

Slowly pulling the curtains apart, Daniel peeked in before sliding into the narrow area beside the bed. Taking a seat, he picked up Da's hand.

"Da, it's me, Daniel." Da didn't move. His breathing remained laboured and irregular. The tubes pumping what Daniel assumed to be pain killers into him looked stronger than the arm they were attached to. A lump rose in Daniel's throat. He'd just have to talk, and trust Da would hear the words. He might not get another opportunity.

Daniel gulped and tried to push the lump in his throat away.

"Da, I'm sorry I ran out yesterday. Silly of me." Daniel fought back his tears. "When I saw you there, and heard you speak about 'seeing the light', and being sorry for what you did to us and Mam, I couldn't cope, and I ran. I'm sorry. I should've stayed. Now I might not even get the chance to speak with you, other than like this."

Daniel paused and took a deep breath, pushing back the tears stinging his eyes.

"Da, open your eyes, please, just once, so I can see you properly. If you can hear me, can you try?" Daniel waited. While he waited, he prayed. His pulse quickened. *Did Da's eyes just flutter?*

"Da, please try again." Daniel squeezed Da's hand tighter and leaned closer to his face. No, he hadn't imagined it. Da's eyes flickered and his hand twitched. Tears welled in Daniel's eyes.

"Da, it's Daniel. Can you hear me?"

Da's eyes flickered open and then closed. Daniel held his breath.

"This is so hard, Da. I didn't want to see you, you know that? But I'm glad I did. Glad I heard you speak yesterday, and I truly believe you're sorry for the past. I would never have believed it if I hadn't seen and heard it myself, but God's done something in me, Da, and I don't hate you anymore."

Daniel bit his lip and forced himself to continue. "Thinking of all the wasted years makes me sad, but knowing you're going to be with God and that He's forgiven you, makes the hurt easier to bear." Daniel took another deep breath as he peered into Da's face. *Come on Da, wake up.*

He pushed back his tears. "Da, I know you didn't mean to hurt us. There's something evil about drink when it takes hold of a person. I know what it's like. Been there myself. I'm just so glad I 'saw the light' now, and I'm determined to stay strong and become a good husband and father. God's blessed me with a beautiful wife, Da. Should see her." Daniel smiled and let out a small chuckle as he thought of Lizzy.

"She loves the Lord, and she's smart, and I love her so much. I've promised never to hurt her again, Da. Makes me sick in the stomach when I think how close I came to losing her. And my little boy, Da. His name's Dillon. Named after our Dillon. Remember him, Da? Only lived a few hours. Broke Mam's heart when he died."

Daniel paused and closed his eyes for a moment. It'd been so hard when Da left, not long after Dillon died. Sure, they all felt safer. There were no more beatings, but despite that, they all expected to see him walk in the door every night. But he never did. Strange, really, because although they hated him and were scared of him, he was still their Da, and the place felt empty without him.

Daniel sighed heavily as he gave Da's hand a light squeeze. "But that's all in the past now, Da. Wish we had more time together, but this is all we've got." Daniel's voice faltered. He had to say it. He swallowed hard and took a deep breath.

"Da, I just want to say that I forgive you, and I love you." His eyes blurred with tears, but when Da squeezed his hand, Daniel couldn't stop them falling. Da had heard him.

No more words were needed. He'd connected with Da, and peace floated through his body.

"Can I pray, Da?" Would Da respond, or had his mind shut down? A small flicker in his eyes. Daniel smiled and squeezed Da's hand gently.

"Lord God, our loving Heavenly Father, we come to You today as men who've known both sides of the track, but are so glad we're on Your side now, Lord God. Thank You for loving us so much, and for forgiving us when we didn't deserve it. Thank You for opening our eyes to the truth of the gospel, and for placing your love and peace deep inside us. Thank You for giving me the chance to see Da before he goes to be with You." Daniel wiped his eyes. "Lord God, You know my heart's breaking, but I know You'll be my comfort in the days ahead. And Lord God, I just pray one more thing. Will You soften Grace's heart? Please, Lord God? Bless Da. Fill him with Your peace, and comfort him. In Jesus' precious name, Amen."

Daniel lifted his head and squeezed Da's hand. As he did, a stronger hand settled on his own shoulder. Caleb stood behind him, tears rolling down his cheeks. Caitlin's arm was around Caleb's waist and she leaned on his shoulder, tears also streaming down her cheeks.

Da's body shuddered, and he took his last breath.

Daniel expected he'd be distraught, but instead, warm calm flowed through his body. The pain on Da's face only moments earlier had now been replaced with serenity. God had answered his prayer.

Daniel leaned down and placed a gentle kiss on Da's hollow cheek.

"God bless you, Da."

He stood and swapped places with Caleb. Caitlin drew him close and hugged him. Wrapped in her arms, Daniel allowed himself to weep.

CHAPTER 11

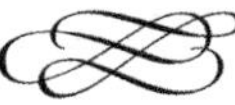

When the doctor finally arrived just after Da died, he'd said Da had been offered a new liver a week before but had refused it. No-one knew. Daniel expected to be annoyed and angry, but instead felt saddened. Da must have been desperate to go home. He could have had a number of years left with his family. But his life had been rough, and Daniel guessed he was tired of living. Daniel prayed he was enjoying his new body, and sent a glance heavenward, letting out a small chuckle.

Da's funeral was held three days later.

"What are you laughing at, Daniel?" Lizzy grabbed his arm and peered into his eyes, a quizzical look on her face.

"Oh, just thinking of Da up there, looking down on us all. He's probably having a good old chuckle too." He grabbed her hand. "Come on, let's go."

They headed into the small chapel. Only immediate family and a few friends were expected to attend. Da had lost touch with all his old drinking buddies, and Michael O'Leary from next door had passed on several years earlier. But the chapel was full. Daniel was shocked. Who were all these people? He led Lizzy to the front seat where Caleb and Caitlin were already seated.

Daniel leaned closer to Caleb. "Who are all the people?"

Caleb's eyes twinkled. "All Da's friends from the centre. Patients and workers. Left his mark on them all, so it seems."

Daniel shook his head and chuckled once again. If only he'd had the chance to get to know Da sooner. But would he have made the trip earlier? *Probably not.*

Daniel leaned closer again and raised his eyebrows. "Grace?"

Caleb shook his head, his shoulders drooping. Aislin and Alana and their partners sat to the right, and Daniel nodded and smiled when he caught their eyes. Should get to know them. They were his sisters too, after all. Beside them, another man sat. Muscle upon muscle bulged in his folded arms, almost splitting his tight fitting shirt. A spark of recognition flickered in Daniel's mind. *Brendan?* Caleb nodded. "They let him out for the funeral."

Daniel turned and faced the front, inhaling slowly. *If only Grace was here.*

Grace paused outside the chapel. She pulled her cigarette case out of her bag and lit up. She didn't smoke often, but she needed one now. Her hands shook as she took a deep drag. It's not too late to get out of here. No-one had seen her. Lizzy's words at dinner last night played over in her mind; *'You'll only get one chance, Grace. Think about it?' One chance...* She'd missed the chance to see Da alive. Could she miss the chance to farewell him in death and live with the guilt for the rest of her life? Even if she held no love for Da whatsoever? *No, I need to be here.*

She took a few quick drags and then ground the cigarette out with the toe of her stiletto, straightened her snugly fitting mid length black dress, and tip-toed into the tiny chapel, taking a seat at the very back just as the minister stood to begin the service. She sat low in the seat to avoid being seen.

The number of mourners was surprising. Were these all Da's friends? Surely not. They all looked normal, not the drunkards she remembered him cohorting with. The minister, wearing the Salvation Army uniform, had a warm and engaging manner. He welcomed everyone, and then prayed. How long had it been since Grace had bowed her head in prayer? Mam used to make them pray every night at the dinner table. As did Aunt Hilda. But Grace had only bowed her head then because she had to. The day Mam's body had been lowered into the ground was the day Grace told God she'd never talk to him ever again. And she hadn't.

Hearing the minister talk about Da was like hearing him talk about someone else. She didn't know the person he referred to. Kind, funny, caring? *Not the Da she knew.* And the stream of people who got up and spoke lovingly about him, saying they'd miss his kind words and encouraging ways. An inspiration. *What? Da? An inspiration? Am I even at the right funeral?*

Caleb stood and faced the gathering. His hands shook, and he blinked rapidly. He cleared his throat and seemed to settle.

"Thank you all for coming today to farewell Thomas Rory O'Connor, Da." His gaze for a moment settled on Daniel, Aislin, Alana and no, don't tell me, is that Brendan? *How did he get out?*

Grace wriggled uncomfortably in her seat.

Caleb returned his attention to the mourners. "Thomas, *Da,* found the Lord just under a year ago, thanks to some of you here who didn't give up on him." Caleb paused and inhaled deeply, his eyes blinking rapidly. He took another deep breath. "For your commitment and dedication to our Da's spiritual and physical welfare, my family and I are truly grateful." Caleb looked around, his eyes soft but steady.

"Da wasn't an easy man to live with in his younger years, as most of you know. He didn't hold back in telling people what a terrible father and husband he'd been, and how he regretted not 'seeing the light' earlier. He's an amazing testimony to the power of God to change people, regardless of their pasts, making them clean and new on the inside. A pity his body let him down in the end, but he accepted that the choices he made as a young man resulted in that, and was prepared to accept the consequences. He knew where he was going, and Da," Caleb glanced upwards, "I know you're probably up there looking down on us and having a good ol' chuckle, but we're going to miss you. We're proud of the man you became, and we just want to say we love you."

Caleb's voice caught, and tears streamed down his face. Daniel rose and stood beside him, placing his hand on Caleb's shoulder.

Grace fought back tears of her own and had trouble breathing. This wasn't expected. She swallowed hard, pushing the lump in her throat away. Her stomach churned. *Should have seen Da when he was alive. Now I'll never have the chance.* She pulled a tissue out of her bag and wiped her eyes. *This is stupid. I hate the man.*

Despite hearing all the testimonies of what Da had been like in the last year of his life, Grace still couldn't accept he'd changed that much. It just wasn't possible. Someone who'd been as despicable as he'd been didn't change overnight. They didn't know what they were talking about. She grabbed her bag and started to stand, but something held her back. The organist began playing a hymn, and the melody tugged at Grace's heart. She'd heard it before. Mam used to hum it as she sat by the kids' beds waiting for them to fall asleep.

'The Lord's my shepherd, I'll not want;
He makes me down to lie
In pastures green; He leadeth me
The quiet waters by.'

Grace stood and listened. She tried to join in, but the words caught in her throat. *The emotion of the moment. Nothing else to it.* But as much as she wanted to leave, her feet wouldn't budge.

~

Daniel lifted his end of the coffin and placed it carefully on his left shoulder. He steeled himself. This wasn't going to be easy. The burden on his shoulder was nothing compared to the burden in his heart.

The organ began playing 'Blessed Assurance' as the three brothers and the minister carried Da slowly towards the hearse waiting outside.

Daniel caught Lizzy's eye, and a hard lump formed in his throat. He swallowed, forcing it down. He stared ahead, but a figure standing at the back caught his eye ... *Grace? Can't be...* His pulse quickened. Had she come after all? He looked more closely. *Yes, it's Grace.* Daniel's heart soared. *Thank you, thank you, God.* Grace lowered her eyes, but not quickly enough. He held her gaze for just a moment. She'd been crying.

Daniel hoped Lizzy would notice Grace. There was nothing he could do, but he prayed Grace would stay.

The short walk to the door through the group of mourners and out to the hearse was the hardest walk Daniel had ever made. Despite the sorrow of the moment, he knew Da wasn't in the coffin. Sure, his body lay there, but his spirit was elsewhere. Da lived on, but with a new body, in a new home. As the coffin was lowered into the hearse, God's peace settled in Daniel's heart. Da was safe and secure in the Saviour's arms, of that he was sure. *Thank you, blessed God.*

With the coffin in place, Daniel turned and searched the crowd for Grace. His heart lifted as he saw her standing with Lizzy. Leaving Caleb and Brendan, he made his way through the gathering towards Grace and Lizzy. He couldn't believe Grace had actually come. An answer to prayer. *Another one.*

"Grace, so glad you came." Daniel placed a kiss on her cheek and hugged her tightly. Grace clung to him. God was doing a work in her life, of that he was sure.

She finally pulled away. Lizzy offered her a tissue and Grace wiped her face and blew her nose. Her mascara had run a little and her eyes were puffy and red.

"I'm sorry," she said, dabbing her eyes.

Daniel squeezed her hand. "It doesn't matter. Are you okay?"

Grace blew her nose.

"Think so." She breathed deeply and straightened herself. In her stilettos, she stood eye to eye with Daniel.

"I didn't think you'd come."

"Hadn't planned on it." She rolled her eyes. "Conscience got to me."

"Glad it did, Grace. Glad it did." Daniel smiled at her warmly. "Will you come to the burial? Be special if you did."

"Don't know. Give me a minute to think."

"No problem, Grace. There's no hurry."

Grace gave him a weak smile, and then turned to Caitlin and Caleb who'd just joined them.

Daniel took Lizzy's hand and stood to the side. He needed a moment to gather himself. Grace turning up had thrown him. But he was so glad she'd come. God really was doing something in her life. But he had to tread carefully. No pushing. If she didn't want to come to the burial, he'd have to let it be. *But God, please let her...*

"You okay, Daniel?" Lizzy peered up at him, concern filling her eyes.

"Yes, my love. A little overwhelmed, that's all." Slipping his arm around her waist, he pulled her close and thanked God once again for bringing Lizzy into his life. She'd become his soul mate. His best friend, and he couldn't live without her. Strange how a funeral brings clarity to everything. Makes you evaluate your own life choices, and as a result, makes you appreciate those most important to you.

Daniel leaned back and studied her. How he loved this woman God had brought into his life. He loved the way she supported and encouraged him and never gave up on him. Sometimes she got a little impatient, but he loved that she cared enough to want the best for him. His heart overflowed with love for her.

"What are you thinking, Daniel?" Lizzy tilted her head slightly, a bemused look on her face.

Daniel chuckled. He'd been caught out, but he didn't care. He lifted her chin with the tip of his finger.

"Lizzy, I don't say this often enough, but I love you."

A small smile came to Lizzy's face and her eyes glistened. "And I love you too, Daniel O'Connor. And I couldn't be prouder of you than I am at this minute."

Leaning forward, Lizzy kissed him gently. He returned her kiss and draped his arm around her shoulder before rejoining the others.

THE GROUP HAD GROWN in size, with Aislin, Alana and their partners joining Caleb, Caitlin and Grace, as well as Brendan and aunts and uncles Daniel hadn't seen for a long time. Daniel stood and listened. These were his family, his roots, but as much as he now realised he loved them, his future rested with the woman beside him. Something stirred deep inside him. He didn't know what they were, but he was impatient to find out what plans God had for their lives. But right now, Da had to be buried.

Daniel moved closer to Grace and gently placed his hand on her shoulder.

"Coming?"

Grace lifted her eyes and nodded.

"I'm glad." Daniel's chest expanded and he smiled broadly.

THE SMALL PROCESSION of cars followed the hearse to Da's final resting place. The family had debated whether Da should be buried next to Mam or not. In the end they'd agreed he should. "Mam never stopped praying for him," Caleb had said. "She loved him, despite all he did to her. I think she'd want him laid to rest beside her."

Not that it really mattered. It was only his body, but to the family left behind, at least they could now remember both parents together.

The grave had been dug the day before, and the rich earthy smell lingered in the air. As Daniel and the other men lowered Da's coffin slowly into the ground, the group began to sing 'Amazing Grace'. Daniel's heart was heavy, but as he joined hands with Lizzy and Grace, the heaviness was replaced with God's peace.

He closed his eyes as the minister gave the final blessing, and squeezing Grace's hand, prayed God would touch her heart.

"In sure and certain hope of the resurrection to eternal life through our Lord Jesus Christ, we commend to Almighty God our brother Thomas, and we commit this body to the ground; earth to earth, ashes to ashes, dust to dust. The Lord bless him and keep him, the Lord make his face to shine upon him and be gracious unto him, the Lord lift up His countenance upon him and give him peace. Amen."

Caleb threw the first shovel of earth onto Da's coffin, the thud echoing in Daniel's heart. Daniel followed. Grace bent down and picked up a handful of earth, and threw it onto the coffin. Tears streamed down her face. Daniel wrapped his arms around Grace and comforted her.

"He's gone to be with the Lord," Daniel whispered as he stroked her hair. *Lord, please let this be a defining moment for Grace.*

The group held hands and sang another hymn before the minister said the closing prayer. It was over. It felt strange. Da was buried. His body was gone, and he would now live on in memory only. Daniel was so glad he'd had the opportunity to speak with Da before he died, and to witness the new life God had breathed into his soul. God may not have healed his body, but he'd done better than that. He'd given him new life. Life that would go on for eternity. No-one could want more than that.

Lizzy slipped her arm around Daniel's waist, and he pulled her close. The two most precious women in his life, wrapped tightly in his arms. What a blessed man he was.

The sound of cars starting up interrupted the moment. Life would go on.

As he walked slowly back towards the waiting cars, Daniel turned his head and looked to his right. Somewhere over there, Ciara and baby Rachel were buried. Another life, another story. Sorrow for all that had happened tugged at his heart, but God had forgiven him and allowed him to move on. He should have supported Ciara in her grief, not deserted her. *What a despicable person I was.* But he'd been young and ignorant. He didn't know how to cope with his own grief, let alone help her. He could allow the sorrow he felt now over what happened to overwhelm him. But it truly was in the past, and nothing he could do now would change it.

"Do you want to go there?" Lizzy asked quietly.

How does she know? She never ceases to amaze me. Daniel took a deep slow breath.

"No, I don't. They're my past, Lizzy. I want to move on. With you." He squeezed her hand and gave her a look that contained all the love God had poured into his heart for her.

Several days later, as Daniel and Lizzy stood leaning on the railings at the stern of the ship heading back to Liverpool, Daniel was deep in thought. He'd become a lot more introspective of late. Maybe it was God's way of talking to him, because he often had thoughts floating through his mind that could only have come from God. But right now, his thoughts were on Lizzy and their future together. He was sure God had something special planned for them, but didn't know what. But he needed to know one thing.

"Lizzy, do you ever regret not having a proper wedding?"

Lizzy spun around, startled.

"What made you ask that?"

"Not sure, really. I was just thinking about all we've been through." He pulled her to him and wrapped his arms around her waist, gazing into her curious eyes. "The way we got married without your parents knowing, the way I treated you so badly, and how thankful I was when you came back and led me to the Lord." He lifted a hand to her face and gently brushed back a lock of hair. "Don't most girls dream of a big wedding? I know you turned your father's offer down, but I sometimes wonder if you're sad about missing out on all that." Daniel tilted his head slightly, his eyes full of love and concern. "Are you?"

Lizzy grinned, letting out a small laugh. "I guess you're right. Most girls do dream of a fairy tale wedding, but you know, it really is just one day. To be honest, I guess sometimes I do feel a little sad, but it's not the fairy tale wedding with all the trimmings that makes a marriage work. It's what comes after that's more important."

"Would you like to have one, anyway? I can sort something if you do."

Lizzy laughed and hit him playfully. "Don't be silly, Daniel. It's too late for all that, and I really don't care that much." Turning serious, Lizzy continued. "But I would like to renew our vows before God one day soon."

"That's a grand idea, Lizzy." Daniel flashed a brilliant smile. "Let's do it now!"

"Now! What do you mean?"

"Like right here, right now. God's here with us. We don't need anyone else to be present. Just you, me, God," Daniel looked down, "and baby Dillon."

Lizzy's eyes twinkled and her grin broadened into a full blown smile. "Okay, let's do it."

Daniel took both of Lizzy's hands and squeezed them, his eyes settling on hers. He took a deep breath.

"Elizabeth, *Lizzy*, before God our Father, who brought us together and gave us the gift of love, I promise to be faithful to you and to love and cherish you as long as we both shall live. Because of you, I laugh, I smile, I dare to dream again. I look forward with great joy to spending the rest of my life with you, caring for you, nurturing you, and being there for you in all God has in store for us."

Daniel leaned forward and kissed Lizzy gently on the lips.

Lizzy wiped her tears and took Daniel's hands in hers. "Have you been practicing that?" She let out a small laugh.

"Maybe..." He grinned at her mischievously.

Lizzy straightened herself and inhaled slowly. "Okay, it's my turn."

"Daniel O'Connor, with God as my witness, I promise to love and cherish you forever. I look forward to dancing with you in times of joy, to lifting you up in times of sadness, to rejoicing with you in times of good health, and to caring for you in times of illness. I promise to turn to you for comfort, for encouragement, and for inspiration. I love you and I know that this love is from God. I'll thank Him every day for bringing you into my life."

Lizzy squeezed Daniel's hands and held his unwavering gaze before kissing him.

Daniel leaned down and lifted Dillon out of his push chair. Lizzy placed her hand on Dillon's head as Daniel cradled him in his arms.

"And Lord God, we thank You for entrusting Dillon, this precious little boy, into our care. Together, Lizzy and I promise to make our home a place where he'll feel safe and loved, and where he'll grow up learning Your ways. Give us wisdom to raise Dillon the way You would have us, to be an example to him of godly love. Let him grow to love You, and may he discover the joy of Your presence in his life. We dedicate him to You now, Lord God. Bless his wee little life, we pray. Amen."

Daniel kissed Dillon's little head and then looked up at Lizzy. His heart overflowed with love for her. What a blessed man he was.

"Lizzy, I don't know what the Lord's got planned for us, but I know He's got something special in mind. I feel it deep within me. There's a real stirring of my spirit." He squeezed her hand and took a deep breath. "I'm so thankful He gave me another chance, and I want to live my life for Him. With you."

"Daniel, that's exactly what I feel. God will show us in His time. We just have to be patient."

Daniel laughed. "Good one, Liz! Coming from you, that's a hoot!"

Lizzy slapped him playfully. Laughing, he pulled her close and lowered his mouth over hers, but had to ply baby Dillon's fingers from between their lips before he could kiss her thoroughly.

BOOK 4 - SECRETS AND SACRIFICE

CHAPTER 1

Belfast 1985

GRACE ROSE, pausing momentarily before marching to the front of the court room. The twelve members of the jury sat in their box, looking weary after a week of listening to the despicable deeds of Donal Patrick O'Malley. Now it was up to her to convince them they should find him guilty of murder.

A hush fell over the court room as Grace cast her gaze over them. She'd prepared for this moment, but would it be enough? Niall would no doubt have a brilliant closing argument. Hers had to dazzle.

Grace took a deep breath to steady herself, but just as she opened her mouth to speak, a tall, thin man with darkish hair, shaved on the sides and spiked on top, entered the room, catching her attention. Grace's body stiffened. *Caleb? No, it can't be. Or could it?* Her brother never came to court, even when she was prosecuting a high-profile case such as this. But it sure looked like him. Grace's heart raced and a feeling of dread flooded her body. He would only come if something bad had happened. Regardless, she'd have to ignore him and focus on the job at hand. Besides, it might not even be him.

Returning her attention to the jury, she began her closing arguments, affording herself the occasional glance at the man. It was Caleb, no doubt about it. His face, normally pale, was deathly white. Something bad must have happened.

Somehow she focused on her speech. She needed to win. No way could she allow O'Malley to walk free after beating his wife to death, but with Caleb sitting in the back, it was a challenge. Finally, she reached her conclusion. "So, members of the jury, after all you've heard, I beg you to find the accused, Donal Patrick O'Malley, guilty as charged. Thank you."

Grace's stomach tightened as her gaze met Caleb's on her short walk back to her seat. She was tempted to go to him, but that would be breaking protocol. She'd have to wait to find out what had happened.

Her head hurt. She'd put everything she had into her speech, and now she felt drained. Normally she could relax a little after her job was done, but now… with Caleb sitting behind her? Impossible.

Bryan leaned over and offered his congratulations. Grace gave him a half smile. Bryan, her trusted assistant and most ardent advocate, would always say she'd done well, even if she hadn't.

Grace inhaled deeply to settle herself as the Judge called for the Defendant's closing arguments. Niall stood, and as he walked to the front of the room, she chastised herself for allowing him to unnerve her. Even after a week of seeing him every day, she failed to treat him like any other man. *Because he wasn't any other man.*

He'd aged a little. Small flecks of grey peppered the dark hair poking out from under his wig, only serving to increase his appeal. He'd also changed. It wasn't just the suit. Or his lean body. There was something else. Grace had seen it from the front of the court room when he'd caught her eye on the first day of the trial. A sadness, and no doubt, she was partly responsible. But it puzzled her—surely three years in London would have given him enough time for him to move on.

He wasn't quite the same man she'd fallen in love with in the heady days of college, but his nearness still stirred something deep inside her.

A tap on her shoulder jolted her, and she looked up into a clerk's concerned eyes.

"Miss, your brother's asking to see you urgently."

Grace spun around. *It must be bad.*

Her stomach churned as she grasped the rail and pulled herself up before making her way as unobtrusively as possible to the back of the room.

Sliding into the seat, Grace grabbed Caleb's thin arm and leaned close to him. She looked into his troubled eyes. "What's happened, Caleb?"

"Come outside, Grace." Caleb took her arm and led her into the foyer as Niall began his closing argument. She shouldn't leave, but this sounded like an emergency, and besides, Bryan was more than capable of taking notes.

"What's wrong, Caleb? It's not Caitlin, is it? Or the girls?" Grace gripped him tighter. "Please don't tell me it's the girls."

Caleb faced her. "If you stop talking, I'll tell you."

Grace pulled herself up. He was right... she needed to stop talking. She was jumping to conclusions. Best get the facts.

"Okay. Who?" Grace's heart beat faster. Was she ready to find out?

Caleb gulped, his protruding Adam's apple bobbing in his heavily tattooed neck.

"Brianna's been found."

Grace's eyes widened and she grabbed his arm again.

"Brianna? Where is she? Is she okay?"

Caleb paused, holding Grace's gaze.

"She can't be..."

"She's alive, Grace, but only just. She was found this morning, unconscious."

Grace covered her mouth with her hand. "I thought you were going to say she was dead…" She let out a huge sigh. Was it wrong to be relieved when your sister had been found unconscious?

"Where was she?"

"In a dingy apartment. Looks like an overdose."

"She promised." Grace huffed and narrowed her eyes. "She promised, Caleb. If only she'd kept her word."

"It's not that simple, Grace. You know that."

Grace sighed heavily. "Yes, I do. Where is she?"

"St. Vincent's. I'm going now. Can you come?"

"Not yet. But I will as soon as I can. Have you called the others?"

Caleb ran his hand along the side of his shaved head. "No—I only just found out and I came straight here. I'll call them now."

Grace pulled a cigarette from under her robe and lit up. She didn't offer one to Caleb. "She'd better pull through." She took several quick puffs.

"Yes, she'd better. Caitlin's at home praying. She said that's the best thing she can do to help."

Grace rolled her eyes. *That's exactly what Caleb's wife, Caitlin, would do.*

Caleb leaned in and hugged Grace. "Come as soon as you can."

Grace hugged him back and held his gaze. "You're a good brother, Caleb."

As she watched Caleb hurry off, she took several more quick drags on her cigarette before grinding it out in an ashtray on the windowsill.

When she re-entered the court room, Niall was towards the end of his speech. Grace remained at the back to avoid creating a disturbance. It was difficult to focus. All she could think of was Brianna, her younger sister, lying in hospital, unconscious. *What if she dies?* Grace needed to get there as quickly as possible. But what could she do to help? At least

Caitlin could pray. Grace couldn't even do that. It didn't matter. Being there would be enough.

GRACE ALLOWED her gaze to follow Niall as he took his seat. Just the look of him stirred her insides. *Why did he come back to Belfast? Surely London would have been more exciting.*

Moving forward quietly, she slid into her seat beside Bryan as a general buzz filled the room.

Bryan lifted his head and looked at her.

"Miss, are you alright?" Bryan's concern for her always warmed her heart.

"Yes, Bryan. Thank you. Just some family issues. I'll be okay." She gave him a weak smile.

Judge Atkinson cleared his throat, and the buzz in the court room died down.

"Thank you, members of the jury. We'll adjourn for now and reconvene at nine o'clock tomorrow for final instructions. Good night, and thank you for your time."

Everyone rose as the Judge stood and exited the room. Gathering her papers, Grace tossed them into her brief case.

"I've got to go, Bryan. But how did he do?" She nodded her head towards Niall who stood with his team on the opposite side of the bench. An unwelcome pang of jealousy stabbed her as a young attractive blond hung on his every word.

"Oh, he did well, as expected, but I think we've got it."

"Nothing's ever definite until the jury comes back. You know that, Bryan."

"Yes, Miss, I do. They can go either way. But if I were a betting man, I'd bet on you."

"Oh Bryan. What would I do without you?" Grace let out a small laugh. "I really do have to fly. I'll see you in the morning."

"Okay, Miss. Good night."

"Good night, Bryan." Grace swept her robe around her shoulders and hurried towards the exit, shooting one quick look at Niall before leaving the room. The blond was standing way too close. Grace sighed dejectedly. *Will I ever get over him?* Stupid, really. It was her fault they'd broken up. She didn't want to get married. He did. *Too late now.* The blond had her hooks into him.

Grace glanced at her watch. She should change, but no, time was of the essence—she'd go straight to the hospital. What if something happened to Brianna in the time it took to return to Chambers?

AS GRACE TURNED into Frew Lane, a biting wind caught her robe and sent it flying. Grabbing it, she pulled it tighter, but as she paused, a deep voice she'd know anywhere called out.

Grace stopped and turned. Niall was jogging towards her. Her heart fluttered. *Drat the man! How does he do that?*

Niall stopped and stood before her, wig in hand, his chest expanding and contracting heavily as he caught his breath.

"Grace, what's happened? I saw you disappear." His warm brown eyes gazed into hers as he touched her arm lightly, threatening to dismantle her resolve to remain aloof. "You don't look too good…"

Grace lowered her eyes. Allowing him back into her life would be asking for trouble. But she could surely do with a friend right now. No. She was strong, and she didn't need anyone. *Especially Niall. Get a grip, Grace.*

She inhaled deeply and lifted her head. "It's nothing, really, Niall. Just a small family matter."

Niall tilted his head, a quizzical look on his way too handsome face. "Doesn't look like that to me, Grace." He knew her too well. "Where are you racing off to?"

Grace shook her head and pulled her robe higher around her neck. A light drizzle had begun to fall. People scurried past, hurrying to get home before the skies opened up. Niall opened the umbrella he'd been holding in one hand and held it over her. The gentleman as always.

"Come on, Grace, let's get out of this. Let me drive you to wherever you're going."

Grace stiffened. Should she let her defences down just a little? If she did, would she be able to put them back up again? Or would she succumb to Niall's charms and let all her resolves fly out the window? She looked into the eyes of the only man she'd ever loved and weakened.

Niall's hand rested on her elbow as he guided her towards the car park around the corner, stopping in front of a silver, 1982 Alfa Romeo Spider. Grace cast her eyes over the tiny sports car and approved. She and Niall had always shared a penchant for fast cars.

Niall's seatbelt clicked. As he turned the key, the Spider sprang to life, the roar of the engine thrilling her. He turned and looked at her. "So, where are we off to?"

Grace had to tear her eyes from his before she did something she'd regret. He was way too close for comfort.

"St. Vincent's." Grace's gaze was firmly fixed on the road ahead. "Brianna's overdosed."

CHAPTER 2

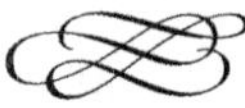

Niall manoeuvred the Spider into a tight car park and turned off the engine, turning his head towards her.

"I can go in by myself, Niall. You don't have to come."

"I'd like to, if you'll let me."

Grace let out a heavy sigh. "I really am okay on my own."

"I know, but I'd like to be there for you." His steady gaze bore into her, unnerving her.

Grace inhaled deeply. How much longer could she resist him? But she had to. Nothing had changed, and she couldn't, or wouldn't, allow her past to possibly destroy the career of the only man she'd loved. He could have the blond. It would do Grace no good to get entangled with him again.

She pushed her door open. "We need to hurry. She's in the Emergency Department."

"Okay then. Let's go." He jumped out of the car and joined her.

Grace strode as fast as she could in her high heels. Niall easily kept up. She knew exactly where to go… how many times had she and Caleb been through this? Not only with Brianna, but with Brendan, their younger brother, too. What a messed up family they were.

Would Brianna make it this time? Or would she finally succeed with her death wish? It didn't seem to matter how many times Grace and Caleb talked to her about making changes in her life, she never saw them through. Of course, Caleb always talked to her about God. "God can help you, Brianna," he'd always say. Grace would roll her eyes, and then go on to tell Brianna to get a grip on herself. Neither approach had worked. Brianna had a death wish. Grace hoped that today her wish would once again be denied.

"She's in there, Miss O'Connor". The nurse at the reception desk tilted her head towards a curtained off cubicle to the right. Not only was Grace a well-known figure in the Emergency Department, she was often featured on the nightly news. The high profile barrister with the drug addicted sister. Both with secrets they'd hidden since fleeing Aunt Hilda's all those years ago... if ever the media got wind of... no, she wouldn't go there. She'd worked too hard to leave it all behind. And she'd done well for herself. No one would have expected poor, motherless Grace O'Connor to amount to anything. She'd shown them. But Brianna? Different story altogether. Brianna was allowing her past to destroy her.

Grace followed the direction the nurse indicated and paused before entering. What would she find? Each time this happened Brianna looked worse. Grace drew a steadying breath. Time to find out...

Brianna lay in bed with a myriad of tubes hanging out of her nose and arm. Her eyes were closed, but she was breathing. Grace sighed in relief.

Caleb squeezed her arm. "Looks like she's going to make it, Grace." Caleb looked better than he had an hour or so ago. Colour had returned to his face, and his troubled look had eased.

"So glad to hear that, Caleb. What did she do this time?" Pulling her scarf off, Grace placed it on the chair beside her bag and took Brianna's hand.

"Tablets. They've pumped her stomach."

Grace sucked in a deep breath and released it slowly. "Silly girl." A wave of sadness flowed through her. Brianna looked so fragile. Her eye sockets had sunk into her filthy face, and her hair looked like it hadn't been brushed for days, possibly weeks. Grace gently pushed back with her fingertips the strands of hair hanging over Brianna's face. "Why, Brianna? *Why?*"

Grace forced back the tears pricking her eyes. She knew why. But how many more times could they go through this? Something had to change. After all they'd been through, she couldn't lose Brianna now. Her heart ached for the sister she'd shared so much with. Life hadn't been fair to either of them, but for Brianna, it had been worse. She wasn't as strong as Grace, and where Grace had determined not to let her past dictate her future, Brianna didn't have the same resilience or determination.

Grace squeezed Brianna's hand and leaned forward, placing a kiss on her sister's hollow cheek. A tear fell from Grace's eye and splashed onto Brianna's cheek, leaving a muddy streak as it trickled down her face.

A hand on Grace's shoulder jolted her. She remained still, hesitant to move, before slowly lifting her hand and placing it over Niall's. Warmth filled her body. Niall knew how close she was to Brianna. How many nights had they gone out searching for her in the past? How many times had she cried on his shoulder when they'd come home without her?

Grace closed her eyes and steadied herself. Niall's hand on her shoulder meant nothing. It was just his way of showing concern. Nothing more. Nothing less. She couldn't have him, or any other man, in her life. It wouldn't be fair to them. She was better off without them, and Brianna certainly was too. If only Brianna hadn't caught the attention of their cousins. Grace gritted her teeth. What they'd done to her little sister still made her blood boil. She should prosecute them. How many times had she pictured it… bringing those pieces of filth to justice? But if she did, her career would be over… Grace had no doubt Aunt Hilda would expose her secret if she did. And meanwhile, Brianna suffered.

Grace inhaled deeply and rose, letting Brianna's hand slip out of hers. Niall moved back, allowing Grace room to turn. As she did, she lifted her eyes and met his gaze. She swallowed hard. Her heart skittered as she looked into those soft-brown eyes she knew so well. *Why are you here, Niall? After all this time?* She brushed against him lightly as she inched along Brianna's bed towards Caleb, who stood at the end of the bed, arms crossed, legs astride, deep in conversation with the doctor.

"Miss O'Connor." Dr Thompson held out his hand. His face was serious and his voice less than friendly. He must be getting tired of treating their sister. Grace took his hand and shook it.

"Hello, Dr Thompson. This is Niall Flannery. A colleague of mine." *A colleague?*

The two men shook hands.

"Your sister had a close call this time, Miss O'Connor, but I think she'll pull through. We'll know more in the morning."

Grace glanced at Brianna lying in the bed and her shoulders fell. If only she could wrap Brianna in her arms and protect her from the demons that haunted her. Lying in the bed, she looked so helpless… so thin, so dirty, so unloved. And yet, she'd been such a beauty when she was young, with her russet locks that bounced on her shoulders whenever she ran and her hazel eyes that lit up every time she laughed. Maybe she'd been too pretty. Maybe that had been her downfall.

Grace breathed deeply and gulped. She'd already made her decision. She looked at Dr Thompson and then at Caleb. "I'd like Brianna to come back to my place when she's released. I want to look after her."

Caleb's eyes widened. "We've talked about this before, Grace. How will you cope with your job?"

"I'll cope. I'll cut back my work load. It'll be fine."

"You know what she's like, Grace." Caleb reached for Grace's hand and held her gaze. Her brother's sensitivity was at odds with his appearance. Always had been. She and Caleb had shared the burden of being Brianna's keepers for years, and Caleb had often taken time off from his job at the shipyards, without pay, to care for her. Brianna had stayed with Caleb and Caitlin and their two young daughters several times, but she'd never lasted more than a few days at a time. It seemed Brianna couldn't handle more than that, and she often disappeared without a word after stealing whatever she could, leaving behind a heart-broken brother, sister-in-law and two little nieces.

"Yes, I do, but I want to do this, Caleb." Grace moved towards Brianna and eased herself onto the bed. Pulling a tissue from a box on the stand, she gently wiped away the dirt caked on her sister's face as she pushed back the tears pricking her own eyes. She would take Brianna home to her apartment and care for her. And once and for all, she'd get Brianna clean.

CHAPTER 3

"Let's get a bite to eat, Grace. Would you like to join us, Caleb?" Grace stiffened as Niall placed his hand against the small of her back as they walked along the corridor towards the car park.

What was Niall doing? She hadn't agreed to go out with him, but the thought of going home to an empty apartment didn't appeal. Despite her resolve, Grace's heart beat faster at the prospect of spending time alone with Niall, even though it couldn't lead anywhere.

Caleb ran a hand along the side of his head. "Thanks Niall, but I need to get home to Caity and the girls. They'll want to know how Brianna is. Besides, knowing Caity, she'll have dinner waiting for me."

"No problem, Caleb." Niall flashed him a smile. "Give my regards to Caitlin, will you?"

"Will do. See you in the morning, Grace." Caleb kissed Grace on her cheek and shook Niall's hand before leaving them and heading off towards his car.

"Well?" Niall tilted his head, a mischievous grin growing on his face as he held the car door open for her. "I know you haven't eaten." One eyebrow lifted, and as much as she tried, she couldn't tear her eyes away from his.

This was happening way too fast. All week she'd tried to avoid him, all the while trying to ignore the fluttering of her heart every time her eyes locked with his, and the stab of jealousy when the blond leaned too close. She angled her head. Weren't they an item? It seemed that way. So what was Niall doing here with her, asking her out for a meal, especially when he knew there was no future for them. She couldn't have made that any clearer when she'd turned down his proposal several years ago. Maybe he was just after a casual fling?

Grace stilled her beating heart. "All right. Let's get something to eat." She slid under his arm and sank deep into the soft leather seat, hoping she'd made the right decision.

The roar of the Spider's engine once again sent a thrill through her body. Niall glanced at her, a wicked grin sitting on his face. He knew her too well. Blow it! She'd relax and enjoy the ride... get her mind off Brianna and the court case for a while. She drew in a breath and laughed as he thrust the gear stick into first and accelerated out of the park a little too fast.

She wasn't surprised when he pulled up outside Molly's Café—their favourite place to chill when they'd been a couple. But they weren't a couple now, and Grace hadn't ventured inside Molly's since the last time she'd been there with Niall, almost five years ago.

Had he chosen Molly's just because it was convenient, or was he trying to revive their relationship? She'd made it clear she'd never marry. And he'd made it clear if she wouldn't marry him, then it was over… so what was he playing at? Had he changed his mind? And if he had, would she let him into her life again? Her heart pounded. This was all so unexpected and unplanned.

Niall opened the door for her. Grace peeled her long legs out of the car and took his waiting hand. Not that she needed help, but it would have been rude to ignore it.

"Thank you." She flashed him a smile, and then, once steady on her feet, let go of his hand and moved aside to allow him to close the door.

Molly's Café hadn't changed. The heavy timber doors were slightly more weathered, but the cheerful exterior still enticed passers-by to enter. Grace followed Niall as he weaved his way through the scattered tables to their usual booth at the back. They'd always liked sitting here, tucked away from the main area, away from prying eyes. But it was all too familiar.

Grace slid into the seat opposite Niall, tucking her bag beside her. The candlelight accentuated the grey flecks in his hair, giving him a distinguished appearance. She lowered her eyes, needing a moment to compose herself.

A young waitress stood before them with pen and pad in hand. Her dark hair was piled in a loose bun, and her green apron, tied at the waist, sat over a plain white blouse and a short black skirt. She could easily have been the waitress who served them five years ago. "Can I take yer orders?"

Niall looked up and smiled. "Not quite ready, sorry. Could you come back in a few minutes?"

"Sure." She gave the table a quick wipe and then scooted off to the next table.

"What would you like?" Niall's voice was so smooth, so familiar.

Grace gulped and picked up the menu, saying, "I'm not sure yet," as she opened it, thankful for the distraction.

She decided on a Chicken Parmigiana, and he chose a Beef and Guiness Pie.

Once their orders were placed, Grace decided enough was enough. She wouldn't let Niall's presence affect her any more. She'd converse with him as if he were any other person she was having a meal with.

Grace lifted her gaze and held it steady. She could do this. "What brought you back to Belfast?"

Niall wrapped his hands around his coffee mug. "I was wondering when you'd ask that." He met her gaze, his expression growing serious. "Father had a health scare recently. He asked me to come back and help so he could reduce his work load. Doctor's orders." He raised his eyebrows. "So here I am."

Grace straightened and leaned forward.

"I'm sorry to hear that. Is he all right?" She didn't like to think that Randal Flannery, a successful barrister known for his skill and tenacity and his passion for helping the down-trodden, would be out of action for long. She enjoyed the time she met him as opposing counsel.

"Yes, but he has to take it easy if he wants to avoid a full heart attack. You know how hard he works."

"Yes, I do." *But don't we all?*

Niall looked down at his mug. "I'm sure he'll be fine. But he won't like not being at work."

"It might do him good, though." Grace sipped her gin and tonic as her thoughts turned to Niall's parents. Niall's mother, Leah Flannery had always welcomed Grace warmly. In many ways, Leah was the mother Grace yearned for after her own mother died when she was twelve and she and Brianna were sent to live with Aunt Hilda. Leah Flannery was everything Aunt Hilda wasn't. Cheery, happy and kind. Aunt Hilda was stern, cold and demanding. The memories of Leah's warmth towards her tugged at Grace's heart strings, and her voice softened. "How's your mother?"

Niall's eyes lit up and he let out a small laugh. "As busy and involved as ever. I don't know where she gets her energy from."

"I'm glad to hear that. Your mother's a wonderful woman." Grace blinked back tears. "You're very lucky."

"I know." Niall paused, his gaze locked on hers. "But I also came back because of you."

Grace froze. *Had she heard right? Niall came back because of her? Why would he do that when he knew she'd never marry him? Plus, wasn't he with the blond? She needed to find out...* "I thought you were with that blond?"

Niall laughed. “Absolutely not!”

Grace raised a brow. “She looks at you as if she owns you.”

“I'm not sure why. I'm definitely not interested in her.”

Grace wasn't sure if she was relieved or not.

Leaning forward and keeping his gaze steady, Niall took her hand in his slender one. His eyes were filled with a curious, deep longing, and she fought to control her swirling emotions. “All the time I spent away, I couldn’t get you out of my mind. I haven’t dated anyone seriously since you, Grace, and seeing you again this week has made me want you more than ever."

Grace let out a shaky laugh. "Niall… don't."

“It’s true. We weren't just lovers, we were best friends, and I’ve missed you so much." His brown eyes didn't waver as he laced his fingers with hers, they just grew softer and needier.

Why was he doing this? He was right—they'd been best friends before they became lovers, and it had taken everything she had to turn down his proposal. What girl in her right mind wouldn't want to marry Niall Flannery? But she'd had no choice. Her past, if ever it came to light, would ruin not only her career, but his as well if they were married. There was no way she could do that to him.

He squeezed her hand. "Can we start again, Grace?"

Grace bit her lip. Why was he putting her through all of this again? He wasn't after just a casual fling, he wanted to revive their relationship, and she couldn't do it. As much as she wanted to, she couldn't. Nothing had changed.

The waitress appeared and placed their meals in front of them, but Grace’s appetite had fled. She downed her gin and tonic and asked for another.

Niall was still waiting for an answer. She had to tell him... it was no use prolonging it. She drew a breath. "I can't do this, Niall. Not now, not ever. I'm sorry." She gulped.

A muscle in his jaw twitched as he held her gaze. "I don't understand."

She shook her head. "I just can't do it. I'm sorry." She couldn't hold his gaze any longer. "I need to go. I'll call a taxi."

As she stood, Niall gripped her hand. "Grace, don't do this."

The desperation in Niall's voice almost made her change her mind. How she hated hurting him like this again, but it was for his own good —he just didn't know it.

"I have to. I'm sorry." Pulling her hand away, she threw her wrap over her shoulder, raced outside and hailed a taxi.

WHEN GRACE ENTERED her apartment a short while later, she headed straight to the drinks cabinet and poured herself a double. Trapped by the secrets of her past, she was defeated. She felt bereft and desolate. Leaning against the cabinet, she squeezed her eyes shut as her heart ached with the pain of lost love.

If only Niall hadn't returned. She'd been doing fine... work had been her solace. But now she'd have to build her walls higher. She drew a long, slow breath and downed her drink before collapsing on her bed.

CHAPTER 4

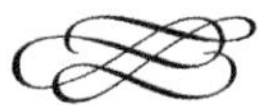

The following morning, Grace entered the powder room at the court house and placed her brief case on the floor. Leaning into the mirror, she inspected her face. She looked better than she felt. The eye drops had worked their magic and her eyes had cleared. She splashed her face and patted it dry with a paper towel before reapplying some face powder and lipstick. Tucking a stray hair under her wig, she studied herself again. She would pass, but only just.

Lifting her chin, she drew a deep breath and re-joined her team in the foyer.

Bryan gave her a warm smile. "Better?"

"Yes, thank you, Bryan." She returned his smile.

Five minutes later, Grace took her seat beside Bryan and forced herself to not even glance at the opposing counsel's seats. Niall would be there by now, and she couldn't risk catching his eye.

Judge Atkinson entered and everyone stood. Grace made herself focus. As well as dealing with Niall's presence, Caleb's phone call earlier that morning weighed on her mind, but she'd have to deal with Brianna's release after the judge had finished his summing up and the jury had been instructed.

Only once during the Judge's summary did Grace steal a glance at Niall. She shouldn't have. The uncomfortable ache in her chest returned at the mere sight of him. Her eyes blurred with tears and she tore her gaze away, forcing all thoughts of what might have been away and focusing instead on the judge.

It didn't take long, and in less than thirty minutes, Grace was heading back to Chambers with Bryan.

NIALL FELT an acute sense of loss as Grace walked out of the court room. He still didn't understand. She had no one else in her life—he'd checked, but Grace had never given him the real reason why she couldn't marry him. He let out a heavy sigh. He'd hoped fleeing to London after she'd turned him down, instead of taking the job with his father's firm in Belfast, would have got her out of his mind, and his heart, but seeing her over this past week had confirmed to him that he still loved her. He'd just have to convince her of that and do everything in his power to win her back.

GRACE CHECKED her schedule and rearranged a few things. She would have to return to court as soon as the jury came back, but that could be days. She got the impression they might be split. She and Niall had both done a good job. Donal O'Malley was guilty, no doubt about it, but had she done enough to convince the jury? Niall certainly had done a good job of attacking her argument and casting doubt. Time would tell. But right now, Brianna needed her.

When Grace entered Brianna's cubicle a short while later, Brianna was sitting up in bed. Her hair was still a mess, but at least her face was clean. “Hey-ya.” Grace leaned down and kissed Briana’s cheek, brushing the unruly hair off her face.

Brianna’s expression remained unmoved.

Grace sighed. This was going to be an uphill battle. She felt like shaking Brianna. Why couldn’t she just kick the habit and get on with life? Grace hated weakness in people, but this was her sister, and if anyone knew what Brianna had been through, it was her. But still, why couldn’t she just sort herself out? It was so frustrating.

Sitting beside Brianna on the bed, Grace took her sister's cold, bony hand. "How are you feeling, Bibi?”

Brianna gave a slight shrug and turned her head away.

Grace bit her lip and glared at her. “Brianna, look at me.”

Forcing herself to remain calm, Grace waited.

Brianna slowly turned her head towards Grace and lifted her dull, lifeless eyes. “Go away, Grace. You’re wasting your time.”

Grace clenched her fist. She wasn't going to let Brianna have her way. “No, I won’t go away, Brianna. I don’t care what you say... I’m not going to let you do this again. You’re coming home with me, and I’m going to look after you.”

Brianna jeered at her. “To your fancy apartment? Yeah, right. What would your neighbours think? I don’t think so, Grace. Just let me be.” Turning her back on Grace, she slid down the bed and curled up, pulling the blankets around her neck.

Grace seethed. She felt like yanking the blankets off Brianna and shaking her. How dare she talk to her like that? “I’m not going anywhere, Brianna. I’ve made up my mind.” It would be so easy to walk out and leave Brianna to her own demise. Grace was sure that’s what Brianna wanted, but she couldn’t do that. Having looked out for Brianna her whole life, she wasn’t prepared to let her go now.

The doctor entered the cubicle and picked up Brianna's chart. After giving Brianna a quick check, he told Grace Brianna was clear to leave.

After the doctor left, Grace rubbed Brianna's arm. "Okay, time to go, like it or not."

Brianna grunted and slowly pulled herself up. "Why can't I go to Caleb's?"

Grace gagged at Brianna's stale breath. "Because you're coming with me." Obviously Briana would have preferred to go home with Caleb, *but tough.* This time she was coming home with her, and this time, she'd get off those drugs if it killed Grace in the process. Caleb was too soft. Brianna needed someone who'd tell her how it is and not just tell her she needed God.

"Let me brush your hair before we leave—it looks like a rat nested in it." But Brianna's hair was so matted that Grace couldn't get a brush through it, instead, she tied it up with a hair tie she found in her purse. "We'll have to sort it when we get home."

After signing the necessary paperwork, Grace led Brianna to her car and helped her in. It wasn't a long drive to her downtown apartment, and within half an hour she was helping Brianna settle into her room.

"There are more blankets if you need them. And the bathroom's just through here. But first, let's give you a wash and sort out that hair."

"It's fine the way it is, Grace."

Grace's blood boiled at the defiance in Brianna's expression. She put her hands on her hips and stared Brianna down. "It is not fine the way it is, Brianna. You probably have bugs, let alone the fact you can't get a brush through it. I'll run a bath and we'll get you clean at least, but then we have to do something with it."

She gave Brianna no choice, and as she sponged her sister's emaciated body, her heart almost broke. What had happened to her beautiful little sister? It was all Da's fault. If he hadn't deserted their Mam, leaving her to raise eight young children on her own, Mam wouldn't have run herself into the ground and died so young. And then she and Brianna wouldn't have been sent to Aunt Hilda's. How Daniel and Caleb had ever forgiven Da before he died was beyond her.

"There… better?" Grace poured warm water down Brianna's back and then rested her hand on her bony shoulder.

Brianna nodded slowly.

Tears rolled down Grace's cheek as she leaned forward and hugged her sister. "It's going to be all right, Bibi. We're going to get you fixed."

BRIANNA SLEPT FOR FIVE HOURS. Grace looked in on her every ten minutes or so. She couldn't relax. What was she going to do with her? If they stayed here in the apartment, Brianna would pack up and leave within days, as she always did at Caleb and Caitlin's. They'd tried putting her into a rehab facility several times, but she'd never lasted. Brianna needed a change of scenery. A complete change. Grace started to formulate a plan. As soon as the jury came back and delivered their verdict, she'd take Brianna on a road trip. They'd drive to the sea. Let the wind and the fresh air blow away all of Brianna's troubles. Yes, that's what they'd do.

Caleb thought it a grand idea. "Why don't I put in for holidays and Caitlin and I and the girls can join you?"

Grace's heart fell. How could she tell Caleb she wanted to do this on her own without hurting his feelings? She just had to tell him. "I'd like to spend time alone with Brianna first, if that's okay with you, Caleb. But maybe you and the girls can join us after a while? Once Brianna's stable?"

Caleb pursed his lips but eventually agreed. "We'll pray for you."

"Thanks Caleb." She couldn't tell him she didn't need his prayers when she'd just told him she didn't want him on the trip.

She hugged him when he went to leave. "You're a good brother,

Caleb. The best." She smiled warmly into his face and their shared history flashed through her mind. Apart from Brianna, Caleb was the sibling she knew the best, and the one she could depend on if ever she needed anything. She just needed to do this trip without him.

"And you're not too bad yourself, sis." He winked at her as he pecked her on the cheek and disappeared down the hallway.

CHAPTER 5

Brianna reluctantly allowed Grace to cut her hair and treat it with bug shampoo. She also allowed Grace to dye it her natural russet colour. She looked in the mirror and didn't recognise the person looking back.

Grace had made her eat small regular meals, and she'd already put on some weight. She hadn't left Grace's apartment since the day Grace had brought her here. The few times she'd asked Grace to let her go out, Grace refused. Apart from jumping off the balcony, there was no way out. She felt like a prisoner.

For the first day or so, they'd spent most of their time watching television. Grace tried to get her talking, but she didn't feel like it. She'd slept a lot, but whenever she was up she couldn't relax. Grace wouldn't let her have a drink, although she was allowed the occasional cigarette. Big deal. What she wanted, *needed,* more than anything, was a hit. Grace had told her she was to go cold turkey. She'd done it before and hated it. As each day passed, Brianna craved her drugs more and more. Her body went into withdrawal. She felt sick. She threw up. She shivered. Grace bathed her body with cool damp sponges. She lashed out at Grace.

Scratched Grace's face. Threw objects around her room. And threw herself onto the bed and screamed.

On the third night, when her body was wracked with cramps, she thrashed her arms about and pummelled Grace's chest. "I can't do this, Grace. Let me go."

Grace caught Brianna's arms and held them above her head. Finally calming, she sobbed into Grace's chest.

"You're almost there, Bibi. You can do this." Grace rubbed Brianna's back and pulled her close. Maybe she could, but she hated it. Why couldn't they just let her be?

THE JURY RETURNED four days after they were dismissed. Grace had Caitlin on call to sit with Brianna while she was gone, and within the hour of receiving the phone call, Grace was wigged up and sitting in court beside Bryan. To be honest, she'd almost forgotten the case was still in progress. She'd hardly given Donal O'Malley a thought since she'd taken Brianna home. And she'd tried not to think about Niall. But there he was, with the blond still looking like she owned him. Grace turned her head away quickly when Niall caught her looking at him, but one moment was enough. Her heart still refused to listen to her head.

Judge Atkinson entered and everyone rose. Donal O'Malley was expressionless as the jury's foreman read out the verdict of guilty. Bryan grabbed Grace's arm and squeezed it. Grace glanced once again at Niall. The blond had her hand on top of his. It was over, and she'd won. She should have felt relieved, elated, but instead, she felt nothing.

Becoming a top barrister had always been her dream, and how hard she'd worked to get there. But now she felt empty. Had it really been worth all the effort? Maybe if she'd spent more time with Brianna rather than studying and working so hard, Brianna might not have ended up in the gutter. At the time it seemed the right thing to do, but now? She was looking forward to the break. Would she miss the court room with all its pomp and ceremony? Would she miss the kick she got from standing in front of a packed court room making witnesses and defendants squirm? Probably, but right now she didn't care. She said goodbye to Bryan and shook Niall's hand as protocol demanded, trying to avoid his eye, but when he slipped an envelope into her hand, she glanced up and met his gaze. He didn't say a word, just looked at her with soft brown eyes that almost made her resolve fly out the window. She gulped and turned away. She didn't trust herself to speak.

WHEN GRACE RETURNED to her apartment, she opened the door quietly and tip-toed inside. Caitlin was sitting on the couch flipping through a magazine and looked up as Grace put her briefcase down.

"How is she?" Grace whispered as she glanced towards Brianna's room and slipped her jacket off.

"She slept the whole time." Caitlin's jolly face seemed to be getting rounder by the day. "Not a peep out of her."

"That's a relief. Coffee?"

"Yes please, that would be lovely." Caitlin eased herself off the couch and joined Grace at the breakfast bar. "When are you planning on leaving?"

Grace stood with her arms folded, leaning back against the counter. "Now the case is over, tomorrow, I hope. Brianna's really fidgety, and I need to get her out of here as soon as I can. We could even leave today." Grace felt brighter at the thought.

Grace had rarely talked to Caitlin on her own. Usually Caitlin was with Caleb, and she let Caleb do most of the talking. But Grace knew Caitlin to be a caring wife and mother, and a devout Christian. Maybe that was one of the reasons Grace had avoided being with her on her own. She'd heard Caitlin had a knack of getting under people's outer layers, breaking through the walls they'd put up. Grace had many walls, and she didn't want Caitlin, or anybody else, getting under, over, or through them.

"Where are you thinking of going?"

Grace lifted two brightly coloured mugs from the cupboard. "We might head north, and then go along the coast, and see what happens after that. Neither of us has seen much of the country, so we'll just take a day at a time."

"Sounds super. Brianna must be looking forward to it."

"Yes, she is, surprisingly. Milk? Sugar?"

Caitlin settled herself onto a stool. "Yes, please. Three sugars."

Grace raised an eyebrow. *No wonder she's stacking it on.*

Caitlin didn't seem to notice. "Have you ever thought of going to Danny's place?"

Grace's head jerked up. "Danny's place?"

"Yes, I thought Caleb would have mentioned it."

Grace joined Caitlin on another stool. "He may have, but I probably didn't take much notice." She always stopped listening whenever Caleb started talking to her about what Daniel and Lizzy were doing since it usually included something to do with the Bible College where they worked, and she simply wasn't interested. The only time she'd ever really listened was when Caleb told her about her new little niece and nephew. And that was over a year ago.

"Well, I think it would be perfect for Brianna. He and Lizzy are managing this place where young people go if they're struggling to fit in or can't stay out of trouble." She paused and took a sip of her coffee. "It's not rehab, and it's not a college—I guess it's somewhere in between. They've had a lot of young people through already with quite a lot of success. The students, as they call them, work for half a day, and then they have lessons for the other half and evening, all the while living in community with counsellors on hand, twenty-four seven." Caitlin's eyes twinkled as she spoke, and her second chin wobbled.

"I guess it's a church run place?" Grace had no doubt, but asked anyway.

"Yes, it's sponsored by the college Daniel worked at. Caleb and I also support it financially, as do a lot of others. It's a great ministry, and I think it'd be perfect for Brianna." She placed her chubby hand gently on Grace's wrist. "Think about it, Grace. I'm sure they'd welcome both of you." Caitlin stopped and laughed. "I didn't mean you as a student... they'd welcome you as a guest!" She let out another chuckle.

Such a jolly person, and she means well, but no, I won't be taking Brianna there. "Thanks for the information, Caitlin. I'll keep it in mind." Grace finished her coffee just as Brianna appeared in the kitchen.

"Hey, Bibi, how are you feeling?" Slipping off her stool, Grace hugged Brianna and kissed her forehead.

"Okay, I guess. Did you win?"

Grace's head jolted up. *The case... she'd forgotten already...* "Yes, we won. It's all over now, and we can head off as soon as we're ready. Do you want a drink?"

"Yes please."

"How are you, Brianna? Doing better?" Caitlin reached out and squeezed Brianna's arm gently as Brianna took a seat beside her.

"I'm getting there, but Grace has kept me locked up." She shot Grace a less than kind look.

"It's worked though, Brianna. You haven't taken any drugs since you were taken to the hospital."

"I almost died, though." She pouted, but took the mug of steaming hot coffee Grace handed her.

"You might have died if I hadn't brought you here." Grace raised her brow.

"I see you two are going to have a fun trip—you sound just like my two! Always bickering." Caitlin let out a jolly laugh. "Anyway, I'd better be off. Ladies luncheon at church today." She paused and looked at Grace. "Guess you don't want to come?"

Grace shook her head. She was right.

"No harm in asking." Caitlin chuckled.

"Sorry. Maybe another time." She was just being polite. She would never go to a ladies luncheon at church. "Thanks so much for coming today." Grace leaned forward and kissed her on the cheek.

"My pleasure, and have a wonderful trip, the two of you." She gave Brianna a huge hug and bustled out the door.

"Phew, I'm glad she's gone." Brianna settled into one of Grace's leather arm chairs with her mug of coffee, tucking her legs underneath her.

"She means well."

"I guess so, but she's so gooey and squidgy."

Grace laughed. "That's one way to describe her!"

Brianna rolled her eyes and joined in with Grace's laughter. It was so good to see the real Brianna finally emerging from the depths of darkness.

"So Bibi, do you want to leave today?" Grace sat down opposite her with another mug of coffee.

Brianna stopped laughing and locked eyes with Grace. "You mean I finally get to leave here?"

"It was for your own good, Bibi. I didn't do it for fun, you know." Grace held her mug with both hands and let out a sigh.

"I understand, and thank you, Grace." Brianna's eyes watered. "I mean it. I can't promise to stay off the stuff forever, but I'll try. I just hope you know what you're letting yourself in for."

Grace shrugged. "I'm tough. I'll cope with whatever."

CHAPTER 6

Grace packed quickly. Brianna had very little, so Grace lent her what she could, and promised to buy whatever she needed along the way. There wasn't much room in Grace's sports car anyway.

Grace was tempted not to take the envelope Niall had given her, but against her better judgment, tossed it into her bag. She'd read it later, although it would do her heart no good.

They headed north out of the city. Brianna's body visibly relaxed when Grace took the A2 and not the M2 towards Londonderry. Neither she nor Brianna had been back to Londonderry since they'd fled Aunt Hilda's house when Brianna was four months pregnant. The memories were too painful, and neither girl dared look down that road.

It was a warm day, and Grace had the roof down. She wore a bright red scarf to help keep her hair in place, but as she'd cut Brianna's hair so short, Brianna had no need of one. She did give her a pair of Oroton sunglasses, though. Grace glanced at Brianna as she accelerated onto the open road and smiled. She hadn't seen Brianna looking so relaxed for a long time.

It was impossible to talk, so Grace just enjoyed being out in the country. It had been way too long. She and Niall used to go for long drives on weekends. In fact, his parents lived just off this road. She peered down Derry Lane as they flew past the intersection, and she just made out the roof line of the large country manor Randal and Leah Flannery had lived in their entire married lives. Thinking of them made her glance at her bag holding Niall's envelope. He probably had nothing new to say… she should have left it behind or tossed it in the bin. But it was a link… a little part of him she could hold close to her heart.

The afternoon drew in, and as they hadn't booked anywhere, Grace slowed down at the next town they came to. The small village of Lorne hugged the banks of the Glendun River, and two pubs, a church, and a few shops lined the road. Signs advertising the local Bed and Breakfast places were scattered here and there. The pubs looked less than inviting, not somewhere to take Brianna on their first night. One of the Bed and Breakfast places would be better.

"Which one, Bibi?" Grace pulled the sports car to a stop as they looked at the signs. Neither one stood out, but as Brianna didn't have any preference, Grace chose the more expensive one. She had plenty of money, and it should be the better of the two.

A short, round lady bustled down the stone steps, bordered on either side with overflowing brightly coloured flowers, and greeted them. She wore a grey, knee-length skirt and a pink twin set with two strings of fake pearls draped around her chubby neck. Her face was round and kindly, and her greying hair was swept up in an old fashioned bun.

"Welcome, ladies! My name's Maeve, and I'm happy to see you both. Come on in and I'll show you to your room." She stopped suddenly. "Did you want one room or two?"

Grace glanced at Brianna. She was hanging back, and her face was blank, as if it was all too much for her. Grace held out her hand and pulled her along. "One room, thanks, Maeve." Grace gave the woman a warm smile. "I'm Grace, and this is my sister Brianna."

"Nice to meet you both. And where have you come from today?"

Maeve bustled ahead, but stopped at the top of the stairs to catch her breath. "Oh my goodness." She patted her chest. "These steps seem to be getting steeper every day."

Grace let out a small laugh to be polite. "Just from Belfast. We had a late start."

"Oh, and where are you heading?"

"We're not sure yet. We'll just drive and see where the road takes us."

"There are some lovely wee towns further north if that's what you're looking for."

"Thanks, we might check them out."

"And now, here's the best room for you. It opens out onto the garden and you can take your tea out there if you like."

The room, halfway down a dimly lit hallway adorned with black and white family photos, reminded Grace of a number of similar rooms she'd stayed in with Niall, except of course those rooms had a double bed. Grace's throat tightened at the memory.

Maeve continued talking. *Did she ever stop?* Grace turned her head. Brianna had paused in the hallway and was looking at the photos. Grace reached out her hand and motioned for her to follow.

'There are more blankets in the cupboard if you need them. And there's a private bathroom just through here." Maeve half opened a door on the far wall of the room. "What time would you be wanting breakfast?"

"Eight o'clock would be perfect." Grace smiled politely.

"Are you right for dinner? If not, I could rustle something up."

"That's very kind, thank you, Maeve, but we might just pop back into the village and see what we can find."

"The Green Leprechaun does meals until nine—that's probably your best option. I wouldn't recommend the Derry Arms—a bit rough for two young ladies like yourselves."

"We can look after ourselves, can't we Bibi? But thanks, Maeve. We might check out the Green Leprechaun."

Grace paid for the night and then closed the door, letting out a huge breath as she flopped backwards onto one of the beds.

"I didn't think she'd ever stop talking." Brianna walked over to the double doors leading out to the garden and looked out. "Feels strange staying in someone's home."

Grace sat up. "Maybe we should have stayed at the hotel. Will you be okay here, Bibi?" Grace stood and slipped her arm around Brianna's bony, fragile shoulder.

Brianna shrugged. "It's too nice for the likes of me."

"Oh come on, Bibi. Stop it!" Grace turned Brianna around to face her and placed both her hands on Brianna's shoulders. She lifted Brianna's chin with her finger and looked into her sister's hazel eyes. "Enough of all that nonsense. This holiday is about spoiling you and getting you better, so get used to it."

"I'm more at home on the streets—you know that." Brianna shook Grace's finger away and looked around the room. "All this frilly stuff." She reached out and fingered the lace edged lamp shade on one of the bedside tables. "I've never seen so many pillows and cushions in all my life. And all these flowers—they'll do my head in."

"Oh Bibi! Just relax and enjoy it! Come outside and we'll sit for a while. I'll make us some tea."

Grace put the kettle on and made a pot of tea while Brianna continued to inspect the room, commenting on everything from the heavy floral duvets on each bed, to the highly perfumed soaps and shampoos in the bathroom.

Grace carried the tray with the teapot, two dainty porcelain china cups and saucers, matching side plates with a homemade scone each, and tiny pots of strawberry jam and cream outside onto their private terrace. Despite the chill in the air, the late afternoon sun peeked in through the vine covered trellis, creating an inviting and warm sitting area. Grace felt right at home, but Brianna shivered as she perched on the edge of a cushioned cane armchair.

"Bibi—just relax and enjoy. Here, let me pour." As Grace poured tea into the dainty cup with delicate pink roses painted on it, she glanced at Brianna's stony face and sighed.

BRIANNA STARED at her tea cup. A set, just like this, sat on a shelf at Aunt Hilda's in that horrible, dingy kitchen that reeked of greasy mutton and stale tobacco. Brianna's heart pounded like it did when her body was waiting for a hit.

She stood, bumping the table and spilling the tea. She didn't care. She ran inside and flung herself onto the bed. This was a big mistake. Why had she let Grace talk her into it? She didn't belong in places like this... she was a drug addict, and she needed a hit, not a cup of tea in a cup she couldn't even hold without getting her fingers stuck.

The bed creaked as Grace sat beside her. Brianna turned her head away. *Why can't she let me be?*

"Bibi, what's the matter?" Grace stroked her hair, just like she used to. But that was years ago. Tears pricked Brianna's eyes as a weight settled on her chest. Where could she start? Everything was the matter. She pushed Grace away and curled into a ball.

Grace leaned over her.

Brianna kicked her away. "Go away, Grace." Tears choked her voice and she could hardly breathe.

Grace grabbed her and held her. Brianna struggled. She didn't want Grace's sympathy. She fought against her, but Grace was too strong and she finally gave in, sobbing uncontrollably into Grace's chest.

"Oh, Bibi." Grace's voice was soft and caring. Brianna hated it. If only Grace would let her be.

Brianna's sobs slowly subsided. Grace dried her face with a tissue, but kept one arm around Brianna's shoulder.

"I can't do this, Grace." She could barely speak.

"Yes you can, Bibi. Look at me." Grace tipped Brianna's chin and held her gaze. Grace's eyes were moist. "I'm here for you. Whatever it takes, okay?"

Brianna drew a shaky breath. She didn't want to do it. That was the problem. She needed drugs because they helped her forget. There was nothing Grace could do that would wipe her memory of those horrid years. Memories that tormented her night and day. Only the drugs sent them away.

Grace tucked a lock of hair behind Brianna's ear. "I'll find those boys and prosecute them."

Brianna slumped. How many times had she thought about tracking them down and making them pay for raping her when she was just fifteen? But Grace had told her she probably wouldn't win, and it might just make it worse, so she'd tried to forget. It was no use. Besides, the thought of facing them in court made her ill.

She lifted her gaze. "No, Grace. I don't want you to."

Grace nodded slowly. "You know I'm prepared to, Bibi, if you want me to?"

"I just want to forget, Grace. That's all I want to do."

"You've got so much to live for, Bibi. You could be anything you want. A nurse, you could go to University, you could work in an office, you could be anything you want."

Brianna's eyes moistened. "How could I do that, Grace? I didn't even finish school."

"Yes, but you can study, just like I did. I can help you. Think about it? It might help you forget."

Brianna shrugged. How could she study when she could barely read?

"Come on. Let's clean up and get some dinner." Grace gave her a big squeeze and then stood.

Brianna let out a deep sigh. *Everything's so simple for Grace, but she doesn't have a clue.*

CHAPTER 7

Later that night, after Grace and Brianna had been out for dinner at The Green Leprechaun, a lively little place with great food, and Brianna was tucked up in bed, Grace reached for Niall's envelope. All day she'd been tempted to open it, but had stopped herself each time she'd reached for it, reminding herself she was trying to forget him. But try as she might, she couldn't get him out of her head.

The light from the bedside lamp was dim, but Niall's handwriting was as strong as ever, and she could make out the words easily. She bit her lip as she read.

Grace,

I'm so sorry for putting you under pressure the other night. We're soul mates—you know that. We can't turn the clock back, but I would love to be your friend if you'll let me, and to be there for you whenever you need someone to talk to. Obviously, I want more than that, but if you won't marry me, at least be my friend?

Call me if you need anything at all. Wherever you might be, whatever the time of day or night, I'm only a phone call away.

I love you, Grace, and I always will. Nothing will change that.

Forever yours,

Niall

Grace flopped against her pillow and held the notepaper to her chest. Part of her wanted to tear up the letter and throw it in the bin. But Niall was right—they were soul mates. Despite the years of separation, there was a bond between them, and her heart still quickened at the very thought of him.

She picked up the letter and re-read it. Her thoughts filtered back to the day she met him... her first day at Belfast University. She wore a long wrap-around Indian style skirt, black knee-high boots, and a blue denim jacket. Niall was wearing skinny jeans and a blue, hand-knitted cardigan. Her first thought was that someone special had made it for him. She laughed when she discovered later that the special person was his mother.

They sat beside each other in their first lecture—Introduction to Law. As he chatted with her, it became apparent he was from a well-to-do family. His father was a high-profile barrister, as was his father before him, and there was never any question about Niall following in their footsteps.

Grace was tempted to make up a story of her own. How could she tell Niall that she'd worked by day and studied by night just to get into University? Or that she was supporting her younger sister whose two-month old baby, a result of being raped by her cousins when she was only fifteen, had just died? Grace gulped. *Or that she herself had blown up ten innocent people when she was only sixteen?* He'd never believe her... In the end, she told him she'd decided to study Law because she'd seen too many violent crimes go unpunished, and she wanted to do what she could to change that. She'd gone home that day with the brown-eyed Niall Flannery on her heart and her mind. And that's where he'd stayed for the next five years. Until the night he proposed.

Brianna stirred. Grace quickly folded the letter and placed it in her purse. She should throw it away, but she couldn't. She switched off the light and hoped Brianna would settle. All afternoon and night Brianna had been restless. Was it a mistake to take her away? Would it be too much for both of them? Grace hoped not, but doubt flooded through her as Brianna writhed around in bed.

Grace finally climbed out of her own bed and climbed in with Brianna, wrapping her arms around her and pulling her close, just like she used to do when they were first sent to live with Aunt Hilda.

Brianna settled for a short while, and then woke with a start, jerking to a seated position.

“Where am I?” The fear and desperation in Brianna's voice tore at Grace’s heart.

Grace flicked on the light and sat up. Sweat dripped from Brianna’s brow, and her bed clothes were damp. Her face was twisted with anguish.

“It’s okay, Bibi. I’m here.” Grace wiped Brianna’s brow. “Were you having a nightmare?”

Brianna nodded and fell back onto her pillow, curling into a ball and sobbing. Grace lay back beside her and held her tight, all the while uttering soothing words until Brianna’s breathing slowed and she fell asleep.

Grace was almost asleep when Brianna jumped out of bed and began rummaging through her bag.

"What are you doing, Bibi?" Grace climbed out of bed and tried to pull her back.

Bibi brushed Grace's hand away. "Leave me alone. I need a hit."

Before Grace could stop her, Brianna upended the bag and began tossing items all around the room.

“Stop it, Brianna.” Grace’s voice was a firm whisper, but panic was setting in. Brianna couldn't give in now.

“Don’t stop me, Grace.” The determination in Brianna's face frightened Grace, but she had to stop her. No way could she let Brianna go into town on her own in the middle of the night.

"No, you're not going anywhere. Stop it now." Grace's pulse raced as Brianna struggled with her. Brianna jerked one hand free and slapped Grace across her face. Grace gasped and her hand flew to her smarting cheek. How dare Brianna hit her! Who did she think she was?

An urgent knock on the door was enough to distract Brianna long enough for Grace to gain the upper hand. "Is everything all right in there?" Maeve called out in a concerned voice.

"Yes, thank you, Maeve. Everything's fine." Grace put on her most convincing voice as she held her hand over Brianna's mouth and tried to keep her still.

"Okay then, dear. If you need anything, let me know."

"Thank you. We will."

As Maeve's footsteps receded, Brianna's body slumped and Grace loosened her hold. Wrapping her arms around Bibi, she pulled her close. "We'll get through this, Bibi, you'll see." Grace's heart tore in two as Brianna sobbed uncontrollably into her chest.

THE FOLLOWING MORNING, Grace had trouble waking Brianna in time for breakfast. In the end, she decided to let her sleep and told Maeve they'd eat in their room. A weaker person would have given in to Maeve's inquisitive glances, but Grace held her ground and didn't say anything other than her sister was still sleeping.

While Brianna slept, Grace took her tea and toast outside and sat in the gazebo. Feeble rays of sun warmed her body as she flicked through the local newspaper Maeve had provided, but her mind was on Niall's letter. Even though she'd only read it twice, the words were etched in her memory and played over in her mind. What she wouldn't give to have him here right now.

Grace glanced towards the room where Brianna still slept. How long would it take for Brianna to be free from her addiction? Grace longed for her little sister to be whole again. She leaned back in her chair and her thoughts drifted to a happier time... the time before Mam died.

Even though they were poor, they'd been such a happy family in the years after Da left. Brianna had always been the fun-loving girl, whereas Grace had been the studious one, but despite that, the two girls had been thicker than mud. The day they got sent to Londonderry to live with Aunt Hilda was etched in Grace's memory. The day of Mam's funeral was cold, wet and miserable. The eight children lined up beside her grave and one at a time threw a handful of dirt on top of the coffin lying in that horrible, deep hole. The minister prayed for Mam's soul, but that was the day Grace told God she would never talk to Him ever again, and she hadn't.

Brianna cried the whole way to Londonderry, and when they were met at the bus stop by Aunt Hilda and Uncle Dougall, Brianna hid behind Grace. They were put in the back room that was no bigger than a broom closet. In fact, Grace initially thought that's what it was. It had no heating, and in winter, she and Brianna clung to each other at night to stay alive.

In all the years they lived there, not once did they feel welcome. They were treated as the poor cousins who'd been taken in and were told they should be grateful for a roof over their heads. *Grateful?* The dogs were treated better than they were.

Grace looked up as Brianna appeared in the doorway, her hair dishevelled and dark circles hanging under her eyes. Grace's heart broke. She held out her hand. "Come and sit."

Brianna took Grace's hand and sat beside her. Grace poured her a cup of tea, and placed it in front of her.

"I'm sorry for last night." Brianna's voice was raspy and faint.

Grace pushed back the tears pricking her eyes. "It's okay, Bibi. We can do this." She gave Brianna an encouraging smile, but wondered if she really believed what she'd said. "It looks like a nice day for a drive along the coast. I thought we could head to Cushendall, but we can just see how far we get."

Brianna shrugged. "Whatever you think."

Grace bit her tongue. It'd be nice if Brianna for once showed some enthusiasm. Maybe once they were back on the road she'd brighten a little.

It didn't take long to finish breakfast, shower and pack. Maeve wore an inquisitive look as they said good-bye, but Grace pretended she didn't notice. As Grace started the engine and pulled back onto the main road, she glanced at Brianna and hoped they'd have a good day.

CHAPTER 8

Five days later, Grace stopped the car on top of a cliff. "Well, go on then. Jump." Grace's nostrils flared as she spat the words at Brianna.

Brianna turned in her seat and reached for the door handle. A gust of wind blew the door back as she tried to open it. She wouldn't let it stop her. Gripping the door with both hands, she pushed it open and climbed out. Another gust of wind whistled past, almost knocking her off her feet. She steadied herself and inched closer to the edge.

Below, angry waves crashed onto the rocks, sending sprays of water into the air. She could taste the salt on her lips. Sucking in a breath, she glanced back at Grace. Her heart was racing. Could she really do this? For the past two days she'd been telling Grace she just wanted to end it all, but now, could she really do it?

It had been over two weeks since her last hit. Surely she was getting to the point where she no longer craved a high, but in the meantime, it was torture. Grace had no idea. Telling her to be strong wasn't enough. Grace had nothing to offer her, and Brianna didn't have Grace's strength or will-power. Never had. Never would.

Grace hadn't been able to save her before, and she couldn't save her now. There was nothing to live for. Nothing. She may as well jump. The nightmares were killing her. Her head ached constantly. Her body was tired. No, she had nothing to live for.

Inching closer to the edge, she lifted her chin. She wouldn't look. She'd just step forward, and then it'd all be over. No more nightmares. No more memories. She'd be free from them all.

"Bibi, don't do it." Grace grabbed her from behind.

"No! You can't stop me." Brianna struggled, kicking and elbowing Grace. Sobs choked her throat and she could barely speak—she just wanted to end it all, why couldn't Grace let her be?

She tried to free herself from Grace's hold, but she was no match for Grace. A heaviness grew in her heart and she collapsed onto the ground. Grace crouched beside her and hugged her. Brianna curled into a ball and wept. She wept for the baby she'd loved and lost. She'd never expected to love him, but when Aedan was born, waves of love and pity flowed through her from the moment she held him.

She didn't even know who his father was—it could have been either of them. Being born prematurely, Aedan had been given a fifty-fifty chance of living, but despite the odds, he survived. Brianna brought him home to the apartment she and Grace lived in, and for two months, she cared for her son. Lying on her bed, she often held him close while he slept. He needed her, and she needed him. But then he got sick.

That night, Brianna woke to Aedan wheezing. She jumped out of bed and shook Grace. Panic set in. "We need to get Aedan to the hospital, Grace." Quickly dressing, she bundled Aedan in a blanket and raced out the door. Grace hailed a taxi. Brianna's entire focus was on coaxing Aedan to breathe, but his tiny body shuddered with every weak breath he took. His face paled to a bluish tinge, and then he stopped breathing.

There was nothing the doctors could do. He'd developed pneumonia and his weak lungs couldn't handle it. She blamed herself. If only she'd looked after him better. If only they'd had better heating. It wasn't Grace's fault… she'd done her best to provide for them after fleeing

Aunt Hilda's, but she was only seventeen and her meagre wage from working at the hotel barely paid the rent. If only Aedan had lived, things would have been different.

A seagull cried overhead, jolting her out of her memory.

"Come on Bibi, we need to go." Grace helped her to stand. The wind had eased, but heavy clouds had rolled in from the sea and rain was falling. She hadn't even noticed.

What was ahead for her? She'd come so close to ending it all, but what now? There was no end in sight—nothing was going to change. *She needed a hit.*

GRACE BREATHED a sigh of relief when she finally got Brianna back in the car. This time she thought Brianna might really do it. In some ways, it would have been easier if she had. How was she going to help her? Grace didn't want to admit defeat, but she had no answers. It would only be a matter of time before Bibi stole money off her and disappeared. She couldn't watch her twenty-four seven. Then what would she do? Start all over again? Grace felt ill at the thought.

Why couldn't Brianna just leave it all behind her and get on with life? Grace took a moment and settled herself before starting the engine. Turning to look at Brianna, her heart softened and she reached out and squeezed Brianna's hand. Tears welled in Brianna's eyes. Grace handed her a tissue. "It'll be all right, Bibi. Not much longer now." But Grace didn't believe it, so how could she expect Brianna to?

Grace stared out at the dark rolling sea. Out there somewhere was Scotland. On a clear day, Grace had been told you could see it. Maybe she should take Brianna to Danny and Lizzy's place after all. Maybe they had some answers, as long as they didn't try to push God down her throat. She'd give it some thought.

Days passed. Grace and Brianna drove through town after town.

They visited castle after castle, drank copious amounts of coffee and spent hours upon hours walking and driving, but one day, when Grace came out of the shower and found the contents of her purse strewn all over her bed and Brianna missing, she'd had enough. She quickly dressed and threw their bags into the car and raced out to find her. It wasn't hard. She headed straight for the local pub. Brianna was there. She hadn't bought any drugs, but it was only a matter of time.

Grace forced Brianna into the car and headed straight to Caleb and Caitlin's.

IT WAS ALL ORGANISED. Brianna had the required medical assessment and got accepted into the Elim Community Centre, the place Danny and Lizzy managed, and within a week, Grace was standing at the airport with Brianna saying goodbye to Caleb and Caitlin. She'd half expected Niall to be there. Scanning the departure lounge, her heart fell. He wasn't there. But why would he be? She hadn't even told him she was back in Belfast after the trip with Brianna. She could have called him, but if she was ever going to be able to forget him, she had to force herself to not even think about him.

"Come here, sis," Caleb pulled her into his arms and hugged her tightly. "We'll be praying for you both."

Grace cringed. She didn't need Caleb's prayers, but hugged him anyway. "Thank you, Caleb." She smiled into his eyes. Caleb meant well, and if he was happy praying, who was she to stop him?

He gave her a kiss and let her go when final boarding was called. She picked up her carry-on luggage and walked slightly ahead of Brianna, giving a final wave before she entered the plane.

Grace turned to make sure Brianna was still following. They'd come this far, she couldn't let Brianna bail on her now. She was there, but she wore a vacant look on her face, as if it was all too much for her. The past week, since the day Brianna had almost jumped, she'd been quiet and withdrawn, as if she didn't care whether she lived or died, and although it'd been easier on Grace, it had also made her angry. Grace had often felt like shaking Brianna and yelling at her. Okay, she'd been through a lot, but why couldn't she just pull herself together? Grace didn't understand.

Brianna shrugged and raised her eyes just enough to meet Grace's gaze. Her eyes were dull and lifeless. Grace had thought flying for the first time might have excited her a little, but no... seemed she didn't care about anything. Grace was starting to doubt whether anything or anyone would ever get through to her. Danny and Lizzy were Brianna's last options. If they couldn't help her, Grace had no idea who could.

CHAPTER 9

Elim Community Centre - outside Fort William, Scotland

"COME ON, Daniel, we don't want to be late." Lizzy drummed her fingers on the door-frame of her husband's office and glared at him. What was he doing at his desk again?

Daniel glanced up and met Lizzy's gaze. "I'm coming—give me a minute." He quickly finished what he was doing and closed his notebook before grabbing his jacket from the back of the door. He placed a kiss on Lizzy's cheek and flashed her a cheeky grin. "What's the matter, love?"

Lizzy humphed, but found it impossible not to return his disarming smile. She couldn't stay angry with Daniel for long, and he knew it. "Nothing, I just want to be early for once in our lives, that's all. And we need to leave before the children come back from their walk."

"Well come on then, let's go." He grabbed her hand and led her out of the house to the waiting van.

As they drove down the rough track leading to the small highland village of Glen Brannie, Lizzy snuggled closer to Daniel and placed her hand on his leg. Mist still covered the top of Ben Nevis, but there was hope the day would be fine and sunny. Lizzy rarely went anywhere these days without their three young children, and rarely did she and Daniel leave the Community alone, so this was a special treat. Not that she minded sharing her husband with the staff and students of the community. She was still in awe of the way God had blessed them.

Nobody had expected their marriage to last. She'd been distraught after Mathew, the handsome student minister she'd loved dearly, broke their relationship without explanation. Daniel had come into her life when she was the most vulnerable and had swept her off her feet and helped her forget about Mathew. *For a time.* It wasn't long before Lizzy knew she'd made a mistake by marrying Daniel. She didn't know him, and when he started drinking and mistreating her, all she could do was trust God to sort out her mess. And sort it He did. God had blessed them abundantly since the day Daniel gave his heart to the Lord following a car accident that almost took his life. Three beautiful children, a wonderful job they could never have dreamed of, and a ministry that gave hope to those who found themselves struggling with life, just like Daniel had. And now they had the opportunity to minister to Daniel's two sisters.

Lizzy's heart warmed as Daniel skilfully weaved the community van along the track that wasn't much wider than the tracks on the surrounding mountains that only the sheep and goats could navigate.

She'd only met Grace once when she and Daniel and baby Dillon went to Belfast for Daniel's Da's funeral just over three years ago. Grace had built so many walls around her, it had been difficult to talk with her, but by the time the week was over, Lizzy felt that she'd connected with Grace just a little, and she and Daniel had hope that one day, Grace might reach out to them. And that day had arrived.

Brianna she had yet to meet. Daniel had told her a little about their early years before all the children were separated following their Mam's death, but he didn't know Brianna as well as he knew Grace. He was nervous about meeting them, even though he said he wasn't. All week he'd been on edge, not his normal, cheery self. He'd cleaned the room they'd set aside for Grace three times. "She won't be happy if there's even a speck of dirt, Lizzy. You've seen her apartment." And he'd gone over the basic programme Brianna would be starting as soon as she arrived no fewer than ten times. Normally, whenever new students arrived, they'd go through a week of settling in before joining in with the main programme, but Daniel wanted to review the whole process. Not because the existing strategy wasn't working, just because it was his own sister who was coming.

She'd told him to stop it and trust God to touch their hearts. They'd prayed for both Grace and Brianna every morning and every night since the day they received the phone call. But Lizzy couldn't blame him for being anxious. Caleb had told them that Brianna was a mess and Grace wasn't much better—she just didn't know it.

"How are you doing, Daniel?" Lizzy turned her head and smiled at him. His dark hair was still as curly and unruly as ever, but she wouldn't have it any other way.

"I'll be better once they're here, Liz. I bet they're nervous too. They have no idea what they're coming to." He chuckled as he changed down a gear to turn onto the A82 towards Inverness. "I can just see Grace's face when she sees the place. She might turn around and leave straight away."

"Stop it, Daniel. It'll be fine. You're underestimating her. She's made the decision to come because she cares about Brianna, so she'll handle it. It's not that bad, anyway."

"It's not that great, either, Lizzy. You know that."

She raised her brow. "It's better than when we came..."

"Yes, but it's not what you'd call a fancy manor house."

"No, but it's warm and welcoming, and that's the most important thing. She'll be fine, Daniel. Stop worrying."

Daniel let out a slow breath. "Okay, love. I'll try." He reached down and squeezed her hand.

"I wonder how the kids are."

"Now you're the one worrying."

"I'm not worrying."

"Yes you are."

She chuckled. "Maybe just a little. I hope Mia's coping with Dillon. He's being a very cheeky four-year old of late."

"She'll be fine with him, Liz. It's only you he misbehaves for."

Lizzy let out a sigh. "I know. I guess it's normal."

"And Mia's great with the twins, so don't worry about them, love." Daniel shot her a smile that gave her confidence that everything would be okay with her not there.

He was right. Mia, the young woman they'd employed to be the children's nanny was the eldest of six children and had a wonderful way with their three. Lizzy had nothing to worry about. Still, they could be a handful at times.

For the remainder of the hour and a half trip to the airport, Lizzy and Daniel chatted about anything and everything, and enjoyed their brief time together knowing that as soon as his sisters arrived, everything would change.

BRIANNA GRABBED Grace's hand as the plane accelerated and began racing down the runway. Her heart pounded and she couldn't move. She was going to die, she knew it. Strange, because when she'd decided to jump off the cliff just a week or so ago, she wasn't nearly as frightened as she was now. Why had she let Grace talk her into this? She braced herself as the plane began to lift. How was it possible for something this big to stay in the air?

Grace squeezed her hand. "It's okay, Bibi. This is normal."

Normal? Who for? The noise was too much. She was going to vomit, or pass out. She closed her eyes and rested her head against the seat, all the while gripping Grace's hand as the plane banked left, and then right before steadily climbing. Her breathing slowed as the plane levelled, and she dared open her eyes. She had the window seat, but she hadn't looked out, until now. Her eyes widened as she took in the city of Belfast. It was so little from up here. And the fields spread out like patchwork. Who would have thought? She couldn't tear her eyes away—this was magic. She should have looked earlier. She'd survived, and it was amazing. Not until land was replaced by sea did she tear her eyes away and settle in her seat.

"See, I told you you'd be fine." Chuckling, Grace patted Brianna's hand.

"It's way better than I thought." Brianna relaxed in her seat, but when the pilot announced they'd be landing in Inverness in less than twenty minutes, she tensed again. "I don't want to do this, Grace."

Grace sighed. "Do what, Bibi?"

"This." She stared Grace down.

Grace didn't flinch. "It's too late, Brianna. Daniel and Lizzy will be waiting for us."

"I'll just stay on the plane. You can't make me get off."

"You can't do that. You have to get off."

Slumping in her seat, Brianna pursed her lips and folded her arms. *Just watch me.*

GRACE FELT THE SAME, although she couldn't say so to Brianna. What had made her agree to this nonsense? How could Danny and Lizzy do what she herself hadn't been able to do? Brianna didn't want to change. How many chances had she had over the years? Caleb and Caitlin had gone out of their way on numerous occasions to help her, but she'd only thrown it back in their faces each time. How many times had they picked her up off the streets and taken her to hospital and then to rehab? None of it had made any difference. Brianna always returned to the gutter.

Grace sighed. Maybe she should have been brave enough years ago and reported those cousins to the police rather than be intimidated by Aunt Hilda's threats to disclose what she knew about the bombing. If Grace had been brave enough, maybe Brianna's life would have turned out differently. But so would have hers. Grace gulped. It wasn't too late. Maybe she should do it and face the consequences, even if that included prison, which no doubt it would if Aunt Hilda followed through with her threats.

It would be Brianna's word against the cousins, but surely Grace's testimony would hold more weight now than it would have years ago. Her stomach tightened. *But not if she was charged with murder.* Aunt Hilda would say that Brianna had encouraged the boys, but it was the opposite. Both she and Brianna hated Uncle Dougall and their cousins. No way would Brianna have encouraged them. She'd just been more trusting than Grace, and she'd paid the price.

The more Grace thought about it, the more determined she became. Proving the two of them guilty of rape would surely free Brianna once and for all from her demons. She'd start the ball rolling as soon as she could. It would mean going back to Londonderry with Brianna, but she'd do it if it put an end to Brianna's problems. And Aunt Hilda's threats? Well, so what if she did have the piece of paper she said she had? It proved nothing. Any good lawyer would get her off, and if they didn't, she'd go to prison so Brianna could be free. Grace closed her eyes as a cold chill ran through her body. *If she was really prepared to do it, why hadn't she done it already?*

The flight attendant tapped her on the shoulder. "Seat up, miss." Grace's eyes shot open. She nodded and then straightened her seat. She took a deep, slow breath and turned to look at Brianna. Her seat was already upright, and her hands were clenched and her eyes squeezed shut. Was she nervous about landing, or about meeting Danny and Lizzy? Or both? It was all a mistake. She shouldn't have brought her here.

Brianna didn't move from her seat until the flight attendant told her she had to get up. They were last off. Brianna dragged her feet the whole way. She vomited in the toilet, and Grace had to drag her along. If there was any way to turn around, Grace would have taken it. They paused before taking the final step. Turning to face her, Grace lifted Brianna's chin and forced her sister to make eye contact. “We won't stay if you don’t want to. Okay? We'll go back whenever you want.”

Brianna's eyes widened. "Are you just tricking me?"

Grace sighed. "No, I mean it. You say the word, and we'll leave."

Brianna narrowed her eyes. "So why can't we leave now?"

Grace sucked in a breath. "Just give it a go, Bibi. You never know. It might just work."

She rolled her eyes. "I doubt it."

Grace stepped forward and hugged her. "Come on, let's go."

CHAPTER 10

Grace squeezed Brianna's hand and drew a deep breath as she and Brianna stepped into the Arrivals Hall. Scanning the waiting faces, she easily spotted Daniel and Lizzy. Daniel had put on a little weight since she'd last seen him, the day he and Lizzy sailed back to England after Da's funeral, but apart from that, he still wore that cheeky grin and she'd know him anywhere. Lizzy, on the other hand, had changed a lot. Her hair was cut shorter into a bob. It suited her. And she'd lost weight. *Must be all the running around after those children.*

There were hugs all round, but Brianna held back. Lizzy seemed to understand and just gave her a warm smile. Daniel put both his hands on Brianna's shoulders, his face splitting into a wide grin. Grace winced. Brianna hated being the centre of attention. But something was happening as Brianna met Danny's gaze, as if scales were falling from her eyes and she was remembering her big brother whom she hadn't seen since she was shipped off to Aunt Hilda's at age ten. Tears rolled down Brianna's cheeks.

Grace forced back tears of her own.

"Brianna—welcome! It's grand to see you after all this time." Danny's eyes sparkled. He leaned forward and kissed Brianna, pulling her into a gentle hug. Brianna hugged him back. Grace couldn't believe it. But then, this was Danny. She should have known that if anyone could get through to Bibi, it'd be Danny.

Then Danny turned to Grace. She'd been determined to remain aloof, but his infectious grin disarmed her, and before she knew it, she was stepping into his arms and hugging him like a long lost brother. When he released her, she wiped her eyes before hugging Lizzy.

"Welcome to bonny Scotland, both of you!" Danny took Brianna's bags while Grace took her own and followed him to an old white van with "Elim Community" printed along the side.

Danny must have noticed Grace's raised brow. "Sorry about the van, Grace... I know it's not quite up to your standard, but it gets us around." He winked as he unlocked the vehicle and began loading their luggage.

She certainly wouldn't be seen dead or alive in a van like this at home. But what did it matter? She wasn't at home.

"Sit up front with me, Grace." He opened the door for her and motioned for her to get in. Grace glanced at Brianna. Lizzy seemed to have taken her under her wing. Grace smiled to herself as she climbed into the front and sat beside Danny.

"Well, this is grand, this is. Three lovely ladies to keep me company." Daniel flashed a smile at Grace and then at Lizzy and Brianna in the back as he clicked his seatbelt and started the engine.

Laughing, Lizzy leaned forward and gave him a flick on his shoulder. "Behave yourself!"

"Always!" He chuckled as he pulled out of the car park and onto the main road.

"So Grace, how's Caleb?"

"He's fine, as usual." She turned her head. "He wanted to come."

Danny shot her a quick glance as he slowed for a red light. "Why didn't he? Would have been grand to see him."

Grace blew out a breath. “I didn’t want him to.”

Danny's brows puckered. “Why?”

Grace glanced quickly at Brianna. Amazing… Lizzy was chatting to Brianna as if she was a normal person. Grace leaned closer to Danny. “It would have been too much for Brianna. Caleb's a bit intense sometimes.”

They locked eyes for a moment. Danny understood.

Grace settled back in her seat. “What’s the place like, Danny? Caleb didn’t tell us much, apart from saying it’s in the middle of the Highlands.”

“Well, he got that right.” Danny chuckled. “We are a bit isolated, but that's a good thing."

"Don't you miss the city?"

He shook his head. "Not at all. Wait until you see it, Grace. It's magic."

A COMFORTABLE SILENCE fell between them for a few minutes. Grace looked out of the window and took in the sights of the city—the steep spire of the cathedral, the old-fashioned stone buildings, the dark waters of the Moray Firth, and the sprawling mountains in the distance. It wasn't that different from some of the towns she and Brianna had driven through, except that she half expected to see a piper in a kilt on every street corner they passed.

Danny interrupted her thoughts as he changed down gears to take a corner. "So, how are you really, Grace?”

The question caught her off-guard. Danny was often direct with his questions, so she should have expected it. Her immediate response was to say she was fine, but if she were honest, she was nothing of the sort. The last few weeks with Brianna had shown her she didn’t have a clue how to help her sister, let alone herself. But she wouldn't admit that to Danny. “I’m fine.”

Turning to meet her gaze, Danny raised his brow. He didn't believe her, but she wasn't prepared to say anything further.

A short while later, Danny slowed the van as they entered the small town of Drumnadrochit on the western side of Loch Ness, and pulled over in front of a row of shops. "Lunch-time, ladies… all out!"

Grace chuckled. Her brother was a charmer, always had been, always would be, so it seemed. His love of life was infectious, and Grace couldn't help but warm to him.

Grace slipped her arm loosely around Brianna's waist as they followed Danny and Lizzy into a café where they were greeted by a short, friendly, middle-aged lady who spoke with a broad Scottish accent. Grace could barely understand a word she said.

The lady directed them to an old wooden table near an open fireplace. Being summer, the fire wasn't lit, but Grace could imagine how cosy it would be in there when it was.

The lady handed menus out to each of them. When she left, Grace opened hers and gagged. Half the menu was filled with Haggis in all different variations. She lifted her gaze to Danny, who was sitting opposite her. "You won't get me eating Haggis, so don't even try."

Danny chuckled. "You don't know what you're missing out on."

Lizzy laughed as she reached out and tapped Grace's wrist. "Don't worry, Grace. I haven't tried it yet, and I don't intend to."

Danny shook his head in mock disgust.

"I don't care." Lizzy glared at him and lifted her chin before bursting into laughter.

Grace relaxed. It was fun being with these two, but she had to be careful. Last time she let them get too close and they'd almost broken through her walls… she didn't want that to happen again.

"Well, I think I'll have the soup of the day." Lizzy placed her menu on the table and sat back in her chair.

"That'll do me, too." Grace turned to Brianna. "Bibi, what do you want?"

Grace's heart fell. Bibi had that overwhelmed look on her face again. Of course Brianna wouldn't know what she wanted... she'd have no idea what all the menu items were. Grace's voice softened as she lowered her face towards hers. "Would you like the soup, Bibi? It's potato and leek."

Brianna nodded, but her eyes were dull and unresponsive. Maybe this wasn't going to work after all.

"Well, I'm going to have the Guiness pie," Danny said, leaning back in his chair and rubbing his tummy.

Grace raised her brow. *So that's how he's put on weight.*

They ordered their meals and Danny and Lizzy began chatting, obviously trying to make both her and Brianna feel comfortable. But their lives were so different to her's and Brianna's. They had no idea. They chatted about the children, which Grace knew was normal, but really meant nothing to her and Brianna. Children were just messy little creatures who put grubby hands on walls and ran around and screamed. But she had to listen and feign interest.

"Dillon's such a little monkey. You wouldn't recognise him, Grace. He runs around all day." Lizzy chuckled. "He doesn't stop, does he, Daniel?" She touched Danny's arm lightly and looked at him with such love and devotion shining from her eyes, it almost made Grace envious of what they had.

"I think they'll need to tie him to his chair when he starts school. If they can catch him!" As Danny laughed, his blue eyes sparkled and Grace could see how much Dillon meant to him.

"The twins try to keep up with him, but their little legs don't go quite as fast." Lizzy laughed as she pulled some photos from her purse and held them out to Grace and Brianna. "This is James and Clare, they're almost eighteen months, and here's Dillon. A little bigger than the last time you saw him, Grace." A proud smile sat on Lizzy's face as she glanced up.

Grace looked closer at the photos. The resemblance between James and Danny was remarkable. Clare was shorter than James, but had the same facial features she herself had at that age. Caleb had given her copies of the few family photos he'd retrieved from the house after Mam died. Not that she looked at them often—just occasionally when she'd drunk too much and hankered back to happier times. She was sure that if she pulled out the photo of her and Danny at about the same age, they could almost pass for James and Clare.

Grace's shoulders sagged as a deep sadness flowed through her. She'd never thought about having children. Just like she could never marry, she could also never have children. It wouldn't have been fair to bring them into the world when her past could be discovered at any time and she could be sent to prison for the rest of her life. Her fate had been sealed the day she went to that bus-stop. No use getting sad about it now. What was done was done.

Grace pushed it all aside as she always did and looked up, giving Lizzy the best smile she could manage. "They're lovely, Lizzy. You must be so proud."

Lizzy nodded, her face breaking into a beaming, beautiful smile. "They're such a blessing, Grace, and we love them to bits. Daniel dotes on all three of them, but little Clare is daddy's girl, isn't that right, Daniel?" Lizzy leaned into Danny and looked up into his eyes as he wrapped his arms around her.

"She reminds me of you, love." He kissed the top of Lizzy's head and pulled her close.

Grace's eyes moistened. She quickly passed the photos to Brianna and ran her hand over her eyes, hoping nobody noticed. She'd never know the love Danny and Lizzy shared. If only she and Brianna hadn't been sent to live with Aunt Hilda, everything would have been so different. It wasn't fair.

Their meals came and before long they were back in the van heading south to the Elim Community Centre. With every mile that passed, Grace became more certain that she and Brianna would be heading home as soon as they arrived. They didn't belong in the Scottish Highlands with a bunch of Christians. Only madness had made her think this was a good idea.

CHAPTER 11

Grace had no idea what she was coming to. She'd imagined a cold, crumbling castle standing amidst a barren, wind-blown moor, but as they rounded yet another bend, her eyes widened. Instead of a crumbling castle, a solid, sturdy stone mansion, covered in creeping ivy, and surrounded by the most beautiful flower garden she'd seen in a long time, came into view. Spirals of smoke drifted lazily into the pale blue sky from a number of chimneys scattered along the roof line.

The house sat on the shore of Loch Linnhe. A small jetty ran out into the water from in front of the house, and a number of row-boats and canoes bobbed up and down in the gentle waves. Why hadn't Danny told her it was so beautiful?

Danny winked at her. "Like it?"

Grace chuckled. "It's stunning. How did you end up in a place like this?"

"I'll tell you one day, if you want to listen." His voice grew serious.

Grace groaned. She knew what he'd say... *God gave it to us...* and she didn't want to hear that rubbish. "I think I'll pass."

"No problem." He brought the van to a stop in front of a smaller stone building to the left of the main house. Long and low, it too was edged with bright, colourful flowers, giving it a very warm and homey feel.

Danny smiled broadly as he opened the door for Grace and then for Brianna and Lizzy. "Welcome to Elim Community."

Three young children burst through the front door of the house and ran towards them. The older one, who Grace assumed was Dillon, was wearing a cowboy outfit and ran around pretending to shoot them all. The younger boy, James, tried to keep up with him, but the little girl went straight to Danny and grabbed his leg. Leaning down, Danny picked Clare up and gave her a big cuddle.

"Hey there little one. Daddy's missed you." As he kissed her, Clare threw her arms around his neck, but when he propped her in his arms and stepped closer to Grace and Brianna, her thumb flew straight to her mouth. "Look who we've got here, Clare. This is Auntie Grace, and this is Auntie Brianna. Say hello."

Clare clung to Danny and buried her head in his chest, but peeked out through her fingers. She really was a daddy's girl.

"They're not going to bite you, Clare."

He tried to pry her head from his chest without success but then just shook his head.

Dillon raced past just then and Danny grabbed hold of his jacket, bringing him to a sudden stop. "Whoa there, Dillon. Settle down—we've got guests. Come and say hello to your aunties."

As Dillon looked up, Grace sucked in a breath. Dillon had Danny's eyes and cheeky grin.

He gave them a quick once over, said hello, and then escaped his father's hold and raced off again.

James stopped beside Lizzy and put his arms up. Lizzy bent over and picked him up and carried him over to Grace and Brianna. He was tongue-tied, just like his sister.

"I don't know what's got into them, they were so excited before."

Lizzy sighed and rolled her eyes. "Anyway, let's go inside and I'll get you a cup of tea." She settled James onto her hip and directed Grace and Brianna inside.

Grace stood in the entry and gazed around her. "This is lovely, Lizzy." The whole place was homely, from the rich rugs on the timber floors to the bright curtains on the windows—the exact opposite of Grace's apartment, which was functional, chic and modern. Danny and Lizzy's house was a family home full of character and love.

"Thank you, Grace. We didn't know if you'd like it or not." Lizzy laughed and glanced at Danny, who was following behind with their bags. "Come into the kitchen and I'll make that tea."

Grace and Brianna followed her down a short hallway into a warm, spacious room. A large wood-burning stove with pots and pans hanging above it from hooks attached to the ceiling sat on the far wall. A heavy timber table and a kitchen dresser covered in all sorts of bits and pieces took up the rest of the space, but Grace's eyes were drawn to the view out the window above the sink. The mountains Grace had admired earlier hovered in the distance behind the loch, but in between the house and the loch, a wooden table with bench seats sat amidst a meadow of daisies. It was beautiful.

"Coffee or tea?" Lizzy asked as she placed James onto one of the chairs and gave him a colouring book and some pencils.

"Coffee, thanks," Grace replied.

"Coffee for me too, please."

Grace's eyes widened. Brianna spoke. *Amazing.*

Grace's eyes widened further as Brianna picked up a pencil and began colouring with James. Never in her wildest dreams had Grace expected Brianna to do such a thing. Who would have thought?

"Would you like to see your room, Grace? I can show you while the kettle's boiling." Lizzy twirled a finger through her hair as her eyes darted to Brianna and back.

Grace got the message, and followed Lizzy back down the hallway and into a clean and tidy room filled with two single beds and an old timber dresser. A bunch of freshly cut flowers sat on the dresser, filling the room with a sweet perfume. Cream fluffy towels and flannels sat on the end of each bed. The room had the same outlook as the kitchen. She'd like lying in bed and gazing out at those mountains. Maybe she could consider climbing them one day. She blinked. Since when did Grace O'Connor climb mountains? She chuckled to herself. It must be the highland air getting to her.

"This is lovely, Lizzy, thank you." Without thinking about it, Grace reached for Lizzy's hand and squeezed it. When she realised what she'd done, she quickly withdrew it.

"Our pleasure, Grace. Danny and I really hope you enjoy your stay." Lizzy's smile was genuine and warm. "You know, ever since Danny found out you were coming, he's been so excited, and a little nervous." Lizzy let out a small chuckle as she sat on the bed and motioned for Grace to join her. Her expression grew serious as she met Grace's gaze. "Is there anything we need to know about Brianna?"

"How long have you got?" Grace raised her brow, but then realised she shouldn't be flippant about such a serious matter. "Sorry… she's a drug addict, Lizzy, but you already know that. Just be careful—she'll steal and lie if she's desperate. Keep a good eye on her." There was so much more she could say, but really, that was enough.

"We've had others like her through here, so we know what to expect. We'll do our best for her, Grace." Lizzy took Grace's hand and squeezed it. Tears pricked Grace's eyes. She was sure Lizzy and Danny would do the best they could for Bibi, but would it be enough? And would she even stay?

Whistling sounded from the kitchen. Lizzy released Grace's hand and hurried back to the kitchen. Grace followed. Brianna was still colouring with James, and a smile grew on Grace's face. Danny arrived with Clare and placed her beside James. Dillon was still running around, but stopped when Lizzy offered him cake.

"Now sit down and eat quietly with your brother and sister," Lizzy said as she placed three plastic plates on the table with a slice of home-made chocolate cake on each. She made coffee and tea, and then placed a larger plate on the table with the remainder of the cake.

"I love this place, Danny. Did you do it all yourself?" Grace asked as Danny took a seat at the head of the table, on either side of Clare and Dillon.

Danny laughed. "No. We had a lot of help from the boys."

"The students, you mean? How many are there?" Grace glanced away and smiled at Lizzy as she took a small slice of the cake she was passing around.

"It varies. Right now we have seven boys and six girls—including Brianna. But we've had up to twenty."

"That's a lot. You must have other people helping?"

Lizzy nodded enthusiastically as she gulped down a mouthful of tea. "We're lucky to have some highly qualified and experienced staff members. I hope you don't mind," Lizzy glanced at Grace and then at Brianna, "but we've asked them over for supper."

Grace glanced at Brianna to check her reaction. Brianna hardly flinched and just kept colouring. *Why would they do that, and on our first night? She really didn't need to meet the staff, but seemed she'd have no choice.* Grace forced a smile. "That will be lovely, Lizzy."

"They're keen to meet you both. It's always good when family members come to visit. Danny and I haven't had any family here since my parents visited a year ago."

Grace sipped her coffee. "Your parents must have enjoyed seeing their grandchildren."

Lizzy sat beside Grace and picked up her cup of tea. "Very much so. And the kids absolutely adored having them here. The twins were only babies, but it was still wonderful. And such a surprise... my father was always so formal and standoffish, but you should have seen him down on the floor giving horsey rides to the twins! They wouldn't leave him alone." Lizzy leaned back in her seat and smiled. "And Mother, well, she was the one who got our garden sorted." Lizzy chuckled. "I'd always wanted a house with a lovely garden, and now I have it."

"You must get snow here in winter. What do you do then?"

"Oh, Mother showed me how to keep the seeds and bulbs to plant in early spring, and it worked! I was so surprised when the first shoots came up. In fact, we had a party to celebrate!"

The chatter continued around the table, but Brianna didn't join in. Instead, she hid herself in the colouring book, just lifting her head occasionally. At least she was still here, that was something, but Grace got the feeling she wasn't okay. She knew her too well. Grace pushed back her chair. "I think we might freshen up before dinner, if you don't mind."

Lizzy jumped up. "Oh, I'm sorry. You both must be tired. Feel free to take a bath or a shower, and have a rest if you like. Dinner for the adults isn't until seven, so there's plenty of time."

"Thanks." Grace smiled at Lizzy as she placed her hand lightly on Brianna's shoulder and motioned for her to follow.

WHEN GRACE and Brianna were on their own in the bedroom, Grace sat beside Brianna on one of the beds and put her arm around her. "What's up, Bibi? Something's wrong. What is it?"

Brianna shrugged and hung her head. "They're all so nice. I won't fit in."

"Oh Bibi, don't feel like that. They're family, and they want you to feel welcome." Grace lifted Brianna's chin and turned her face towards her. Brianna's eyes were filled with tears. Grace pulled her close and hugged her, brushing her hair with her hand. "I'm sure it'll be okay, just give it time. But I'll keep my promise and take you home if you want to leave."

Brianna didn't reply. Instead, she pulled away and curled up on the bed, hugging a pillow to her chest as she closed her eyes.

As Grace looked at Brianna's pitiful frame, hopes of ever getting her well faded and despair for her sister's future grew.

CHAPTER 12

An hour or so later, Grace managed to get Brianna showered and dressed, and they headed back towards the kitchen. The rest seemed to have done Brianna good—at least she was prepared to leave the room and come for dinner. The sound of a piano playing drew them into a cosy living room where Lizzy sat at a piano beside Dillon. He was propped on a cushion so he could reach the keys, and he looked so cute. And could he play! He and Lizzy were playing together, and whilst Lizzy was the better player, Dillon was doing a great job for a four-year old.

Grace and Brianna stood at the door listening until Lizzy must have sensed their presence and turned around.

"Don't let us stop you," Grace said. "You're both great!" The cheeky smile on Dillon's face made Grace laugh. "I don't know how you got him to sit still for so long, though."

"That's part of the bargain. If he wants to run around like a tornado, he also has to do piano lessons. No lessons, no play. It's that simple, isn't it, Dillon?" Lizzy ruffled his hair and he nodded eagerly, looking up into his mother's face with a cheeky grin, just like his father's. Lizzy and Danny were so lucky to have such lovely children. Who would have thought that her brother, Daniel O'Connor, ex-alcoholic, would turn out to be such a model husband and father, and manager of a place such as this. Amazing.

"We were just finishing up anyway. It's almost bed time for the children. Come and tuck them in with me." Lizzy stood and closed the piano lid, and then led Grace and Brianna into the children's bedrooms. Dillon ran ahead, grabbing Grace's hand and dragging her with him.

"Come on, Auntie Grace, you can read me a story."

Grace shuddered, but chuckled at the same time. What could she do? She didn't have a choice.

Lizzy sprinted after him and grabbed his pyjama top, managing to stop him just before he reached his room. "Whoa there, Dillon, slow down. You'll pull your auntie's arm off!"

Dillon had his own little room next to the twins' room, and he pulled Grace in there and directed her to sit on his bed while he chose a book from his bookshelf. His floor was covered with toy trucks and cars. Dillon jumped onto the bed and presented her with his book of choice. Grace groaned. Of course it would be a Bible story book.

She rarely read to Caleb and Caitlin's girls, but when she did, they usually chose Bible stories too, and Grace always struggled to read them, mainly because of the memories they brought back. Memories of happier times when Mam was still alive, and she'd gather the children around at bedtime and read to them all. Mam loved her Bible stories, but what made it worse, she actually believed them. Mam had a simple faith, and it annoyed Grace. God hadn't saved her in the end, so what use was He? Surely if He loved her like Mam said He did, He would have healed her, and then they all could have stayed together as a family, and she and Brianna wouldn't have gone to Aunt Hilda's. And Brianna wouldn't have been raped by her cousins, and Grace wouldn't have...

"Are you going to read it, Auntie Grace?" Dillon's little voice interrupted her thoughts.

"Yes, I'm sorry, Dillon." Grace quickly opened the book and began reading, pushing her memories away.

When Grace reached the end, Dillon promptly asked if she could read another.

"I don't think so, I think it's time for bed. I can hear your Mum finishing up with the twins. Do you need to clean your teeth and go to the toilet?"

Dillon pushed his bottom lip out. "I don't like cleaning my teeth.

"You need to look after them or they'll fall out."

His little face lit up. "That's what Da says."

Grace sucked in a breath. Dillon's reference to Da brought a sudden memory of her own Da. That horrid man who'd caused all their problems. Just as well Danny was nothing like him.

Just then, Danny appeared at the door and Dillon jumped up and ran into his arms. "Daddy, you made it!"

"You bet I did, little man." Danny spun Dillon round and then plonked him down on the bed beside Grace. "Have you been good for Auntie Grace?"

"I'm always good."

Danny laughed. "Yes, right... and did she read to you?" Danny glanced at Grace and winked at her.

"Yes, she read me Noah's Ark."

"That's about the hundredth time you've had that book read to you. Maybe you should pick a different one tomorrow night."

"But it's my favourite, Daddy."

"Yes, I know, and it's a grand story. Anyway, I believe it's bed-time, so off you go. Toilet, teeth and bed."

"And prayers."

"Yes, and prayers."

"Can Auntie Grace pray with me?"

Grace stiffened. *Please don't ask me to do that...*

Danny glanced at her, briefly meeting her gaze. "I'm sure Auntie Grace would love to pray with you, Dillon. Wouldn't she?"

Grace narrowed her eyes and glared at Danny. He knew she wouldn't want to pray. The hide of him to put her on the spot like that! As much as it irked her, she'd have to go along with it to keep Dillon happy, so she put on a happy face but spoke through clenched teeth. "Of course I'll pray with you, Dillon. Just as soon as you've cleaned your teeth and been to the toilet."

In the next room, Lizzy was doing much the same with the twins. Brianna was with them, and Grace had heard James ask if she could read to them, but Lizzy had stepped in and said maybe Auntie Brianna could read to him another time. Thank goodness Lizzy seemed to understand where Brianna was at.

Dillon cleaned his teeth in record time and was back in the room waiting for Grace to say prayers with him. Danny had gone into the twins' room, so Grace had no option but to get down on her knees beside Dillon, but there was no way she was going to steeple her hands like he was doing.

"Will you go first, Auntie Grace?" He looked at her with his sweet innocent face, almost melting her heart. How had she gotten herself into this position? Grace O'Connor, barrister, atheist, murderer, kneeling on the floor with a four-year old, praying to a god she didn't believe in?

She couldn't do it. "Why don't you go first, Dillon?"

"Okay." He squeezed his eyes shut and began. "Dear Lord Jesus, thank you for bringing Auntie Grace to stay with us. And the other Auntie, I can't remember her name. Mam says she needs Your help, so Lord Jesus, can you please help her? I'm sorry for being naughty for Mia today, and please help me to have a good sleep tonight. Thank you for loving me, and for giving me my Mam and Da, and James and Clare. I love them lots. Amen." He looked up and smiled. "It's your turn."

Grace gulped. How could she pray? She'd vowed she'd never talk to

God again after Mam's funeral. And she hadn't. But this little four-year old had put her on the spot, and she'd have to break her promise. "Okay, close your eyes."

She gulped. This was not going to be easy. "Dear God. Thank you for Dillon, and for his love of life. And thank you for bringing me here so I can spend time with him and with his mum and dad. Watch over him tonight as he sleeps, and let us have a good day tomorrow. Amen."

Grace quickly brushed unexpected tears from her eyes, but not quickly enough.

"Are you crying, Auntie Grace?" Dillon's little face peered up at her.

"No." She brushed the last tear away and sucked in a breath. "Come on, let's get you to bed."

"I need my animals. I take three to bed... Mouse, Rabbit and Fred. Here they are." He put the three stuffed animals under his blankets and snuggled down with them. "Good night Auntie Grace. I love you." As he smiled up at her, tears pricked her eyes again.

She bent down and kissed him on the cheek. "I love you too, Dillon. Night night. Sleep tight."

"Good night."

She stepped back and tip-toed out of the room, flicked the light switch, and bumped into Danny just outside the room.

"You did good, Grace. Dillon's taken with you." He squeezed her hand as he whispered. "I knew he would be."

Grace shrugged. "I don't know why."

"I told him you're a very clever person and that you wear a wig when you're at work, and that you're my little sister, just like Clare's his little sister." Danny stepped towards her and hugged her before drawing back and meeting her gaze. "And that did it for him, Grace. You're now his favourite Auntie."

Grace couldn't help it. She blinked back unwelcome tears that sprang to her eyes as mixed emotions assailed her.

Danny brushed her tears away with his thumb and drew her close.

"It's so good to have you here, Grace." His voice was soft and caring, and she knew he meant it. But drat the man. He had a knack of getting through her carefully constructed walls and exposing her inner feelings, and she couldn't allow that to happen.

Grace sucked a deep, slow breath and regained her control. "Thanks Danny, it's good to be here."

"Come on now, supper must be almost ready, and there are people waiting to meet you."

Grace groaned. A nice quiet evening with Danny and Lizzy would have been preferable. Now she'd have to put up all her defences since no doubt all the people waiting to meet her and Brianna were Christians. And that was not something she looked forward to at all.

CHAPTER 13

Grace followed Danny down the hallway into a larger room she hadn't noticed before. Tucked away at the other side of the kitchen, it served as a dining room and lounge room all in one. Brianna was already seated on the edge of an old brown leather couch, looking very uncomfortable. Lizzy, perched on the arm of the couch beside her, was talking to another shorter, chubbier young woman who wore a pleasant smile. Brianna looked up as Grace entered the room and shot her a plea for help.

As Grace stepped closer to Brianna and Lizzy, a man, possibly in his early forties, entered from the door at the far end. Her heart skipped a beat. Acutely conscious of his tall, athletic physique, her eyes were drawn to him like bees to a honey pot. His smile was wide and warm as Danny clapped his arm around the man's shoulders. "Ryan, great to see you. Come and meet my sisters."

Grace quickly pulled herself together as Danny steered Ryan towards the group at the couch, but she couldn't stop the ripple of excitement that flowed through her as his brilliant blue eyes met hers.

Danny smiled as he made the introductions, seemingly unaware of the undercurrents flowing between her and this hunk of a man. "Grace, Brianna, meet my good friend and co-worker, Ryan MacGregor. Ryan, these are my sisters, Grace, and Brianna."

Grace raised her brow slightly as she took Ryan's outstretched hand, which was firm, warm and masculine.

"Nice to meet you, Grace." His voice was just as warm as the touch of his hand. With a name like MacGregor, she'd expected a broad Scots accent, but instead, he spoke with an English one. She was almost disappointed.

"And nice to meet you too, Ryan." Her voice was low and husky as she held his gaze.

"I've heard a lot about you, Grace." His blue eyes sparkled, and his hand remained in hers slightly longer than would normally be expected on occasions such as this.

"All good, I hope?" She gave a small laugh.

"Of course. Danny wouldn't have a bad word to say about anyone." Ryan elbowed Danny gently in the ribs and chuckled.

"I can always count on you to build me up, Rye old man." Danny gave Ryan a playful punch on the arm.

Grace laughed at their friendly banter. Supper with the staff might be fun after all.

Still very much aware of Ryan's presence beside her, Grace tore her eyes away and glanced at Brianna as Ryan shook her hand. Grace winced as Brianna only managed a cursory smile.

Brianna certainly gave the impression she didn't want to be here, but then, Danny and Lizzy would be used to that, from what Lizzy had said.

The chubby young woman, who was introduced as Emily, sat beside Brianna and began chatting when Lizzy excused herself.

Grace returned her attention to Ryan, quirking her eyebrow. "And what do you do here?"

Danny squeezed her shoulder before Ryan could answer. "I'll leave you to it, sis—I need to help Lizzy." He promptly disappeared into the kitchen, leaving her alone with Ryan.

Amusement flickered in Ryan's face. "I'm in charge of the outdoors programme."

Of course... that would make sense. "What types of things do you do?"

He shrugged. "Depends on the season, but in summer, like now, we do all sorts... mountain climbing, hiking, abseiling, rafting, rowing, and in winter, tobogganing and cross-country skiing, but there's also an indoor gym, so most of winter's spent in there."

Grace angled her head. "The students get to do all that?"

Ryan nodded. "Yep. It's often the first time any of them have done anything like this, so it can be a real challenge for them, but they usually love it once they get over their initial fear." He smiled at her, sending another ripple of excitement flowing through her. "Can I get you a drink, Grace?"

"Thought you'd never ask. Gin and tonic, thanks."

Ryan laughed as if he was sincerely amused. "You won't get one of those here, Grace, sorry. It's soft drink or punch."

She let out a frustrated sigh. She should have realised. Of course they wouldn't serve alcohol here... what was she thinking? She drew in a breath. "Guess I'll have a punch."

He steered her towards a table where a punchbowl sat and poured two glasses before handing her one.

"First time in the Highlands?"

She nodded.

"I can take you into the mountains one day if you'd like."

She raised a brow. "Hiking?"

"We can drive if you prefer." His eyes twinkled.

She chuckled. "Driving sounds good... let me think about it." She took a sip of her punch.

Stepping closer, he lowered his voice. "Danny told me a little about your sister. She's come to the right place."

Grace rubbed the back of her neck and blew out a breath. "She doesn't want to be here."

"Most of the new students say that when they first arrive, but it usually just takes a day or two, and then we can't get them to leave!"

Grace shrugged. "Guess we'll see."

"Come on, supper's served." He cupped her elbow with his hand and directed her to the table, where he pulled a chair out for her before taking a seat next to her.

Brianna sat on the opposite side of the table between Emily and Lizzy. Danny sat to Lizzy's right, and then another older woman, who introduced herself as Rosemary, sat on his other side. Rosemary had a broad Scottish accent, and taught sewing and piano. She also oversaw the female students' general welfare and was the first person they should see if they had any issues or concerns. Emily was in charge of the kitchen and other domestic duties. The last person at the table was David, Rosemary's husband. Like Rosemary, David also had a broad Scottish accent. He was in charge of the Bible school, and also oversaw the male students' welfare. Grace learned during the course of the evening that Lizzy also taught basic literacy skills in the school, as often students arrived without being able to read or write, but the one who surprised Grace the most was Danny. He taught classes in basic Christianity.

"So who funds all of this?" Grace asked Ryan during a break in the meal, which was being served by two of the students. It was a blunt question, but someone had to be paying for it all, and Grace was curious. The students obviously weren't paying.

Ryan chuckled before sipping his drink and leaning closer. "A lot of people wonder that… David and Rosemary own the property, and a number of interested people provide financial support, and I've got my Army pension, so we get by."

"You were in the Army?" Grace's eyes shot open.

"Yes, for just over twenty-two years." Grace did a quick calculation. That would make him in his early forties, depending on when he joined.

"Where did you serve?" She held her breath.

Ryan angled his head. "You really want to know?"

Grace nodded. She didn't, but she couldn't help herself. She had to know… what if he was in Londonderry when the bomb went off?

"Well, the British weren't involved in Vietnam, thank God, but I was in the Aden Conflict, and then I got tangled up with the Troubles in Ireland in the late sixties and early seventies."

Grace felt the blood drain out of her face. Her heart raced and she bit her lip. She had to get a grip on herself. She couldn't allow even a smidgen of concern to show. Besides, he was probably in Belfast, not Londonderry.

"And I was in Malaysia, and also the Falklands." He leaned closer. "Best not make this public, but I was in the Special Forces."

Grace's eyes widened. Why was he telling her all of this? And why would a man like Ryan, who'd obviously seen so much action, choose to come and work in a place like this, with a mob of drug addicts and drop-outs? It didn't make sense. Surely he'd be bored stiff. She would be. She was already missing the challenge of the court room, and that was nothing like the adrenalin rush she imagined Ryan would have gotten from being in the field.

"So how are you finding it here? It must be tame after what you're used to." She tried to keep her voice calm, natural.

"Yes, it is, but the thrill of helping these kids, and seeing them face challenges they've never dreamed of facing before, is worth it. It's such a rewarding job, especially when most of them come to know God."

Grace blinked. *God?* Surely this burly ex-Special Forces soldier didn't believe in God? Surely after all the evil and hatred he would have seen, he'd be more cynical about God than ever. But here he was, talking about God as if it was the most natural thing in the world. Something told Grace that Ryan meant it, and just like Lizzy and Danny, his faith would be utterly genuine.

Dessert was served, saving Grace the need to provide some kind of answer to Ryan's last statement. *For now.* If she got the chance to spend more time with him, no doubt it would come up again, and she'd have to have a response ready.

Following dessert, Ryan pushed his chair back. "Sorry folks, I'm going to have to leave you. Early start in the morning and all." He smiled at everyone, and then leaned closer to Grace, whispering in her ear, "Let me know when you want to do that hike." And then he was gone.

The evening was finished as far as Grace was concerned. She had no inclination to strike up a conversation with any of the others, especially the older couple who she guessed could be quite boring, especially after Ryan. Who wanted to talk about Bible school, sewing and piano? Or cooking or domestic duties? No, the only person of interest here was Ryan. Apart from Danny and Lizzy, of course.

"I think I might head off, too if you'll excuse me." Grace wiped her mouth with a napkin and pushed her chair back. "It's been a lovely evening, thank you all." She nodded to each person in turn, and then made eyes at Brianna.

"I need to go to bed, too." Brianna took the hint. She stood and thanked everyone, before leaving with Grace.

Grace turned as Lizzy caught them just outside the kitchen. Grabbing both their hands, Lizzy gave them a warm smile. "I hope you both sleep well. Let me know if you need anything."

"Thanks, Lizzy. I'm sure we'll be fine." Grace returned her smile. "Thanks for a lovely evening."

"Our pleasure, Grace. I'm so glad you enjoyed yourselves." Lizzy leaned forward and hugged and kissed them in turn before saying goodnight.

. . .

ONCE IN THEIR ROOM, Brianna climbed into bed fully dressed.

"Are you okay, Bibi?" Grace eased herself onto the bed and brushed the hair off Brianna's forehead with her fingers.

Brianna sighed and closed her eyes. "I'm tired. And I'm sick of talking. That's all they seem to do." Her voice trailed away as she rolled over and faced the wall, curling into a ball as she always did, as if she just wanted to hide from the world.

Grace leaned over and hugged her. "It'll be all right, Bibi. Just get some sleep." She rubbed Brianna's back gently until her breathing slowed and her body relaxed.

Grace tip-toed away and prepared for bed, but as she lay in bed, sleep eluded her as her mind drifted back to the day that had haunted her for so long. She'd only been sixteen. Young and rebellious, and looking for a cause to follow. Something that would relieve the boredom of life in Londonderry…

CHAPTER 14

Londonderry, 1969

"Fergus has agreed to meet you after school," Grace's best friend, Samara whispered to her one boring Wednesday lunch-time in the school cafeteria.

Sixteen-year old Grace's face lit up at the prospect of something new happening in her life. Aunt Hilda treated her and Brianna like they were servants, not relatives, and Grace was sick of it. She didn't care if she got into trouble for being late to do her chores. Samara had been telling her about Fergus for some time, and finally she was getting the chance to meet him. Not that she believed for a second that was his real name. But that only added more to the intrigue and mystery.

"That's great, Sammy. Will you be there too?"

"Yes, I'll come. Meet me at the main gate and we'll catch the 3.11 into town."

Grace smiled at her. "I'll be there."

As they alighted from the 3.11 in downtown Derry and made their way first along Bishop Street and then through a rabbit warren of narrow alleys full of overflowing rubbish cans, stray cats and ancient crooked buildings, Grace's heart beat with anticipation. Finally she was getting a chance to do something exciting. Ever since she and Brianna had come to live with Aunt Hilda and Uncle Dougall after Mam died, she'd been longing for some excitement to replace the everyday drudgery of life in the tiny house in the suburbs of Londonderry.

The Troubles had begun a year ago, but having been kept on such a tight leash by Aunt Hilda, Grace hadn't seen any of it first hand, although, explosions and gunfire could often be heard in the distance, and occasionally, helicopters would fly overhead. But she wanted to see it for herself. And now she was sixteen, she was prepared to stand up to Aunt Hilda and get a life.

Sammy finally stopped in front of a nondescript door in a narrow alleyway and knocked three times. A voice from inside called out some unintelligible word, and Sammy replied with the word 'potato'. Seemed it was the word the person inside was looking for, because the door creaked open. Grace squinted. The shades were drawn over the solitary window, and she gagged at the smell of stale cigarettes and beer. Steeling herself, Grace followed Sammy inside. Sammy stopped in front of a table littered with wires and cables and bits of tin and metal. On the other side of the table sat a man with a big bushy beard and a cap drawn low over his eyes.

"Fergus, this is my friend, Faith."

Grace clenched her hands and inched closer to Sammy and the table. Her heart raced. Now the moment was here, could she really go through with it? What would Sammy think if she pulled out now? No, she had to hold herself together and go ahead with this meeting and prove to Fergus that she was capable of doing what was required.

Fergus leaned back in his chair, folded his arms, and sized her up.

Grace bit her lip to stop it quivering.

"So, Faith, what makes you think you might be of use to us?" His voice was deeper than she'd expected, and slightly gravelly, as if he was trying to disguise it.

Sammy pushed her forward. Grace swallowed hard. "Well, sir, I believe in the cause, and I'm smart, and I'm quick." Her voice was less confident than she'd hoped it would be.

"Smart, huh? Mary here has told me you're top in your class. Bit of a whizz kid."

"I don't know about that, sir, but I think I've been blessed with a decent brain."

Fergus continued to study her. Grace forced herself to stand still, although she was itching to turn around and flee.

"Mary said we can trust you. She'd better be right." He paused, as if he was weighing up whether he really could trust her or not. He lit a cigarette and blew smoke out of the corner of his mouth. The glow from the cigarette highlighted the red in his beard. Grace jumped as he leaned forward and folded his arms on the table. "You'll have two classes, and after that you'll be given your first assignment. You're not to say a word to anyone. Mary's already been chastised for talking to you." He glanced at Sammy. "We normally do our own recruiting."

Grace gulped. "Thank you, sir." She got the feeling that something was going on between the two of them and she felt sick in her stomach at the thought of it. Sammy had never said anything directly, but a few things she'd said now made sense. *How could Sammy do that?* Fergus was a disgusting creep.

"One thing, don't call me 'sir'."

"Okay, thank you, sir. Sorry, *Fergus*." Grace needed to get out before she vomited. She was panting, and couldn't steady her breathing.

"Read this and memorise it. You've got ten seconds and then I'll have it back."

Grace took the paper and read it carefully. Details of her classes were scrawled in untidy capital letters. She committed them to memory and handed the paper back. Fergus lit a match and held the paper up, making sure it was alight before tossing it in the bin.

"That's all. Good afternoon, ladies." He glanced at Sammy and ever so slightly nodded his head at her. Was Sammy planning on coming back later? What excuse did she give her Mam for being out so often? Grace gulped. Did she really know what she was getting herself into?

Once back outside in the alleyway, Grace gulped in lungfuls of air and steadied her breathing. If only she'd pulled out then... but she couldn't lose face with Sammy, and so she pretended she was impressed with Fergus, and feigned her excitement about the classes.

The following day she told Aunt Hilda she was going to Sammy's place after school to work on a joint assignment, but instead she went to her first class. Being clever, Grace picked up the art of bomb making very quickly. But what interested her the most was finding out which wire to pull out so it wouldn't go off. She couldn't ask directly, but by the time she'd completed her second class, she'd worked it out herself. And with that knowledge, she left the class with details of her first assignment scribbled on a piece of paper.

RIGHT FROM THE moment the girls arrived, Hilda resented them. She'd never wanted to take the girls in, but Dougall had spoken and she had no say in the matter.

"They're just poor wee little lassies without a Mam or a Da, Hilda, love. We have to offer them a home." He wrapped his stinking arms around her and breathed his foul breath on her, and then told her he'd earn extra money so they could afford to feed and clothe them. What a fool she'd been to believe him. Whatever extra money he might have earned, he spent at the pub on the way home. She never saw a penny of it.

She rarely spoke to the girls, apart from giving them chores to do.

The boys resented them too, and made faces at the girls, especially the youngest one who was much quieter than the older one. She sat in the corner and sucked her thumb even though she was ten when they arrived. She wet her bed every night too. Hilda made the older girl wash the stinking bedding. Why should she have to do it?

But Grace was the sly one. She was too smart for her own good, and Hilda despised her even more with every day and year that passed. She knew Grace was up to something when she was quieter than usual one morning at the breakfast table. She'd grown into quite a striking teenager, and Hilda had noticed Dougall's not so discreet interest in her. But what did she care? She couldn't stand the man touching her anymore, so if he was able to satisfy his needs with this young hussy, she should be grateful. But the airs and graces that girl put on! Who did she think she was? She should leave school and get a job, that'd bring her back to earth, but Dougall wouldn't allow it. "She's the clever one, Hilda, love. She can become anything she chooses. Leave her alone."

But Hilda kept watch, and this morning she had a feeling she was onto something. After the girls left for school, she quietly opened the door to their tiny back room and closed it behind her. No one was home, but still, it paid to be careful. She scanned the room. Rarely had she come in here, just on the odd occasion when she had extra jobs for them to do, but then she'd only stand in the doorway. The room was barely big enough for the two girls.

As she eased her large frame onto the bed, it squeaked and sagged in the middle. At least the bedding was clean. On the faded timber book-case, a lone photo sat in front of a row of books. Hilda reached for it and studied it. The woman must be their mam. She held a babe in her arms, and was surrounded by seven other children ranging in ages from about two to early teens. Hilda peered closer. It must have been taken not long before she died. She picked out Grace and Brianna and was tempted to tear the photo up. Instead, she replaced it carefully.

Her gaze moved slowly around the room. There had to be something. The girls were surprisingly neat. But then again, they didn't have much to be untidy with. Her gaze settled on a notebook on the desk. She picked it up and flicked through it. Nothing. Then a scrunched up piece of paper in the bin caught her attention. Hilda leaned over and picked it up. She smoothed out the creases and tried to read the few words that had been written in neat handwriting. She wasn't that literate, but could make out a few of the words. *'Friday 13th November Stop 20 4pm'*. Somehow she knew this was what she'd been looking for. She shoved it into her apron pocket, and after standing, smoothed the bed covers and backed out of the room with a smile on her face. She'd catch that young hussy out once and for all. Studying with Samara, sure. *And the Queen's my mother.*

ALL DAY AT SCHOOL, Grace couldn't concentrate. She glanced at the clock on the wall every few minutes. Every now and then Sammy kicked her and she turned her attention back to the algebra she was supposed to be doing, or the Shakespeare she was meant to be reading. Finally, the bell rang, and Grace quickly packed her books into her backpack. Her stomach convulsed. She just made it to the toilet block before vomiting violently into the bowl. Anyone who saw her probably thought she was pregnant. But that was impossible. Despite all Uncle Dougall's attempts, she'd never once given into him. Her acrid tongue and sharp words had somehow kept him at bay. But it had backfired, and he was now paying Brianna attention. Grace wasn't sure if Brianna was strong enough to hold him off much longer. But that was the least of her concerns right now. She stood slowly and wiped her mouth. Sweat dripped off her forehead despite the chill of the day.

"Grace, are you okay?" Sammy called from the other side of the door.

Grace inhaled slowly and forced herself to reply. "Yep, coming."

Sammy didn't know today was the day. Nobody knew, apart from her and Gregor, her teacher. *And Fergus, no doubt.*

"I've got to go home today, Sammy," Grace said when she finally opened the door. "I just remembered Aunt Hilda needed me to do extra chores this afternoon. Sorry." She planted a smile on her face and hoped she hadn't given anything away. "I'll catch you Monday, if not before."

Sammy narrowed her eyes but didn't say anything. She probably guessed, but what did it matter? "Okay then, see you Monday." As she began to walk away, she stopped and turned. "Come over tomorrow if you want."

Grace lifted her hand and smiled. She could see it in her eyes. Sammy knew.

Left on her own, Grace returned to the toilet cubicle and opened her back-pack. So many times she'd played this over in her mind, but now she had to do it for real. Carefully lifting the device she'd made during her class out of her back-pack, Grace set the timer for four p.m. Less than thirty minutes to get to the bus stop, plant it, and get out of the area. Before replacing the package in her back-pack, Grace did one more thing. She carefully picked up the white wire, but instead of connecting it to the terminal, she left it hanging. Maybe she'd be excused for not tightening it up properly since it was her first mission. But Grace doubted Fergus would let her off that easily... she'd be expelled from the group, but she couldn't do what they were asking. She'd just have to suffer whatever penalty he doled out if he realised what she'd done.

CHAPTER 15

Elim Community, 1985

GRACE SPRANG UP IN BED. Her heart pounded like a hammer drill and sweat dropped from her forehead in beads, landing on her already sodden bed clothes. Where was she? She held her hand to her chest and calmed her breathing. The first rays of daylight peeked in through the window. In the other bed, Brianna stretched and turned over. Grace remembered. She was at Danny and Lizzy's, and meeting Ryan must have triggered that horrible memory.

If only she hadn't gone to the bus stop that afternoon, everything would have been so different for both her and Brianna. The bomb shouldn't have gone off. Her stomach convulsed again just recalling the images of bodies flying through the air. And the noise. It shouldn't have happened. How had she made the mistake? She knew which wire to leave off. She knew what she was doing. It was quite simple. But somehow she'd made an error. A fatal error. How had she lived with herself all these years knowing she'd killed all those innocent people?

She'd been a hundred yards away when the bomb went off. She stopped and turned as if it was all happening in slow motion. Her heart stopped beating for what seemed ages as people ran all around her trying to get as far away as possible. Someone pulled her along, but she kept turning her head to see what was happening. Within seconds, sirens screamed as response teams raced to the site. Soldiers intermingled with Police as the area was cordoned off, and then Grace was pulled around a corner and could no longer see the devastation she'd caused.

"Best get home quickly, miss," a man said. She had no recollection of what he looked like; the only image in her head was of bodies lying on the ground amongst the debris, along with the memory of the smell of the smoke and dust that stung her nostrils. She could never forget.

She found the nearest train station and ran into the toilets where she retched violently into the putrid bowl until nothing was left in her stomach. How long she remained there she had no idea. Finally, she cleaned herself up and made her way home.

AUNT HILDA WASN'T in the kitchen. Strange, since she was always there. Grace breathed a sigh of relief and went straight to her room, closing the door behind her. Brianna lay on the bed, curled in a ball and sobbing. Her clothes were ripped and strewn over the edge of the bed and the floor.

Grace's heart pounded again. Throwing her bag down, she bent over Brianna, turning her over slowly. She peered into Bibi's eyes. "Bibi, what's happened?" Grace could barely speak.

Brianna's sobs increased, and Grace gently pulled her up and hugged her until she settled. Grace had a feeling she knew what had happened. Uncle Dougall had finally had his way. Her blood boiled. She'd report the brute to the police. But when Brianna finally spoke, and whispered "the boys", Grace could hardly believe it. She pulled Brianna closer and hugged her tighter.

"Both of them?" Grace asked quietly.

Brianna nodded.

Grace's chest heaved with anger. If only she'd come straight home from school, this wouldn't have happened. "I'm going to report them."

Brianna shook her head. "No...please don't." Her voice was barely a whisper.

"Why not, for heaven's sake? They've raped you, Brianna!"

A fresh round of sobs assailed her, and Grace pulled her close once more. "Well, I'm going to tell Aunt Hilda for a start." Grace gently laid Brianna back on the bed and tucked a blanket around her. "I'll come back and clean you up in a minute."

Grace left the room and strode into the kitchen. This time Aunt Hilda was there, and she had a smirk on her face. Grace's blood boiled. She strode straight up to her and stood over her. She was already a foot taller than her aunt. "Do you know what your boys have just done?" She didn't recognise the voice coming out of her mouth, it was so determined and full of hate and anger.

Aunt Hilda didn't reply, but she held her ground and met Grace's angry gaze.

"Well, do you?" Grace stepped closer. "I'll tell you what they've done. They've just raped Brianna, that's what. And I'm off to report them."

Aunt Hilda laughed. "You do that, missy, and I'll tell them who planted that bomb."

Grace sucked in a breath and stopped dead. She stared at Aunt Hilda. How did she know? Grace's whole world crumbled. They couldn't stay here a moment longer.

She gave Aunt Hilda one final stare and then turned and fled.

"Come on Bibi, we've got to get out of here." She helped Brianna up, quickly cleaned her, and helped her dress.

"What's happened, Grace? Why do we need to go?" Brianna's voice was weak and weary.

"Trust me, you don't want to know. We just need to get out of here." Grace pulled a bag from under the bed and quickly threw in as much as she could. Changing out of her school uniform, she climbed into a pair of jeans and put on her thickest shirt and jacket. "Okay, let's go." As she pushed Brianna out the door, she glanced in the bin. A heavy weight landed in the pit of her stomach. The scrunched up piece of paper she'd tossed away in disgust wasn't there.

She swallowed hard. It was too late. They snuck out the back door and into the narrow lane-way that ran behind the houses. Darkness had set in along with the chill of the night. Grace had no idea where they'd go. They just had to get as far away as possible. *And quickly.*

DOGS BARKED as they passed behind each of the neighbouring houses. Grace wished they'd stop. Would Aunt Hilda come after them? Or worse still, would she send the boys? Grace's heart was already thumping, but the thought of facing those two disgusting vile creatures made her blood boil. She dragged Brianna along with her until they reached the end of the lane. They headed the opposite way they'd normally go, and weaved in and out of the lanes running through the area until they reached the main road out of town. Grace put out her thumb and hoped they'd be picked up by someone quickly, praying that whoever picked them up wouldn't take advantage of two young girls out on their own on a cold winter's night.

Brianna stirred, bringing Grace back to the present. Brianna rubbed her eyes as she pulled herself up onto her pillows.

"Good morning, Bibi. Did you sleep okay?" Grace forced herself to sound normal.

Brianna shrugged. "Same as usual."

"I know, Bibi." And Grace did know. Neither of them had had a good night's sleep since that fateful day. They were each tormented by their own demons, they'd just handled them in different ways. Grace became so obsessed with study she stayed up late each night cramming for her next exam. Brianna turned to drugs. But now Brianna had the opportunity for a fresh start, and Grace hoped she'd grasp it with both hands. For both their sakes.

"I don't want to do this, Grace." Tears rolled down Brianna's cheeks.

Grace slipped out of bed and climbed in with Brianna, wrapping her arms around her like she used to do. "Give it a chance, Bibi, you've got nothing to lose."

As they lay in each other's arms, Grace tried to erase from her memory the horror of what she'd done, but it was no use. She knew she'd be tormented forever. It was her punishment.

A SHORT WHILE LATER, once they'd woken again and freshened up, Grace and Brianna made their way down the hallway to the kitchen where the children's happy voices could be heard.

Grace peeked in before entering. Dillon's little face lit up as he caught sight of her. He hopped out of his chair and ran over to her, hugging her around the middle.

"Steady on, Dillon," Lizzy called out from her seat opposite James and Clare. "Give your auntie some space."

"It's okay, Lizzy." Grace smiled at her as she leaned down and hugged Dillon.

Dillon grabbed Brianna's hand, and walked between the two of them to the table. "You sit here, Auntie Grace, and you sit here, Auntie…" He glanced at Brianna before looking to his mother.

"Brianna," Lizzy said.

Dillon turned his focus back to Brianna. "Bianna."

Everyone laughed. Dillon's face dropped.

Grace gently hugged the little boy. "It's okay. Dillon. I call her 'Bibi'. I'm sure she won't mind if you call her that too."

"Auntie Bibi." He flashed a charming smile at Brianna.

Brianna's lips lifted at the edges into a small smile. Even Brianna couldn't help but warm to this little boy.

As Grace and Brianna took seats on either side of Dillon, Lizzy stood and collected the children's dirty breakfast dishes and carried them to the sink. "What can I get you for breakfast? There's cereal and toast, or I can cook eggs… whatever you like."

"Just toast and tea for me, thanks Lizzy," Grace replied. She could never stomach breakfast. What she needed was a cigarette and a stiff drink.

"Same for me, thanks," Brianna added quickly.

"Did you sleep well? I hope the beds were comfy." Lizzy popped two pieces of bread into the toaster and turned on the kettle.

Grace blew out a breath and smiled. "The bed was great, thanks. Took a while to get to sleep, but that's normal." *So normal that I haven't had a good night's sleep since before that horrible day...* Just as well she'd learned to survive on next to no sleep.

"The mountain air should fix that pretty quickly." Lizzy flashed her a quick smile as she grabbed the toast. Smoke drifted into the air and the smell of burnt toast reached Grace's nostrils. "Just as well I don't do most of the cooking here." Lizzy tossed the burned pieces into the bin and started again.

After breakfast, Mia, the children's nanny, came to take the children outside. "Come and play with us, Auntie Grace and Auntie Bibi," Dillon called over his shoulder as Mia led them out the door.

Grace laughed. "Maybe later, Dillon. Have fun!"

Once on their own, Lizzy poured herself another cup of tea and sat down, letting out a contented sigh.

"They're lovely kids, Lizzy." Grace smiled warmly at her. She really meant it.

"Thank you." Lizzy returned Grace's smile. "They can be hard work sometimes, but we love them to bits." She took a sip of her tea and placed her cup on the table. "So, Brianna, are you ready to see your new quarters?"

Brianna's face paled. Grace squeezed her hand. "She'll be fine, Lizzy." Grace turned her head and gave Brianna an encouraging smile. "Won't you, Bibi?"

Brianna's shoulders slumped. Grace drew a slow breath. This was Brianna's last chance to start a new life. She had to take it. She narrowed her eyes at Brianna and pursed her lips. "She's ready."

CHAPTER 16

Brianna's heart thudded as she walked between Grace and Lizzy along a gravel pathway leading to the students' quarters in the huge stone mansion. Never in her wildest dreams had she imagined she'd be living in a place like this, but would she fit in? She doubted it. It was too nice a place for the likes of her. She was more at home in a gutter or a dingy apartment than a grand place like this.

Lizzy directed them towards a side door made of heavy timber. The door stood open, and they followed Lizzy up a spiral staircase. Brianna paused half way to catch her breath.

"Are you okay, Bibi?" Grace stopped behind her.

Brianna nodded. She held one hand against her chest and took several deep breaths. A pleasant aroma wafted down and tickled her nose. She'd expected the mansion to smell like some of the buildings she'd lived in, dank and musty, but this smell was different... it was nice. She drew a deep breath and continued on.

At the top of the staircase, a bunch of fresh flowers sat in a beautiful painted vase on a highly polished timber dresser. That's where the smell came from. Brianna's gaze turned to the area to the right of the staircase. A bookcase filled one wall, and an old piano another, but her attention was caught by the three over-sized couches covered with lap rugs and brightly coloured cushions, and the large coffee table sitting between them. A pile of magazines sat on one corner of the table, and on another corner, a pile of board games. Another smaller bunch of perfumed flowers sat in the middle, making it cosy and inviting.

The couches faced a large open fireplace, and Brianna could imagine herself curled up on one of those comfy couches, flicking through a magazine in front of a roaring fire. There was something about this room, and a sense of serenity flowed through her. Three large, religious posters hung on the far wall. She didn't have many thoughts either way about religion, but she hadn't seen much good come out of it. Grace, on the other hand, never hesitated to tell anyone who'd listen that she didn't believe in a God who'd let the mother of eight young children die an untimely death. If pushed, Brianna tended to agree.

"Ah, there you are." The kindly lady from last night bustled towards them, reminding Brianna a little of that lady at the first place she and Grace stayed at on their trip, but this lady seemed much nicer. Before Brianna could remember her name, the lady held her arms out and drew Brianna to her ample chest. "Ah Brianna, lassie, so good to see you. I hope you slept well." When she released Brianna, the smile on her face was as warm as her voice.

"Yes, thank you." Brianna's voice quivered, and she struggled to say anything more than that, but she liked the lady even though she spoke funny. The lady then hugged Grace and Lizzy with just as much warmth as she'd hugged her.

"How are you, Rosemary?" Lizzy returned the lady's smile. *Rosemary. That's her name...*

"Oh, I'm fine, lassie. How are your wee bairns this morning?"

"As active as ever, but they're off with Mia for the day."

"And what a jolly lassie she is. But come, we need to show Brianna around." Rosemary took Brianna's hand and patted it while she talked.

"As you can see, this is the female students' lounge area. There's a television in the corner, but the reception's bad and so it barely gets used. But don't worry, lassie. The girls find they don't miss it—there's plenty of other things to do.

"This hallway leads to the girls' dormitory." As Rosemary led the way, she continued chatting. "The kitchen and dining room are downstairs, but the classrooms are further along this hallway, in the front of the building. I'll show them to you later." Stopping in front of a closed door, Rosemary squeezed Brianna's hand. "This is where you'll be staying." Her double chin wobbled. "There's room for four girls, but there's only three at the moment, including you."

Brianna's heart raced. What if they didn't like her?

Grace's hand settled on her back and Brianna relaxed a little.

As Rosemary opened the door, Brianna's eyes widened. She'd expected to see double bunk beds, or at least a row of single beds close together, much like they'd grown up with, but instead, there were four separate areas, each with their own single bed, dresser and wardrobe. Each bed was covered with a soft, thick duvet, and more pillows than she'd know what to do with. On top of each dresser sat a lamp and more fresh flowers. The room was lovely. Tears flooded Brianna's eyes. She hadn't felt comfortable in Grace's modern apartment, but here, in this warm, friendly room, maybe, just maybe, she might be happy.

"This is your bed over here, Brianna." Rosemary directed her to the area in the far left hand corner. Brianna gasped as she gazed out at the mountains that seemed so close she could almost reach out and touch them. She stepped closer to the window. In front of the mountain was a lake with row boats tied up to a wharf. This was a dream, surely. It couldn't be happening to her. She pinched herself to make sure it was real.

Grace stood behind her, placing her arm around Brianna's shoulders. "It's lovely, isn't it, Bibi?"

All Brianna could do was nod as more tears slipped down her cheeks.

Rosemary handed her a tissue. "There, there, lassie. It has that effect on all of us." She chuckled. "The other two lassies are eager to meet you. They'll be back from morning duties shortly, but let's have a cup of tea and a chat while we wait."

"I'll leave you to it, Rosemary." Lizzy leaned down and placed a kiss on Rosemary's cheek before turning to Grace, arching an eyebrow towards the door. "Come with me?"

Brianna's eyes shot open. As much as she liked Rosemary, she didn't want to be left alone with her. She held her hand out to Grace and pleaded with her eyes for Grace to stay.

Grace held Brianna's gaze for a second, but then tore it away and looked at Lizzy. "Yes, I'll come with you." She placed Brianna's bag on the bed and then stepped closer to Brianna, brushing the tears off her cheek with her hand. "You'll be fine, Bibi. I'll be back soon." She squeezed her hand, and then turned and left with Lizzy.

Brianna crumpled. How could Grace just leave her like that? Tears stung her eyes again, and her bottom lip quivered.

Rosemary closed the gap between them, drawing Brianna into a hug, and smoothing Brianna's hair with her hand. "You'll be fine, lassie. The first day is always the hardest." Her voice was soft and kind. Rosemary pulled a white, scented handkerchief out of her pocket and gave it to Brianna.

Brianna sniffed, then blew her nose. She drew a steadying breath and lifted her head slowly to meet Rosemary's kind gaze. She managed a small, tentative smile. "Thank you." Her voice was no more than a whisper.

"You're more than welcome, lassie. Come now, leave your unpacking until later. Let's go and have that cup of tea."

Rosemary guided Brianna into another room at the far end of the hallway, passing two more rooms along the way that Rosemary told her were the other girls' rooms. "We have beds for twelve girls altogether, and this my office."

Brianna followed her into a room that looked more like a sitting room than an office. A small desk sat in one corner, but two comfy looking couches, positioned at right angles and both with a view of distant mountains, grabbed Brianna's attention.

"Take a seat, Brianna. I'll put the kettle on." Rosemary opened a cupboard and pulled out a kettle, two large mugs and a tea pot. She placed three heaped teaspoons of tea leaves into the pot before joining Brianna on the opposite couch.

"So, what do you know about the place, Brianna?" Rosemary gave her an easy smile as she perched on the edge of the couch.

Brianna shrugged. "Not much."

Rosemary chuckled. "Well, you're in for a treat." Her face expanded into a beaming grin. "There are so many things to do here. It's a wonderful place to learn new skills. Most of the girls love the cooking lessons, and some prefer gardening to piano, but there are so many options, and you can try them all to start with and see what you prefer."

The kettle whistled and Rosemary bounced up and turned it off. She poured the steaming water into the teapot, and then placed a colourful tea cosy over it, just like Mam used to do. The sudden memory brought tears to Brianna's eyes. She rarely thought of Mam, but when she did, she always grew sad. She missed Mam so much. Why did she have to die? She brushed her tears away quickly with the handkerchief before Rosemary could see them.

Rosemary poured two mugs of tea, placing them, along with a jug of milk and a sugar pot, on a small table between them. As she looked up, her expression changed. She sat beside Brianna, placing her arm around her shoulder. "What's wrong, lassie?" Her voice was gentle and soft.

Tears returned to Brianna's eyes. She clenched her hands and tried to squeeze them back. She wasn't a cry baby. What was she doing? She sucked in a breath and gulped. "It's nothing."

"Ach, lassie, if you don't want to talk, that's fine, but something's unsettling you, I can see it in your wee, bonnie face." Rosemary spoke in a gentle voice with a lilting Scottish burr, and as she brushed Brianna's face lightly with her warm fingertips, tears streamed down Brianna's face.

Sniffing, Brianna lowered her eyes and balled the handkerchief in her hands. "Mam had a tea pot and cosy just like yours."

“How old were you when she died?”

Brianna sniffed again. “Ten.”

Rosemary pulled her close and rocked her. “Poor wee lassie." Her voice was soothing, like the sound of a dove cooing to its young. “There’s no need to talk about it now, lassie, but when you're ready, I’m a good listener.”

Brianna was tempted, but she wasn't ready. Straightening, she blew her nose and slowly lifted her eyes to Rosemary's. “Thank you.”

"You're welcome, sweetheart. Would you like some shortbread? Handmade by the girls, and it's very good." Rosemary held the plate out to her.

Brianna took a piece and nibbled it. Rosemary was right, it was really good.

“Do you like cooking, Brianna?”

Brianna blinked. “I've not done any, so I don't know."

“Would you like to learn?”

Brianna blinked again. “I’ve never thought about it, but maybe.”

Rosemary smiled as she took a bite of shortbread and settled back further on the couch, balancing her cup and saucer with one hand. "I think you'll like it here, Brianna. It's a place where hurts from the past can be slowly healed. Daniel will give you a full run down on the programme this afternoon with the other new students." She glanced towards the door as two girls stopped in the doorway. One was thin and had shoulder-length brown hair and very narrow, arched eyebrows. The other girl had dark hair and pale skin, and a heart tattooed on her neck.

Rosemary's face expanded into a beaming smile as she extended her hand to the two girls. “Come in, lassies, and meet your new room-mate."

The two girls stepped into the room. Rosemary put her tea cup down and patted spots on either side of her on the couch. As the girls sat, Rosemary placed her arm around the thin girl on her left. “Brianna, this is Maggie. Maggie comes from London, and has been with us just under a week.”

Maggie gave Brianna a half smile and fiddled nervously with her hands.

Rosemary then placed her arm around the other girl, the dark-haired girl with the tattoo. “And this is Susan, and she comes from Glasgow. She’s been here just under a week as well.”

“Hi-ya.” Susan sounded just like Rosemary, and her smile was warmer than Maggie’s.

“Hi.” Brianna gave a small smile before lowering her eyes.

“I’ve been telling Brianna a little about the place, and she’s seen your room, but hasn’t unpacked yet." She patted both their legs. "Why don't we head back there and I can leave you girls to help Brianna settle in before you meet with Daniel?” Rosemary smiled at them both, her double chin wobbling as she turned her head.

The two girls agreed and they stood, waiting for Brianna to do the same.

Brianna swallowed hard. She was just getting used to being with Rosemary, and now she was expected to spend time with girls she didn't know. She wasn't ready for this, but seemed she had no choice.

“Where are you from, Brianna?” Susan asked in her Scottish burr as they walked along the hallway together.

“Belfast.” It was all Brianna could manage.

“You’re going to love it here. It’s such a cool place, and the people are great. Wait…” Susan turned and placed her hand on Brianna’s shoulder. “Daniel’s your brother, isn’t he?”

Brianna's shoulders slumped. She didn't want to be known as the manager's sister, but it seemed everyone knew already. She sighed. What did it matter? "Yes, but I hardly know him. Last time I saw him, I was ten."

"Really? Wow!"

They reached the room before Susan could say more. Rosemary glanced at her watch as she stopped in front of them. "Okay girls, you've got half an hour before you need to meet Daniel down in the meeting room." Turning to Brianna, Rosemary rubbed her arm. "Are you okay, lassie?" Her eyes were soft and warm as she met Brianna's gaze.

Brianna sucked in a breath. Was she okay? She really didn't know, but surprisingly, in the few short moments she'd spent with Susan and Maggie, something had clicked with Susan in particular, and for the first time in a long time, Brianna thought she might end up having a friend. She nodded, giving Rosemary the biggest smile she'd given anyone in a long time. "I think so."

"That's grand, lassie." She pulled Brianna in for another hug before releasing her. "I'll see you there soon. Have fun!" She turned and bustled down the hallway, leaving the girls alone with each other for the first time.

CHAPTER 17

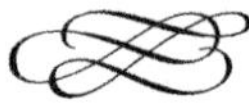

For the next half hour, Susan and Maggie helped Brianna unpack and set up her area of the room. Brianna discovered that Susan had been trying to kick her drug habit for the last two years without success, and it was her mother who'd heard about the Elim Community and arranged for her to come. She'd been clean for three weeks, and was eager to be clean for the rest of her life. Maggie's problem was different. She'd been brought up in foster care all her life, and didn't seem to fit anywhere. A care worker from the local parish recommended the Elim Community to her. Brianna found herself opening up with the girls. She told them she'd been on drugs since she was sixteen, and that it was her sister who'd brought her here in the hope of getting her clean. She didn't tell them about being raped or losing her baby. Some secrets were just too deep.

"It's time to go," Susan said as she glanced at the clock beside the door. "We can help you finish later, Brianna."

The girls headed along the hallway and down another spiral staircase similar to the one Brianna had gone up earlier. Brianna had no idea where they went after that. The building was full of narrow hallways that twisted and turned and went up and down, but finally they arrived in a room that looked much like a classroom, except that the chairs were placed in a semi-circle and not straight rows. Daniel looked up as the girls entered.

Brianna hung back, but Susan grabbed her hand and pulled her in. Brianna's heart raced again. What was she doing here? This was crazy. Brianna O'Connor in a classroom, with Daniel, her brother, as teacher? She shook her head and blinked. She must be dreaming. But no, Daniel strode over to her, and taking one of her hands, kissed her on the cheek. Her face grew warm. Why would he embarrass her in front of everyone like that?

He smiled easily, and his eyes sparkled. "Brianna, great to see you." She felt like hiding. He then turned to Susan and Maggie. "And good to see you both." He gave them a warm smile but didn't hug or kiss them. "The boys are on their way, but in the meantime, take a seat."

Just as they were sitting, two young men entered. Brianna's eyes popped. *Brayden McCafferty! What's he doing here?* The boy all the girls crushed on in school… the boy everyone expected to go places, to be someone. She peered at him… *yes, it's him, but he's different.* His eyes were dull and lifeless, and his head hung low, but she would have known him anywhere. Every night in that horrid room Aunt Hilda had called their bedroom she'd dreamed about him as she and Grace huddled together to keep warm, but now he was in front of her, all she wanted to do was hide.

"Boys, come on in." Daniel waved Brayden and the other young man in and clapped both of them on the back.

As Daniel introduced everyone, Brianna's heart pounded. What if Brayden recognised her? What would happen then? But there was no recognition in his face. Brayden didn't remember her. Brianna breathed a sigh of relief.

Grace had said that their brother had a way with people. Brianna wasn't sure what Grace had meant by that until now, but when Daniel stood in the front of the room, all eyes were on him. Even Brayden's.

He cleared his throat. "Well, good morning, everyone." His eyes and voice were bright. "Most of you have been here for a few days already, and I hope you've started to settle in, but now you're all here, it's time to kick off properly. Welcome to Elim Community, a place of hope and new beginnings." He paused and caught each student's eye as his gaze travelled around the room. "We've all messed up. You and me, both. I've been where you are today, and okay, I'm not perfect by a long shot, just ask my wife, but I can assure you that my life now is so much better than it was just a few years ago. What we have here in this community is a place where you won't be judged. You'll be offered hope, love and understanding, and you'll have the opportunity to learn skills that will help you live a more fulfilling life than you've ever dreamed possible." Daniel took a mouthful of water, and pulling his chair closer to everyone, leaned forward.

As Brianna listened to Daniel, she caught a little of his infectious enthusiasm. Her heart quickened. Maybe, just maybe, this place might hold the answers to questions she didn't even know she was asking.

Daniel angled his head. "What makes us different from other places you might have been to? For a start, you're living in a beautiful mansion in the Scottish Highlands. That has to be different." He chuckled. "But apart from that, being away from the city and your normal environment helps give a different perspective on life. How many of you have ever sat on the top of a mountain you've spent all morning climbing and gazed out into the distance in awe?" He waited, but no one claimed they had. In fact, they all shook their heads. "How many of you have rowed along a loch in the early morning when the water's so still and glassy you can't tell where the loch ends and the mountains begin?" They all shook their heads again. "And how many of you have had someone you can talk to who'll listen without judging or trying to tell you what to do?" His voice had an infinitely compassionate tone, and all eyes were fixed on him.

"You've all come here because you've tried other places or programmes, but nothing so far has worked. You're still struggling with your demons, whatever they are, and you've come here, possibly as a last resort." He smiled. "We don't offer any guarantees, but we know that if you're committed to turning your life around, it's more than possible to do that here. We're a Christian community, but we don't force religion down your throat. We expect you to go to classes where you'll have the chance to find out what Christianity is all about, but then it's up to you to make the decision. You won't be judged either way. You'll also meet with either David or Rosemary at least once a day to chat about how you're doing. They're great people, and you'll find them both easy to talk to." He took a sip of water. "Our programme also includes outdoor and indoor activities, such as hiking, rowing, abseiling, sailing, metal work, carpentry, gardening, cooking, piano lessons, painting... basically whatever you want to learn, you can learn here.

"We also expect students to work for several hours a day to help cover their board. Apart from daily chores, we have several small businesses running, and you'll be assigned on a roster basis to help out with each of them in turn." Daniel paused, letting his gaze travel around the students again. "So, you'll be kept busy, but what you get out of this place will depend on how much effort you put in. I have great hopes for all of you." He smiled at them before glancing towards the door. "And now, here are David, Rosemary, Ryan and Emily. Let me introduce each of them properly."

The four staff members briefly spoke as Daniel introduced them one at a time. When Rosemary stood and smiled at Brianna, warmth trickled through Brianna's body.

"Okay, then," Daniel said once the staff members had finished. "Lunch, and then you get to choose an activity. Ryan's running a beginner abseiling class, and Emily's holding a cooking class. Shepherd's Pie's on the menu, and I believe we'll be eating that for dinner."

Emily nodded.

"And then after that, you'll have some free time, and after dinner we'll have our first class. Sound good?" Daniel glanced around the group as he stood.

Everyone nodded, apart from Brayden.

"What are you going to choose, Brianna?" Susan asked as they walked to the dining room together.

That was a good question, but since she had no idea what abseiling was, there really wasn't an option. "Cooking."

Susan smiled broadly and linked her arm through Brianna's. "Me too."

Maggie walked ahead with Rosemary, and Brianna felt a pang of jealousy run through her.

The afternoon passed, and Brianna enjoyed her first cooking class ever. Emily was a patient teacher, and Brianna was proud of the pie she'd made—she hoped everyone would like it. During her spare time, she finished unpacking and settled into her room.

Later, sitting in the classroom and hearing Daniel talk about God and Jesus, it was like a switch flicked in her mind. Daniel said to forget all they'd heard and been taught about religion. Jesus had come to offer peace, hope and forgiveness, and all the fighting over religion just showed how many people had missed the true message. Over the coming weeks they'd be studying the Gospel of John, but any questions they had along the way would also be addressed. They all left with their very own copy of the New Testament.

Brianna glanced at Brayden as the students shared supper after class. The other boys chatted together, but he barely said a word. *What happened to you, Brayden McCafferty?*

Meanwhile, Grace spent the morning with Lizzy and helped with her jobs, all the while keeping a lookout for Ryan. Her pulse quickened when she caught a glimpse of him just before lunch as he jumped out of his truck and sprinted into what Lizzy told her was the meeting room.

"I saw you looking at him, Grace." Lizzy's face twisted in an amused grin, and her eyes sparkled.

"No I wasn't." Grace turned quickly and composed herself.

"I hope you do better than that in court." Lizzy chuckled. "Still no one special in your life?"

Grace shook her head slowly. *There never will be...*

"He's a nice man. You should get to know him."

Letting out a sigh, Grace's shoulders slumped. But Ryan had been a soldier and had probably killed a hundred times more people than she had. Maybe she could risk it. She drew a breath. "We'll see."

CHAPTER 18

One morning, several days later, Grace was sitting outside in the garden wrapped in a blanket, trying to read a John Grisham thriller she'd found amongst all the Christian books on Lizzy's bookshelf, but she was finding it hard to relax, and was wishing she was back in the courtroom. A movement distracted her, and looking up, Grace saw Brianna coming towards her with a smile on her face. Putting her book down, Grace held out her hand. "Hey, Bibi, this is a nice surprise. How are you?" Pulling Brianna onto the seat beside her, she gave Brianna a big hug.

"Good. Really good." Brianna's eyes were brighter than Grace had ever seen them. Even her voice sounded more alive.

Grace smiled into Brianna's eyes as she brushed some hair off Brianna's forehead. "That's great. What have you been doing?"

Brianna let out a small chuckle. "I've been learning how to cook." Her eyes sparkled as she held out a covered plate. "I made an apple pie this morning, and I brought you some." The proud smile on Brianna's face brought tears to Grace's eyes. Was this the same girl she'd left in Daniel's care just three days ago?

"It smells wonderful!" Grace lifted the cloth and took a peek.

Brianna smiled, her eyes glistening. "I've done some painting too, and I've been canoeing on the loch. I didn't even fall in."

Shaking her head, Grace laughed. "I don't believe it."

"Here's something you really won't believe." Brianna's expression grew serious and she glanced down at her hands before meeting Grace's gaze. "I've been taking the Bible classes Daniel runs, and he's amazing. You should hear him."

Grace stiffened. "Don't tell me they've brainwashed you already?"

"No, Grace. It's not like that, really. There's no pressure. We're allowed to make our own minds up, but I'm starting to understand about God, and how He can fix my life if I let Him. I've still got a lot to learn, but so far it makes sense."

"Well, it's great to see you so excited." Grace smiled at her but let out a sigh. *At least she's off the drugs, for now...* "You know I don't believe in all that, but if you want to, that's up to you."

Brianna grabbed Grace's hand. "You should come to one of Danny's classes and see for yourself."

Grace pursed her lips. "I don't think so, but thanks."

"Tomorrow Ryan's taking us hiking, and he said to ask if you wanted to come."

Grace's eyes widened. *He hadn't forgotten.* "Who's going?"

"All the new students. There's five of us—three girls and two boys. Oh, I forgot to tell you—one of the boys was in my class at school, but he doesn't remember me." Brianna's smile slipped. "He's not doing too well."

"But you are, Bibi, and that's all that matters." Grace squeezed her hand.

Sighing, Brianna glanced down at her hands. "Yes, I know, but everyone else is doing well, apart from him." She looked up, her face brightening. "Danny's coming too."

Grace ran her hand through her hair. "I'll think about it." But she'd already made up her mind. She'd go.

“We’re leaving at nine if you decide to come.” Leaning forward, Brianna gave Grace a hug. “Thanks for bringing me here, Grace.”

Tears stung her eyes. Was it possible that Bibi was finally getting clean? Straightening, Grace smiled into Brianna's eyes and tucked a stray lock of hair behind her ear. "I'm glad you're happy here, Bibi. I really am."

Brianna nodded and gulped. "See you in the morning?"

"Maybe."

A spark of hope grew inside Grace as Brianna walked away with a spring to her step. It had only been a few days, but already Brianna was a changed person. *But would it last?*

Lizzy poked her head out the kitchen door. “Lunch is ready, Grace.”

"Coming." Grace folded the blanket, picked up her book and headed inside. The children were already seated at the table, as noisy as ever.

“Come and sit here, Auntie Grace.” Dillon jumped up and grabbed her hand, pulling her towards the seat next to him.

Grace laughed as she let Dillon drag her along. How could she resist his charm? He was just like his father. “Have you had a good morning?” Grace asked as she sat beside him.

“Yes, we played lots of games and we did some painting. I did this one for you.” He jumped off his seat again and scrambled through a box of bits and pieces, finally pulling out a folded piece of paper which he handed to her.

Carefully opening it, Grace swallowed hard. Dillon had painted himself holding her hand. “It’s lovely, Dillon. Thank you.” She swallowed again as she gave him a big smile. "I'll take it home with me and put it on my wall."

"Really?" His whole face lit up.

Grace nodded. It might not fit her decor, but it would take pride of place in her living room.

“That’s enough now, Dillon.” Lizzy placed a tray of sandwiches cut into triangles on the table.

“He’s fine, Lizzy. Let him be.” Grace chuckled as she folded the painting and slipped it into her book.

“We did some too.” Little Clare spoke timidly, her big round eyes serious as she looked at Grace.

"Did you? You’ll have to show me.”

Clare nodded as she stuck her thumb in her mouth.

Lizzy joined them at the table, and reaching out her hands, took hold of the boys' hands. "Let's give thanks before we eat."

Having been there three days already, Grace was used to this, so she took Dillon's other hand and gently plied Clare's thumb from her mouth, and bowed her head while Lizzy gave thanks. It was a pointless routine, but she had no choice.

Lizzy raised her head and began placing sandwiches on the children's plates. "Please help yourself, Grace."

"Thanks." Grace smiled and reached for a ham and tomato sandwich.

“Was that Brianna I saw leaving just a while ago?” Lizzy looked up.

Grace nodded. “Yes. She seems to be doing really well.”

“Daniel said she’s doing great. You must be so relieved.”

Grace released a slow breath. “I just hope it lasts.”

“I know what you mean. I used to get my hopes up with Daniel all the time.” Lizzy let out a heavy sigh before brightening. “But he got there in the end, and so will Brianna.”

“I hope so.” Grace toyed with her napkin. If anyone knew what she was going through, Lizzy did. Her's and Daniel's marriage had almost fallen apart because of his addiction to alcohol. “She asked if I wanted to go hiking with them tomorrow.”

Lizzy’s eyes widened. “You should go, Grace. You’ll love it.”

“I was thinking I might. Some exercise might do me good.”

"Cup of tea?” Lizzy held up a teapot and raised a brow, an amused smirk sitting on her face.

Grace ignored the smirk. “Yes, please, that would be lovely.”

. . .

LATER THAT EVENING, when Grace was preparing her hiking clothes for the morning, she came across the letter Niall had given her before she left Belfast. Sitting on the wing chair under the window, she toyed with the letter. She knew the contents by heart, but opened it anyway. She shouldn't have, because her thoughts were drawn back to the night he'd proposed…

She was twenty-four when they both graduated from Law School, and to celebrate, Niall had booked a table at the fanciest restaurant in Belfast, on top of the Riverside Tower. Grace would have been happy just to go to the local pub, but he'd insisted. He was paying, so she agreed.

He looked so handsome that night—but he always did. He had such style, and that evening, in his freshly pressed navy trousers and crisp white shirt, Grace was acutely aware she was with the most eligible bachelor in town. Her heart skipped a beat when he placed his hand on the small of her back and led her into the elegant dining room.

As the waiter directed them to a window seat, Grace's gaze was automatically drawn in the direction of Londonderry, almost a hundred miles away. Would there come a time when she didn't think about the events of that afternoon and evening? She doubted it, but Niall would never know. No one would.

"Spectacular, isn't it?"

Grace blinked. She had to focus on Niall and on the present, and not on events of the past. Turning towards him, she planted a smile on her face and nodded. "Yes, it is."

All through dinner they chatted easily, talking about life after University, and the jobs they were going to. Niall was going to work in his father's practice, defending the innocent. She'd be working for the Department of Public Prosecution, prosecuting the guilty. It was highly likely they'd cross each other in court some day in the future. They laughed when they discussed who'd be most likely to win.

After dinner, Niall took her hand, squeezing it and looking deeply into her eyes. A quick and disturbing thought flashed through her mind as he reached into his pocket, drawing out a small red box and placing it on the table between them. She gulped.

"Grace, you know how much I love you." Niall's voice, strong and deep, sent a quiver of excitement through her, but she couldn't go there. She steeled herself as he continued, rubbing his thumb gently along her hand. "You won't agree to live with me, so I'm hoping instead that you'll agree to marry me." His Adam's apple bobbed as he swallowed, and his eyes, filled with hope, remained locked on hers. Her stomach churned. He squeezed her hand tighter. "Grace, will you marry me?"

Tears slipped down Grace's cheek as a deep ache grew in her heart. Niall was the perfect man and she loved him, but she could never be his wife. She had to live with her past, but she couldn't expect anyone else to. Looking at him now, she wished she'd never gotten involved with him. She could never commit to a permanent relationship, with him, or anyone.

Sniffing, Grace wiped her tears with a napkin and lowered her gaze. She was about to break his heart, and there was nothing she could do. If only things had been different. Taking a slow breath, Grace looked up and met his quizzical gaze. "Niall..." She gulped. "I can't marry you. I'm so sorry. Not now, not ever." She swallowed hard. If only she could have said "yes".

Niall's face paled. He leaned closer, gripping her hand. "Grace... why not? Please tell me. We can work through whatever the problem is... please don't do this." His voice was shaky, pleading, distraught.

Grace shook her head and fought back her tears. "No, Niall. We can't." Images of bloodied bodies strewn on the pavement flashed through her mind. There was no way they could work through that together.

"Grace... please tell me." He gripped her hand. She couldn't bear the pain in his eyes, but there was nothing she could do. *Nothing.* The suffocating sensation of loss gnawed at her, overwhelming her. This was the end for them. She had to make a clean break. She couldn't allow him any hope.

She squeezed his hand and forced her tears back. “Niall, I can’t marry you, not now, not ever. I'm sorry.” Tears streamed down her cheeks as she pushed her chair back and stood. "I've got to go, I'm sorry." She could barely speak. She fled towards the elevator, and when she got home, she drank a whole bottle of gin and cried herself to sleep.

Sitting in the chair under the window in Lizzy's cottage, tears streamed down Grace's cheeks. She'd tried to bury the pain and despair of that night in her work, but nothing had changed. Niall coming back into her life had proven that. She still loved him, but she still couldn’t marry him, or anyone else. Those innocent people's lives were on her head, and would be until the day she died.

Sleep eluded Grace as usual. Memories circled in her head like vultures, each eager to take a piece of her. But that was nothing new, and so the following morning, she was ready to leave by half past eight.

Grace shivered as she walked the short distance along the path that joined the cottage and the mansion. Mist hung in the air like a damp blanket. Why had she agreed to go? Right now, a courtroom held way more appeal.

As Grace rounded the corner and approached the main entrance, her breath caught. Ryan was leaning against the centre's minibus, his arms folded and one ankle crossed over the other as he chatted with Danny. He was a good-looking man, and her heart quickened, not only at his ease and self-confidence, but also at the muscles bulging under his ribbed khaki sweat shirt.

Since Niall, she'd only had casual liaisons, and the thought of a casual dalliance with Ryan appealed. It wouldn't have to be serious, just a short fling. And it might help rid her of Niall's lingering memory.

Ryan lifted his gaze as Grace approached, his eyes sweeping over her face approvingly. "You decided to come?"

"Yes." She tilted her chin, but her heart pounded.

"It's a great day for a hike." An easy smile played at the corners of his mouth.

"You could have picked a better one." Grace glanced at the mist hanging over the mountains. "It'd better not rain."

"A bit of rain never hurt anyone." He chuckled, his eyes twinkling.

Grace raised a brow.

"Ryan's right, Grace, you get used to it." Leaning forward, Danny placed a kiss on her cheek.

"We'll see..."

Ryan winked at her as he began loading the students' backpacks into the bus.

Shortly after, sitting in the middle beside Brianna, surrounded by Brianna's new friends, Grace felt like a fish out of water, but she fixed her eyes on the broad shoulders and the curly reddish-blond head of hair in front of her.

As Ryan drove skilfully along the single-track winding its way above the eastern shore of Loch Linnhe, the mist began to lift and Grace glanced out the window at the rugged, bare hills dotted with sheep and the occasional herd of highland cattle. She had to admit it was kind of beautiful in its own way.

Ryan stopped the bus on a heather covered meadow on the crest of a hill and everyone piled out. Ryan and Daniel handed out the packs, and when Grace took hers from Ryan, her fingers brushed his. Lifting her gaze, she angled her head and looked into his blue eyes, once again wondering what a man like him was doing in a place like this.

They set off in single file, Ryan in the lead and Daniel at the tail. Grace chose to walk with Daniel—she'd make her move later when it was more appropriate, and besides, from the back, she could keep her eye on Ryan.

The winding path led across bare foothills dotted with rocks, heather and sheep. Below, to the right, the loch reflected the grey of the sky, and the remains of an old castle sat on the far side, bearing witness to times gone by.

Up ahead, Brianna chatted with her new friends. Grace knew she should be happy for her, and she was, but it only highlighted her own unhappiness. Brianna might be able to shake off the shackles of the past in religion, but Grace could never do that. She needed to return to work, immerse herself in it. That was the only way she could survive, by prosecuting scum, because in some cathartic way, every case she took, she was prosecuting herself...

"You're very quiet, Grace. What's up?" Daniel asked from behind.

She shrugged. "Nothing, just enjoying the view."

CHAPTER 19

After hiking for an hour, Ryan stopped on a grassy knoll, removed his back-pack, and turned around, pleased to see that everyone had kept up, even Grace. He looked at her with a heavy heart. She needed the freeing power of Jesus's love in her life just as much as these drug addicted kids did, she just didn't know it. It didn't matter that she was a wealthy barrister, or gave the appearance of someone who had it all together, he'd seen through her facade the moment he'd laid eyes on her. Maybe it was his training, but he had a gift of knowing what made people tick, and Grace O'Connor had a ticking time bomb inside her. He sent up a quick prayer for her.

Brayden stopped behind him. Ryan smiled at the troubled young man. "Keep up okay?" Brayden's face was still deathly pale and disengaged, but it was early days. Ryan was sure that the enthusiasm of the others would rub off on him in time, and that the Holy Spirit would touch the young man's heart, softening it, drawing him slowly but surely to the Healer of broken lives.

Every night the staff prayed for the students, and the guests, like Grace. In the two years he'd been with the Elim Community, Ryan had witnessed miracle after miracle as God's healing touch changed the lives of those who came. Something wonderful happened when troubled youth distanced themselves from the hustle and bustle of city life and came face to face with the raw beauty of God's creation. He expected the same would happen for both Brayden and Grace, just like it already had for Brianna.

Brayden shrugged, barely giving a grunt.

Squeezing the young man's shoulder, Ryan gave him an encouraging smile. He was going to be hard work, but God was able to break through his barriers, it might just take time.

Everyone else stopped and took out a snack—oatcakes made by the students, and water. Ryan had several flasks of coffee, and after offering some to the students, held out a mug to Grace. "Like some?"

"Thought you'd never ask." She let out a small chuckle as she took the mug. Throwing her pack onto the ground, she lowered herself gracefully onto a rock, stretching her long, slender legs in front of her, and took a sip.

"Mind if I join you?"

She looked up, her hazel eyes travelling lazily up his body. "Please do."

He ignored her play-acting and sat on the ground beside her. "So, Grace O'Connor, what do you think of the Highlands so far?"

Tilting her head, she met his gaze and took her time in answering. "They have their good points."

He chuckled. "They certainly do." He held out a container full of oatcakes. "Like one?"

She shook her head. "No thanks."

"Come on Grace, you're not watching your weight, are you? And besides, your sister made them."

Grace grunted, and reaching out, picked out one of the cookies. "I don't normally snack."

"Too busy, huh?"

Grace shrugged. "Something like that."

"Well, if you stay out here long enough, you'll not only develop a good appetite, but you'll feel better. Maybe you need to slow down a little."

"I'm perfectly fine, thank you."

He studied her before speaking. She was a beautiful woman, there was no doubt about it. Her rich auburn hair lay thick on her shoulders, and although her profile was strong and determined, underneath that facade lay a soft heart, of that he was sure, otherwise, why would she have brought her sister here? "Are you really fine, Grace?"

She took another sip of her coffee and lifted her chin. "Yes." Her eyes flickered as she dug her heel into the ground.

He gave her a warm smile. "If you ever want to talk, I'm a good listener."

Grace angled her head. "And what about you, Ryan MacGregor? Are you fine? What are you really doing here?" She raised her brow, an amused look on her face. "Hiding from something? *Or someone?*"

Ryan laughed. "I can see why you're good in the courtroom." He held her gaze as his expression sobered. "I'm here because I want to be." He drew a breath and released it slowly. "I love these kids, and I want to help them." Her gaze didn't waver... she was assessing him, just as she'd assess a witness in one of her high-profile cases. He had nothing to hide. Not any longer, anyway. His past was just that—his past. God had cleansed him and forgiven him, praise the Lord.

Grace's eyes narrowed. "That's a very glib answer."

"It may be, but it's true. I love it here. It's peaceful and it's rewarding. And I'm not hiding from anyone or anything."

"Everyone has something in their past, Ryan, including you."

"Perhaps, but when you have God in your life, He gives you a clean start, and your past can be left where it belongs... in the past."

She went silent.

Something had happened to Grace, and it still haunted her. He'd say an extra prayer for her tonight. "Well, it's time we made a move." He jumped up and held his hand out. The touch of her skin triggered an unexpected response, one he hadn't felt for a long time. Her hand remained in his a moment longer than necessary. She was still flirting with him, but this time he looked at her with fresh eyes. He could easily fall for her… but not until God did a work in her heart.

Grace walked beside Ryan until they stopped for lunch. She was tempted to quiz him, to ply him with questions about his past, but refrained. Instead, she quizzed him about the highlands and about the countryside they were walking through, anything that wasn't personal or about God.

"We're all going to the Highland Games on Saturday. Will you still be here then?" Ryan asked as they walked along the grassy trail with plenty of room for two high above Loch Linnhe. The mist had lifted completely, and the loch shimmered in the bright sunshine.

"I was thinking I'd go home since Brianna seems settled."

"Why don't you stay, Grace? At least until after the weekend. You can't come to Scotland and not go to a Highland Games."

"That's what Lizzy said." Grace shrugged. "I'll give it some thought."

"You'd enjoy it. It's a really fun day, and there's a Ceilidh in the evening… you can't miss that."

"I can't dance, Ryan." She chuckled at the very thought of doing a Highland Fling.

"I can teach you."

Grace turned and looked at him. If things were different, she could easily fall for this man. His easy, relaxed manner was so refreshing, but nothing had changed in her life, and all she could offer him would be a few fun times together and then she'd have to walk away. But maybe she could go to a Ceilidh with him… and then afterwards…. who knew what might eventuate?

"You're very convincing. Okay, I'll stay."

His face broke into a wide, open smile, lighting up his eyes that were as blue as the loch below them.

WHEN GRACE RETURNED to the cottage later that afternoon, Lizzy and the children were sitting on a blanket out on the grass having a picnic. Lizzy waved her over. "Come and join us, Grace."

Dillon's face lit up. He jumped up and ran towards Grace, throwing his arms around her waist. "I missed you, Auntie Grace."

Grace couldn't help herself, and a laugh bubbled up from deep within. Dillon's infectious enthusiasm warmed her heart. It really was nice being wanted, even if it was only by a child. "And I missed you, too, Dillon." She bent down and gave him a hug before he grabbed her hand and led her to the rug.

"Sit down, Auntie Grace, and have a gingerbread man. I helped Mummy make them."

Grace caught Lizzy's amused look and grinned. "They look lovely, Dillon, but I don't know if I could fit one in."

The expression on his little face fell.

Grace let out a breath. She'd said the wrong thing. "On second thought, I'd love one."

His smile returned and he quickly picked a gingerbread man out of the container and held it out to her.

"Put it on a plate for Auntie Grace, Dillon," Lizzy said in a stern voice.

He giggled. "Sorry." He picked up a small plate and after placing the gingerbread man on it, handed it to Grace with a sparkle in his eye.

"Thank you, Dillon, it looks great." Grace took a bite just to be polite, but it actually tasted so good she took a bigger bite. Maybe Ryan was right and the highland air had given her an appetite.

"So, how was the hike?" Lizzy leaned back, resting her hands on the ground behind her.

"It was actually much easier than I thought it'd be, but I think I could do with a rest. I'm not used to all this physical activity."

Lizzy gave her a warm smile. "Plenty of time before dinner. Oh, I almost forgot to tell you... there was a phone call for you. I wrote the number down inside."

Grace's face fell. It couldn't be Caleb, because Lizzy would have said so. *It had to be Niall.*

SHE FINISHED her gingerbread man and managed to ease Clare off her lap. For some reason, the little girl had taken a liking to her and took whatever opportunity she could to sit on her lap. Grace thought it cute, in fact, everything about Clare was cute, from her big round eyes and adorable blond hair cut in a bob, to the thumb that perpetually lived in her mouth. "Auntie Grace has got to go, Clare. I'm sorry. I'll see you at dinner, okay?"

The little girl nodded.

Grace walked into the cottage and found the note Lizzy had taken. Yes, it was Niall's number. She glanced at her watch. He'd called more than three hours ago. Strange he'd be calling on a work day. Something must have happened—perhaps to his father. Why else would he be ringing? Nothing had changed between them, and he knew that.

She dialled the number, and he answered within two rings.

CHAPTER 20

"Grace, thanks for calling back." Niall's voice sounded so familiar, so calm, so steady.

"I only rang because I thought something must have happened to your father."

"No, nothing like that... sorry to have caused you worry. I was just ringing to let you know that O'Malley's appeal has been scheduled for next week. I know you said you wouldn't be back for it, but I just thought I should let you know, in case you changed your mind."

Grace held the receiver tighter against her ear. Her heart rate increased. The pull of the courtroom was strong, and hadn't she been thinking about returning anyway? It was tempting... very tempting. She let out a slow breath. "I'll think about it, Niall. Thanks for letting me know." She paused, her eyebrows furrowing. "Would we be against each other again?" How would she ever convince him they had no future together if they kept seeing each other?

"Yes. Come back, Grace. I've missed you." His voice had lost its calmness, and had grown thick and unsteady.

Grace slumped against the wall and held her hand against her head.

There it was... the real reason... She exhaled slowly. "Nothing's changed, Niall."

He didn't reply. Most likely he'd be sitting at his desk holding a photo of her. If only he'd let go of her. She wasn't any good for him, and he deserved better. *Way better.* He was a good man. A lovely man. A caring man. Grace closed her eyes as the acute sense of loss overwhelmed her again. Maybe she could live with him and keep her secret hidden? No, he'd find out somehow. He was a barrister, and he'd whittle it out of her eventually. She couldn't drag him down with her if ever she was discovered. She had to stay strong, keep her walls up. Even going back for the appeal would be asking for trouble... but then, she'd have to go back sometime. She'd just have to learn to live in the same city as him without allowing him back into her life. Difficult, when they'd meet in court every other day.

"How's your father?" She had to say something.

"Doing okay. How's Brianna?"

"Good." She swallowed hard.

Silence.

"I'll think about the appeal. I need to go."

"I love you, Grace." His words came out quickly.

"Niall... don't..." Tears pricked her eyes and she could barely speak. "I have to go..." She hung up and made her way to her bedroom. Falling onto her bed, she sobbed into the pillow until she fell asleep.

Sometime later, Grace woke to soft knocking on her door. Her head felt thick like concrete, heavy and lifeless.

"Dinner's ready, Grace." Lizzy's voice came to her through her fog.

Grace struggled to lift her head. There was no way she could drag herself to the table. "I'll be down later, Lizzy." Her voice belonged to someone else. Not to Grace O'Connor, Barrister.

"Are you all right?" Lizzy's voice held concern.

Grace forced herself to reply. "Just tired."

"Okay. I'll keep your dinner warm."

Rolling onto her back, Grace lifted her hand to her forehead and stared at the ceiling. What did she have to live for? Brianna no longer needed her, now she had Danny and religion. She couldn't marry Niall, she could never have children, not that she wanted any, hadn't even thought about it until being with Lizzy and Danny's kids, but maybe if things had been different... all she had was work. Which meant she needed to go back. Only work would provide the answer to her deep despair and loneliness. But then she'd have to see Niall... she had no choice—she'd just have to learn to ignore him. She'd have that fling with Ryan MacGregor, and then go back.

THE NEXT COUPLE of days passed. Grace put up her walls and pretended everything was fine. She was good at that. She even feigned joy when Brianna told her that she'd given her heart to Jesus. Grace hugged her and wished her well, but she didn't know this new Brianna. In some ways, she was more comfortable with the old Brianna. At least she understood her then, but now? It was like Brianna's past had never existed. Grace doubted it would last. It had happened too quickly. How could Brianna forget about being raped and the death of her baby just like that? Grace guessed she hadn't told anyone about either, and it would only be a matter of time before she was back on drugs. But then, she'd be Danny and Lizzy's problem, not hers.

Grace had told everybody she'd be leaving on Monday to attend the appeal—she had no doubt the guilty judgment would be upheld, but it was an excuse to leave. She was tempted to go earlier, but everyone insisted she go to the Games on Saturday. Besides, spending the day with Ryan still held attraction. She might get to have that fling with him yet.

The morning of the Games, Grace went with Danny, Lizzy and the children—Ryan said he'd meet her there as he was transporting the students in the mini-bus. The light, misty rain, which Danny told her was called *smirr*, didn't seem to worry the crowd already filling the football field.

As Grace stepped out of the van, Dillon took her hand. "Can you take me to the rides, Auntie Grace?" His little face was full of excitement and expectation. Grace swallowed hard. As much as she tried to pretend she wouldn't miss the children, she would. They'd broken through her walls with their innocence and honesty, *and love*. The sooner she could return to work, the better.

"Dillon, leave Auntie Grace be. Daddy will take you a little later, okay?" Lizzy ruffled Dillon's dark, wavy hair and raised her brow.

"It's all right, Lizzy, I can take him."

Dillon jumped up and down and whooped without letting go of Grace's hand.

Grace couldn't help herself and let out a laugh. If only she could wind the clock back…

"Can we go now?" He was still bouncing, and his little face pleaded with her.

"All right, Dillon. But what about James and Clare?"

"They're too little. Come on, let's just you and me go."

Ryan appeared from in front of the van, looking as relaxed and handsome as ever in his faded blue jeans and red, white and blue checked shirt. He met Grace's gaze, his eyes twinkling in amusement. "And where is this young man taking you?"

Grace chuckled, but Dillon replied before she could. "To the rides. You can come too." Dillon grabbed Ryan's hand and tried to drag both Grace and Ryan away from the van.

"Whoa, little man. Let's see if that's okay with your mum first."

"I said I'd take him, Ryan, it's okay." Grace's heart quickened as she looked into his blue eyes.

"Okay then, let's go. We'll meet up with you later, Liz."

"Thanks Ryan. Good luck with him. And you behave, Dillon... okay?" Lizzy chuckled as she raised her brow again, shooting Dillon another warning look.

"Okay, Mummy." His voice was so cute, Grace's heart came close to melting.

IT SEEMED SURREAL, walking through the food stalls where delightful aromas of freshly baked treats filled the air, rubbing shoulders with burly Scotsmen proudly wearing their Clan's tartan, and listening to the bagpipe music blaring from the hill, but what was more surreal was that she was holding a little boy's hand and Ryan held the other. Grace fought the overwhelming sense of loss which had been surfacing more every day she stayed. She needed to go home, away from this place that just served to remind her of the life she might have had if only things had been different.

"Would you like a coffee, Grace?" Ryan asked as they passed an area set aside with tables and chairs at the far end of the food stalls.

"I'd love one, but we'd better take Dillon on a ride first."

"You're right. We'll come back."

They headed for the children's rides and let Dillon pick which ride he wanted to go on. He chose the merry-go-round, and he wanted both Grace and Ryan to go with him.

Grace laughed. "I've never been on one of these."

"Well, it's time you did!" Ryan dragged her onto the merry-go-round, and after he'd helped Dillon onto a dark brown horse with a cream mane, he helped Grace onto the horse to Dillon's left, a white one with a bright pink mane. Ryan took the horse to Dillon's right. As the music began and the horses rose and fell while circling the carousel, Grace almost forgot herself. How many times as young children had she and Brianna looked with envy at the other children riding the carousel at the local fair? Mam could never afford for them to go on any rides, and

Aunt Hilda never let them go. Joy welled in her heart at the pure excitement on Dillon's face, but when her eyes met Ryan's smiling ones, warmth trickled through her body from the tips of her fingers to the bottom of her toes.

"Can we ride it again?" Dillon asked, his little face fully animated.

Laughing, Ryan ruffled Dillon's hair. "Maybe later. Auntie Grace would like a drink, and so would I. Would you like one, Dillon?"

"Can I get a milkshake?" His eyes sparkled, just like his dad's.

"Of course." Ryan smiled and took Dillon's hand.

It was tempting to slip her hand into Ryan's, but she refrained, and instead, took Dillon's spare one.

Seated at a table covered with a red and white checked plastic tablecloth and a vase with a sprig of heather sitting in the middle, Grace found it difficult to look Ryan in the eye, instead, she paid attention to Dillon. There was something unnerving sitting here with Ryan, almost like they were playing happy families. Nothing was further from the truth.

"I like you being here, Auntie Grace. Why can't you stay?"

Grace sighed, clasping her hands together and staring at them before slowly lifting her eyes. "You know why, Dillon. Auntie Grace has to go back to work."

Ryan raised his brow. They'd already had this conversation, and she guessed Ryan knew she was running away, and that she didn't really need to go back.

"I'm going to miss you."

Grace swallowed hard. "I'm going to miss you, too, Dillon."

Lifting her gaze, she met Ryan's magnetic blue eyes and her heart pounded. His mouth twisted in a grin that told her he knew exactly how she was feeling and what she was thinking. She held his gaze for a long moment before tearing her eyes away. He was the most infuriating man. She hated that he had the uncanny knack of seeing through her.

"We should go find our seats. The events will be starting soon." Ryan toyed with his coffee mug.

"Good idea." Grace downed her coffee and stood. "Come on Dillon, let's find your parents." She took his hand and didn't wait for Ryan. She needed the safety of numbers. It was foolish to think she could flirt with a man like Ryan and not get hurt. She was falling for him, and fast, and she couldn't let herself go there.

THE STADIUM WAS a-buzz with anticipation as the massed pipe bands prepared to enter the grounds. Sitting with Lizzy on one side of her, Ryan on the other, and Clare on her lap, Grace should have been happy. Brianna was sitting with her new friends, including Brayden, and looked happy and relaxed. Happy faces were everywhere. Happy faces belonging to happy people. She didn't belong amongst them.

Somehow she got through the day. Bagpipes, drums and Highland flings gave way to caber tosses and hammer throws. Grace laughed and clapped and chatted, but inside, she was empty. It was all meaningless. None of them had any idea of the weight she was carrying. How could they? She'd told no one, not even Brianna. Why it had resurfaced of late, she didn't know, but her nightmares had increased, especially since being here with such good, kind people. *And Ryan.*

"Coming to the Ceilidh tonight?" Ryan asked her as they all made their way back to their vehicles after the main events had finished. He held an umbrella over her head as the *smirr* grew heavier, and she had to fight the overwhelming temptation to slip her arm through his. If only she could welcome his friendship, let everything go. All day her swirling emotions had tormented her, as all her loneliness and guilt welded together to the point she just had to get away or else she'd explode. One more day… she took a deep breath and put on a bright face. "Yes, I'm looking forward to it."

"Great! And I'm looking forward to seeing you in tartan!" His eyes sparkled as he opened the door of the van for her.

Grace's forehead puckered. "I don't have any tartan."

"I'm only joking. You can wear whatever you want."

She let out a small laugh. "Okay, I'll see what I have. See you tonight."

As she settled into her seat beside the children, Grace let her gaze linger on Ryan as he walked around to the mini-bus and chatted freely with the students as they all climbed in. He was so relaxed and happy—something she could never be.

"Have you had a good day, Grace?" Lizzy asked as she finished buckling up Clare.

What could she say? *"No, it's been torture...?"* She couldn't say that. She smiled at Lizzy. "Yes, it's been great."

"And you're going to the Ceilidh with Ryan, I hear?"

"So it seems." Grace gave a small chuckle. How had she gotten herself into this situation?

"He's a nice man, Grace. You could do worse for yourself."

Grace shrugged. "I'm not interested."

Lizzy laughed. "Yeah, right."

Grace met Lizzy's gaze. "I'm not interested in him, Lizzy. In him, or anyone."

Lizzy's expression slipped. "Okay, sorry. I was only having a bit of fun."

"Well, don't." Why was she talking to Lizzy like this? It was like someone else had taken over her tongue and words she didn't mean tumbled out. She had to get away. She didn't mean to snap at Lizzy of all people.

Thankfully, the children's chatter filled the van on the short drive home. When they arrived, Grace excused herself and began packing.

~

"WHAT'S UP WITH GRACE?" Lizzy asked Daniel when they sat down for a cup of tea after dinner before getting ready for the Ceilidh. David and Rosemary were putting the children to bed, having offered to mind them so Daniel and Lizzy could attend the dance.

"What do you mean?" Easing back onto the sofa, Daniel angled his head, and slipping his arm around her shoulders, pulled her close.

"I don't know, but she seems kind of… troubled, I think that's the word. She snapped at me in the car." Lizzy ran her hand slowly along Daniel's leg.

Daniel straightened. "Grace snapped at you? What on earth made her do that?"

Lizzy shrugged. "I just told her she could do worse than Ryan."

Daniel laughed. "You should know better than that, Lizzy. I remember a time when you told me off for asking her if she had anyone special in her life."

Lizzy let out a sigh. "Yes, you're right. I shouldn't have said anything. But even without that, she seems on edge more than normal."

Daniel rubbed her arm. "We just have to keep praying for her, Liz, you know that. We don't know what's going on inside her, but God does."

"You're right, Daniel." Lizzy straightened. "Maybe we should pray for her now?"

He smiled. "Good idea. Let's do it." Taking Lizzy's hand, Daniel bowed his head. "Dear Lord, we bring Grace before You. We'd hoped that by being here, amongst those who love You, and amongst Your great creation here in the Highlands, that she might have let her walls down and opened her heart to You. We feel saddened that this hasn't happened yet, but Lord, we trust You to continue working in her heart, drawing her to Yourself, chipping away at the walls she's put up. Lord, we pray that she'll open her heart to Your love and peace, and that she'll give whatever's troubling her over to You, the great Comforter and Healer. Open the eyes of her heart to the truth of the gospel message;

may she embrace the sacrifice Jesus made for her when He gave His life on the cross so that she might live. Lord, bless her this day, we pray, in Jesus' name, Amen."

"And Lord," Lizzy cleared her throat, "give us wisdom to know what to say to Grace, especially as she's planning on leaving soon. I'm sorry for being so thoughtless with her this afternoon. And Lord, we thank You so much for the change in Brianna's life. Thank You for healing her hurts, and giving her hope for the future. We're so glad she's opened her heart to You. Continue to strengthen her on a daily basis, so that she won't succumb when temptation comes knocking on her door, as it's bound to do. Amen." Lizzy let out a slow breath as she brushed tears off her cheeks.

"We have to leave her in God's hands, Liz."

"I know. I just wish He'd hurry up."

"Patience, Lizzy, patience."

"You know that's not my forte."

Daniel lifted his hand and brushed her cheek. His blue eyes twinkled, sending her senses into a tailspin. "Yes, but you've come a long way, Lizzy O'Connor."

Lizzy chuckled. "I guess I have, but He's still got a lot of work to do on me."

"As He does on me."

Lizzy smiled at him. "I love you, Daniel. And I love that God brought us to this place. It's hard to remember what life was like before we were here. I feel like we've come home."

"Home is wherever you are, Liz."

"You're such a big softie, Daniel." She chuckled as he lowered his lips against hers, but she pulled away before he could kiss her properly. "If we're going dancing, we need to get ready."

"I guess we do." He gave her another quick kiss and then fixed his eyes on hers as he traced her hairline with the tip of his finger. "Later?"

Nodding, she stretched up and gave him a slow kiss.

CHAPTER 21

When Grace asked Lizzy what she should wear to the Ceilidh, Lizzy suggested jeans and a comfortable top, but in her designer jeans and soft cream silk shirt, Grace knew she would still turn eyes.

Ryan ran his eyes over her when they all met up outside the main building before leaving. Despite not wanting to go at all, Grace found it hard to take her eyes off him too. Wearing black trousers and a long-sleeved black shirt with the cuffs rolled up, he was devastatingly handsome. His compelling blue eyes and confident set of his shoulders, coupled with the tantalising smell of his after-shave, sent her pulse racing.

"Would you like to sit up front with me, Grace?" Ryan held his hand on the sliding door and looked at her as she stood beside Lizzy and Daniel. Danny had his arm around Lizzy's waist, and she got the impression they didn't want to be separated.

"Go on, Grace, it's fine." Danny said, giving her a nod.

Grace let out a breath. Why not? She smiled at Ryan. "Okay, thanks."

The students were already in the back, and Ryan slid the door closed after Daniel and Lizzy climbed in, and then held the front door open for her. "You look lovely tonight, Grace."

As she lifted her eyes to his, a ripple of excitement flowed through her. She gave him a grateful smile, but didn't trust herself to speak as she climbed in as elegantly as she could.

The Ceilidh was being held in the local hall, and even as they pulled up, the sounds of accordions, drums and fiddles filled the air. Grace had to admit that the music was stirring, possibly even more so than the Irish music that often floated out of the hotels near Chambers. Despite not expecting to enjoy herself, her heart quickened in anticipation.

The drizzle had stopped, and people gathered inside and out while they waited for the official start, but some eager couples were already dancing to the music. Ryan's light touch on her back sent tremors through her body. "Can I get you a drink?" He had to shout as he guided her through the crowd.

Turning her head, she lifted a brow. "Gin and tonic?"

He shook his head and chuckled. "We've been through this before, Grace. Water, soft drink or tea..."

Grace raised her other brow. "Whisky?"

He chuckled again. "Sorry."

She let out a sigh. "Guess I'll have water."

He handed her a glass. "I need to check on the students. I'll be right back."

She smiled at him. "Okay. I'll stay with Lizzy."

Ryan left with Daniel and headed towards the students who were all standing together in a huddle. The old Brianna would never have been seen dead or alive at a gathering such as this, but what would the new Brianna do? Grace kept her eye on the two men as they stood with their arms folded talking with the group. Half of the students looked like they didn't want to be there. Brianna was talking with Brayden, who had a sullen look on his face.

Daniel and Ryan returned just as the band stopped playing and someone blew into the microphone.

"Welcome everyone to tonight's Ceilidh. Take your partners for the first dance of the night, a Gypsy Tap."

Ryan held out his arm. "May I have this dance, Madam?" His eyes twinkled, warming Grace's heart.

"Thank you." She took his arm, as solid and firm as a tree trunk. The smell of him made her flesh tingle.

"Do you know this dance?" he whispered into her ear.

"No."

"Don't worry, it's easy." They joined the circle of other couples before an older man wearing a kilt stood at the microphone and gave instructions. Within moments, Ryan slipped his arm around Grace's back and his left hand took her right one. His face was close enough for her to feel the warmth of his breath on her cheek. Against her better judgment, she allowed herself to relax. The music played, the man called the steps, and the dance began. Ryan was right—it wasn't difficult, and within a couple of sequences, Grace had it sorted. He hadn't told her it was progressive, and too soon she found herself with men she'd never met, each paying her a compliment. She was sure they said the same thing to all the women, but it boosted her spirits, nevertheless. When she came to Brayden, she tried to jolly him along. She was surprised he was up dancing at all. She glanced around the circle and found Brianna. She was laughing, and it looked like she was having the time of her life. The change in her was still so hard to believe.

Once the Gypsy Tap finished, Strip the Willow was called. Ryan headed straight for Grace, and taking her elbow, placed her opposite him in a long row that stretched all the way from the front of the hall to the back. She had no idea what she was letting herself in for, but by the time it was hers and Ryan's turn to "Strip the Willow", she had a good idea she was going to embarrass herself in front of everyone, but Ryan's arms were so strong, and he made sure she didn't fall over, and every time she swung out into his arms, he steadied her. By the time they'd finished stripping the willow, she was breathless, but couldn't stop laughing.

"You did well, Grace," Lizzy stepped close to her and shouted into her ear.

"Thanks!" Grace's chest heaved as she tried to catch her breath. On the other side, Ryan winked at her, and a warm fuzzy feeling surged through her.

The rest of the evening passed all too quickly. Grace had never danced so much in all her life, nor had so much fun. Before she was ready, it was time to leave.

As she sat beside Ryan on the way home, instead of after-shave filling her nostrils, masculine body odour oozed from him, but she didn't find it offensive, in fact, it had the exact opposite effect on her. She found it intoxicating, and had to fight her overwhelming desire to be close to him.

When he stopped the bus in front of Lizzy and Danny's cottage, her hopes for a romantic evening flew out the window. He jumped out, jogged around the front, and opened the door for her. Instead of sweeping her up in his arms and kissing her as she'd hoped he would, he just took her hand and smiled. "I enjoyed myself tonight, Grace. I hope you did, too."

She forced a smile. "Yes, I had a lovely time, thank you."

"Will we see you in church in the morning?"

She fought her automatic response of "no", and instead answered "maybe."

"You'd be welcome." His smile widened, and her heart once again fluttered as his eyes twinkled at hers.

"I'll think about it." But she'd already thought. If he was there, she'd go.

"Thanks for coming, Grace. I'll look forward to seeing you tomorrow." He leaned forward. She held her breath as he placed the lightest kiss she'd ever had on her cheek. But just the touch of his lips was enough to send her heart into a spin.

AS LIZZY, Daniel and Grace waved good-bye to Ryan and all the students, Grace's throat clenched. Nothing could happen between her and Ryan, but seeing him drive away just accentuated her loneliness. It would have been nice just to talk with him, if nothing else.

"Come inside and have a cup of tea, Grace." Danny placed his hand gently on her back. "Did you enjoy yourself tonight?"

She let out a sigh and nodded, turning her head slightly to smile at him. "Yes, it was fun, thanks."

"It was good to see you laughing." He left his hand on her shoulder as they walked inside.

Rosemary and David greeted them with tired smiles as they all entered the kitchen.

"How were the children?" Danny stepped to the stove and picked up the kettle.

"No problem at all. They're all sound asleep in bed, which is where we should be." Rosemary chuckled.

"Sorry we're so late, Rosemary." Lizzy hurried over and gave Rosemary a big hug. "Thanks so much for looking after them."

"Our pleasure, Lizzy. Hope you all had a good night."

Lizzy beamed. "The best. It was so much fun."

"Ceilidhs always are."

"You'll have to come next time."

"Not sure about that." Rosemary chuckled. "I don't think I could strip the willow any more than I could climb Ben Nevis! No, we were happy to mind the children so you could go."

"And we appreciate that, we really do."

"As I said, it's our pleasure, but we really must be going. We have to be up early in the morning to prepare the flowers for church."

After Rosemary and David left, Danny pulled out a chair for Grace and they both sat while Lizzy began making tea.

Grace toyed with the spoon that had been left sitting on the table. The feeling of loneliness that had crept through her after Ryan drove away still sat heavily inside her.

"So, one more day..." Danny angled his head and looked at her.

"Yes. One more day."

"The kids will miss you." He paused. "We'll miss you."

Grace swallowed hard, her shoulders sagging under the weight of her loneliness and confusion. She finally lifted her head and met Danny's gaze. "And I'll miss you all, too." Her words caught in her throat.

Danny leaned forward and squeezed her hand. "You don't have to go, Grace. You're very welcome to stay as long as you want."

His kind eyes unnerved her further. She glanced down at her lap and tried to compose herself.

Finally, she lifted her head and met his gaze. "I don't know, Danny. I don't know what I want to do."

"Why don't you stay, then? Surely somebody else can step in for you."

Shaking her head, Grace sucked in a slow breath before releasing it. Her shoulders slumped. “I really don’t know.” She swallowed hard. And that was the truth. She didn’t know. If she went back to work, it would all be the same. She’d get caught up with high profile cases that might help her forget for a while, but seeing Niall on an almost daily basis would be a constant reminder of what she could never have. If only she’d never got tangled up with Samara and Fergus. The only real way out was to confess and pay the penalty. But could she really do that now, after all this time? And how would she cope being in prison with those she’d put there? Grace shuddered at the thought. She was caught between a rock and a hard place. The only way forward was to push it all away again and not think about it. Bury it. Hide it. Pretend it had never happened. She could do that. She’d done it before, she could do it again. *But staying a while longer was tempting.*

Danny squeezed her hand again. "Think about it?"

She shrugged. "Maybe."

Lizzy placed three steaming mugs of tea on the table and sat down opposite. "Dillon would love it if you stayed longer." She lifted her eyes and smiled. "And so would I, Grace. It's been lovely having company."

Tears sprung to Grace's eyes. If she ever wanted a friend, Lizzy would be a great choice. Oh, blow it! She'd stay. Sniffing, she let out a small chuckle. "Okay, you talked me into it."

Lizzy's eyes popped. Jumping up, she threw her arms around Grace's neck. "That's fantastic, Grace."

Grace laughed. "I didn't know I was so popular."

"You'd better believe it." Smiling, Lizzy took her seat and touched Grace's wrist lightly. "The kids adore you, Grace."

"I don't know why."

"Oh, I think it's because you look like their dad, and they love him to bits." Lizzy's eyes shone with love and devotion as she slipped Danny a smile.

Once again, the pain of knowing she'd never share such a moment with anyone special tore at Grace's heart. But being loved by Danny and Lizzy's children was some compensation at least… *or was it?*

"Well, now that's sorted, let's drink our tea." Danny winked at Grace as he lifted his mug. Did he ever miss drinking anything stronger? She knew she did… but she'd have to do without while she was here.

Taking a sip of her tea, Grace leaned back, and wrapping her hands around the mug, angled her head towards Danny. "Do you think Brianna's going to make it?"

His expression grew serious. She'd caught him off-guard with her direct question. He cleared his throat and steadied his gaze. "Yes, I think she will."

"What makes you so sure? She's stayed off drugs before for weeks at a time, and then she's gone back onto them. What's different this time?" She raised her brow. "And don't tell me it's because she's found God."

Danny drew a slow breath, put his mug on the table and folded his arms. "I can't guarantee she won't go back on them at all, Grace, but I do know that she's sincere about wanting to stay clean. I know you won't want to hear about her conversion experience, but you should ask her someday. I believe it was real, and that God has filled the hole in her heart that's been there all her life. He's given her a new start, Grace. He's washed away all the dirt from her previous life, and cleansed her from the inside out. She's still going to face challenges, as we all do, but she's got God in her heart now, and He'll give her the strength to get through whatever comes her way."

Grace remained silent. It was a lot of rubbish as far as she was concerned, but she couldn't deny Danny's sincerity, and the change in his own life. "Has she told you what happened to her?" Grace's eyes narrowed as she angled her head.

Danny leaned back in his chair. "No, she hasn't, but I can see she's been hurt in the past." He turned his head and met Grace's gaze. "Was it terrible for you at Aunt Hilda's, Grace? I've always wanted to know, but you've never wanted to talk about it."

Grace shook her head. "You really don't want to know."

"I feel guilty that you and Brianna were sent away when Mam died, Grace. I wished you could have stayed in Belfast with Caleb and me. I'm sure there would have been room for you at Aunt Moira's."

"But you didn't have such a good time either, from what I hear."

Danny sucked in a big breath. "No, you're right. I messed up badly."

Lizzy reached out and squeezed his hand.

He looked up and smiled at her, causing Grace to gulp. He shifted in his seat and turned back to Grace. "Would you like to hear about it?"

Grace shrugged. "Okay. I've only heard bits and pieces from Caleb, so I may as well hear it from you."

He drew a slow breath, as if he was steeling himself. "You already know Aunt Moira and Uncle Desmond took Caleb and me in."

Grace nodded.

"I was fourteen, and angry about Mam dying, and even more angry about the way Da had treated her." He shrugged. "I started drinking when I was sixteen, but then one night I got so drunk I ended up in hospital. I was given an ultimatum, either start going to church with the family, or move out. They'd had enough of me." He paused. "I wasn't ready to move out, so I started going to church, and I met a girl... her name was Ciara."

Danny's eyes moistened. "She was beautiful. She had long, flowing hair, and she was always smiling. For some reason, she liked me, and we started dating." His expression grew serious and he wiped his eyes. "She got pregnant, and her parents made us get married. We lived in a room at the back of their house. It was hard, but we loved each other." He closed his eyes and sucked in a deep breath.

Grace reached out and touched his arm. "You don't have to tell me if you don't want to..."

He opened his eyes. "No, it's okay. I want to."

As she gave him a smile, her heart went out to him.

"The baby was born. A little girl... we named her Rachel. She was the most precious little thing, and we loved her so much." He swallowed hard. "Having a baby to look after made me grow up. I got a job, Ciara and I moved out into a place of our own, and everything was great for six months, until one night, Rachel died in her sleep." His eyes moistened again, and his body shuddered. "I can still remember that night..."

Lizzy rubbed his back.

Grace pushed back tears of her own as memories of the night Brianna's little baby boy died flooded back. But she couldn't tell Danny about that. It was up to Brianna to tell him if she wanted to.

"I couldn't handle it and started drinking again, heavily. I went on binges, and one night when I came home, my cousin Liam had his arms around Ciara. I lost it, and beat him until he was almost dead. I went to prison for it." He lifted his head. "Ciara left me after that. I don't blame her. But this is the worst bit, Grace." Tears flooded his eyes. "A few years later, Ciara took her life." Tears rolled down his cheeks. "I should have been there for her when Rachel died, instead of beating Liam up and landing in jail."

Tears streamed from Grace's eyes. She reached out and pulled him close. She'd had no idea. Why hadn't Caleb told her? Maybe he had but she just hadn't listened. "I'm so sorry, Danny."

He sucked in some big breaths and released them slowly. "It's okay. It's part of my past, and it doesn't haunt me anymore. Meeting Lizzy was the best thing that happened to me. Well, the second best. She led me to Jesus, and He changed my life. I know you don't believe in Him, Grace, but I can testify for a fact that He's real. The gospel message is real. Jesus died for my sins so that I can live with Him forever, and while I'm here on earth, He's given me peace, joy, purpose, and forgiveness. That's what Brianna's found, and I pray that you'll find it too."

Grace didn't know what to say. She couldn't deny Danny's experience. But how could Jesus ever forgive her of murder?

CHAPTER 22

The following morning, Grace rose and dressed for church, something she hadn't done since Mam died, almost twenty years ago. Danny's story had haunted her all night. Something about it had stirred her heart. If God had relieved him of his guilt over Ciara's death, maybe there was a way of getting rid of her own. Maybe she didn't need to tell anyone, other than God, what she'd done. Brianna hadn't. She'd go and hear what they had to say, because if there was a way out of this hole, she was starting to think she should look for it. Anything had to be better than the hell she was living in.

The children were already sitting around the table eating breakfast when Grace entered the kitchen. Lizzy smiled brightly and the children all called out for her to sit beside them.

Grace laughed. She really had no idea why they liked her, but she had to admit it felt nice to be wanted. She just hoped they'd never find out that the auntie they seemed to love so much was a murderer. She chastised herself. She had to stop thinking like that.

"Let Auntie Grace pick her own seat." Lizzy shook her head at the children but laughed along with Grace, catching her eye as Grace chose a seat at the foot of the table on either side of James and Clare. "Coffee?"

"Yes, please."

Lizzy smiled warmly as she poured Grace's coffee and placed a mug of the steaming brew in front of her before taking her own seat beside Dillon. Lizzy knew better than to ask if she wanted breakfast, but the toast sitting on a plate in the middle of the table smelled good, so she reached out and took a slice.

"How are you feeling this morning? My muscles are really sore after all that dancing."

Grace chuckled. "The same... I could hardly move when I got up."

"Sounds like we need to do more exercise."

Grace grimaced as she buttered her toast. "I'm not sure my body could handle much more."

"Me either, but it was fun." Lizzy glanced at the clock on the wall. "Danny's already left to help prepare for the service, and we need to be leaving shortly."

"I'll just finish this and then help you with the children."

"Thanks, Grace." Lizzy met her gaze, a genuine smile on her face. "I'm glad you're coming."

Grace drew a breath and released it slowly. Going to church was so normal for Lizzy, but for her, it was anything but. The only memories she had of church angered her. Eight children and Mam, sitting all in a row on a hard pew, with Mam doing her best to keep them all quiet. Why she'd bothered, Grace really didn't know. It seemed more trouble than it was worth, especially since God hadn't stopped Mam from dying. If God had kept her alive, then Grace and Brianna would never have gone to live with Aunt Hilda, Brianna wouldn't have been raped or fallen pregnant, and Grace wouldn't have set that bomb and killed all those innocent people. So really, it was all God's fault. *So what was she doing going back on her vow never to set foot in a church again? What had changed?*

Grace nibbled her toast while the children chattered around her. Could she go through with this? She remembered Da's funeral. She hadn't wanted to go—she hated the man. The way he'd treated Mam was despicable. An abusive drunkard, he'd disappeared when Grace was eight, leaving Mam to look after all eight kids, including a baby. And then when he reappeared years after Mam died, Caleb and Danny had the gall to forgive the man. They said Da had 'found God', and that he was sorry for what he'd done. She didn't see him before he died, but she remembered the words spoken about him at his funeral.... it was like they were talking about a different person, not the Da she remembered. But something had happened inside her that day—a few chinks in her walls had been chipped away although she'd rebuilt them since. *Was she ready if that happened again?* No, she wouldn't let it. It was just emotion. She'd put on her lawyer's hat and assess everything. She wouldn't let herself get caught up in all that like Brianna had.

"Auntie Gwace..." A small voice came to her. How long had Clare been tapping her arm?

Grace blinked. "Sorry Clare, what did you say?"

Clare stuck her thumb in her mouth and giggled.

"Clare, don't put your dirty fingers on Auntie Grace's shirt." Standing, Lizzy grabbed the cloth. "Here, let me wipe it for you, Grace."

"Don't worry, Lizzy, it's fine." Grace waved her off. "It's just a bit of jam."

SHORTLY AFTER, Lizzy and Grace walked with the children into the small chapel sitting on the far side of the main Elim Community building. Built of stone, it had once been a barn, but several years ago it had been renovated and made into a simple place of worship, and now it even had stained glass windows. It wasn't just the students and staff of the Community who attended. People came from miles around as the small church's reputation for preaching God's word without compromise had spread over the years.

The chapel was already half full when they took their seats at the back. "I have to sit back here because of the children," Lizzy whispered to Grace.

Suited her… she could hide back here... well, almost. Her heart quickened when Ryan caught her eye and lifted his hand in a wave. An easy smile played at the corners of his mouth, and in his pale blue jeans and white polo shirt, his toned body looked so masculine and appealing. It probably wasn't appropriate in a place like this, but her flesh tingled at the memory of being in his arms last night as they danced. She nodded and returned his smile.

Brianna and the other students sat towards the front. They had chapel every day, so this would be nothing new for them, but Grace was surprised that as well as a piano, a small band filled the left front of the church. A young girl with a violin, another with a flute, a young man with a guitar, and yet another young man sitting behind a set of drums. At least there wasn't a bagpipe.

Clare climbed onto Grace's lap, but when the music began playing a few moments later, everyone stood. Awkward… what should she do? She glanced at Lizzy. She'd stood and had James in her arms. Grace guessed she should do the same. Standing, she lifted Clare up and positioned the little girl on her hip. It felt strange, but kind of nice. How did Lizzy normally do it on her own? At least Dillon seemed happy to stand on his own, although he jumped up and down on the seat behind Lizzy. *Mam would never have let us get away with that.*

Although the songs were unfamiliar, the tunes were catchy and the band played well, but Grace was determined not to join in. Singing was just one of the ways they got at vulnerable people. Instead, she studied the congregation as her gaze travelled from one side of the building to the other, but her gaze got stuck on Ryan and Danny, who both stood near the front on the opposite side to the band. More masculine men would be hard to find, but here they both were, singing, clapping, and waving their hands in the air. Unbelievable.

Grace drew a breath and smiled at Clare as the little girl played with Grace's earring. She was such a precious little girl, and Grace's heart softened.

The singing continued, probably a little too long for Grace's liking, but then Danny stepped to the front and welcomed everyone, and then he asked everyone to join him in prayer. Grace swapped Clare to her other hip. She didn't know how Lizzy could hold them for so long.

Instead of closing her eyes, Grace kept hers on Danny. Was he play acting? She had to know. After hearing his story last night, she seemed to think he wasn't. Danny's remorse over what he'd done had certainly sounded genuine, as did his belief that Jesus had forgiven him and given him new life, but was he deluded? As he prayed, he held one hand in the air, but it didn't look like he was acting. Grace got the impression he was in awe of the God he was praying to, and His words confirmed that.

"Lord God, our Heavenly Father, we stand in Your presence today, in awe of what You have done, and who You are. You're the Almighty God, the creator of heaven and earth, and we bow before you in humble adoration. There is none like you, oh God. Open our hearts and minds to Your love, and speak to those who don't know You yet. Those who are struggling with things in their past that are weighing them down, those who are carrying guilt over actions and thoughts that have created a barrier between You and them. Let them know the freedom of forgiveness that Jesus bought for them when He died on the cross for them, and the joy of the new life that is waiting for all those who believe. Please be with us today, dear Lord, and be with Ryan as he brings us Your message. In Jesus' precious name, Amen."

Grace gulped. If he was making it up, he was a very good actor.

Danny sat and Ryan took his place at the front. Grace straightened, fixing her eyes on Ryan, mesmerised by his warm, genuine smile and his relaxed demeanour. He radiated a vitality that drew her like a magnet and her whole being waited eagerly to hear what he had to say.

Resting his hands on the lectern, Ryan gazed around the congregation, his eyes soft and caring. Grace's heart quickened when his gaze lingered on hers momentarily.

"Let me start by asking a question." He paused and took a sip of water. "I don't ask this lightly or in judgment, but because it's important. Even if you've accepted Christ into your heart, you might not be experiencing the full freedom that Jesus came to give you. Jesus came to this earth to free you from the bondage of sin and death, to give you new life here and now." He paused, casting his gaze around the congregation. "But are you experiencing that new life and freedom, or are you chained to the past? Is there something you've done, something you've thought, or has something been done to you, an insult, a slur, a put down, or even worse, have you been rejected or abused, that's set like some immovable dead weight in your soul and every time you try to move forward in your life, spiritually or emotionally, this incident just chains you to the ground?"

Grace shifted uncomfortably in her seat. Ryan's question pierced her heart like an arrow. Had he planned this just for her? She gulped. *Did he know about her past?*

Ryan continued. "If you're carrying guilt over something, or if you feel you're unworthy of love because of the shame of what might have happened to you, or you believe you're a failure for whatever reason, let me tell you, *Jesus is your freedom*. He has the power to break the bondage of the past, whatever you've done, or whatever has happened to you. *He can free you from it*.

"You might be asking how He can do that, especially if you've already asked Him into your life and you still feel the weight of that bondage. Firstly, if you're in bondage because of something you've done, you need to receive the Lord's forgiveness. Come to the cross of Jesus, and realise afresh, or perhaps for the first time, the power of the cross in your life. The cross is our freedom. It doesn't matter what you've done, it doesn't matter what's in your past, how ugly, how brutal, or how violent it is, it doesn't matter how badly you've messed up, the cross can set you free. Let me read from Colossians chapter 2, verses 13 and 14: "... God made you alive with Christ. He forgave us **all** our sins, having cancelled the charge of our legal indebtedness, which stood against us and condemned us; he has taken it away, nailing it to the cross." Do you understand what God's saying here? *All* our sins are forgiven—not just some, but *all.* We stand holy and blameless before our Lord because of the cross. Jesus died for **all** our sins."

A hush fell over the chapel. Grace couldn't take her eyes off him—he really meant this stuff, and her heart pounded.

Ryan's voice softened. "If you're chained by something that was done to you, you might need to be healed at a deeper level, but know that as you have a new identity in Christ, you're not chained to whatever happened to you, because Jesus buried your past forever and has given you new life. You're in a new place, and you're no longer a slave to anything in your past. I want to encourage you today to take God at His word. If He says you're a new creation because you've accepted Jesus as your Saviour, that's what you are. The old has gone, the new has come. The bondage of your past is broken, and you can live in the freedom that Jesus bought for you on the cross. If you don't know that freedom, come to the cross today. While we sing the last song, come, but before we sing, please join me in prayer." He held his hand up as he bowed his head.

"Lord God, thank you that Jesus died on the cross for all our sins, not just some of them. There is nothing that any of us can't be forgiven of, and there's nothing that's been done to any of us that can't be healed by the love of Jesus. Help us to grasp the fact that the cross is our freedom, and that Jesus came so that we might have new life, here and now. In Jesus' precious name, Amen." He looked up slowly and smiled. "Let's sing, and while we sing, come forward if you need to do business with God."

The band started, and everyone stood. Grace's heart continued to pound. Ryan had been very convincing, and she was almost tempted to go forward, but she wouldn't. How did she really know it wasn't just some kind of emotional manipulation? But she had to agree that it certainly sounded good. To be free of guilt, how would that feel? Instead of going forward, she'd talk to him about it. She had to do something.

The song mimicked Ryan's sermon…

Would you be free from the burden of sin?
There's power in the blood, power in the blood
Would you o'er evil a victory win?
There's wonderful power in the blood.

There is power, power, wonder-working power
In the blood of the Lamb
There is power, power, wonder-working power
In the precious blood of the Lamb

Tears stung Grace's eyes as Brianna and Brayden, along with some others walked forward and knelt down on the steps at the front. Danny, Ryan, David and Rosemary knelt with them, placing their hands on their shoulders.

Grace glanced at Lizzy... her eyes glistened. Lizzy reached out her hand and Grace took it.

Lizzy squeezed it and then slipped her arm around Grace's shoulders, pulling her close. Clare touched Grace's cheek with her chubby fingers.

"What's wrong, Auntie Gwace?"

"Nothing, sweetheart. Auntie Grace is fine." Grace pulled Clare closer and hugged her. She wasn't fine, and she knew it.

The song continued, and Grace's heart still raced. The weight of her burden was so heavy, and growing heavier by the minute. But she couldn't do it. She drew in a slow breath and steadied herself as the song came to an end. She was a barrister, and she wasn't going to be drawn in unless she could prove it all true, but deep in her heart, she prayed that it was. But could she really expect God, *if He existed,* to forgive her of murder?

THE SERVICE ENDED. Grace dabbed her eyes with a tissue and hoped her mascara hadn't run. Many people remained in their seats while the band continued playing, a lot of them with bowed heads. Others hugged each other, and others walked out quietly.

Lizzy gathered the children's books and placed them in a bag, and then stood, giving Grace a warm smile. "Are you ready to go?"

Grace nodded. Standing, she lifted Clare back onto her hip and followed Lizzy and the other two children outside. Yesterday's *smirr* had returned, but nobody seemed to mind. It was so fine it was barely noticeable.

Lizzy stopped and turned to Grace. "We normally have lunch with the students after church. Do you want to do that, or would you rather go home for lunch?"

Grace was in two minds. She needed to talk with someone, but who? Lizzy, Danny, Ryan? Could she face being amongst all the students and pretend everything was fine, or should she go back to the cottage with Lizzy? She'd rather talk with Ryan, but he was still busy with other people. Maybe talking with Lizzy was the thing to do now. She could talk with Ryan later.

"Can we go back to the cottage? Would you mind?"

Lizzy rubbed Grace's arm. "Not at all, Grace. Dillon will probably want to stay—he loves Sunday lunch at the Hall, but we can take these two." Lizzy glanced at James and Clare and smiled at them.

"Thanks, Lizzy. I appreciate that." Grace was struggling to speak.

Shortly after, Grace and Lizzy settled into Lizzy's comfortable and homely living room with mugs of hot coffee and a sandwich each. Lizzy put a children's programme on the television for James and Clare to watch, and then turned her attention to Grace.

"I'm a good listener, Grace. I can see something's going on inside you, but I also know how hard it can be to talk about things. I hope you'll trust me enough to share what's on your heart, but just tell me what you want, nothing more, nothing less. Danny and I would just love to see you free from whatever's troubling you."

Tears pricked Grace's eyes. She drew a deep breath. Now the moment had come, she really had no idea where to start. Her pulse raced. So many years of building walls, and now they were crumbling around her. But Lizzy was the first real friend she had, and so there really was no better time to start.

She let out her breath. "I don't know where to start, Lizzy. There are things in my past I've never told anyone, and I still can't." She looked down at the bright red mug in her hands. "The service was moving, and Ryan spoke well… he was very convincing." She looked up and smiled. "He could almost be a barrister. I was tempted to go forward, but I need to know that what he was saying is true. I'm not just going to blindly believe."

"Nobody would expect you to do that, Grace." Lizzy sat forward and smiled. "There's plenty of proof that Jesus existed, that He really did come to earth and lived here amongst us. There's also plenty of proof that He died on the cross and that He rose again, but the main proof is in the lives He changes and their testimonies. Believing is one thing, but accepting and following is another. It's not until you take that step of faith that you really know, because something changes in your heart that nothing can explain. It's spiritual, and it's like nothing you've ever experienced before, but I can understand where you're coming from." Lizzy straightened. "How about you and I do a study of John's gospel? We can take our time, and you can ask as many questions as you want, and we can do research as well as we go. I've also got some other books you might like to read. Apologetic type books that provide arguments for and against God's existence and Jesus's death and resurrection, as well as a lot of other issues that people ask questions about. How does that sound?"

"I think I'd like that, Lizzy. I need to do something, because I don't think I can go on like this much longer." Grace covered her face with trembling hands as tears streamed down her cheeks.

Lizzy moved swiftly and sat beside her, wrapping her arms around her, comforting her. "It's okay, Grace. I'm here for you… God's here for you."

Grace sobbed until she could sob no more. Her heart felt constricted, heavy. She felt ill.

"Can I pray for you, Grace?" Lizzy brushed Grace's forehead with her fingers as she peered into her eyes.

Grace nodded. She couldn't speak.

Lizzy took her hand and squeezed it. "Dear God, You know what's in Grace's heart. You know the hurt that's in her life, the despair she's feeling. Lord, I ask that You gently draw her to Yourself. Wrap her in Your love, and give her freedom from the burdens that are weighing her down. Let her know it's between You and her, and no one else. Touch her in her deepest parts, dear Lord, heal her, make her whole. She's your precious daughter and You love her so much. Let her know that You love her in a truly personal way, dear Lord. Open her heart and mind to You. Thank You for her life, and for the care she's taken of Brianna. So many hurts from the past, dear Lord, but we know that the cross of Jesus provides freedom, no matter what's in the past, the cross of Jesus is enough. Lord, please bless us as we study Your Word, open

Grace's eyes to the truth of the gospel message. In Jesus' precious name, Amen."

Grace drew a steadying breath, and opening her eyes, squeezed Lizzy's hand. She gulped and let her breath out as she dabbed her eyes. "Thank you, Lizzy. I needed that."

"You're welcome, Grace. God's going to do a mighty work in your life, I just know it." Warmth flowed from Lizzy's eyes as she gave Grace a hug.

"We'll see about that." Grace let out a small chuckle.

"Do you want to start now? We've got time before Danny gets back."

Grace shrugged. "I guess so."

Lizzy stood and pulled a Bible from the bookshelf behind the couch and handed it to Grace, and then picked up her own Bible from the lamp table beside her as she sat back down. "Guess you've never opened one of these before?" Lizzy's brow lifted as she leaned forward, an amused but friendly grin on her face.

Grace shook her head. "Never."

"Okay, John was one of Jesus's disciples, and he gives a first-hand, eye-witness account of Jesus's life. He wrote it so that people might believe that Jesus is the Messiah, the Son of God, and that by believing they might have life, so it's a great place to start. It's the fourth book of the New Testament, about two-thirds of the way through… "

Grace opened the Bible and flicked through until she found it.

"That's it. Shall I start reading?"

Grace shrugged again. "Okay."

"Stop me whenever you want." Lizzy smiled before lowering her eyes to the book on her lap. "John Chapter 1… 'In the beginning was the Word, and the Word was with God, and the Word was God. He was with God in the beginning. Through him all things were made; without him nothing was made that has been made. In him was life, and that life was the light of all mankind. The light shines in the darkness, and the darkness has not overcome it.'"

As Lizzy continued reading, Grace interrupted occasionally and asked a few questions, but she was mainly happy just to listen. Somehow the words soothed her spirit, and the questions could wait. Grace had never heard such words before, and she was hungry to keep reading, but the programme finished on the television too soon and James and Clare wanted her to play.

"We can pick up again later, Lizzy, besides, I'm going to need time to digest all of this." Grace chuckled as Clare tried to drag her off the couch.

"Okay, to be continued." Lizzy smiled warmly as she stood and gave her a hug.

CHAPTER 23

For the rest of the afternoon and evening, Grace devoured not only the gospel of John, but dug into the Apologetic books Lizzy had given her. She was used to reading fast, and always read with an analytical mind. She approached the Bible and these books no differently, but there was something different about the Bible—when she read it, her heart quickened, as if it wasn't just words she was reading. Lizzy told her it was because the words came from God, and that God was speaking into her heart. Grace was starting to believe that Lizzy was right.

Grace telephoned Niall on Monday morning and told him she wouldn't be coming back for the appeal. The disappointment in his voice ripped her heart apart, but she couldn't give him what he wanted. She also called the Prosecutor's Office and told her boss she didn't know when she'd be returning.

Lizzy set aside as much time as she could to spend with Grace, but on Tuesday, Lizzy suggested Grace attend Daniel's evening class.

"I'm not sure I'd fit in, Lizzy. Are you sure it'd be all right?"

"Absolutely. Daniel's a great teacher, and it'll be good for you to be amongst others who are also seeking. Besides, I'm sure Brianna would be excited to have you there."

"I'll think about it." Grace closed her Bible and drained the remains of her cup of tea.

"Do that, Grace. I'm sure you'll enjoy it. But now, I've got a trip to town. Would you like to come?"

"I'll pass, if you don't mind. I think I'll take a walk."

"No problem, Grace. Enjoy your day." Bending down, Lizzy gave her a hug and then left.

THE DAY WAS warm by Scottish standards, and Grace was eager to get out amongst the hills and have time to think by herself. There was something magical about the wide open spaces, so different from the hustle and bustle of downtown Belfast with its heavy traffic and constant noise. Out here amongst the hills of heather, the only sounds came from the occasional bleat of a sheep and the squawk of red kites as they soared in the air.

Sitting on a rock above Loch Linnhe, Grace breathed in the clean, fresh air and tried to settle her heart and mind. As she gazed out at the hills in the distance, one of the verses she and Lizzy had studied that same morning came to mind. John chapter 5, verse 24: "I tell you the truth, whoever hears my words and believes Him who sent me has eternal life and will not be condemned; he has passed over from death to life." She drew a breath and shook her head. *God, I find that really hard to believe. How could you not condemn me for murder?* The old battle surfaced, and tears streamed down her cheeks. *All those people, blown to shreds. God, I don't deserve your love and forgiveness.* Drawing her knees up under her chin, she wrapped her arms around them and rocked back and forth and began to sob. The sobbing increased the more she remembered. *All those people. God... I'm so sorry...* Gut wrenching sobs that had been building for so long rose from deep inside her. *I didn't mean to kill them. You know that...* She rolled onto the grass, curling into the fetal position as tears spilled down her cheeks. Deep, guttural weeping rose from her innermost being until she could cry no more, but neither could she move. Maybe she should stay here and let the buzzards fight over her body—that was all she was good for.

RYAN WAS out for his afternoon walk when he saw someone lying on the grass up on the hill above the loch. If it hadn't been for the deep agonising wailing coming from that direction, he would have missed seeing the person altogether, but he immediately hurried up the hill in case the person was in trouble.

As he approached, he gasped. It was Grace! He bent down on one knee and brushed the hair off her face. "Grace, what are you doing here?"

Her face was damp, and when she opened her eyes, pain and anguish filled them. His heart ached for her. *Lord God, please bless dear Grace. Whatever's going on with her, help her to give it to You, dear Lord.* "Grace, can you hear me?" Sitting down beside her, he stroked her hair. Her body shuddered with deep, heart-wrenching sobs.

She lifted her head slowly and looked into his eyes. "God will never forgive me for what I've done." Her voice was raspy and weak, and her head flopped back onto the ground.

"That's not true. It doesn't matter what you've done, nothing's too big for God to forgive."

She shook her head and began weeping again.

Ryan looked at her shaking body. God was working on her, that was for sure, but what had she done that was so bad? *Lord God, please give me words that will reach her heart.* He continued stroking her hair. "I thought that once, too, Grace, but God's offer of forgiveness covers all sin, no matter how big or small. Can I tell you my story?" He swallowed hard.

Very few people knew the full details of his past, but he wanted to tell Grace. In the short time he'd known her, something had been happening inside him, and he wondered if this might be the beginning of something special. If he wanted her to trust him, he had to start by trusting her.

Grace sniffed and nodded weakly.

He sucked in a breath. This wasn't going to be easy... "I didn't leave the army by choice."

Grace's head jolted up. "What do you mean?"

He blew out his breath. "It all started when I was sent to Aden. Do you know where that is?"

She nodded.

"It was 1964, and I was in my second tour of duty. I'd never wanted to join the army, but it was expected of me. My family has a military background, and my father encouraged me to join as an Officer. I joined when I was eighteen, straight from school. Aden was like something I'd never seen before... hot, dry, and full of families living in the most basic of houses, if you could call them that. I would have much preferred to have been sent there as an aid worker, not as a combat soldier, but I did what everyone else did, and put on a stiff upper lip, and did my job. Whenever I was faced with a kill or be killed situation, I never looked the person in the eye before I pulled the trigger. I could never come to terms with taking someone's life, but it was him or me, so I had no choice.

"My family was proud of me. I was promoted, and offered a position in the Special Services, but I was living someone else's life, not mine. I kept it hidden. My father, in particular, would have been devastated if he knew how I felt.

"When I was sent to the Falklands in '82, I snapped. I'd kept everything bottled up all those years, but I just couldn't do it anymore. I had a breakdown, and was sent to hospital. It was the most humiliating time of my life. I'd let myself down, my family down, my country down." He squeezed his eyes shut and shuddered. "I was medically discharged. Pensioned out, as my father calls it."

Grace straightened and touched his wrist. She'd stopped crying, but her eyes were etched with red. "I'm so sorry, Ryan. That must have been awful."

Ryan shrugged. "Yeah, it was at the time, but I got to talking to the chaplain while I was in Rehab. A guy by the name of Rob." He smiled and gazed out at the mountains. "Rob was a cool dude. He talked to me about God, and how He could help me to forgive myself. I felt like I was a failure, and I felt guilty about all the people I'd killed, even though I was just doing my job. That guilt weighed me down for so many years. Over several months, Rob helped me put the pieces of my life together, and I was finally able to forgive myself when I asked God into my life.

"Rob explained to me about Jesus dying on the cross for my sins, and that if I believed, and asked Him into my life, He'd forgive all my sins, and would give me a new heart and a new mind, and free me from all that guilt." Smiling, Ryan looked down at Grace. "So I did. I can't explain what happened, but it was like a load was lifted from me, and in that moment I was finally free from the guilt and despair that had been with me for years. My recovery after that was quick. I was discharged from Rehab within three weeks, and went home to my family a changed person. My father still doesn't understand, but I don't judge him for that." He paused, and looking into her eyes, brushed tears from her face.

"You can trust Him, Grace. He promises to forgive all sins, even the big ones, because in His eyes, they're all the same. No sin is any different or worse to God. We're all sinners in need of His saving grace. He sees what's in our hearts. If we truly believe in Him, and we're truly sorry for our sins and ask Him for forgiveness, He wipes our slates clean and gives us brand new beginnings." Ryan paused again and looked deeply into her eyes. He prayed her heart would be open to God's cleansing love. "Will you do that, Grace? Will you take Him at His word and give your heart to Him?"

Tears gathered in the corners of her eyes and one by one rolled down her cheeks as she nodded. "Yes." Her voice was soft and barely audible. She straightened further, and shuffled to sit beside him. "Yes, I will, Ryan." Her voice grew in strength and conviction.

"That's wonderful, Grace, you won't regret it." His whole face spread into a smile as he took her hand. "Just say this prayer after me, okay?"

GRACE NODDED her head as Ryan bowed his head and began the prayer. "Dear Lord, I know I'm a sinner, but I also believe that You sent Your Son, Jesus Christ to this earth for one purpose, to die a sinless death on the cross to bridge the gap between God and man."

Grace repeated Ryan's words in a quiet but sincere voice. It was like someone else praying, but she knew it was her, and something was happening deep inside her.

"Lord God, I repent of my sin, and ask You to forgive me for all my sins." Her voice caught in her throat as tears trickled down her cheek. "I want to take Jesus as my Lord and Saviour, and to live with You as my Lord and King." She took a slow breath. "Please fill me with your Holy Spirit, and give me a new heart and a new mind. Thank you, Lord Jesus. Please help me to live my life in a way that will bring honour and glory to You. Amen."

Ryan pulled her close as tears streamed down her face. "You're now a child of God, Grace, forgiven, clean, and perfect in God's sight. He's living in your heart, now, and you don't need to carry that burden anymore." He released her and peered into her eyes. "How do you feel?"

Grace sucked in a breath and let it out slowly. How did she feel? Lighter? Certainly different. It was like a load had been lifted from her... something inexplicable had happened, something she'd never expected. She wiped her face and returned Ryan's smile. "I feel strange... different. It's like you said, I don't know how to explain it." But it was true. God had taken the load of guilt off her, and she was cleansed and new. "I need to tell Lizzy and Danny. They'll be so excited."

Ryan smiled at her as he gently took her hand in his, his gaze holding firm. "Brianna will be excited, too."

"Yes, of course." Grace made no effort to retrieve her hand. Her heart pounded. Was it wrong to hope he'd kiss her moments after she'd given her heart to the Lord?

"Grace, I've been waiting for this moment since the day you arrived. I can't tell you how happy I am that you've given your life to Jesus. It's just the beginning of a whole new life for you. God has great things in store for you." As he paused, he rubbed his thumb gently along the top of her hand. "We've only known each other for a short time, but there's a connection between us. Do you feel it too?"

Swallowing hard, Grace nodded. She didn't trust herself to speak.

"If you're willing, I'd love to get to know you better, and see where God might lead us." His eyes were sincere and gentle, just like his voice.

Was she hearing right? Ryan wanted to get to know her better? This strong, handsome man she thought she'd like to have a quick fling with, wanted to get to know her? To spend time with her? She gulped. That was all very well, as long as he didn't expect her to give up her secret. God may have forgiven her, but what would Ryan do if he found out what she'd done? He might understand she hadn't meant to do it, but he was a soldier, and she'd been in one of the radical groups they were fighting against. In fact, he might even have been there that day the bomb went off. She gulped, and then she remembered… God had forgiven her, and she had no need to think about it ever again.

A smile trembled over her lips. "I think I'd like that."

He squeezed her hand and gave her a smile that sent her heart racing. If only he'd kiss her…

CHAPTER 24

Neither Grace nor Ryan were in a hurry to return that afternoon. For Grace, it was a magical time of new beginnings, and for the first time ever, she felt blissfully happy and fully alive. The colours in the sky and the hills and the loch seemed so much brighter, the air so much fresher. She was wrapped in a silken cocoon of euphoria as she clung to Ryan's warm, strong hand.

Several times they stopped, and just sat and talked. One time, as they sat beside a bubbling brook, Grace asked him more about his family, about where he'd grown up, and what had brought him here to the highlands. He told her his family lived in the south of England, but they had Scottish heritage, which is what had drawn him to this place.

Grace angled her head to study his profile as she twiddled a piece of heather between her fingers.

"After Rehab, I was ready for a new life, and to be honest, I've never had any regrets about being here. I get to help people who are struggling just like I was, and I get to go hiking, abseiling and rock climbing as much as I want. I love these highlands." He smiled at her as he chuckled.

"I think they're in my blood. I should have been born here, not in southern England."

"It *is* lovely countryside, and there's so much history."

"You're not wrong. I'll have to take you exploring."

"I'd like that."

She dreaded him asking about her childhood. He didn't… instead he asked why she'd become a lawyer, but that was almost as difficult to answer without giving away hers and Brianna's secrets.

She leaned forward and hugged her knees, her thoughts filtering back to those days when she and Brianna survived on next to nothing, just so she could get through her course and become a lawyer. *Why had she done it?* Why had she put herself through such stress and pressure? Grace knew the answer, but could she tell Ryan? She drew a breath. He'd entrusted her with things from his past he'd probably rather not have shared, so she probably should share a little… just a little...

"Things happened to Bibi and me when we were staying at our aunt's and uncle's place in Londonderry after Mam died." She lifted her head and stared at the water gurgling down the brook's narrow path. "It wasn't good. I can't really say what happened unless Bibi has already told you…"

Ryan put out his hand and touched Grace's arm. "I know part of it, Grace. She opened up last night at her inner healing session."

Grace's eyes widened. "Did she tell you she'd been..." she couldn't say it…

Ryan angled his head. "Raped?"

Grace nodded.

"Yes, she did." His eyes were as soft as a doe's.

"Did she tell you who did it?"

Ryan shook his head. "No, but she said she had a baby who died."

Tears pricked Grace's eyes and she lowered them. It was one thing talking about it with Bibi, but totally different talking about it with Ryan…

"It must have been so hard on you both."

Nodding, Grace pushed back her tears and swallowed hard. "It was so sad. And that's what made me determined to become a barrister. To put people like..." she stopped mid-sentence. She couldn't disclose who'd raped Bibi without opening herself up to questions about why they hadn't reported their cousins. About Aunt Hilda's threat to expose her secret if she ever told anyone who'd raped her sister.

"You've done well for yourself, Grace. I looked you up... the youngest female to work as a barrister for the DPP. Impressive."

She shrugged. "It seems kind of surreal sitting here talking about it. It's like a different life."

"Are you missing it?"

She turned her head and looked at him. His blue eyes were compelling, magnetic. Her heart pounded. *Not when I'm with you...* She gave him a small smile. "It's been good to have a break."

"How much longer have you got?" His soothing voice gently probed.

"As long as I want." She could hardly lift her voice above a whisper as her heart hammered in her ears. If only he'd kiss her. She longed to be wrapped in his arms.

"Well, let's make it count." He put his arm around her shoulder and drew her close, kissing the top of her head. "I think I'm falling for you, Grace O'Connor."

RYAN'S WORDS sent waves of joy through Grace's body—she thought she might burst. In his arms, she felt safe, secure and loved, wrapped in an invisible warmth. Tilting her face, her heart lurched as she gazed into his eyes. "And I think I'm falling for you, Ryan MacGregor." His face was so close, his breath warm.

He lifted his hand and traced her hairline slowly with the tip of his finger. "You're very beautiful, Grace."

She raised her brows playfully. "You're not bad yourself."

"I shouldn't do this, but I really want to kiss you."

Her heart beat wildly. "You have my permission."

His kiss was slow and tender, and she never wanted it to end. When he lifted his mouth, her lips were still warm and hungering for more, but somehow she knew she'd have to wait. This wasn't going to be the quick fling she'd hankered after, instead, it was going to be a relationship that grew slowly, with purpose and control. *How would she cope?*

"We'd best get back." Ryan stood and held his hand out to her. Drawing her up, he wrapped his arms around her and held her tight as he whispered into her hair. "I'm looking forward to getting to know you, Grace."

Her heart steadied as a warm glow of content flowed through her. Somehow, this felt right.

SOON AFTER, as the sun slipped behind Ben Nevis, Grace and Ryan returned to the cottage. Stepping inside, Grace's hand shook a little as she walked down the hall towards the back of the house where the children's happy chatter came from. Two momentous events to tell Lizzy about, and for some reason, Grace felt a little nervous. Ryan's hand on the small of her back as he walked beside her helped steady her nerves, but she couldn't help but wonder what Lizzy would think about her and Ryan. Yes, Lizzy had been encouraging it, but now it had actually happened?

Lizzy glanced up as Grace entered, her eyes popping as her gaze shifted to Ryan and then back to Grace. She left her grocery bags on the table and stepped forward, taking Grace's hand. "Grace?"

Grace's eyes misted over and a lump appeared in her throat as she gave Lizzy an enthusiastic nod. "I gave my heart to Jesus, Lizzy."

Lizzy's eyes widened further and her whole face lit up. "Really? That's wonderful news, Grace." Lizzy threw her arms around Grace and hugged her, jumping up and down on the spot like an excited schoolgirl.

Grace laughed.

Lizzy finally stopped jumping, but left her hand on Grace's arm. "We'll have to tell Daniel… he'll be so excited." She glanced at the clock. "He should be home any time now."

"I thought I might go to his class tonight."

"Great idea, Grace. Now, let me get you both a cup of tea…" Her gaze travelled to Ryan again, her eyebrows arching.

Crossing his arms, Ryan leaned against the door-frame. "Guess you're wondering how I came to be with Grace?"

Lizzy nodded. "Yes."

Grace's hands twisted nervously in front of her, but Ryan flashed her a grin that dismissed any concern she might have held.

"I came across her while we were both out walking."

"Yes… and is there more you want to tell me?" Lizzy's eyes held an amused glint.

"Maybe…" He reached his arm out to Grace, and slipping it around her shoulders, drew her to his side. "We might just be an item." His face split into a broad grin.

Squealing, Lizzy jumped up and down again on the spot. "No! That is the second best news of the day!" She threw her arms around them. "That's wonderful. I'm so happy for you both."

"Mum, what's so exciting?" Dillon raced in from the play room and looked up at her and then at Grace and then at Ryan.

Grace laughed at the innocence in his eyes and leaned closer to Ryan, cocooning herself against his strong body.

Ryan chuckled. "Auntie Grace and I have become good friends, Dillon my mate."

As Ryan pulled her closer, Grace had never felt so contented and loved.

. . .

LIZZY MADE TEA, and soon after, Daniel walked in. Lizzy told him about Grace coming to the Lord, and like her, he was overjoyed. "This is amazing. Two sisters, both coming to the Lord. How special is that?" As he hugged her, Grace felt his body tremble. Tears rolled down his cheeks, but his eyes were filled with joy. "Can I pray for you, Grace?"

Grace smiled as she let out a small laugh. "If you want to."

He smiled. "I'd love to." Leaving his hand on her shoulder, he bowed his head. "Lord God, we rejoice that both Grace and Brianna have given their hearts to You. Thank You that they know Your love in a real way, and that you've cleansed them and given them hope for a bright future with You as Lord and King. Be with Grace in the days ahead as she learns more about You, and as she grows closer to You. Guide her as to what You would want her to do with her life. Thank You so much, Lord, I'm just so excited and grateful that both Grace and Brianna have come to know You. You are indeed a mighty God. In Jesus' precious name, Amen."

Grace wiped the tears off her face and then gave Danny a hug. "Thanks, big brother."

"My pleasure, Grace." He smiled at her. "You know who we need to call?"

Grace angled her head. "No... who?"

Danny chuckled. "Caleb. He's been praying for you for so long."

Grace smiled. She could just imagine the look of shock on Caleb's face when he heard.

"I've already told him about Brianna. He won't believe you've finally given in, Grace." Danny chuckled again.

"No, he probably won't."

Danny draped his arm across her shoulder. "Come, let's call him now."

"Okay..." She cast a backward glance at Ryan as Danny led her out to the back room where the phone was and chuckled. *Wait until Caleb hears I'm seeing someone...*

As expected, Caleb was just as over-joyed as Danny. "That's great news, Grace. Welcome to the family. I can't wait to tell Caitlin."

"Thanks Caleb. Thanks for praying for us both for all those years."

"It was nothing, Grace. We knew it would happen one day. This is really special." The sincerity in Caleb's voice warmed her heart and made her miss him. "So when do you think you'll be coming home? I thought you were coming back for the appeal?"

Grace's grip on the receiver tightened. She'd been dreading that question... what could she say? "I... I changed my mind, Caleb. I'm not sure what I'm doing right now, but I'll let you know, okay?"

"Okay... but you might need to call Niall. He's been coming around to visit a lot. He's like a lost kid without you here, Grace."

Grace's heart fell. She lowered her voice. "I've told him countless times it's over between us, Caleb." For some reason she couldn't bring herself to tell Caleb about Ryan. Not that she was embarrassed, but all of a sudden she felt coy.

"Well, he doesn't think it is. He's determined to get you back."

She let out a heavy sigh. "I'll call him again."

"Good... you do that."

"I will." How could she tell Niall she'd taken up with someone else? It'd break his heart.

"Thanks for calling, Grace, it's been great talking to you, and I'm so glad about your news."

"You're welcome, Caleb. Give my love to Caitlin and the girls."

"Will do."

Grace hung up the receiver and slumped against the wall.

Looking at her with drawn brows, Danny placed his hand on her shoulder. "What's wrong, Grace?"

She let out another heavy sigh and rolled her eyes. "Men problems."

Danny laughed. "What do you mean? I didn't know you had anyone in your life."

Danny's laugh cheered her and she let out another small chuckle as she glanced at Ryan in the other room. "There's two, actually. One's right here in your kitchen, and the other's back home." She spoke quietly so Ryan couldn't hear—she'd tell him about Niall later.

Danny's eyes widened. "You mean...? You ... you and Ryan?"

A coy grin grew on her face as she nodded slowly.

"When did that happen?"

"This afternoon. It was Ryan who led me to the Lord."

Danny ran his hand through his hair. "Wow. I had no idea. And who's the other?"

"Niall. You don't know him, but I've known him since university days. He's a barrister, and he asked me to marry him years ago. We met up again recently."

"Why didn't you accept him?"

She shrugged. "It just wasn't right. I didn't want to get married." She couldn't tell him the truth.

"But he's not taking no for an answer?"

She shrugged. "Seems like it."

"Well, you'll just have to tell him about Ryan."

"Guess I will."

Lizzy came out and slipped her arm around Danny's waist. "What's going on out here? Can I join?"

Danny kissed the top of her hair. "Course you can. Grace is just telling me about her men problems."

Grace glared at him before glancing towards the kitchen. She breathed a sigh of relief... Ryan was engrossed with Clare and James, colouring at the kitchen table.

Danny lifted his hand to his mouth. "Sorry."

"What's this about *men problems*, Grace," Lizzy whispered, her brows drawn. "I didn't know there was someone else."

Grace let out a breath. "I was just telling Danny about this barrister friend of mine—he asked me to marry him recently, and I turned him down, for the second time.... seems he's not taking no for an answer."

"Oh dear… what are you going to do?" Lizzy's eyes softened.

"I'll have to call him. And I'll also have to tell Ryan about Niall."

"Good idea."

"But not now—I'll call later. I couldn't handle it right now."

"Let's get some dinner, and then it'll be time for Danny's class… if you're still going?" Lizzy raised her brow.

"Are you coming to my class, Grace?" Danny's face lit up.

"Thought I might." A playful grin grew on her face.

"Sweet."

CHAPTER 25

That evening, Ryan stayed for dinner, and then held Grace's hand as they strolled to the main building for Danny's class. Being late summer, it was still light, even though it was almost half past seven. Grace shivered as a cool breeze came off the loch, and Ryan put his arm around her.

"This still feels really strange, Ryan, but I like it." She snuggled closer to him.

He chuckled. "I know what you mean... I do, too." Turning his head, the beginning of a smile tipped the corners of his mouth.

Brianna's eyes popped when Grace followed Ryan into the classroom a few minutes later. She was sitting between Brayden and one of the girls. Jumping up, Brianna hurried towards Grace, holding her arms out. "Good to see you, Grace! What made you come?"

Steering Brianna to the back of the classroom, Grace told her quietly about giving her heart to the Lord that afternoon.

Brianna's eyes glistened as she threw her arms around Grace. "We can both leave the past behind us now and start afresh. I'm so excited about it all." Stepping back, she grabbed Grace's hands and met her gaze with eyes full of excitement. "I had prayer and counselling last night, and you know what?"

"No. What?" Grace angled her head.

Brianna's voice lowered to a whisper. "I think I can almost forgive those boys for what they did to me."

"Oh Bibi..." Tears sprung to Grace's eyes. "I'm not sure I can do that yet, but that's good for you. Do you feel better?"

She nodded. "I don't know why we didn't listen to Caleb years ago."

Grace lifted her hand to Brianna's face and tucked a stray piece of hair behind her ear. "We both coped in our own ways, Bibi."

"I guess so." She glanced down quickly before lifting her eyes again. "And you know what?"

Grace shook her head. She hoped Brianna wasn't going to say that something was going on between her and Brayden. He still seemed like such a lost soul, even though he'd walked forward at church the other day.

"I don't even want drugs anymore."

Relief flowed through Grace's body as she smiled at Brianna. "That's great, Bibi."

"I know I've still got a long road ahead, but so far, so good."

Danny cleared his throat. "Would you two at the back like to take your seats?"

Spinning around, Grace caught his amused gaze and grinned. It was such a strange situation—to be in a classroom with her brother as her teacher and her sister as a fellow student, but it felt good. And what was even better? Ryan would be waiting for her outside.

Grace took her seat behind Brianna and her friends, and was surprised when Ryan joined her. Angling her head and arching her eyebrows, she leaned close to him. "What are you doing here?" She kept her voice low.

His eyes sparkled, radiating a vitality that drew her to him like a magnet. "Thought I might learn something from your brother."

Already her feelings for him were intensifying, and she couldn't stop the warmth spreading through her body when he winked at her.

She tore her gaze from his and forced herself to focus on Danny. That's what she was here for, after all.

"Welcome, everyone, and a special welcome to our newest student, my sister, Grace." As Danny held his arm out in Grace's direction, a grin stretching from ear to ear grew on his face.

Grace forced herself to smile when everyone turned and looked at her, but she wished he hadn't done that. *Brothers.*

"Okay, let's open in prayer, and then we'll begin."

Everyone returned their attention to the front and bowed their heads. Danny prayed a short prayer, asking God to open their hearts and minds to His Word and to the truths it held.

Grace shifted in her seat. Ryan's presence beside her was unnerving. How could she focus on God's Word with him so close? She felt like a school-girl with her first crush. *Take some breaths, Grace... focus...*

Danny cleared his voice. "Tonight we're looking at the two commandments that Jesus said were the most important, and how they apply to our lives here and now. Let's open our Bibles to Matthew chapter 22, verses 36 to 40."

Grace panicked. She had no idea where the book of Matthew was—she'd been reading John. She began flicking through the pages when a hand touched hers. She looked up and met Ryan's gaze. He didn't have to say anything... he took the Bible and opened it for her and smiled.

"Okay, Matthew 22, verses 36 to 40: ""Teacher, which is the greatest commandment in the Law?" Jesus replied: "Love the Lord your God with all your heart and with all your soul and with all your mind. This is the first and greatest commandment. And the second is like it: Love your neighbor as yourself. All the Law and the Prophets hang on these two commandments.""

Danny leaned forward in his chair. "For many of you, love is a foreign concept. I get that. You might have felt unloved by your parents, or maybe you were moved around between foster parents, and there was never anyone you could really call a parent. You might have been abused, or you might have been told you'd never amount to anything. Your concept of love has been tainted by this world and the experiences you've had."

Grace couldn't meet Danny's gaze… he was too close to the truth.

"Jesus came to show what true love really is. In I John chapter 4, verses 7 and 8, we read: "Dear friends, let us love one another, for love comes from God. Everyone who loves has been born of God and knows God. Whoever does not love does not know God, because God is love." To understand true love, we have to know God.

"There's no better way to get to know God than by studying Jesus's life here on earth. Jesus showed love and compassion to all people—not just those who were nice. He loved the unlovely; He loved the weak; He loved the sick; He loved the hurting; He loved those who'd been shunned because of their backgrounds or lifestyles; He loved sinners. He didn't judge them; He didn't tell them to clean themselves up before He would love them—He loved them as they were, and that's what He asks us to do—to love not only our friends and those people who are easy to love, but also to love our enemies, for want of a better word."

Looking up, Grace raised her brow. *I hope he doesn't mean I have to love Aunt Hilda…*

"In Matthew Chapter 5, verses 43 to 48, Jesus says: "You have heard that it was said, 'Love your neighbor and hate your enemy.' But I tell you, love your enemies and pray for those who persecute you, that you may be children of your Father in heaven. He causes his sun to rise on the evil and the good, and sends rain on the righteous and the unrighteous. If you love those who love you, what reward will you get? Are not even the tax collectors doing that? And if you greet only your own people, what are you doing more than others? Do not even pagans do that? Be perfect, therefore, as your heavenly Father is perfect.""

Grace's shoulders slumped. *That's exactly what he means... I can't do that...*

Danny shifted in his chair and began gesticulating with his hands. "We can't do this in our own strength—it doesn't come naturally. We must call on the power of the Holy Spirit living in us to grow the fruit of the spirit—love, joy, peace, patience, kindness, goodness, faithfulness, gentleness and self-control, inside us, so that we can love like Jesus."

He paused and took a deep, slow breath. "The more we love God with all our hearts, souls and minds, the more we'll love our neighbours, even the unlovely ones, like Jesus commands us to. Love is laying down your life for your friend, like Jesus did for us when He died on the cross." He let out a small chuckle. "We're not expected to do that literally, but by putting other's needs before our own, we're effectively laying down our lives for them. We become focused on the well-being of others instead of concentrating on our own. God blesses those who care for others, who treat others with kindness and compassion, who go out of their way to make sure they have food, shelter and feel loved and wanted."

A genuine smile grew on his face. "This journey we're on is an exciting one. There's so much hate in the world because people have turned their backs on God. They don't know Him, and they don't love Him, and therefore they don't love with His love. As His people, let's commit to loving God with all our hearts, all our souls, and all our minds, and to treating each other how we'd like to be treated ourselves. Let's be kind to each other, and let's find ways to bless each other... maybe we can do something nice for someone without letting them know who did it, and we can speak nicely with each other, respecting each other, uplifting not tearing apart. The more we can practice that here, surrounded by friends, the easier it'll be to do out there amongst people we don't know."

Pausing, his gaze travelled around the room. No one made a noise. "I hope this has given you some idea of what it means to be a follower of

Jesus. There aren't any rules or regulations apart from loving God and each other, but if we truly want to follow Him, we need to follow His example, and do it gladly." He smiled. "Let's pray." Raising his hand, he closed his eyes and bowed his head. "Lord God, help each of us to love You with everything we have, and to love both our neighbours and our enemies alike, just as you commanded. This doesn't come easily, as most of us have been bruised and battered by this world, but we come to You, the author and finisher of our faith, and we ask You to help us to love like You do. In Jesus' precious name, Amen."

Grace brushed tears from her eyes as Ryan reached for her hand. Where had Danny learned to speak like that? Amazing. But it wasn't only *how* he said it, it was *what* he said. After having such a challenging childhood and youth, to be able to talk about loving your enemies like he had was almost too much. It could only be God working in his life, and now she had God in her life too. Although she was excited about what He was going to do in her, she wasn't ready to love Aunt Hilda or those cousins yet, but maybe, in time... who knew?

At supper a short while later, Grace sat down with Brianna and had the best talk they'd ever had. Brianna had a clear head, and Grace had a soft heart. Brianna apologized for all the trouble she'd caused Grace and Caleb over the years, and Grace apologized for being so impatient with her. They hugged and cried, and then hugged and cried some more. Danny joined them after a while, and for the first time ever, the three of them talked about Mam and remembered just how much she'd loved them all and how much she'd given up for them.

Ryan joined them, placing his hand lightly on Grace's shoulder.

Brianna's eyes widened, her gaze travelling between the two of them. Finally, she fixed her gaze on Grace, angling her head and asking the question with her eyes.

Nodding, Grace let out a small chuckle as she lifted her face and smiled into Ryan's eyes that were caressing her with softness, sending a gentle stream of warmth through her body.

Shortly after, Ryan walked Grace back to the cottage. Darkness had set in, but the moon was trying its best to peek through the wispy clouds overhead, causing the surface of the loch to shimmer whenever it came out. His fingers were laced through hers, and his hand felt strong and firm. Gravel from the path crunched underfoot, and in the distance, a curlew called.

When they reached the cottage, Ryan turned Grace to face him and rubbed his hands on her upper arms as he gazed into her eyes. "I have to work tomorrow, but I have the following day off. I'd love to spend it with you, Grace. We could take a drive and see where we end up." He raised a brow, his grin irresistibly devastating. "Deal?"

She broke into a smile and laughed. "Deal." She couldn't think of any better way of spending a day.

His blue eyes twinkled before his expression sobered. She held her breath. Would he kiss her again? His nearness made her senses spin and her heart lurched madly. She was tempted to reach up and pull his face towards hers, but something held her back. Whilst she longed for his kiss, she'd allow him to take the lead, and she'd be patient. *Even if it killed her.*

He brushed the hair from her neck as he gazed into her eyes. Her body tingled at the touch of his hand.

He smiled into her eyes. "I'll look forward to it." He lowered his face slowly and pressed his lips against hers before gently covering her mouth in a slow, tender kiss. She longed for more, but she would not spoil this.

When he pulled away, he gazed into her eyes before kissing her forehead and turning away.

GRACE SNUCK INTO HER ROOM, flopped on her bed and closed her eyes, lifting her finger to her lips, still tingling from the sweetness of Ryan's kiss. She sighed contentedly before sitting up and bowing her head. *Lord*

God, thank you for bringing me into Your family. I don't deserve Your love and forgiveness, but I'm extremely grateful for it. Help me to be all that You want me to be. And thank You for Ryan. Help me not to mess it up. Amen.

THAT NIGHT, Grace fell asleep with Ryan on her mind and warmth filling her heart.

CHAPTER 26

The next morning, Grace rose early to telephone Niall before he left for court. She hesitated as she picked up the phone. Would it be fair to call him on the morning of the appeal? Even though he wouldn't win, he'd need a clear head, and it wouldn't be right to upset him. No, she'd wait until later in the day.

She put the phone down and climbed back into bed, plumping her pillows so she could lean against them, and picked up her Bible. She flicked it open, but so many thoughts flitted through her head it was hard to focus. She should be in court today—O'Malley was her case. He was unlikely to win his appeal… he was as guilty as they came, *but what if he did?* Niall wouldn't have encouraged the appeal without some new evidence.

And then there was Ryan. A sense of anticipation flowed through her. She still had to pinch herself... but where would it lead? It was still early days, but would she marry him if he asked? She'd turned Niall down, but that was because marrying him could have jeopardised his career if her past was ever discovered, but could she, in all honesty, marry Ryan without telling him what she'd done? Could she even encourage their relationship without telling him? Would it be fair on him not to? But what if she did, and he decided to end it before it really began? Already she was lost in his charisma, good looks, and strength of character. A tumble of confused thoughts and feelings assailed her.

She let out a heavy sigh and closed her Bible. *God, what should I do? I have no idea what's ahead... but I guess You do. You're the only one I can talk to about this, so please show me what I should do. I don't think I've told you this, but I'm really sorry for what I did. I feel so bad for all the people I killed, and all their families.* Her throat thickened as tears stung her eyes. *Lord, I didn't mean to kill them, You know that.* Her breathing grew heavier as she squeezed her eyes shut and tried to rid her head of the images bombarding her mind. Images she'd been trying to erase for so long without success.

Curling into a ball, she sobbed herself to sleep.

SOMETIME LATER, Grace woke to soft knocking on the door. She glanced at the clock. Her eyes sprung open. *Midday... how did that happen?*

"Grace, are you okay?" Lizzy sounded slightly worried.

Grace sat up and pushed her hair back off her face. "Yes... sorry, I slept in. I'll be out in a minute."

"No problem. Just checking to make sure you were all right."

Grace smiled. It was nice having someone care. "Thanks. I'll be out soon." She slipped out of bed and opened the curtains. No wonder she'd slept. Rain tumbled down and a thick mist hung over the loch, giving it a kind of ethereal look. Ben Nevis was invisible. A great day to curl up with a good book. Or to sleep.

She dragged herself out of bed and stepped into the shower, turning the heat up slowly until the water was hot on her skin. She stood there for a few moments longer than she should, but it felt so nice. She still had no answer as to what she should do, but the hot water flowing over her body helped calm her thoughts. God would show her. Wasn't that a perk of being one of His children?

Shortly after, Grace entered the kitchen where Lizzy was preparing a lunch of toasted sandwiches for the children. They all looked up with eager faces, each wanting her to sit beside them.

Grace laughed. "I think it's James's turn."

Clare and Dillon both let out a wail.

"Clare, Dillon, stop it." Lizzy turned around and glared at them. "Auntie Grace might decide to go home if you keep that up."

The two children quietened momentarily as Grace took her seat beside James, opposite Clare and Dillon.

"Where's your home, Auntie Grace?" Dillon asked in his cute little voice.

"You know where Auntie Grace lives, Dillon."

"No I don't." He flashed Lizzy an annoyed look.

Grace chuckled. "I live in Ireland, where your daddy comes from."

"Is that why you speak funny?"

Grace laughed again. "I guess so."

"Dillon!"

Grace smiled at Lizzy. "It's okay, Liz. I don't mind."

"Okay..." Lizzy glared at him again as she placed a plate of steaming sandwiches in the middle of the table and took her seat at the end. "Dillon, it's your turn to give thanks."

"Okay." He held out his hands and took Lizzy's and Clare's before bowing his head.

"THANK you for the world so sweet,
Thank you for the food we eat,
Thank you for the birds that sing,
Thank you God for everything."

. . .

"Amen", everyone said in unison. Grace let go of James's and Lizzy's hands, and sat back in her chair and smiled. The children were so sweet.

Lizzy began handing out sandwiches, and the children began chattering, even Clare.

Lunch passed, and the children went into the living room to play before taking a nap. Lizzy made a pot of tea and returned to the table where Grace was still sitting.

Folding her arms, Grace angled her head. "Liz, how does God talk to you?"

Lizzy's brows lifted as she took her seat. "Interesting question, Grace. What makes you ask?"

"Oh... I've just asked Him something, and I'm wondering how He'll answer."

Lizzy leaned forward, her eyes bright. "Is it about Ryan?"

Grace chuckled. "Not directly. But I'd rather not say... I just want to know how He'll answer, that's all."

"All right..." Lizzy poured two mugs of tea and handed one to Grace. "You probably won't hear a physical voice, rather, it'll most likely be a quiet assurance that one answer is right and the other, wrong."

"Kind of like your conscience?"

"Kind of, except that you'll hear God better the more You know Him, and come to understand His ways. Answers will often come when you're reading His word, so spending time studying the Bible is a great way to learn to hear His voice. When you spend time with Him, don't just talk with Him about what you want or need. Be still before Him and listen."

Lizzy paused and sipped her tea. "I hope this is helping."

"Yes, it is. Thanks." Grace smiled at her as she replaced her mug on the table.

"Also, He'll never want you to do anything that goes against His principles, so often, all we need do is ask ourselves what Jesus would do in a particular situation, and we have the answer, because if we're honest, we probably know what He'd do."

Lizzy leaned back in her seat. "Other times it might not be as clear cut as that, but basically, if we pray for His guidance, and if our hearts and minds are committed to doing what He wants us to do, we then just have to make the best decision possible, and trust that that's His answer. Often our own needs and desires get in the way, and we don't see things from God's perspective, and we end up making wrong decisions. God is just, and He's kind. He wants the best for people, so if we use that as a guide, chances are we'll do the right thing. Sometimes you might get a real sense that He's leading you, and other times you just have to trust that your faith and understanding of what He wants will ensure you make the right decision." Lizzy paused. "Does all this make sense?"

Grace let out a sigh. It wasn't as easy and simple as she'd hoped. If only God would give her a straight answer. "Yes, it does. I guess I was just hoping He'd just tell me."

Lizzy chuckled. "Don't we all! Is it something we can pray about, Grace?"

Grace swallowed hard. This was getting a little too close for comfort. "Not really... I think it's something I have to work through on my own."

"Okay, but if you want to chat about it or pray about it together, let me know."

"Thanks, Liz." Grace sipped her tea, her hands wrapped around the mug as she gazed out the window at the mist. This thing was going to haunt her all her life. God may have forgiven her, but would Ryan ever forgive her if he found out after it was too late, presuming their relationship developed? Maybe Lizzy was right and she already knew what she had to do. Jesus would never have kept such a huge secret from someone He loved—not that she loved Ryan yet, but she might come to love him soon. He deserved honesty, even if that jeopardized their relationship and she might end up in jail. She felt ill in her stomach. "I think I need some time alone, Liz." Grace pushed her chair back and stood.

"No problem. I'll be praying for you, Grace." Lizzy rubbed Grace's arm and then hugged her. "Whatever's troubling you, God will help you through it. Okay?"

"Okay. And thank you." Grace gave Lizzy a grateful smile and then left the kitchen, sneaking past the living room to avoid attracting the children's attention. As much as she loved them, she needed to sort this thing out.

BACK IN HER ROOM, Grace opened her Bible randomly at the book of Ephesians and began reading from the beginning. Sometime later, when she reached Chapter 4, verse 25, her eyes popped. "Therefore each of you must put off falsehood and speak truthfully to your neighbor, for we are all members of one body." Her heart thumped, but she knew… the answer was clear. She had no choice. She had to tell Ryan.

For the remainder of the afternoon, Grace read the Bible and prayed. Her senses were heightened, because for more than fifteen years, she'd vowed she'd tell no one what she'd done. She'd even chosen not to report Brianna's rape so she wouldn't be found out, and sacrificed marriage with Niall because of it. And now she was potentially sacrificing a relationship with Ryan. But she had to. She had no choice. God had spoken. No more secrets. She had to speak truthfully with Ryan before they got serious. She gulped. *While he had time to back out...*

Ryan would have to report her. If he was the honest Christian he professed to be, he'd have no choice. She suppressed the urge to vomit as her stomach heaved at the prospect of being charged with murder. Grace O'Connor, Barrister, Prosecutor, *murderer*. Why had she thought she'd get away with it? Even after all these years, she constantly expected a knock on her door, but it had never come, and now here she was, about to give herself up. Maybe she could ask Niall to represent her. Then he'd know the reason she'd turned him down. *Niall!* She'd planned on calling him…. she couldn't do it now. *Tomorrow...*

She fell to her knees. "God, I feel so sick. I know this is the right thing to do, but why is doing the right thing so hard? Please help me to tell Ryan tomorrow about what I've done. I know he'll understand how I'm feeling, but he won't understand why I did it. Give me strength to face the consequences of my actions, even if that means going to prison. God, steady my heart, and help me do what's right in Your eyes. Amen."

If she had any cigarettes left, she would have smoked one, but as she hadn't bought any since arriving, that wasn't an option. Instead, she told Lizzy she was going for a walk, put on a rain jacket and wellies, and stepped outside. What did it matter if she got wet? She had to do something to get her mind off what was about to happen.

THE GROUND WAS MUDDY, sodden and slippery as she made her way along the track beside the loch. The rain was a grey blanket around her, but at least she could see the foothills of Ben Nevis, and the sheep still grazing as if the rain didn't matter.

Even though she knew what she was about to do was right, a heaviness hung in her heart. Maybe this was how Jesus felt when He knew His time on earth was coming to an end, not that she could compare herself to Jesus, but at least He would know how she was feeling. *But He hadn't done anything wrong.* She had, and she deserved her punishment.

She walked for more than an hour. When she came to a fast flowing burn, she stopped—it would be folly to try to cross it. But then, maybe dying out here would be better than going to prison. She sucked in a breath. *Where did that thought come from?* She sunk to her knees and sobbed. *I'm sorry, God. I didn't mean that.*

She half expected Ryan to come along like he had yesterday. Had it only been a day since he'd led her to the Lord? It seemed much longer. He didn't come. She pulled herself back up and retraced her steps. The words from one of the songs they'd sung at church on Sunday played through her mind... "What a friend we have in Jesus, all our sins and griefs to bear, what a privilege to carry everything to God in prayer." She sang the words out loud as she stepped over rocks and logs, and tried to stay upright on the slippery grass. The words began to cheer her, and she prayed about the conversation she'd have tomorrow with Ryan, and decided to leave the outcome with God.

THAT NIGHT she didn't need to put on a happy face. She had confidence that God would sustain and bless her because she was doing what He wanted, even if it might mean losing Ryan and going to prison.

CHAPTER 27

Despite having peace in her heart, Grace had trouble sleeping, so sometime during the night she rose and wrote Niall a letter. She owed him that much at least. When she confessed to the Police, as no doubt she'd be doing in the next few days, she'd make sure he got it then. At least then he'd know why she hadn't agreed to marry him. She also read more of her Bible, clinging to the comfort it provided that God would uphold and bless those who did right in the sight of the Lord.

Morning finally came. When Grace drew back the curtains, instead of a grey, misty morning, the sky was bathed in a glorious blue, and below, the loch shimmered in the early morning sunshine, warming her heart. It was going to be a lovely day, but how would it end? Grace's heart pounded once more, but as she gazed out at the beauty of God's creation, she reminded herself that God was with her, and would uphold her. Calmness returned to her soul.

As much as she loved Lizzy and the children, Grace breathed a sigh of relief when she entered the kitchen to discover it empty. She turned the kettle on and made her herself a strong coffee. A note on the table caught her attention, and she picked it up.

Dear Grace,

Sorry we missed you—I didn't want to wake you... I've taken the children into town to see the doctor. I hope you're okay and that you have a nice day. We'll see you tonight.

Lots of love and God bless,

Lizzy

A nice day... Closing her eyes, Grace gripped the edge of the table and drew a long, slow breath. *If only...* Releasing her breath, she sat, resting her head in the palm of her hand. How many times had she played over in her mind how she'd tell Ryan, and imagined the look of shock in his eyes when she did? But she had to do it, and God would be with her. Maybe they could have a nice *morning*... and then she'd tell him.

Grace drank her coffee and poured another. Taking the mug back to her room, she placed it on her dresser while she showered. Ryan was picking her up at nine, so she had less than twenty minutes to be ready. She chose a pair of dark blue designer jeans, a red collared shirt, and matching red ballet flats. She threw in a denim jacket just in case.

Looking in the mirror, she applied a light coat of foundation, some blusher, and some red lipstick to match her shirt. She decided to leave her hair down. She peered into the mirror. Would anyone pick her as a murderer? She'd looked into the eyes of many a killer, and they all had a look about them. *Did she?*

She closed her eyes and swallowed. *God, please be with me today. I need Your strength more than ever to do this.*

If they were to have a few hours of enjoyment before she dropped the bombshell, she needed to pull herself together before Ryan arrived. She'd done it before, and she could do it again. Drawing a deep breath, she steadied herself and opened her eyes, downed the rest of her coffee, picked up her bag, and went outside to wait for him.

. . .

He turned up on the dot of nine in an old, olive-grey Land Rover. Not quite the car she was used to, but then, this was the Scottish Highlands, not downtown Belfast. Pulling up in front of the cottage, he jumped out and jogged around to where she stood in front of the white, picket fence.

Grace's heart skipped a beat. So ruggedly handsome in blue jeans and white polo shirt, she struggled to tear her eyes away from Ryan's powerful, well-muscled body.

He stopped in front of her and gave her a smile that sent her pulses racing. At the same time, her heart was crumbling. Taking her hands in his, he smiled into her eyes. *The eyes of a murderer.* "It's great to see you, Grace. Are you ready for today?"

She swallowed hard and returned his smile. "Absolutely. Where are you taking me?"

A mischievous look came into his eyes. "You'll have to wait and see." He chuckled. "Come on, let's go." He let go of one of her hands and led her with the other to his truck before opening the door.

He must have seen her raised eyebrows as she clambered inside. "Don't you like it?" He wore an amused grin as he climbed in beside her.

She cast her gaze over the basic dashboard, the long gear stick, the torn seat, and the metal floor in the back. "What makes you think that?"

He shrugged as he let out another chuckle. "I have no idea."

Their eyes locked. Grace's heart pounded. Leaning towards her, he lifted his hand to her cheek. "You look lovely today, Grace." His voice was soft, tender. He leaned closer, brushing his lips gently across hers, teasing her.

"Thank you." She could hardly lift her voice above a whisper. She so desperately wanted him to kiss her. His nearness was overwhelming.

He pulled back but left his hand on her cheek. "We'd best go."

Her heart fell as he straightened and turned the key in the ignition. She studied his profile with sadness. They'd have so little time together.

Ryan pointed the Land Rover northwards on the A82 towards Inverness, but soon after turned right onto the A86.

"So, where are we going?" She had to speak loudly to be heard over the engine, and she didn't really care where they were going. It was just nice sitting beside Ryan, watching his strong arms handling this beast of a truck, but she guessed she should have some idea.

Turning his head, Ryan leaned towards her. "Thought we'd take a drive into the Cairngorms, stop at Aviemore for a coffee, and then decide where to from there."

"Sounds good." Grace smiled at him and then returned her attention to the countryside, all the while praying for strength for the conversation they'd soon be having.

Half an hour later, Ryan pulled off the road and headed onto a smaller track.

Grace angled her head and laughed. "Is this the right way?"

He chuckled. "I know a short cut."

She raised a brow. "I hope it doesn't turn into a long cut."

"We'll be all right. Don't you worry."

They bounced along the rough track, climbing steadily until they reached a plateau. Ryan pulled over and killed the engine. "Come on, I want to show you something."

Grace climbed out as gracefully as she could and took the hand Ryan offered. The clean, crisp air took her breath away. All around were mountains dotted with sheep and heather, craggy rocks and the remains of old stone buildings. So peaceful, so quiet, so beautiful. "Where are we going?"

"I found the remains of one of my ancestor's cottages a while ago. There's not much to see, but it's still interesting."

"Do you still have family around here?"

"Some. Distant relatives, but they've made me feel part of the clan, even though I'm a Sassenach."

Grace laughed. "What would they think of me?"

"They'd love you, Grace." His eyes flashed warmly as he wrapped his arm around her.

She chuckled, but the heaviness in her chest was growing. *They won't when they know all about me...* But with Ryan's arm around her she felt safe, and she tried to push away the impending situation and just enjoy the present. "Tell me about them."

She listened eagerly as he talked about the clan MacGregor, the most famous member being the one and only Rob Roy MacGregor.

"The outlaw?" Grace laughed.

"Yep."

She looked more closely at him. "Ah, I see the resemblance..."

He hit her playfully, and then stopped all of a sudden, gathering her in his arms. He flicked some hair off her shoulder and gazed into her eyes.

Her heart thudded noisily.

"I enjoy being with you, Grace. We understand each other." His voice was soft and warm, and sincere.

His look was so galvanizing she almost melted in his arms. "Yes, we do." Her voice caught in her throat. An undeniable magnetism was building between them, and the mere touch of his hand against her cheek sent a warming shiver through her.

Her knees weakened when he lowered his face and pressed his lips against hers. His kiss was slow and gentle, and she savoured every moment of it as if it were the last kiss she'd ever receive. When they parted, it was as if they'd entered a whole new world together. *If only she didn't have to spoil it...*

He took her hand as they continued along the track in comfortable silence.

When they reached the pile of rocks which Ryan told her were the ruins of a crofter's cottage that he believed belonged to one of his ancestors, she laughed. "You brought me all the way up here to show me a pile of rocks!"

"They're special rocks. Can't you see that?" He bent down and picked one up.

She looked at the rock in his hand and laughed. "It's just a rock!"

He chuckled. "I guess so. But it's kind of cool to think my ancestors used to live up here." He turned around and gazed out at the bare mountains that stretched into the distance.

"It must have been a hard life." Grace's tone sobered.

"They were a tough lot, but yes."

"Ryan..." Grace's heart pounded.

As Ryan turned to face her, his expression changed. "What's wrong, Grace?" He stepped closer, placing his hands on her shoulders.

"I... I need to tell you something." Her pulse raced. She swallowed the lump in her throat.

"What is it?" His eyes held concern as they peered into hers.

Her shoulders slumped. "I wasn't going to tell you until later, but I can't wait any longer. Can we sit?"

"Sure. How about over there?" He pointed to a flat grassy patch to his right.

Once seated, she took his hand and looked into his eyes. "I don't know how to tell you this, Ryan, but I need to, because once you hear it, you may not want to be involved with me."

"Grace, it's okay. I don't get shocked easily."

She grimaced. "No, but this might be the exception." Her bottom lip quivered as tears stung her eyes.

He wrapped his arm around her shoulder and tilted her face towards his with his fingers. "You don't have to tell me, but if you feel you need to, I'm not going to judge you. Okay?"

Blinking back tears, Grace's body shuddered as she drew a big breath. "Okay." Her voice was barely a whisper. She took several more breaths. "When I was sixteen, I did something really stupid." She gulped. "I got involved with a radical group." She gulped again. How could she do this? Her chest heaved.

"It's okay, Grace. Take your time." Ryan stroked her hand and pulled her closer to him.

She sucked in a steadying breath. Now she'd started, she had to continue. "I... I think I was just looking for something to be part of." She blew out her breath. "Being at Aunt Hilda's was horrible for Brianna and me, and I was angry we were there. I was just looking for something. *Anything*."

Her body shuddered. "A friend introduced me to this group." She lifted her eyes and met Ryan's gaze. "It was exciting, and I jumped in head first." She gulped again, but held her gaze steady. "I went to bomb making classes without Aunt Hilda or Brianna knowing, but then I was given my first assignment." She swallowed hard as tears stung her eyes. "I had to place my bomb at a bus stop. Maybe I was naive, but I'd never really thought it through properly. I didn't think I'd be planting a bomb that would kill anyone. There was no way out if it, I had to place the bomb, otherwise who knows what would have happened to me, but I left a wire loose so it wouldn't go off. Only, it did." Tears streamed down her cheeks.

"Ten people were killed, including three children." She wiped her cheeks with her fingers. "Somehow I got out of there without being picked as the one who'd planted it. I guess being in a school uniform helped. When I got home, that's when I discovered Brianna had been raped by our cousins. I was going to report them, but Aunt Hilda had found the piece of paper I'd stupidly thrown in my bin that had the time and place of the bombing on it." Grace sucked in a breath as the smug smirk on Aunt Hilda's face flashed through her mind. "She knew it was me who'd placed that bomb, and she vowed that if I ever reported her boys to the police, she'd report me." Grace clenched her fists. "Brianna and I fled, and we've never been back since. I changed my appearance and kept a low profile. Nobody other than Aunt Hilda knows, not even Brianna. She only knows something happened, but still doesn't know what." Grace lifted her gaze again. "But now that I'm a Christian, I know it's time to face the consequences." Her hands shook and her body felt cold. "So if you don't want to have anything more to do with me, I understand. And I'm ready for you to take me to the police."

RYAN WAS UNABLE TO SPEAK. He'd known Grace was holding things back, but he'd never in his wildest dreams imagined anything like this. And he knew about the bombing… he'd been in Londonderry when she was sixteen, having been sent there as part of a special task force to help combat the Troubles.

But Grace? Caught up in that? Grace, Barrister, upholder of the law… maybe it wasn't just Brianna's rape that had motivated her to become a lawyer. Maybe she was putting herself on trial every time she stood up in court.

What should he do? God had forgiven her, but he'd have to report her. If only she hadn't told him… but no, she had to, he could see that. It was better he knew. But he was falling for her… and now she'd given her heart to the Lord… but if what she was saying was true, she was responsible for the deaths of ten innocent people. He knew what that was like… how had she been able to keep it secret all these years without going crazy?

He drew a deep breath. His heart was breaking as he gazed at Grace. *God, please help me. Show me what to do.* He squeezed her hand and then dabbed her cheeks with a tissue he drew from one of his pockets. "Grace, you're not a killer."

Her eyes widened. "Yes, I am."

"No, you might have killed people, but that doesn't make you a killer. You never intended to kill them."

Her body shuddered.

"I find it strange that no one came after you. The police were good at tracking down rebels back then."

She angled her head. "How do you know?"

His voice softened. "I was there, Grace. I was in Londonderry when that bomb went off."

Her face paled even further. "I've been expecting a knock for more than fifteen years."

"I bet you have. It must have been terrible."

She nodded. "I should have handed myself in straight away. The longer I left it, the harder it became."

"Are you sure it was your bomb that went off?"

She nodded again. "The job was given to me. I was the only one there."

He let out a heavy sigh. "We'll have to go the police."

"I know."

"I'll stand by you, Grace."

"You don't have to do that, Ryan. We barely know each other."

"Yes, but I want to know you better."

"Even now?"

"Nothing's changed that. From the moment I met you I felt a bond between us."

"What if I'm sent to prison?"

"We'll cross that bridge if we come to it."

Tears spilled down her cheeks. She threw her hands over her face and burst into tears.

He pulled her close, tucking her head into the hollow between his shoulder and neck as he gently rocked her back and forth, brushing her hair with his hand. "Shh... it'll be all right." He had no idea how, but thank God, He did.

CHAPTER 28

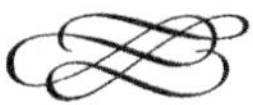

Ryan suggested they continue with their day out and not rush into anything. "It's been so long already, Grace, another day isn't going to make any difference."

"Are you sure?" Grace couldn't believe what she was hearing. Ryan had said he'd stand by her, and that there was no hurry, and they could continue their day out, almost as if nothing had happened.

"Yes. As soon as you go to the police, they'll take you into custody, you know that."

She nodded.

"We need to think this through, because something doesn't seem right to me. Did you follow the story in the news to see if they arrested anyone?"

"No. After Brianna and I left, we kept our heads down and tried to stay out of trouble. I never looked it up, and I knew Aunt Hilda wouldn't report me because if she did, I'd tell the police about the rape."

"I think that's where we need to start."

She drew her brows together. "Why? What are you thinking?"

"I'm not sure. We just need to do some digging, that's all."

"Okay. How do we do that?"

"You're the lawyer..."

"Yes, you're right... but not for much longer."

Ryan squeezed her hand. "Don't say that, Grace. Don't give up hope." He smiled at her as he traced her hairline with his finger. "I think we should pray about it."

"That's all I've been doing."

"Another prayer won't hurt."

"You're right. Thank you." She gave him a grateful smile before bowing her head, squeezing tears from her eyes as Ryan prayed for her.

"Dear Heavenly Father, we come to You with heavy hearts. I thank You that Grace has come to know You, but as a result, she now has to face the consequences of her past. Please give us guidance and wisdom to know how to handle this, and if there's anything we need to know, please guide and direct us, but most of all, I pray that You'll bless Grace's honesty, and that she'll feel Your loving arms around her, no matter what happens. In Jesus' precious name we pray, Amen."

Sniffing, Grace gave Ryan a weak smile. "Thank you."

"You're welcome." He pulled her tight and gave her another hug as he kissed the top of her head. "Now, let's leave these rocks and grab a coffee. I sure need one, and I bet you do."

"Where are we going to get one of those? I don't see any cafés around here." Grace chuckled. She felt lighter somehow, as if the weight she'd been carrying for so long had lifted. It was strange to think that after all these years of hiding it, her secret was finally out.

"Oh, I have my secret places."

"Really?" She chuckled again. "Did you bring a flask?"

"No, but I should have." He jumped up and held his hand out to her. "Come on, there's a place not far from here."

"I'll believe you when I see it."

'You'll just have to trust me."

Tucking her hand into the crook of his elbow, she smiled up at him. "I will, won't I?"

"Yes."

As she walked, Grace thought about what Ryan had said. Never had she doubted it was her bomb that had gone off... no one else had been there. But it might be worth doing some research. Easier said than done, out here in the middle of the Scottish Highlands. Niall. *Niall!* She hadn't called him... Her stomach churned and she let out a sigh. Well, at least now she could tell him why she hadn't married him rather than letting him read it in a letter. And surely he'd help her... but maybe not if he knew about Ryan... Only one way to find out.

"I know someone who can help."

Ryan turned his head. "Who?"

"A lawyer back home. He fights for the bad guys."

"You're not a bad guy, Grace."

"So you say, but I guess we'll see when everyone finds out."

They reached the truck and climbed in. Ryan pulled back onto the heavily rutted track.

"I really hope this leads somewhere."

"Don't worry, it does."

He was right. In less than five minutes they reached a cross road, and directly in front, on the main road, sat an old stone building with a 'Café Open' sign hanging out front. Ryan pulled up in front of the building and jumped out, running around to open the door for Grace. "I told you I knew somewhere."

"Okay, you win..."

Ryan took her hand and pushed the door open. The café doubled as a souvenir shop, and the front section was filled with all things Scottish, from postcards of Edinburgh Castle and Fort William, to Tea Towels adorned with Scottish recipes and pictures of Ben Nevis and Loch Lomond, to miniature pipers, complete with bagpipes and kilts, but in the back, the café was warm and friendly, with a view to die for.

The waitress directed them to a table beside a huge picture window and handed them each a menu.

Ryan glanced at the menu and then looked up. "I think we should have lunch… there's no hurry."

"Okay. What do you suggest?"

"There's a Haggis Lasagne on the menu." He raised a brow.

"Absolutely not. You'll never get me to eat it."

"Never?"

"Never."

He leaned closer and lowered his voice, a grin forming on his face. "Even if that's all you'll get in prison?"

Grace's eyes widened. "Don't joke about things like that!"

He looked bashful. "I'm sorry. It really was just a joke."

She let out a sigh. "It's okay. I'm sorry I got upset."

"I won't do it again."

"Thank you."

"So, will you try it?"

"No!"

He snickered as he lowered his eyes to the menu. "Okay, I guess that's a no for Haggis. How about a Smoked Haddock Crepe?"

Holding his gaze, she didn't say anything, she just sat there with folded arms and a raised brow.

"Okay, what about Crumbed Scampi and chips?"

She smiled. "That sounds better."

"At last." He chuckled. "I can see why you're a good barrister."

She gave a small shrug. "And I can see why you're so good at your job."

He angled his head. "How's that?"

"You're easy to be around."

His face softened. "That's nice of you to say that, Grace."

"It's true. I like being around you."

"And I like being around you too."

She drew a breath. "It's such a pity we're going to be separated." Her bottom lip quivered. "I'll have to go back to Ireland."

He leaned forward and took her hand. "Don't look too far ahead. A day at a time. Okay?"

She nodded. "Okay."

Ryan gave the order to the waitress and then returned his attention to Grace. "This friend of yours... when can you call him?"

"As soon as we get back."

"Could you call him from here?"

"How?"

"I'm sure they have a phone. We can tell them it's urgent, and pay extra."

"I thought you said we weren't in a hurry?"

"We're not, but the sooner we can get some information, the better."

"I guess you're right. Okay, let's ask, but he might be in court, I don't know how the appeal went."

"Wait here, I'll see if I can find the owner."

She smiled at him. "I'm not going anywhere."

While Ryan was gone, butterflies appeared in Grace's stomach. Could she really tell Niall everything after all these years? Would he understand? And would he help? She felt ill. *Oh God, please still my heart. Give me the words to say.*

Moments later, Ryan returned and gave her the okay sign. "She said yes—the phone's in the back room."

Grace gulped as she stood and followed Ryan to a poky little office filled with overflowing bookshelves and benches littered with paperwork. The telephone sat on the wall, an old fashioned one that Grace doubted would even work.

"Do you want me to stay?"

Grace drew a breath. She'd love for Ryan to stay, but what she had to say to Niall was for Niall's ears only. "I think I need to talk to him alone. Do you mind?"

"Not at all. I'll wait outside."

She smiled. "Thanks."

She drew another steadying breath as she picked up the hand set and dialled the number for Niall's office.

His receptionist answered.

"Mairie, this is Grace O'Connor. Is Niall available?" She held her breath.

"You've just caught him, Miss. I'll put you through."

Grace's pulse raced.

"Grace, this is unexpected. Are you calling about the appeal?" His voice was so familiar.

She drew another breath. "No. This is personal. Can you talk?"

She could imagine him leaning forward in his large swivel chair, eager to hear what she had to say. She was about to break his heart… again.

"Yes, what's up, Grace? Have you changed your mind?"

"No, but I'm about to tell you why I can't marry you."

Silence.

"Niall… are you there?"

"Yes… you threw me, that's all. What's going on, Grace?"

"It's a long story, and you may not believe it, but it's true. Remember when you met me at University and you always said you thought I was hiding something?"

"Yes…"

"You were right." She gulped. "I was involved in a bomb blast that killed ten people when I was sixteen."

"No…"

"Yes. And I'm about to go to the Police."

"No…"

"Yes. I need you to do something for me, Niall. Can you help me?"

"Of course. I'll do anything."

"Can you look into it for me? After Brianna and I fled Londonderry on the day it happened, I was never game to read anything about it. All I heard was that ten people were killed, and they were looking for those responsible. Nobody has ever come knocking on my door, even though I've been waiting all these years. So we just want to know if anything was ever found. Can you do that for me, Niall? I can't do it easily from here."

"Give me the details."

"Friday the thirteenth of November, 1969. That's all you need to know."

"I'll get right onto it. Where can I call you?"

"At Danny and Lizzy's. You have the number."

"I'll call as soon as I have something. When are you going to the Police?"

"Tomorrow. We'll be back at Danny and Lizzy's late this afternoon, best not to call before then. They don't know yet."

"You said *we*. Who are you with?"

Grace gulped. "A friend."

Silence.

"Niall..."

"Yes..."

"Thank you, and I'm sorry. You can see now why I couldn't marry you."

"I guess so. How could you have done something like this, Grace? The media will have a field day."

"I know." She bit her lip. "I was young and stupid, but the bomb shouldn't have gone off."

"I don't understand."

"I chickened out, Niall, and I left a wire loose, or I thought I had... it shouldn't have gone off."

"I don't understand, but I'll do it anyway. By the way, O'Malley lost his appeal. They wouldn't even look at it."

"I'm sorry."

"Not sure why you're sorry, Grace. You won."

"I'm sorry for you, Niall."

"Yes, well, such is life." His voice was clipped.

"I guess so."

"I'll talk to you soon."

"Thanks." As she hung up, her heart ached for him as she pushed back tears. Niall didn't deserve this. *God, please bring someone special into Niall's life, and help him to move forward.*

She wiped her face and took another moment to steady herself before opening the door.

Ryan was sitting at an old table reading a newspaper, and looked up when she stepped towards him. "Okay?"

"Yes. He'll do it."

Ryan held his hand out. "You've been crying."

She dabbed her eyes again and nodded. "Years ago, Niall asked me to marry him. I turned him down, and he never knew why. He does now."

"The poor guy."

"I feel sorry for him."

"He must still be a good friend if he's prepared to help you out."

"I hope so. He was my best friend, *my only friend,* at University."

"I'm sorry, Grace."

She shrugged. "It's okay. It's just what happened. I hope he can move on."

The waitress popped her head around the corner. "Sorry to interrupt, but your meals are ready."

Ryan lifted his hand in acknowledgment and smiled. "Thanks."

He stood and squeezed Grace's hand. "Come on, let's eat."

THE REST of the afternoon passed in a blur. So many mixed emotions ran through Grace. The joy of being with Ryan, knowing they shared a connection that was real, but unsure of what would happen if and when they went to the police. She tried not to think about it, but it was impossible not to. Her whole life was about to change. And then there was Niall... he'd sounded so desolate on the phone, as if his whole world had also been shattered. Her heart ached for him. They could have been happy together, if only...

Ryan ran his thumb along Grace's hand. "What are you thinking about?"

Taking a slow breath, Grace tore her gaze away from the window she'd been staring out. "Just everything."

"It'll work through, Grace. Whatever happens, God's with you, and I'll be there for you."

She released her breath and gave him a grateful smile. "Thank you. I know I shouldn't, but I can't help thinking about it all."

"It's understandable, but you need to get your mind off it for a while. There's nothing we can do until we hear back from Niall."

She angled her head. "What do you have in mind?"

He chuckled. "A game of mini golf might be fun..."

She drew her brows together. "And where are we going to do that?"

"There's an old course just outside. Hasn't been used for a while, but I asked Sheila, and she said we could use it."

"Who's Sheila?"

"The owner."

"Is she a friend of yours?"

"She is now."

Grace laughed. "Okay, you win. Mini golf it is. But I can't play..."

Ryan's eyes twinkled. "It doesn't matter. I'll have fun teaching you." He raised a brow, a playful look on his face.

"I get the picture." Grace's heart fluttered at the thought of Ryan standing behind her helping her hold the golf club.

. . .

SHORTLY AFTER, once Ryan had paid for the meal, they ventured outside with a golf club each and several golf balls. Ryan was true to his word and showed Grace how to hold the club and how to swing. Competitive by nature, Grace took it seriously, although several times she had to tell herself to focus on the ball and not on Ryan, leaning back with his arms crossed, studying her with an amused grin on his face. When it was his turn, she admired his easy style and his ruggedly handsome good looks. She just wanted to wrap her arms around him and stay here forever.

But finally they had to go. Ryan chose the circuitous route through the quaint town of Aviemore and then through to Inverness, where they stopped at a small traditional café for an afternoon tea of scones with clotted cream and mouth-watering pastries. Grace tried not to think it might be her last meal out before being incarcerated. She was in no hurry to return to the cottage—they'd agreed she should tell Danny, Lizzy and Brianna, but the thought made her ill.

The whole way back, Grace had her hand on Ryan's leg, and when he could, he held it. They chatted easily about lots of things, but when they arrived at the cottage just before dinner time, and Danny was coming through the gate, waving to them, Grace's butterflies returned.

She forced a smile and returned his wave as she climbed out.

Danny strode towards them, and when he reached Grace, gave her a hug. "Enjoy your day?" He winked at Ryan.

"Yes, it was fun, thanks."

"Staying for dinner, Ryan?"

Ryan shrugged. "If there's enough."

"I'm sure there will be. Come inside."

Ryan took Grace's hand as they walked inside with Danny.

Dillon, followed closely by James and Clare, raced down the hallway. Danny swept Clare into his arms and kissed her. Clare clung to him and put her thumb in her mouth as she looked down at Dillon and James with a smug look. Ryan swept James up into his arms, and Dillon tugged on Grace's hand.

It was all so surreal. Happy families. Her news would shock them.

Lizzy appeared, looking flustered.

Danny bent down and kissed her. "Got enough food for Ryan?"

"Always." She blew some hair off her forehead. "Oh, Grace, that friend of yours called a few minutes ago. I told him you'd be back soon."

The blood drained from Grace's face. Ryan placed his hand lightly on her shoulder.

"Thanks. I'll go call him."

"Okay. Dinner will be ready in ten minutes."

Grace extricated herself from Dillon's hold, and Ryan placed James back on the floor and followed Grace into the back room and closed the door.

"They'll know something's going on." Grace's hands shook as she picked up the receiver.

"We'll tell them after dinner. I'll call the centre and ask Brianna to come over." Ryan held her gaze, his voice softening. "Are you okay, Grace?"

Grace shook her head. Her chest felt constricted and she could barely breathe.

"Take some slow breaths." He breathed with her. "That's the way."

Her heart still pounded, but she tried to steady herself with her breathing. "I'm scared to hear what he's found out."

"Do you want me to talk to him?"

She sucked in a long breath. "No, I need to do it. But thanks." Her hands shook as she dialled the number.

With each ring, her heart rate increased. Maybe he wouldn't answer. She gulped when he answered on the fifth ring. "Niall…"

"Grace, thanks for calling back. I made some enquiries, and no one's been charged... they didn't find the bomber."

Grace's heart plummetted. "Because it was me."

"I did come across something that might be of interest. The reports suggest there might have been two bombs, but looks like only one went off. Might be worth pursuing."

"Two bombs? I only planted one."

"I don't know, Grace. I'll keep checking. Is it possible somebody else planted one as well?"

"I guess it's possible, but I wouldn't have thought so."

"What will you do?"

Gripping the receiver, she sucked in another breath. "Go through with it."

"You'll need a lawyer. I know a good one."

"Are you offering?"

"Of course. I'll do whatever I can. I'll be there in the morning."

Grace gulped. "You don't have to do that, Niall."

"I want to."

Grace's throat burned, and she could hardly get her words out. "Thank you."

"You're welcome."

WHEN GRACE HUNG UP, she lifted her gaze slowly to Ryan's. "Did you hear?"

He placed his hands on her shoulders and returned her gaze. "Yes."

"He's coming."

"I know."

CHAPTER 29

After dinner, Ryan made the call to the Centre and asked Brianna to come over. Ryan and Grace were still sitting at the table when she arrived within ten minutes of the call.

"You look like somebody's died." Her gaze travelled between Ryan and Grace as she took off her coat and joined them. "What's happened?"

"We need to wait for Danny and Lizzy. They're just putting the children to bed." Grace was glad Ryan answered, because she couldn't. What would Bibi think after all these years? If it hadn't been for the bombing, she would have prosecuted those cousins and they'd still be in prison. Would Bibi ever forgive her?

Ryan made small talk. Grace said the occasional word, but her heart thumped so loudly it was a surprise Bibi didn't hear it.

She offered to make tea, but Ryan took over. Finally, Danny and Lizzy returned.

"Brianna, good to see you." Danny smiled warmly, but his forehead was puckered. It wasn't usual for Brianna to be here after dinner. "What do we owe this to?"

It was Brianna's turn to look puzzled. "Ryan called me over."

All eyes turned to Ryan as he cleared his throat and squeezed Grace's hand. "Grace has something she needs to tell you."

Lizzy and Danny both took a seat.

"Sounds serious, sis. What is it?" Danny's voice softened.

Tears stung Grace's eyes. How could she tell them? She wrapped her hands around her mug of tea, and inhaled slowly. She lifted her gaze to Danny's. "It is."

As she relayed the story, silence filled the room. Three sets of eyes looked at her in disbelief.

"I'm sorry." She swallowed hard and shifted her gaze to Bibi. "I'm sorry Bibi. I should have told you." Tears streamed down Grace's cheeks.

Brianna pushed her chair back and stormed out.

"I'll go." Ryan stood and followed her.

Grace fiddled with her hands. Seconds passed. *Why weren't they saying anything?*

Tears streamed down Lizzy's cheeks. Reaching for the tissue box, Lizzy handed one to Grace and kept one for herself.

Danny ran his hands through his hair. "You've been hiding it all this time? Does Caleb know?"

Grace shook her head. "Nobody knew until today."

"And you're going to hand yourself in?"

Grace nodded. "I have to." She swallowed hard, forcing down the lump in her throat.

Standing, Lizzy walked around to the other side of the table, and slipping her arms around Grace, gave her a big hug. "What you're doing is very brave, Grace, and God will honour it."

Grace swallowed again as she dabbed her face. "I hope so."

Ryan re-entered with Brianna.

Grace lifted her gaze and held her hand out to Bibi. "Will you forgive me, Bibi?"

"Yes, but I wish you'd told me." Tears welled in the corners of her eyes.

Grace stood and hugged her. "I'm so sorry, Bibi. Please believe me."

"If only we hadn't gone to Aunt Hilda's." Brianna's voice caught in her throat and tears streamed down her cheeks.

Grace closed the gap between them and hugged her. "Everything would have been different, but we can't change what's happened, and I'm prepared to face the consequences of what I did. And you know what this means?"

Brianna pulled away and shook her head.

"Aunt Hilda won't have anything over me anymore, and we can report those boys for what they did to you."

Bibi's bottom lip trembled. "I… I'll have to think about that. I don't know if I want to go through it all again now I'm moving on."

Grace squeezed her shoulder. "Just think about it?"

Bibi nodded and then looked up. "Will you really be sent to prison?"

Grace drew a breath. "Unless Niall can get me off. But I did it, so that's where I deserve to be."

Tears streamed down Brianna's cheeks again. "I can't believe it, Grace."

"I know. It seems like another life, but I can't live with it anymore. I have to hand myself in."

"I'll be praying for you."

Grace choked. To hear those words come out of Bibi's mouth was too much. The tables had been turned. God had changed her little sister so much.

"I think we all need to pray." Ryan slipped his hand onto Grace's shoulder.

"Good idea," Danny agreed.

Everyone gathered around Grace and took it in turns to pray for her, even Brianna. Grace knew she was doing the right thing, and peace settled in her heart, slowly replacing the anguish that had threatened to overwhelm her. Whatever happened, God would be with her.

~

NIALL BOARDED the plane for the flight from Belfast to Inverness with a degree of hope. If he could help Grace, maybe she'd agree to marry him after all. He didn't really care what people thought, or if being associated with her damaged his career. He loved her, and that was all there was to it. Besides, with the information he'd gathered, he felt confident he could get her off. He couldn't get there soon enough.

Grace and Daniel had agreed to meet him at the airport, and they'd go on from there to the Police Station.

He still couldn't believe that Grace had been involved with terrorist activity. What was she thinking? And then to hide it all these years? And then to take the oath as a barrister? He shook his head as he gazed out the tiny window. What made her decide to hand herself in now? She'd obviously been hiding it well… in fact, she probably could have gotten away with it forever… if she'd done it, that is. He opened his folder and pulled out his notes. There was certainly room for doubt. He'd make it difficult for any jury to convict her, if it got that far.

Before he could finish his cup of tea, the plane began its descent into the small city of Inverness. He should have been looking at the magnificent scenery, but only one thing held his interest, and that thing was meeting up with Grace O'Connor.

Holding his chin up, Niall stepped into the Arrivals Hall and scanned the waiting crowd. He felt a little overdressed in his dark, tailored suit, but impressions were everything. He was meeting Grace as a client for the first time.

Grace stood with a man he assumed was Daniel. As she lifted her hand in a wave, a ripple of excitement flowed through him. Grace needed him, even if she wouldn't admit it. As he stepped closer, his gaze travelled over her face and then searched her eyes. His heart went out to her. She was different. Gone was the confident barrister. Her face was pale, and dark circles sat under her eyes. She mustn't have been sleeping. Not surprising, really.

Placing his brief-case on the ground, he reached out his arms and drew her close. His heart warmed when she returned his hug. "Good to see you, Grace. And don't worry… I'm going to get you off."

Pulling away, she gave him a warm but slightly shaky smile. "Thanks for coming, Niall." Turning to the man beside her, she extended her arm. "This is my brother, Daniel."

NIALL TOOK Daniel's hand and shook it. "Good to finally meet you. I've heard a lot about you."

"All good, I hope." Daniel let out a small chuckle, lighting up his eyes which were the same as Grace's, mesmerizing.

"Of course." Niall tried to be jolly, but he just wanted to hold Grace and talk with her, not with her brother. He returned his focus to Grace. "Are you sure you want to go ahead with this?"

"Yes, I am."

"Okay. We need to go through some things first. Can we grab a coffee while we chat?"

"Yes, but not in here, it's too noisy. Let's find somewhere quieter."

"Good idea."

"I know a place," Daniel said.

"Okay. You lead the way."

Niall walked beside Grace as they followed Daniel to the car park. Niall raised his brow as they stopped beside an old van with 'Elim Community Centre' plastered over it.

Daniel chuckled. "It's not quite a sports car… sorry…"

Niall chastised himself. "It's fine, Daniel. I've been in worse."

Grace drew her eyebrows together. "Have you? When?"

It was Niall's turn to chuckle. "You don't know everything about me, Grace."

"I guess I don't." Grace's expression sobered. "You'll have to tell me some day."

"It's a deal."

Daniel unlocked the van and held the passenger door open. "We can all fit in the front if you like."

Niall motioned for Grace to go in ahead of him. He climbed in beside her. He longed to put a protective arm around her. There was something fragile about her, something vulnerable, and he just wanted to be there for her. Instead, he asked her about Brianna.

"She's doing well, thanks to Danny and the others." Grace's voice lifted.

"So it was a good move?"

"Absolutely. She's a different person."

He smiled. "I'm pleased to hear it."

Danny pulled up outside a row of shops, one of which was Aggie's Bakery. A few people sat inside, but it was much quieter than the airport café. They ordered a coffee each, and Daniel insisted on getting some pastries.

Once seated at a table away from the other customers, Niall pulled out his folder and opened it. "Grace, I need you to tell me everything. Right from how you got involved until when the bomb went off. The more you can tell me, the more prepared I'll be."

She drew a slow breath and gave him a nod. "Okay, I'll start at the beginning..."

RELAYING the whole sordid story to Niall was hard, but Grace had to do it. She also had to tell him about Ryan. She'd seen the look of hope in Niall's face when their eyes met at the airport. The way his gaze travelled over her face... but her heart now belonged to another, and she'd have to break that news to him sooner rather than later. *After she finished telling him what she'd done.*

She felt ill relaying it all in minute detail, especially with Danny listening. The meeting with Fergus, the elation she'd felt when she'd been accepted into the group. The challenge and secrecy of the bomb making classes, the sinking feeling when she realized what she'd gotten herself into. The nerves she felt when she decided to leave a wire loose. Vomiting into the toilet on her way to the bus stop to plant the bomb. Planting it… and then watching in horror as it exploded. *It shouldn't have gone off. How had it happened?*

"There was another bomb, Grace. Somehow we have to prove that yours wasn't the one that went off. You need to give me every minute detail about it. And you need to be prepared to disclose the details about Fergus and anyone else who was involved."

Grace gulped. She'd expected to be going to prison, why hadn't she thought about the implications? Could she betray Sammy, wherever she might be? And would Fergus come after her if she testified against him? Probably, but wasn't she a barrister, and hadn't she lived with the possibility of that happening with every case she prosecuted? Niall had done his homework. He'd raised her hopes… maybe she hadn't been responsible for all those deaths after all.

"Okay, I think I've got enough to make a start." Niall closed his notepad and drained the last of his coffee. "Are you ready to do this, Grace?" His voice was gentle, and his gaze as soft as a caress.

Grace drew a long, slow breath and nodded. Now the moment had come, she just wanted to get it over with. To face whatever was before her. But she still had to tell Niall about Ryan. The longer she left it, the harder it would become. She could see the longing in Niall's eyes, and she felt so sorry for him. If he decided not to represent her, she wouldn't blame him.

She put out her hand and touched his wrist lightly. "Niall, there's something else I need to tell you before we go."

He angled his head. "What is it, Grace?"

She swallowed hard. "I don't know how to tell you, so I guess I should just come out with it..." She swallowed again. "I... I've been seeing someone."

The colour drained from Niall's face.

Pain squeezed Grace's heart as a muscle clenched along his jaw. "I'm sorry, Niall, I really am. If you decide not to help me, I won't blame you."

"I don't understand, Grace. If you couldn't be with me because of this, how can you be seeing someone else?" The hurt in his voice tore her apart.

"It just happened, Niall, I'm sorry... I told him it'd be best if we weren't together with all of this happening, but he wouldn't listen. It won't hurt his career like it would have hurt yours."

His eyes narrowed. "Shouldn't you have let me decide that?"

Grace gulped as tears stung her eyes. He was right. She'd decided for him. She hadn't even told him why she couldn't marry him. Maybe if she had, he would have stuck by her, just like Ryan was. What kind of person would do that? It was all such a mess. Her chest heaved as her breathing grew more laboured. It was too late for them... she couldn't turn the clock back. Guilt and sorrow flowed through her. "I'm so sorry, Niall. You're right. I should have trusted you."

"Yes, you should have." His voice was short and filled with pain.

She squeezed his wrist. "If you decide to leave, I'll understand."

He shook his head. "I'm man enough to see it through, Grace. But I have to say I'm disappointed."

"I know. I'm sorry."

He lifted his chin. "So, who is this person you're seeing?"

Grace glanced at Danny. He hadn't said a word, which was unusual for him, but as he caught her glance, he sat forward and gave her a supportive smile.

Grace shifted her gaze back to Niall. How she hated hurting him. He didn't deserve this. "He's... he's one of the leaders at the centre. He used to be in the army... and he was actually in Londonderry when all this happened. He was the one who said we needed to find out more."

Niall straightened, his eyes narrowing further. "So you told him, but you wouldn't tell me?"

"It was different, Niall. I had to tell him... I couldn't go through the same thing I went through with you." She squeezed back her tears. "You don't know how hard it was. I wanted to marry you, to say yes, but I couldn't. I just couldn't do it to you."

He let out a heavy sigh. "I guess it's too late?"

She nodded slowly. "Yes. I'm sorry."

"Okay. We'll do this professionally, and I'll treat you like any other client." He reached for his brief case and stood. "Shall we go?"

"Yes." Standing, she met his gaze and then reached up and placed a gentle kiss on his cheek. "I'm sorry, Niall."

His eyes moistened. "And so am I. Let's go." Placing his hand on the small of her back, he followed behind her as she weaved through the tables now bustling with lunch time diners, to the door and then outside to face whatever lay ahead.

CHAPTER 30

The desk sergeant's eyes widened as Niall told him that Grace wanted to confess to a serious crime that had occurred fifteen years ago in Londonderry. He made a phone call and then ushered Grace and Niall into an interview room. Danny was asked to wait outside.

It was like many a room Grace had been in—they were all much the same, cold and impersonal, but it was the first time she'd been the one being interviewed. The interviewing officer quizzed her and she answered all his questions. Niall had told her to be cautious with what she said, but she'd told him she just needed to be honest. She didn't want to hide anything. After hours of interrogation, she was charged with being involved in an act of terrorism and was remanded in custody. A bail hearing was scheduled for the following morning.

Sitting in her cell after Niall and Danny left, Grace determined to be strong, but the reality of what she'd done sat heavily in her stomach, making her feel ill. What if Niall couldn't get her off? Could she survive in a cell like this for perhaps the next twenty years? Bile rose from her stomach and she vomited into the toilet. Wiping her mouth, she fell onto the floor and sobbed. It was too much... what had she been thinking? How could she survive in a tiny cell like this?

Her panic slowly subsided, and she pulled herself up off the floor and sat on the hard, narrow bed. She'd known this would happen, but the stark reality of it was worse than she'd ever imagined. Inhaling slowly, she closed her eyes. Right now she needed to hear from God, to know that He was with her. What had Lizzy said? Learn to listen... be still before God.

She bowed her head, resting her forehead on her upturned hands. *Okay God, I'm here, and I'm listening. Please help me get through this, and help me trust You, regardless of the outcome.* As she hummed the songs she could remember from the Sunday service, peace slowly filled her spirit, and although she didn't hear God's physical voice, she sensed His presence. He truly was close in times of trouble, when everything else was stripped away, and there was nothing else, just her and God. Nothing to get in the way. No television, no one to talk to. She was used to being on her own, but at least at home she had books to read, a television to watch, music to listen to. The silence of her tiny cell would drive her crazy if God hadn't been there with her.

The night passed. She barely slept. Not surprising, really. The guards came for her an hour before the bail hearing and placed handcuffs on her. Not that she was a threat, but they didn't know that. Dressed in drab prison clothes, Grace walked between them down the hallway and to the waiting van.

As she was taken into the court room and placed in the dock, for the first time ever she knew what all those men and women she'd prosecuted over the years felt like... and it wasn't good. There was nothing good about this. She scanned the court room for Niall. Her mouth went dry. Maybe he'd changed his mind. But Danny and Lizzy weren't there either. *Nor was Ryan*. Had they all deserted her? Her chest tightened. No, they wouldn't do that. Something must have happened.

The clerk stood and walked forward, whispering something to the judge. If only she could hear.

Moments passed. She'd be returned to prison shortly if Niall didn't appear. It was most unlike him. He was always on time or early. Never late. And then she recalled the verse Lizzy had suggested she memorise... "Cast all your care on Him because He cares for You." *Okay, God, I'm casting my care onto You. I'm really struggling here... please help me to trust You. I'm sorry for panicking.*

Moments later, heads turned towards the door and Grace breathed a sigh of relief as Niall entered, looking very professional once again in his smart, dark suit. She caught his eye, but he didn't smile. He just met her gaze and nodded his head before he stood in front of the judge and apologised for being late.

Danny, Lizzy and Brianna followed him in. Grace met each of their glances briefly, but she really only had eyes for Ryan, who brought up the rear. As she met Ryan's gaze, she pushed back tears of embarrassment. How terrible that he should see her like this. Her bottom lip quivered, and her breath stuck in her throat. But his eyes told her what she desperately needed to know. He was there for her.

The four of them took their seats towards the back. The judge called the prosecutor to state his case. It was all so familiar, but so surreal... like an out of body experience, as if it was happening to someone else, not to Grace O'Connor, Barrister. And then it was Niall's turn. Grace's heart fluttered as he adjusted the buttons on his suit jacket. How many times had she seen him do that? He looked so smart, and as he addressed the judge, his voice was strong and confident. If anyone could get her off, it was Niall.

Niall's argument for bail was strong. She wasn't a flight risk... she'd handed herself in. She was a lawyer, and she knew the penalties for breaking the terms of bail. Plus, there was reasonable doubt that she hadn't actually placed the bomb that had gone off.

She got bail—Ryan put up the security. She left the court a free woman, but only for two months when her case would be heard in Belfast. What a spectacle that would be. Grace O'Connor, Barrister for the Department of Public Prosecutions, being prosecuted by her own department. No doubt she'd be relieved of her position as soon as she told them.

Ryan walked on one side of her, with his arm lightly around her waist, and Danny, Lizzy and Brianna flanked her other side as they all followed Niall out of the court house to face the waiting media. Niall was the spokesperson, and he firmly stated his belief that Grace was innocent, even though she'd handed herself in. Microphones were flung in front of Niall's face as reporters bombarded him with questions, all the while, Ryan, Danny, Lizzy and Brianna huddled around Grace, protecting her from the gazillion cameras flashing in the crowd.

Danny slipped away to get the van, and finally Niall was able to convince the media that he had no more for them. With his long arms, he shepherded Grace and her protectors away from the crowd and towards the car park exit where Danny was waiting with the van running.

Everyone, including, Niall, climbed in, and Danny took off. He'd very smartly covered the Elim Community sign, so at least the world wouldn't know where she was, for a while, at least.

Danny turned the van onto the road leading to the airport. Of course, Niall needed to return to Belfast—he had work to do. Work for her. Should she go back as well and help? But how could she leave Ryan? She leaned closer into him and gazed up into his blue eyes. No, she'd stay here with Ryan unless Niall needed her to go. Niall would do his job, and she'd pay him. It wasn't what he wanted, but it's all she could offer him.

When they arrived at the airport, Niall opened the front passenger door and climbed out.

Grace squeezed Ryan's hand. "I need to say good-bye."

Meeting her gaze, he returned her squeeze. "Of course."

Grace stood quietly as Niall said good-bye to everyone. When he turned to her, she looked up into his eyes, watching the play of emotions run through them. He was hurting, but he hid it well. Her eyes clouded with visions of the past. They'd shared so much, but in that moment, she knew she didn't love him. Her heart belonged to another. Gulping, she reached out and took his hand. "Thanks for being here, Niall." She struggled to speak.

He remained silent, his face expressionless.

She gulped again. "I'm sorry, I really am."

"So am I, Grace. I hope you'll be happy together."

"Can we still be friends?"

He let out a small chuckle and shook his head. "I'm not sure."

"I hope we can."

"We'll see."

"I'll stay here until the trial, unless you need me before then."

"I'll be in touch." He turned to leave.

She grabbed his wrist, and he turned back. She gave him the best smile she could manage. "Thanks." Her heart was breaking for him, but there was nothing she could do.

When she climbed back into the van, Ryan slipped his arm around her shoulder and pulled her close. Everyone was quiet, even Danny. They understood the awkwardness of the situation. Once they reached the outskirts of the city, Danny glanced around and asked if anyone wanted to stop or just head back. No one wanted to stop.

Grace fell asleep in Ryan's arms and woke to him gently shaking her shoulder as they pulled up outside Danny and Lizzy's cottage. She blinked as she straightened. "I had no idea we were here."

"You slept the whole way."

"I'm sorry."

"It's not a problem. I caught a bit of shut eye too." He kissed the top of her head. "Anyway, it's time to get out." Holding her hand, he helped her out of the back seat.

"Will you stay for a while?" She almost pleaded with him.

"Yes, of course." He placed his arm around her shoulders as they followed the others inside.

Lizzy already had the kettle on by the time they reached the kitchen. "Sit down, Grace, Ryan. Danny's just grabbing the sandwiches Mia prepared for us."

Grace sat at the table between Ryan and Brianna, still in a daze. Lizzy chatted, but Grace barely heard her. Brianna said something, and Grace replied. Danny returned with the sandwiches. Lizzy placed a mug of tea in front of her. Ryan kept squeezing her hand. But none of it was real. It was like a play going on around her, and she was just an observer. She tried to join in with the conversation, but her mind was floating. Eventually she excused herself. "I'm sorry, but I need to rest."

Lizzy's eyes widened as her hand flew to her cheek. "Of course you do, Grace. We're sorry, we should have realised."

"It's okay. I just haven't slept much the last few nights."

"Let us know if you need anything."

Grace pushed her chair back and stood. "Thanks. I'm sorry to have put you all through this."

"Grace! You're family… you don't need to apologise!" Lizzy shook her head.

Tears pricked Grace's eyes. "You don't know how much that means."

"I agree," Brianna said quietly.

Grace placed her hand on Brianna's shoulder and squeezed it.

Ryan stood, and leaning close, kissed her cheek. "I'll come back later after you've rested."

Looking into his wonderful, caring eyes, she gave him an appreciative smile. "Thank you."

CHAPTER 31

When Grace closed the door, she spent a few minutes on her knees before climbing into bed. She didn't deserve to be back here with Danny and Lizzy, amongst family and friends who loved her, she should have been in prison, because, regardless of what Niall said, she was still guilty of being involved in a terrorist activity, and she should be punished. But the memory of that tiny cell sent shivers through her body. If she was found guilty, that would be her life for the foreseeable future. Now she knew what it was like, she'd be better prepared next time, but still, it would only be because of God living in her that she'd survive in there.

Images of a tiny cell and Niall's sad face drifted through her mind, but it was the comfort of being wrapped in God's arms that finally calmed her spirit enough to allow her to sleep.

When she woke later that afternoon, an envelope was sitting on her floor near the door. Slipping out of bed, Grace picked it up and lifted it to her nose. It held a faint perfume, and on the front, her name was written in an unfamiliar hand. Taking it back to her bed, she sat down and carefully opened it, scanning straight to the bottom to see who it was from. *Ryan...* a smile came to her face as she read.

Grace, I want you to know that I'm here for you. I'm looking forward to spending the next two months with you, getting to know you, having fun together, but most of all, growing together in the Lord. I don't know what God has planned for us, but I know it's something good. God will honour your bravery and obedience, and you have the opportunity to be a witness to the world of how He can change a person. You did so well today, and we're all proud of you. Stay strong in God, Grace, and He'll uphold you with His right hand.

All my love,

Ryan

Grace wiped the tears from her eyes. Yes, she had the opportunity to be a witness to God's amazing love as the case progressed. But to do that, she'd have to be steadfast in her faith. No more anxiety, no more self-pity. She was a child of God, and she was being obedient. Even though in God's eyes she was forgiven, the incident had happened, and many people's lives had been changed forever. The families who'd lost loved ones deserved closure. If she could help Niall and the police discover the truth of that day, she'd be doing them all a service. And if it meant she had to spend time in prison, well, so be it. She'd failed last night, but she'd be stronger next time. Being such a high profile case, she had the opportunity to show that there was a different way… a better way. She'd do it. She wouldn't wallow in self-pity. Now was the time to be strong.

She threw the curtains open. The weak Scottish sun was sinking slowly over Ben Nevis, washing the sky in soft hues of pinks and oranges. Out on the loch, the students were bringing a number of canoes into shore. Ryan was amongst them, and her heart fluttered with excitement at what the next two months might hold. God was indeed good, and she couldn't wait to see it all unfold.

. . .

Ryan did indeed keep his word. Every spare moment he had he spent with Grace. He took her on long hikes, they went on drives through the countryside, discovering quaint villages and cute cafés. He took her to Edinburgh and to Glasgow and to Inverness, and to all the towns in between. They walked on Culloden Moor, the site of the final Jacobite rising in 1746, where thousands of brave Highlanders fought the English and lost, but they also studied the Bible and prayed together. Ryan told her that if their relationship was going to stay strong, it had to be built with God at the centre, and Grace was more than happy to do that. The more she learned about God, the more in awe she became of His amazing greatness. Not only was He the God who'd created this amazing world, He was the God who lived inside her, giving her new life and hope for the future. She might have lost her identity as a barrister, but she'd gained a new one—she was a child of God, washed clean by the blood of Jesus, loved and cherished as if she were a precious only child.

When the time came to travel to Belfast for her trial, Grace knew with certainty that her strength came from the Lord, and that she would face whatever came her way with God on her side. She'd be a witness to His amazing love as she stood in the dock and testified. She'd be gentle and kind with the media. They wouldn't understand, in fact, Ryan had warned her they'd most likely be sceptical of Grace O'Connor's conversion, and would try to disparage her name. She didn't care. She was standing for the truth, and that's all that mattered.

She'd been in contact with Niall on and off for the entire two months. With the information she'd given him, he believed she'd be acquitted of murder, although she might be found guilty of being involved with a terrorist group, although he was hopeful she might be acquitted altogether. The prosecution maintained that even though her bomb might not have gone off, her intention was to kill.

They hadn't found Fergus, despite Grace providing as much information as she could, all the while knowing he might come after her. The police had been trying to find him and other members of that group for years without success, but armed with the new information Grace had provided, they were hopeful he'd eventually be found. Grace was saddened to discover Sammy had been killed in another bomb blast several years after Grace fled Londonderry. She wasn't surprised she hadn't heard anything from Aunt Hilda or the cousins, but no doubt they'd be worried she'd report the rape some time soon.

As she placed her hand on the Bible and took the oath that day, Grace knew that whatever happened in the days ahead, God would uphold her. Never had she thought she'd be on this side of the court room, but as she listened to the prosecuting barrister's opening speech, one thing she knew for sure, she no longer wanted to prosecute. Yes, for the justice system to work, there was a need for the prosecution, but her heart was no longer there. Her need to punish had been replaced with a heart of love and compassion. The thought crossed her mind that if she was found to be innocent, she could join Niall's firm as a defence lawyer, but then when she looked at him and saw the sadness that still hung heavy in his eyes, she realised that wouldn't work. If he was to ever move on, it was best they didn't see each other after the trial ended. Besides, who knew what God had planned for her and Ryan? But first, she had to get through the trial.

It lasted for three days. The media were relentless, but Grace stayed true to her promise. Unable to speak to them herself, she'd instructed Niall about what to say. He didn't understand either, but she didn't care. She wanted the world to know that truth was more important than self-preservation. That God's forgiveness didn't mean she was exempt from paying whatever penalty she would be handed if found guilty. That providing answers and closure to those family members who'd lost loved ones was more important to her than saving her own skin, and that she was sorry she hadn't come forward earlier.

The prosecution was good, but Niall was better. But that didn't matter. What mattered was that the truth was revealed, and Grace believed it was, although she was stunned as the full realisation that her bomb hadn't gone off finally hit her. All those years believing she'd killed those people. But the evidence was there—they'd found the remnants of a crudely made unexploded bomb amongst the rubble, and it matched the description she'd given. The bomb that had exploded was more complex. Someone else had planted it without her knowing. Had Fergus doubted her ability to follow through? Probably. He was right… how had she ever imagined she could do it?

The jury took just under four hours to find her not guilty. The relief she felt was immense, although she'd been prepared for a guilty verdict. At least now, with all the extra information she'd been able to supply to the police, the actual bomber might be found and brought to justice.

Reporters jostled to get close to her as she exited the courthouse surrounded by Niall, Ryan, Danny, Lizzy, Brianna, and Caleb and Caitlin. The main questions they asked were how she felt and what she would do now. Would she be returning to the bar now she'd been acquitted?

Now she could speak for herself, she was almost tongue-tied, but this was her opportunity, and she needed to take it. A hush fell over the crowd as she lifted her chin and began speaking. "Firstly, I need to thank my lawyer, and *friend,* Niall Flannery, for the superb job he did." She turned and gave him an appreciative smile. Her voice caught, but she quickly regained control. "Niall helped unravel the truth about that awful day, and now the police are a step closer to finding the real culprit. I pray with all my heart that he's found, and that the families of those who've suffered all these years can finally find closure. I've lived for the last fifteen years thinking I'd done it, so I know a little of what they're going through."

A microphone was shoved in front of her face. "So why did you plant it in the first place?"

Grace gulped. The question she'd been dreading. She looked the young female reporter directly in the eye. "I was young and insecure, looking for something to follow. I truly regret my actions."

"So is it true what they're saying? Grace O'Connor has found God?"

"Yes, it's true. Finding God was the catalyst for me coming forward. I didn't want to hide my secret any longer, especially as I believed I was responsible."

"Will you be going back to work for the DPP now?"

"No."

"Will you be staying in Belfast?"

"I'll be considering my options. I don't know at this stage."

Niall leaned in front of her and pushed them away. "That's all for now, folks. Give Ms O'Connor some space."

After the crowd dispersed, the family group gathered at Caleb and Caitlin's house for a celebratory meal. Caleb had invited Niall, and Grace was pleased to see that he'd come, with the blond hanging off his arm. She wasn't sure if the blond was the right woman for him, but she didn't know her, so who was she to judge? But she really wanted the opportunity to share her faith with Niall at some point, and she prayed she'd get the opportunity before she headed back to Scotland, because she was surer than ever that that was where God wanted her.

Niall introduced her formally to Roisin, and Grace discovered she was actually a nice person. Maybe he wasn't dating her just because he couldn't have Grace, maybe he really did like her. Grace prayed that was the case—she didn't want to see him hurt again.

Before dinner was served, Danny gathered everyone together to give thanks. Grace leaned against Ryan's strong, firm chest, with her arm slipped around his waist. It had always been possible she would have been found guilty and sent to prison, but here she was, surrounded by all those she'd come to love and appreciate so much. She brushed back tears of gratitude. God was indeed good.

CHAPTER 32

Six months later, Grace opened the door to her new premises in downtown Glasgow. "Place of Hope" was where rape victims could come for counselling and support. It wasn't flashy by any means, in fact, unless anyone knew it was there, they'd probably just walk straight by. Grace wanted it that way. She wanted to make it as easy as possible for those who needed help to come, and not feel threatened.

After her court case was over, Grace had undertaken an intensive counselling course so she could offer rape victims the best help possible. Brianna had also begun studying a Diploma in Counselling and would be Grace's assistant. But Brianna brought something more than just head knowledge—she brought first-hand experience. She knew what it was like to be raped. The disgust and shame of it all. It had almost killed her, but praise God, thanks to the cleansing power of the cross, she'd come out the other side and was a new person, filled with God's love and compassion for others.

Soon after her court case finished, as part of her preparation for leaving Belfast and moving to Scotland, Grace had written a letter to Aunt Hilda confirming that Brianna was not planning on reporting the rape, and had in fact forgiven the boys. She wasn't surprised she hadn't heard back, but she prayed for them often, because they'd be carrying guilt over what they'd done, and needed God's healing touch in their lives, even if they didn't know it.

As she turned the sign on the door from "Closed" to "Open", a delivery van pulled up in front. The driver jumped out and ran around to the passenger side. He slid the door open, and pulled out a huge bunch of flowers, and then, after looking at the tag, walked straight towards her. Grace chuckled. She knew who'd they be from... Ryan had been sending her a bunch of flowers every week since the court case had ended. It must have been costing him a fortune. But he'd gone all out on this one... it was huge! She thanked the driver and took the bouquet inside. She opened the card and smiled.

Dinner tonight? Pick you up at 6. I love you, Ryan. PS All the best for today.

Her heart skipped a beat. Ryan hadn't planned on coming to Glasgow this week, in fact, she thought he was busy with a new intake of students. She wasn't complaining... dinner with Ryan was something she always looked forward to and didn't do often enough, even though they tried to see each other as much as they could.

The day passed in a flurry. They had four scheduled appointments and two walk-ins. All were women who needed someone to talk to, someone who'd listen without judging, and could offer them hope that one day they'd get through this.

Grace wished Ryan had told her where they were going for dinner so she'd have an idea of what to wear. Casual or formal? She guessed casual, but went smart just in case. She never knew with Ryan. He'd surprised her so often in the past months. They'd had so much fun getting to know each other, but it was hard being apart. He was still the head instructor at the Elim Community, and she'd moved to Glasgow a month after the trial ended.... almost three hours by road each way. It was almost a long distance romance, but in some ways that made the anticipation of their time together even sweeter.

She stood in front of the mirror and checked her make-up. Not that she wore much these days, in fact, she rarely wore more than a lick of mascara and lipstick. She'd even stopped colouring her hair and had returned to her natural light brown. It took her a while to get used to it, but Ryan had told her countless times he loved her regardless of how she looked, and now that Fergus had been found and charged, she had no need to disguise herself any longer.

But she did wonder where their relationship was going. Ryan had never mentioned marriage, and neither had she. She guessed, like her, he was cautious. It was a huge thing for him, especially having lived his whole adult life on his own or with other men. But she felt she was ready to commit. Now her past had been cleared and she didn't have any secrets to hide, she was ready. Or she thought she was. Maybe tonight would be the night he'd ask...

Right on the dot of six the buzzer for Grace's small apartment in a not too salubrious part of town rang. She checked the mirror one last time and then pressed the button to speak through the intercom. "I'll be right down." Grabbing her jacket and bag, she stepped out the door, closed it behind her, and then pressed the lift button. As the lift descended the five floors, she wondered again where he was taking her, and she felt giddy like a breathless girl of eighteen going on her first date.

The lift opened, and he stood there with a beaming smile on his face.

A ripple of excitement ran though her body. She stepped into his arms and lifted her face to his. "I didn't expect to see you so soon."

He cupped her chin and looked deeply into her eyes. "It's a special day, Grace, and we needed to celebrate. It's not every day you start a new career." His eyes sparkled, and she felt enveloped in an invisible warmth.

"That's true." She smiled. "Thank you for the flowers."

"You're welcome."

"You must own shares in a florist shop by now."

Ryan chuckled as he slipped his hand gently behind her neck and drew her face to his. His eyes twinkled. "I can't think of a better investment." As he lowered his mouth against hers, her knees weakened.

"Come on, we'd best get dinner or I might do something I'll regret." Pulling away, he placed his arm around her shoulder and directed her out of the building and towards his Land Rover.

"So, where are we going on this chilly night?" Grace rubbed her arms after she'd done her seatbelt up.

He chuckled again. "I thought you'd be wondering. I've booked a table at The Arthouse."

"You haven't!"

"I have."

She laughed. "And you're going to drive us there in this?"

"What's wrong with my Drover?"

She snickered. "Nothing, but the other diners might raise their eyebrows."

"Let them. I don't care."

She leaned over and kissed his cheek. "I don't either. But can you turn the heat up. It's freezing in here."

"It's as high as it goes, you know that."

"I should have put on an extra coat."

"There's a rug in the back."

As she stretched around to grab the rug, he slipped his hand onto her shoulder and turned her to face him. The only light came from a dim street light, but his eyes still sparkled in the semi-darkness. Her heart raced.

His eyes peered deeply into hers as he took her hands, stroking her skin gently with his thumb. "Grace, I love you so much. I don't want to spend any more time apart." He paused, but his gaze didn't waver.

Grace's heart thudded. For a long moment, she felt as if she were floating, drifting on a soft cloud of euphoria. Was this really happening?

"I want us to do life together, so Grace," his face broke into the most beautiful smile and his eyes lit up, "will you marry me?"

Grace's heart danced with joy. "I thought you'd never ask!"

"So is that a yes?"

"Of course it is!" She threw her arms around his neck, and as his mouth found hers, she gave herself freely to the passion of his kiss. She longed for more. To fall asleep in his arms, to wake up beside him every morning, and to share every aspect of his life. And now, it was about to happen. He'd asked her to marry him, and she'd said yes! It was really happening!

Finally pulling away, he tilted her chin upwards with his finger, as a grin as large as she'd seen grew on his face. "One more thing before dinner." He reached into his pocket and drew out a small box, snapping it open with his thumb and forefinger. Inside sat an elegant sapphire and diamond engagement ring.

Grace gasped and held her hands to her face. "Ryan! It's gorgeous! How did..."

He held a finger to her lips. "Shh... just put it on." He took the ring out of the box and slipped it onto her finger. It fit perfectly.

Grace pushed back tears of joy as her gaze travelled between the ring and his eyes. "Ryan, thank you. I love you so much."

"But not as much as I love you." He smiled as he lowered his lips to hers and kissed her slowly and tenderly.

As they drove to the restaurant a short while later, Ryan turned to Grace and slipped his hand onto her leg. "Now we've got three things to celebrate."

Grace's forehead puckered. "Three? What's the third?"

"Oh, didn't I tell you?" He wore a playful look on his face.

Grace grabbed his hand. "Tell me what?"

He chuckled. "I've got a permanent job in Glasgow... starting tomorrow."

Her eyes popped. "Really? Why didn't you tell me?"

His eyes sparkled. "I wanted to surprise you."

"You certainly did that! Are you going to tell me about it?"

"Over dinner."

"You never cease to amaze me, Ryan MacGregor."

"That's me... full of surprises!" He chuckled again.

RYAN KEPT HIS PROMISE, and over dinner told Grace that he'd been accepted, as a Chaplain, into one of the high schools which had a high rate of troubled youth. He'd be given free rein to implement programmes he felt would benefit the teenagers, and help keep them off the street and out of trouble.

"That's great, but what's Danny going to do without you?"

"Don't worry about that, Grace. He's got a new fellow lined up. In fact, he's starting this week."

"Anyone I know?"

"Maybe." His eye held a glint.

She let out an amused chuckle as she folded her arms. "So, who is it?"

"Just your other brother."

She shot forward. "Caleb?"

He nodded. "Yep, Caleb and Caitlin and the girls have just moved over."

"How come I didn't know?"

"It's just happened, and besides, Danny said he wanted to keep it as a surprise for you and Brianna."

"You're not too good at keeping secrets."

"It's not good to have too many secrets, Grace. You should know that."

Drawing a deep breath, her expression grew serious. "You're right. Unless they're good ones that are kept for a reason."

"And was this a good one?"

"Absolutely. Does Danny know you've told me?"

"I did mention it would be hard to keep it quiet..."

"So, does he know you were going to propose?"

"Maybe..." She didn't like the mischievous glint in his eye.

"What do you mean by that?"

He pulled a face. "I hope you don't mind, but I asked a few friends to come and celebrate with us."

Grace turned around as a group of people appeared out of nowhere, shouting their congratulations all at once. Danny, Lizzy, Brianna, Caleb, Caitlin. She laughed. So much for a romantic dinner... but she didn't mind. Dinner with her family was always special, and now Caleb and Caitlin were here, it was extra special.

The waiters quickly added more tables, and what Grace had expected to be a quiet dinner with just the two of them turned into a loud, fun-filled evening. They'd all taken the following day off work, and the children were all being minded by Rosemary and David, so the party continued into the wee hours. Grace had no idea how she was going to get up for work the next morning, but she didn't expect to sleep, so it wouldn't be a problem.

Despite the cold, when Ryan dropped her off outside her apartment, she didn't want to get out of the truck. She just wanted to stay with him, encircled in his arms.

"I need to go, Grace—we'll freeze if we stay here, but let's not wait long to get married. We're both sure, and so I propose we get married as soon as we can."

Her eyes widened. "Like in a few weeks?" Her heart raced. Could this be true?

"If you're happy to do that, yes."

"I won't have a dress, or time to do all the normal wedding preparation things."

"I can't imagine you bothering too much with all of that anyway."

She chuckled. "You're right. I can't imagine myself being a typical bride."

"No, you're anything but typical." He brushed the hair off her forehead and looked into her eyes. "So, what say you, Grace O'Connor? Will you become my wife on the first possible date we can make it?"

"Do you need to ask?" She raised a brow.

He chuckled. "Not really… I take that as a yes."

"It's definitely a yes." She threw her arms around him, and knowing she wouldn't have too many more times to do this, tore herself away from him after he'd kissed her thoroughly, and caught the lift to her apartment on her own.

THEIR WEDDING WAS SCHEDULED for midday on the fifteenth of April at The Elim Community chapel. Grace decided it was her turn to surprise Ryan, and found a wedding gown she felt comfortable in, and knew Ryan would like. It fitted her figure perfectly, and although simple in design, it held an understated elegance.

The ceremony was also simple, but she and Ryan planned it to be all they wanted… a committal of their love to each other and to God. They'd both been through so much in their lives, they didn't need all the frills that normally accompanied a wedding.

Danny walked down the aisle with Grace, and then took his place beside Ryan as Ryan's best man. Lizzy and Brianna were Grace's only attendants, but looked stunning in their pale blue suits. Little Clare was her flower girl, and James and Dillon were the page boys. Nothing was too fancy, but the service was perfect in every way.

As Danny stood to pray for them after David pronounced them

husband and wife, Grace gazed into Ryan's eyes, still not quite believing that all this had happened. Less than a year ago, Brianna was close to death and hooked on drugs. She herself was hidden behind the walls she'd put up, bitter from the hand that life had dealt her. Yet now, both she and Brianna had new lives, ones full of hope and promise, filled with God's love and forgiveness. They had hope and a future. And Grace had a husband she adored, one she could never have imagined meeting anywhere, let alone in the Scottish Highlands. She had no doubt life with Ryan would be filled with fun and excitement, but most of all, she knew that their marriage would be strong because God would be at the head of it. She smiled at him before bowing her head when Danny placed his hands on their shoulders.

"Dear Heavenly Father, we come to you with joy in our hearts as we witness the joining together of Ryan and Grace in holy matrimony. We're excited for where You're going to lead them, as they both seek to follow You and to live for You. We thank You that they found each other. We love seeing them together, their joy of life is infectious, but their love and compassion for others is what sets them apart. Bless their ministries, dear Lord. Use them to bring hope to those who've lost hope, and let them lead many into Your Kingdom. Bless Ryan and Grace as they start their new lives together as husband and wife, In Jesus' precious name, Amen."

"Amen." Grace lifted her face and gazed into Ryan's intoxicating blue eyes. As their eyes locked, her heart thudded as he lowered his lips and kissed her for the first time as her lawfully-wedded husband, something she had never in her wildest imaginings expected to happen.

"Give thanks to the Lord, for He is good; His love endures forever."
I Chronicles 16:34

BOOK 5 - A HIGHLAND CHRISTMAS

CHAPTER 1

Glasgow, Scotland December 23, 1988

After almost three years of working full-time with rape victims, Brianna deserved a holiday. But instead of going with her friend, Susan, to the south of Spain, where the weather would be mild and possibly even warm, she was going to the Scottish Highlands to spend Christmas with her Irish family she barely knew. *Argh!* No, that wasn't quite true—she did know and love some of them, *but the others?* She barely remembered her younger siblings, Aislin, Alana, Brendan and Shawn, after being separated from them when she was just ten following their Mam's untimely death.

Drat Danny for organising this. The one year she'd planned a real holiday. She blew out a breath as a familiar car horn sounded from the road. Drawing back the thin, sheer curtain, she glanced out the window of the two-bedroom semi-detached terraced home in downtown Glasgow she shared with Susan. Although less than eager, she was packed and ready to go, so she flicked the television off, slipped her coat on and stepped outside, closing the door behind her. As the damp air hit her face, she shivered and dreamed of warmer climates.

Lifting her hand, she waved at her brother-in-law, Ryan, as he climbed out of his large SUV and jogged up the stairs towards her. He gave her a quick kiss before grabbing her bag and placing it in the boot. She slid into the back seat behind her older sister, Grace, rubbing her hands together.

Grace turned around and extended her slender hand, giving Brianna's a squeeze. "Hey, Bibi, how are you doing?"

Brianna shivered, her lips tight. "Wishing I was in Spain." She sounded petty, and she had to get over it, but at least she could be honest with Grace.

"Don't we all?" Grace laughed lightly as she patted Brianna's hand. "Never mind, it'll be good to see everyone after all this time."

Brianna humphed as she strapped herself in. "I don't know about that. I'd been looking forward to having a real holiday for once."

"Next year, maybe." Grace gave an understanding smile before facing the front and cranking the heat up, while Ryan jumped in and pulled away from the kerb.

Brianna stared out the window as dreary terraced houses flashed past. She was being immature. Grace was probably right... spending Christmas together with all her siblings for the first time in more than twenty years should be cause for celebration. She just didn't feel it. She didn't want to rake over the past—goodness knows she'd done enough of that and now she'd moved on. In fact, she'd even been thinking of leaving the Rape Centre she and Grace ran together, although the courage to share that thought with Grace was presently lacking. Besides, what would she do if she left?

With no other option, she settled into the soft leather seat for the two and a half-hour drive to Fort William and the Christian community her older brother, Danny, and his wife, Lizzy, managed, and dreamed she was in a plane heading for Spain, not a car heading for the Highlands in thick, damp fog.

"YOU NEED TO LEAVE NOW, Daniel, or you'll be late." Lizzy folded her arms and studied her husband with amusement as he stood in front of the mirror combing his dark, wavy hair.

"I know, love, I'm almost ready." Daniel caught her eye in the hallway mirror and winked as he slipped the comb into the back pocket of his faded blue jeans and turned to face her. "Sure you can't come?"

As he lifted an eyebrow while rubbing her forearms and gazing into her eyes, Lizzy almost changed her mind. But no… she had to stay home and finish the preparations. "You know I can't come. Mother and Father will be here soon. Besides, the children are looking forward to going to the airport with you."

Daniel stepped closer and drew her into an embrace, nuzzling her neck. "Okay, but I'll miss you."

Lizzy chuckled and shook her head. "Don't be silly—you'll only be gone a few hours." She pulled back and looked into his crystal blue eyes, her voice growing serious. "Just take care on those roads, especially in this fog."

"I fully intend to." Daniel lowered his face and placed a soft kiss on her lips. "Sorry I won't be here to help with everything."

"No, you're not! Since when did you like cooking?"

Daniel laughed. "You're right."

"Thank you. Now, off with you!" Lizzy pushed him away and stepped into the living room where the children were running around chasing each other. The noise was deafening. "Dillon, James, Clare, calm down. Daddy's ready. Come and give me a hug."

They all ran towards her at once, wrapping their arms around her, almost toppling her over. She laughed and met Daniel's amused gaze. "I think I'm glad I'm staying here. It's going to be a noisy trip!"

"It's all good, love. I can make as much noise as they can."

"I know. That's what I mean." She let out another laugh, but a tinge of sadness flowed through her. It would have been fun to take a drive with Daniel and the children, but there was a ton of cooking to do, and besides, her parents were coming, and no doubt they'd be early. She bent down and pulled the children into a group hug. "Have a nice time together, darlings, and I'll have some surprises waiting for you when you get home."

Five-year-old Clare pulled on her arm. "Surprises, Mummy? Like what?"

"It wouldn't be a surprise if I told you. Now, give me another hug and off you go."

She helped the children into their coats and into the bus belonging to the Elim Community, the Christian community she and Daniel had managed for the past five years. She waved as Daniel headed the bus towards the main building to collect his older brother, Caleb, who lived in the community with his wife, Caitlin, and their two daughters. Caleb was going with Daniel and the children to the airport in Inverness to meet the four siblings arriving from Ireland. She stopped waving within seconds as the tail-lights disappeared into the thick pea-soup fog they'd woken up to. As she stared into the thick mist, Lizzy shivered and prayed for their safety. Not even the grand manor house was visible… she'd never seen it so thick.

With Daniel and the children gone, she quick tidied the toys and games lying scattered over the lounge room floor. Once the house was in order, she scurried down the flagstone path that led to the impressive stone mansion now used as a community home for young people struggling with life's problems. She and Daniel and the children lived in the smaller cottage that had once been the estate manager's home.

Through the fog, Lake Linnhe was barely visible, but the gentle lapping of the waves against the shore confirmed that the large body of water was indeed only a stone's throw away. As she approached the sturdy mansion covered in creeping ivy, and normally surrounded by a beautiful flower garden, she realised how much she would miss it, if and when they left. Not that anything was planned, but both she and Daniel had a sense that God was about to lead them onto something new.

She ducked around the side of the mansion and pushed open the heavy wooden door, the servants' entrance in years gone by, but now the entrance used mostly by the students. She made her way down the hallway, following the aroma of freshly baked bread all the way to the kitchen where her sister-in-law, Caitlin, was busy at work. She and Caitlin were spending the morning in the big kitchen, and had planned to bake lots of meals and treats in readiness for everyone's arrival.

Caitlin looked up as she entered, her round, jolly face lighting up. "Come and warm up, Liz. The teapot's still hot if you'd like a cuppa."

"Thanks. I'll grab one in a moment." Lizzy headed straight for the wood stove, holding her hands in front of it, and shivering again as warmth spread slowly from the tips of her fingers, up her arms, and into the rest of her body. She rubbed her hands together and glanced out the window where Ben Nevis, the tallest mountain in Great Britain, would normally be visible in the distance. "It's such a dreadful morning."

"You're not wrong. A great welcome for everyone." Chuckling, Caitlin opened a bag of onions, pulling several out.

Lizzy stepped away from the fire and poured herself a mug of tea. She lifted the pot in the air and looked at Caitlin. "Like a top-up?"

"No thanks, I'm on my third already. How long until everyone starts arriving?" Caitlin blew some hair off her face as she diced the onions for the shepherd's pie they'd decided to serve for dinner.

"Three hours, maybe less if the fog lifts." Lizzy cupped her hands around the mug and blew on her tea.

"The girls will be down in a minute." Caitlin looked up, brushing her watering eyes with her sleeve. "I almost forgot to tell you—Andrew also offered to help."

Lizzy rolled her eyes. "Wow, we'll need to be on our toes." Andrew, a chef at one of the top restaurants in Glasgow, and the son of David and Rosemary McKinnon, the owners of the property, had arrived the previous evening to spend Christmas with his parents.

"I think it'll be fun. I've always wanted to cook with a real chef."

"It's all right for you. I struggle just to do the basics." Lizzy took a sip of tea before placing the mug on the kitchen table and donning an apron, tying it securely behind her back.

"I'm sure it'll be fine, but you can work with the girls if you'd rather."

"I thought they might have gone to the airport with Daniel and Caleb?"

"No… twelve going on twenty. You know what it's like." Caitlin chuckled. "They spend hours in front of the mirror these days."

"They're lovely girls. You and Caleb have done a great job with them."

"Thanks. They're going to miss it here when we go back to Belfast." Caleb had been the Activities Co-ordinator at the community for the past several years, but the family was returning to Belfast because Caitlin's mother had taken ill.

"They must be looking forward to seeing their friends again."

"They'd rather be here with their new friends." Caitlin wiped her face again.

"They'll adjust quickly." Lizzy took out a mixing bowl and grabbed the ingredients to start making a triple-sized bread and butter pudding. With so many mouths to feed, they'd chosen easy to prepare meals they could make ahead of time.

"I hope so. It's a hard age to uproot them." Putting the knife down, Caitlin grabbed a handful of tissues and blew her nose.

"They can always come back for a visit."

"I'm sure they'd like that." Caitlin threw the tissues into the bin and washed her hands, then turned to the doorway, her face lighting up when Imogen and Tara, both wearing hot pink sweat shirts, dark blue jeans and black joggers, appeared. She held out her arm. "And here they are."

Lizzy chuckled. How could she still not tell them apart after almost two years? She gave them a smile. "Hi, girls. Are you excited about Christmas?"

The girls both nodded as they entered together and stood in front of the free-standing island bench where Caitlin had resumed dicing the onions.

"Cat got your tongue, girls? Answer your auntie."

One of them, maybe Imogen, turned and looked at Lizzy. Her eyes, although dark like her mother's, were innocent and clear. "Sorry, Auntie Lizzy. Yes, we're very much looking forward to Christmas."

Lizzy smiled. "My three certainly are. They can't wait. Every morning they check the tree for new presents."

Caitlin tipped the tray of onions into a large pan on the stove. "Come on, girls, you need to get to work. You're on vegetables."

"Mum..." Their shoulders slumped.

She stirred the onions as they began to sizzle, filling the kitchen with a wonderful aroma. "Only joking. You can bake some gingerbread men and then help with the trifle."

The face of the twin who'd answered earlier lit up. "That's better. Come on, Tara, let's get started."

Lizzy smiled to herself. For once she'd guessed right!

Soon after, as Imogen and Tara were busy mixing dough for the gingerbread men and Lizzy buttered bread for the pudding, Andrew knocked on the door and poked his head in. "I believe this is where it's all happening. May I come in?" The words rolled off his tongue in a soft Scottish brogue.

Caitlin looked up. "Please do! We've been expecting you."

Andrew took the apron she offered and slipped it on. As he rolled up his sleeves, Lizzy couldn't help but notice the curly ginger hair on his fair arms. With that tawny-gold hair with a hint of ginger, and his warm hazel eyes, Andrew McKinnon would be a great catch for someone, *if he were available.* Lizzy's mind ticked over. *Brianna?* She chuckled as she returned to her pudding. Yes, Brianna. It was time Daniel's younger sister had some love in her life, and the softly spoken, ruggedly handsome Andrew McKinnon might just be her perfect match.

CHAPTER 2

As Lizzy expected, her parents, Roger and Gwyneth Walton-Smythe from Wiveliscombe Manor in the south of England, arrived first. While she greeted them at the main door, a dark coloured SUV turned into the driveway and pulled up behind her parents' BMW. The front passenger door opened, and Grace, Daniel's sister who was closest to him in age, stepped out, her long legs easily reaching the ground as she quickly slipped on her dark red coat. Grace then opened the back door for her younger sister, Brianna, who, by the way she stretched, looked like she'd just woken up. Grace's husband, Ryan, lifted their cases out of the boot and followed the women to the main entrance.

Lizzy greeted everyone and made the introductions, and after they'd all removed and hung their coats, she ushered them into the drawing room. The log fire Andrew had lit earlier that morning crackled in the huge fireplace, the smell of pine needles filling the room with a reassuringly familiar smell.

Without Daniel and the children there, Lizzy wondered how the next hour or so would go, but she had nothing to worry about. Grace, as confident and charming as ever, engaged her mother in conversation, but Brianna headed straight for the kitchen. Although she had grown in confidence since kicking her drug habit and giving her heart to the Lord almost two years ago, there was no doubt she'd feel intimidated by Roger and Gwyneth. Lizzy's parents couldn't help the way they spoke, but she knew many considered them *posh*. It wouldn't worry Grace, who'd been a high-profile prosecuting barrister prior to her marriage to Ryan, but Brianna? A different matter altogether.

Lizzy sometimes wondered if Grace missed the challenge of the court room now that she was managing the "Place of Hope". She and Brianna had opened the rape and support counselling centre in Glasgow following her acquittal of involvement in a terrorist attack. Seeing the way Grace and Ryan looked at each other, Lizzy decided that Grace was content with her new life, especially as she now had no secrets to hide and her slate had been wiped clean by the blood of Jesus.

She sat down and joined the conversation between her mother and Grace, while Ryan stood with his back to the fire and chatted with her father. Caitlin poked her head into the room. Despite her face being flushed from cooking, she still wore a cheery smile.

"Caitlin, come in and say hello." Lizzy held her hand out and motioned for her to join them. "You remember my mother, Gwyneth?"

"Of course I do." Caitlin smoothed her hair and straightened her apron before stepping closer and taking her hand. Lizzy hoped Caitlin wouldn't curtsy and breathed a sigh of relief when she leaned down and placed a kiss on her cheek. "Nice to see you again, Gwyneth. How was your trip?"

Gwyneth smiled politely. "Not too bad, considering the weather and the time of year. We only came from Edinburgh this morning, so we didn't have far to come."

"No, but the fog was terrible, and it still hasn't lifted." Grace stood and gave Caitlin a hug. Tall and elegant as always, Grace towered over her short, pudgy sister-in-law. "How are you, Caitlin?"

"I'm fine, thanks. Good to see you, Grace." An easy smile played at the corners of Caitlin's mouth as she took Grace's hands in hers. There had been a time back in Belfast before Grace met the Lord when she barely acknowledged Caitlin's existence, but things had changed. God had transformed Grace's life so much that Lizzy still had to pinch herself occasionally to believe it had really happened.

Caitlin let go of her hand. "Can I get everyone a drink before lunch?"

Gwyneth smiled. "A cup of tea would be lovely, thank you. I'm sure Roger would like one, too." She glanced at him, but his back was turned and he and Ryan were engrossed in conversation.

"I'll make a pot and bring it in." Caitlin took a step backwards towards the door, her head bobbing.

"I'll give you a hand." Lizzy went to stand.

"No, stay there. Brianna and Andrew can help." Caitlin's mouth twisted into an infectious grin as she motioned for Lizzy to remain where she was.

Lizzy suppressed a chuckle. It was happening already, and she hadn't done a thing…

BRIANNA'S EYES had widened when she entered the kitchen. A man with the most gorgeous gingery golden hair stood at the sink washing dishes. She began back pedalling when Caitlin gestured for her to come in.

Jolly as always, and totally unaware of Brianna's hesitancy, Caitlin drew her into an embrace. "Great to see you, sweetheart. How are you doing?"

Brianna blinked, momentarily tearing her gaze from the man at the sink to return Caitlin's hug, but her gaze had a mind of its own and kept darting back to him. *Who is this man? And what's he doing standing at the sink, washing dishes, wearing an apron?* She blinked again and answered Caitlin's question, forcing herself to smile at her sister-in-law. "I'm good, glad to be having a break."

Caitlin held Brianna's gaze, her eyes smiling. "Danny will be pleased you're here."

Brianna sucked in a breath. "Yes, well, he owes me a trip to Spain."

Caitlin chuckled. "You never know with Danny; he might just surprise you. Anyway, come and meet Andrew, Rosemary and David's son."

Brianna's eyes widened again. *Of course...* Rosemary, the owner of the property and the support person for the female students, had mentioned her son several times while Brianna had been a student at the community. Rosemary had even proudly shown her some family photos, but she'd had taken little notice at the time. Now she wished she had. Caitlin grabbed her hand and drew her towards the most disturbingly attractive man she'd ever laid eyes on. As Andrew McKinnon turned around, her gaze was drawn to his hazel eyes, soft, warm, and dancing with amusement.

She averted her gaze quickly, but it was too late. He'd seen her reaction. If only the floor would open up and swallow her now.

"Brianna, is it? Nice to meet you." Goose bumps ran over her skin as the soft Scottish inflections rolled off his tongue.

She was too surprised at her reaction to do more than nod, but she had to say something. She offered him a small, shy smile. "Yes, nice to meet you, too." Her throat was tight, her voice shaky.

He extended his hand. She reluctantly reached out and took it. As their skin touched, her flesh tingled. His hand, firm and strong, was surprisingly tender, like nothing she'd felt before. The nearness of this man overwhelmed her, and she quickly withdrew her hand and stepped back.

"Did I hear you were going to Spain?" He reached behind his back and undid the apron. As he removed it, she took in his tall, athletic physique and tried to remember what Rosemary had said about him.

"Ah, ah… yes..." She was stuttering, but couldn't help herself. "I… was going with a friend, but I cancelled because of the family gathering."

"You'd love Spain. You should go one day." He hung the apron on a hook behind the door.

With his back turned, she took the opportunity to get Caitlin's attention. She needed help, but Caitlin just grinned, her eyes glinting.

"I'm going to say hello to everyone. Can you make a pot of tea, Brianna? I'm sure they'll want one after their drive."

Brianna's eyes widened. What was Caitlin doing? Surely she wouldn't leave her here alone with Andrew? Caitlin knew she wasn't any good with men.

Caitlin didn't wait for an answer. She grinned mischievously and bustled from the kitchen.

Brianna's heart raced. Caitlin had given her no choice. She'd make the tea and try not to embarrass herself, and then she'd escape. Quickly grabbing the cannister of tea from the shelf beside the window, she heaped spoonsful of the black leaves into the tea pot.

"You know your way around this kitchen." Andrew leaned back against the bench with one ankle crossed over the other and his arms folded.

Brianna swallowed hard. She'd have to tell him she used to be a student here, but as soon as she did, she'd be giving him a glimpse of her past. Only people with problems came to the community, and since his parents owned the place, he'd know that. She took a deep breath. What did it matter? God had healed her deep inside, but it was still hard talking about her past, especially with such a disturbingly handsome man. But it would come out eventually. Rosemary would no doubt say something, so she may as well get it over with.

She plopped another spoonful of tea into the pot and kept her head down. "I used to be a student here."

He angled his head. "Really?"

She wasn't sure if her answer had surprised him or not, but the tone of his voice suggested it hadn't. She nodded. "Yes, a couple of years ago."

"You'd know my mum, then."

She looked up and smiled. Her heart warmed every time she thought of the kindly Scottish woman who'd taken her under her wing on the day she arrived. "Yes, your mum helped me so much."

"She's a special lady." He picked up the large kettle whistling on the stove and poured the steaming water into the teapot.

She was acutely aware of his masculine body and cologne as he stood near her filling the pot. His closeness was both confronting and disturbing. She breathed a sigh of relief when Caitlin returned.

"They all would like tea. Andrew, would you mind taking the tray in with the cups and saucers? Will you be okay with the pot, Brianna? I'm going to call the girls."

"I'll be fine." Brianna forced a smile. Caitlin was putting her on the spot, and she knew it. What if she spilled the tea on Lizzy's mother? And Grace would notice her unease straight away. She'd poured tea hundreds of times before, *but never with a man like Andrew McKinnon by my side.*

LIZZY GLANCED up as Brianna entered the drawing room. Looking uneasy, she carried the tea pot covered with a brightly coloured tea cosy, but Andrew, hot on her heels and wearing a wide grin, appeared to be enjoying himself.

"Thanks Brianna, Andrew. Just put it on the side board. I can pour." She stood, and after they'd placed the tray and pot down, gestured for them to join her. "Andrew, come and meet everyone." She made the introductions, and then, after they'd all exchanged pleasantries, took orders. Andrew joined Ryan and her father in front of the fire, and Brianna helped distribute the cups of tea as she poured.

As she poured the last cup, Caitlin and the girls joined them, and everyone continued chatting while sipping tea and nibbling shortbread, but she kept an amused eye on Brianna and Andrew. Sparks were flying between them, and it gladdened her heart. It was beyond time Brianna had someone special in her life, but it would challenge her. In Brianna's entire thirty-four years, she was yet to have a proper relationship with a man. Raped by her cousins at age fifteen, and losing her baby at age sixteen, she'd turned to drugs. Jesus had since healed her, but she would need God's grace and strength to get close to a man. *Any man.* But from what Lizzy had seen of Andrew McKinnon, she was convinced he would be perfect for her. With his mother's gentle spirit and his own zest for life, Andrew McKinnon could be exactly what Brianna needed. *Unless he already had someone special in his life...* She'd just have to pray he didn't.

After a short while, she suggested everyone freshen up before lunch. She showed her parents to the upstairs room. Normally they would stay in the cottage, but Daniel had thought it would be fun for them all to stay in the big house, so Lizzy had prepared a room for them in the east wing, where she, Daniel, and the children would also stay.

As they climbed the spiral wooden staircase, she turned her head and smiled at them. "I'm glad you were able to make it. The children can't wait to see you. In fact, they should be here any minute." She glanced at her watch. *Where were they?*

Her mother's expression grew wistful. "It's a pity your brother couldn't make it. One of these years we'll spend Christmas all together."

"I haven't seen Jonathon since he visited briefly last year. He seems to just do his own thing, or at least that's the impression I got."

"He's so caught up in his world, I don't think anything else matters to him anymore. Especially family."

Lizzy slipped her arm around her mother's slim waist. "Don't worry, Mum, you've got us."

"Yes, but look how far away you live."

Lizzy sighed. Her mother was right, they did live a long way apart, and as much as she loved the ruggedness of the Highlands and being involved in the community, she missed being close to her parents.

Surprising, really, after all the years when she and her father could barely share a civilised word. But things had changed so much, and her father now didn't just approve of Daniel, he loved him. "Let's not think about that now."

She paused at the top of the stairs where the bunch of fresh flowers she'd bought at the local florist the day before sat on a highly polished timber dresser.

Her mother's gaze swept over the large room the students used as a lounge area. A bookcase, overflowing with books of all sorts, filled one wall, and an old piano another. Three over-sized couches, covered with lap rugs and brightly coloured cushions, faced a large open-fireplace. A large coffee table sat in the centre. Lizzy had tidied the pile of magazines the students had left behind, and they now sat neatly on one corner of the table. Board games were piled on another, and in the middle, a smaller bunch of fresh flowers.

"This is very cosy," her mother said approvingly.

"I'd forgotten you hadn't been up here before. I'll have to give you a tour, or maybe Rosemary can."

"I'd like that."

"Your room's down this way." Lizzy motioned to her left and led her parents down a long hallway lit with old-fashioned wall sconces and decorated with oil paintings and tapestries, stopping outside a door on her right which she held open for them to enter. "I hope you'll be comfortable here."

As her mother stepped inside the large guest room, her gaze travelled around the best room in the house. Lizzy had made sure everything was perfect… her parents liked nice things, and so she had gone shopping and bought an expensive, high quality duvet cover, matching pillow cases and new fluffy towels. She'd even contemplated updating the long, slightly faded drapes, but that would have been going too far. "It looks wonderful, doesn't it, Roger?" Gwyneth slipped her hand into the crook of her husband's arm and looked up at his face.

Although he gave her a warm smile, he still stood rigidly. "Perfect. Thank you, Elizabeth."

Lizzy stifled a chuckle. When would her father give in and shorten her name like everyone else did? "Great. Let me know if you need anything."

Her mother's eyes moistened as she grabbed Lizzy's hand. "Thank you, dear. It really is good to see you."

Lizzy stepped forward and gave her a big hug. "And it's good to see you, Mum. I'm sorry it's been so long."

Soon after, as Lizzy left her parents to freshen up, she checked her watch again and tried to ignore the lump growing in the pit of her stomach. *Where are they?* Daniel had called when he and Caleb arrived at the airport, but that was hours ago. She blew out a breath and hurried down the steps. *God, please keep them safe, wherever they are...*

CHAPTER 3

Daniel and Caleb and the children arrived at Inverness Airport half an hour later than planned due to the heavy fog, and were relieved to discover that the plane carrying their siblings from Belfast had also been delayed and had only just landed. They waited in the Arrivals Hall for another half an hour before the group of six emerged.

Aislin clutched her husband's hand. Alana held three-year-old Quinn's hand, and Shawn and Brendan, looking like body guards, brought up the rear. As they wandered out, their eyes scanned the crowd.

Daniel drew a breath and sent up a quick prayer. *God, please bless our time together...*

Each of his siblings had their own unique stories, but none, apart from Aislin and Alana, who'd lived together for most of their lives until Aislin had recently married her long-time boyfriend, Joel, really knew each other. Shawn was a mystery to them all, having travelled the world for most of his adult life, rarely returning to Belfast. It was a miracle he was home and had agreed to join the family for Christmas. It was also a miracle Brendan was out of jail. How would these two in particular cope with staying at a Christian community? Would they feel uncomfortable? Would there be arguments and disagreements? How much of the past would be raked through? What would these four, plus Joel, think about the other four siblings, including himself, who'd given their hearts to the Lord? Would they consider them soft and weak?

Daniel had asked God to bless their time together and trusted He'd smooth the way, but had he been too ambitious? He released his breath and raised his hand, catching Brendan's eye. Brendan nodded in acknowledgment, but his expression remained unchanged. Daniel gulped. What had he gotten himself into? Brendan was a hardened criminal who mixed with other hardened criminals, yet when he attended Da's funeral several years ago, he had a tear in his eye as the coffin was lowered into the ground. There was hope for even the toughest of criminals—no one was beyond God's saving grace, and didn't Daniel know that.

He shifted Clare to his other hip and pushed his way through the crowd. Caleb held James' hand and followed closely behind. Seven-year-old Dillon raced ahead, darting around groups of people and stopping only when Daniel called out.

The men shook hands, Daniel and Caleb kissed and hugged the girls, and Quinn clung to his mother, studying everyone with big, round eyes covered by lashes too long for a boy.

"Welcome to Scotland, everyone. Great to see you all. Thanks for coming." Daniel spoke too fast, and his chest was tight.

Caleb clapped Daniel on the back and stood beside him. "It means a lot to both of us that you've come. It really is great to see you all."

Alana's eyes misted over. She quickly wiped them with the back of her hand and pulled Quinn tighter.

Aislin smiled. "We're all glad to be here, aren't we?" Clinging to Joel's arm, she glanced at each of her siblings in turn, urging them to agree.

Brendan looked down at his shoes before raising his head, his expression softening. "Yeah, I'm glad to be here."

"I am too, I think." Shawn stood with his hands in the pockets of his red bomber jacket. Despite his years of travelling, he hadn't lost his Irish accent.

Alana just nodded. Black streaks from tears mixed with mascara ran down her cheeks.

Daniel gave her an extra hug, but if he made too much of a fuss, he too could end up in tears.

Caleb rubbed his hands together. "We'd better get moving. The fog's started to lift, but it'll still take about two hours to get home." He headed for the exit and everyone followed.

Daniel unlocked the twenty-seater community bus, and after he and Caleb stacked the suitcases in the back, they ushered everyone into their seats. Clare clung to him, wanting to sit beside him in the front. He probably should have left her at home with Lizzy, but she'd been excited to come. It was a different story now… not surprising, really. Brendan and Shawn would intimidate anyone.

"It's okay, Danny. I'll sit in the back." Caleb knew what it was like to have a shy daughter. He had two.

"Thanks, man, appreciate it."

Daniel's hopes for a drive home filled with happy chatter soon flew out the window. Engaging everyone in conversation was hard work, a lot harder than he'd expected. Aislin and Joel chatted on and off with Caleb, as did Shawn, but Brendan and Alana barely said a word. And he had to concentrate on the road.

At just under the half-way mark, when the crumbly remains of Urquhart Castle and the deep, dark waters of Loch Ness came into view on their left, Daniel rounded a corner and slammed on the brakes. A truck on its side blocked the road. The bus skidded and fish-tailed. Clare screamed. Daniel pressed harder, trying to bring it to a stop. A deathly hush filled the back of the bus. The bus stopped inches from the truck. Daniel blew out a deep breath and reached for Clare, pulling her close, comforting her, and very glad she'd been wearing a seat belt. He turned around and cast his gaze over the rest of his passengers. "Is everyone okay?"

One by one they either nodded or said quietly that they were, but all their faces were pale. He thanked God silently that no one had been hurt, but then his thoughts turned to the driver of the truck. "Clare, Daddy and Uncle Caleb have to go outside and look at the truck. Can you climb into the back with your aunties?"

"I want to stay with you, Daddy." She shot several quick glances into the back but then buried her head in Daniel's shoulder.

He gently pried her head up and looked into her eyes, wiping her damp face with his fingers. "I know, sweetheart, but it's cold outside, and I won't be long. Will you do it for me?"

Looking at him with a serious expression, she nodded. "Okay, but come back quickly."

"I will, sweetheart. Thank you." He hugged her and then helped her climb over the centre console into the back. Aislin reached out and lifted her onto the seat beside her that Joel had just vacated. Joel, Caleb, Shawn and Brendan had already jumped out and were sprinting to the truck. Daniel quickly reversed the bus away from the wreck, switched on the warning lights, and then followed them, pulling his beanie over his ears as a blast of icy wind hit him.

Approaching the truck, which lay on its side, Daniel wondered what they would find. Many years ago, when he and Lizzy had just met, he was an orderly at a hospital and had seen many traffic accident victims wheeled in with various degrees of injury, and he and Caleb had both taken emergency first-aid courses as part of their jobs at the community, but even with all that preparation and training, dread filled him. He prayed the driver had survived, but held little hope as the cab had almost completely crumpled when it hit the stone wall bordering the road.

As more people stopped at the accident, the potential danger grew. Steam hissed from the engine, and there was every possibility the truck could burst into flames any second. It was too dangerous for any of them to go inside, but Caleb and Brendan had already scaled the crumpled side and were on top. A sinking feeling, like being swept out to sea in an ebbing tide, flowed through him.

He took a moment to catch his breath as he reached Joel and Shawn who were holding people back on the other side of the truck. "Has anybody called emergency services?"

"Someone drove back to that town we just passed to make the call," Joel replied.

Daniel ran his hand over his beanie. "It'll be at least half an hour before any services can get here, if not longer. Do we know if the driver's okay?"

"Not yet. They just got up there." Joel glanced to the top of the cab where Caleb and Brendan had been moments earlier, but were no longer in sight.

"I'll go and help." As Daniel moved closer to the truck, Joel grabbed him.

"It's too dangerous, stay here. They'll call if they need help."

Daniel paused. Joel was right. What if the truck exploded? Caleb and Brendan were risking their lives up there. He prayed for their safety and returned to stand with the others. At least there wasn't another vehicle involved. He looked at the road and scratched his head. How had it happened? *Must have been speed.* But why would a local carrier, who knew the road and the conditions, speed along here, especially with visibility so low? *Crazy.*

A bang made them all jump. Daniel's heart thudded. *Oh God, please keep Caleb safe.* What would he say to Caitlin and the girls if Caleb didn't make it home? No, that wasn't going to happen. He rushed forward and started climbing. "Caleb, get out of there. It's not safe."

"He's alive, Danny. We've got to get him out." Caleb's voice was desperate.

Daniel bit his lip and continued climbing as another bang split the air. "I'm coming up." He clambered up the wrecked metal, grabbing hold of whatever he could until he reached the top and then peered in through the smashed window.

"Danny, help us get him out. Grab his head and shoulders and we'll support his body." Caleb's face, smeared with blood, wore determination like Daniel had never seen.

"Okay, let's do this." Daniel manoeuvered himself into a better position. As Caleb and Brendan carefully lifted the man up, he bore the weight of the man's upper torso until his whole body was clear. Daniel yelled down to where everyone stood. "Joel, Shawn, come and help."

The two men raced over and took the weight of the man from Daniel as Caleb and Brendan clambered out of the smashed-up cab. They laid him onto a patch of grass beside the loch moments before the truck exploded.

Daniel gazed in awe at the fireball and thanked God for His perfect timing before returning his focus to the man. His face paled. He knew him. Fraser McAdams. He lived in Fort William and his wife, Niamh, was due to give birth any day. *That's why he was speeding.* Fraser must have gotten word she was ready to deliver. "Okay, let's have some room. Is there a doctor here?"

Everyone in the gathered crowd looked at each other, but no one came forward. "What about a nurse?" Still no one stepped up. Daniel met Caleb's gaze. "Looks like it's you and me."

"We can do this." Caleb knelt down on the opposite side of the man and lowered his face. "Fraser, can you hear me?"

Fraser moaned.

"Where does it hurt?"

Fraser groaned louder.

Caleb glanced up at Daniel, the muscles in his neck taut. "We need to check his airways."

Daniel carefully tilted Fraser's head back, opened his mouth and peered inside. "Clear."

"We need to make him comfortable and stop that bleed." Caleb raised Fraser's bloodied shirt and gagged. He lowered the shirt and then looked at the crowd. "Has anyone got a towel?" His voice was desperate as he held his hands tightly over the oozing wound.

"I have," someone called out. "I'll get it."

Moments later, the person handed Daniel a towel which he folded quickly into a pad and carefully slipped under Caleb's hands to stanch the bleeding. Daniel kept pressure on the wound and prayed. Fraser couldn't bleed to death. Niamh would be devastated. Minutes ticked by until sirens sounded in the distance. Daniel breathed a sigh of relief.

A fire engine and an ambulance arrived at the same time, followed closely by a tow truck. The paramedics took over but praised Daniel and Caleb for their swift actions which most likely saved Fraser's life. They lifted him onto a stretcher and into the ambulance and whisked him off to the hospital. The fire fighters took another twenty minutes to fully extinguish the blaze, and it took two tow trucks almost an hour to right the wrecked vehicle and get it onto one of them before the road was re-opened.

Almost two hours after their trip was interrupted, the men headed back to the bus to re-join Aislin, Alana and the children, who were huddled together with blankets wrapped around them watching the proceedings from a safe distance.

Clare ran towards Daniel. When she stopped, she looked up at him, her eyes big, round and full of concern. "Will the man be okay, Daddy?"

His heart melted. Bending down, he rested one knee on the ground to level his face with hers. "Yes, sweetheart. The doctors will fix him and make him better."

"Can we ask God to help, too?"

"That's a great idea. Shall we do that now?"

Clare nodded, thumb in mouth.

"Would you like to pray?"

"Okay." As Clare bowed her head, Daniel placed his hand on her shoulder to steady himself and then bowed his head, too. Clare's little voice was so sweet. "Dear God, please help the man get better before Christmas so he can be home with his family when Santa comes. Thank you that Daddy was able to help him. Amen."

Daniel added his own request. "And dear God, please be with the man's wife as she brings their new little baby into the world."

Clare's head shot up. "Are they getting a baby for Christmas?"

Daniel laughed. "You could say that."

"Can we get a baby for Christmas, too?"

"Not this year, sweetheart."

"Next year?"

"Maybe." Standing, he ruffled her hair and took her hand. "We need to go home now. Mummy will be wondering where we are."

"Okay." She smiled sweetly as they walked back to the others.

"Would you like me to drive?" Shawn asked as Daniel approached.

"That would be super, thanks." Clapping him on the back, Daniel gave him a grateful smile.

Brendan joined Shawn in the front, while Daniel joined the children in the back. He wasn't sure what had happened, but everyone seemed closer. Maybe witnessing such a terrible accident had made them appreciate their own lives and family more than before. Whatever it was, he felt blessed to be surrounded by his family, and thanked God for bringing them all together.

CHAPTER 4

When the bus pulled up outside the main building, Lizzy dashed outside with Caitlin right behind her. They'd heard about the accident near the castle on the news and figured Daniel and Caleb and the others had been caught up in it. Everyone back at the community had been relieved it was a truck, and not a bus that had crashed, and then immediately Lizzy and Caitlin felt guilty. When they heard the injured man was Fraser McAdams, they felt even worse. His wife, Niamh, belonged to their Wednesday Bible study group, and they'd heard she was in the early stages of labour. They'd all gathered together and prayed for both her and Fraser, and had been waiting eagerly for Daniel and Caleb to return with the rest of the family.

As Daniel climbed out of the side door of the bus with Clare's arms wrapped around his neck, Lizzy's heart filled with gratitude—it could so easily have been them. She quickly closed the gap between them and threw her arms around Daniel. He reeked of smoke, grease and dried blood, but she didn't care. She held him close and pushed back the tears stinging her eyes. "Thank God you're all safe. We were so worried." She leaned into his chest before pulling back and looking into his eyes. "Will Fraser be all right?"

"We prayed for him, Mummy." Clare reached out and twiddled a strand of Lizzy's hair.

"That's wonderful, Clare. I'm sure God will look after him."

"And Daddy said they're getting a baby for Christmas!"

Lizzy fought the urge to laugh. "Yes, they *are* getting a baby for Christmas. Let's pray Fraser will be home before it comes."

"Is Santa bringing it?"

Lizzy gently shook her head as she touched Clare's cheek. "Not really, but let's talk about that later, okay?"

"Okay."

She and Daniel had debated about whether to tell the children the truth about Santa or not, but hadn't been able to agree. He couldn't see the harm in letting the children find out in their own time, but Lizzy wanted to tell them, and moments like this just confirmed to her they should.

Daniel kissed the top of her head and then eased himself from her arms. "Everyone's okay, love, that's the main thing. And we've got guests to think of now."

He was right. They could have this conversation later. She smiled into his eyes and then turned to greet the family. After everyone hugged and kissed, she and Daniel led them inside and introduced her parents to the family from Ireland. Grace and Brianna hugged their brothers and sisters, and then everyone sat down for a cup of tea and a chat.

Lizzy kept an amused eye on Brianna and Andrew. Brianna sat on the couch beside Aislin and Alana, but every now and then she shot a coy glance at Andrew, who was talking with Ryan, Brendan, Shawn and Daniel. And every now and then, Andrew shot a glance at her, but their eyes never met. Maybe they needed a little help after all. She'd sit them together tonight at dinner.

After everyone had finished their tea, Caitlin and Lizzy took the new arrivals upstairs and settled them into their rooms. Lizzy wondered how Brendan and Shawn would cope living so close to everyone, but then, these accommodations would be luxury compared to a jail cell, and Shawn would be used to bunking down with others, so she quickly put her concerns to rest.

She excused herself after a while. Daniel had taken the children to their rooms, and although he was more than capable of looking after them, she wanted to make sure they were all okay after witnessing the accident. "Feel free to take a wander around, have a rest, whatever you like. Dinner will be at six in the main dining area. Call out if you need anything before then."

"We'll be fine, Lizzy. We're all big people and can look after ourselves." Grace said, lifting her gaze from the magazine she'd been flicking through as she sat on one of the couches in front of the fire. She leaned against Ryan with her long legs elegantly crossed on the coffee table.

Lizzy laughed. Grace would never have done that in her fancy apartment. How far she'd come to be so relaxed. "I know, I'm sorry. We just want everyone to have a nice time."

"And we will. Off you go and look after your family." Grace dismissed her with a wave of her hand and a playful grin.

"Thank you." Lizzy chuckled as she headed down the hallway with a plate of freshly baked gingerbread men to where the laughter and giggles of happy children, *and Daniel,* spilled out of the room next to her parents. Hopefully putting them so close wasn't a mistake.

BRIANNA WAS SHARING a room with Alana and Quinn. That morning, when she'd arrived with Grace and Ryan, Lizzy had asked if she minded staying in her old room, the room she'd shared with Susan and Maggie when she'd arrived at Elim Community as a suicidal drug addict more than two years ago. The room hadn't changed a bit. It was still as cozy and lovely as it had been on the day she first saw it, and the view of the mountains, still shrouded in mist, took her breath away. Living in the city, she missed the mountains—she'd never thought she would, but there was something special about them… calming, yet at the same time, awe-inspiring. Brianna had already unpacked, and now she sat on the chair with Quinn on her lap while Alana unpacked.

She hardly knew Alana. When all the siblings had been separated after Mam died, Brianna and Grace, ages ten and twelve, were sent to Londonderry to stay with Aunt Hilda, but Aislin and Alana, the two youngest girls, stayed in Belfast with another aunt and uncle. Now, more than twenty years later, they were both adults. Brianna looked at her younger sister and saw a lifetime of sadness in her eyes. Working with rape victims every day, Brianna had come to know a lot about the human heart, and how if someone said they were okay, often their eyes told a different story. Alana may not have been raped, but she was hurting, and Brianna's heart wept for her. Maybe God had put them together so she could share God's love with Alana, just like Rosemary had shared His love with her not that not long ago in this very room.

Brianna pulled Quinn closer. Holding him made her think of her own little son who'd died when he was only two months old. Even after all this time, she still felt the pain of loss, but it wasn't as fresh anymore. God had healed the bitterness and hurt she'd carried for many years, but if she wanted Alana to feel comfortable with her, Brianna had to earn her trust, and as painful as it might be, sharing the part of her life that Alana would relate to might help.

"Quinn's a beautiful little boy. You must be proud of him." Brianna's smile shifted from him to Alana.

Alana looked up from her suitcase, her face splitting into a wide grin. "He's the best thing that's happened in my life."

"I had a son…" Brianna's smile slipped as she took a slow breath.

Alana angled her head, her forehead creasing. "I didn't know that. What happened to him?"

Brianna's tears were just below the surface as the memory of her beautiful little boy returned. "Aedan died of pneumonia when he was two months old."

Alana sat on the bed and lifted her gaze. "I'm sorry. That must have been horrible."

"It was a long time ago, but yes, it was." Brianna closed her eyes for a moment, remembering the last time she held Aedan, just moments before he died.

"Were you ..." Alana's voice trailed away.

Brianna grimaced. "Raped?" She mouthed the word so Quinn wouldn't hear it.

Alana nodded, her eyes wide.

"How did you know?"

Alana shrugged and looked down at her hands, fidgeting with them. "I kind of guessed, you working at that Rape Centre and all." She looked up, her eyes sad.

Brianna released a deep sigh. "It was all such a long time ago, and I try not to think about it much, although it's hard not to, considering where I work."

"I don't know what I'd do if I lost Quinn." Alana reached out and squeezed Quinn's hand, her eyes moistening.

"What happened to his father?" It was a risk asking, but if Alana didn't want to talk, that was fine.

She lowered her gaze and picked at her nails. "He left when I was seven months pregnant. He said being a father scared him." She raised her head. "Being a mother scared me to bits, but I didn't have a choice. I thought he was excited about having a baby. He was at the beginning. We'd been together for a long time. I obviously didn't know him as well as I thought I did."

"Where is he now?"

Tears filled Alana's eyes. "Living with some chick on the other side of the city."

Brianna quickly moved beside Alana and wrapped an arm around her shoulder, pulling her close. Quinn wriggled onto the floor and stood in front of his mother, looking up at her with enlarged eyes.

Alana reached out, and sitting him on her lap, pulled him close. "I love you, Quinny. Mummy's okay. Don't worry." As she rocked him and kissed the top of his dark, wavy hair, her voice choked.

Brianna prayed silently for them as she held Alana tight. *Dear Lord, please help me show Your love to Alana and Quinn. She's hurting so much. Please help her open her heart to You this Christmas, dear Lord, and give her new life full of hope and peace. Please bless her, dear Lord.* Brianna wiped her eyes, and straightening, she rubbed Alana's back and put on a happy face. "Come on, I'll help you unpack, and then maybe we can take a walk now the fog's lifted."

Alana brushed her eyes with the back of her hand and nodded. "I'd like that."

Shortly after, dressed in warm coats and walking boots, Brianna, Alana and Quinn headed outside. The top of Ben Nevis was still covered in low-lying clouds, but the sky had cleared to a pale blue, and the sun, although low on the horizon, shone weakly on Loch Linnhe, drawing them to the water's edge. Several row boats, tied securely to the jetty, bobbed up and down in the gentle waves, making a splashing noise.

Quinn's face lit up. "Can we go for a ride?"

"It's a bit too cold, Quinny. Maybe tomorrow," Alana replied.

Quinn's little face fell and his bottom lip protruded in a pout. "I'm not cold."

Alana laughed. "Yes, you are. Your lips are blue and they're quivering."

"I think we need to play chasings to warm up," Brianna said as she began to run. "I bet you can't catch me," she called over her shoulder.

Quinn let go of Alana's hand and chased after Brianna, giggling when he caught her.

Brianna laughed. "You're such a fast runner. Okay, let's see if we can catch you."

Quinn took off, squealing and laughing. Within moments, Dillon and James came racing down from the big house. "Can we play too?" Dillon called out.

"Sure." Brianna stopped and pressed her hand to her chest. She'd just caught her breath when she felt, rather than heard, footsteps stop behind her. Her heart thumped. Somehow, she knew who it was—or did she just hope it was Andrew?

"Mind if I join in?" His voice held a trace of laughter and sent a tingle down her spine.

Her heart pounded, but not from running. She turned around and met Andrew's twinkling eyes. "Sure. You can be it." She tore her gaze away and called out to the children. "Hey, everyone, Andrew's it. See if you can catch him."

Andrew's athleticism amazed Brianna. He dodged James and Quinn, and outran Dillon. He laughed when she tried to catch hold of his coat as he zipped past, teasing her. Alana was the clever one, waiting for him to turn his back before leaping towards him and slapping him on the back.

It heartened Brianna to see Alana join in. The fresh, crisp air of the Highlands would do her good, just as it had done her not that long ago.

After a few more turns, they all collapsed onto the damp grass and caught their breath, but within minutes, the children wandered down to the edge of the loch.

"Don't get your boots wet, Quinny," Alana called out.

"You either, Dillon and James," Brianna called as loudly as she could.

Andrew chuckled. "Leave them be… they're boys."

"Yes, but they can still get sick." Brianna turned her head and met his gaze. Her pulse quickened.

"They'll be fine... leave them be." His gaze locked on hers.

She gulped. She'd never expected a man to affect her like this. Could she open her heart just a little and see what might happen? She'd witnessed both good and bad relationships. More bad than good if she were honest, but Danny and Lizzy, Caleb and Caitlin, and Grace and Ryan were all happy. Could she dare hope that she might also find happiness and love? Was it asking too much?

Brianna drew her gaze away and focused on the boys sploshing in the mud. There was only one way to find out, but the thought scared her to death. She'd convinced herself she would never get close to any man—it wasn't worth the risk. But now? Did she dare let her guard down just a fraction and see what might eventuate? The thought both thrilled and terrified her.

CHAPTER 5

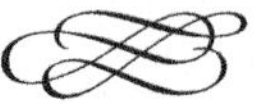

Brianna's long wavy hair, bouncing softly on her shoulders, mesmerized Andrew as she walked ahead of him into the dining room that evening, but he couldn't stop his gaze drifting to her shapely figure. Snug plaid trousers and a cream cashmere sweater accentuated not only the brilliance of her hair, but her very attractive figure. He inhaled her sweet perfume wafting in the air, but then pulled himself up. Brianna was gorgeous, but he couldn't fall for her. What was he thinking? He had far greater things to deal with right now... but maybe it wouldn't hurt to spend a little time with her. She seemed different from the shallow, vain girls he mixed with—a downfall of his job. Apart from her looks, her fragility and tenderness attracted him. There was depth to Brianna O'Connor. If nothing else, she could be a good friend.

Brianna's eyes widened as he darted ahead and pulled the heavy wooden chair out for her. She gave him a shy nod and thanked him demurely. When she sat, she looked straight ahead with her hands folded in her lap. Her sister, Grace, and brother-in-law, Ryan, took the seats opposite. Her brother, Shawn, sat on Andrew's left. Andrew smiled when his parents took the seats beside Lizzy's parents at the top end of the long table.

He could easily feel like a gate-crasher. When he agreed to spend Christmas with his folks, he hadn't realised it actually meant spending it with the O'Connor family as well, but at least he'd have time to think. *And pray.* He released a sigh and pulled his thoughts back to the present. Time enough for that later.

Grace began chatting with Brianna, asking her about her afternoon. Grace, with hair much darker than Brianna's, was also a looker, but she was classy, sophisticated. Andrew had heard she'd been a lawyer. He was just about to join their conversation when Ryan caught his eye. "What do you do for a living, Andrew?" Ryan asked.

Andrew tore his attention from Brianna and Grace and answered Ryan. Before long, Ryan drew Shawn into the conversation, and within moments, they were chatting like best friends, especially when Andrew discovered both men had also travelled extensively.

Soon after, Brianna's older brother, Daniel stood at the head of the table and dinged a glass. "Can I have everyone's attention, please?"

Hush fell around the table as everyone turned their attention to him. He flashed an engaging smile as he cleared his throat. "I'd like to officially welcome you all. It's fantastic you could all come, and Lizzy and I are really looking forward to spending time with every one of you. Christmas is a season of celebration, and I'm so glad we can finally celebrate it together after all these years. Without any more ado, let's give thanks for this wonderful meal that my beautiful wife and sister-in-law have prepared." Daniel slipped his hand onto Lizzy's shoulder, sharing a smile with her before bowing his head to pray.

Andrew felt, rather than saw, Shawn shift uncomfortably in his seat. Giving thanks obviously wasn't something he was used to. Andrew could understand that. Although his parents were devout Christians, for many years he'd rejected the message of the gospel and felt uncomfortable when anyone gave thanks at the meal table. Shawn and the others would get plenty of that here. He hoped they'd cope, and that maybe their hearts might open a little to God's love over this festive period.

Once Daniel finished praying, Lizzy and Caitlin stood and headed for the kitchen. Andrew excused himself and joined them, reappearing moments later with trays of the shepherd's pie and vegetables they'd prepared that morning, placing the dishes at intervals along the table.

"Please help yourselves," Lizzy said as she placed a steaming dish of the pie in front of her parents.

Retaking his seat, Andrew picked up the server and cast his gaze around those nearby. "Can I dish out for everyone?"

Grace chuckled as she held her plate out. "You can be my mother any day."

He laughed. Surely she wasn't flirting? He scooped a medium-sized portion from the dish and placed it carefully onto her plate. "More?"

A mischievous grin brightened Grace's face. "Thank you, that's plenty."

Andrew then turned to Brianna. When their eyes met his heart-rate increased, and for a moment, he forgot to speak, her eyes mesmerising him until she averted her gaze. He blinked and shifted in his seat. "Can I dish up for you, too, Brianna?" He spoke softly.

Lifting her gaze, she gave him another shy smile and held up her plate. "Yes, please."

As he spooned a similar-sized portion onto her plate, he stole a glance at her full mouth and her long, slender neck. She was truly beautiful. He cleared his throat. "Is that enough?"

"Yes, thank you." Her eyes lingered on his for a moment before she lowered them, her long, dark eyelashes fluttering.

He continued serving, but Brianna's delicate features were indelibly imprinted in his mind. When he finished serving everyone else, Andrew served himself and then paused before he began eating. All around him, chatter continued as people interspersed eating with talking. Ryan and Shawn discussed Shawn's adventures in Africa, and Grace talked with

Brianna and Alana, seated on Brianna's other side, about recent happenings in Belfast. He tried listening to both conversations, but ended up chatting with the men. Just being near Brianna was enough. For now.

~

LATER, following dessert, Brianna offered to help with the dishes on the off-chance that Andrew might offer his help as well. All through dinner she'd been wanting to talk with him, but didn't know how. She stood and began collecting the dirty dishes, her heart racing when he did the same. Grace and Ryan followed them to the kitchen, loaded with dirty dessert bowls and coffee mugs. The others adjourned to the main lounge area while Lizzy and Alana put the younger children to bed.

Brianna stacked the dishes ready for washing as Andrew filled one of the sinks with water. His nearness made her senses spin… she could easily drop the dishes if she wasn't careful.

"Tell me about yourself," Andrew said, as his eyes, gentle and soft, found hers.

Brianna laughed nervously, averting her gaze. "There's not much to tell."

His mouth tipped in a smile as he thrust his hands into the hot water. "I'm sure there is."

She blew out a frustrated breath, annoyed with herself. Grace and Ryan were chatting together at the other sink, and she'd gotten what she wanted—the chance to talk with Andrew. She talked easily with the women who came into the Rape Centre, but something about this man left her tongue-tied. It was silly. She had to pull herself together. Another opportunity like this might never come along. "You're right, but I don't know where to start." She grabbed a tea-towel and began wiping the dishes.

Andrew paused for a moment and looked at her with kind, understanding eyes. "Well, tell me where you live and what you do. That's a good place to start."

His easy-going manner relaxed her a little. The first question she could answer, but the second? Brianna swallowed hard and decided not to be embarrassed about what she did. Why should she be? He already knew she'd been a student here. "Okay, then. I live in Glasgow with a girlfriend, Susan. She was the one I was going to Spain with."

"How long have you lived in Glasgow?" His soft Scottish burr calmed her, but her gaze settled on his arms. Elbow high in water, ginger hairs glistened on his fair skin like gold sparkling in sunlight. She blinked and lifted her gaze. "Going on three years. Ever since I left the community."

"And what do you do in Glasgow?"

Brianna stiffened. It was the question she'd been dreading. Inhaling slowly, she picked up another bowl and began wiping it. "I work with Grace at a support centre called the Place of Hope."

"Really? With Grace?" His head tilted.

"Yes, with Grace. We started the centre when I left here." She paused. "It's a Rape Support Centre." Brianna held her breath while she waited for Andrew's reaction.

He didn't flinch. He just looked at her, eyes soft. "I wasn't expecting that. It must be a hard job."

Brianna released her breath and nodded. "We see some really sad cases."

He stopped washing and leaned back against the sink, drying his arms before folding them. "How do you manage?" His tone, filled with awe, surprised her further. But then, she shouldn't have been surprised—Rosemary had the same caring, gentle nature.

"I try not to bring it home, but it's hard not to. Some of the stories just stay with you, it doesn't matter what you do." She shrugged, trying not to meet his gaze, hoping he wouldn't ask the obvious question.

"I can understand that."

"I pray for them all, and I do things to get my mind off it. We try to take a break every few weeks. Grace makes sure we do that." Brianna let out a small, nervous chuckle as she glanced at her sister.

"Where do you go?"

"Mainly here to visit Danny and Lizzy." Brianna picked up another dish and held his gaze. "So now it's your turn. Tell me about you."

Andrew's face flickered before a playful grin lifted the corners of his mouth. "I wondered when we'd get to that." He turned back to the sink, but his voice had grown serious. Was he hiding something?

Brianna studied his back. "I should have made you go first."

"I'm surprised you didn't."

Why hadn't she thought of that? Too late now. She angled her head. "So?"

"Not much to tell."

Brianna shook her head, her mouth curving into a smile. "Really, I've heard that before."

Andrew chuckled. "Yes, you have. Okay, well, I grew up here, in this house, but when I was nineteen, I went travelling. I wanted to see the world."

"Where did you go?"

"Just about everywhere."

"Like Shawn."

"Yes, like Shawn."

"How long did you travel for?"

"Three years."

"Wow. I'm lucky if I get away for two days."

"You should try it sometime. Travel widens your horizons."

"I was going to Spain, remember?"

"That's right, you were." Andrew stopped washing and looked deep into her eyes, sending her heart-rate flying. "You should go in the spring. It's lovely then."

Brianna's heart thudded as the thought of going with him flitted through her mind. She bit her lip. How could she be even thinking that?

She barely knew him, but a longing she'd never felt before took hold within her. *To be close to a man*. It had always frightened her, but she'd never met anyone like Andrew McKinnon. Could God help her to open her heart after all this time? She fought to regain her composure. "I might just do that." She held his gaze, unable to tear away, her heart pounding with a warmth she'd never felt before.

"Hey you two. Have you finished?"

Brianna's eyes widened and she felt her face flush. Grace had caught them staring at each other. She immediately faced the sink and continued wiping the dish in her hand, trying to steady her heart-rate. "Almost." Her voice came out high and shaky.

"Well, we're done. We'll leave you to it."

Brianna glanced over her shoulder. Grace's grin caused her cheeks to flush a second time. "Okay…"

Once Grace and Ryan left, Brianna and Andrew glanced at each other and burst into laughter. His eyes twinkled, and for a long moment they looked at each other and smiled in earnest. "Come on, let's finish up and find a cosy corner to chat."

Was this really happening, or was she dreaming?

CHAPTER 6

Andrew chose a corner in the drawing room near the fire, and he and Brianna talked for hours, drinking copious amounts of hot chocolate while Christmas carols played in the background and the others chatted and played games. The more she learned of him, the more she was drawn to him. She surprised herself and told him about her rape and the baby she lost, her years of drug addiction, and then how his mother, Rosemary, had led her to the Lord, right here, in the Elim Community.

In his soft Scottish brogue, Andrew told her about the years he'd spent away from the Lord, and how close he'd come to getting drawn into the world of drugs and alcohol, but something had stopped him—he believed it was God and the prayers of his parents.

He told her about the walk he did in Spain, where he met God for real. Brianna decided she'd like to do it herself. It sounded awesome, hiking through small villages and across huge mountains. But not alone—*with him.* Andrew exuded all the qualities she could ever want in a man but had never expected to find. Soft-spoken, kind and gentle, and so good-looking. And his job… chef in one of the fanciest restaurants in Glasgow! Not a restaurant she'd ever been to, but she'd heard about it. It was the place people went to for special occasions, where the meals were amazing. But above everything, *he loved God.* And it seemed he liked her… a lot, which made her heart sing. But was it right? Was she racing ahead? Was it what God wanted for her? And there was also the feeling that he was keeping something from her.

As Brianna lay in bed later that night, her heart danced with excitement and anticipation, sleep eluding her as images of Andrew McKinnon played through her mind. But when sleep finally came, her soul was filled with peace. If this was meant to be, she had no doubt that God would lead and guide her.

The following morning, Brianna woke with a start. Someone was staring at her, touching her… Her eyes snapped open, her heart racing, and then she laughed. "Quinn, what are you doing?"

"Mummy won't wake up." His voice was so little, and his dark eyes were round and anxious.

Brianna shivered as she sat. The first hint of daylight peeked through the gap in the curtains. Slipping her gown over her shoulders, she glanced at the clock on her nightstand. Seven a.m. Nothing to worry about, but Quinn obviously was concerned.

"Come and sit up here with me, Quinny. Mummy's just asleep, that's all." Brianna hoped that was all—surely Alana hadn't taken anything? Her brows pinched together. *But what if she had?* She should have spent the evening with her sister, not with Andrew. What had she been thinking? But the thought of Andrew's soft voice and caring eyes sent her heart spinning afresh.

Quinn climbed onto the bed, snuggling close.

Brianna put her arm around the little boy, smoothing his messed-up hair and placing a kiss on top, surprising herself at how natural it felt. "Does Mummy often sleep in?"

Quinn nodded.

"What do you normally do when you wake up?"

"I look at her until she opens her eyes."

Brianna's heart melted. She hated to think how long he stood there.

"Mummy must get tired. I'm sure she'll wake up soon."

"Can you read me a story?" Lifting his head, Quinn looked at her with anticipation.

"Sure. Have you got a book?"

"Yes, I'll go get it." Slipping out from under her arm and onto the floor, he ran around the divider into the partitioned off area he shared with his mum. While he looked, Brianna also poked her head around the divider to allay any fears about Alana. From what she saw, Alana was just asleep. Moments later, Quinn stood up with several books in his hand, and they both returned to Brianna's bed.

"Which one would you like me to read?"

He looked at each of them in turn, and then held up a well-worn copy of *The Poky Little Puppy*.

Memories of Mam reading this very same book to her and Grace when they were little flashed through Brianna's mind. *Surely it's not the actual book?* She quickly flicked it open to the inside front cover and her jaw dropped. Her name, scrawled in messy hand-writing, confirmed it was. Tears welled in her eyes as she lifted a finger and ran it over the scrawl. It seemed like just yesterday she was snuggling close to Mam. She could hear Mam's soft, gentle voice reading the story, feel Mam's arm around her... it wasn't fair that she'd died so young. Brianna sucked in a breath and brushed at her eyes.

Alana and Aislin had been even younger than she and Grace when they all got separated. They probably didn't even remember Mam. What had it been like for them to be sent away at such a young age? Brianna shuddered as she recalled the years she and Grace spent at Aunt Hilda's and prayed that Aislin and Alana had fared better, but somehow, doubted it.

Renewed compassion grew in her heart for her younger sisters,

Alana in particular. Only God had saved Brianna from the self-destructive path she'd taken, and only God could heal the deep-seated hurts Alana carried. More prayer was needed.

"Auntie, are you going to read?" Quinn looked up again as he pulled on Brianna's arm, bringing her back to the present.

She hugged him. "Sorry, Quinny. Let's start." Locating page one, she began reading the words she knew so well.

"Five little puppies dug a hole under the fence and went for a walk in the wide, wide world. Through the meadow they went, down the road, over the bridge, across the green grass, and up the hill, one after the other..."

Immersed in the story, Brianna didn't notice Alana leaning against the wall until Quinn held his arms out and asked her to join them.

Smiling, Brianna patted the empty space on the bed. "Come on, Alana, come and join us."

Alana hesitated for a moment, but then walked to the bed and perched on the edge.

Quinn scrambled up and threw his arms around her neck.

"Quinny, be careful or you'll knock Mummy off the bed."

Alana gave a small chuckle as she hugged him. "He's okay. I love my morning cuddles." She rested her head against his and smiled at Brianna. "Thanks for reading to him." Her voice was soft but hoarse.

"You're welcome. I'm glad you had a lie in."

Alana nodded. "I don't get much of a break now that Aislin's married."

"You must miss her."

Alana nibbled her lower lip. "Yes. We've never been apart until now."

"Much like Grace and me." Brianna rubbed Alana's arm, the sadness in Alana's eyes tugging at her heart. "You'll have to tell me what it was like growing up, but later." She nodded her head towards Quinn.

Alana sniffed and gave Brianna a small, grateful smile.

"I can hear noises downstairs. We'd best go down."

Alana blew her nose and nodded before lifting Quinn's head off her chest. She gently brushed the hair off his forehead and looked into his eyes. "Ready for breakfast, Quinny?"

"Can we finish the book first?" He looked at her with pleading eyes.

She hugged him to her chest, rocking him like a baby. "Later. Okay?"

"Okay." His voice was so sweet, so innocent.

Alana stood and placed Quinn on the floor. Taking his hand, she turned and gave Brianna a nod. "We'll be ready in a few minutes."

Brianna gave her a warm smile. "No hurry."

BRIANNA SAT on her bed and bowed her head, her heart heavy with compassion for Alana. She knew what it was like to be lonely, and she prayed her sister might find peace and love, just like she had when she met Jesus. Rising from her bed, she slipped on a soft-pink cashmere sweater and her favourite pair of jeans, brushed her hair, and applied a little blusher and lip-stick. Her mind drifted to Andrew as she dressed and her heart skittered, but then she grew guilty for thinking about him after seeing how deeply lonely Alana was. But only God could truly fill the empty vacuum in a person's heart. The prospect of being loved by someone special was exciting, but faded in comparison to being loved by God. She prayed Alana might come to know that truth for herself.

Shortly after, Brianna, Alana and Quinn headed downstairs for breakfast, each woman taking one of Quinn's hands as they descended the steps. He wanted to be swung, but Alana told him it would be too dangerous, so he just walked down between them. By the time they arrived, just about everybody else was seated at the long table eating breakfast and chatting.

Caitlin looked up from her position near the door and waved them forward, her face jolly as always. "Come in, come in. There's coffee and tea on the sideboard, as well as cereal and toast. Fresh eggs are coming in a moment."

"I'm happy with tea and toast, thanks." Brianna smiled as she headed for the sideboard, but her gaze darted around the table until it connected briefly with Andrew's. She gave him a small nod before turning her attention to the toast and tea, but she couldn't help the tingle of excitement rippling through her.

She poured tea for herself and for Alana, and then popped a piece of pre-cooked toast onto a plate before heading for the vacant seat beside Andrew, surprising herself with her forwardness.

"Good morning. Sleep well?" His soft burr and warm eyes made her heart skitter afresh.

"Yes, and you?"

His eyes twinkled. "Och aye, I fell asleep with a sweet lassie on my mind."

Brianna giggled. The only other person who'd ever called her 'lassie' was Andrew's mother, and she loved the way it rolled off his tongue.

As she sipped her tea, Danny stood, rubbing his hands briskly together. "Good morning, everyone. Hope you all slept well."

Generally favourable responses moved around the table.

"Great to hear. I've got two pieces of good news for you. The first one is that Fraser McAdams is stable in Glasgow Hospital, and his wife gave birth to a healthy baby boy last night. She's been transferred to Glasgow Hospital to be near him."

Audible relief shifted from person to person.

"And here's some other good news… snow fell on the mountains last night, so skiing will definitely be on the agenda for today."

Once again, everyone reacted positively, apart from Brendan. He leaned back in his chair, folded his arms, and stared at Daniel. "I'd rather go to the pub." Silence fell around the table as all eyes turned to him. It was almost like he was laying down a challenge.

Daniel didn't react. Instead, he just shrugged. "Suit yourself, but we'd like you to come." He sipped his coffee, making a slurping noise, then wrapped his hands around his mug as he glanced out the window. "Should be a good day, although the weather can change at any time. I suggest we head off as soon as we can and make the most of the day, given how short it is this time of year. There's gear in the storeroom for anyone who wants to try their hand at skiing. Otherwise, just grab some thick jackets. If the wind picks up, it can get freezing up there."

"Sounds great, Danny," Grace said, shooting a severe look at Brendan as she pushed her chair back. If anyone could take him on, it would be Grace. "Brendan should be on dishes if he's not coming."

He sighed. "I'll come. I was just stirring."

"Good. But you can still do the dishes." Grace's tone of voice left no room for argument.

"I'll help," Shawn said as he began gathering the dirty plates.

Brianna watched everyone interact as she finished her tea. Not much had changed since they were all children, sparring in the kitchen together at meal times. Grace had always been the boss, and she still was. A tinge of sadness washed over her as she thought about all those lost years. But they were together now, and somehow, they'd all survived. Now she was beginning to feel glad she hadn't gone to Spain after all. She did know them... they were her siblings, her family.

Within half an hour, everyone was ready to leave. Andrew was waiting by the bus for Brianna when she arrived from upstairs with Alana and Quinn. It amazed her how every time his gaze met hers, her heart turned over in response. She gave him a smile and joined him as they climbed into the bus. Despite the cold, she felt wrapped in an invisible warmth as she sat beside him for the short journey to Aonach Mor.

CHAPTER 7

As Brianna sat in the bus with Andrew beside her, Ben Nevis had never looked so majestic. Covered in snow, the bare slopes of the huge mountain dominated the horizon, but it was Aonach Mor, just two peaks from Ben Nevis, they were headed for. In the seat in front, Quinn jiggled on Alana's lap and peeked over her shoulder, smiling coyly at Brianna. When she returned his smile and reached out, tapping the tip of his nose, he giggled and her heart warmed.

Daniel brought the bus to a stop in the parking area already filled with tourist coaches and motorhomes. Everyone stood and began filing out. Brianna's heart missed a beat when Andrew placed his hand briefly on the small of her back as she slipped past him.

Although she wore her thick winter jacket, she shivered when a blast of bitter wind buffeted her as she stepped out of the bus. The Cairngorm range, with snowy peaks towering all around, was much colder than Glasgow.

She smiled when Dillon ran up to Andrew, taking his hand and chatting excitedly as they approached the ticket booth. Andrew didn't seem to mind—in fact, by the way he chatted back, he seemed to enjoy the interaction.

With the tickets bought, they all joined the line of people waiting to catch a gondola up the mountain to the ski fields and restaurant. Daniel allowed everyone to go ahead of him and stood with Andrew and Dillon at the rear. Aislin, Joel, Grace, Ryan, Brendan and Shawn hopped into the first gondola. Caleb, Caitlin and their two girls climbed into the second one. Lizzy, James, Clare, and Lizzy's parents were next in line, leaving Daniel, Andrew, Dillon, Alana, Quinn, and Brianna in the last one.

Daniel motioned for her, Alana, and Quinn to enter first. Brianna followed them in and sat beside Alana. Andrew climbed in and sat directly opposite. Their eyes briefly met, and as they shared a smile, her pulse skittered alarmingly. She'd never seen a man look so good in a hand-knitted beanie and matching scarf. As the gondola jerked and began its journey upwards, she swivelled in her seat to look at the magnificent view, but every now and then her gaze found Andrew's, and each time, a quiver surged through her.

The ride only took fifteen minutes. When the gondola reached the top station and they all began to exit, Brianna tripped and almost lost her footing. Strong hands on her arms steadied her. She turned around to offer her thanks, but as she looked into Andrew's eyes, her voice caught and all she could do was offer a coy grin.

Andrew struggled to tear his gaze away from Brianna and listen to Dillon after they exited the gondola. Her shyness and innocence mesmerised him, but Dillon tugged on his sleeve, pulling his attention away. He looked down at the little boy as Brianna walked ahead and joined Grace and Ryan.

"Can you take me skiing, Andrew?" Dillon grabbed his hand and dragged him to the fence where skiers were lining up for the chair lift.

"We'll have to talk to your dad about that. Have you skied before?"

Dillon nodded enthusiastically. "Dad took me last year."

Andrew grinned. "I bet you were good."

"I fell over three times, but I didn't get hurt. Can you take me, please?" He jumped up and down on the spot.

Andrew ruffled Dillon's hair and chuckled. "If you dad says yes, I'll be happy to."

Dillon whooped. "I'll go ask him."

As the boy dashed off to find Daniel, Andrew headed back to the group, his gaze searching for Brianna. When he found her, for a long moment he studied her, drinking in her rosy cheeks and full lips as she crouched in the snow, busily making a snowman with Quinn while everyone else stood around discussing their options. He'd never seen anything so beautiful.

Dillon waved Andrew over to where he was trying to get Daniel's attention. Andrew was torn. He wanted to join Brianna, but didn't want to let Dillon down. He shouldn't have promised. Blowing out a breath, he joined him and Daniel.

Daniel looked up as Andrew approached. "So, I believe Dillon's asked you to take him skiing." Daniel patted the little boy's shoulder. "Don't worry, I'll take him. I'm sure you don't want to be stuck on the beginner slopes."

"I don't mind, really." But that wasn't true… he'd rather build a snowman. He could go skiing anytime he wanted.

Daniel shrugged. "I wouldn't mind going on the red run with the others, so maybe we can take it in turns?"

Andrew bit his lip. "Sure. You go now, I'll go later."

"Thanks. Just keep an eye on him. He thinks he's better than he is." He winked at Dillon and clapped Andrew on the back before moving off to the chairlift with Grace, Ryan, Caleb and Shawn.

A few members of the group left for the beginner slopes, while others headed to the restaurant for hot chocolate and shortbread. Lizzy had joined Brianna and Quinn in the snow, as had James, Clare and Alana. Lizzy motioned for Dillon to join them. "Come on, Dillon, we're making snowmen. Come and join us so Andrew can go skiing."

Brianna looked up with a puzzled but pleased expression. She'd obviously expected him to go skiing with the others.

"It's okay, I'm happy to take him." Andrew placed his hand on Dillon's shoulder, and after shooting Brianna a quick glance, he bent down and looked Dillon in the eye. "How about we make a snowman first, buddy?"

"Yeah, come on Dillon. Come and help us," James called out as he patted a lump of snow onto the snowman's body.

Dillon glanced at the ski field and then at the snowman. "Okay." He threw his skis down and scooped up a big handful of snow, slapping it onto the snowman James was making with Lizzy and Clare.

Andrew put his skis down and hesitated. Dillon seemed to have forgotten about him, and there were four in that group with Lizzy and only three in Brianna's. It was a no-brainer. He crouched down and joined Brianna.

BRIANNA ALMOST HADN'T DARED hope that Andrew would join her, so when a shadow fell across the snowman she was building with Alana and Quinn, she took a quick, sharp breath.

He knelt beside her and winked. "Like some help?"

A giddy sense of excitement rushed through her.

Quinn nodded eagerly, saving her from answering. "You can build his arms."

"We'll have to find some sticks for that," Andrew said. "Do you want to come look for some with me?"

"Okay." The little boy stood and took Andrew's hand, angling his head to peer up at the tall man. "Where will we find them?"

"I'm not sure. We might have to look really hard… there aren't many trees around."

"Why aren't there?" Quinn's eyes narrowed and his forehead scrunched.

"That's a long story," Andrew answered as they walked off together.

The way Andrew took all of Quinn's questions in stride warmed Brianna's heart. All the kids loved him, and he seemed to love them. She recalled reading somewhere that you could tell a person's character by the way they treated children and animals. If this was anything to go by, Andrew McKinnon was a good man.

"He's nice," Alana said quietly, as she patted more snow on the snowman's body.

Brianna blinked. Had Alana read her thoughts? "He is."

"He likes you."

Heat raced up Brianna's neck and into her face. "What makes you say that?"

"The way he looks at you."

Brianna shrugged as she balled more snow, all the while keeping her gaze averted. "I hadn't noticed."

Alana chuckled. "Come on, Brianna. Of course you have."

She looked up, unable to hide the grin on her face. "You're right." Maybe she shouldn't be saying this to Alana—it might just make her loneliness more obvious, but then, maybe being honest and sharing would help seal their relationship. "I think I like him too."

Alana focused on the snowman before meeting Brianna's gaze. When she did, her eyes were filled with longing and regret. "I'm happy for you."

"Thanks, but nothing's happened yet."

"It will, I can tell."

"You miss Conall, don't you?"

Alana nodded, wiping a tear from her eye.

Brianna gave her wrist a gentle squeeze. "I'm sure there's someone better out there for you. He doesn't deserve you after what he did." Brianna would have preferred to tell Alana that Jesus loved her, but it was too premature—they barely knew each other, and somehow it didn't seem like the right time. *But when was the right time?* She prayed God would let her know.

She glanced at Andrew chatting easily with Quinn while the two of them looked for sticks. A tinge of guilt flowed through her. She quickly put it aside.

When Andrew and Quinn returned moments later with some small twigs, Brianna couldn't deny the spark of excitement rising in her.

The next half hour or so passed happily. Brianna laughed and joked with everyone, including Andrew. When it came time for judging whose snowman was the best, they all agreed they were both great in their own way and both were winners.

Lizzy stood and brushed snow off her jacket and pants. "It must be time for a hot drink. It's freezing out here." She rubbed her hands together briskly.

"Can't we go skiing, Mum? Andrew was going to take me." Dillon pleaded with her.

"After we've had something to eat and drink, Dillon. Okay?" Lizzy gave him a stern look.

Dillon hung his head. "Okay."

They gathered their belongings and tramped through the snow up to the restaurant. After placing the skis in the racks, they headed inside into the warmth of the restaurant, joining Lizzy's parents, and Caitlin and Brendan, at a table near a large picture window with a panoramic view of the ski fields.

Dillon headed straight for the window and stared out at the skiers weaving down the mountain. James, Clare and Quinn joined him.

When Andrew pulled a chair out for her, Brianna's mouth curved into a smile before she lowered her gaze. It was nice having a handsome Scotsman look after her.

The adults ordered coffees, and the children, hot chocolates. Scones with clotted cream and strawberry jam were ordered all round. They'd just finished eating when the skiers returned.

"How was it?" Andrew asked, when they all traipsed in and pulled up chairs to join the group.

"Great," Danny replied, shrugging off his jacket before he sat. "How was the boy?" He nodded towards Dillon.

"We just built snowmen." Dillon leaned on Daniel, his bottom lip protruding in a pout.

Daniel picked him up and plopped him on his lap. "That must have been fun."

"Not as much fun as skiing."

"It was my fault. I wanted to make a snowman," Andrew confessed.

Daniel held in a chuckle.

Brianna picked at her nails to avoid looking at him. Danny would easily figure out why Andrew chose to make a snowman over skiing. She hoped he wouldn't joke about it in front of everyone.

A child screamed at the next table and everyone turned to see what had happened. A toddler had fallen off his chair and landed heavily on the floor. By the time he stopped crying, the previous conversation had been forgotten, and Brianna relaxed when everyone started chatting amongst themselves.

A little later, when Andrew leaned close and whispered in her ear inviting her to ski one of the runs with him, she agreed without a second thought.

CHAPTER 8

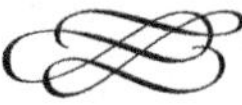

After Brianna quickly organised a set of skis, she and Andrew hurried to the chairlift where Grace, Ryan, Caleb, Shawn, Joel and Aislin stood in a group chatting.

Ryan looked up as they approached. "About time! We were just about to go without you."

"Sorry we held you up," Andrew said, his voice low and humourless.

Grace nudged Ryan in the ribs. "We weren't about to go. Ryan was just trying to be funny."

He clapped Andrew on the back and chuckled. "Like Grace said, I was just being silly. It's all good. Thought we'd do the blue run this time. Sound all right?"

"Is it an easy one?" Brianna asked.

"You worried, Bi?"

Straightening, she lifted her chin. "No…" But if it hadn't been for Andrew inviting her, she most definitely would not be standing there about to ski down a mountain, no matter how easy the run might be.

"Okay, let's go." Ryan led the way and they all skied to the line. Within a matter of minutes, Brianna was sitting beside Andrew, being swept upwards over the dazzling white snow, skis swinging in the air below the seat.

"Are you okay?" He turned his head and searched her eyes.

She felt a ripple of excitement. Was Andrew about to hold her hand? Kiss her? How romantic would that be? How had this happened? White snowy peaks, brilliant against the pale blue sky, fresh mountain air brushing her face and heightening her senses, a gorgeous, caring man seated beside her, gazing into her eyes... *Was she okay?* She was more than okay. She surprised herself and smiled easily. "Yes, but I have to confess I'm not good at skiing."

"That's okay. I've done a bit of skiing. I can help."

Brianna let out a happy sigh. Warmth flooded her body, and she pulled her gaze away to look at the scenery. Minutes later they disembarked and joined the others, but as she stood beside them, a lump grew in the pit of her stomach as the reality of what she'd committed herself to hit home. *Why had she thought she could do this?*

Grace adjusted her goggles, nodded to Ryan, and together they took off down the mountain, looking like pros. Caleb and Shawn went next, followed by Joel and Aislin. When just the two of them were left, Andrew looked at Brianna and tilted his head. "Ready?"

She steeled herself but her insides quivered. "I... I guess so." She lowered her goggles and eased forward. Her heart pounded. The hill was so steep. *Why was she doing this?* As her speed increased, she tried to remember how to snow plough, but she panicked and angled her skis to the side, coming to an abrupt stop and landing headfirst in the snow.

Lifting her head, she brushed snow off her face as tears pricked her eyes. She shouldn't have come.

Andrew stopped beside her and bent down, his face etched with worry. "What happened, Brianna? Are you hurt?"

"No, but I shouldn't have come. I'm sorry." She tried to sit, but her skis were so long and she couldn't get them into the right position. She flopped back into the snow, close to tears.

Andrew reached out his hand. "Let me help you up. I didn't realise you couldn't ski at all. But it's okay, I can show you."

Brianna shook her head. "No… I'll climb back to the top and go down on the chair lift."

"They won't let you. Here, take my hand—I'll help you." His voice was so kind and sincere, and he didn't sound annoyed.

She took his hand. Finally getting her skis facing the right direction, she slipped when she tried to stand and collapsed back onto the snow. This time, instead of crying, she laughed as her skis went in opposite directions. "I'm sorry. I really am useless."

Andrew laughed with her. "No, you're not. Use your poles and I'll steady you. Bend your knees and keep your weight low. It's all about your centre of gravity."

"Okay… I'll try again." She sat, then slowly eased herself up with Andrew's help until she was upright and stable. "Thank you."

"My pleasure." He grinned at her. "Now, tell me what you know."

"Not much, I'm afraid."

"Okay, we'll take it really slowly. We'll need to keep out of the way of the faster skiers, but it'll be fine. We'll just do short runs, and we can take a break whenever you want."

"I'm so sorry."

Andrew gave her a smile that made her knees even weaker, if that was possible. "I don't mind. We can take as long as you need. Ready?"

She nodded.

"Okay, we'll just go a few metres, then we'll stop, turn, and go another few metres until you get the hang of it. I'll go first and I can help you stop if needed." He lowered his goggles and effortlessly skied a short distance before stopping and turning, and waited for her to reach him.

Brianna inched forward, trying to keep the skis angled in a little as she steadied herself with her poles. Going sideways was much less frightening than going straight down. As she approached Andrew, she slowed and then stopped.

"How was that?"

She smiled. "Better."

"Good. Now we need to change directions. It's easier to do when you're moving, so we'll keep going in this direction, then when you're ready, turn your left ski first, bend your leg, then bring your right ski around until they're parallel again. We won't go fast, so it'll be okay. I'll go first."

Andrew made it look so easy. Brianna squared her shoulders and steeled herself. Surely she could do it. She inhaled slowly then eased forward. Her heart ricocheted in her chest as she began turning her left ski. What if she couldn't bring it around and she ended up going straight down? She could kill herself. *No... don't think like that... concentrate. Bend your knees. Bring the skis around.* The tension in her body eased a little when she was facing the opposite direction.

Andrew rested one arm on his pole and gave her a high five as she pulled up next to him.

"I did it." Her gentle laugh rippled through the air.

"You did." His eyes sparkled and her heart skipped a beat. "Ready to do another one?"

"Yes," she replied, feeling a lot more confident.

"Let's go."

She followed him down a slightly longer run, but her ski got stuck and she tumbled, landing at his feet, face first in the snow once again. She lifted her head slowly, wiping snow off her face.

Andrew bent down and helped her sit. "Are you okay? Nothing broken?"

Brianna felt her ankle. It was a little tender, but not broken. "I'm fine. Just embarrassed."

"It was a very elegant fall."

"No, it wasn't! How can a face-plant be elegant?" She broke into an involuntary giggle.

"Depends on who's doing it." His eyes sparkled with merriment.

Brianna's breath caught as their eyes met. The magnetism between them was growing, and it scared and excited her at the same time. "You're... you're such a good skier. Where did you learn?"

"Italy, mainly. It's great over there. Bigger ski fields than here. Lots of runs." He reached out and flicked some snow off her hair. "You should check it out."

Brianna giggled. "Bigger runs wouldn't be any good for me, but I'd love to go to Italy. It must be lovely."

"It would be even lovelier when sharing it with someone special."

Her heart beat faster. Was he just flirting, or was he for real? He'd have the pick of any number of girls in his line of work. Maybe he wasn't serious at all and he was just amusing himself with her. Filling in time. He seemed genuine, but really, what did she know about him? *Zilch.*

She jumped when a spray of snow hit her in the face. Grace and Ryan pulled up in front of them, looking anxious. "Bibi, we've been looking everywhere for you."

Brianna angled her head. "Why? What's wrong?"

"A storm's coming—didn't you notice?" Grace's annoyed glance darted between her and Andrew.

"No." But a quick look at the sky confirmed Grace was right. A thick band of cloud hovered threateningly over Ben Nevis and was heading their way. How had they missed it? "Thanks for letting us know. I got stuck, and Andrew's been helping me. We'll follow you down."

"Good. Don't waste any time. We're off to find Aislin and Joel and we'll be right down."

"We won't—we'll come straight away." Brianna grabbed her poles.

"See you there." Grace lifted her hand in a wave and propelled herself forward. Ryan followed, and within moments, they were out of sight.

Brianna looked at Andrew. "How did we miss those angry-looking clouds?" But she knew… they'd been so distracted with each other they hadn't noticed it.

Andrew shrugged and looked apologetic. "I should have paid more attention. We'd better get moving." He sounded worried. Quickly standing, he offered her his gloved hand.

Brianna took it and tried hard not to get her skis tangled as he helped her up. "I hope we make it back in time. The sky looks menacing." Her chest tightened.

"We'll be okay, but we'll need to go faster." A muscle in his jaw quivered.

"I'll do my best." Taking some deep breaths, she tried to avoid looking too far down the hill.

"You'll be fine. I'll be beside you the whole way."

"Thanks." Brianna gave him a nervous smile and eased carefully forward. As her confidence grew, she took longer, steeper runs before changing direction, but was still unable to go straight down like the other skiers. Before reaching the half-way mark, wind gusts carrying icy bullets of snow and ice pummelled them, reducing visibility and sending the temperature plummeting. When the lights from the restaurant pierced the cloud, she released a huge sigh of relief. She thought she was never going to make it.

Daniel waved frantically as they approached the gondola station, motioning them to hurry. "Quick, the last gondola's about to leave." His voice barely reached them.

Brianna dipped her chin against the wind and skied the short distance to join him. He gave her shoulder a squeeze and then peered behind her, his forehead puckering. "Where are Grace and Ryan?"

Brianna's forehead creased. "They went looking for Aislin and Joel."

"Aislin and Joel are fine—they caught the last gondola with the others, but Grace and Ryan aren't here." Daniel's voice was thick with emotion. He peered up the mountain as the gondola operator ushered them onto the landing. Turning around, he pushed against the man. "There's two more to come... we have to wait." Brianna had never seen Daniel so agitated.

The short, chubby man shook his head. "We can't wait, sorry. This is the last one going down. I'll report them as missing and send a team out. Just give me the details."

Brianna's eyes popped open. *Missing? Grace and Ryan?* The gondola lurched when she stepped into it, and without thinking, she grabbed Andrew's arm.

Daniel held his ground. "I want to stay. I'm sure they'll be here any minute." His usual kind voice was surprisingly curt.

But even his charm didn't work on the man. "Like I said, I'll report them as missing. The Mountain Rescue Team will go looking for them and will bring them down. Where were they last seen?" He ushered Daniel into the gondola as he spoke.

Daniel looked to Andrew.

Andrew took the cue. "They were about three hundred metres from the start of the blue run when we saw them. They're good skiers, so I don't know what would have happened."

"We'll find them, don't you worry." After the man closed the gate and pressed a button, the gondola lurched forward.

Daniel ran his hand over his thick woollen beanie as they began to descend, his eyes wide and glassy. "I don't believe this has happened."

Tears pricked Brianna's eyes. It was all her fault. What if something happened to them? She'd never forgive herself. She brushed her tears away quickly, but too late, because Andrew had noticed. He took her hand and squeezed it. "They'll be okay. Ryan seems resourceful and he knows these mountains, and your sister's strong. They'll be fine."

She nodded, wanting to believe him, but she couldn't help but fear the worst as the wind gusts increased and visibility reduced to zero.

CHAPTER 9

With the wind buffeting the gondola, the ride down Aonach Mor was scarier than the rides at Alton Towers. Daniel, Brianna and Andrew held hands and prayed not only for their safety, but that of Grace and Ryan's. Brianna could barely utter a word, but her heart pleaded with God to keep them safe. If only she hadn't gone up there in the first place. What had she been thinking? She owed her life to Grace. A heavy weight settled in her stomach. How many times had Grace dragged her out of the gutter after she'd overdosed following the loss of her baby? Sat beside her in hospital when she should have been at work? Cared enough to bring her to Danny and Lizzy's when neither of them believed in God's power, but it was the only option left? Brianna squeezed her eyes shut and fought back tears. Surely God wouldn't let anything happen to Grace now after all they'd been through?

As they approached the bottom of the mountain, she inhaled deeply and tried to leave her worry with God. Bible verses she'd committed to memory challenged her to trust Him, but could she? Trusting God in small things was one matter, but now her sister's life was in danger. That was a different story. She had no doubt God worked in people's lives—He'd worked in hers, but would He answer their prayers and keep Grace and Ryan safe in this blizzard? Did he really answer prayers like that?

The gondola came to a stop, and Daniel and Andrew both motioned for her to alight first. Snow swirled on a freezing wind, virtually blowing her off the step. When Andrew grabbed her arm and steadied her, Brianna looked up and gave him a weak, but grateful smile.

Joel, Aislin, Shawn and Caleb stood huddled together and looked up expectantly as the three of them approached. The questions in their eyes quickly changed to alarm as Danny conveyed the news that Grace and Ryan were still on the mountain.

"We need to report them as missing," Caleb said, his eyes large and wild. "It's supposed to get worse."

"The report's been made, but I don't know what's happening. We need to find out." Daniel rubbed his arms briskly as his glance shot to the Aonach Mor Ticket office, now shrouded in heavy cloud.

"I'll come with you." Caleb turned to the others. "Get in the bus and go home. We'll wait here until they're found."

Brianna shook her head. "I want to wait too."

Caleb placed his hand on her shoulder. "No, Bi. You're better off at home, out of this. It could be hours."

"Caleb's right, Bi. We'll let you know as soon as they're found. Go home and pray." Danny's voice was firm, and even though she would rather have stayed, Brianna allowed Andrew to guide her to the bus, the only vehicle remaining in the car park.

A hush fell amongst those waiting inside the bus as the five of them entered. It must have been clear from their faces that something was amiss.

When Andrew cleared his voice, everyone turned their attention to him, Brianna included. With Danny, Caleb and Ryan absent, Andrew took charge, and despite the situation, her insides glowed with pride.

He gave the group a reassuring smile. "I don't want any of you to worry, but Grace and Ryan didn't make the last gondola."

Stunned silence filled the bus.

"Will they be okay?" Dillon's little voice came from one of the front seats.

Andrew looked down at him. "The Mountain Rescue Team will find them." He spoke with quiet confidence.

"Will they come down by helicopter?"

"Maybe."

"Where's my daddy?"

"He and your Uncle Caleb are waiting here until they come down the mountain. He said for the rest of us to go home and get warm and dry."

"Can I stay with them?" Dillon's little voice inched higher.

"Dillon!" Lizzy glared at him. "That's enough. We're going home like Daddy said."

"Okay." Dillon's shoulders slumped.

Andrew rubbed his hands together. "We'll need to get the chains on the tyres—it's going to be a hairy ride home. Everyone understand?" His gaze travelled around the bus. There was a general nod of consensus. Maybe it was because he was Scottish and this was his home, but it seemed that everyone, not just Brianna, was relieved that he was taking charge.

"I'll help." Brendan stood and headed for the front. Brianna was surprised he could walk straight given the number of drinks he'd had, but then, this was Brendan.

"Wait for me." Shawn stood and joined him.

Andrew nodded in appreciation. "We won't be long."

After the three men exited the bus, those remaining talked in hushed tones. Brianna learned that Lizzy's parents had left early, taking James and Clare with them. Concern grew when Aislin and Joel stated they hadn't seen Grace and Ryan on the mountain. Brianna's chest grew heavy once more until she remembered God was looking after them.

~

GRACE MOANED as she lay flat on her back in the snow, wincing as pain shot through her right shoulder when she tried to move. Snow swirled all around, and she could barely see a foot above her. Tiny darts of ice, like needles, pelted her in the face. Her chest tightened as panic set in. *Ryan... where's Ryan?* She called out, but the howling gale stole her voice. She placed her hands over her stomach and bit back tears. Cold seeped into her body and she shivered uncontrollably. How had this happened? One minute they'd been skiing down the hill looking for Aislin and Joel, and the next, a mighty gust of wind blew her off-track and sent her flying… now she had no idea where she was, nor where Ryan was, and she couldn't move.

Ryan had to be all right. After everything she'd been through… the horrid years at Aunt Hilda's, Brianna's rape, the bomb… and then finding God, and Ryan. No, she couldn't lose him now, *especially now...* Trying to pull herself up again, she cried out as pain shot across her shoulders and down her arm. No, she couldn't move. Ryan would have to find her. She whimpered. *God, please help him find me...*

Sometime later, Grace thought she heard a voice calling her name. A glimmer of hope washed through her but quickly faded. She must have been hallucinating. But then, moments later, relief flooded her body when Ryan's face loomed over hers.

He cupped her face and planted kisses all over it. "Grace… thank God." The warmth of his breath was like nothing she'd ever known. She stifled a scream as he covered her body with his, transferring his heat to her. Life slowly returned to her bones. She wouldn't die out here after all.

Lifting his head, Ryan stroked her face and gazed lovingly into her eyes. "I looked everywhere for you. One minute you were beside me, next minute you were gone. Are you hurt?"

Grace looked back at him, nodding as best she could. "My… my shoulder…"

"I'm sorry, darling, I'm leaning on you." He eased himself off her. "Which one?"

"Right."

"You can't move?"

She shook her head ever so slightly. Despite Ryan's gentle manner, Grace flinched as he felt the injured area. She didn't need him to confirm she'd broken something. The look on his face when he straightened said it all. But at least they were together.

"Any pain in your back?"

"I don't think so. Just my shoulder and arm." Her lips were so cold she could hardly move them.

"I think you've broken your collarbone."

"Oh…" Her voice was small. "What are we going to do?"

"Get you off the snow for a start. It'll hurt, but I've got to lift you off it or you'll freeze to death. I'll grab some branches and place them under you. Are you okay while I go find some?"

She blinked, and it felt like her eyelashes were frozen. "Don't be long."

Lowering his face, he kissed her gently, warming her lips. "I'll be right back, but before I go, I'll wrap you in this." Taking out a small package from his backpack, Ryan removed a thin, silver piece of plastic which flapped wildly in the gale until he managed to secure it around her.

"I should have known you'd come prepared." Her teeth chattered.

"Once a soldier, always a soldier." Blue eyes she'd come to love so much winked at her. "Better?"

She nodded and gave him a weak smile. "Thank you."

"You're welcome. Now, I'll go and grab those branches. I'll be back in a jiffy."

Although she knew Ryan wouldn't go far, fear of losing sight of him outweighed any pain she might experience by turning her head and keeping him in sight. She bit back pain as she watched him stumble through the fresh snow to reach the pine bushes only metres away. Despite the emergency blanket blocking most of the wind, Grace still shivered uncontrollably. Ryan was right… they could die out here. Visibility was so low no one would find them, and early dark was already setting in.

Breaking off several branches, he carried them back and knelt beside her. "I'm going to put these under you. I'll try not to hurt you, but I can't promise."

Grace nodded and tried to prepare herself for the pain, biting down on her lip to stop screaming as he rolled her gently onto her left side. He slid the branches under her before rolling her back. The relief of being off the freezing snow was worth the pain.

"I'll grab some bigger branches now and make a shelter."

She looked up at him with pride. "You're… quite the boy scout." Her voice wobbled as her teeth continued to click together.

His mouth twisted in a smile. "Survival training, Grace."

"I'm glad you know what to do."

"I'll be back in a minute."

After Ryan returned with some larger branches, he wedged them into the snow and huddled down beside her, careful not to hurt her as he placed an arm across her body, drawing close to her as he gazed into her eyes. "I thought I'd lost you."

Her throat was so cold and sore, she could barely reply. "I thought I'd died."

"Thank God you didn't. I love you, Grace."

"And I love you, Ryan." She swallowed hard. "There's something…" She swallowed again. "There's something I need to tell you…"

"What is it, love? What's the matter?"

"I... I was keeping it as a Christmas present, but you need to know. Just in case..." She sucked in a breath and felt a sharp pain in her chest.

In the rapidly fading light, she could just make out his furrowed brow.

He stroked her cheek. "Tell me love, what is it?"

"I... I hope nothing's happened..." Her lips trembled. "I'm... I'm pregnant."

Ryan's eyes enlarged. "Pregnant?"

Grace nodded, pushing back the tears stinging her eyes. "I hope I haven't lost the baby."

"Oh Grace, I'm sure he or she will be fine. Pregnant? Really?" Intensity radiated from his bright eyes.

"I shouldn't have gone skiing."

"You didn't know this was going to happen." He traced her cheek with his finger before kissing her forehead gently. "That little baby is well protected in there."

"It was supposed to be a surprise."

He gave her a smile that spoke straight to her heart. "It is a surprise. Telling me a day early hasn't spoiled it at all." He stroked her hair. "And you know what?"

Grace shook her head.

"We'll remember this moment forever." Leaning closer, Ryan kissed her softly on the lips before cradling her head against his chest. He began to hum the tune to *Silent Night, Holy Night* as the wind howled around them.

"All is calm, all is bright..." Grace's voice was quiet and weak, but the words of the carol filled her with peace. Everything would be all right—God was on their side.

Sometime later, Grace didn't know how long, a flicker of light penetrated the darkness and an overwhelming wave of relief washed over her. *Thank you, God. All is calm, all is bright.*

CHAPTER 10

Back at the house, the atmosphere was subdued as the family sat around the kitchen table. Even Brendan, who'd had more than a few drinks up on the mountain, was quieter than normal. Having two of their group missing in a blizzard was the last thing anyone had expected when they'd set off that morning for a day in the snow, and everyone's thoughts and prayers were with Grace and Ryan.

Lizzy forced herself to remain positive. When the phone rang, she raced to answer it, placing her hand over the mouthpiece to let everyone know it was Daniel. But there was no news, other than to let her know that the Lochaber Mountain Rescue Team was out searching for Grace and Ryan. Daniel was annoyed and disappointed that he and Caleb hadn't been allowed to accompany them.

Lizzy turned her back, keeping her voice low. "Did you really expect they'd let you go with them?"

"Yes. We know what we're doing."

Her hands tightened on the receiver. "Let them do their job, Daniel. They're trained to do this." Sometimes her husband was just too sure of himself, even though he meant well.

"It's just annoying, that's all. We could be out there helping." She could imagine him raking his hands through his hair.

"What, and put yourselves at risk?"

Silence. She was pushing the boundaries, casting doubt on Daniel's abilities, but surely, he'd see it was better for him and Caleb to stay safe. They were both fathers, and the Mountain Rescue Team did this type of thing often. Putting themselves at risk needlessly would be foolish and possibly even selfish, although Lizzy was sure they didn't see it that way.

"You're right, Liz. I'm sorry. You know how bad I am at waiting." He sounded apologetic, slightly downcast.

Lizzy let out a relieved sigh. "I know." Daniel would go stir-crazy if they had long to wait. "Hopefully they'll be found quickly."

"That's what we're praying for."

"As are we." Closing her eyes, she sent up another silent prayer. "Keep us posted, Daniel."

"I will."

When she turned around, all eyes were on her. She gave a small shrug and shook her head, biting back the pent-up emotion welling within her. What if Grace and Ryan weren't found quickly? What if they lay injured somewhere and weren't found until it was too late? Lizzy wrung her hands. No, she couldn't allow herself to think like that. They *would* be found. God was with them and was looking after them. She just had to trust. How important, in times like these when faith was tested, to truly practice what she believed. She prayed she wouldn't be found wanting.

Lizzy forced herself to sound positive when Clare asked if Auntie Grace and Uncle Ryan would miss Christmas. "I'm sure they'll be back soon, sweetheart," she answered, lifting Clare onto her lap and pulling her close.

. . .

Andrew's parents, Rosemary and David, had joined the group in the kitchen while Lizzy was on the phone. Having lived in the area all their lives, they knew the procedures for a search and rescue, and did their best to assure everyone the Mountain Rescue Team knew what they were doing and would find Grace and Ryan as quickly as they could. "However, saying that, we should continue praying. Conditions often change rapidly in the mountains," David said, his thick Scottish brogue doing little to soften the sobering statement.

Caitlin and Gwyneth, who were busily making cups of tea for everyone, stopped and took a seat. Lizzy glanced around the table. No doubt Brendan and Shawn, and possibly the girls and Joel, would feel uncomfortable, but surely with the seriousness of the situation, they'd put their discomfort aside and stay.

They did. "I'll start if you like," Lizzy said. Bowing her head, she took a slow breath. "Dear God, our hearts are filled with worry over Grace and Ryan, out there somewhere in this blizzard." Her voice was soft and she struggled to speak. "You know where they are. Please wrap your arms around them and protect them from danger. Fill them with your peace, and keep them safe." The inside of her mouth felt as dry as sawdust. "Please help the Mountain Rescue Team find them and bring them home in time for Christmas. Lord, give us peace at this special time of the year as we prepare to celebrate the birth of Jesus. May we truly see your power and might at work in this situation. In Jesus' precious name, Amen." She wiped her eyes as a round of subdued *Amens* followed.

Roger cleared his throat and began praying. Even to Lizzy, her father sounded posh. She prayed the others wouldn't care. "Our dear Lord and heavenly Father, we beseech You to bring Grace and Ryan back to us safely. And be with the rescue team. Guide them and lead them to wherever Grace and Ryan might be. And please bless those of us who are waiting for news. Help us to trust You and to keep Grace and Ryan in our prayers and close to our hearts. In Jesus' name, Amen."

Lizzy brushed another tear from her eye before lifting her head. Never in a million years had she expected her well-bred, arrogant father to have his heart softened by the Almighty God, but she should have—because wasn't that what God did? It was the message of Christmas… God reaching out to a fallen world by sending His perfect son, Jesus, to earth, offering all those who believed in Him new hearts and new lives.

David prayed next, followed by Andrew, who was holding Brianna's hand. Tears streamed down her cheeks. From what she'd told Lizzy when they arrived at the house, Lizzy knew she was blaming herself, but she shouldn't. It was no one's fault that Grace and Ryan were missing.

After the prayer time ended, Caitlin and Gwyneth resumed making tea. Everyone remained at the table chatting quietly, expecting the phone to ring at any minute. It wasn't how Lizzy had planned to spend Christmas Eve. Instead of the roast chicken dinner she and Caitlin had thought they'd be serving, they had toasties and tatties with grilled cheese. Everybody's appetite had fled.

THE PHONE RANG AGAIN as the dishes were being cleared after dinner. Lizzy sprang and answered. Her eyes lit up and she nodded. "That's fantastic news." Covering the mouthpiece with her hand, she shared the news that Grace and Ryan had been found. Loud cheers shattered the air. She returned her attention to Daniel on the other end of the phone.

"They think Grace has broken her collarbone," he told her.

"Oh, no. That's terrible. Poor Grace. Has the wind dropped up there?"

"It's dropping, but it's still too risky for the helicopter. They'll bring her down on the snowmobile and rush her to the hospital."

"Well, it's great news they've been found. I guess you and Caleb will stay with her and Ryan?"

"If we're not needed at home."

"The children are missing you, but you need to be there for Grace."

"Yes, we agree."

"A great way to spend Christmas Eve." Lizzy grimaced as she thought about all the fun things they'd planned for the evening.

"Better than stranded on a mountain."

"You have a point," Lizzy conceded.

"I'll keep you posted, Liz. Tell the kids they need to go to bed early so Santa will come."

"Daniel!" Lizzy turned and faced the wall so the others wouldn't hear.

"Only joking."

"Well, don't! Not now..." She let out a frustrated sigh but then followed it with a small chuckle. Did it really matter?

"Sorry, love." He sounded apologetic.

"Apology accepted."

"I need to go. Love you."

"Love you, too." Lizzy hung the phone up and sent up a prayer of thanks.

BRIANNA COULDN'T HELP IT. As she listened to Lizzy on the phone, tears spilled down her cheeks. It was the best news ever. *Grace was safe.* She silently thanked God, and apologised for doubting Him. She wasn't the only one with tears. Alana also wiped her eyes, as did Caitlin.

When Lizzy turned around, a broad smile filled her face. "I'm sure you all heard that. Grace and Ryan are safe. Grace has a broken collarbone, but apart from that, they're both okay. She'll be taken to the hospital as soon as the rescue team can get them off the mountain, and hopefully she'll be home for Christmas."

The children whooped, and everyone visibly relaxed. In an instant, the feeling in the room changed from worry to relief.

"We need to thank Jesus," Dillon stood quietly beside Lizzy and locked eyes with her.

"Yes, we do. You're right. Let's do that now." Her gaze travelled quickly around the table before she placed her hands on his shoulders and bowed her head. "Dear Lord, thank you so much that Grace and Ryan have been found, and that they're both all right. Thank you for looking after them and for leading the Rescue Team to them. We're very grateful. In Jesus' name, Amen." Her voice was so much more upbeat than in her earlier prayer.

A round of enthusiastic *Amen's* followed. Brianna was surprised to hear Brendan and Shawn utter the words.

The children were eager to go to the hospital, but Lizzy told them they needed to go to bed early.

"So Santa will come?" Clare asked.

"Can't we go to the hospital and sing Christmas carols to all the sick people?" Dillon asked. "Santa isn't real anyway."

James and Clare looked up, their eyes questioning. A hush fell over the room as everyone waited for Lizzy's response.

"That's a great idea, Dillon, and yes, you're right... Santa isn't real." She reached out and squeezed James' and Clare's hands. "But it's fun to pretend he is."

Clare burst out crying. "Does that mean we won't get any presents?"

"Oh sweetheart. It doesn't mean that at all. You'll still get your presents, and if you want to believe Santa's real, that's okay."

"Why did Dillon say he's not real?" Clare flashed her brother an angry look as she mixed her words with sobs.

"Maybe because of what's happened with Auntie Grace. Sometimes when serious things happen, we say things we might not normally say."

"Is Auntie Grace going to be all right?"

"She's going to be fine."

She nodded and wiped at her damp cheeks. "I don't mind if Santa isn't real as long as Auntie Grace is here."

Lizzy pulled Clare back onto her lap and hugged her. "She'll be here when you wake up in the morning."

"That's good. Can we go and sing to her?"

Lizzy kissed the top of her head. "It's too late to do that, sweetheart, but we can sing Christmas carols here. We can light our candles and hang our stockings, just like we planned."

"But Daddy isn't here."

"No, but Grandfather is, and Uncle Shawn, and Uncle Brendan, and everybody else. We'll still have tons of fun, and we can light extra candles for Daddy and Uncle Caleb and Auntie Grace and Uncle Ryan."

"Okay."

Brianna brushed at her own eyes. Andrew slipped a warm hand into hers, squeezing gently and rubbing his thumb lightly over her skin. The sensation filled her with warm fuzziness.

She didn't want the moment to end, but as they all gathered in the drawing room and sang Christmas carols, lit candles and hung stockings, Brianna grew more certain she was smitten with Andrew McKinnon. Not only was he handsome, but watching him lead the singing and read to the children made her wonder if there was anything he couldn't do.

CURLED up in a corner of a couch, surrounded by assorted cushions and lap blankets, her gaze was fixed on Andrew on the floor with Clare perched on his lap, and James, Dillon and Quinn leaning on him as he told them the story of the Three Wise Men seeking Jesus. But she still sensed he was hiding something. She couldn't put her finger on it, but the occasional shadow that crossed his face hinted that something concerned him. He seemed weighed down, although he hid it well.

But she didn't know him, and she didn't want to get hurt. Maybe it was best to forget about him... Brianna's mind whirled with confused thoughts, but when Andrew's eyes lifted and caught hers, her heart lurched afresh and she knew she couldn't. All she wanted was for him to hold her, to kiss her... Her pulse raced.

Brianna looked up as Rosemary sat on the couch next to her and smiled.

Rosemary patted her leg. "I haven't had a chance to talk with you much, Brianna. How are you doing, lassie?" Her soft brogue warmed Brianna's heart as it always had.

Straightening, she blinked and gathered her thoughts. Had Rosemary noticed her attraction to Andrew? Of course, Rosemary would have... but did she approve? "I'm... I'm doing well. Especially now that Grace has been found."

"I could see you were worried."

"It was my fault." Brianna's voice wavered as she shot a quick glance at Andrew.

"Nobody thinks that, lassie. Don't blame yourself." Rosemary also cut a glance at her son on the floor, her mouth twitching with amusement. "I can see you're taken with each other."

Brianna felt the heat rushing to her face. "I... don't know what to say..."

"You don't need to say anything, lassie. Just let it happen. I'm happy about it."

Relief washed through Brianna. She was getting ahead of herself, but if things worked out, Rosemary could become her mother—how wonderful would that be! To have a mother after all these years. And not just any mother, it would be Rosemary! God was indeed good.

When Andrew finished his story, Brianna quickly gathered her thoughts and gave Rosemary a grateful smile. If Andrew could read her mind it could all come undone. She'd need to be more careful, because what if he didn't feel the same way?

Lizzy announced it was bedtime for the children, and they all asked Andrew to put them to bed. Brianna's cheeks flushed again when he invited her to join him. He must feel the same way, but there was little chance of keeping whatever they had private. She stood, taking Quinn's and James' hands, while Andrew held Clare's and Dillon's. Lizzy and Alana followed behind, chatting quietly as they all walked down the hallway towards the bedrooms.

After settling the children, and assuring them that Auntie Grace and Uncle Ryan would be there in the morning to watch them open their presents, Andrew grabbed Brianna's hand. He held her back, letting Lizzy and Alana go on ahead down the hallway. In the subdued lighting, Brianna's heart pounded, her imagination running wild. Was Andrew about to kiss her? Her heart thumped as she looked expectantly into his eyes, a shiver rippling through her body. The breath caught in her throat. The anticipation was almost unbearable.

But instead of kissing her, he asked if she'd like to go to the hospital to be there when Grace arrived. Brianna bit back her disappointment. Of course he wasn't about to kiss her... what was she thinking? She blinked and quietly said, "That would be great."

His eyes were tender and soft. "I know how much you want to see Grace."

A fresh wave of respect for him washed through Brianna as she chastised herself. He wasn't just handsome and great with the children, he was sensitive as well. "Yes, I do."

"Then, let's go. We'll let the others know on our way out."

"Should we ask if anyone would like to come?" If she were honest, she didn't want them to. The thought of spending time alone with Andrew was more than appealing, but asking would be the right thing to do.

His eager expression changed as his eyes searched hers. "I guess we should." He stroked her hand with his thumb. "Come on, let's go."

He kept hold of her hand as they strode to the top of the staircase. Stopping abruptly, he swung her to face him, his hands gripping her upper arms, the expression on his face a mix of eagerness and tenderness.

Brianna's pulse skittered as Andrew lowered his head and pressed his lips against hers, gently covering her mouth. Shocked by her fervent response, she tried for a moment to pull away, but then gave in and returned his kiss, disappointment filling her when he ended it.

Andrew's chest heaved as he gazed into her eyes. "I've been wanting to do that all day. I'm sorry." He sounded breathless.

Brianna's eyes widened. "Don't be sorry. You can do it again if you like." Her boldness surprised her.

His gaze intensified before lowering his mouth hungrily over hers.

Returning his kiss with reckless abandon, Brianna was transported on a soft, wispy cloud to another world she never knew existed.

When Andrew released her, her lips tingled, and it was the best feeling in the world. She'd been kissed by the man she loved.

Andrew grinned. "Come on, we'd best go." Brushing a gentle kiss across her forehead, he slipped an arm around her shoulder. "They'll be wondering where we are." As he winked at her, a tingle of delight ran through her body.

Slipping her arm around his waist, she leaned into him. "Maybe we won't ask anyone to come with us to the hospital."

He kissed the top of her head. "Good idea."

EYES WIDENED when Andrew announced to everyone that he and Brianna were driving to the hospital.

"You're not going out in this weather, surely?" Disbelief punctured David's thick voice.

"We'll be fine, Dad. I've driven in much worse."

"I know you have, son, but still… it's Christmas Eve."

Andrew placed his hand lightly on Brianna's shoulder. "Brianna wants to be there for Grace."

Grins formed on Lizzy's and Caitlin's faces. A flush crept up Brianna's neck and into her cheeks. There was no hiding it now.

"Well, take care, son. We don't want any more accidents."

"I will, Dad. Don't worry."

"Give our best to Grace," Lizzy said. "Tell her she needs to be home by morning or the children will be disappointed."

"We will."

They bid everyone good-bye and escaped out the side door, and were immediately blasted by a biting wind.

CHAPTER 11

Grace clung to Ryan's hand as the rescuers placed her onto a stretcher. She steeled herself for the journey down the mountain. A helicopter would have been preferable, but as the wind was still gusting, the snowmobile was the only way down.

Fergus, a short, stout, ruddy-faced man dressed in high visibility rescue gear, assured her they'd take it slowly, and would make the ride as comfortable as possible. An ambulance would be waiting at the bottom to take her to the hospital.

Ryan sat close to her as the snowmobile began its descent. When the snowmobile became airborne and landed hard several times, Grace thought she would pass out as pain shot through her body, but they finally came to a stop. They'd made it.

As promised, an ambulance was waiting, along with Daniel and Caleb. Her brothers' faces were a welcome sight. The drive to the hospital took forever. Ryan told her it was because the road was slippery and they wanted to get there safely. That was fine with her… she was drifting into numbness now that the pain relief had kicked in.

Grace opened her eyes as the lights of Fort William flickered through the ambulance windows. "Are we almost there?" Her voice sounded tinny and far away in her ears.

Ryan smoothed her brow with his hand. "A few more minutes."

Her eyes fell shut again.

The sound of the ambulance door opening aroused her. The stretcher was lifted out and wheels snapped into place as it was lowered to the ground. Bright lights hurt her eyes as she was rushed inside. She tried to lift her hand to cover them, but her arms were secured in place. She began to panic, tried lifting her head, looked around. Then she remembered—she wasn't in prison, she was in the hospital.

Ryan spoke gently. "It's okay, Grace. You're safe."

BRIANNA SNUGGLED CLOSE to Andrew as he shoved the gear stick of his father's four-wheel-drive into first and headed down the rough track leading to the tiny highland village of Glen Brannie. She still couldn't believe he had kissed her. Reaching up, she pressed her fingers to her lips—there was no question about it. Her heart sang with delight, a warm glow filling her body as snow chains rattled and pine branches heavy with snow scraped against the vehicle.

Andrew drove in silence, concentrating on the road. The tyres skidded and the vehicle fishtailed as he made a run up a steep hill, but they made it out of the pine forest without any drama. Approaching the small village, an array of Christmas lights flashed from the roofs of old stone cottages, reminding her it was actually Christmas. The only shop in the village, a general store she knew well from her time living at the community, sold everything from bread and milk to all things Scottish, including home-made shortbread and tea-towels adorned with Scottish recipes and pictures of Ben Nevis and the Loch Ness Monster. The shop was closed, but a Christmas tree sat in the window, lights twinkly and cheery.

Brianna glanced at Andrew as he turned onto the wider road leading to Fort William, recently salted and gritted after the snowplough had been through. The clear-cut lines of his profile stood out against the moonlight now reflecting off the dark waters of Loch Linnhe. Her heart filled with warmth. He was a most handsome man.

When the lights of Fort William came into view, Andrew slowed to turn into the road leading to the hospital. He parked in the almost empty car park, not surprising since it was Christmas Eve. He offered his arm to help her along the slippery path leading to the entrance. It felt nice. As his hand closed over hers in a squeeze, a wave of contentment flowed through her.

When the automatic doors opened, the comforting sounds of *Silent Night* played through the hospital's speakers. A giant Christmas tree, decorated with colourful baubles, white and silver tinsel, and flashing lights, dominated the small waiting area. Daniel and Caleb sat on chairs against a wall. They looked up with mouths gaping. "We didn't expect to see you here." Danny stepped forward and hugged Brianna.

"It was a spur of the moment decision." She gave Andrew a coy look. "Andrew's suggestion."

"Well, Grace will be happy you've come."

"How is she? Can we see her?"

"The doctor's with her now, so we'll have to wait. She was in a lot of pain, but she's had some meds, so she should be feeling better soon."

"We were so worried..." Brianna choked out, pushing back the tears welling in her eyes.

Andrew wrapped his arm around her and rubbed her arm. Danny and Caleb both took notice, but she didn't care. It felt good being cared for by Andrew. And why wouldn't they be happy for her?

"I'll grab some tea." Caleb headed to the self-service drink dispenser.

"How did you get here?" Brianna asked Daniel. Sniffing, she reached into her pocket and drew out a tissue. If she could keep the conversation away from Grace and her injury, she might not break down and embarrass herself.

"A lift with one of the rescuers."

Of course. "Where's Ryan?" She looked around, having almost forgotten about him.

"In with Grace and the doctor. Come and sit down, Bibi." Danny gestured to the chairs he and Caleb had vacated.

Caleb handed her a polystyrene cup filled with hot, sweet tea. She brought it to her mouth and took a sip. It was just what she needed.

"The children wanted to come in and sing Christmas Carols to the patients." Brianna forced herself to chat.

Danny chuckled. "Of course they did."

"Will Grace make it home for Christmas?" Brianna's voice quieted as she met Danny's gaze.

He released a slow breath and skimmed his hand through his hair. His eyes were watery and slightly red. "Not sure. We'll know more once the doctor comes out."

Brianna grimaced. That wasn't what she wanted to hear. The children would be devastated if Grace wasn't there in the morning. They really needed that miracle.

"Let's go and visit the other patients while we wait. Sing some carols," Andrew suggested.

His happy face cheered her, pulling her out of her self-pity.

Danny rubbed his hands together. "Not so sure about the singing, but yes, visiting the patients is a grand idea."

"Will we be allowed?" Brianna asked.

"Of course. It's Christmas Eve, and besides, I know the sister on duty." Danny winked.

Brianna shook her head. Of course Danny would know the sister on duty. Danny knew everyone.

After he checked with the sister, who said they were more than welcome to visit the patients, Brianna followed the three men into the women's ward. The foursome offered Christmas greetings to five older ladies who were spending Christmas in hospital. Danny knew four of them, and they were very pleased to see him.

Andrew had just finished leading a surprisingly melodious rendition of *The First Noel,* when Ryan found them. Like Danny, he too looked tired, but his grin was so wide it nearly slid off his face. "They're letting her go home."

Danny gave him a bear hug. "That's great news."

Brianna hugged him too, pushing back relieved tears.

"She'll be ready shortly." Ryan spoke to Brianna. "I didn't know you were coming in."

"We wanted to be here for her."

"She'll be glad to see you." He smiled and then turned his head as a nurse pushing Grace in a wheelchair stopped at the entrance to the ward.

They bid the ladies a merry Christmas and then left to approach the nurse. With her arm in a sling and still in her ski clothes, Grace looked a little worse for wear, but she still managed a weak smile.

Brianna gave her a gentle hug, taking care not to hurt her injured shoulder. Despite her intention to be strong, tears sprang from her eyes. "I'm so glad you're coming home."

"So am I, trust me. It wasn't easy convincing them I'm okay—they wanted to keep me in. Anyway, let's get out of here." She looked up at the nurse and thanked her. "I'll be all right from here, thanks."

"No, I'll push you to your car. No argument, thank you."

"I'll get the car," Andrew said.

When Andrew left, Ryan whispered to Brianna, "So, what's going on between you two?"

She stiffened. "Nothing." Her voice was small but defensive.

Ryan chuckled. "Yeah, right."

Grace reached out her good hand and smacked Ryan playfully.

"Leave Bibi alone. I think it's lovely." She reached out her hand to squeeze Brianna's.

With her brothers, brother-in-law and sister in the car on the way home, Brianna sat further away from Andrew than she had on the drive there, but every now and then she shot him a glance, and each time she did, her heart did a little skip.

CHAPTER 12

It was nearing midnight when they arrived back at Elim Community. The storm had completely cleared, and instead of dark, angry clouds and a howling gale, stars shone down from an unusually clear sky. When Andrew helped Brianna out of the car and offered his arm, she was tempted to suggest a stroll to the loch, but it was so cold her nose was running. Instead, she pulled her coat tighter and leaned in close to him.

Ryan carefully carried Grace the short distance to the house. Lizzy and Caitlin greeted Daniel and Caleb at the door, quickly ushering them inside. Andrew slipped his arm around Brianna's shoulder as they followed.

The grandfather clock struck midnight as Andrew closed the door. They were alone in the foyer. He drew her close, the tenderness of his gaze sending her pulse racing. "There might not be any mistletoe, but I think it's time for another kiss." His breath was warm and moist as his lips feather-touched hers. Brianna's knees weakened with longing. She still could not believe this was happening. Brianna O'Connor, kissed by the most gorgeous man ever. Unheard of. But it was real. She drank in the sweetness of his kiss, lost in the magic of the moment. "Merry Christmas, lassie." Gazing into her eyes, he tenderly traced the line of her cheekbone and jaw with his finger.

She smiled dreamily into his eyes. "And to you, Andrew."

Lowering his head, his lips had just touched hers again when, in front of them, someone cleared his throat. "Come on, you two. You can't stay there all night." Danny's voice held amusement as he stood in the hallway with his arm draped around Lizzy's shoulder.

A flush crept into Brianna's face—she hadn't heard them sneak up.

"Leave them alone, Daniel." Lizzy spoke quietly as she looked up at him. "We're off to bed… no doubt the children will be up early. Good night, and merry Christmas."

"Merry Christmas to you both, as well. And no, we won't stay here all night. Don't you worry about that," Andrew replied.

"Good night, then." Lizzy smiled before dragging Daniel away.

Brianna knew she should go to bed, but she didn't want this night to end. Even with Grace's accident, it had been the best day she'd ever had, so when Andrew asked if she'd like a hot chocolate, she didn't think twice. "And shortbread?"

"Whatever you like." He lifted his hand, tucking a lock of hair behind her ear before popping a kiss on her lips and leading her to the kitchen.

Brianna sat on a stool and watched as Andrew made the most amazing hot chocolate ever. Rich, velvety and topped with whipped cream, she thought she'd died and gone to heaven.

"Like it?" He angled his head.

"Love it."

"Let's find somewhere cosy to sit."

"Okay."

He led her into the drawing room where he re-stoked the fire, put on some quiet Christmas music, and joined her on the couch. "I'm not in any hurry to go to bed." He slipped his arm around her shoulder and kissed the side of her head.

She leaned into him. "Neither am I."

"We might see Santa come down the chimney."

Brianna giggled. "He's not real, remember. Besides, he might get burned if he comes down this one."

"You have a point."

"Tell me more about your travels."

"What do you want to know?"

"Everything."

"It might take all night."

"I don't care."

"In that case..."

For the next few hours, Andrew told Brianna about all the amazing places he'd travelled to, but the one she was most interested in was the walk he'd done in Spain.

"So what made it so special?" she asked him as the clock stuck three.

"I was at a low point in my life. A girl I'd been with for a few years had just ditched me for someone else, and I was looking for something." He released a slow breath as he stared into the fire. "I felt empty. I could have come home, but I wasn't ready for that. I'd heard about the walk, and something about it appealed, so I decided to do it."

He ran his finger around the top of his mug. "I was in Barcelona working in a restaurant, so I packed up and headed for *Saint Jean Pied de Port* and began walking." Pausing, he turned to look at her. "It wasn't so much the scenery, although some of it was awesome, or even the people I met along the way. It was the time I spent alone, just walking, that made it special."

"I've never done anything like that. Hiked on my own."

Andrew squeezed Brianna's hand, rubbing his thumb gently over her skin. "It wasn't easy. I had to push myself often, but I learned the most about myself at the places that were most challenging. That was when God got through to me." He smiled. "Every night I read a chapter of the Bible and asked Him to be real to me, because even though I'd grown up in a Christian home, I didn't *know* Him, I just knew *about* Him. And every day I prayed David's prayer from Psalm 63 verse one: '*O God, You are my God; I shall seek You earnestly; My soul thirsts for You, my flesh yearns for You, In a dry and weary land where there is no water.*'

"And one day, somewhere high in the mountains of *O Cebreiro* when I was thirsty, hot and tired, with blisters upon blisters on my feet, God spoke to my heart, and I knew then, beyond a shadow of a doubt, that He was real. I sat on a rock, all alone apart from some bleating sheep, the air so clean it hurt to breathe, and something moved in my heart. I began to cry. I fell on my knees and gave my life to God there and then."

Brianna let his words sink in a few moments before she replied. "That's amazing. I can understand your experience, because mine was similar. Something happened inside me the day your mother led me to the Lord, and any doubt I had that God cared was blown away. I knew that God loved me and wanted me for His own. It still amazes me that He did that. I was the worst person ever."

Andrew shook his head. "No, you weren't."

"I felt like it. I couldn't understand for a while why He'd bother with me. I was a nobody. A drug addict. A thief. But he loved me enough to send Jesus to die for me." Brianna pulled out a tissue and dabbed her eyes. "It still blows me away."

"Me too. His love is amazing, and it must break His heart that so many shun Him, because He just wants to give them a new life. A fresh start. I know it breaks my heart."

"Mine, too." Brianna thought of all the rape victims she'd shared her faith with, but how few welcomed God's message of hope and love. They couldn't understand His love, and yet, if they only admitted their need, she knew that God would take their hand and give them a much better life.

She leaned her head against Andrew's chest and he tenderly stroked her hair. She sat up abruptly when Alana crossed her mind. "I'd really like to pray for Alana. I think God's working in her heart, but she knows so little about Him, and she's hurting badly. I've been praying for the right time to share with her, but it never seems to happen."

"Sure." He smiled warmly. "That's a great idea."

Andrew bowed his head and listened to Brianna pray. Her voice, so soft, so caring. Just like everything about her. He'd fallen for her, and it seemed she'd fallen for him, but would that change once she knew the truth? Like it or not, he needed to tell her. He should have told her already.

Brianna said *Amen* and raised her head. In the light of the embers, her eyes flickered and shone. He had to tell her. Taking her hand, he stroked her soft skin with his thumb. "I… I need to tell you something. I don't know how to say it, so I'll just blurt it out."

Brianna's eyes widened. "What is it, Andrew?"

A knot twisted in his stomach. Not even his parents knew. He'd been planning on telling them, but hadn't found the right time, but he couldn't keep putting it off. He ran his hand through his hair. Gosh, he was still coming to terms with it himself. Still digesting the news that had thrown him for six only weeks before. He still wondered if it was true or not, or if he was just being set up. *Used.* But somehow, he knew it was true. He had a son. An eleven-year old son. *Andy.*

He braced himself and gazed into Brianna's eyes. "Brianna, you're everything I've ever wanted in a woman… I love your heart, the way you care. I love your gentleness, your depth of character. But I can't lead you on without telling you that…" His gaze dropped to his lap. Was this the right time to tell her? Was it premature? Presumptuous? Should he wait? If he told her, it could mean she'd run a mile, and he wouldn't blame her. Or it could galvanise their relationship when maybe it shouldn't. *What if she decided to date him **because** he had a son, compensating for the one she'd lost?* Would he ever know? *Would it matter?*

He had to trust his instincts. His heart. Somehow, he knew Brianna was genuine. She wouldn't abuse the situation. Besides, he'd already started the conversation and couldn't very well drop it now. He lifted his eyes slowly, meeting hers. "I have an eleven-year-old son."

Hazel eyes held his without blinking; the only sound was the hissing from a log that crackled in the fire. Brief moments passed. He tried to smooth his face into an emotionless mask, allowing her time to digest this news.

She finally blinked. "Where is he?" Her voice was soft, just like her eyes.

"With his mother."

"Tell me about him."

Andrew closed his eyes. Images of a sandy-haired boy who bore his own facial features flitted through his mind. Yes, Andy was definitely his son. He opened his eyes and looked up. "Remember that girl I mentioned?"

"The one who ditched you?"

He nodded. "She contacted me a month ago. Came to the restaurant, in fact. She'd seen a feature article in a newspaper with my photo, so she said. She asked for me, and to cut a long story short, we had a drink after work, and that's when she told me about Andy."

"You didn't know until then?"

"No." He held her gaze.

"Wow. Why now, after all this time?"

"She's sick. Dying." An ache pierced his chest at saying the words aloud. "She's got cancer."

"Cancer? That's terrible."

"Yes." He could see Brianna's mind ticking.

"So, what did she want?"

Blood surged through his veins. "She wants me to look after Andy."

Brianna's gaze remained steady. *What was she thinking?* She angled her head. Moistened her lips. Took her time. She looked deeply into his eyes. "How do you feel about that?" Her voice was gentle. Caring. Nonjudgmental. He could imagine her asking a similar question of her rape victims.

He relaxed and answered honestly. "Excited. Scared. I know nothing about raising a kid."

Her face broke into a wide smile and she clasped his hands. "But you're great with them. And they love you."

Andrew let out a nervous chuckle. "That may be, but I'm sure it would be different being a full-time parent."

"Have you met him?"

He nodded. "Just before I came up here."

"Do your parents know?"

He grimaced.

"I take that as a no."

"I haven't known how to tell them."

"I'm sure they'll be thrilled to have a grandson."

"Maybe." He raked a hand through his hair, blinking rapidly.

"It would be a great Christmas gift for them."

"I should tell them."

"Yes." She held his gaze.

"I've been praying about it non-stop," Andrew admitted. "There's still a lot to work through, but yes, I think I'll take him." He'd said it. *Finally.* And it felt right.

"You'll make a great father, Andrew."

Tears pricked his eyes. Until recently, he'd never thought about having children. Yes, it was true he loved kids, but he'd never had full-time responsibility for any. Never pictured himself being a father, *especially to an eleven-year old*. Andy would be a teenager soon. *What did he know about raising a teenager?* Andy seemed like a good kid, but he'd have issues. What kid didn't? And how would he cope when Shelley died, because die she would, and soon, unless God performed a miracle. But Shelley didn't believe, so not much chance of that happening. He brushed his eyes and gave Brianna a grateful smile. "Thanks."

He wanted to ask her how she felt about the news and if this would change anything between them. Not that there was anything between them, *yet.* Just a few kisses that might not have meant anything to her. Although he sensed they had. Brianna might have been swept up in emotion. He sensed she'd never been kissed before, at least not in the way he'd kissed her, but despite that, she seemed to genuinely care for him. It had been wrong to put her in this position. He should never have let his attraction to her get the better of him. But it had happened, and now here she was, finding out he had a son he was about to take full responsibility for. *Would it change anything?*

He took her hand again. "I know we've only just met, but I really like you, Brianna." She started to speak, but he shooshed her. "Please let me finish."

She nodded.

"I don't know how you feel about dating a man with an eleven-year old son he doesn't really know, but I'd love it if you'd give it a shot. But I'll understand if you'd rather not have anything more to do with me."

A few beats passed before she spoke. "Are you asking me to go out with you? To be your girlfriend?"

"Yes…" Andrew sucked in a breath. Was he about to get the best Christmas gift ever?

"Of course I will!" Her eyes lit up as she threw her arms around his neck.

"Even with an eleven-year old appendage?"

"Even with an eleven-year old appendage."

Their eyes locked. He couldn't believe this was happening. He didn't want to think too far ahead, but an image of the three of them together filled his mind, and deep peace filled his heart.

He lowered his head and was about to kiss her when he heard a noise. He raised his head and chuckled. Four small bodies, all wearing colourful flannelette pyjamas, stood about a foot from them.

Brianna also chuckled, amusement flickering in her eyes as she held out her arms to them. "What are you four doing up?"

"Seeing if Santa's come," Clare said, hugging her precious stuffed elephant close to her chest as she slid onto Brianna's lap.

"We haven't seen him yet, but he probably won't visit while we're here and awake. We might need to go back to bed so he'll come."

Dillon began to speak, but Brianna gave him a warning look.

"Is Auntie Grace home?" Clare asked.

Brianna pulled her close and smoothed the little girl's hair. "Yes, Auntie Grace is home."

"That's good. I prayed she would be okay."

"And God heard you." Brianna kissed the top of her head.

The three boys moved to the fire and one of them started prodding it with the poker.

Andrew quickly hopped off the couch. "Best not to stir it up if we're going back to bed."

"Can't we stay up?" Dillon asked. "You're up."

"Yes, but we were just about to go to bed."

"No you weren't. You were just about to kiss Auntie Brianna."

Ruffling Dillon's hair, Andrew stifled a laugh. "Maybe I was, but we need to get to bed now or we might all get into trouble."

Standing, he took Dillon's and James' hands, while Brianna placed Clare on the floor and took her hand along with Quinn's, and they all tiptoed up the stairs, trying not to make any noise. After delivering Dillon, James and Clare to their rooms, Brianna stood on tippy toes and placed a kiss of promise on Andrew's lips before leading Quinn into the room she shared with him and Alana.

As Andrew walked back into his parents' wing along the long hallway, his feet felt lighter and his heart overflowed with hope and anticipation. It seemed God hadn't just given him a son, but He might also have given him someone to share his life with. He was getting ahead of himself, but so far, this was the best Christmas ever.

CHAPTER 13

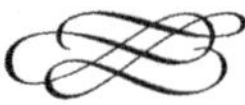

Slipping into bed, Brianna pulled the duvet around her neck until she was snuggly and warm. Her heart sang. Blissfully happy, she felt fully alive, *and awake*. Sleep was needed, because no doubt the children would wake again soon, and she didn't want to miss the joy and excitement of Christmas morning. But how could she sleep?

Andrew had a son. *A son!* That's what he'd been hiding from her. What kind of Christmas would young Andy be having? The last one with his mother… Brianna's heart ached for him. If anyone knew what it was like to lose your mother as a pre-teen, she did, and she wouldn't wish it upon anyone. The poor little boy… he must feel so alone and scared.

But filling her thoughts more than that, was that Andrew had asked *her* to be his girlfriend. *To date him!*

Suddenly, reality hit her. *If* things progressed with Andrew, and *if* he went ahead with his plans of caring for Andy full-time, then she could become the mother of an eleven-year old. Perspiration dampened her body. Throwing off the duvet, she lay flat on her back, gazing at the ceiling. It was one thing to have fallen in love when she'd never expected to, but completely another when it might lead to being an instant mother. What did she know about raising a child? Maybe it was too much. Maybe she should end the relationship while she could. Before it got too hard.

The more Brianna thought about it, the more her mind spun. How could she let Andrew go now? But how could she continue? She released a huge sigh. Prayer was needed. If this was what God wanted, He'd give her whatever skills were required.

Sitting up, she pulled her bed-jacket around her shoulders, bowed her head and prayed quietly, asking God for guidance and wisdom. She also prayed for Andrew, and for Andy. Lastly, she prayed for Shelley, that in her final days before passing, she might open her heart to God's love, and would experience His peace in her life.

Resting in the knowledge that God would give her the direction and guidance she needed, Brianna finally drifted off to sleep.

SOMETIME LATER, her eyes snapped open when little hands shook her.

"Auntie Bianna, wake up. It's Christmas." She just made out Quinn's face in the dark room.

Quickly sitting, she threaded her fingers through her hair and glanced at the clock on the bedside table. *Six o'clock.* Not bad. She must have gotten a few hours' sleep.

Moments later, a knock sounded on her door, followed by Danny's cheery voice. "Everybody up. Merry Christmas!" He sounded as excited as a five-year old.

"Is your mummy awake?" Brianna clicked on the bedside lamp and smiled at Quinn.

He shook his head.

"Why don't you see if you can wake her? I'll grab my gown then I'll come help. Oh, and by the way, merry Christmas!" She pulled the little boy close and gave him a big hug.

He ran off to wake Alana, although Brianna suspected he might need help. Alana certainly was a heavy sleeper.

Slipping out of bed, she shivered and quickly grabbed her thick, quilted gown and slippers. A quick glance in the mirror told her she needed more sleep. Running her hands through her hair again, she tied it back loosely, then ducked into the bathroom before stepping into Alana's side of the room. Alana was stirring and opened her eyes as Brianna approached. Quinn just stood there looking at his mother, melting Brianna's heart.

"Merry Christmas, Alana," Brianna said softly as she smiled at her sister, recalling the prayer she'd prayed just hours before, that today Alana would experience God's love in her life.

Alana yawned, stretched, then pulled Quinn in for a hug. "Merry Christmas, Quinny." As she kissed the top of his dark, messy hair, she returned Brianna's smile. "And merry Christmas to you."

"Can we go downstairs, Mummy?" Quinn hopped up and down like a bunny.

"Yes, Quinny. Just let Mummy get dressed. I'll only be a moment." She plopped him on the bed and then grabbed her gown and visited the bathroom.

Once both Alana and Brianna had changed out of their night attire and into warm, fleecy pants and thick sweaters, the three of them headed downstairs, drawn by the happy sounds of the other children.

Danny, Lizzy and the children were already in the drawing room where the fire that Andrew had put out only hours before was now blazing. Quinn let go Alana's hand and skidded onto the floor to sit beside James and Dillon. Clare sat on Danny's lap.

"Merry Christmas," Danny and Lizzy said in unison. Brianna leaned down and gave them both a hug before sitting with Alana on the same couch she'd sat on with Andrew only hours before.

Andrew wasn't there yet, but every time someone entered, she looked up expectantly. When Grace and Ryan entered, a hush fell over the room. Grace's arm was in a sling, and several bruises on her face had darkened. Clare jumped up and wrapped her arms around Grace's middle. "Merry Christmas, Auntie Grace. Is your arm sore?"

Grace let out a small laugh. Brianna knew her sister was fascinated by Clare's attraction to her, but neither she nor Grace had any idea what had caused the little girl to single Grace out as her favourite auntie. Whatever the reason, Grace loved it. And she loved Clare. They had a special relationship. Strange, really, because Grace had never shown much interest in having children of her own. She bent down and hugged Clare as best as she could with one arm. "It's just a little sore, but I'm okay. Thanks, sweetie."

"Can I sit with you?" Clare's little voice was so adorable.

Grace face lit up. "You sure can."

The chatter in the room returned, escalating when Lizzy's parents, Brendan, Shawn, Aislin, Joel, Rosemary, David, Caleb and the girls all arrived. But no Caitlin, *and no Andrew.* Brianna tried to still her thumping heart. Just the memory of his kisses made her blush. She couldn't wait to see him, but then there was still the question of Andy... *what if God said no?* She prayed that wouldn't be the case. Somehow it felt right. *But where was he?*

Moments later, when the children were getting restless and wanting to open their presents, the door opened and Andrew and Caitlin entered carrying trays of steaming coffee, croissants and pastries. Brianna's gaze immediately went to his, and when they met, her heart-rate accelerated.

He began offering coffee to everybody, but when he stopped in front of her, joy bubbled inside her. How could a man like Andrew McKinnon have fallen for her? Even though he had a past, and now a present that included a son, he was everything Brianna had never known she'd wanted until now. Her heart pounded as she gave him a shy smile and took a coffee from the tray.

When he walked on, Alana whispered in Brianna's ear. "Did I just see something between you two?"

Brianna couldn't hide it if she tried. She nodded, knowing her eyes shone, but not trusting herself to speak.

"I thought so. That's wonderful, Brianna. I'm happy for you."

She squeezed Alana's hand. "Thank you."

"He's a good catch."

"He is..."

As Andrew offered the coffee tray to his parents, Brianna wondered when he'd tell them about Andy, *their grandson.* Would they be excited, or would they be disappointed? If she knew them as well as she thought she did, they'd welcome the boy into their family with loving arms.

Andrew put the empty tray down on the side buffet, grabbed a coffee for himself, along with a croissant, and then sat on the floor at Brianna's feet. They shared a smile as he tilted his head, and then she sat back and watched with amusement as Danny distributed all the presents, with Dillon and James acting as little helpers.

The delight in the children's faces and voices was contagious, and the atmosphere in the room was such a happy one. Just like Christmas should be. Once all the presents had been opened, and the room was littered with wrapping paper, toys, games, clothing and other assorted gifts, Danny announced that following breakfast, a short church service would be held in the chapel, and he hoped everyone would attend.

Brianna turned to Alana, trying to gauge her reaction. *Nothing.* She needed to say something. With firm resolve, she met Alana's gaze. "I'd love you to come to the service, Alana? Will you? Quinny will enjoy it. Danny's got things planned for the children."

Alana shrugged. "I guess so, although I'm not really a church-goer."

Brianna squeezed her hand. "It doesn't matter. I think it'll be fun." She turned her head and rolled her eyes. What was she saying? *Fun?* Church wasn't normally fun, but maybe today it would be. Especially if Danny was leading the service.

Andrew stood and offered his hand to help her up. Brianna still had to pinch herself that this had happened. It was like she forgot, but then when she saw him, or they touched, a wave of warmth swept over her, reminding her that something indeed was happening between them.

When he returned to the kitchen, where no doubt he was concocting something amazing for breakfast, Brianna helped clean up the mess. As she shoved the last of the paper into a huge garbage bag, Grace caught Brianna's eye and patted the spot beside her on the couch. She adjusted her position and looked Brianna in the eye. "So, are you going to tell me?" Grace raised a brow, a grin on her face.

'Tell you what?"

"Come on Bibi, you can't hide anything from me, you know that."

Grace was right. They'd shared everything from the time they were young. Nothing was hidden between them. Besides, by the grin on her face, Grace already knew. Brianna let out a small chuckle and glanced at the ceiling. "I think you already know."

Grace's face lit up. "I'm so happy for you, Bibi. He seems like a good man."

Brianna nodded. If she could talk to anyone about 'the complication', it would be Grace. "Yes, but don't tell anyone…" She leaned closer and lowered her voice. "He has an eleven-year old son."

Grace's forehead creased. "Is that a problem?"

Brianna's shoulders sagged and she looked down at her hands. "I'm not sure." Lifting her head, she met Grace's uneasy gaze. "Andrew only found out about him a month ago, but the boy's mother is dying, and she wants Andrew to take him."

"Oh." For once, Grace seemed lost for words. Moments passed. The fire crackled. One of the children laughed. Brianna could see Grace's mind working. Finally, she spoke. "And is he going to take him?"

"I think so."

"How do you feel about that?"

"I've prayed about it."

"And?"

"I don't know yet, but I think I'm okay with it." Shrugging, Brianna fidgeted with her hands. "It's early days, anyway."

"Yes, but I've seen the way you look at each other. I can tell." Her eyes grew dreamy. "It was the same for Ryan and me. There was something special, different, and you just know. I can see it in you two."

"Really?" Brianna thought she might cry from happiness.

Grace nodded and tucked a strand of hair behind Brianna's ear.

"I can't believe all this has happened."

With her good arm, Grace drew her close and stroked her hair. "Bibi, God only wants good things for us, and I think this might be His good thing for you."

Brianna squeezed her eyes shut. It was almost too much… all those years of heartache, and more recently, the years of working with rape victims but not really living a life of joy and fun. Although she was so grateful that God had given her new life, and she was content, but if she were honest, she longed to be loved by someone special as well. Someone other than her siblings and friends. She'd accepted that might never happen, and she'd been scared of getting close to anyone. But now that love was a possibility, she was delighted, albeit, in shock.

"I think you'll be a great mum."

That did it. Tears streamed down Brianna's cheeks. Grace handed her a tissue. Brianna blew her nose. "Thank you."

"I mean it, Bibi. I think it's great." Grace leaned closer. "Can I tell you my secret now?" Her face lit up.

"You have a secret?" What was Grace hiding?

Grace's smile widened. "Don't worry—it's nothing bad. Ryan and I are expecting a baby."

Brianna's eyes popped. "You're not!"

"We are!"

"I didn't think you wanted children."

"Until I met Ryan, I didn't. Then everything changed. True love can do that for a person."

Brianna threw her arms around Grace, taking care not to hurt her sore shoulder. "That's fantastic news, Grace. Congratulations." Drawing back, a thought occurred to her. "Yesterday… the fall… is everything okay?"

"Yes, praise God. I'm perfect except for the collarbone and shoulder."

"I'm so sorry, Grace. If I hadn't gone skiing, you wouldn't have been worried about me and gone out looking for us."

"Don't say that, Bibi. It's all good."

"But it could have ended badly."

"It didn't, so no more. Okay?"

Brianna gave her a grateful smile. "Okay. So, who knows about the baby?"

"Only you."

"Oh. Okay, I won't say anything." Briana lowered her voice.

"We're planning on announcing it at lunch."

Brianna smiled again. "Everyone will be excited. I won't say anything until then."

"Thanks." Grace hugged her again. "We'd better go in for breakfast before it's all eaten. That man of yours is cooking something special, so I hear."

Brianna giggled. *Man of hers?* She liked the sound of that!

CHAPTER 14

With Caitlin acting as apprentice chef, Andrew had indeed prepared a special Christmas breakfast. French toast with mixed berries and whipped cream, pancakes with blueberry-plum syrup, and the tastiest little quiches Brianna had ever eaten. She patted her stomach as she thought how much weight she might put on if Andrew kept cooking like this.

After a very jolly breakfast and a quick clean-up, Danny gave a reminder about the service. Everyone, including Brendan, Shawn, Aislin and Joel, and Alana, said they'd be there.

After promising Alana she'd walk with her to the chapel, Brianna hung back in the kitchen and helped Andrew with the final clean-up. Andrew slipped his arms around her waist and gave her a slow kiss. "I've been wanting to do that all morning." His breath was warm and sweet and filled her with longing.

"Have you had any sleep?" she asked.

"No…" He kissed her again. "Too much on my mind."

Brianna pulled back. "Like telling your parents about Andy?"

"How did you guess?"

She shrugged. "That's got to be the biggest thing on your mind right now. So, when are you going to tell them?"

His shoulders slumped. "After church."

"I'm sure they'll be fine once they get over the initial shock."

"I hope so." He glanced at the clock on the wall. "We'd best go or we'll be late."

"I promised to walk with Alana. Save me a seat?" The prospect of sitting beside him in church filled Brianna with joy and anticipation. If their relationship was to develop, God had to be their focus, and what better day to start than Christmas Day?

"Yes, but hurry," he said. A thrill of excitement raced through her when he lowered his head and brushed his lips over hers. Would she ever get used to this?

"I will." She gazed into his eyes for a moment longer before tearing herself from his arms.

Brianna took the steps two at a time, praying that Alana hadn't changed her mind. She smiled to herself when she reached the room. Quinn was seated on Alana's bed, hair brushed, face wiped, and wearing the new set of clothes Aislin and Joel had given him for Christmas—dark blue corduroy trousers and a hand-knitted red sweater. He looked adorable. And Alana had applied a little make-up... amazing how much difference it made to her appearance. Brianna was pleased Alana wanted to look her best for church. Not that it mattered. With the amount of snow they'd had, most likely it would only be family attending, as well as David, Rosemary and Andrew. But the fact that she'd taken care with herself heartened Brianna.

"You look nice, Alana." She flashed a warm smile and then squatted in front of Quinn, getting down to his level. "And you look so cute in those new clothes, little Quinny."

His face beamed. "Auntie Ash made them for me."

"She's a very clever auntie."

He nodded as he inspected the trucks and tippers Aislin had knitted into each wrist band. She'd obviously taken a great deal of care.

Straightening, Brianna glanced in the mirror. A little make-up was needed to camouflage her lack of sleep. "I'll just be a minute." Darting into the shared bathroom, she smoothed her hair and brushed her teeth, then threw on some blusher, a light coat of mascara, and a quick lick of lipstick. That would have to do.

"Ready?" she asked, re-entering the bedroom.

Alana nodded, took Quinn's hand, and they followed Brianna out the door.

THE SMALL CHAPEL sat on the far side of the main Elim Community building. Built of stone, it had once been a barn, but quite a few years ago it had been renovated and made into a simple place of worship, and now it even had stained glass windows. Although mainly intended for the students and staff of the Community, people now came from miles around. The small church's reputation for preaching God's word without compromise had spread over the years.

The chapel was more than half full—people had braved the weather after all. Brianna's eyes searched for Andrew, and when she caught sight of his tawny-gold hair her heart skipped a beat. Would she ever be able to look at him without having palpitations? Somehow, she doubted it.

She ushered Alana and Quinn forward, directing them to the pew on the left, midway down the small chapel, where Andrew sat with his parents. Alana motioned for her to sit beside Andrew, while she and Quinn took the spots nearest the aisle. When Andrew slipped his hand into hers, squeezing gently, a thrill raced up her spine. There had been many times when she'd looked at Danny and Lizzy and Grace and Ryan sitting close to each other in church that she wondered what it was like to sit with someone special while worshipping God together. She was about to find out, but so far, she liked it.

Danny and Lizzy and the others had done a great job of decorating the chapel. A nativity scene, complete with a small make-shift barn, hay, cows, sheep, the three wise men, and the baby Jesus with Mary and Joseph, took pride of place at the front of the chapel. Dillon played *Joy to the World* on the piano while Lizzy stood and turned the pages. Although he barely reached the pedals, he played brilliantly.

The other children sat in the front pew beside Grace, Ryan and Danny. When Dillon finished playing, Danny stood and welcomed everyone, inviting the congregation to stand and sing the carol that expressed the joy of Christmas.

Brianna glanced at Andrew and smiled before turning to Alana.

She had picked Quinn up and placed him on her hip.

Brianna leaned closer. "Are you okay?"

Alana nodded, a small smile lifting the corners of her mouth.

"Let me know if you'd like a break."

"Thanks."

Brianna inched closer to Andrew and began singing.

The service was everything she had expected and more. Danny and Lizzy had a special gift when it came to running a service, and they had planned songs and a short activity just for the children in which they all played a part, even Quinn. Caleb and Caitlin's girls took turns reading the Bible verses, telling the story of Jesus' birth in the manger, and there was lots of singing. When Danny stood at the lectern to start the sermon, Brianna shifted in her seat, growing a little anxious. Normally she loved listening to Danny preach, but with Alana beside her, and Brendan, Shawn and the others not far away, she hoped he'd make it short and to the point.

When he started by promising not to speak for long, Brianna breathed a sigh of relief and relaxed, but prayed silently that God would speak through him to everyone there. Danny had never formally trained as a preacher, but he spoke from the heart, and that, combined with his easy-going nature, meant that whenever he spoke, it was entertaining but meaningful, and God used him to touch peoples' hearts. Brianna prayed that today would be no different.

"Christmas is just the best time of year, isn't it?" he began. "And this Christmas it's even better having all my family here. To me, that's what the message of Christmas is all about... *connecting.* God connecting with man, people connecting with people, families connecting with each other. Love, acceptance, new beginnings, *hope.* We can all do with that, especially hope. God sent His only son, Jesus, to earth as a baby for just that reason... to give hope and a future to all those who believe."

As Danny continued to speak, Alana brushed her damp face with the back of her hand. Brianna reached out, placing her hand gently against Alana's shoulder while sending up another prayer. God was touching Alana's heart, and Brianna couldn't have been happier.

Danny finished his short sermon by asking everyone to bow their heads while he prayed. From the corner of her eye, Brianna noticed Alana sniffle as she closed her eyes. Brianna slipped an arm around her shoulders, pulling her close while Danny prayed.

Fresh tears continued to slide down Alana's cheeks. When Danny finished praying and everyone rose to sing *'Hark, the Herald Angels Sing',* Brianna offered to take Quinn. The little boy clung to her while staring at his mother with his thumb in his mouth.

As the carol ended, Brianna leaned closer to Andrew and whispered, "I'm going to stay here with Alana for a while. Okay?" Their eyes held for a second, and she knew he understood.

Nodding, Andrew held his arms out to Quinn. "Come with me?"

The little boy quickly climbed across, wrapping his arms around Andrew's neck.

Brianna smiled her thanks. "I'll catch you soon." For a moment, she thought Andrew might lean across and kiss her, but she was very relieved when he didn't. They hadn't formally told his parents they were dating yet, although she assumed they'd guessed. Andrew and his parents left the pew in the opposite direction, leaving her with Alana.

Memories of Rosemary sitting with her not that long ago flashed through Brianna's mind. God's first touch on a life was such a precious time… inexplicable, but real, nonetheless. She sat quietly with her arm around Alana's shoulder, giving time for her sister to compose herself before saying anything. When Alana raised her head slightly, Brianna searched her eyes. "Are you all right, Alana? Would you like to talk?"

Alana nodded, sniffing.

"God's affecting you inside, isn't He?"

Alana nodded again.

"I'd love to pray for you, and then maybe we can spend some time chatting. Would you like that?"

Another nod. Another sniff.

Bowing her head, Brianna paused before beginning. Her heart was filled with gratitude that this moment had finally arrived, and she didn't want to spoil it. She took a slow breath and began in a quiet voice. "Dear God, thank You for my precious sister, Alana. You know what's going on inside her, the hurt she's experienced, the disappointments, the lack of hope. Thank You for gently reaching out to her, showing her how much You love her, how precious she is to You. Lord God, I pray that today, as we celebrate the birth of your son, Jesus, who came into the world so that all who believe in Him can have eternal life, I pray that You'll touch her in a real way, and that she might open her heart to You and to Your healing. Lord God, I pray special blessings upon her life, and I thank You so much for her precious little boy. Bless Quinn, dear Lord, and may he also come to know You. I ask all these things in Jesus' precious name, Amen."

Brianna wiped her own eyes as she raised her head and gave Alana a big hug.

Sniffing, and with eyes moist, Alana hugged her back. "Thank you."

"You're more than welcome."

Alana blew her nose. "I've… I've never really believed in God too much. I guess I always assumed He was there, but never thought He was of any use in my life. But since being here, with you, and Danny and Lizzy, and all the others, I can see that He's changed you all, and I think I want what you've got." Tears streamed down her cheeks again.

"That's the best thing I've heard all day." Brianna handed Alana a clean tissue. "It's really simple. You just have to be sorry for all the things you've done wrong, and then claim the forgiveness that Jesus brought when he died on the cross, and then ask Him to come and live in your heart. It sounds a bit mysterious, but Jesus, being perfect, took on the sins of the whole world when He died on the cross, so that anyone who believes can be made clean in God's sight and have new life. It's a lot to take in, and we can talk about it more, but that's basically it."

"It sounds great, but I think I need to understand a little better before I make a decision."

"That's perfectly fine. It's a big thing, and you shouldn't do it lightly, but having an open heart is the first step. That's all He asks of you, to open your heart and your mind, and He'll gently lead you to Himself when you're ready. But let me tell you, when you do, it's like a whole new world opening up. I couldn't believe how free I felt after all those years of drug addiction and self-hate. God has made such a difference in my life, and He can in yours, too."

"I really want to know more. I'm tired of living like I do." Alana blinked back tears again.

Pulling her close, Brianna rubbed Alana's back, rocking her like a baby. "I know. Believe me, I know."

They sat there for several more minutes before Brianna straightened. "We can chat more later, okay?"

"Yes, thanks." Alana dabbed her nose and nodded.

"Let's grab a coffee."

"Sounds great."

Brianna stood first and helped Alana up. Although the chapel was now empty, a special sense of God's presence filled the air.

CHAPTER 15

Andrew followed his parents out of the chapel with Quinn perched on his hip and shot a backwards glance to Brianna. His heart was with her, but Alana would be more comfortable chatting with her sister alone. *Besides, there was that talk with his parents.* He walked behind them, gathering his courage. How would his parents take the news that they had an eleven-year-old grandson? Would they be excited, as Brianna had suggested, or would they be disappointed he'd fathered a child out of wedlock? Or maybe both? He guessed the latter. For years his mother had been at him to find a nice girl and settle down and to give her some grandbabies... *but Andy was no baby;* he was almost a teen. But his parents loved God, and they loved people, and so there was no reason why they wouldn't love Andy. They might just be in shock for a while.

Last night, unable to sleep after Brianna went to bed, Andrew had spent the rest of the night in the kitchen preparing not only breakfast, but all the vegetables and everything else for Christmas lunch. He'd told Caitlin earlier what still needed to be done in case he got held up, and while he diced carrots, potatoes and pumpkin, he thought through what it would be like to be a father to Andy. *A real father,* not just a biological father. The prospect scared, yet excited him.

He not only thought, but he prayed, asking God for wisdom. Not only with regard to Andy, but also with Brianna. Andrew hadn't been looking for an instant family, but it seemed highly likely that God had been planning it. Brianna would be the perfect mother for Andy. Kind, caring, understanding, and empathetic. She might not have had any experience with teenagers, but Andrew was sure she'd rise to the challenge. *But was he only interested in her because he'd soon be responsible for a motherless child?* The more he thought and prayed, the more he realised how much he already liked her… dare he say it, *loved her?* But could you love someone you've only just met? All these thoughts and more still ran around his head as he exited the chapel, and he almost bumped into his parents who'd stopped at the door and were putting on coats and scarves.

Andrew pulled himself up, placed Quinn on the stone floor, and helped him into his little coat. Although the chapel was only a short distance from the main house, the day had dawned bitterly cold, and dark, heavy clouds filled the sky. The family had started scampering back to the house to freshen up before Christmas lunch, so as Andrew and his parents followed along behind, he cleared his throat. "Mum, Dad, can we have a chat?"

His parents both slowed. "Sure, son, what's up?" his father asked.

"Let's grab a coffee when we get into the house and find somewhere to talk."

"Is it about you and Brianna?" His mother sounded hopeful.

"Kind of…"

"That sounds promising." Her eyes sparkled.

Andrew gulped. *Yes, but wait until you hear the rest of it.* "I'll make some coffee and we can sit and talk. In the small drawing room?"

"Sure. Sounds intriguing, son." His father angled his head, placing his hand lightly on Andrew's back.

"Yes, well… let me make that coffee. Mum, can you take Quinn? Maybe see if he can play with the other children?"

"My pleasure." His mother flashed a smile and then bent down and took Quinn's hand. "I love the trucks on your sleeves, Quinn."

"Auntie Ash made them." Quinn pointed to his sleeves proudly.

"She's a very clever auntie."

Nodding, Quinn walked off happily with Rosemary.

Andrew headed straight to the kitchen, poured three cups of coffee from the percolator Caitlin had ready, popped them on a tray along with three generous slices of Christmas cake, and walked to the smaller drawing room where his father had already retreated. He stood with his back to the fire. Andrew placed the tray on the coffee table as his mother came into the room. His parents took a seat on the couch while he sat in the single armchair.

"So, son, what is it you need to tell us?" His father leaned back and crossed his legs.

Andrew picked up his coffee and took a slow sip before lifting his gaze, shifting it between his parents. "Do you remember a girl called Shelley that I used to date?"

His mother's brow puckered. "I'm not sure I do." Rosemary turned and looked at her husband, her head tilting in question. "Do you remember her, love?"

Shaking his head, David leaned forward. "Anyway, son, what about her?"

Andrew cleared his throat. "She contacted me recently." Adrenaline surged through his body like a locomotive. Best just to blurt it out and be done with it. "I have an eleven-year old son."

His mother's jaw dropped, her eyes widening. "What do you mean, an eleven-year old son? How do you know he's yours?"

"I thought you'd ask that. I've met him… that's how. He looks exactly like I did at that age. And I've also had a DNA test done."

"So why did this, what did you say her name was?" his father asked, his brows pinching together.

"Shelley... her name's Shelley."

"So why did this Shelley just tell you now? Does she want something from you?" His father sounded disbelieving. Annoyed.

Andrew's shoulders sagged. "Yes, she does." He stared into his coffee mug. "Shelley's dying, and she wants me to take the boy." His heart beat fast as he studied his parents' reactions.

Tears welled in his mother's eyes. "Does the boy know his mother's dying?"

Andrew shook his head. "Not yet, but I'm sure he knows something's wrong."

"How long does she have?" his father asked, taking Rosemary's hand, his voice softening.

"Not long... maybe two months."

"Are you going to take him?" Rosemary dabbed her eyes.

Andrew swallowed hard. "I'm not sure, but I think so."

His father released a heavy sigh. "We never expected this, son, and it will take a while to sink in, but if he *is* your son, then you have to take him. I gather there's no one else lining up for him?"

"No... she hooked up with someone else after we went our own ways, but it didn't last."

"What about her family?" Rosemary asked.

"She hasn't had anything to do with them for years. Her parents are divorced and basically disowned her. Shelley is adamant. She wants me to have him."

His father narrowed his eyes. "How do you feel about that?"

Andrew looked down at his hands. "I was shocked to start with. And angry." Shaking his head, he lifted his gaze, remembering back to the last time he'd seen Shelley. He'd had no idea she was expecting. "If she'd told me she was pregnant, we might have stayed together." Blinking, he wondered whether it would have worked. They were both pretty messed up back then.

"We broke up not long before I went on that walk, but she never said a word."

"It must have been a real surprise." His mother reached out and squeezed his hand.

Andrew nodded. "It took a while, but I finally agreed to meet him. We met in a park, but Shelley didn't tell Andy, that's his name, that I was his dad. She just said I was a friend." Pausing, Andrew glanced out the window before turning and meeting his parents' stunned gazes. "He still doesn't know… she's waiting on my answer before she tells him the truth."

His father's gaze was steady. "And have you decided?"

Andrew's heart pounded so hard he was sure his parents could hear it. Now, it wasn't just something that *might* happen… it was happening. "I've been praying about it a lot, and I feel God wants me to. I'm scared, but excited at the same time."

His father gave him an understanding smile. "I can understand that, especially being on your own."

His mother leaned forward. "How does Brianna fit into the picture. Does she know?"

Andrew blinked. His mother was very perceptive, but was putting him on the spot. "I thought you'd ask that."

"She's a nice girl, Andrew, but can you expect her to be interested in you if you have a son?"

"That's what I thought, but I told her last night, and she's okay with it."

His father's brow furrowed again. "Your having a child by another woman doesn't concern her?"

Andrew shook his head. "No." A slow grin replaced the grim line of his mouth as he recalled the genuine warmth of her reaction. "In fact, she was happy for me."

"Well, sometimes God surprises us with His plans." His mother chuckled as she dabbed her eyes again. "I was starting to think you were never going to give me any grandchildren, and now we've got an instant one. I'd love to meet him, Andrew. He'll always be welcome here."

Tears stung Andrew's eyes as a deep sense of peace filled his heart. Maybe this really was God's plan for him. "Thanks, Mum. He'd love it here."

David angled his head as a gong sounded. "Is that the dinner bell?"

Andrew glanced at his watch. "I think so. We'd best be going." He stood and raked a trembling hand through his hair. "I'm sorry I shocked you… I was sweating on telling you."

"We all have things in our lives that would surprise others, son." David eased himself up from the couch and then helped Rosemary up. "You needn't have worried." He slipped his arm around her shoulder. "This news has made your mother's day. It's the best Christmas present you could have given her."

Andrew chuckled. "That's what Brianna said you'd say."

"Brianna's a clever girl." His mother moved closer, her eyes shining. "Let me give you a hug." Pulling Andrew close, Rosemary rubbed his back. "You'll make a great father, Andrew."

Coming from his mother, those words were music to his ears. "Thanks, Mum. I appreciate your confidence."

"Come on you two. I don't want to miss my Christmas lunch." David moved to the door, and as he opened it, a flash of red caught Andrew's eye. *Brianna*.

Andrew hurried to the door and poked his head out to call her name. Brianna and Alana both paused and looked back down the hallway. Alana squeezed Brianna's hand and whispered something to her before stepping away and continuing on her way. As his gaze met Brianna's, his heart did a quick flip. Yes, he'd fallen for her big time. He smiled and extended his hand. "Got a second?"

Nodding, Brianna stepped towards him, her gaze shifting between his and his father's.

Andrew slipped an arm around her shoulder and motioned for his father to go back into the room. "Brianna, I've just told Mum and Dad about Andy, and about us..."

"And we're thrilled." His mother stepped forward and gave her a big hug, bringing tears to his eyes. Every minute that passed confirmed this was God's doing.

Letting out a small laugh, Brianna winked at him as she returned his mother's hug. "It's a weekend of surprises."

"It is indeed." Rosemary agreed.

David headed to the door again. "I truly like all this love and togetherness, but we're going to miss our Christmas lunch if we don't go now."

The other three laughed, then they all headed for the dining room.

As Lizzy listened to the happy chatter at the Christmas table, her thoughts drifted. What would life have been like had she married Mathew Carter instead of Daniel? Not for one moment did she regret marrying him, but Mathew had been her first love, and she'd been so looking forward to supporting his ministry as his wife. So much water under the bridge, but there'd been a time when she thought she'd made a mistake marrying Daniel, as had everyone else, given his alcoholism and abuse issues. However, God had brought them through that time, and now she couldn't imagine life without him.

The chat they'd just had following the service made her realise that God had a sense of humour. Daniel had found her when everyone was filing out of the chapel, his eyes alight and full of excitement. "Lizzy, Lizzy love, wait up. I've got something I want to run past you."

She'd stopped and angled her head. "What?"

"I think I know what God wants us to do."

Her eyes widened. They'd been praying for His guidance, but until now, no clear direction had been forthcoming. "Are you going to share?"

"Yes. I think He wants me to be a preacher."

Lizzy laughed. Preaching was a perfect job for Daniel. He loved talking, he was great with people, and he loved God. He was a born communicator, *and God did have a sense of humour.* She, Elizabeth O'Connor, née Walton-Smythe, would be a minister's wife after all. Just not Mathew's wife, but *Daniel's.* Her heart soared, it felt so right. "You'll make a wonderful preacher, Daniel. So... you're thinking Bible College? Four years of study?" Her brow lifted.

"I guess so. I haven't thought that far, but if that's what it takes."

"There's a college near Mother and Father's... maybe we could consider that one?"

Slipping his arms around her waist, Daniel gazed into her eyes. "You'd like that, wouldn't you?"

Lizzy nodded. She loved Scotland and the ruggedness of the Highlands. She loved the people and the ministry they had here, but she missed her home, and her parents would love their grandchildren living near them. "I think it would be perfect."

Daniel leaned forward and kissed her. "Let's pray about it, shall we?"

"Yes. If that's where God wants us, I'm sure He'll show us the way."

"I love you, Liz. Thank you for standing by me when things were bad."

"I love you too, Daniel. God's been good to us."

"He has. Amazingly good."

"So, do we say anything?"

"Not yet... let's keep it our secret for now, but you're on board?"

"Absolutely. You're a born preacher, and God will use you mightily. It feels so right."

When Ryan stood and dinged his glass, Lizzy's thoughts returned to the present. When he announced that he and Grace were expecting a baby and everyone clapped and laughed with elation, Lizzy was so glad she and Daniel had decided not to say anything about their idea just yet. Time enough for that once they were completely sure, although in her mind, there was no doubt.

Over the next few days, while everyone either relaxed indoors or ventured outside when the weather allowed, more news came out. Everyone was initially surprised to hear about Andrew's son, but he and Brianna looked so happy together, it was almost assumed they'd be an instant family before the year was out.

When the time came for everyone to leave, they all agreed it had been the best Christmas ever and they should do it again. Lizzy didn't say she and Daniel might not be here next Christmas, but the thought raced through her mind that they could have an O'Connor family Christmas at Wivelscombe Manor, her parents' large manor home in the south of England. Wouldn't that be a turn-around!

CHAPTER 16

Brianna stood in Lizzy's bedroom in the small cottage at the Elim Community three months later. Lizzy and Grace fussed over her as they adjusted the beautiful lace bridal gown Grace had helped her choose after Andrew proposed less than two weeks after Christmas. She was marrying Andrew McKinnon today, that they were leaving in the morning for their honeymoon in Spain, and that Andy, their eleven-year old son, would be staying here with his new grandparents, Rosemary and David for a holiday in the Highlands. What a whirlwind it had been!

The day Andrew told Andy he was his father was etched in Brianna's memory. Andrew had agreed to meet Shelley and Andy at the restaurant he was the Executive Chef. The day after he returned to Glasgow after the Christmas break, he'd booked the table with the best view of the city —having made the decision and not wanting to waste any time. Shelley would break the news of her terminal condition to her son.

Andrew had asked Brianna to join them, but she believed he needed to do it on his own. He was so nervous that morning, she had to tell him countless times to trust that it would be okay... God was with him and would give him the right words. Brianna promised to stay at her home and pray for them all.

After Andrew left, and all afternoon, Brianna's thoughts and prayers were with them. She tried catching up on some paperwork for the centre to help pass the time, but her heart wasn't in it. Instead, she put on a thick coat and went for a walk, and as she walked, she prayed. Despite the chill of the day, she didn't feel cold. Her focus was totally on Andrew, Shelley and Andy. She pictured how the conversation would go... Andrew's nervousness, and the shock and sorrow in Andy's eyes when he discovered his mother had only months to live. She also imagined his reaction when told that Andrew was his father. Her heart ached for the boy, but she knew that God would wrap him in an invisible blanket of love, protecting his heart. Yes, he'd be sad about his mother, but Andrew was a good man, and would be a great father. He would see Andy through this difficult time.

When Andrew returned to Brianna's semi-attached terraced home several hours later, she'd just put the kettle on and was about to make a pot of tea. As she opened the door, she immediately knew God had answered their prayers. Andrew's eyes sparkled.

She gave him a smile that came from her heart. "So, it went well?"

He nodded enthusiastically, his eyes moistening as he reached out and pulled her close. "Andy said he'd already figured it out."

Brianna couldn't help herself and chuckled. "He sounds like one smart boy."

Andrew pulled back and gazed into her eyes. "He is."

"I'm so glad it went well. What about Shelley? How is she?"

"Are you going to invite me in, or do we have to stand here for all the neighbours to see?"

Brianna chuckled again as she glanced down the street. "Sorry. Come in. I was just making tea. Would you like a cup?"

"Love one."

She'd grabbed his hand and pulled him inside before closing the door. "So, Shelley?"

"He knew about her condition, too. He'd seen her medication and guessed."

"And how is he handling it?" Brianna asked as she poured steaming water into the tea pot.

"Better than expected. But maybe he's putting on a tough front."

"Probably." She took two mugs from the shelf.

"I want you to meet him, Brianna."

She'd turned around and faced him. "Isn't it too soon?"

Andrew had stepped toward her, rubbing her forearms with his, and gazed deeply into her eyes. "I know we haven't known each other long, but I love you, Brianna. I love everything about you, and I want to spend my life with you. I just know it deep down that this is right. Brianna, will you marry me?"

Her palm had flown to her chest, where she felt her heart lurch. Never in a million years had she expected their relationship to accelerate so quickly. But she'd agreed… it seemed so right. Joy bubbled in her laugh as she'd nodded eagerly. "Yes, Andrew McKinnon, I'll marry you!" she'd exclaimed. She'd gazed into his eyes, and as his arms encircled her, she'd buried her hands in his hair, lifted her face, and waited for his passionate kiss. Her knees weakened as his lips, warm and sweet, met hers.

Two days later, Brianna met Andy and she loved him immediately. He was just like his father, not only in looks, but in personality, soft and gently spoken, courteous and polite. But she knew deep down there would be sadness and loss, and plenty of challenges to overcome. She prayed that God would help her and Andrew to be sensitive, and to help Andy through the difficult days ahead.

They agreed not to wait to marry. They were both sure, and so now, here she was, preparing to marry her perfect man.

"There," Grace said as she stood after adjusting Brianna's long train.

"You look beautiful, Bibi." Holding her at arm's length, Grace gazed into her eyes. "I'm so happy for you."

Brianna forced herself not to cry—she didn't want to ruin her make-up. Instead, she swallowed hard and returned Grace's smile. "Thank you, Grace. For everything. I mean it."

"Come on now, enough of that, or we'll both be blubbering messes. Time to get you hitched."

Brianna laughed gently. Yes, it was time to get hitched.

LIZZY SAT in the Elim Community chapel, her heart overflowing with love and gratitude as Daniel walked down the aisle with Brianna's arm tucked through his. She was a beautiful bride, her face was glowing, and it warmed Lizzy's heart to see how much in love she and Andrew were.

Brianna's eyes were firmly fixed on Andrew, looking ruggedly handsome in McKinnon clan tartan, but when Lizzy caught Daniel's eye as he and Brianna passed and he winked at her, she couldn't help but smile. New beginnings were everywhere. Brianna was marrying Andrew, eleven-year old Andy had a new family, Grace and Ryan were expecting their first child, and she and Daniel were looking forward to moving closer to her parents and him starting Bible College in a few weeks' time.

And then there was Alana. Caitlin had taken Daniel's younger sister under her wing when they both returned to Belfast after Christmas, and Alana seemed at peace. Happy, even. God was working in her life as He no doubt was in the lives of the others. They might not have responded to Him yet, but Daniel and Lizzy prayed for Shawn, Brendan, Aislin and Joel every night, along with all his other siblings. They'd become so close since Christmas, and even Brendan had flown back to Scotland for Brianna's wedding, having managed to stay out of jail for the longest time ever.

So many things to be thankful for. So many blessings. So much to look forward to. Lizzy sighed with contentment as Daniel joined her and squeezed her hand. They were indeed blessed beyond measure.

"Every good and perfect gift is from above, coming down from the Father of the heavenly lights, who does not change like shifting shadows." James 1:17

NOTE FROM THE AUTHOR

I hope you enjoyed Brianna and Andrew's heartwarming story as much as I enjoyed writing it.

Make sure you don't miss my new releases by joining my mailing list. **Visit www.julietteduncan.com/subscribe** to join, and as a thank you for signing up, you'll also receive a **free short story.**

Enjoyed The Shadow Series...Here's another book I think you'll enjoy! Safe in His Arms. Read a preview below.

Finally, could I ask you a **favour**? Would you help other people find this book by writing a review and telling them why you liked it? Honest reviews of my books help bring them to the attention of other readers just like yourself, and I'd be very grateful if you could spare just a minute or two to leave a review.

With gratitude,
Juliette

Safe in His Arms

THEY WERE TRAPPED.

Panic rose inside Junia as the reality of the situation sunk in. The adrenalin that had kept her going through the crazy events of the last hour had subsided. In its place, terror curled in her stomach.

Below, smoke blanketed the horizon, darkening the sky and thickening the air. Above reared the mountaintop, high and forbidding against an azure sky. She swallowed hard, fighting to keep her cool, but her body began trembling uncontrollably. Their route off the mountain was blocked in every direction except up.

"Junia," Max said, his voice low but urgent, and threaded with pain from his gunshot wound, "Did you hear me? The radio signal isn't coming through...I can't get hold of my brothers."

She sucked in a breath. If only her thighs and hands would stop shaking. "What do we do?" Her voice sounded muffled.

"We have to go higher so we can get around the other side." His mouth was set in a grim line.

She gave a slow nod, trying not to voice her immediate fear. They could only go so high. She was no mountain climber, and if the fire came in their direction, it would catch them in minutes.

"Will we get a signal if we go higher?" She was grasping at any slight hope. If they could get through to Joseph, who worked in Mountain Rescue, to give him their location, the Rescue helicopter could pick them up.

"Maybe. We'll keep trying. Come on."

But she couldn't move. Her ears still rang from the gunshots which had seemed impossibly loud on the quiet mountain. They had no idea where the gang members had gone, if they were looking for Max to finish him off, or if they'd managed to catch Tasha.

Where was she? A fresh wave of panic surged through Junia. The girl was as trapped as they were, but she was alone with no survival skills, and the gang members were after her, intent on dragging her back to the city.

Even worse, she'd fled straight in the direction of the fire.

Junia stared at Max, her lip trembling. "I'm...I'm scared."

He held her gaze, and for a moment she thought he might hug her. But of course, he wouldn't. They'd only known each other a week, and she'd already gleaned that he was far from a touchy-feely person. Instead, he narrowed his gaze. "I'll look after you. We'll be fine." His voice was gruff but held a small amount of compassion. *But how could he be so sure they'd be fine?* He suffered from a gunshot wound and a raging bushfire was hot on their heels.

"We need to pray," she said. Only God could help them out of this mess.

He nodded. They might not see eye to eye on everything, but they both had faith in God. That was something. Taking her elbow, he led her to a rock where they sat next to each other.

He enclosed her shaking hands with his. This token of empathy was totally out of character for the gruff wilderness guide who'd kept himself at arm's length all week. If they weren't fearing for their very lives, being close to him could have been pleasant. In that moment though, she was simply grateful for his strength.

She swallowed hard, closing her eyes and trying to go within, to reach the peace that was always there, deep down, but terror welled up in her again. Throwing herself on God's mercy, she prayed aloud for them both.

"Lord, lead us through this danger to a place of safety. Guide our steps that we might find rescue and refuge. Calm the fires with Your mighty hand. Heavenly Father, watch over Tasha. Keep her safe from her pursuers. Blind their eyes so they don't find her. In Jesus' name, we pray. Amen."

"Amen," Max echoed.

Raising her head, Junia met his gaze. Pain filled his eyes. She lifted one of her hands from his and placed it gently over the roughly bandaged wound in his shoulder.

"Lord," she prayed again, *"send Your healing to Max. Bind his wounds and*

heal his flesh. Take his pain from him. I beseech You in the name of Your Son. Amen."

He drew a deep breath and released it slowly, as if allowing God's healing presence to touch the injury, before lifting his gaze and nodding. "Thanks. It feels a bit better."

Still seated, with one of her hands in his, Junia sensed something had changed between them. Perhaps because they faced a common enemy. Their gazes held, and she felt her face warm as she suddenly realised how close they were. They both dropped their hands and gazes at the same time, and an awkward silence filled the space between them.

Max coughed and stood, and the moment was gone. "Come on," he said briskly. "We need to move. The further we can get away from that smoke, the better. Even if the fire doesn't reach us, the smoke will kill us."

With his words, Junia was again reminded of how desperate their situation was. They had to go up before they could go down, because there was no way they could traverse the sheer cliffs on either side. They couldn't go back, because that would put them in the direct line of the fire.

As she followed him up the mountain, she tried not to think what would happen if help didn't come soon. They were truly in the wilderness, and right now, there was no escape.

One week earlier

"OKAY GUYS, WE'RE HERE." Junia stepped down from the minivan and waited for the young people she was responsible for to follow. One by one they climbed out and waited for the driver to get their bags from the luggage hold while she looked around. Eastbrooke Mountain Retreat looked just as the brochures had pictured. A small ranch at the bottom of a forbidding looking mountain, just two kilometres out of the small town of Eastbrooke, it had seemed the perfect place to bring the teens for a ten-day retreat, where they would learn team building and practical survival skills of a different sort to the ones they were used to. These were kids who knew how to survive on the street, but she wondered how that would translate to the wilderness. Her hope was that this retreat would boost their self-esteem, as well as teach them gratitude for the simple things of life.

Not to mention burn off some of that adolescent energy. Chuck, an angelic looking blond boy with ADHD and a previous tendency to set things on fire, jostled Gavin, a brooding boy with a prominent gang tattoo on the side of his neck.

These were her kids, not just her work. They were her vocation. After her own struggles in childhood, Junia had always known she'd become a youth worker, and she couldn't imagine doing anything else. She loved her job, as challenging as it sometimes was.

She cast her gaze over the group. Four boys, two girls, all with their own stories to tell, challenges to overcome, and potential to be watered into bloom. As well as Chuck and Gavin, there was Marley, a quiet girl with purple braids, Sonny, the joker of the group, and Kevin, a youth offender who was determined to turn his life around and was the unspoken leader.

And then there was Tasha. With her slight frame, huge green eyes and high cheekbones, the girl was both fragile-looking and beautiful, but her appearance was deceptive. Having run away from an abusive home at the age of twelve, she'd ended up in the midst of gang life. She was as hard as nails and about as forthcoming. Although she'd been with Safe Harbour, the Christian youth charity Junia worked for, for less time than the others, Junia was surprised she'd lasted even this long. Yet, Tasha had seemed excited about this trip. Junia guessed it was the closest thing she'd ever had to a holiday.

"Okay guys, everyone got their bags? Let's go in, shall we?"

She bid goodbye to the minivan driver, who reminded her that he'd be in Eastbrooke for the weekend if they needed to go anywhere. She made a mental note to ask about churches since it was Sunday the next day and it'd be nice to take the guys to a service if possible. Not all of them were Christian, but they all seemed to enjoy the worship sessions Safe Harbour ran each week.

As they walked towards the main building, a slight, fair-haired guy of about thirty came out and greeted them.

"You must be Max," Junia said, stepping forward and smiling, although his voice wasn't as deep as she recalled when they spoke on the phone.

"No, I'm Jay, Max is in there." He indicated behind him and held out his hand.

"Well, I'm Junia. Nice to meet you." She shook his hand.

"I can show the kids to the dorms while you check in if you like," he said, shoving his hands in his pockets.

"Thanks. That'd be great." Junia smiled again and gave the youth cohort a gentle, encouraging push before she followed the signs to reception. Reaching the steps, she glanced over her shoulder before entering the small, log building. The teens didn't need her to hold their hands every moment of the day, but this was new to them. She prayed silently they'd be polite and would show gratitude to the young man, not give him a hard time as they tended to do. She blew out a breath, walked up the steps, and opened the door.

A small bell jingled as she pushed it open. A dark-haired man, who'd been sitting with his head down behind the desk, looked up.

Now, *this* man's looks matched the deep voice on the phone. With dark hair, piercing blue eyes, sensual lips that were at odds with his chiselled face, and a wiry, muscular frame, Junia was momentarily tongue-tied.

He lifted a brow. "Can I help you?"

She felt flustered, almost lost for words. "Yes, sorry. I'm from Safe

Harbour. Your worker, Jay, took the young people to their dorms." She extended her hand over the counter. "You must be Max Carlton."

Standing, he nodded and shook her hand, his grip firm and cool. "And you're Junia Fox. How was your trip?" His voice matched his grip and confused her. She'd expected a warmer welcome. After all, they were paying guests.

"Oh, it was fine..." she began, but then her voice trailed off when he began rifling through a drawer as if he wasn't at all interested in her reply.

He looked up moments later with a key in his hand. "We've prepared a separate room for you. It's small and basic, but basic is how we do things here. Or did you want to sleep in the dorm with the girls?"

Junia chewed her lip. She wanted to keep an eye on the youth in her care, but she also wanted them to enjoy the experience and have some time to themselves. It also didn't seem fair that the boys would get to board on their own if the girls didn't.

"I'll take the room. Thank you."

"I'll show you where it is." He stepped from behind the counter and headed for the door. She was surprised when he held it open for her, but once outside, she struggled to keep up with his long, lean stride. He took her to the main building, which was also made from rough-hewn logs, and had a long, covered walkway down the middle. She followed him to a small room opposite the dorms.

He was right. The room was definitely basic, but it had a cosy feel. There was a small single bed with a mattress that looked clean, a wooden chair with a navy-blue chair pad under the window, a sink and a small cupboard. The floor was timber, as were the walls. It was clean, and the view from the window was stunning, the mountain rearing up like a sentinel standing guard.

"It's lovely," she said, setting her bag on the floor and glancing at the clock on the wall. It was already four in the afternoon. It had been a long drive, and she would have loved a short nap, but doubted there'd be time. "Is there a schedule for today?" she asked, swinging her gaze back to him.

He stood in the doorway, arms crossed. He was close enough for her to see the stubble on his face which glinted in the late afternoon sunlight streaming along the verandah. "Dinner's at five-thirty in the hall. Jay's wife Sonia does the cooking. I'll do some fire-building with the group tonight before they head off to bed. There's a schedule in reception. I meant to give you one."

"I'll come back with you and get it," she said.

He shrugged and headed down the steps, leaving her scurrying to catch up with him again. Despite his reticence that bordered on rudeness, there was something about the wilderness guide that made her curious. He seemed to be a man of few words, but there was no harm trying to make conversation.

"It looks like an amazing place. What inspired you to start the retreat?" she asked as they walked across the yard towards the reception cabin. Or rather, he walked, she half jogged.

He shrugged again. "I like the outdoors. The place used to be my father's." He didn't offer any more, and although she burned with curiosity, she sensed he wouldn't appreciate her prying.

Back in reception, he handed her a few copies of the schedule, printed simply on plain paper. As she cast her gaze over one of them, a flicker of excitement coursed through her. She was a city girl, and this was her first wilderness retreat as well, and the schedule looked amazing.

The next day, Sunday, was relatively light. Sonia was scheduled to take them for a short hike in the morning, followed by Sunday lunch and a recreation afternoon, but the week was filled with everything from high ropes, to bush craft, to foraging. For the last few days, they'd venture up the mountain for a three-day hike and camp where they would implement the skills they'd learned over the course of the week.

"It looks great," she said, smiling. "Everything the brochure promised."

"Good," Max replied, retreating behind the counter to sit in front of the computer, effectively dismissing her.

"Right, I'll see you at dinner then," she murmured.

He lifted his gaze momentarily. "I eat in my rooms. I'll see you for the fire-building session."

"Okay, well, bye then." She headed for the door.

He grunted inaudibly, making her wonder why he was a retreat leader when he had such limited people skills. She shrugged. Maybe he was simply having a bad day. She'd learned not to judge people by first impressions in case something had happened to make them act differently to whom they really were. She'd so often seen troubled teens judged for their poor behaviour when they were simply crying out for help, but most people didn't see that.

Reaching the path, she remembered she hadn't asked about a church. She started to head back inside but decided to ask later rather than disturb him again now. She got the impression he'd rather not see her again so soon.

Instead, she headed for the dorms to distribute the schedules. The four boys were lying on their bunk beds listening to music. Their bags were strewn on the floor, half unpacked, and already the room smelled like rotten socks.

The boys sat up when she handed out the schedules. Chuck was excited about the fire-building, although the other boys teased him, albeit in a good-natured way. Even Gavin seemed relaxed.

In the girls' dorm, looking lost amidst six bunk beds, Marley was tutting at her phone while Tasha stood by the window, staring out of it.

"I can't get a signal. This sucks," Marley grumbled.

Junia raised an eyebrow. "You do remember you weren't supposed to bring a phone, right?"

Marley sighed as Junia held her hand out, but she passed her the phone anyway. "I forgot," she mumbled.

"Of course, you did," Junia said with a grin. She walked over to Tasha, who was still staring out the window. "You okay, hon?"

Tasha lifted her shoulder without turning. "Yeah, suppose."

Junia lowered her voice. "You can come and talk to me anytime if you need to, you know. About anything."

"I know," Tasha mumbled, still not looking at her, although her face softened a little.

Junia smiled sadly. Tasha reminded her of herself when she entered foster care at the age of thirteen, desperate for someone to love her but too fearful and distrusting to show it or allow anyone to get close. She'd been lucky. She'd been adopted quickly by a lovely Christian couple she now called Mum and Dad. A lot of children in care never got that opportunity. Not enough people wanted to take on a troubled teen; people wanted cute little kids.

She left the schedules on a spare bunk bed and returned to her room to unpack and prepare for dinner, wondering just what the next ten days had in store.

THEY WERE GATHERED around the fire pit, a collection of wood stacked on one side. Max studied the faces in front of him. The boys looked curious and ready to learn some skills, the girls less so. That was fairly typical. City girls often had little interest in wilderness pursuits, but if they ever got lost in the wild, the elements were no respecter of gender.

This evening was simply an introduction to fire-building. Later in the week he'd teach them about gathering materials. He'd found that city kids had little idea how to set and light a fire they could cook on and that would last for hours, but he gained great satisfaction from teaching them those basic survival skills.

Junia sat on the ground amongst the group of teens. He was carefully avoiding her gaze, but that was easier said than done. Her sudden appearance in the cabin that afternoon had unnerved him. The group had arrived early, but it wasn't that. He hadn't expected her to be drop-dead gorgeous.

To be honest, he hadn't given any thought to her before she appeared at the door. She was simply a name on an email and a voice on the phone, but the moment she stepped inside, she'd pretty much swept the breath from his chest. She was wearing a white V-necked top paired with faded jeans that accentuated her slim figure, but it was her eyes that captivated him. Deep hazel, brimming with tenderness and compassion.

He'd been short with her. Rude, even, but it had been the only way to control the unexpected, and unwelcome, reaction of his heart.

He was resolutely single and had been for some years. He loved solitude and the freedom that living in the wilderness gave him. If he was ever lonely, his mother and three brothers weren't far away. He didn't need people around him...and he carefully avoided any exploration into why that might be. As a result, he didn't think much about women, or feel the desire for a relationship.

And so, his immediate reaction to Junia had thrown him. Now he had to act professionally and not give any hint that she'd bowled him over. It wasn't just her looks, though. There was a light about her, what his mother would describe as 'spirit'. He found her intriguing, and even felt an urge to get to know her, which was pointless, because she was here as a paying customer with her bunch of teens, and she'd be gone in ten days and he'd never see her again. So, he had the next ten days to get through without making a fool of himself.

He hunkered down in front of the fire pit and began to talk, demonstrating as he did so. "If you're ever lost in the wild or find yourself having to stay outdoors without resources for any reason, then knowing how to build a fire could save your life," he told the group, his serious tone immediately grabbing their attention.

"Fire's your friend in those circumstances, but it can just as easily be your enemy. Up there, on the mountain, you won't have a fire pit like this to contain it, and fires can get out of control fast. You must respect fire, and never take its power for granted." He paused, letting his words sink in, then gave a rare grin. "Right. Who knows anything about building one?"

The lad called Chuck raised his hand eagerly. Judging from the sniggers the others gave, Max gathered that the boy's experiences with fire were less wholesome than a course on survival skills.

He motioned him over. "Okay." He gestured to the pile of firewood. "What would you start with?"

Chuck hesitated, then pointed to one of the bigger logs. "Uh, with that?"

"And what would you light it with?"

"A lighter."

"And what if you didn't have one?"

He shrugged. "Dunno."

His eyes widened when Max pulled a flint from his pocket and demonstrated how to get a spark. "Want to have a go?" Max asked, offering the flint to the lad.

"Sure." He took ten tries, and then frowned. "This isn't going to light that log, is it?"

"No," Max said with a small chuckle, "it isn't." He picked up a handful of bark. "We start with stuff like this. It's less dense and burns easily, especially when it's dry. When we go on the hike, you'll strip it from the trees yourselves, but I'll show you how to do that so you don't take too much and harm the tree. I'll also show you how to use an axe to create kindling, but this evening, this will do just fine."

As Max helped Chuck get the tinder going, a look of achievement grew on the lad's face. Max then took the smaller logs and showed the group how to make a smaller teepee fire. They all had a go at lighting the flint, and then with his help, each built their own teepee fires in smaller, pre-prepared pits. By the time he showed them how to ensure their fire was properly extinguished and how to cover the ground so that no trace was left, the sun was disappearing over the mountains.

"That was great!" Chuck enthused as the group began heading back to the dorms.

Max grinned. Fire-building was always a winner. For someone so resolutely solitary, he was always surprised by how much he enjoyed teaching, especially youth, and how seeing city kids loosen up was so rewarding.

Junia hovered at the back of the group, her hair glowing rose-gold against the sunset. He tried not to think how close she was, or how pretty she looked in the soft evening light.

"They absolutely loved that, thank you so much." Her smile lit up her pixie-like face and sent his heart spinning as he fell into step beside her.

"I'm glad they enjoyed it," he said, swinging his gaze ahead of him, while very conscious of her beside him.

"I wanted to talk to you about tomorrow's schedule."

"Yes. What did you want to ask?"

"We're supposed to be going for a hike in the morning."

"Yes, with Sonia. I'll be at church."

She turned her head and stared at him. "Really? I was going to ask if there was a church in town that I could take the kids to. We normally do a church service on Sundays back at Safe Harbour, but it'd be good for them to go to a proper church for a change. That is, if you're happy for us to tag along. Although we're supposed to be going on the hike. We couldn't change that, could we?"

He blinked. How had this happened? She was intending on bringing the teens to his quiet, little church? *What would everyone think?* But that wasn't the real problem. *She'd be with them.*

He raked his hand across his head and met her gaze. "Ah… I guess it would be okay. We could change the hike to the afternoon."

"That would be great. Thank you." She smiled, then an awkward silence followed as they stared at each other for a moment.

He quickly averted his gaze and breathed a sigh of relief as the dorms came into view. "Good night." He lifted his hand as he veered towards his cabin.

"Oh, okay, then. Goodnight." She sounded miffed.

He didn't blame her. He'd been rude again. But what else could he do? He was way out of his depth. As he walked off, he felt sure she was staring at his back.

Go here to continue reading: www.julietteduncan.com/heroes-of-eastbrooke-christian-romantic-suspense-series

OTHER BOOKS BY JULIETTE DUNCAN

Find all of Juliette Duncan's books on her website: www.julietteduncan.com/library

Heroes Of Eastbrooke Christian Suspense Series

Safe in His Arms

Some say he's hiding. He says he's surviving.

Under His Watch

He'll stop at nothing to protect those he loves. Nothing.

Within His Sight

She'll stop at nothing to get a story. He'll scale the highest mountain to rescue her.

Freed by His Love

He's driven and determined. She's broken and scared.

Water's Edge Series

When I Met You

A barmaid searching for purpose, a youth pastor searching for love

Because of You

When dreams are shattered, can hope be re-found?

With You Beside Me

A doctor on a mission, a young woman wrestling with God, and an illness that touches the entire town.

All I Want is You

A young widow trusting God with her future.

A handsome property developer who could be the answer to her prayers…

It Was Always You

She was in love with her dead sister's boyfriend. He treats her like his kid sister.

My Heart Belongs to You

A jilted romance author and a free-spirited surfer, both searching for something more...

I'm Loving You

A young widow with an ADHD son. A new pastor with a troubled family background...

A Sunburned Land Series

A mature-age romance series

Slow Road to Love

A divorced reporter on a remote assignment. An alluring cattleman who captures her heart...

Slow Path to Peace

With their lives stripped bare, can Serena and David find peace?

Slow Ride Home

He's a cowboy who lives his life with abandon. She's spirited and fiercely independent...

Slow Dance at Dusk

A death, a wedding, and a change of plans...

Slow Trek to Triumph

A road trip, a new romance, and a new start...

Christmas at Goddard Downs

A Christmas celebration, an engagement in doubt...

The Shadows Series

A jilted teacher, a charming Irishman, & the chance to escape their pasts & start again.

Lingering Shadows

Facing the Shadows

Beyond the Shadows

Secrets and Sacrifice

A Highland Christmas

True Love Series

Tender Love

Tested Love

Tormented Love

Triumphant Love

Precious Love Series

Forever Cherished

Forever Faithful

Forever His

A Time For Everything Series

A mature-age Christian Romance series

A Time to Treasure

She lost her husband and misses him dearly. He lost his wife but is ready to move on. Will a chance meeting in a foreign city change their lives forever?

A Time to Care

They've tied the knot, but will their love last the distance?

A Time to Abide

When grief hovers like a cloud, will the sun ever shine again for Wendy?

A Time to Rejoice

He's never forgiven himself for the accident that killed his mother. Can he find forgiveness and true love?

Transformed by Love Christian Romance Series

Because We Loved

Because We Forgave

Because We Dreamed

Because We Believed

Because We Cared

Billionaires with Heart Series

Her Kind-Hearted Billionaire

A reluctant billionaire, a grieving young woman, and the trip *that changes their lives forever...*

Her Generous Billionaire

A grieving billionaire, a devoted solo mother, and a woman determined to sabotage their relationship...

Her Disgraced Billionaire

A billionaire in jail, a nurse who cares, and the challenge that changes their lives forever...

Her Compassionate Billionaire

A widowed billionaire with three young children. A replacement nanny who helps change his life...

The Potter's House Books...

Stories of hope, redemption, and second chances.

The Homecoming

Can she surrender a life of fame and fortune to find true love?

Unchained

Imprisoned by greed — redeemed by love.

Blessings of Love

She's going on mission to help others. He's going to win her heart.

The Hope We Share

Can the Master Potter work in Rachel and Andrew's hearts and give them a second chance at love?

The Love Abounds

Can the Master Potter work in Megan's heart and save her marriage?

Love's Healing Touch

A doctor in need of healing. A nurse in need of love.

Melody of Love

She's fleeing an abusive relationship, he's grieving his wife's death...

Whispers of Hope

He's struggling to accept his new normal. She's losing her patience...

Promise of Peace

She's disillusioned and troubled. He has a secret...

Stand Alone Books

Leave Before He Kills You

When his face grew angry, I knew he could murder...

The Preacher's Son

Her grandmother told her to never kiss a preacher's son, but now she's married to one...

Promises of Love

A marriage proposal accepted in haste... a love she can't deny...

The Madeleine Richards Series

Although the 3 book series is intended mainly for pre-teen/Middle Grade girls, it's been read and enjoyed by people of all ages. Here's what one reader had to say about it: *"Juliette has a fabulous way of bringing her characters to life. Maddy is at typical teenager with authentic views and actions that truly make it feel like you are feeling her pain and angst. You want to enter into her situation and make everything better. Mom and soon to be dad respond to her with love and gentle persuasion while maintaining their faith and trust in Jesus, whom they know, will give them wisdom as they continue on their lives journey. Appropriate for teenage readers but any age can enjoy." Reader*

ABOUT THE AUTHOR

Juliette Duncan is a USA Today bestselling author of Christian romance stories that 'touch the heart and soul'. She lives in Brisbane, Australia and writes Christian fiction that encourages a deeper faith in a world that seems to have lost its way. Most of her stories include an element of romance, because who doesn't love a good love story? But the main love story in each of her books is always God's amazing, unconditional love for His wayward children.

Juliette and her husband enjoy spending time with their five adult children, eight grandchildren, and their elderly, long-haired dachshund, Chipolata (Chip for short). When not writing, Juliette and her husband love exploring the wonderful world they live in.

Connect with Juliette:

Email: author@julietteduncan.com

Website: www.julietteduncan.com

Facebook: www.facebook.com/JulietteDuncanAuthor

Printed in Great Britain
by Amazon